"Enormous . . . Cloete bends all his skill and talent to a major story where incident is piled dramatically on incident and people such as the world has not seen for years love, live, die, hope under the pressure of the new-born twentieth century . . . Cloete is a master"

Cleveland Plain Dealer

"Cloete at last has written the epic of the struggle for the South African veld. His vast panoramic novel is as monumental as the land it covers . . . a magnificent saga crowded with full dimensional characters . . . a great novel with all the ingredients of love, war and death which make an epic"   Detroit Press

RAGS of GLORY
STUART CLOETE

AN AVON BOOK

AVON BOOKS
A division of
The Hearst Corporation
959 Eighth Avenue
New York, N. Y. 10019

Dedicated to
TINY

With grateful acknowledgments to Lee Barker and Naomi Burton for their superb and sympathetic editing and encouragement, and to Major Geoffrey Tylden for his help in obtaining rare material.

INTRODUCTION

THERE are many parallels between the United States and South Africa. Both began as distant overseas colonies in the seventeenth century. Both Cape Town and New Amsterdam were founded by Hollanders within a few years of each other. Both fought savages for the possession of the land. Both threw off the British yoke. Both trekked into the wilderness to found new states. Both had a civil war. Both had the same initials, the U.S.A. and the Union of South Africa, till South Africa became a republic.

The Indian and Zulu wars were fought by similar men. The American wagon trains and movement to the West had the same inspiration and motives as the great Boer Trek to the north.

The Anglo-Boer War combined some features of both the American Revolution and the Civil War. As in America, it was a war of cultures. In Africa it was England with her colonies of the Cape and Natal fighting the two little republics of the north. A civil war in which brother was against brother, in which, as in America, an industrialized people attempted to force a material and alien culture upon farmers who were fighting for a way of life.

S.C.

CONTENTS

PART THREE
LOVE AND WAR
*[South Africa and England—October to December 1899—
Summer]*

PART FOUR
THE TURN OF THE TIDE
*[South Africa and England—December 1899—March 1900—
Summer and Fall]*

PART FIVE

THE CAPTAINS

[April—July 1900—Winter]

PART SIX

METHODS OF BARBARISM

[South Africa—July to December 1900—Winter, Spring, and
Summer]

PART SEVEN
THE TRAITORS
[South Africa—January to December 1901—Summer]

PART EIGHT
THE SCARECROWS
[South Africa and England—December 1901—June 1902—
Summer, Fall, and Winter]

PART ONE

"BLOOD MUST FLOW"

—Adriaan de la Rey

[South Africa—September and October 1899—Spring]

CHAPTER 1

WHAT IS A MAN?

CATALINA MARIA ELVIRA DU TOIT had been a beautiful girl. Dark, vivacious, with the large brown eyes of her Huguenot ancestry. This darkness, these genes, popped in and out continually among her race, which was in general blond, skipping a generation or two and then throwing back to a man or a woman who in appearance and character was almost French.

She was still good-looking. Like wine, she was one of those women who mature well. The fiery, slim slip of a girl who had married Petrus Paul van der Berg had turned into a serious woman, with faint wrinkles about her eyes and mouth, where life had left its marks—the crowfoot spoor of work and sorrow.

Servas had been eleven and Boetie two when her husband had been killed. Since then, till Servas had been old enough to help her, she had run the farm alone. Both boys were fair. Elsa, two years younger than Servas, had had her coloring. Her sudden death had hit her hard. At the time she had felt she could take no more blows. But she was going to have to. She was sure of it. There would be war.

She dressed carefully, putting on her best plum-colored taffeta, which was shot with brown. She was going to call on the President. She hoped he would remember her, or, if not, Petrus, who had been his friend's son and was his godson. She wondered how many godsons he had. Dozens. Hundreds perhaps.

She knew everyone wondered why she had never married again. That was one reason she left the farm so seldom. She did not like to be talked about. Perhaps she was too strong, too decisive. She had once contradicted Oom Paul when he said the world was flat. The President did not like or care for opposition, particularly from a woman. But the incident might bring her back to his mind.

At last she was ready.

"Have the horses put in, Klaas," she said.

"Where are we going, Ma?" Boetie asked.

"We? Who said you were coming?"

"I say so." He was fifteen years old, with gray eyes like his father's. His sunburned face was dotted with freckles. He stood, his legs apart, as immovable as rock, nearly as tall as she. How children changed. It seemed only yesterday that he had been an infant in her arms, clutching and pummeling at her breasts. Then a baby, round, hard as a nut, rolling about on all fours among the dogs. Then, almost overnight, he had become a little boy, sturdy, fearless, adventurous, clamoring for a horse of his own, a gun of his own. A real one. She had given him a gun when he was ten. His brother had taught him to use it.

"Very well, Boetie," she said.

"I will drive, Ma. We will take four horses. *Ja*," he said, "when I drive my Ma we go in style and fast."

"Put in four horses, Klaas," he shouted. Then he turned to his mother. "Where are we going?"

"To the dorp, Son. We are going to see Oom Paul."

"The President?"

"*Ja*, the President."

"He will see us?"

"He will see us, Boetie. He sees all men. Besides he knows me." He would remember that she had been there with Petrus when Captain Slocum said he had sailed the *Spray* around the world. "Also," she went on, "he was your father's father's friend, and your father was his godson."

How strange it was that her husband should have come back safely from battle and then been killed in a hunting accident. Franz Brand, who had been with him, had brought back the buffalo horns, his last trophy. "*Ja, mevrou*," he said, "he slew it. They died together."

Some people did not understand her having them there over the door that led to the sitting room, the great black scimitars, joined by their flattened boss, that had killed her man. But either they did not have sons or did not understand the way she was bringing them up. They must be men. He would have been pleased.

Yes, she thought, I have made a good job of it.

Too good a job, perhaps, the way things were going.

How strong was a woman, really? How strong am I? she wondered. If only Petrus were still alive . . . and then, she thought, if he were he would go. He would have gone already. How strange a world in which you could no longer regret the dead. Petrus's troubles were over. Who was she to wish more suffering upon him?

Mevrou van der Berg slipped on her dust coat as the Cape cart came to the door with a jingle of harness and crunch of iron tires. The four bay horses arched their necks and rolled their eyes, eager to go, to run at a trot and canter. With four good horses a two-wheeled Cape cart could make twelve miles an hour on a short trip. Two stable boys held the horses' heads. The reins were in Klaas's hands. The whip, its thong rolled around a long bamboo stock, stood like a lance in its bucket on the dashboard.

Boetie climbed up and took the reins. His mother settled herself beside him.

"Ready?" Boetie asked. She nodded. "Make loose!" he shouted. The boys let go. The horses sprang forward in a gallop. Jonas, the boy who had held the leaders, ran behind the cart and, grasping the tailboard, sprang up. They were off.

The country slid past them. The veld, velvet green, rolled like a carpet over the low hills. Here and there an outcrop of reddish dolomite broke the surface like the back of a fish leaving the sea. Here and there were patches of trees—blue gums, black wattle, thorns gnarled with years and painted with clusters of golden bloom.

The red dust of the road rose in a low cloud to the horses' knees and hung dragging like a scarf behind the cart. A kestrel hovering in the sky shot downward upon some small unseen prey. Three mounted men with rifles slung to their backs were overtaken, greeted, and passed.

How often had she been on this road? Catalina wondered. The first time had been when she had been driven over to meet Petrus's parents by the friends she was staying with. No one had mentioned a young man, or if anyone had she had not remembered it, her heart being at that time occupied with thoughts of another man. But when she had seen Petrus the other man had ceased to exist. Her heart had been wiped clean of him as a black-board is wiped clean of chalk in a schoolroom.

And after that, and after marriage, how many times? For this road was the road of her life, the road into it and out of it. All that the farm produced went to Pretoria, everything they bought came from there. As they got nearer there were more houses. Small farms, gardens, people.

How well Boetie drove—holding the four heavy reins as if they were ribbons, shouting to the horses as he called them by name. How beautiful the country was. She turned her head to look back at a group of weeping willows that stood, like women washing their hair, in the dark water of a dam.

Then suddenly, before she was ready for it, her mind still lost in dreams and memories, they were among the wagons in the square. Never before, even at a *nagmaal*—a communion—had she seen so many wagons lying wheel to wheel. All tented, they looked like great white cocoons bursting with people—whole families had come to the capital with their men.

Slowly, almost imperceptibly, as the President exchanged note after note with the British Government, Pretoria had become an armed camp. Batteries of guns rattled down Church Street. Shoppers ceased to comment on the rifle shots that came from the men practicing in the hills that surrounded the town. Things, even simple things, became hard to get because the train service was disorganized by troops being sent to the Natal border, and English refugees making for the safety of the colony.

British troops were massing on the frontier of the Transvaal, more troops were said to be on the water. But there was still a continual coming and going of deputations from the Cape Colony, trying to effect some settlement, some compromise that would be acceptable to both sides.

There were armed men everywhere, some mounted, some on foot. Catalina was astonished to see grandfathers and their grandsons, even great-grandsons, riding side by side.

But if she saw them with one eye, Boetie saw them with another. All Africa was here. Farmers, traders, fresh-faced high-veld boys, and hunters and transport riders from the north—lean, sweated-out men, yellow with fever. Big, small, fat, thin, old, and young, drawn from all over the republic like iron filings to the magnet of her danger.

Boetie saw only the romance of it, of all these strange men united in a common purpose—to defend their land. *Ons Land,* as they called it.

His mother saw the women left at home to guard and work the farms, left as she had been in 1880. Not yet widows, but more anxious in a way, for a widow had no more to lose.

A battery of Staats Artillery passed them, their gun mouths black, menacing, ready to spit death. The gunners, smartly uniformed in blue with white helmets, were the only uniformed, paid troops in the South African Republic. And then the bays, black now with sweat, curded with soapy foam where the harness touched their chests and flanks, pulled up as Boetie whistled to them to halt. This is the way horses and mules are brought to a stop in Africa, by long whistles before the reins are pulled, for they have no mouths for the snaffles they are driven on.

"We're here, Ma," he said, tying the reins to the dashboard as Jonas went to the leaders' heads. One boy could hold them now. The steam was out of them. They had had their fun.

The President's little tin-roofed house in Church Street boiled like a pot as men came and went. Burghers in field clothes, men in top hats and black coats, elders who looked like undertakers. Horses were tied everywhere or held in groups by horse holders. A dog yelped as it was kicked.

Boetie got down to help his mother. She took off her dust coat and drew a feather duster of gray ostrich plumes from under the seat to dust her shoes. Boetie took off his hat and wiped the sweat from his face and neck. It was hard work driving four fresh horses twenty miles.

"I'm not coming in," he said. "You'll be better alone, Ma, and I am not clean enough to see so great a man."

Catalina did not argue with him. Perhaps it was better to go alone than to have Boetie overcome with shyness shuffling his feet at her side.

"I'll not be long," she said, wondering if she would be

any time at all. The President might be too busy to see her. She walked past the men loitering in front of the house, between the two white marble lions, a gift of Barney Barnato, the mining magnate, that flanked the entrance.

How absurd they looked in front of that little house, surrounded by stolid, pipe-smoking men. Men already separated from their women and their homes; men enveloped in the cloak of war, lost in its folds, detached from the past, awaiting the future among their comrades patient as yoked oxen. None uniformed except for the two armed artillerymen who stood by the door. But these burghers were stolid, as immovable as rocks.

Yes, she thought, as she passed them, stones. These men could not be defeated—only killed. A strange citizen army of farmers such as the world had never seen. Most of the older men had been out on commando before—to fight the English, to recover stolen cattle from the Kaffirs. But except for the War of Independence and the Jameson Raid these had all been local affairs of small importance.

"The President," she said to a man standing in the passage of the little house. "I have come to see Oom Paul. Say it is Catalina van der Berg, the wife of Petrus, his godson."

How many others, she wondered, had used this method of introduction.

The man left her standing and went into a room to his right. A moment later he was back. "The President will see you." He opened the door.

"Oom Paul," she said.

"*Ja, ja,*" he said. "I am the uncle of all the world. And you," he went on, "I remember you. You are the widow of Petrus, who was killed by a buffalo. One nearly got me. But I was young then, and the Lord gave me strength to wrestle with it, and hold its nose in the mud of the vlei until it died. But the smell of it is still in my nostrils"— he touched his great nose with his forefinger—"and the fear of it still in my heart, though I have killed many a one since then. You are also the woman who was here with the blasphemous American who said he had sailed around the world. You agreed with him. But because you are a woman I forgive you, for women have no sense. That is the way the Lord made them."

He loaded his big meerschaum pipe, stained brown with much smoking, with a handful of loose Boer tobacco that he took from his pocket. She noticed the missing thumb he had lost in a gun accident. His strong, thickset figure. Even in old age, and he was then seventy-three, he remained formidable; his bloodshot eyes gleaming like those of a bush pig brought to bay by dogs.

Before him on the desk were papers, an inkpot, and several quills. On his right lay a great black Bible bound in leather with two brass clasps.

"How can I help you?" he asked.

"I want advice, Oom Paul, and counsel."

He laughed—a deep rumbling sound.

"Advice," he said, "is cheap. It is also something nobody takes, for it is like medicine, bitter on the tongue. Listen, *mevrou,* my child. All I can tell you to do is to pray. Pray for the land, for your men, and for me. Today no man needs more prayers than I. War is being forced upon us. In '37 we fled the English. I was a child then and came north with my father. Once over the Vaal we thought we were safe. That it was over. But it was not over. They came again, came after us like dogs on a blood spoor. In '80 we fought them and beat them. Your Petrus was with us. I remember him. In '96 Rhodes's jackal Jameson sprang when he thought our backs were turned. And now they come again." He stopped speaking as a heavy-set old man with a long gray beard came in.

Catalina got up. "I will pray," she said.

"You know General Joubert," the President said. "He is in command of our forces."

"Only his name, Oom Paul."

The old general put his hand on her arm. It was the strong hand of a farmer, brown with sun and blotched with the dark spots of age. "I knew your man," he said. "He served under me."

"His son will serve under you, if there is war," Catalina said.

"There will be war," the President said. "The sword is drawn."

"He has good blood, *mevrou,*" Joubert said. "The best. The grandson of a *voortrekker.* We shall welcome him."

Catalina shook hands with them both. She did not know what she had expected the President to say. She only knew that she had wanted to see a man and had seen one. Old, savage, a man of iron who, like a prophet of old, was leading his people. She was glad she had met Joubert. Petrus had said he was a great leader and brave, but that was twenty years ago. Was he not too old to command an army today? Would he not be too cautious?

She wondered now how she had dared to come to interrupt such great affairs for no real reason. None but the one the old man had given. He was Oom Paul, uncle to all the world. She had not come to interrupt a president, but to get comfort from her uncle, and he had given it to her. "Pray," he had said. "Seek help from God."

As she got to the door the President said, "Go and see Tante Sanna. Drink coffee with her. She sees too few women these days."

Catalina went to the kitchen in the back of the house. Suzanna Kruger, a dumpy little woman, stood by the wood-burning stove stirring an iron pot with a long wooden spoon.

"I am Catalina van der Berg," she said, holding out her hand.

Sticking the spoon in the pot and pushing it to the back of the stove, Mrs. Kruger came forward, smiling. She was rather fat, with the flat, high-cheekboned face of the Low Countries. Her gray hair was parted in the middle and drawn back into a bun. She was dressed in black silk as if it was Sunday, and wore a white cap. As if she guessed what Catalina was thinking, Mrs. Kruger smiled sadly. "So many people we see now," she said, "important people, that I always dress this way."

"These are terrible times, Mevrou Kruger," Catalina said. What was she to say to this little woman who had borne the President nine sons and seven daughters? Why had Oom Paul sent her here?

"Sit," Mrs. Kruger said. "We will have coffee. We will forget the war. We are women. Ah," she said, "how stupid I am. As if women could forget war.

"But we will talk of other things. Look," she said as they drank. "Look at that picture." It was a photograph of the statue of the President that had been put up in the square. He was wearing a top hat. "Do you know," Mrs. Kruger said, "what I wanted when they first showed me the picture? They said, 'That is what it will be like, this statue.'

I said, if they make a little basin inside the top of the hat—hollow out the inside of it—it could be used as a drinking fountain for the birds. Everybody laughed, Mevrou, but I still think it would have been a good idea."

"A beautiful idea," Catalina said. This was a good woman. They had been married more than fifty years, and now in their old age there was this trouble, this culmination of everything they had tried to escape when they fled the English in their childhood.

In the small yard beyond the back stoep three red cows were being watered. Mrs. Kruger ran a little dairy business, selling milk to her neighbors.

"Did you hear about the hospital, *mevrou?*" Mrs. Kruger said. "The Russians offered one if there was war. But Piet Joubert refused it, for he said our *bossiemiddels*—herbal remedies—are enough and that we Boers do not hold with newfangled ideas. You see," she went on, "it is impossible not to think of war. It weighs very heavily upon us in our old age. Long years ago I came to the Transvaal with my parents on the Great Northern Trek. If I were to tell you the troubles and hardships we went through! When I remember how we women and children had to hide many a night in the reeds, half in the water, hiding from bloodthirsty Kaffirs who would not hold back from the most atrocious deeds to white women. When I think how these worries and other troubles have continued ever since, my heart feels sore that the evening of our lives should be darkened by this awful, this unnecessary bloodshed between people of our kind and race. But we have gone far enough. We can go no farther. We must stand."

Catalina finished her coffee. "I must get back to the farm," she said, and held out her hand.

"Good-by, Mevrou van der Berg," Mrs. Kruger said.

"Good-by, Mevrou Kruger. Till I see you." The Boer good-by. But how long would that be?

There were tears in Mrs. Kruger's eyes as she burst out, "Do you know how many of my men will go? Five sons, six sons-in-law, and thirty-five grandchildren, all in the field."

Catalina went out the back door, through the yard, and into the street. Boetie and Jonas were talking to some men. The horses had their bits out of their mouths and

were eating the oat forage that had been slung in a bag
under the cart.

"You were so long, Ma, I thought I'd feed them. We
can water them at the drift on the way home."

"I am sorry I was so long." She had forgotten that he
was waiting there. She had been in another world. On the
very edge of the great world. Its final extension. Pretoria
was where civilization ended in Africa. In one direction,
to the south, were roads, railroads, towns—Cape Town,
the ocean, and Europe. In the other, scattered farms like
their own Groenplaas, and then nothing. It was true that
the President had built a railroad to Delagoa Bay so that
the republic would have an access to the sea that was not
English. But it was an empty land the track ran through, a
wilderness of low veld, and many had died of fever in its
construction.

She had to hoist her skirt and petticoat high to reach
the step as Boetie helped her into the cart. She was embarrassed to do so before so many men. But they did not
see her. She belonged to the world they had left.

The rested horses sprang forward, filled with life again
as their heads were turned homeward. Home to Groenplaas. To water, a rubdown, and more green oat forage.

Catalina saw nothing on the drive home. Her mind was
filled with her thoughts of the President, Oom Paul, standing like a lion at bay. Without doubt he was the ugliest
man she had ever seen. She had forgotten how ugly he was.

His eyes were dark brown, almost black. They had
heavy bags beneath them, his left eyelid drooped, both
eyes were inflamed and he held them partially closed. His
eyebrows were heavy, his nose prominent, with wide
nostrils. He had big ears. His mouth was large. He held
his lips tightly compressed. His face was clean-shaven
except for a gray beard that went from ear to ear below
his chin. His expression was melancholy. His head, in
comparison to his great body, was small. His most striking
characteristic was his voice, a deep double bass. When
irritated he used it with terrifying effect. This was Oom
Paul. A man. It was a man she had come to see. The husband of two wives, father of sixteen children, grandfather
of a hundred twenty.

His Bible was always with him. It was not a book to

him, not even a holy book. It was his life's guide. Still the farmer, he rose at daybreak. His first action was to go to his study and read a chapter of the Bible. Then he had a cup of coffee. After that he sat on the stoep staring across Church Street at the little Dopper Church, where he preached every Sunday and waited for those who wished to see him. He received all comers.

At meals the women and girls of his household had to sit with their heads covered. He ate fast and suffered from indigestion. He ate no rice and no vegetables. He liked bread soaked in milk. He did not drink. He suffered from asthma and heart disease.

He smoked heavily. His favorite pipe was the meerschaum with a curved stem that she had seen in his hand. He drank a great deal of coffee. There was always a spittoon near his chair which he generally missed.

He always dressed in a long black morning coat and top hat. He wore a green sash of office, and *klapbroek,* flap fly, trousers. If someone annoyed him he would pound his Bible with his fist and shake the room with his roars. Everyone knew all this, but having seen him again made it all come back.

Ugly, hideous, terrible, his looks were at once forgotten, so great was the strength of his personality.

An old man utterly set in his ways, rooted in his religion, in his belief in the Old Testament God. In his land and his people. He epitomized the Boers' character, which may have accounted for his power as a leader. He had all their virtues and all their faults. Brave, inured to hardship, a farmer, hunter, and citizen-soldier since boyhood, generous and hospitable, a good friend and a dangerous enemy.

He was like his fellows, obstinate and opinionated, bigoted and mule stubborn. Anything that was not in the Bible was untrue. Giraffes were camels because there were no giraffes mentioned in the Holy Writ. The world was flat. The Garden of Eden a real place. For the Boers there was no myth, no allegory. All was true—the Tower of Babel, the Flood, the Fiery Tablets, Jonah and the Whale. The Bible was their book of law, their natural history book. It was from it they got their science and astronomy. It was upon it they based their lives—an eye for an eye, a tooth for a tooth; increase and multiply; the belief that

the black children of Ham were condemned to hew wood
and draw water forever.

Oom Paul saw the Boers as Israelites, the Transvaal as
Canaan, the English as Philistines, and Johannesburg as
Sodom and Gomorrah rolled into one.

Catalina thought of Oom Paul's life. It was the life of
all her people. His history was the history of the South
African Republic across the Vaal.

It was some time since Groot Adriaan de la Rey had
shouted, "Blood must flow!" to Cecil Rhodes.

To which Rhodes had replied, "Give me breakfast."
There was no blood after breakfast. Rhodes stayed with
De la Rey for a week and became the godfather of his
grandchild. But Rhodes was now discredited. Milner, who
was running things now, gave the orders and declined to
negotiate.

The second Boer war for independence was about to
begin.

Without a word to anyone, Catalina went into the
house. The President had said, "Pray for me." She could
do no less.

CHAPTER 2

THE BIRTHDAY

IT WAS the eleventh of September, 1899, and Boetie—
Louis Petrus van der Berg—was sixteen years old. It was
a great day. The greatest in his life so far, for today childhood and boyhood were behind him. Now he was a man,
a· full burgher.

With his father dead, Ma had run the farm alone till
Servas was old enough to help, and now that he was a
man too, her worries were over. The two of them together
could run a bigger place than this, unless there was war.
Either way, he was now a man with a man's responsibilities. He walked through the violets to the path where he
had left his shoes. He always took off his shoes when he
walked through the big violet bed, partly because it

crushed them less, partly because he liked the feel of the leaves on his legs and the moist soil beneath his feet.

Boetie's pony looked up and nickered when he went into the stable carrying a bucket of cold water. He stroked its neck and mousy nose. "You'll soon be well now, Pasha," he said. He loosened the bandage, dropping it like a khaki-colored snake into the water to soak. Bubbles of air rose to the surface and clung to the black floating hairs from the pony's leg. Pasha had been given to him by a British officer, Captain Turnbull of the 2nd Hussars, two years ago, when he had gone back to England. He'd thought how rich a man must be to give away a pony. He could have sold him easily.

He'd said, "Why don't you sell him?"

"Yes, my boy, I could," the captain had said, "but you never know, do you, when you do that? He's a pet, you see, and I want him to have a good home. You're a good boy with horses, you talk to 'em. That's what they like— conversation. They are like women: talk to 'em, stroke 'em, and they'll go to the ends of the earth for you." That's what he had liked about the captain. The way he spoke to him as if he was a man. Even if he did not understand it all.

Now that he was older, he could see the pattern. The captain, as he still called him in his mind, had not gone back to England till Elsa, his pretty sister, had died. A swift fever that in forty-eight hours had sweated the life out of her, the color out of her cheeks, and left her lying waxen, hardly breathing in her bed. And then, not breathing. Gone. The captain had come galloping when he heard the news of her illness, but had been too late. Boetie had held Servas's hand but had not gone in. He had watched them from the door. He could not bear to be there with them. Later he had crept in alone. It was hard to believe she was dead. She was so beautiful. But she was cold. That was the difference, the living were warm and the dead were cold.

"They'll go to the ends of the earth for you." That was what Elsa would have done for the captain. Gone to England with him.

It had begun with the captain leading his horse, a big

brown gelding, to the farm. He had cast a shoe and the
captain had asked if they would lend him a mount to ride
back to town. He had been dressed in riding clothes,
coat, breeches, and boots. He was in Pretoria with a commission of some kind investigating something. But when
the others had gone he had stayed on. That was after he
had seen Elsa for the first time. She had seen him, too.
From that day she had changed. The snap and sparkle
had gone out of her brown eyes, and they had become
as soft as a heifer's. She had become quiet in her ways,
demure, neater in her appearance, and so stupid that she
could not remember anything for more than a few minutes at a time.

It was he, Boetie, who had taken the big hunter to be
shod, and later ridden him to Pretoria. Never had he been
prouder, sitting like a king on a blood horse that stood
sixteen two, with a hogged mane and a banged tail. He
had never ridden an English horse before, nor sat in a
hunting saddle, nor had two reins—a bit and bridoon
—in his hands. The horse—Ranger had been his name—
had played up a bit, pig-jumping in the freshness of the
morning air. But that had not worried him. He had talked
to him first in Taal, which the horse had not understood,
and then in English. Before they reached town they had
been friends.

Boetie had never liked anyone so well as the captain.
This was really strange, because he was English.

His father had fought the English, and it looked as if
he might now do so too, and among them would probably be the man who would have become his brother. He
had heard it said that many British officers had married
Boer girls at the Cape.

Servas was riding back from the dorp. He had been in
to get the latest news, to bring back the papers and gossip.
The people had not been working. They went through the
motions of their accustomed activities in a kind of excited
dream, as if reality, as they knew it, were about to end.
None of them doubted that war would come. The fiasco
of the raid had been one thing, but this was another.
This would be a real conflict—a final war of liberation
and a test of strength. The nation was aroused and prepared. Oom Paul had seen it coming; they had thousands

of new rifles ready, millions of rounds of ammunition, and big guns from Le Creusot and Krupp. Pretoria was fortified. This was the news he was bringing back. But he was heartsore and ill at ease. He thought of Captain Turnbull, who had given Boetie his bay pony, of how nearly they had become brothers. What would Elsa have made of it? Of her loyalties, of her love of a man as a woman, and her love of her country as a Boer girl? How torn she would have been! How torn he was himself, but in his heart he knew that within a month he would be out on commando to defend the republic. Ma and Boetie would run the farm. The boys were good. The little world he would leave behind would be secure—something to fight for, and return to. His home. His land was his love.

His horse's hoofs were muffled in the red dust of the road. He wondered if he would be afraid. He would take General, the black stallion he had trained as a shooting pony, and a pack horse. He patted his horse's neck. "The war is no place for you," he said. No place for a white horse like Witbooi. Witbooi had belonged to his sister. He had broken him in for her, and seemed nearer to her on his back. Elsa's death had made a big hole in his life.

His mother met him in the yard and said, "What news, Servas?"

"Bad, Ma. There is no hope of peace." He was still on his white horse, his hands on its withers, looking about him. War. How impossible it was to believe there could be war, looking at this peaceful scene. At the yard he had known all his life. At the cattle being driven into the kraal, at the chickens pecking about his horse's feet, at the dog sitting beside his mother, slowly wagging its tail as it looked up at him, at his mother, and young Boetie standing in front of her. At a peacock spreading its tail. Peafowl had been his father's hobby.

"They say there was a great scene in the Volksraad, Ma. De la Rey spoke against Oom Paul and the war party. The President taunted him and those who were with him as 'cowards.'

"Then De la Rey spoke again. He said, 'I shall do my duty as the Raad decides.' Then he turned on the President and said, 'You will see me in the field, fighting for our liberty, long after you and your people, who make war with their mouths, have fled the land.' "

His mother licked her lips. "Then we must fight," she said.

"*Ja*, we will fight." All the men of the republic must ride out as one and drive the English back into the sea. He had forgotten Turnbull, and his other English friends, now. He saw only Africa, free at last, with the Vierkleur flying in the breeze from the Cape to the Zambesi.

"You too, Servas?" His mother's voice was so low that he hardly heard her speak. Servas, she thought. Her first-born. Of course she had known it, but the ways of God must always be strange to women. Her husband gored to death. Her beloved Elsa dead before she flowered. And now Servas . . .

Boetie said, "Pasha is nearly well, Servas. There is no heat left in his leg." He wanted to change the subject to take the burden of conversation off his mother for a moment.

"That's a pity," his brother said.

"A pity, Servas, why?" What could his brother mean?

"They'll take him," he said. "They said in the dorp that tomorrow they would collect all horses in the district for the commandos."

"My horse? They shall never take my horse."

"You wait and see, young man."

"They cannot," he said.

"Oh, can't they?"

"No," the boy said. "You have forgotten something. They cannot take a burgher's horse. I'll ride him to war myself."

"Boetie!" his mother cried.

"*Ja*," Boetie said, drawing himself up to his full height. "I was sixteen today. I am a man." And it was true. He felt it in himself. A change had taken place in his heart. When he had gone barefooted in the violets he had been a boy, almost a child. Now he was a man, a burgher of the South African Republic.

His mother threw her apron over her face. "Not Boetie, not Boetie," she cried, running into the house.

The brothers looked at each other.

"*Magtig*," Servas said, "My God, I had forgotten your birthday. I have no gift for you."

"Ma," Boetie said, "Ma is upset," and it dawned on him that what for him was the beginning of a great adventure was the end of the world for her.

"War is hard on the women," Servas said. He threw his leg over Witbooi's neck and slid to the ground. *"Kom, jong,"* he said. "We must get ready if we are to ride out."

They went to the stables together, the white horse and the dog following at their heels. "We shall need coats, blankets, water bottles, *veldkos*—biltong and rusks—rifles and ammunition. We will take two horses each."

"Yes," Boetie said, "two horses."

"I shall take Witbooi, Boetie." Servas had changed his mind.

"Why, Servas?"

"Because he belonged to Elsa, and will be safer with us than with a stranger." He had changed his mind about Witbooi.

In her bedroom Catalina knelt by the bed to pray. "God give me strength," she prayed. "God give me strength to stand alone. Please, God, bring them safely home." Thousands of women must be offering up the same prayers; all the women and girls and children in the Transvaal and the Free State must be praying. Surely God would hear them, hear their wordless cry, that their men should come home safe. Each praying for her own, each, in her wickedness, hoping that if anyone were killed, it would not be one of her men. Praying that the sweet fruit of her womb would be preserved, that her bed would not be forever empty. Yes, she thought, there will be many wives weeping in their beds alone. Many girls with their faces swollen thick with tears.

Suddenly she became strong. It is our land, *Ons Land*, she thought. We took it with our blood, with our blood we will hold it. God is just. God is with us. "Damn the English!" she cried aloud. "God damn them! If we had no gold under our soil they would leave us alone." It was as Oom Paul had said years ago, when gold and diamonds were first discovered: "These are not riches for us. We do not want them. They will only bring us blood and tears." Already there had been blood and tears, but now it would run in rivers. Yes, there would be rivers of blood and buckets of tears.

She went to the garden by a side door. I must be alone, she thought, alone to commune with God and my memories.

The jacarandas, blue, almost mauve, were painful in the intensity of their beauty. Nearly invisible against the blue sky. They made holes in the wooded landscape of black wattles and the olive pillars of the gums. Each stood in a bright azure lake of its fallen petals, like girls with their clothes lying at their feet. Bees came and went on transparent wings in an endless two-way stream to drink at the fountain, where the drops overflowed the green-stained edge of the stone basin.

Birds came too: doves, wagtails, white-cheeked sparrows, yellow weaverbirds. She saw a hoopoe raising its black, white-spotted crest. A hammerkop on slow brown wings came to hunt frogs in the furrows. Except for the hum of the bees and the cooing of the doves, the world was silent, sun-struck, drunk with the promise of summer. But soon guns would be firing, and men dying, their bright blood staining the veld. In her mind she saw them riding out from the farms. Fathers and sons, brothers like my Servas and Boetie. Old men, grandfathers, and boys scarcely strong enough to hold a rifle, such as she had seen in Pretoria. Parties of friends and relatives, riding in, who would fight together, without uniforms, without pay, riding their own horses, carrying their own guns. Forming into bigger groups, into commandos. Fathers, husbands, sons, lovers, all united under one flag, under the protection of one God. Now it was no longer a dream. The nightmare had become reality.

She remembered standing beside Petrus when he had planted the jacarandas. "They will be beautiful one day," he said. "When we are old we will see them flower, and standing hand in hand will remember this day."

Yes, she thought, I remember it. And this day, too, is a day I shall never forget.

She turned her back on beauty. Today her Boetie had become a man, and she had been turned from a woman into a thing of stone. There was no more time for sorrow.

How strange that she had not thought of Boetie's going. She had bought him a birthday present, a little New

Testament. She had known he was sixteen, but it had only been a word. Her mind had been on Servas, who was a man, not on her baby. And even with Servas she had felt it could not be really true.

CHAPTER 3

THEIR FATHER'S SONS

SEPTEMBER 29 was another beautiful spring day, no different from those that had preceded it except that it was warmer and lovelier, really summer. The white almond blossom was over. But some of the peach orchards were still a faint misty haze of pink, though the little green marbles of fruit were beginning to form. There had been more nice rains, and young green spears of grass were piercing the black stubble of the new burns. In the bushes and the trees, the birds were busy with their nests.

From the lands came the shouts of the drivers to the plowing oxen. Behind the spans, the soil lay in furrows as rich and moist as butter, crying out for seed. The doves bowed and cooed in ecstasy. From the kraals and stables came the usual sounds. A hungry calf called for its mother. A cock crowed. A bull roared out his loneliness.

Everything was as it had always been on Groenplaas, where life was tuned to the slow pulse of the seasons, till a dusty man on a chestnut horse galloped up to the house. Pulling it into a rear, he shouted, "Get your horses, *kêrels*. We are trekking."

The day had come.

In that instant, by those words, the little private world of the farm was shattered, broken like an egg dropped upon a stone. Half an hour later Servas and Boetie were on their horses, rifles in hand, with Jonas leading the two pack horses that carried their spare blankets, gear, and cook pots. After their swift good-by they rode without looking back, without a wave of the hand, with their rifle

butts on their hips, enveloped in the soft red dust that
rose like wool from their horses' cantering feet.

The messenger had not paused, but swung his horse
around and galloped on to raise more men.

The boys' cries of "Jonas, Jonas, saddle up," as they
ran to the stables where their horses stood ready, seemed
to echo in the trees. The swift embrace. Catalina still
felt their strong young bodies against her. Still heard
the scuffle of their horses' hoofs, overfresh from confinement, rearing and plunging as they mounted. And then
they were gone.

Boetie had had tears in his eyes. "Do not look back,"
Servas said.

Their dust still hung low and incandescent in the sunlight. But the boys were gone.

I'll wait till it settles, Catalina thought, as she stared
down the road as if the dust was part of the men that
had raised it.

The last time she had watched a man ride to war it
had been her husband. But then she had not been alone.
Her children had stood at her side, and now she realized
what a little war that had been. This would be a big one
—a long one.

In the history of the world, how many women had
stood like this? How many in the future would do the
same? Were men always destined to go and the women to
wait at home?

Catalina stood long after the red dust had sunk. The
boys had gone. Boys . . . The man Servas. And Boetie—her
baby—suddenly, because he was sixteen, a man by law.
But if he had been only fourteen he would have gone.
She knew she would not have been able to hold him back.

One minute they had been there—her sons and Jonas.
The horses—General and Pasha, Witbooi and the two
pack horses. Three men and five horses. A group against a
background of trees and shrubs. Now only the background
was left, but she saw them still, like ghosts in the sunlight.

She went over to where they had stood curveting and
milling with freshness. Nothing was left but their spoor—
hoofmarks and some little heaps of dung already dotted
with flies. She stood looking into space the boys had filled
as they rode away, looking into it as if she could penetrate

time, see into the future, make time pass, and see them come back riding toward her.

At whatever their age, beyond infancy, her sons would have gone. No one would have been able to hold them if there were war. Since the age of five they had been men— male, at least—bold, resolute, and impossible to control by force. How proud she had been of her little thickset sons, who even at that age would stand up to anyone who seemed to threaten what they considered to be their rights! It's their father's blood, she thought. That was why I married him, why he swept me off my feet. Someday they would do the same with the girls they courted. They were both their father's sons.

Groenplaas, now bereft of white men, for the two foremen had left soon after the boys—on the same day—settled down despairingly as a hen whose eggs have been stolen—sits on nothing out of habit.

The work went on, but slowly, under the direction of ɔld Klaas, the Basuto who had been Petrus van der Berg's friend and servant.

To all appearances the farm was unchanged, but the spirit of the place, as invisible as the soul of a man, had gone out of it. Groenplaas was not dead but in a state of suspended animation.

The parting of the two bywoners from their families had been different from that of the Van der Berg boys. Both in their late thirties, they had been on commando before. This was no adventure for them, only a severing of roots, only another pruning that cut away the dead wood of petty misunderstandings and left the bare branches of their love clear and unencumbered.

Herman Prinsloo, who for days had been silent and preoccupied, knowing what was to come, had taken his wife Martha in his arms and said, "My heart, my heart." She had her boy child Japie in her arms. The two little girls, Sara and Anna, clung crying to her skirts, their white *kappies* awry, their mouths puckered, their grubby faces streaked clean with tears. They did not know why they cried, for they had never been without their father. Japie, infected by their misery, began to howl. His mother, still in Herman's arms, rocked and patted him.

"Take care of yourself," she said.

Take care? As if care were possible in war. "*Ja,* I will take care."

Inarticulate, overcome by their feelings, they said nothing more in words but communicated as animals do, by touch, by smell. The sweet smell of his wife's hair, the milky smell of her full breasts, the acrid smell of her sweat were in Herman's nostrils. The smell of her fear and anxiety, so different from the smell of happiness. He thought of elephants he had hunted as a young man —how their stand places smelled sweet when they were unafraid and how this scent changed when they were chased. How strange to be holding his wife and thinking of elephants. How strange to be leaving them all, and this peace, for war and the society of men. There was no valor in his soul, only an anger that would, when the time came, amount to the same thing.

Jan Bothma, saying farewell to his wife and children, was silent. The children—Frikkie, Hendrik, Susanna, and Catalina—stood grouped near their father's saddled horse as if to make sure he would not escape them. They understood better, had some concept of time and the unprotected loneliness of the days to come. So they stayed together, close as the berries on a bunch of grapes. Serious, tearless, silent, each lost in a world of his own imagining. Frikkie, who was twelve, was the only one torn two ways. It was his intention before long to steal a horse from Groenplaas, take his rifle—he had had one for a year—and find his way to the war. But against this intention was another. He was the oldest man on Groenplaas, or would be in an hour—Kaffirs did not count— and there were women and children to be protected, even Ouma Catalina at the big house, so he must stay and do his duty. His father had told him to, and his father was always right.

He watched his parents go into the house, his father's arm around his mother's waist. By the time they came out together, his mother straightening her dress, the horse was restless with standing.

There was a dazed look in their eyes as his parents came toward him. He was old enough to know by instinct what they had done, what men and women did. He even understood why it had been done.

This act of love would be performed by many couples in their last hour, so that its memory would be held by both, pressed like a flower in a Bible, browning with time, but still holding its form, though two-dimensional now—flattened by the weight of absent days: but there, to be turned back to and regarded in the light of the campfires, in the dawns that crackled with gunfire, and thought of in the cold, long, lonely night bright with the same stars that had shone, utterly without feeling, upon the Israelites in the Wilderness, upon the Lord Jesus on the Cross—upon all history.

The men's houses were close together. Without orders the boys holding the horses brought them nearer till they stood side by side. A bay and a blue-roan with black points. The women, driven by the same force, had come together like two bits of flotsam in a whirlpool, their children with them.

The men mounted, swung their horses, and, turning in the saddle, waved their hats in a gesture of good-by and defiance. *"Tot siens,"* they shouted. "Good-by. Till we see you again." No one knew how long it would be. Perhaps it would never be. They rode off slowly, stirrup to stirrup, the black tails of their horses switching at the flies that bothered them. When would they ride back? What lay between the now and the then?

These were not adventurous boys, but men—family men —riding out in anger.

Still standing grouped, as if they were frozen, the women and children waited till the riders were out of sight hidden behind the trees in the bend of the road. They waited to see them again for an instant on the horizon— two mounted men no bigger than ants, dark against the sky. Then they turned, and went into their houses, their children trailing behind them.

Jacoba Bothma flung herself on the tumbled bed and sobbed. The children stood like a frieze beside it, watching their mother as people stand by the beds of the sick, the dying, and the dead. Wordless, they watched her paroxysm, her hands grasping the pillow to her breast as if it was her man, her body shaken with gasps, with the movements of love against the emptiness of the mattress Jan would no longer share.

The bed of a woman is a precious thing, more to her than to a man. It has sanctity, a symbolism of conception and childbirth.

Then, as suddenly as she had flung herself down, she got up.

"It is over, children. We are Boers." Her long brown hair had come loose and hung down her back to her waist. Her eyes were not the eyes they had known all their lives, but agate hard. Her mouth was firm.

"Your father has gone to war," she said. "Your father. My man. Now till he comes back we are alone, with only God to help us. But we will stand firm. You are no longer babies—even you, Catalina. There is no place for children in our land today. You are people." She licked her dry lips and went on: "You have seen a terrible thing— a man torn from his wife's arms, from his family. You have stood by your father's horse while I loved him. *Ja*," she said, "I am shameless before you. For this is a woman's last gift to her man. The gift of herself. One day you will understand this thing, this bond of the flesh. Perhaps he has given me a son. Perhaps even now a brother to you all is hidden in my belly that I may have to bear alone. Now go," she said, "and leave me, for I must pray."

These events on Groenplaas were no isolated tragedies. They were taking place all over the Transvaal and the Free State. Everywhere there were men riding away from their homes. Men alone. Men in groups that coalesced into larger groups riding over the veld along tracks and roads that led inward, like the spokes of a wheel, to the commando assembly points. They had come, leaving behind them all they possessed but their horses and rifles.

Most of them were poor men. The richest were far from wealthy. None had been here long—only about sixty years. They believed themselves a chosen people under the special protection of God. Many were related by blood and marriage. All were brothers in religion and in outlook. They loved this terrible country—for only small parts of Africa are fair—with a fanatical love. It was their promised land that they had bought with their blood. For a thousand miles to the south whence they had fled, the great *trekpad* was dotted with the graves of men and the bones of the stock that had died by the thousand on the way.

It was over this land, with last year's yellow grass brushing their stirrup irons and the young grass on the burns lawn green, that the Boers rode. It was in this bare country that they would fight. In no place, in no battle that was to come, was there not one man at least who knew the country like his mother's face, having lived in it and hunted over it since childhood.

Like bees whose nest has been disturbed the Boers swarmed to their land's defense. Filled with rancor, the sting of their rifles in their hands, and a belief in God in their hearts. No one, as they rode to war, still dreaming of the homes they had left, realized how formidable they were.

The British Queen and her ministers were not apiarists. To them the Boers were a handful of recalcitrant peasants that a few battalions of regular troops would soon subdue. The same mistake had been made a little more than a hundred years before, when the British underestimated George Washington. His men had been farmers and tradesmen too.

CHAPTER 4

A FLAG GOES DOWN

MEVROUV VAN REENAN was in Pretoria, one among the many, on October 11, when the Union Jack was hauled down from the British Consulate. From now on the American Consul would watch over British interests. She only wished her daughters had been with her. Her husband and her son were already with the Boer forces.

A kind of sigh like a little breeze went through the people as they watched two hands reach out to grasp the lanyard and take it in. The last British flag in the South African Republic had gone.

Dora van Reenan drove back to Sunnyside slowly. She

was thinking not of the war, which was now a fact, but of side issues, human issues, the woman's side of it—her own. The men at war. This would be a civil war. Many South African girls had married British officers, civil servants, and farmers. The Boers and the British had shared so much, so many hardships, so many dangers. Wars with Kaffirs, pestilence, and storms. Both had such a stake in Africa, in this tip of a continent. Her own sister at the Cape was married to a member of Parliament. What was Anna thinking now? Which side would she be with? How could the human heart be split down the middle like this, as if it were a log split with a wedge driven into it by the hammer of war?

She herself had been educated at an English school in Cape Town. Many of her friends were English, some even in England. And yet, knowing it meant war, she had rejoiced at seeing the alien flag go down, even though it was only on the consulate and had no authority. What madness was this?

When she got to the house, she did not go in. She did not want to see the girls just yet. In a curiously objective way she thought about her daughters, of their heredity, their different natures, and the fact that they were both pretty and already attractive to men. But how different they were. Louisa—dark, slim, fiery, passionate—utterly unreliable, utterly selfish and self-seeking, but so charming that no one could believe that so many of the things that went her way had been carefully engineered by this apparently flighty and gay young lady. Louisa thought of only one thing, herself, her looks and her desires. To gain her ends, she was steadfast, her will iron, and her apparent unreliability, her capriciousness, only marked the points where she changed her course—sometimes even reversing it completely.

Renata, a year younger, had almost honey-colored hair and golden, sherry-colored eyes flecked with golden spots. Her skin was a light apricot, always a little sunburned, with a red flush of blood darkening her cheeks. It was funny that when Dora thought of Renata she always thought in terms of something to eat. Honey, sherry, apricot. The French had a phrase for it: *"Jolie à croquer."* Pretty enough to eat. They made pretty phrases. She was glad she had learned to read it. Renata was not as slim as

Louisa. She was more rounded, her body a series of smooth curves that blended into a delicious whole. Louisa was a dark flame that burned everyone about her including herself. If a cleverly and charmingly disguised selfishness was the keynote of the one girl's character, a steady, unbreakable kind of integrity was that of the other. It could also be called obstinacy. But since childhood, if Renata made up her mind, nothing would change it. Perhaps this was the only thing the girls had in common, strong wills that would lead them in strange and probably opposite directions. A will, she knew, because she had one, was a dangerous thing. Once the will was set, the mind made up, it was like a bullet speeding toward its mark. Like hounds in full cry on a hot scent. Once they had started nothing could stop them.

She was sure a girl was better off if she was just nice-looking rather than pretty, only fairly intelligent rather than clever, and adaptable rather than ambitious. A will of one's own or strong feelings did not lead to happiness.

She went in to tell the girls the news. The shuttered house with its thick walls was pleasantly cool. For an instant, her eyes still dazzled by the sunlight, she saw nothing. She only felt the welcome coolness; the security of the home she had always known closed about her, shutting out for an instant all thought.

The girls, both in white, came toward her. "Mother, where have you been? Mother, we heard you come in and were looking for you. Where did you go?"

"I was in the garden."

"What were you doing?" Louisa said.

"Thinking."

"What about?" It was Louisa again, eager, excited, having to know everything even before it happened.

Renata said nothing.

"About what I have just seen."

"What have you seen?" Louisa was upon her, against her, thrusting her young body at her. Her mother stepped back away from her.

"I saw the English flag go down at the consulate. It has begun."

"Oh!" Renata gasped.

"Then it is really war," Louisa said excitedly, her dark eyes dancing.

"It is war," their mother said. What could she tell these girls? What did she know that she could tell them?

"Let us pray," she said, and they knelt on the carpet and closed their eyes. Pray to a God in whom she did not fully believe. Pray to a God who permitted war? Who tore men from their wives' beds and boys from their mothers' sides.

If the Book of Genesis was wrong, if there had been no Creation, how much was right? Still she prayed, out of habit, as an example to the girls, because if it did no good it could do no harm.

She supposed that in England women were praying too for their men—their husbands, sons, and lovers—praying that no harm should befall them, praying for victory. She could not pray for that, only for peace. Pray that at the last minute before the first shot was fired some event would intervene, some person—God.

But the first shot had been fired. Amid the good-bys at the station during the singing of the National Anthem and the cheers that sped the Pretoria Commando on its way. Among the volley of blanks fired by the Boers, as was their custom, a young farmer had been wounded. Some burgher who had forgotten to take the bullet out of a cartridge to blank it had wounded him in the arm. The first blood had flowed. A Boer had shot a Boer. The war that would turn into a civil war with brother against brother, before the end of it, had begun, while the three women prayed, kneeling on the carpet of their home.

Outside in the yard a dog barked. A hen cackled. She had laid an egg. The dog was Chaka, a big black mongrel. The hen was white, one of their Leghorns. The egg would be white. Later she would go and collect it. One of them would eat it for breakfast.

Everything was the same—the dog and the hens, the garden she had just left, the swimming goldfish and the cooing doves, the pictures in the room—the furniture, the carpets—but nothing was the same. Nothing would ever be the same again.

The girls had changed before her eyes. Louisa, unstable as always, was thrilled by the excitement of war, of action, of blood. Renata had grown up. One phrase had been enough to turn her from girl to woman.

And I? she thought. What about me? She felt numb. Later, when the time comes, it will be revealed to me what I must do. If not by God, then by my heart.

She got up and smoothed her dress, once again a married woman of thirty-five with two nearly grown daughters, the mistress of a house.

On whose side was God? That was the question. She wondered how he would decide, by what means, since he could not be on both.

CHAPTER 5

COMMANDO

SERVAS AND BOETIE were riding away from their home without any idea of when they would return to it, or even if they would return; though this was only vaguely in their minds, for all men, even in action, believe death will pass them by. Even in their fear they all feel, "It will not be me." If they felt anything else, there could be no wars.

They thought of Groenplaas, their *woonplek*—living place—as the Boers call their homes, of their mother, who was part of it, their first home in her belly; the two could never be disassociated. The woman, the house, the trees, the land. It was for this they fought, though by not fighting, by giving in, their homes would be even safer. There was nothing so terrible about British suzerainty. There would be peace, order, and even greater prosperity. This would not be difficult, since, except for the mines, the South African Republic was in a state of perpetual insolvency. The Boers did not see why they should pay taxes, and paid such as they did with the greatest reluctance.

Boetie was crying softly. He said he was not sad. He was only excited, but the tears still formed in his eyes and ran down his cheeks. Both boys wondered what the other men they would serve with would be like. Some, a few, they might know, but they had not met a great number of people, or at least did not know any of them well. Every three months they went to communion, *nagmaal,* in Pretoria, one family among the many who outspanned their wagons in the square to attend the service. There they moved among a multitude of other farmers who came in with their wives and children to worship God, trade a little, and exchange news. For the young people this was a chance to do some courting, to seek a *mooi meisie,* a pretty girl; or a fine young man to father sons. But in general the association was superficial. They knew the names of some of the people they met at *Nagnaal* even the names of some of their farms, but that was all. Servas, though he was of an age when most Boers were already married, did not have an eye for the girls who pursued him. The only young woman in his life had been his sister Elsa. She was his model, and no girl he had ever seen could approach her for looks or charm. No wonder the English captain had been captivated by her. That was another thing. He hated the English, the abstract English, but had liked the ones he had met. He worried about the farm; the farm and the land were his life. About Boetie. He should not have come. The first call up was for eighteen to sixty. He need not have come.

"You should not have come, Boetie," he said. "You should have stayed and helped Ma on the farm."

"It's a bit late now to say that."

"Ja, it is late, and I wanted you to come. It will not be so lonely for me among strangers. But I was wrong. I was just thinking of myself."

"How could I have stayed, man?" Boetie said. "I saw them in Pretoria—you saw them—boys that could not be fourteen. Besides," he went on, "how could I miss this thing? It will be over before I am eighteen. Look at the War of Independence. A few months and it was finished. Then, sitting like a girl on the farm I should have seen nothing. How could I have held up my head? Who would believe when I was thirty that I had been too young?" He leaned forward and patted Pasha's neck. The pony turned back one ear and arched his neck.

"Well, you're here and we're together," Servas said.

"Servas, are you afraid?" Boetie asked.

"Not yet. I am worried a little about meeting so many

strangers. But afraid, no. Not yet, for there is nothing to fear. What I am afraid of is being afraid. Then I think, I am Servas van der Berg. My father fought the English and the Kaffirs and his father made the trek with Oom Paul as a boy! All we can do, Boetie, is to count on our blood, which is good. We are like horses before a race. They must be afraid, all in a sweat with excitement and fear. But when the race is run the blood comes out, the hot blood that makes them gallop till they drop. That is all we have now, Boetie, our blood, each other, our horses and our guns—no home, no mother, no men but Jonas."

"I am glad we are together," Boetie said. "That may be why I came. I have never been parted from you. I do not think I could stand alone. I am still too young." Sixteen might make him a man technically, but a month ago he had not been sixteen. It was only a few days ago that he had stood barefoot among his mother's violets, tearing off streamers of blue-gum bark and playing with them, cracking them as if they had been whips.

They rode on in silence, knee to knee, Servas on the offside, Boetie on the near, Jonas and the two pack horses behind them, all of them, boys and horses, white and black, bred on Groenplaas.

They saw a horseman waiting at a small branch road. When they came up he joined them. He was riding a buckskin, a yellow horse with a black mane and tail and the beginning of a black donkey stripe down his shoulders from the withers, and black points that ended in zebra markings on his forelegs. They noticed the horse before the man. They looked at it first, seeing at first glance he was a stranger, and, overcome with shyness, they avoided his eyes. This was a mature man, clean-shaven, forty perhaps, burned almost black by the sun, a hard man who certainly had known war. His clothes were old but good, his bandoleer well worn with use. The rifle slung over his shoulder seemed a part of him, as if it grew there. In his slouch hat he wore a black ostrich plume. On his belt he had a sheath knife in a sheath of tiger skin.

When they pulled up beside him, for he had not moved toward them, they saw his eyes were black.

"Moolman," he said. "Dirk Moolman from the Zoutpansberg."

"Van der Berg," Servas said. "Brothers, from Groenplaas ten miles behind us."

"We will ride together," Moolman said, and joined them, his yellow horse on the offside so that now they rode three abreast.

Both boys felt better with this man. He was experienced. He would advise them. They would do what he said. It was a great relief, a weight was lifted from their hearts, particularly from Servas's, because he knew he was not as wonderful as his brother thought him.

"You are farmers?" Moolman asked.

"*Ja*, we farm."

"Where is your father?" Moolman asked.

"Dead," Servas said. "He fought the English in '80 but was killed by a buffalo later. Our grandfather was a *voortrekker*, a friend of Oom Paul's when he was a boy." Then he was silent. It was up to Moolman now. He wondered why he was here, not with the Zoutpansberg Commando.

"I hunt," Moolman said. "I was here selling my ivory but stayed on with a friend, being sure there would be war. I fought the English in '80 too. I was a boy like you then. Do you know what is bad about war, *kêrels?*"

"What?" Servas said. "The danger?"

"No. In danger you forget danger. You fair before and after. The worst thing in war is boredom, day after day doing nothing—just riding about and waiting. Also the food is bad. Also you are not your own master. That is why I hunt. I have no master. You will say you have none. But I say your farm is your master. You think it is yours but it is not so. You belong to the farm, like the rest of the livestock." He laughed at them. He had a good laugh. There was some mockery in it, some bitterness, but it was directed at himself. "I know," he said. "I too had a farm once, and a wife and children. I was respectable man of property. Then it went, they went, everything went, and my heart too. I was on commando. The Kaffirs had been raiding cattle. When I got home nothing was left. My wife and two little boys were dead, horribly dead. I buried what was left of them and became a hunter, a killer of elephants and men. Nothing can hurt me now. There is nothing to fear. I seek death so that I may join those I love. That is Dirk Moolman, the man you ride with."

After his outburst Moolman was silent. He was surprised at himself. What he had said he had never put into words before. He had not even known it of himself. But now that it was out he knew it was true. Francina's death, the mutilated bodies that he had buried in the bush veld, had changed him from a man into a beast. He supposed some men would have killed themselves. He had thought of it, turned the idea over in his mind, and rejected it. Certainly he could farm no more. Not only could a man not farm without a wife, but he had no heart for it, so he had hunted elephants; there was a good living in it and a good chance of getting killed. A hunter's death carried no stigma. He had been out on commando several times since then and had been reprimanded for reckless behavior. But evidently his time had not come yet; perhaps he had been preserved for this war. And what had he done? He smiled sardonically. By God, Dirk, he thought, you've got a couple of sons again. For he knew in his heart these boys were his as surely as if he had sired them. Somehow, by some strange circumstance, a ridiculous relationship had been established in a few minutes between two lost, fatherless young men and a man who had lost his sons.

He turned to the boys. "If you are willing, we will stay together."

Servas looked at Boetie, saw his smile, and said, *"Ja, please let us stay together. We will do what you say."*

So on the road to Pretoria a curious consummation was accomplished, a bond of blood still to be spilled was forged. All is not evil in war. Men can learn to love, as brothers, men they would never have met but for war. There can be much beauty in this love, surpassing that of women, for it is love without lust or possession.

In Pretoria the boys and Moolman found their commando quartered in and about the station. They watered and fed their horses and went downhill to the square. The town seethed like an anthill with men, women, and children, many more women and children than before. They had come to see their men off or go with them. Mevrou Joubert, the commandant general's wife, always accompanied him to war, to cook for him and take care of him. The Van der Bergs saw many men they knew by sight. Moolman met a friend, from the north, a man named Cornelis Nel, who went back to the commando with them.

Nel was a heavy-set dark man of thirty-odd who stood six feet four. He was uncertain of his own age and unable to read or write. He had a big black beard, wore his hair long, and tied it with a thin red ribbon. He said he sometimes parted his great beard and fastened it with ribbons to his hair. His arms were hirsute as a baboon's. Unless excited he was very silent—of a peaceful disposition—very still except for his eyes, which were never still. He too was a hunter and a cattle trader among the Kaffirs of the north, the Bapedi, and even the Matabele.

When they got back they found the two Groenplaas bywoners waiting for them and formed a little group, sharing their food and sleeping in their blankets side by side. Nel, who said he had no friends here, asked if he could stay with them. They were only too pleased, for he was another old campaigner. "My problem," he said, "is to find a horse to carry me." He had one horse, a thickset brown, but he was worried about what he would do if anything happened to him. "Man," he said, "a horse for me is hard to replace."

The organization of the South African force was a loose association in which the men chose their officers and decided for themselves under whom they would serve. A commando consisted of two field kornetcies, each of approximately two hundred men, which was again divided into eight corporalships of approximately 5 men each. But these figures were theoretical. A popular officer might have twice as many men as an unpopular one. Moolman found he knew a corporal named Johannes Brink—a good man, he said—and they decided to serve under him. The group almost at once, since four of them came from the same farm, were known as the Groenplaas Kerels—or "Green Place Boys." Moolman, though he had no official rank, was the leader of the group, and Nel second-in-command. Little groups like theirs were forming everywhere, friends sticking together and pooling their resources, and were recognized as military units. The issue of food was simple. The field kornet knew about how

many men he had, and sent a detail to the food depot
to draw the needed rations, which were loaded on a wagon
and dumped near the men, who then took what whole-
meal flour, sugar, salt, and coffee they needed. The meat
was alive, on the hoof, the cattle being slaughtered as required.

When someone shouted, "Rations up!" Boetie lined up
with the others to get the chunks of raw meat issued by
the *vleeskorporaal*. The flesh corporal was a well-fed man,
like most butchers, and, to avoid anyone's accusing him of
favoring his friends, stood with his wide back to the
burghers and handed out lumps of dripping meat, still
warm from slaughter, to the eager hands that grasped
them. Boetie got a piece of ox neck and Servas some liver.
The others got chunks of fattier flesh.

The eight days' rations they had brought with them, as
they were compelled to do by law, were held in reserve.

Boetie grilled his meat on a forked twig cut from a nearby tree. Moolman had a four-pronged fork made of fencing wire, and impaled a piece of fat and a piece of lean
alternately to make what the Boers called a *bout span*,
the word they used to describe a span of oxen that were
not all the same color.

Moolman taught the boys how to cook the flour they
drew in boiling fat. These delicacies were known as
stormjagers or *maagbommen*, that is to say, storm hunters
because they were rapidly cooked, or stomach bombs,
owing to their effect on the digestion.

This rough food was about all most of them had at
home, and it seemed to satisfy everyone. Everything was
very free and easy. There was no discipline except that
which was self-imposed or imposed by public opinion.
These men wore their own clothes, rode their own hores,
carried their own guns, and received no pay. It was true
that they had been called up, but they were really volunteers, free burghers who felt they had the right to come
and go, choose their leaders, and argue every decision.

The next day was spent in a parade that ended with their
handing in their own rifles and getting new German
Mausers of a Spanish design with five-cartridge, clip-load-
ing magazines.

Hunters like Moolman and Nel were loath to give up

the guns that had served them so well shooting game in the bush veld, but saw the sense of it because, in their corporalship alone, hardly two rifles were of the same make or even caliber.

Much of the evening was spent in discussing the merits of their weapons, and with morning came the order to entrain. The horses were the most trouble, many of them never even having been in a stable or under cover of any kind. But eventually they were loaded, dragged in by their bridles, or with a twitch on an ear or a lip, and pushed from behind. The guns were loaded on flatcars. Ammunition, baggage, and rations were stowed. The train filled up amid shots, shouts, cheers, and the tears of those who had come to see it off. The Transvaal National Anthem was sung by both the soldiers and those they were leaving behind them. And then they were off; the umbilical cord was cut with a whistle and a clash of couplings.

Everyone settled down, the strain of partings over, the uncertainty of where they were going bothering no one. They were on their way somewhere. Gay, filled with ardor as soldiers going to war have always been—playful as boys. Some of the men who came from the town had no training at all, even in horsemanship or the use of a rifle. On the journey Moolman taught the boys what he could of tactics and basic strategy. You are never safe in war, he said, but when you know your trade you are safer and more comfortable than when you don't. Old soldiers are always the last to die.

They rattled and clanked along, stopping for no apparent reason and starting off again with a series of tooth-rattling jolts. They stopped to cook and water the horses once a day, at places where ramps had been built for detraining the animals. On the third day they got to Sandspruit, a few miles from the Natal border. This was as far as the train would take them.

When the horses were detrained and the guns grounded, the commando rode to their halting ground, where they offsaddled and built their cooking fires. When they had eaten they sat about smoking, all but Boetie, who did not smoke yet, and then turned in—rolled in their blankets, their heads on their saddles, to spend the first night, of the many hundred that were to come, sleeping in the open.

Boetie and Servas lay side by side next to the two bywoners; on the outside of the Groenplaas men, one on each flank, were Nel and Moolman. Jonas slept near them.

Boetie stared up at the stars, bright pinpricks in the blue bowl of night. He had slept out before, but never like this, just hunting with his brother—never in the company of thousands of men. Never had he seen so many fires. No voices could be heard clearly, but there was a murmur of sound, hardly audible, but there, like a distant brook, running over stones. The veld for a square mile or more was carpeted with sleeping men, with men sitting by the fires, talking of the past and future. An aura of thought hung over the tall grass heads like an invisible mist. In a day or so there would be no more grass. It would have been trampled down by a thousand feet and ten thousand hoofs, but now, at ground level, turning his head sideways, Boetie saw the grass stems like black spears against the starlit night.

Boetie and Servas woke with the cold of predawn. The sky was dove gray to the east. The sun was coming up over Natal, where the English lay, where they would fight, coming up out of the sea—the Indian Ocean—into which they would drive their enemies. The others, the old campaigners, slept on.

But they were not the only ones. As the gray turned to rose, the boys saw others stirring, young men like themselves who still missed their mothers and their homes. Fires were lit and kettles put on.

"We will make coffee," Servas said, and went to draw water from the water cart. Now as the sun came up the whole camp came to life. They saw the dust of the horse and cattle herds as they were driven to the river to drink.

Only now did they take in the vast camp properly. Yesterday they had been too excited and too tired to do more than just see it with their eyes. It had made little impression on them.

On both sides of the railway line burghers were already camped. The veld was dotted with tents and wagon laagers. Not far from them was a big marquee tent over which the Transvaal Vierkleur floated lazily in the morning breeze. This was Joubert's headquarters. His wife was cooking the general's breakfast.

Jonas fetched their horses from the herd and they rode

over the countryside to see the neighboring camps, to watch more men and horses detrained, and meet the long lines of dusty men and horses that were riding in from the countryside. For ten days they lay there.

It was said that there were fifteen thousand horsemen here ready to ride into Natal. As far as one could see there were men and horses. Surely nothing could stop this flood of men, nothing could prevent their reaching the sea, driving the English like buck before them.

Everywhere groups of men were maneuvering. The sound of shots was continuous as the Boers practiced with their new rifles.

The Boers were spread from horizon to horizon. The air was a blue haze of smoke from a thousand cooking fires that merged into the rusty dust clouds thrown up by the horse herds. Fifteen thousand stallions neighing, shrieking, fighting, grazing, always in movement—being driven to the water and back again, in great patchwork quilts. From a distance they looked like game, their colors merged into a dark, neutral tone. But when they were approached, their infinite variety was apparent. With the coming of the summer they had lost their winter coats and shone like metal in the sunshine. The Groenplaas horses stuck together and were easy to find, with Witbooi, one of the few whites, among them.

Moolman, Servas, and Boetie were watching two stallions fight half-heartedly—half in play and half in anger. "If there were mares here they would kill each other," Moolman said. Mares were property. That was what men and horses fought for. His herd of mares was to a stallion what his farm was to a Boer, his very life, something he must fight to hold. Also there was the show-off part of his nature—his pride, which must be demonstrated in front of a female. Man, horse, or lion. That was a strange thing, how well males got on alone—great *klompies* of them could live together with hardly a serious quarrel till a female came along. Then things changed.

Moolman was thinking of women. A loved and special woman was like a drug to which one became addicted, like drink, like some nectar that, when it was withdrawn, sent men mad, into a fury at God, a fury at everything, into moods that alternated between anger and the greatest melancholy.

Moolman knew himself to be one of the few among all these thousands who did not believe in God. To most Boers, God was all-powerful, omnipresent, and terrible. He had told the Van der Berg boys, in that strange confession of his, that he wished to be killed so that he could join his wife and sons. But was this true? If there were a God and a heaven, they would be there. If there were no afterlife, they would not. What he had meant was that he wished to be where they were. To join them in heaven or in nothingness, at least to quit the world from which they had gone.

Servas and Boetie were happy with Moolman, secure with him, sure that whatever they got into he would get them out of. They did not mind his long silences. The Boers were by nature somewhat taciturn and had a limited vocabulary, their language a mixture of the biblical and bucolic. Solemn sometimes, magnificent in oratory, often crude and earthy. Biblical Dutch blended into the Taal of their home language, a kind of Flemish-German derivative of the Low Countries, from which they came, spiced with Portuguese, carried over from the East Indies by the slaves the Dutch East India Company had brought from there when they first settled the Cape of Storms as a revictualing halfway house to the Orient.

The boys' minds, as yet unformed and inexperienced, worked on reflexes like those of animals. They were aware of things they could neither name nor analyze; of love, of danger, of a coming storm. Living so close to nature, all Boers, except those of the towns, were a part of it, almost psychic in their apprehension. There were real mystics among them. Old General Christiaan de la Rey; Oom Paul, who in his youth, until he felt it sinful and no longer used the gift, had been able to tell where game was long before it was seen. He would say, "Go northeast or southwest and you will find game." Often he even named it. Eland. Wildebeeste, and so on.

Taking his pipe out of his mouth, Moolman turned to them suddenly. "There is something we must do," he said. Two pairs of eyes met his.

"You must train your horses to come to a whistle like mine does."

They did not know his buckskin came to a whistle. They had never seen him call it.

"We have not seen you do it," Boetie said.

"I do not want everyone to know the trick. If everyone whistled the horses would become confused."

They had left their horses with trailing reins behind the crest of the hill on which they sat. This was something Moolman taught them. "Leave the horses, lie down before you reach the top, look well, and if you see nothing, creep over and do not stand up till you are well below the skyline on the other side."

Boer horses were trained to stand if the reins were thrown over their heads. This was done by tying the reins to a heavy weight until they learned not to move.

Moolman whistled one note sounded continuously. He whistled loud so that the sound would carry back over the brow of the hill. A moment later the buckskin's dark nose was nuzzling his back.

"How do you do it?" the boys asked.

"With food. Save little bits of food in your pocket—bread, mealie meal, a little sugar, salt. Then feed it to your horse from your hand and whistle while you do it. The horse learns to associate the sound with the food and hearing the sound comes to seek what goes with it."

They were lucky to be with Moolman. To be a soldier was a new trade. One had to learn it and the better it was learned the better the chance of survival.

Boetie took the New Testament his mother had given him out of his pocket and began to read. Servas went to sleep on his back with his hat over his face. Moolman continued to stroke his horse's nose and stare out over the veld.

If there was a God who watched over every sparrow, why had he let Francina and the boys be killed?

He found no answer.

By now the Groenplaas group had another recruit, a young, newly married man named Jan Beyers of Boskop. He had asked to join them and had been accepted. He was twenty-five, and thought of nothing but his wife. His farm was in the Waterberg near Nylstroom, the village near the little river the Boers had named the Nile when they discovered it, thinking they had discovered its source, since it was the first watercourse they had found in Africa that ran north. This seemed logical to their biblical way of thinking.

There was nothing remarkable about Beyers except his voice. He was a good singer of sad songs. He sang as if his heart would break. And his beard, which was very full for so young a man, and which he combed night and morning. "It was for my beard my wife married me," he said, "my beard of gold, the finest in the Waterberg."

He had a passion for cattle and hated to see a good beast slaughtered for food. Somewhere along the line he had acquired a dog that he called Rand because he had found it, or it had found him, on a ridge. It sat beside him by the fire and slept against him at night. It kept him warm. "*Ja*, man," he said, "it keeps me warm. But not like a young girl. There is nothing as warm as a young girl." No one was prepared to argue with him, certainly neither Boetie nor Servas, who had never known such delights.

Rory O'Brien, the Irishman who had left Blake's Brigade to join them, was twenty-six. He had worked in the mines in Johannesburg and had been brought up on the stories of the famine of '48 and the brutality of the English landlords. His father had brought him to Africa from the old country when he was six. But he remembered it—the green of the Irish fields, the soft, moist beauty of it, the whitewashed cottages, the great hedges of fuchsia that lined the lanes of Kerry. The little black cows and gray-eyed women of Erin were half remembered and half invented, but real to him—as real as his hatred of the English.

"Why did you want to leave the brigade?" Moolman asked him.

"Too many damn Irish," he said. "There it's all Irish. Here I am a rarity. And I don't want to be Irish any more. It's behind me. I want to be a burgher of the republic. So I'd sooner fight the damn English with you." And they had taken him in.

That made the lot of them. Moolman, clean-shaven; Nel, a giant with a coarse black beard and long hair; Japie Beyers with a splendid golden beard; Bothma and Prinsloo with nondescript beards; O'Brien with a black imperial; Servas with a short reddish beard, and Boetie with yellowish fuzz like the down on a peach on his chin and cheeks.

Bearded and beardless the men and boys of Moolman's section, with Jonas the colored boy half servant and half mascot to the lot of them.

On October 10, a glorious day as hot as full summer but with a cool breeze from the south, there was a great parade for the President's birthday.

It was a magnificent sight to see the commandos, one after the other, ride past the commandant general— heavy, gray-bearded, sitting his big black horse beneath an embroidered banner, with his staff behind him.

In columns of four, their rifles held butt on knee, the Boers rode toward the saluting point under the kornets and corporals, but once there, unable to control their enthusiasm, they all shouted and waved their hats and rifles.

Then, having marched past, they formed up again in a series of lines, charged up the slope shouting wildly and cheering as they came to a halt in front of the commandant general.

Joubert addressed the troops. The Groenplaas corporalship was too far back to hear what he said, but the gist of it was passed from mouth to mouth.

An ultimatum had been sent by the presidents of the two republics to the British, giving them twenty-four hours to withdraw their troops from the border. The alternative was war.

The burghers stood up in their stirrups. They shouted and cheered. General Joubert raised his hat. Those who were near enough to see said he had tears in his eyes. Then, as the men became too hoarse to shout any more, he turned his horse and rode back to his tent, to his old wife and the coffee she would have ready for him.

The excitement continued till dawn; all around the Pretoria Commando the fires of the other camps burned bright as candles in the dark, with the noise of men shouting and singing there was no chance of sleep, so they discussed the enemy, their position, strength, and the chances and hazards of war.

Next day the English accepted the challenge. There was more excitement, more speeches were made. General Joubert commended the men to God, assured them that He was with His chosen people, and that right, unquestioned right, was on their side. Five days' rations of meal and biltong were issued. The transport wagons were to be laagered and left behind.

The Boer War had begun.

With a splendid gesture, this tiny nation of "do it yourself" soldiers rode into Natal to face the might of the British Empire.

It was October 11.

CHAPTER 6

GOD'S FINGER

VOLKSRUST was reached by early afternoon. Here the force was split up, and the Pretoria Commando joined General van der Merwe's force of fifteen hundred men. Servas, who was sent to him with a message by his corporal, described him as a tall, saturnine, dark-complexioned man dressed in a black claw-hammer coat and wearing a low top hat trimmed with black crepe. This, as they were to find out later when they saw more of them, was the usual garb of a Boer general. The men looked like the farmers that they were, and the generals like church wardens at a funeral. No wonder the British were contemptuous of them.

That night it rained. Shivering, without tents, they made a poor best of it, sitting on the low ant heaps that abounded to keep their bottoms dry, or, lying down, tried to sleep in the mud. It was a matter of taste. Moolman sat, the others lay. It was still raining when dawn broke, so there were no fires and no coffee. They moved off, soaked to the skin, tired and dispirited.

"You see," Moolman said, "this is war: discomfort, cold, boredom, hunger." He laughed at Boetie. "Cheer up. Before long you'll look back on this night with regret. Things can always be worse. We are all well and our horses are sound."

They were going through the mountains. The rain came down in torrents. It ran off the sides of the hills as if it was being poured onto their crests out of a kettle. The road was a flood of red-brown water up to the horse's pasterns.

Then the sun came up and its heat brought on a mist so thick that they moved through it like ghosts, the horses almost invisible but for their heads in the white blanket that rose up from the steaming ground. That night it rained again, and again there were no fires, no cooking, and no coffee. Supper was biltong from the saddlebags and a handful of uncooked meal. To add to their discomfort, a bitter wind blew up from the Drakensberg Mountains— the dragon mountains—which are the backbone of South Africa.

Next day it cleared, and before long they saw the plains of Natal lying spread out below them, with the Buffalo River a silver ribbon running between low rolling hills. This was the Promised Land, Natal, which had been stolen from their fathers by the English.

That night they camped on the hills near Newcastle, and their fires—at last there were fires—burned like stars on every hill.

In the morning they rode through the village, passing the sullen English inhabitants who lined the streets to wish them ill. Most of the day was spent halted, and another night march was ordered.

By now the army had closed in again, having come through the mountain passes, and a pincer movement around Dundee was planned. In the black of night they marched through broken, muddy country that was occasionally lit by the flashes of lightning, and finally arrived at the foot of a mountain, which they climbed, leaving their horses behind them.

From this mountain, when they took it, they would be able to look down on the British camp below.

"It will be held," Moolman said.

Nel, who was beside him, laughed. "But we will take it."

Boetie felt Servas grasp his arm as if to give him strength.

"I am not afraid," he said, and he wasn't, not very afraid. Now that he must do it he felt he could, as excitement mastered him. He felt his blood hammering in his veins as he climbed, expecting to be fired on at any moment. At last, ready for anything, they reached the top and there was nothing. The wide, flat top of the mountain was deserted.

It was again pouring with rain. Everyone stood about. No one knew what to do. The letdown, when keyed for action, struck them like a blow. At dawn the rain ceased and the mountaintop became shrouded with mist through which the men moved belly deep. When asked for orders Van der Merwe was silent. They could not see fifty yards, but could hear the English below them. They heard shouts and the rumbling of wagons. Surely they would be led down to attack. But no order was given. Suddenly there was the sound of gunfire, and the sharp rattle of rifle shots.

Boetie thought his heart would leap out of his body. This was his first sound of war. Any moment now he would be in it, immersed in action as if it were an element like water. They heard the rat-tat-tat of a Maxim. But the action was all taking place to a flank. Nothing happened in their vicinity. Suddenly Nel shouted, "Look back there!"

Across the plain they had crossed in the dark, in the bright sunlight that had burned away the ground mist, they saw three hundred British horsemen, the first enemy they had laid eyes on. No one could understand how they came to be in the rear of the whole Boer army, with thousands of horsemen between them and their main force. Had the mist held they might have made it. But Boers began galloping toward them, firing from the saddle and driving them before them as if they were sheep, away from their own people.

"Come on!" Moolman shouted as he led the Groenplaas men leaping down the mountain, up to their horses. They galloped toward the English, who had decided to make a stand at a farm.

The English bullets began to whistle around them. Some high ones cracked like whips, some sounding like hornets hissed past them or landed in the ground, throwing up little spurts of dust. There was nothing to see but an occasional glimpse of a khaki helmet. It was like riding toward a nest of angry insects that got more plentiful and furious as they approached.

Jan Bothma was hit in the arm as they crossed a spruit. They left their horses with him and went on. A

Creusot gun began to shell the English and a white flag
went up.

On the stoep of the farmhouse was their commanding
officer—Colonel Moller. That the English were dressed
in khaki instead of the red coats disappointed Boetie
very much. The English had worn red coats in 1880,
much to the joy of the Boers, for in red coats with white
crossbelts they made splendid marks.

There were some dead. Neither Servas nor Boetie had
seen dead men before. There was something revolting
about their white faces, staring eyes, and sagging jaws.
They looked like big broken dolls, like something thrown
away. Big patches of blood, brown on their khaki uniforms, looked like spilled gravy. There was no dignity
in death. But Boetie was happy. He shook hands with his
brother as if they had been parted, as indeed they had,
for all men in battle are alone. "Now we have been in
action, *jong*," he said. "I was not as afraid as I thought
I should be."

"There was no time to be afraid," Servas said as they
rode back to the commando.

The Boers' encircling movement had failed and the
English had retreated to Ladysmith.

Next day Moolman was told to take his men into Dundee but to exercise caution. There might still be a rear
guard there. But before they reached the town the rest
of Van der Merwe's commando caught up with them and
they all galloped in together.

This was the first English town they had taken. They
swarmed over it like baboons, smashing windows, looting the shops, and throwing things into the street. Caught
in the hysteria, Boetie and Servas were as bad as any.
They knew they could carry nothing away with them, but
gave way to these instincts of destruction that are the
heritage of a prehuman past. Boetie opened drawers full
of ladies' underclothes and examined them. They were
the first, other than his sister's hanging on the washing
line, that he had ever seen. Drawers edged with lace that
had ribbons threaded through them—some pink, some
blue, some white. There were silk stockings. These he
had never seen before, and shoes with high heels.

On the outskirts of the town there was a large military

camp with great stocks of canned food, streets of tents filled with camp beds, blankets, and sleeping bags. The commando collected enough food for a tremendous feast. They took clean shirts and socks and an extra blanket each. After living on half-cured, that is to say, half-rotten, biltong for days, the English army food seemed wonderful. What was wonderful, as Moolman pointed out, was the lack of mobility of the English forces owing to all these luxuries, which they regarded as necessities. Perhaps the most curious of these were some crates of ladies' saddles. These, with their two crotches, the Boers could not figure out at all till one of the more sophisticated explained their use. Saddles for girls. What girls? Did they imagine Boer girls would use them? Go riding with them? Were they so sure of victory?

Moolman and Nel did no looting, but amused themselves watching the others. It took several hours for General van der Merwe to restore order and resume the trek to Ladysmith. They camped ten miles from the town, with the commandos strung like pearls on a string around it. With darkness the pearls burst into a thousand flames as the Boers' cooking fires were lit.

It was here they got news of the Elandslaagte disaster, where the Johannesburg Commando under Viljoen had been routed by the British cavalry, who charged them with lance and saber.

"Sticking us like pigs as we ran, chopping off arms and legs as if we were not human beings," a man who had been there said. The only previous experience any Boer had of the *arme blanche* had been a Kaffir spear, a very different thing from the thundering hoofs of charging lancers and dragoons.

The Boers moved forward next day. Thousands of horsemen breasted the slopes that surrounded the town almost simultaneously—a splendid sight that warmed Boetie's heart as he watched the English soldiers nervously building redoubts and trenches. But there was no action. That day neither side seemed eager to come to grips.

The Boers took possession of two heights. Bulsana Kop and Lombaards Kop. They also held a line from Pepworth Hill to Nicholson's Neck.

It was thought that the British had some ten thousand

to twelve thousand men in Ladysmith, including those
who had returned from Dundee, leaving their stores behind them.

The Pretoria Commando was ordered to Pepworth Hill
and set to work entrenching itself. As the sun rose they saw
the English on top of Nicholson's Neck. They were building sangars of stone. Although they were out of accurate
range the Boers shot at them and the sound of the shots
roused the Boers who occupied the forward crest that
overlooked the plain. Then the Free State Commandos
attacked the English. In a countermove several columns
of English infantry, enveloped in clouds of dust, came out
of Ladysmith toward Pepworth Hill. A Creusot Long
Tom (six-inch gun) and some smaller guns that had been
mounted by the Staats Artillery began to fire, the shells exploding among the English, sending up pillars of earth
that grew like trees out of the ground but failed to stop
the advancing troops.

As if it was only a spectacle Servas and Boetie watched
the battle develop below them. Soldiers no bigger than
match heads deployed, advanced, and fell dead or
wounded as the Boer guns took effect. Tiny batteries of
horse artillery—toy guns—were galloped up, unlimbered,
and went into action, the teams galloping back to safety.
It was all quite unreal until suddenly English shells began
to explode around them on Pepworth Hill.

This was something new to the Boers, even veterans
were shaken by the noise of the bursting shells, the yellow clouds of smoke and the smell of lyddite. The noise
was unbelievable. Thousands of rifles were being fired.
The Boer guns were being fired from behind them, their
shells screaming like trains through the air. The English
covering fire became fiercer. But as they approached more
and more men fell, and before the English got to within
a thousand yards so many were down that they hesitated
to face this rain of bullets and came to a halt.

Boetie's rifle was hot in his hand. His shoulder was
bruised by the recoil of the many rounds he had fired.
His mind was curiously blank, empty of content. He just
lay there, reloading clip after clip, firing at individual
Englishmen, concentrating on one till he stopped him,
either wounded, dead, or hiding behind an ant heap,
afraid to continue his advance.

Boetie looked at the men about him as they moved forward. Their faces had changed since the order had been given. They were hard, as if carved out of some close-grained, dark brown wood. He ran his left hand over his own face. It felt strange to him. He knew it must resemble the faces of those about him. This was the face that men put on to conquer fear—a mask of iron that disguised all feeling, even to themselves. He felt that he was no longer there, that he was an observer, more than ever conscious of the beauty of the scene about him; of the rolling hills spotted with patches of dark thorn; of the olive-green veld; of the blue sky; of the aak-aak of a korhaan—the bustard—that rose vertically in front of them, disturbed by the battle. The very stones at his feet assumed a curious importance as if each said, "Observe me. You may never see the like of us again. We are Africa, we are your land, we are what you are fighting for." So were the rough red patches of dolomite and the harsh tufts of last year's grass that crunched beneath his feet. He thought of his pony in the safety of the valley behind them. How much easier it was to be brave on the back of a good horse! You were never alone on a horse. I am afraid, he thought. But also I am not afraid, because I am not here. I stand afar, watching this line of Boers advance, watching Boetie—young Louis van der Berg—moving forward and wondering how he will take it.

There was a sharp crackle of fire from a *kopje* on their right, a sound like the crack of a whip as a bullet passed him. Bullets were hitting the ground in front of them, sending up little spurts of dust and hitting rocks with the violence of hammers. The English had not got their range yet, and were firing short. A hundred yards away he saw a tall Boer spin around and fall. Another man staggered and fell to his knees. He saw a battery of artillery gallop up and open fire before the teams of horses were clear. None of it was real. None of this was happening. How could these little men, the size of ants, hurt him?

Shells began to burst about them. They had the range. "Get down!" Moolman shouted. "Get down and open up on them."

Now it was real. There was an object again, a target. The rifle lived in his hand as it recoiled with the explosion of each shot he fired. There was something beautiful in its power, in the smooth working of the action. Fear had left him with the first round he fired. With a weapon like this in his hand, what was there to fear? A sense of strength overwhelmed him as his fingers pressed the trigger. Moolman, lying beside him, said, "Good lad. Take it quietly. There is nothing to fear. They cannot shoot like us."

The Boer shells were screaming over them. Three of the British guns were knocked out. They were good men, those Staats Artillerymen.

The British teams were coming back at the gallop to get the guns. Boetie saw a direct hit on one team. The men and horses disintegrated in a cushion of dust. Two horses were dead, the others seemed to be wounded. One of the drivers who was unhurt was cutting a horse loose of its harness. Two other guns were being galloped away, their limbers bouncing behind them. The lone soldier was still occupied with his wounded horses. No one fired at him. He must have loved them, Boetie thought. Moolman must have thought the same. "He could have left them," he said.

The English were getting the worst of it, for the Free Staters were among the best shots in an army of good shots. The moment an English soldier put up his head to shoot he was hit.

It was terrible to Boetie to hear the smack of a bullet hitting a human skull. The English were driven slowly back. As they advanced the Boers came upon the English dead and wounded. There was one behind almost every rock. At last, when the sun was high, casting no shadows, a bugle sounded over the noises of battle. Clear and clean as the crow of a cock in the morning. A white flag was put up and hundreds of Englishmen, their rifles at the trail, walked toward the Boers. One thousand prisoners were taken. They were Irishmen, their regiment the Dublin Fusiliers. The Boer commander of this little battle, a small segment of the whole engagement, was Commandant Mentz of the Heilbron Commando. But the man who had led the fight was Field Kornet Adriaan de la Rey, the member of the Raad who had been against the war and had stood up to Paul Kruger and the war party. Boetie had seen him in the action, moving from point to point quite fearlessly, as he encouraged his men—a man with dark, fierce eyes who seemed inspired.

After the surrender Boetie and Servas were talking to the captured officers. They were the only two who spoke good English in the corporalship.

"Your men can certainly shoot," one of them, who was tying a bandage around his leg, said.

"Yes, we can shoot," Servas said.

"You know," the Englishman said, "we didn't think you could shoot any more. Not like your fathers did in the eighties. That's what we were told. They said now that there is so little big game left you would have forgotten."

Moolman, his eyes blazing, said, "Why should we forget? There is our land and there are still the English and the Kaffirs who wish to take it."

"I did not know you spoke English," Servas said.

"I don't," Moolman replied. "It is a *verdomde* tongue. I know it but I will not speak it unless I must."

There was a cry from another officer, a captain.

"Good God! Just look at that!"

They looked where he pointed, and there, enveloped in a great cloak of dust, was the rest of the British force in full retreat.

Dead and wounded soldiers lay all around on the veld. Some sat propped against boulders, dragged there by their companions. Medical orderlies were giving what help they could. Most bore their injuries bravely without a whimper. But some moaned, and a boy who seemed to be about Boetie's age held his side and cried, "Mother, Mother." All seemed surprised at the outcome of the engagement. The officer to whom Servas was talking said, "We never thought you could face regular troops, with no discipline, no proper officers and no uniforms."

"Well, you know now," Servas said.

Then a man dressed as a Boer burst into a great cry. "Mother of God," he said, "the Dublin Fusiliers. Our own boys. Jesus and Mary, we've been a-killing of our own boys." It was Rory O'Brien, the Irish Volunteer. This was something he had not foreseen, something his hatred of the English had got him into.

The Boers were helping the British troops with their wounded, giving them water from their bottles and helping to bandage them.

Not one man of Moolman's group had been hit but
Bothma. The Free Staters had nine dead and fifteen
wounded. The English had lost two hundred killed and at
least as many wounded.

Boetie felt himself a veteran, a real Boer, a man who
had seen war and killed men before he was seventeen.
This had been a battle, not a skirmish. They had beaten
the English and the war was almost won. If I had waited,
he thought, it would all have been over before I was called
up.

What surprised him most was the mess on the battlefield. Not only the scattered dead, but the equipment, the
bloodstained bandages, the contents of the dead men's
packs scattered by the action. How could there be so
much paper on a battlefield? Letters, pay books, photo-
graphs of women and children, and newspapers littered
the veld.

The English were in full retreat. When were they going
to get the order to follow them?

Boetie looked at the battlefield again. Ma would not like
this, he thought. She would not like the bodies and the
blood. She would not . . . she was so tidy.

He turned to Servas and said, "Our ma would not like
this," and began to laugh, to laugh till tears came to his
eyes, and then he cried, the laughter and tears coming
together. "Ma," he said. Before God, how he wanted his
mother. It was nonsense to think he was a man just because he had been in a battle. He was a boy. A boy. A
boy.

Moolman slapped him. "Shut up," he said. "You have
done well. You are a man today."

Only now that the firing had died down and his blood
no longer thundered in his ears did Boetie hear the moans
of the wounded and their cries for water. A soldier near
him was holding a wound with his hand. The blood
spurted between his fingers. "Mother of God," he said,
"Mother of God, Jesus Mary, hasn't anyone got a dressing?"

The Boers were gaping with amazement. General White
had retreated without firing another shot. The English
who had marched out of Ladysmith were marching back
again, with ten thousand men unblooded.

"Magtig," Moolman said, "now we have them—they are ours." They ran for their horses and rode back to the main force, eager to be in at the death—in the wild, charging battle that would end the war.

They found Boers massed and ready to go, just waiting for the order.

General Joubert, his head sunk on his chest, sat on his black horse staring at nothing, with his staff, mostly relations, around him. He was near the Pretoria Commando. Boetie could see him clearly and hear what was being said.

A dozen field kornets who were strangers to him were urging Joubert to attack, to ram the victory home, for it was victory, and turn the retreat into a rout. "Let loose your riders. For God's sake, loose your riders," the kornets said, echoing each other.

For a while Joubert said nothing, sitting heavily hunched on his horse. At last he said, "I will not go on. When God gives you His finger it is wrong to take the whole of His hand."

Adriaan de la Rey, the hero of the little battle they had just left, rode his chestnut almost into the general's black and cried, "For the sake of God, *los jou ruiters. Los jou ruiters.* Loose your riders, in the name of God."

The others echoed him, more boldly now that they had a leader, but he was the most urgent and trembled with rage. His feelings were those of the burghers. If he had charged, shouting, "Follow me!" they would have followed him. But that was not the Boer way. He, the man who had pleaded with the President in the Raad, against the war, was now pleading again. First he had wanted to stop the war's beginning. Now that it had begun he wanted to end it with a great British defeat.

But the commandant general remained unmoved.

Restlessness swept over the whole Boer force. Every moment counted. The horses, sensing their riders' excitement, reared and neighed, eager to be off.

No order came.

"Loose your riders," De la Rey cried once more.

"Loose us. Let us go!" the burghers echoed.

All the commandant general did was to say again, "When God gives you a finger you do not take the whole of His hand."

And the horsemen, who had waited trembling, eager as hounds to go, now sat watching the British escape. This they felt had been their great chance. God had delivered the Philistines into their hands. They could have swept them into the sea. But Joubert had misinterpreted God's message. He had only taken God's finger when he had been offered the whole hand.

He had sat still with fifteen thousand riders behind him watching the English go in a retreat that by a single word could have been turned into a rout.

Ja, Boetie thought, our ma was right. He is too old. But another chance would come. God had shown them whose side he was on.

PART TWO

THE HEART OF EMPIRE

*In London the Heart of Empire
beat faster. Rudyard Kipling was
in full and heartening cry.*

[England—August to November 1899—Fall]

CHAPTER 7

THE ENGLISH CAPTAIN

Captain John Elphinstone Turnbull of Queens Own 2nd Hussars was hot and bad-tempered. He hated London in August. He should have been on leave shooting grouse on the moors in Scotland. This was what most of the upper class, the landed gentry of England, were doing. For the first week of August, Euston Station was alive with men in tweeds, with valets in bowlers, with dogs—flat-coated retrievers, curly-coated retrievers and spaniels —the platform piled with leather gun cases and with ammunition boxes. Grouse shooting began on the twelfth and with it the London season ended. No one was left in London, though except in Belgravia and Mayfair this was hardly noticeable.

The thermometer stood at eighty, and eighty in London was a heat wave. The trees in the park looked tired. They drooped as if exhausted by carrying the heavy dress of their foliage for so long, as if they looked forward to the autumn, when they could drop their clothes at their feet and stand naked, waiting for the cool hand of winter.

In the Transvaal it would be cold now, rainless, clear, with occasional bitter winds sweeping across the high veld from the south. The country would be parched, the tall grass as yellow as straw, the rivers almost or completely dry.

And that was why Turnbull was here, supposedly an expert on South Africa—in London in August, seconded from his regiment in Colchester. There in the cavalry barracks a few officers would be in charge—the rest were in Scotland. He thought of the moors, the butts. That's where he ought to have been with his pair of Holland & Holland guns, with his loader behind him, and Queenie, his flat-coated bitch, at his feet, while they waited for driven birds. But he was one of the few officers in the British Army who

knew the Transvaal and the Boers. He had been engaged
to a Boer girl who had died. And because of it he was
working at the War Office—a desk wallah. A number of
British officers had married Dutch South African girls
when they were stationed at the Cape, but they had been
Anglicized, some of them had been at school in England
and finished in Paris, Brussels, or Lausanne.

Elsa had not been like that. That had been her charm,
her utter naturalness, her goodness, her complete incapac-
ity for doing harm. He had never been in love before, and
had hardly really looked at a woman since, though plenty,
both married and unmarried, had thrown themselves at
him. Every so often he visited a discreet house in Bays-
water that was very popular with the cavalry for an hour
or two. Mrs. Fitzherbert—of course that was not her real
name—ran the place well. The girls were young, clean,
and gay, the wine expensive but good. So were the girls.
But they never seemed real to him. Pretty, beautiful—
dressed or undressed—they were toys that served their
specific purpose. That they might have lives of their own,
mothers, fathers, homes, or interests, never occurred to
him. He never wondered how they got there or where
they would end. Girls had little protection in England.
Gin-soaked mothers still sold their daughters into prostitution, though things were better than they had been a few
years ago. He knew men who went to places where no girl
was over fourteen. He knew of men who were reported to
pay high prices for virgins, and was revolted by it, as he
was revolted by men who were bad horse masters and
knocked their hunters about. But that any of these girls
could have anything in common with Elsa, or with the
girls and women of his own class, was beyond his compre-
hension. Insulated by wealth and upbringing, he regarded
them as something completely apart.

In those hypocritical late Victorian days there were only
good women and bad. A divorced woman was cast out
of society. It was less a matter of having committed adultery than having been found out. Adultery was common.
At most of the great weekend house parties there was a
great deal of stepping into and out of other people's bedrooms. But it was secret, guessed at by intimate friends;
known only to the chambermaids who did the rooms.
They knew the signs and looked for them. They were the

basis of most of the gossip in the servants' halls of England. Who slept with whom and when? The chambermaids, the ladies' maids, and valets all had stories to tell about the men and women they served.

In the center of this web many a butler, sitting in his pantry, wove a pattern of gossip into a blanket of possible blackmail. Many a man who set himself up letting chambers to bachelors in the West End had been a butler once.

Turnbull's mind went back to his love, to Elsa. To his astonishment when he had met her. Within a few minutes his life had been changed. He had arranged to stay on in the north when the rest of the mission returned to the Cape. He had done some shooting, that was his excuse, and had courted Elsa. The world had been more beautiful than he had ever known it before, the sunshine brighter, the scent of the flowers sweeter, the song of the birds more poignant, just because of her.

Then a boy had come on a sweating horse with the message from her mother—a letter. "Come at once. Elsa is ill." Within fifteen minutes they were on their way, galloping hard. He had given the boy a fresh horse, but they had got there too late. Elsa, his little dark-haired girl, was dead, her brown eyes closed. He had stood there beside her bed with her mother and Servas. Boetie, his little friend, had refused to come in.

It had been summer. December 15. Ten hot days before Christmas.

"She will be buried tomorrow," Catalina had said when he asked. "At eleven o'clock."

At eleven o'clock on December 16—Dingaan's Day—the great Boer festival that celebrates the defeat of the Zulus and the breaking of their power.

"I will be there," he said as he pressed her mother's hand, squeezed Boetie's shoulder, and said good-by to Servas. Then he had gone, riding back slowly through the dusk. He had watched the great African moon, red as blood, come up from behind the hills and turn slowly white. He had gone on up the road, through a black world bathed in moonlight. Last full moon he had walked among the violets with Elsa, talking of their marriage. It was to have taken place at the church in Wynberg. The whole family would come down to the Cape. A military wedding. They were to have come out of the church to the waiting carriage beneath an arch of swords, down an alley whose walls would have been his brother officers, its roof a ceiling of bright steel. This she wanted badly.

"I have never seen you in uniform," she said, clasping her hands together. And now it was too late.

Next day the few people who were about in Pretoria at six-thirty in the morning stopped in astonishment to see a captain of hussars in full uniform, his saber at his side, his saber tache dangling from his belt, his plumed busby on his head, riding a splendid dark-brown charger slowly down the street. From the horse's headstall a scarlet fox-tail dangled. The brasswork of the saddlery shone like gold. The curb chain and bit jingled as the big horse, his belly full of corn, pranced, angry at this restraint.

He knew it was against the law, against every regulation, for an officer to wear uniform in a foreign state. But he had not cared. It was his method of showing respect, of showing the dead what he had not been able to show the living. He had been up much of the night polishing his gear. Full dress and horses had been brought up by all the officers in the mission in case they might be needed for some official function, as if fine feathers such as these would impress the Boers. For even then there had been trouble pending.

As a soldier he welcomed war, but not one against his friends. All soldiers, before the present era, welcomed the excitement and the possibilities of decoration and promotion. A peacetime army was static; promotion came slowly with the retirement or death of senior officers. In war promotion was accelerated.

A regiment was like a family of brothers whose father was the colonel. No one could wish for the death of a brother, but should he die the inheritance might be promotion. Besides, a regiment was a tool forged for war, a composite weapon of squadrons and troops that was built for use, eager for more glory, for more battle honors on the standard; the first, in the 2nd Hussars, was Blenheim, and the last Balaclava. The 2nd had been in the Light Brigade. Only twenty men had reached the Russian guns. Only eight had survived, and no officers.

When he got to Groenplaas he had handed his horse

over to a popeyed stable boy and gone into the house, his sword under his arm, his busby in his hand, the rowels of his spurs clinking with every step. The yard had been full of Cape carts, tied horses, and the colored boys who had come with their masters.

They were waiting. The coffin, a deal box mounted on two trestles, was covered with bunches of flowers and homemade wreaths of roses, violets, and lilies. The perfume of the roses was very strong. Every time he smelled a rose it all came back to him. Mixed with the roses was the smell of Sunday clothes, of black that always seemed to have an odor of its own, of people—of sweat, their personal smells, the odor of humanity and naphtha. Except for Cátalina there were no women. In South Africa women did not attend funerals.

No one spoke. Servas had taken the head of the coffin, and Klaas, the old Kaffir, the foot. Mrs. Van der Berg and he walked behind it with Boetie crying quietly between them. Behind them came the two bywoners, the sharecropping foremen, and the other mourners. It was Jan Bothma who had made the coffin out of planks that had been destined for a new wagon bed. Behind the white people came the Kaffirs—the house servants first, then the stable and boss boys, then the farm workers, who were followed by their women and children.

In front, leading the procession to the farm graveyard, was the predicant, dressed in black with a white tie. His head bowed as he read from a little prayer book in High Dutch. The grave had been dug the previous day. Turnbull remembered thinking how deep the topsoil was—more than four feet of black alluvial loam lay over the yellow gravelly clay.

The graveyard was among the trees—syringas, chinaberries—that dappled it with leopard shade. Elsa would lie here with her grandfather and grandmother. There was a stone with her father's name on it, the dates of his birth and death, but no body. Petrus van der Berg lay in the northern bushveld where he had died, near a giant cream-of-tartar tree.

The coffin was lowered into the grave by Servas, Klaas, and the two foremen. The servants and farm workers filed by and threw in the bunches of common flowers they had picked. The mourners each in turn dropped a handful of earth upon the flowers as the predicant began to read the service. . . . The doves in the trees cooed as if they too were sad. But doves always sounded sad. The predicant closed his book. Servas, Boetie, and the foremen took the spades the boys had been carrying and filled in the grave.

Then they had gone back to the house to eat. Catalina and the servants must have been up all night to prepare the feast—hams, suckling pigs, chickens, with tarts and *konfyts*.

This was the Boer tradition of hospitality, a breaking of ceremonial bread to welcome a new baby into the world or to speed a departing soul.

They stood as the predicant said grace, and then everyone helped himself from the trestle tables set up under the trees in the yard.

Turnbull had looked like a peacock among crows, with his blue-frogged tunic and dark red breeches with a canary stripe, his sword, boots, and spurs. But they knew him, or many of them did, and knew why he was here dressed as he was. These people hated the English, but not all Englishmen. Only a few of the most bitter mumbled that this was judgment—that God had taken this young Boer maid to his bosom rather than see her lie in wedlock with this rooinek soldier.

At Wynberg he had asked for more leave and gone back to England. Six months later, the regiment, its tour of foreign duty over, had come back and he had rejoined it.

And now, when the past was buried, softened by time, it was being dug up again as he worked at Whitehall trying to correct the impressions the top brass had of the Boers and the terrain over which the war, if it came to war, would be fought.

In June, when he had presented himself at the War Office, he found that there was no general staff. There were no accurate maps. A handful of officers were responsible for the intelligence service of the entire colonial empire. The infantry were trained to fire in volleys because it was by volleys they had defeated Napoleon at Waterloo. For a war that would inevitably be fought by cavalry, the army had only sixteen thousand sets of saddlery, with under five hundred in reserve.

Only recently had breechloader guns and magazine rifles come into use. They had not existed in the Crimea. There

were also machine guns—Maxims, as they were called—
and some junior officers were being trained in their use, but
there were too few of them.

No one believed him when he talked of Boer mobility
or the accuracy of their shooting. The Boer military system of commandos seemed laughable to the regular soldiers of that day. The cavalry, his own hussars included,
now carried carbines. This was a concession to modernity,
but reliance was still placed on the *arme blanche*—the
white weapons of lance and saber. This time the army was,
at least, not going to be dressed in red tunics and blue
trousers as it had been in the first Boer war. They were
going to wear khaki—such as was worn by the Indian
troops in the field. The name came from a Persian word
that meant dust.

There were some other inventions that would be tried
out somewhat hesitantly. Shrapnel had been invented by a
lieutenant of that name, and a Scots Presbyterian minister
called Forsyth had perfected a chemical detonator that
made the cartridge possible. Smokeless powder was new,
too. But none of these weapons had really been tried out,
and the Boer war, which daily seemed more and more inevitable, would be their great testing ground.

The infantry was armed with Lee-Enfields or Lee-
Metfords Mark Two, capable of rapid fire, the only difference between the two being in the rifling. It was in
general believed that this deadly array of modern weapons
was capable of dealing with any enemy, and certainly of
overcoming a rabble of peasant farmers.

No one even believed in the efficiency of the German-
trained Staats Artillery. No one believed anything he told
them. Above all, no one believed that these new weapons
required new tactical concepts, or that this war could
not be fought as the Crimean War had been forty-three
years ago. Nor would anyone believe that mounted troops
were essential to deal with the Boers, and when the self-
governing colonies offered to send men, the War Office,
which liked only regulars, showed little enthusiasm and
stressed "unmounted preferred." This, for the only other
people in the world who could ride and shoot like the
Boers themselves—the British colonials.

This refusal to believe what he told them accounted for
John Turnbull's temper as much as did the heat and miss-

ing the shooting in Scotland, which was reported in the *Times* as being exceptionally good. He was a rarity—a keen and dedicated soldier.

Walking down the Mall, he almost laughed as he thought of his father's conversation with Hiram Maxim. The old man had been talking about his invention of the machine gun.

His father had said, "But this is a most terrible and inhuman weapon. Men will be mown down like sheaves of wheat."

"That's it," Maxim had said, smiling. "It's so terrible that war will no longer be possible."

August 1899, two years after the Queen's Jubilee, was the height of Britain's power, its very apogee. (The only other great powers were France, Germany, and Russia.)

But times were changing. Not merely in new armaments. The "week-end" had come in. African gold and diamond magnates had set up establishments of unbelievable grandeur in Park Lane. Some of them were Jews. People smoked cigarettes, a habit the army had brought back from Egypt. A vulgarizing process had begun. Bicycles were the rage. Women, the "new women," rode them, shamelessly, in bloomers.

This was the time of Oscar Wilde, Huxley, Millais, Leighton, Burne-Jones, Kipling, Pushkin, Arnold, Morris, Landseer, Tod Sloan, Sigmund Freud, Buffalo Bill, Swinburne, and Darwin. All were alive or newly dead, their influence a living thing in this society, which, having reached its maturity, was about to begin its slow decline. From empire to commonwealth. The common man and the black man would come into their own in Turnbull's lifetime. Czars, kaisers, sultans, kings, and rajahs would topple like ninepins from their thrones. Pomp, ceremony, and manners would be lost in the chaos of equality. There would be great social gains, but these had to be balanced against the losses. There were already some motorcars, electric lights, telephones, none of them very efficient yet, but there, and improving daily.

The streets were filled with horse-drawn vehicles: vans, buses, drays, butchers' traps, cabs, and hansoms. Private carriages drawn by magnificently matched pairs that showed the status of their owners. The smarter and faster the horses, the faster and smarter their possessors. The coachmen and grooms of commissioned officers wore black cockades on their top hats. Those entitled to a coat of arms had it discreetly painted on the doors of their carriages. This was a period of snobbery, extravagance, and immense wealth. The gentleman, the horse, and the common sparrow still lived in symbiotic association.

CHAPTER 8

GOD BLESS ELSIE

ANYONE seeing John Turnbull walking back from the Horse Guards would have known him for what he was. A soldier in plain clothes, with a bowler hat, a black jacket, striped trousers, gray spats over buttoned boots, a gray silk ascot tie with a pearl pin, a dark red carnation in his buttonhole, and a neatly furled umbrella. He might have been a senior civil servant. That was till you saw his back. It was straight, a soldier's back up to the shoulder. Then it took a cavalry stoop. The shoulders sloped forward at an angle, bent by hours spent in the saddle. This was confirmed when he went down any stairs. He went down sideways. Even in civilian clothes he wore spiritual spurs.

It was a pleasant walk to Albany, but he was preoccupied. He could not help worrying about the Van der Bergs, the boys who would have been his brothers-in-law. What would happen to them if there were war?

When he opened his front door, his man Vincent was waiting for him.

"I was waiting for you, sir."

"So I see."

"There's a young person here."

"Person?"

"A young female, sir. Sit down, sir," he said as he took the hat and umbrella and gloves. "I'll get you a brandy and soda, sir."

He brought them on a silver salver.

"Well?" Turnbull said.

"I've got her in the kitchen, sir."

"Well, let her out. We'd better see what it is all about."

"It's not very nice, sir. I mean to say . . ."

"Bring her in, Vincent."

Vincent left the room. Turnbull heard him say, "Come this way," and a moment later the young person, a very pretty dark girl in a big hat with a black ostrich feather and wearing a black dress and shoes, came in. He could not place her, but she seemed familiar.

"You can go, Vincent," he said.

"I don't think so, sir," Vincent said. "You might want a witness. Not that I couldn't lie, sir, for you, that is, but I prefers not to." When he was upset Vincent's English lapsed.

"All right," Turnbull said, and turned to the girl. "What can I do for you, young lady?" he asked.

"I'm Elsie," she said.

"Elsie who?"

"Just Elsie. Elsie from Mrs. Fitzherbert's. You've slept with me five times, sir. You always ask for me."

"The little dark one. So that's who you are."

"That's it, sir," she said.

"And . . . ?"

"And I've come for help, sir. You're the only one that ever treated me decent."

"So decent I didn't even know your name?" Or recognize her, he thought, with her clothes on. "Sit down," he said, "and tell me your troubles. Give her a brandy, Vincent, and have one yourself."

"Thank you, sir," Vincent said as he poured out the drinks.

"Would you like a cigarette, Elsie?" Girls of her kind smoked, he knew.

"Thank you," she said.

"Get the cigarettes, Vincent." Vincent got the cigarettes. She took one and he lit it for her.

"Now," Turnbull said, "what is it?"

"I don't know how to tell you, sir," she said. "They beat me."

"Why?"

"Because I wouldn't go with that man on a boat. She sold me, that's what she did, to a South American. And they beat me, beat me black and blue. But I was artful. I didn't say nothing. I just dressed and went out. Who could I go to? 'Turnbull, the captain,' I says to myself. 'He always acted decent—the only one!' I made you happy, didn't I, sir? Didn't I?" She stamped her foot, her brown eyes blazing, bright with tears. "She didn't tell me nothing, the madam didn't. She had me licked because I refused, sir. I wouldn't let that man touch me. The first time ever. But he was 'orrible. Like a toad, with hairs on his back. Hairs all over his back, chest, and arms, like a bloody monkey, and I said no. So they took me downstairs and beat me. But it was Betty who told me he wanted to buy me for a thousand quid. She heard it listening at the door and tipped me off. That's when I ran, sir. We're allowed out, you know, to shop and so on, but we come back—afraid not to."

Vincent gulped his brandy. "Let me talk to her, sir," he said. "I'm glad I stayed. Let me take her into the kitchen. You don't know this sort, sir. Blood horses and blood women you're used to, sir. But she's common. Cold blood, light draft, but I know 'em, sir. They're not our kind.

"Come along, miss. You come and talk to Vincent." He led her away by the arm.

"Now," he said when the green baize door to the kitchen closed, "you tell me, you little bitch, and no bloody nonsense."

"You want to know, do you?" she said. "Well, you'd better look, and see it's no lie. Come on," she said, "undo me." There seemed to be a thousand hooks and eyes to her dress. The bodice fell like an apron in front of her.

"Me stays," she said. They were black, laced tightly from below her hips.

"I can't do that," Vincent said.

"You do it," Elsie said. "I'm just a whore. Do you think I've never been undressed by a man before? I'm twenty-two," she said, "and the first man had me ten years ago. He was my dad with Ma there laughing drunk as she looked on."

Slowly, with clumsy fingers, Vincent unlaced her.

"Christ!" he said when he saw her back. "You told the truth." She was a mass of black-and-blue bruises and stripes. In two places the white skin was broken. The corset had rubbed the scabs and thin trickles of blood ran down her back.

"I've been licked before, mister," she said, "but not like this. They meant to break me," she said, "to break me. Now call him, call him in."

"Sir," Vincent called, "it's true, sir. Will you come in, sir?"

As he came in Elsie turned her back to him. "My God!" he said.

Then she faced him, her breasts naked, her bosom heaving, her eyes full of tears.

"If you don't help me what'll I do, sir? They'll catch me. They followed me here. They're waiting outside—two in Piccadilly and two in Vigo Street."

"Come into the other room," Turnbull said. "We need more drinks, Vincent."

"Yes, sir."

The girl followed him. She did not pull up her dress. What did she care? He'd seen her naked often enough.

"Sit down, Elsie."

She sat on the edge of the chair. "I won't lean back, sir," she said. "You don't want blood on your chairs, do you? Even if it's only whore's blood."

"What do you want?" Turnbull said.

This was a strange turn of events. When he'd seen the girls at Mrs. Fitzherbert's, he'd chosen her. "That little dark one," he'd said. "You've got good taste, Captain," she'd said. And after that it had always been the little dark one. He'd ridden her like a hired hack. If you hire a horse you don't ask its name. A curious shame flooded over him. She'd said he was the only one who'd treated her decent. Those were her own words. How had he treated her decent? He had not hurt her or insulted her. That was all. And if that was all, what had the others done?

"What can I do to help you, Elsie? What do you want?"

"Want?" she said. "I want you to keep me. You like me. I give you what you want. I'll be straight with you. Christ," she said, "I'd be straight with any man who'd treat me decent."

That word again. Why had he chosen her out of Mrs. Fitzherbert's riding stable? Because she was pretty and small and dark and gay and looked a bit like Elsa.

My God, he thought, that's it. I never laid a hand on

Elsa, I felt so pure about her, but it just shows what I really thought. What I felt when I found a girl like Elsa in a brothel. Then I touched her. Then I took her and never even asked her name. I never asked, because in some hidden part of me I was having Elsa.

"Now," he said, "what about now? You can't stay here. Not for the night. They're fussy about these things here."

Elsie sipped her drink. "Please yourself," she said, "but they won't get me. I'll kill myself first."

"I could take care of her," Vincent said. "My friend Marshall—Corporal Marshall's wife—would take her. I know that. He was in the Eighteenth with me, sir. We could leave her there."

Turnbull lit a cigar. Why not? Why not chance it? It might be the answer. A woman, not a wife, of his own.

"Can you do without men, Elsie, for a year or so?"

"Men!" she said. "I hates them!"

"Vincent," Turnbull said, "I've been worrying about you. I'll be going to South Africa soon. If I took a little house would you take care of her for me and no nonsense?"

"Nonsense, sir? It's horses I like, not women."

"You'll have the horses, too. I don't want to leave them in a livery stable when I'm away. You'll have to exercise them."

"I'll do that, sir, and take care of this young person, too."

That was how Turnbull got Elsie, a pretty young woman of his own.

When Vincent came back after having fixed Elsie up with Corporal and Mrs. Marshall, he said, "She was right, sir. They was waiting and we had a bit of a scuffle. They turned tail but it was lucky I had me little stick. And do you know, sir, I don't think you're making a mistake to have a bit of your own, sir. She's got blood, even if it's the wrong side of the blanket. Her dad's Lord Fenton. Her ma was a maid at Fenton Hall. That's what she told me, and I believe her."

Fenton. That was amusing. Turnbull knew him. He was a member of the Athenaeum, in the Treasury, and had been in the Cabinet.

"It's her pasterns," Vincent said. "That's where blood shows."

It was true. Elsie did have good ankles and high insteps. He remembered her body now. The slim legs, fine flanks, and small, neat breasts the size of a Cox's orange pippin, the finest apple in the world.

Getting clothes for Elsie was the next problem. She had only what she had on. Turnbull told Vincent to tell Mrs. Marshall to get her what she needed. Vincent was only too pleased. There'd be a nice little fiddle here.

But real clothes, dresses and so on? What could Turnbull do about that? And then he thought of Peggy de Vere. She'd married a chap called Barlow, a stockbroker. He went to his desk and wrote her a note.

Two days later he got a reply. "Come to dinner Tuesday."

Peggy had been one of his first affairs. It had been broken off by her very simply after supper one evening. She'd said, "Johnny, this is the last time. I'm getting married to George Barlow."

"I'm sorry," he'd said. "We've had a nice time."

"A lovely time, Johnny, but it couldn't go on and I'm sick of lovely times with lovely young men that go on till they want to marry. The boot's on the other foot this time. And I've told him everything."

"Everything?"

"Pretty well," she said. "You see, he was bound to find out and he's a good chap. Do you know what he said? He said, 'I don't give a damn about what you did before. It's what you do afterward I care about.' He said, 'Will you play the game with me, Peggy?'

"I said I would, and I will. I'll be a good wife to him. I'm sick of it, Johnny. The stage—the chorus. Dance, dance, dance, kick your bloody legs in the air and try to catch the fancy of some chap."

"Like me," Turnbull said.

"Like you, Johnny. You weren't the first by a long chalk. But you're the last. I'm going to be a respectable woman now."

He hadn't seen her since. He wondered how much she had changed.

The Barlows lived in Wetherby Gardens. It was a nice

house. Very well, if somewhat vulgarly, appointed. Everything in it was new and expensive. They had no menservants. The door was opened by a nice-looking parlormaid in a cap and apron. She served the dinner. It was the kind of house that could be run with only four servants.

Peggy looked well. She had taken care of herself and not put on much weight. Her husband, George Barlow, was as Peggy had described him—a nice chap, a typical stockbroker. Medium height, inclined to be fat, with a reddish, fleshy face and blue eyes. The kind of man who had never been on a horse or had a gun in his hand.

"So you are one of Peggy de Vere's old friends?" he said when they had been introduced to show that he knew.

"And one of Mr. and Mrs. Barlow's new ones, I hope."

They all laughed. The ice was broken. The dinner was the usual soup, fish, entree, sweet, and fruit. The fish was Dover sole, the meat sirloin, which Barlow carved. The wines were passable—an excellent Barsac followed by a mediocre Beaune.

"We'll have coffee upstairs," Peggy said as she went out.

The two men settled down with the decanter of port. Barlow was a good judge of port.

He said, "I've been very happy with Peggy. I hope you haven't come to muck things up." He'd drunk quite a lot and was emotional. "You know, Turnbull," he said, "I'm not out of the top drawer. But if you hurt her I believe I'd kill you."

It was all very un-English, very middle class. A man might feel like that, but he didn't say it. Another kind of man would probably have said, "I think, my dear chap, it would be a mistake to create any kind of difficulties."

"Don't worry, Barlow," Turnbull said. "I've come for advice."

"I'm glad, because I like you. Peggy said you were a good friend when she needed one. Have another glass of port." He passed the decanter.

Upstairs in the drawing room Peggy was waiting. She looked at them anxiously as they came in, and then, seeing they were friends, she smiled.

"You take it black with one lump, don't you?"

"What a memory you have, Peggy."

"For some things, John." Her husband went over to her and put a pudgy hand on her shoulder.

None of this was being played by any rules that Turnbull knew. But it was touching in a way. They were happy, united, and ready to fight.

"What did you want to see me about, John?" Peggy asked.

Turnbull put his cup on a small occasional table and stood up. He talked better that way.

"I want advice."

"What about?"

"A girl."

"You never used to need advice about that sort of thing, Johnny. Experts at seduction, the lot of you." Her tone was sharp.

"It's not that," he said. "It's clothes. She's got no clothes."

Peggy burst out laughing. "You've got a naked girl?" she said.

"In a way." He paused. This was going to be difficult. "She ran away and is afraid to go out alone. And I want someone—you—to buy her everything she needs."

"A trousseau?"

"In a way," he said again. How absurd the phrase sounded.

"Tell the whole story, John. It's no good in bits. It'll come out in the end anyway." Peggy was a great believer in things coming out, a very straightforward sort of girl.

When he'd done, both of them were serious.

"You're going to set her up?" Barlow said.

"I am."

"I wonder if you are wise. I mean . . ."

"He means," his wife said, "if a girl comes out of a whorehouse will she run straight?"

"I'm going to take a chance," Turnbull said.

"Very decent of you," Barlow said, "considering . . ."

"I don't know that most people would put it quite that way, but I could hardly turn her out, could I? They were waiting for her outside. My man had a scuffle with them, two thugs with a growler waiting."

"A cab," Peggy said. "My God! I've heard things. You do on the stage, you know." She went over to Turnbull, stood on tiptoe, and kissed him. "I'll do it," she said. "What woman wouldn't? Fancy buying clothes like that! Anything we want?"

"Anything you want, Peggy," Turnbull said, "and I think you'll like her."

"You don't mind, Barlow, do you? I mean Peggy going out with a girl who . . ."

"I don't mind," Barlow said, "but I think we need another drink. I'll go down and get the port."

"I'll have brandy," Turnbull said, and poured some into his glass.

As her husband left the room Peggy said, "You're a good boy, Johnny. You always were. I only hope you're never sorry."

While he looked for a house to set up what Vincent, now very romantically inclined, called his establishment, Elsie stayed with Corporal and Mrs. Marshall and he saw very little of her. Vincent fetched her two or three times and took her back in the morning. She was afraid to go out alone. He didn't worry about any difficulties with the management now. A fiver to the head porter and commissionaire smoothed out any possibility of trouble.

"Your sister, sir," the porter said. "Why not? Lots of young gentlemen have their sisters to spend the night with them. The thing is, though, sir, that all our gentlemen have such pretty sisters. You'd think there'd be one ugly one, wouldn't you, sir? But there isn't. Not one. And it's a pleasure to watch them come and go. One young gentleman—I won't mention his name, sir—has a lot of sisters and every one of them a beauty. Funny, I call it."

"And profitable," Captain Turnbull said.

"Oh yes, sir, very." They both laughed.

These nights with Elsie convinced Turnbull he was making no mistake. She had the makings of a wonderful mistress—charming, good-tempered and accommodating.

He still did not regard her as a woman, or perhaps he did as a woman in that sense, but certainly not as a lady; certainly not as an individual, a person whose feelings were in any way to be considered. The making of her into a mistress was like schooling a hunter. Bringing her up to the bit, teaching her to change feet by the pressure of alternate rein and leg.

Eventually he found the house and furnished it. He told her it was going to be a surprise, and she smiled, not really believing him.

"You'll not see it till it's ready and waiting for you," he said. "Cook-general, and all, with the larder and the cellar stocked." It was a good yarn, Elsie thought.

"You'll carry me over the doorstep, won't you?" she said, smiling up at him. "I could just pretend, couldn't I? I've heard that's what men do to their brides." She wanted to show him that she had a sense of humor too. But sometimes she felt a bride, a virgin. What, after all, was a ceremony? Why should a few words make so much difference? And the past had gone. She scarcely remembered any of it now.

"I'll carry you," he said. What a romantic little creature she was. But he liked carrying her, picking her up with one arm around her waist and one under her knees. A warm, pliant little bundle of nonsense, with her arm around his neck, her cheek pressed against his chest.

He was amused at Vincent's enthusiasm for this change in his life. He understood it, too. Vincent's great fear was that he should get married. This was the great fear of all gentlemen's gentlemen who were neither valets nor butlers. They could not fit into a staff. Their position was one of confidence. They were at once servants and companions, well aware of every secret in their masters' lives. They read their letters, they saw their bankbooks, all in a spirit of pure co-operation. The more they knew, the more they could help. They did the ordering of the wine, of the little expensive meals they cooked for the discreet visits of lady friends, and with the ordering came the perks. Never less than 10 per cent. On top of that he would gain status among his peers from having a master who'd set up a woman in a house. There'd be perks there too. A little cut in the servant's wages and in her perks—say fifty-fifty, and then there would have to be a vehicle. He would suggest it. "More convenient, sir, if you had a conveyance, say a private hansom, sir. A nice blood horse." He knew the very thing. The horse, and the coachman, and the cab.

Vincent had known men who'd tried to stay on after their masters married. It never worked. When they married, even if it was a girl straight out of the schoolroom, presented at court and married, within a month, they all had the nature of a detective. You found, however stupid she was, that she'd learned some arithmetic. She might not be able to do long division, but she could add and subtract. That was enough. Life was no longer worth living. So this was a good idea. A very good idea. A girl like Elsie, with her experience, would keep him busy.

The whole affair was providential. Vincent was a devout man who saw the hand of God in everything, even the strangest things. God, it seemed to him, took a particular interest in the light cavalry, and why not? Weren't they the finest and most beautiful of His creations? What could please God more than to see squadrons of hussars and lancers wheeling on parade? Beautiful, that's what it was. Beautiful. The very fact of light cavalry made this Darwin business nonsense. As if such men could have been fathered by monkeys.

There was no doubt in Vincent's mind that God had sent Elsie, that His hand was in it, plucking her out of a house of ill fame, saving her from this cruel fate, and at the same time arriving at the very moment thoughts of marriage were flitting through the captain's head. This gallant man had been talking about settling down, having an heir, going to live at Turnbull Court, the place in Surrey he had inherited but seldom visited, except to shoot. Good God, what an idea! The possibility of war had postponed things and then Elsie had come into their lives.

But he'd not said anything, not he. He'd said, "Such things come into a man's mind, sir, when he's lonely. Would you consider it impertinent if I asked who the lady is?"

"No, Vincent. It's no secret. It's Miss Amelia Broughton."

"Ah," Vincent said, "that's the only daughter of Sir Charles and Lady Broughton of Wilton Place, is it not?"

"That is correct, Vincent. You are very well informed."

"Young, sir, isn't she? Just out?"

"You've got to get them young, Vincent."

"That's true, sir. I married a young one."

"I had no idea you ever had a wife."

"I had one once, My Lord." Vincent had a tendency at times to revert to the appellation of his first master. It came easily to him because, like all his kind, he loved a lord and he felt it flattered the commoners whom he addressed this way, making them feel that he at least felt they should be peers.

"So you were married?"

"Yes, sir. A pretty little piece she was—and a hot one. Well, that's not so bad in a horse, but in a wife, sir, that's another thing. Always hot under the collar. Say a word and she was up, kicking and rearing. I should have known better, sir. Her showing the whites of her eyes. But I was lucky, sir, very lucky."

"What happened, Vincent?"

"She ran off, sir. Imagine that. Leaving me for a heavy. A retired dragoon that owned a pub. Very happy she is, I understand, and in high condition. Fat, sir, in other words, or so they tell me." That was what he had said to the captain, and God's will it was. God bless Elsie.

Elsie was a godsend.

CHAPTER 9

THE MADAM

MRS. FITZ was annoyed. She'd been sent for by Samuel Tupper. The note had been very precise but nonetheless menacing.

Dear Mrs. Fitzherbert:
   I should be much obliged if you would call at my office tomorrow at exactly eleven o'clock to discuss a matter of some importance.

Yours truly,
Samuel Tupper

Tupper was the only man in the world she was frightened of, and she was not alone. The bastard! she thought. It was this bloody little Elsie business. Well, she supposed she'd better go over it all again before she saw him.

She rang the bell. A very pretty little hussy of a maid knocked and came in. A redhead in black with a very frilly apron and a cap. Her bodice was cut lower than usual in servants and her skirt shorter. It showed her ankles and the beginning of her calves.

"Sometimes I think you're in the wrong profession, Betty," Mrs. Fitz said.

"I'm a good girl, ma'am."

She certainly didn't look it. But there was no point in going further. She had a father who drove a coal cart, and two brothers who worked as porters in Covent Garden. Mrs. Fitz was only interested in girls who had no family, or at least none near London. But she couldn't help sizing up every girl she saw.

"Tell Bill to come up."

The girl bobbed her head and went out swishing her skirt.

A moment later Mrs. Fitz heard heavy steps coming up the stairs.

"Want me, ma'am?" Bill Evans lumbered into the room. He was an ex-pug, with two cauliflower ears, a broken nose, and a drooping eyelid. There were other scars on his body that were hidden—one bullet wound and three knife marks. Trouble was Bill's other name. But behind that bashed-up mug of his was a sharp, scheming brain. He acted stupid because it paid him, but he was smart—very smart.

"Sit, you big ape," Mrs. Fitz said.

"Yes, ma'am." He sat down gingerly.

"Now I want the story again."

"Story, ma'am?"

"Yes, you bloody fool. The whole bloody story of what went wrong with that Elsie business. By God, if we'd caught her I'd have taken the hide off her."

"It wasn't my fault, ma'am. Who'd have thought she wouldn't be alone."

"Two of you," she said, "two at each entrance. Picked men. And you mucked it. One man, a small man too, I hear. What happened? I want it again. A thousand bloody quid we lost on that deal. A thousand."

"They comes out," Bill said, "and we goes up to them. I 'ad me 'and on 'er arm. She was set to squeal, began like, so I clopped me other 'and over 'er mouth."

"People?" Mrs. Fitz said. "There were people about, weren't there?"

"They didn't notice nothing. No one very near. Besides, people generally mind their own business when they sees the likes of us." He clenched his big hands and flexed his muscles till they bulged the sleeves of his blue serge suit.

"Well?" Mrs. Fitz said.

"Well then the man turned as quick as a cat and poked at Joe. Never seen anything like it," he said. 'E didn't 'it at 'im. 'E just poked 'im straight in the eye. 'E's lost 'is eye. I suppose you knows that?"

"I know, and I don't give a damn. What happened next?"

"Joe clops one 'and to 'is eye and grabs the stick with the other. It comes off in 'is 'and. 'E thinks 'e's busted it. That's wot I think too but 'e ain't. Instead of the stick there's a bloody little sword. 'Id inside the stick, it was. And 'e comes at me. I lets go of the girl. She screams like a stuck pig. People comes running and we runs."

Mrs. Fitz said nothing. It all seemed reasonable. You could hardly expect them to stay there and be killed.

"A shame, ma'am," Bill said, "a bloody shame. It was all set up beautiful. The growler ready. Chloryform and a pad inside it. And the same on the other side in Piccadilly. All as easy as kiss your 'and. We'd 'ave 'ad 'er 'ere and in the room in an hour."

"Well, it's too late now," Mrs. Fitz said. "You can go, Bill."

There were no flaws in the story. The other man had confirmed it. That was what she'd have to tell Mr. Tupper. And there'd be a black mark against her. Fine her probably. That hurt. When you weren't young any more, taking your money hurt you. When you were a kid, it was a hiding you were afraid of. She'd had plenty and given plenty. That was what the room was for.

Mrs. Fitz had come up the hard way. Seduced at fifteen, put into a "house" by her lover, she had fought her way up to the top. From the kid who had to take the men the others wouldn't touch to top girl in a big house where she could pick and choose. To a little house of her own. That was before Tupper had taken over the small houses in London. And now this. The madam of the finest place in England. The very top of the tree.

Mr. Samuel Tupper lived in Dulwich. He was a pillar

of the church—a deacon in fact. He had a nice wife and two children—a girl of fifteen and a boy of twelve. He drove to town every day in a carriage and pair that were put up during office hours and took him home in the late afternoon. His office was not in the city. It was a small house in Knightsbridge that looked like a private residence. This was the center from which he spun his web, not only across England but over the world, with ramifications in South America, France, and the Levant. His business was the import and export of women, and their exploitation. He could not have been described as a pimp. He was too big for that. He was a businessman concerned with supply and demand, and a very good judge of the goods he handled in so objective a manner.

This Elsie affair had annoyed him. It was more than the thousand pounds, considerably more. That was the figure he had given Mrs. Fitz. Why should she get a commission on more? The man, an Argentine, was mad about the girl. He'd certainly put the fear of God into Mrs. Fitz. It had been a great disappointment. Mr. Tupper hated to be disappointed.

After Betty had told Bill that *She* wanted him (that was the way Mrs. Fitz was referred to at No. 20—*She* says . . . *Her* orders are . . .) she climbed four flights of stairs to her room under the eaves. "The young ladies," as they were called, were all asleep on the second and third floors. Betty and the two other maids, Eliza and Alice, had served their breakfasts in bed as they always did. They did not go back for the trays till late afternoon so as to avoid disturbing them. The maids all had three hours off after lunch to rest, because they too were busy most of the night, tidying rooms and changing linen.

The gentlemen were often in the rooms while they worked. The young ladies rang when they were finished, and the girls saw a lot when they went in. The young ladies naked or half dressed in evenings gowns that had to be hooked up or buttoned properly before they could go down to the drawing room to entertain new guests. The men in evening trousers putting the links back in their cuffs or tying their clean ties. At No. 20 each young lady had a drawer full of clean men's handkerchiefs and fresh ties. A white tie could be tied only once.

Very little that went on escaped Betty's pretty brown eyes. She knew about *the room*. She hated Bill. She hated *Her*—Mrs. Fitz. But she liked the tips and the excitement of the place, the wickedness of it; this playing with the fire that scorched others and only warmed her. She knew what was in *Her* mind when *She* looked at her and she knew she was safe because of her dad and brothers. It was she who had tipped Elsie off. She'd heard Mrs. Fitz talking to a man in a top hat who pretended to be a doctor with a black bag and stethoscope.

"You'd better run away, Miss Elsie," she'd said. "They're going to sell you for a thousand quid. Fancy being worth that much." She'd stood quite close as she talked, hooking up her dress.

"Where'll I go, Betty?"

"To one of your men. There must be one of them that'll help you. I've heard them talk. They like you."

"Most of them are married," Miss Elsie said. Then she'd said, "What about the captain, Miss Elsie—Captain Turnbull?" And that was what she'd done.

But if they ever found out . . . that she'd been listening at the door. If *She* found out she'd tipped Miss Elsie off . . .

When Betty had undressed, she looked at herself in the glass

I'm a pretty bit of stuff, that's what I am, she thought. Pretty all over. When I've saved up enough I'll go into a hat shop and learn the trade. Then I'll open one of me own. That's what I'll do.

Her pretty head was screwed on right. She knew her own mind and was careful with money. What she knew of the world was its seamy side, but after all there was more of that than the other. She put a hand up to her cheek and pulled down a lower eyelid as she looked in the glass. No green in your eye, is there, my girl? And she laughed at her own reflection. Laughed at the freckled face with its brown eyes, turned-up nose, and big mouth that laughed back at her. Betty was all right. That she was.

When she reached Knightsbridge, Mrs. Fitzherbert was shown straight up to Mr. Tupper's office. "He's expecting you," the man who let her in said.

He was seated behind his desk when she knocked and

went in. He did not get up but stared at her with veiled, cold gray eyes. They were utterly without highlights or expression.

"I am disappointed, Mrs. Fitzherbert," he said, "very disappointed. Disappointed in the loss we have sustained, and in you, in whom I had the greatest confidence. Never before have you failed.

"How did the girl get away? Why did she run away? She must have heard something. Someone has been indiscreet. Someone has been spying. Your commission would have been a hundred pounds, the usual ten per cent. As a fine I shall deduct five hundred pounds from your emoluments, at a rate of one hundred pounds per month, which you will agree is very fair. But it is not the monetary loss that affects me so profoundly. It is the fact that a plan has gone awry. And the loss of good will.

"I know once the girl got away you did your best. You did very well. All that was possible. The men you sent were good men but they met with an unexpected obstacle in this sergeant of hussars, Captain Turnbull's valet, and could do no more than they did."

"So you know the story," Mrs. Fitz said.

"Of course I know it. I have ways of finding things out. Do you think I could run a business of this magnitude without an espionage system of my own?

"No, my dear Mrs. Fitzherbert, since I have suffered no pecuniary loss and as it has never been my habit to cry over spilled milk, let us forget the matter and go on to other and more profitable things.

"I have a consignment from which you will make your selection downstairs. You are the first to see them and you will select only one. They are waiting at the agency. You are Mrs. Lawley, a respectable married woman living in Ealing. You are in need of a parlormaid.

"The girls will come in one at a time as usual. You talk to them. Then, when you have seen them all, you will have the one you select called back.

"There is a cab waiting for you. And please, before going down, remove all that vulgar jewelry. It is not what a respectable married woman from Ealing would wear." He looked at her hand. "No wedding ring? Really, Mrs. Fitzherbert, you are getting careless." He took a handful from a drawer. "Choose one that fits and report progress in a week's time. I shall expect a favorable report."

The agency was situated next door. Except for a communicating door in the attic the two houses were quite separate, though they shared an inner wall.

The agency, as it was called, was dedicated to finding suitable work for young women of the lower and lower-middle classes. As long as the girls were unattractive it was legitimate, and they were found places as domestics in various categories. The pretty ones or those with good figures were separated—the sheep from the goats—and Mrs. Fitz and the other madams came to pick them in order of seniority, that is to say, according to the type of establishment they ran. Expensive, medium-priced, or low (within the price range of a bank clerk or shop assistant).

The agency also had a small, very select theatrical section. But this dealt with export only.

It ran advertisements for both in the papers, but never the same paper and never the same day. They usually ran as follows:

Domestic Help: We find good places for personable, healthy young women. Good homes guaranteed.

or

Dancers & Singers: Must be young and attractive. No previous experience wanted. We will train you if suitable and pay while you learn.

Mrs. Fitzherbert rang the bell and told the maid she was expected. "I am Mrs. Lawley. I need a parlormaid."

"Come in, ma'am, and step this way." The girl did not know her because the servants were paid off every month.

She went into a comfortable parlor. It was very home-like, with an aspidistra in a pot on a bamboo table and a clock and two Staffordshire dogs on the mantelpiece. There was nothing here to frighten anyone.

Mrs. Humphries, an old friend, came in acting like a stranger.

"I have some nice girls, Mrs. Lawley," she said, looking at the slip of paper in her hand. "I'm sure we shall have someone who will suit you."

"I hope so, I'm sure. Will you please send them in one at a time."

Six girls came in one after the other. Jane, Mary, Ellen, Madge, another Jane, and an Alice. All nice girls. Plump, healthy-looking, and agreeably on their best behavior, but nothing here for No. 20. Nothing with any style till the seventh girl came. She was a beauty, with dark, almost black hair, big brown eyes, and a splendid figure. She carried herself beautifully.

Mrs. Fitz asked her age.

"Eighteen, ma'am."

"Previous experience?"

She'd had some. She had helped the parlormaid in her last place and thought she would pick it up.

"And what is your name, dear?" Mrs. Fitz asked.

"Dorothy."

She'll be Dolores, Mrs. Fitz thought. "Where are your things, Dorothy?"

"I've got my basket here. Mrs. Humphries said to bring it. She was sure she'd get me a place today."

"Go and get it. I've got a cab waiting outside."

"Oh," the girl said. "I've never been in a cab before."

On the drive, to the slow plodding of the horse's hoofs, Mrs. Fitz told her about the house in Ealing. "But tonight we're stopping in town," she said. "I've got some more shopping to do and I'm going to a play. A friend's house," she said. "I'm sure you'll be happy there. You won't mind a room in the basement, will you, just for one night?"

"Oh no, ma'am."

"Then get your basket out while I pay the man." She opened the door. "Come along, Dorothy," she said, and led the way downstairs. "This is your room, dear." The girl went in and Mrs. Fitz closed the door and shot the bolt.

The girl began to scream and beat on the door. It was thick and padded with green felt. She was screaming, "Let me out! Let me out!" They all did, but you could hardly hear her.

After taking off her hat and gloves and washing her hands, Mrs. Fitz rang the bell. Betty answered it.

"Tell Bill I want him," she said.

He came in and touched his forelock. "You wanted me, ma'am," he said.

"The room, Bill," she said. "And let me know when she's ready. It should not take you more than three days. We're shorthanded, you know, with Elsie gone."

"Yes, ma'am," he said.

This was the work he liked. It meant more to him than the pay. The pay was good, but this was better— breaking in a young one. He took off his coat and hung it on a peg in the basement and unbolted the door of the room.

In his office Mr. Tupper was thinking about a new dance troupe he was sending to Alexandria. The Golden Dozen. They were all fair or dyed blond. Less than a dozen did not pay, and besides twelve girls gave each other confidence.

The procedure had been the usual one. The girls had been collected and boarded out. A small hall, a choreographer, and a three-man orchestra had been hired. They had been trained in a simple routine and were sailing tomorrow in charge of their director, a good-looking young man in his employ. He would entertain them on the voyage, keep them happy. In Alexandria they would be driven to a pension that belonged to a colleague. When the door closed on them, it would not open again. The buyers would be waiting. It was a simple operation.

He never hired the same hall or used the same choreographer or orchestra again. He did not use the same steamship line or even the same port of entry for a year or more. There were plenty of ports. Alexandria, Algiers, Tangier, Constantinople. Plenty. He supposed some of his girls were scattered around in harems all along the North African coast, Arabia, and Turkey, all over Asia Minor, as the Middle East was then called.

But it was a shame about Elsie. That had been worked out too. Again the usual way. She would have been drugged and taken on board on a stretcher with the doctor at her side. He would accompany his patient to Buenos Aires and have her carried off the ship in the same way as she came onto it. He was taking her to her parents, who wanted to nurse her at home. Kept under sedation the whole time, she would come to when suitably incarcerated in the New World. Who would question a doctor? A man in a top hat with a stethoscope around his neck, carrying a small black bag as he walked beside his patient's stretcher. A very nice, quiet man who spent most of his time in his patient's cabin, even sleeping in it on the couch. A man who tipped very freely for every service.

Mrs. Fitz, when she got into the waiting cab with the girl she was going to call Dolores, had not noticed a coal heaver putting a nose bag on a big black Shire with white points. Nor was there any reason why she should have.

Mr. Tupper was pleased with his letter he had just written to Mrs. Fitzherbert. It was at once clear and cryptic.

Dear Madam:
Re our recent conversation every effort should be made to recover the goods that have been mislaid. The fact of their loss is a reflection on the efficiency of our organization and a bad example to others. If this can happen once it could happen again. I am convinced that somewhere there is a leakage of trade information that might do a great deal of harm. This source should be traced and dealt with.

The parcel, when recovered, should be put back on the market though perhaps not here, or, if too seriously damaged, destroyed. I would recommend some consideration of the old adage about one bad apple spoiling the barrel. We can afford no bad apples. Should you require specific help in the recovery of this parcel once it has been located, you have only to apply to this office for any assistance you may need, even for its disposal if necessary.

I remain yours faithfully,

Samuel Tupper
Managing Director

The letterhead was "Imports and Exports, Ltd.," the address a small fruit-importing firm that Mr. Tupper owned in Maiden Lane. He had bought it for this purpose, partly because it was near Covent Garden and partly because of the name of the street in which it was situated. Mr. Tupper was not without humor, though he amused no one but himself.

When Mrs. Fitz received the letter, she went into what

was described at No. 20 as one of her "states." Her face
became suffused with blood and swelled so that she resembled an infuriated turkey. Her dyed red hair became
disheveled as she ran her hands through it. Her whole
body seemed to thicken as though inflated and threatened to burst out of its whalebone stays and split the
black satin dress she wore like a uniform.

She knew where Elsie was, but saw no chance of recovery. She was guarded by two ex-soldiers and had maidservants in the house as well. She never went out alone.
The little bitch had certainly fallen on her feet, set up in a
house like a bloody princess. Not only had she lost an
excellent girl who was a good draw to the house—she
had lost a customer. Who was going to buy milk when he
had a cow of his own? God damn her! The little whore.
Who did she think she was? Still, she'd keep an eye on
her. She might make a slip and Captain Turnbull, like so
many of her clients, was bound to go to South Africa
when the war broke out.

Hers had been almost exclusively an army house. She
catered specially to officers of the cavalry. But if there
were war and the soldiers left, she'd have to change, take
businessmen, married, fat, unvirile, who wanted oddi-
ties. The girls, who were used to the other type—clean-
cut, dashing, free spenders, and quick on the job—would
kick up a fuss. But a little visit downstairs would soon
cure that. Still it was a nuisance and a matter of regret
even to her. She still liked to see nice gentlemen about
her house.

That Argentine had been an exception, but he had come
with special recommendation from "you know who," as
she called him to herself sometimes. In her heart, which
was still that of a high-class prostitute (after all she had
her memories, which no one could take away), she understood Elsie's revulsion. And if Elsie had known what was
in store for her, if she had known he intended to buy
her, how much greater it would have been.

This was the point. Evidently she had been tipped off.
Someone had told her about the deal. *He* thought there
was a spy in the house. In my house. God help her if she
caught her, that was all.

She went back to the phrase "disposed of." Well, it had
been done before. It was not difficult if you knew how.

A barrel of beer was delivered and an empty picked up. Only of course it was not empty. Some distance away it was transferred to another cart and driven into the country, where it was interred in a hole that had been prepared for it by an obliging farmer, who asked no questions and reploughed the field. There were no difficulties except that of finding the girl concerned. The blood had gone from her face now, her body shrunken to its usual rather stout dimensions.

She decided to send for a barrel of beer. It wouldn't be wasted. They could always drink it. If it were needed before it was empty, the beer could be run out. Bill would be pleased. He was very fond of beer. Too fond. She'd have to warn him to control himself. She laughed. That gorilla control himself. No, the best plan would be to keep it locked up and dish it out herself. She'd give some to the girls with their lunch, and to the maids.

The maids, she thought. By God, that might be it.

Those happy days of freedom when there were no restrictions of any kind and women could be moved from country to country like other merchandise were gone. White slavery was no longer at its peak. There were laws against it, but, provided that care was exercised, they could be evaded. In most European countries brothels were publicly controlled; in almost all, brothels and red-light districts were tolerated. The prostitute was regarded as a necessity, the only safeguard of good women from the lubricity of unmarried, thwarted men. There were, however, no passports, no controls at the ports of entry, and there were no exchange difficulties. Gold was good everywhere, and no gold better than a British sovereign.

Children were sold by their mothers, unwanted babies farmed out to women who slowly starved them to death or smothered them. Death certificates were easy to obtain from venal doctors. This was the field in which Samuel Tupper and his like still reaped their corn—the harvests of cruelty, sin, and lust.

London was no worse than any other great metropolis, perhaps better, but it was from London that this mode of life had reached South Africa—Johannesburg, the Sodom and Gomorrah of the Calvinistic Boers. It was London and the wealth of the mines that had set up these daughters of the horseleech on the cold, clean high veld that even fifty years ago had known no greater evil than the lion's roar or the innocent massacres of the Matabele whose spears had drunk blood across it.

It was against this the Boers fought as much as for freedom, for it was part of their freedom. They fought for God against Moloch, for their way of life against the English, for the security of their bucolic pastoral life. They were against all modernity, against all progress, all business, all wealth. For wealth they saw as the source of all evil. They saw the civilized world as a spoiled orange —its skin was beautiful, but below it the flesh was rotten.

CHAPTER 10

THE LOVE NEST

THE LITTLE HOUSE Turnbull bought for Elsie on Acacia Road was a very attractive Regency two-story cottage with large windows and a white marble Adam fireplace.

Facing the road were the hall, drawing room, and dining room, a small sitting room that had a door leading into the main bedroom, and a bathroom that had been added later. On the second floor there were four bedrooms, a box room, and a linen closet. In the basement there were the kitchen, scullery, pantry, and a good wine cellar. It was in fact a very nice small house, almost a country house of the kind that was then described as a bijou residence and ideal for its purpose. It had been built by a royal duke as a love nest and had continued as such, always inhabited by beautiful women and their protectors.

No. 7 Acacia Road had an atmosphere of sophisticated coziness, of cottagey secrecy, an odor quite the opposite of sanctity. It smelled, if the term can be architecturally applied, less of temporary passion than happy illicit love. It was a happy house. No one in it had been cruel or wicked. They had merely not been moral. Above all, it was gay. Her predecessors and their friends would have liked Elsie. She was their own kind of girl.

The street was shaded by sycamores and the back rooms faced a half acre of garden. It had a fountain with a lead

Cupid riding a dolphin in the center of a tiny circular lawn that was surrounded by shrubs and trees. Roses and honeysuckle climbed a trellis against the house, which also had a small lean-to greenhouse. At the end of the garden, which was walled, there was a door that led out onto Primrose Street. Here, cutting into the garden but opening onto the street, was a stable, with sleeping quarters above.

At last the day came. The little house was ready like Napoleon's army, to the last button on the last gaiter. The cook-general, Ellen, a fat, good-natured woman in her fifties, was there in a black uniform with a white apron and cap. The larder and cellar were stocked. There were flowers in the vases. Bottles of perfume on the dressing table. The big double bed was made up with two hot-water bottles in case the sheets were not sufficiently aired. The garden was neat as a toy. A jobbing gardener had been told to spend one day a week keeping it in order. Only one thing remained to complete the household—its mistress.

Turnbull sent Vincent to fetch her. "Tell her to dress up," he said.

"What is it?" she said when she came rustling in. She was wearing white. She had on a big white hat with a white ostrich plume, carried a white parasol, white kid gloves, and a white reticule. Her button boots were white kid.

"It's the house," he said. "It's ready and we're going there now."

He had not told her how things were going. He had not mentioned it again after having said he would set her up in a house of her own.

"What!" she cried, jumping up and down like a child with excitement. "You mean . . ."

"I mean we're going there. That's why I told you to dress up. Vincent's coming later with your things. Mrs. Marshall will pack them."

"Oh!" she said. She put her hand to her heart. "I think I'm going to faint."

He pulled her to him. "Wait till we get home," he said.

"Home." Tears came into her eyes. "I've never had a home."

"Come along, Elsie, the carriage is waiting."

"You've got a carriage?"

"A victoria with two good horses."

"I've never been in a carriage."

"Well, you're going in one if I can ever get you out of this place."

Now she could hardly wait.

It took half an hour to drive there. When they arrived he dismissed the carriage.

"You don't want me back, sir?"

"No, thank you." Turnbull put a gold sovereign into the coachman's gloved hand. He nodded at the footman, who sat beside him. "That's for both of you."

"We'll drink your health, sir, and that of the young lady."

"Thank you," Turnbull said. With Elsie beside him he watched the carriage turn and drive away.

"Now," he said as he opened the gate in the low wall, "now you're home." The front garden was only a few yards wide. It was flagged and the border of purple iris was in full bearded flower. They climbed the steps. The front door was painted apple green.

"A green door," Elsie said.

"Here." Turnbull gave her a latchkey. "Open it," he said. "It's your house."

Elsie turned the key, pushed the door open, and stood staring into the hall—at the carpet, at the pictures on the wall, at the staircase that swept upward in a beautiful curve. She stood frozen with astonishment. A house. She'd never seen a house like this, and she was going to live in it. She felt Turnbull's arms about her. She felt him bend over. His left arm went under her knees. He raised her. A minute later he had put her down on the carpet and closed the door

"Oh, oh!" she cried. "You didn't forget." She burst into tears and ran forward into Ellen's arms. Ellen held her and patted her as if she was a child.

"Leave her to me, sir," she said. "I'll take her into the kitchen and give her a nice cup of tea."

Then began an idyll that Turnbull found at once absurd and enchanting. God knows he had made love to Elsie often enough as the little dark one, as his mistress that his manservant had brought to his rooms and taken away

when he had finished with her. But this was another girl—
a child. So much a child that he was embarrassed by her
and by Ellen's solicitude for their comfort. Ellen was romantic by nature. "Just like a story, it is," was her way of
expressing it. " 'Im so rich an' 'ansome an' 'er so little
and pretty." He was embarrassed by Vincent's knowing
look. Vincent acted as if he was responsible for this happy
state of affairs, and Elsie's pleasure in everything. In her
ivory hairbrush and hand glass, her little jars and glove
stretchers, all with her initial, a simple E, in black on them.
At the cut-glass, silver-topped bottles for oddments, at
the tiny china tree with short, stubby branches.

"What's this?" she said, picking it up.

"For rings."

"I've got no rings," she said.

"You will have one day, my pretty one."

She opened every closet. She turned on the water in the
bath. She flushed the toilet, laughing, her dark eyes bright
with tears.

She ran into the garden and picked flowers. She had
never picked a flower before. "We must put them in water
before they die," she said. She seemed to think flowers
wilted and died in a few minutes if they were not attended
to.

She dressed up in the new dresses that he had not
seen, everything Peggy had bought for her, and modeled
them, strutting up and down like a child dressed up in
grown-up clothes. She dressed and undressed a dozen
times a day. She put on lacy nightdresses, peignoirs, and
dressing gowns. She draped herself naked in a white
feather boa.

A child—a woman—using every talent of provocation.

Of course it could not last. She would get tired of play-
acting and he would become bored. She would begin to
want things. More and more things. More clothes, jewels,
furs, money. This was all a trick, a woman's wiles designed to soften him up. He had heard of it all from
other men who had kept girls. How they went on bleeding
them. That was the pattern. It always started out all right.
But he might as well enjoy himself while the going was
good.

At this moment it was wonderful to be alone with a
beautiful girl who said she loved him and denied him

nothing. To be out of Mayfair, out of London. To sit quietly in the garden and listen to a blackbird sing, yellow-beaked, sharp-eyed, his feathers as smooth and shiny as a new top hat. To sit there with Elsie beside him, her hand in his.

The roar of the traffic in London was tremendous. Every wheel that turned, except those of the private carriages, was iron-tired. The buses, drays, vans, carts, all rumbled on iron-tired wheels. The ironshod hoofs of the horses rang on the roads, many of them still paved with cobbles, striking sparks. The butchers' two-wheeled traps drawn by small, well-bred ponies were driven fast. The butchers in dark blue linen aprons and straw hats were proud of the way they handled the ribbons, and the sharp tap of their ponies' shoes was easily recognizable. If someone of importance was ill, golden wheat straw that came up to the horses' knees was strewn in the street to muffle the noise of hoofs and wheels.

It was quiet in St. John's Wood and Elsie always knew the butcher's trap. When she heard the pony coming she got sugar ready to take out to him. His hoofs had the quick tap of a woman's high heels on a parquet floor. The hansom-cab horses, mostly thoroughbred culls, had a fast hoofbeat too. A horse that could not be driven any other way was quiet enough in a hansom. The driver, perched ten feet up in the air, had immense leverage on the horse's bit. The reins, running through the hames of the collar, went up at an angle of forty-five degrees to the cabby's hands. Blood carriage horses, half-breds, and so on, hard to control, were restrained with bearing reins that held their chins almost onto their chests, forcibly arching their necks in a manner that was sometimes cruel. The more staid Cleveland bays and Yorkshire coach horses were easy to manage, being of much colder blood.

The streets were spotted with horse dung that the street cleaners swept up into little handcarts. In every West End street there was a mews where the local carriage horses were kept. Each had a coach house for the family vehicles and a flat above for the coachmen and the grooms. Many people kept hacks in London, either in mews or boarded out at a jobmaster's stables.

It did not take Elsie long to learn all this, with Vincent talking horses and manners most of the time. That first time in the Albany kitchen he had called her Elsie and told her to call him Mr. Vincent. Now she was Miss Elsie and he was Vincent, but he still intimidated her with his knowledge of correct behavior. It was he who taught her what knives and forks to use before Turnbull came to dinner, he who taught her how to order meals and what wines went with what. He even took her into the park to see how real ladies dressed and walked. "No wobbles please, Miss Elsie. I know the master likes it but keep it at home for him." He minced no words and spared no pains. To him she was like a young horse that must be schooled, and she took to it as a woman will. A man has to be bred to be a duke, but any chorus girl can become a duchess tomorrow and in a year she's learned all the tricks.

Vincent got Elsie a French maid. He told Celeste the truth more or less. That Elsie was no lady, that she was kept—the girl would have found out anyway—and that she must teach her about clothes and the mysteries of a woman of fashion. "Outside, Celeste," he said, "I can manage, but underneath it is up to you, and you do your job or get sacked."

"*Oui, monsieur,*" she said.

"Now run along like a good girl and get started."

He had employed her without informing the captain, or the master, as he called him sometimes, but when he told him he said, "That was a good idea. Put the frills on her, Vincent. She can carry them."

A lot of the things Vincent and Celeste taught Elsie the captain never knew about, seeing only the results.

There were more clothes, more corsets, corset covers, drawers, chemises, camisoles, silk stockings, negligees, more petticoats, nightgowns, slips.

"Wear this one tonight, Mademoiselle," Celeste would say. "It is taffeta and rustles like the leaves of a tree. That is something men like. It makes them think of nature. Also the tap of high heels is good—like a deer walking on the rocks. All men are hunters. The chase excites them. Of course Mademoiselle is too young to understand men fully, but she will learn."

Elsie said, "I hope so, Celeste," as inside she bubbled with laughter, though all that had gone before was nothing, was forgotten in her new love. The only love in her life was the captain. She knew he had no idea what he had done to her. He had just been kind, but kindness to a girl who had never known it was like a revelation of God. It did not seem strange to her that God should turn out to be a captain of hussars. Her religious education had been neglected.

There were liberals in England, pro-Boers. Lady Balfour, the sister of the leader of the House of Commons, wrote in one of her private letters: "I never feel easy about our pursuit of the Boer. If gold were not under him we should leave him alone."

Even the Foreign Office subscribed to this idea and did not see how public opinion should be expected to endorse a war upon the South African Republic in order to secure a franchise for a certain number of British subjects who chose to live in the Transvaal. A Welsh lawyer, Lloyd George, became vitriolic at the iniquity of a war. This was the first time anyone had heard of the little man.

The idea of making war for the capitalists, for the Rand lords, was unattractive, and there was an uneasy feeling even among the patriotic "My country right or wrong" boys that if there had been no gold there would be no war.

Kruger had made two mistakes. The first was to cross the border with his commandos, for public opinion in England would never have let the British forces take the initiative and attack him. The second was, having crossed the border, not to have sent his horsemen galloping to the sea. Natal was in his pocket. Had he done this the population of Cape Colony, predominantly Boer though British subjects, would have risen almost to a man.

The Boer population of South Africa had never been consulted about becoming a British colony. The Cape had been the booty of another war, handed over to England with other territories after the defeat of Napoleon, whose unwilling Dutch allies had fallen with him. The Boers did not feel themselves British subjects and had no desire to become so. But to most people in England, the English who did not support their country and the Dutch who were British subjects at the Cape were traitors, the whole damn lot of them. This was the time of black or white, of wrong or right. Few people could see gray or recognize finer shades of opinion.

Like all soldiers Turnbull was supposed to be without political opinions. Soldiers had no vote, they were servants of the Queen. Their duty was to obey, not to question or to think.

Turnbull, knowing he would sail soon, spent as much time as he could with Elsie, always expecting her charm to pall. But it palled no more than the charm of a kitten. He began to take her out, not caring if he was seen. He took her to dine at Frascatti's and the Trocadero. He took her to see *The Belle of New York* and *Florodora*. She had never been to the theater and her naïve pleasure amused him more than the show. They would drive back in a hansom.

When they got home late Elsie would make him tea. She didn't like him to drink brandy.

"I'm afraid of it, sir," she said.

"Don't call me sir."

"Captain," she said.

"Don't call me Captain. Call me John."

"I couldn't do that," she said.

"Why not?"

"Because I'm not a lady."

This lady business got on his nerves. "There are plenty of ladies who aren't ladies," he said. "You're more of a lady than lots of them, and getting more like one every day."

"I'm learning," she said. "Mr. Vincent and Celeste are teaching me."

"Don't call him Mr. Vincent."

"He says that too, and I try not to, but he's so respectable."

"He's not as respectable as you think. No one in the cavalry is respectable. It's not commensurate with the cavalry spirit."

"What's commensurate?"

"Part of, going with, that kind of thing." Then she'd come and sit on his lap. Later he undressed her. "I'm as good as Celeste, aren't I, Elsie?"

"Better, sir, I mean John," she said.

Turnbull couldn't reconcile himself to Elsie. He couldn't place her. Could not find the exact niche she occupied in his life—mistress, pet, chattel, child, daughter, part object of art, hobby, amusement, charity, luxury. He could put no exact word to it. All he knew was that he was going to miss her. That he would worry about her when he left. Except for Elsa he had never worried about a woman before. Any others that he had known had been well able to take care of themselves.

Suddenly he realized that he loved her the way he had once loved a dog when he was a boy—a fox terrier called Nelly. Not because she was a companion who thought he was God, but because he could love her without fear of betrayal, because she could accept the love he had to offer.

Since Nelly there had only been Elsa; when she died there was no one, nothing, only the regiment. It was curious that though so many people talked about love nobody wanted it. They wanted admiration, adulation, flattery, no matter how gross. They wanted presents. Flowers, perfume, furs, jewelry, money. They wanted attentions of all kinds, but not love. And they didn't want it because the responsibility of accepting it was too great.

That was his problem. Nelly, he thought—I mean Elsie —loves me and damned if in a way I don't love her back. This was a pretty kettle of fish. It's a good thing I'm going, he thought. Though he hated the idea of it as a man with a new woman, and longed for it as a soldier. If only he had been going with the regiment instead of the General Staff. If he had not fallen in love with Elsa, he would not have stayed on in the Transvaal. He would not have learned Dutch. He would not have been an expert on Africa.

All he could hope for now was that in the excitement of war he would forget Elsie. But he knew he wouldn't. There was the possibility that with him away she would be unfaithful to him and take up with another man. But he didn't want that really, and he didn't think she would. She was like Nelly. Nelly had been a one-man bitch. It was a hell of a mess to be in.

He did not want to be in love again. He'd had no idea he had such a lot of it bottled up inside him, just waiting to be poured out on someone. But it was embarrassing, even more so if you thought about who and what she was. Besides, he'd never heard of anyone being in love. Elsa had been different, like a young, lovely wild thing,

not like a woman at all, not a trick in her. And that was
what she and Elsie had in common, as well as their coloring. Among his kind, men had a woman when they needed
one and paid for it, or they kept someone. That was a
smart thing to do—like driving a tandem or having a
coach and four. Then when the time came and they found a
nice, well-bred girl with some fortune and settled down at
stud in the country, they paid their mistresses off. But
love . . . He'd always thought it was for common people
—country bumpkins spooning in the lanes. Servants and
policemen. Sentimental balderdash. Elsa had been the exception. It always came back to that.

He supposed if it went on and he got married Elsie
wouldn't kick up much fuss. On the other hand, if he
offered her money she'd probably throw it in his face.
Perhaps she'd not mind his being married. He'd still be
able to see a lot of her. Plenty of men did that.

Still, there was lots of time. There was the war and it
would not be the walkover so many people thought it
would be. They did not know the Boers as he did.

Elsie had guts. Only Celeste and Vincent knew how
much she cried.

"Do you know, Celeste," Vincent said one day, "I believe the little bitch loves him, damn me if I don't."

"Say that again and I'll slap your face," Celeste snapped,
her eyes blazing. "That is a good girl, a brave girl. I don't
care where she came from, or what she has done. She is
like my sister."

"Your sister a tart?"

She did slap him, and stamped her foot.

"Your bloody language," she said. "I mean to me she is
like a sister. In six weeks I love her. There is no bad in
her. No cruelty. I should know about women. Not only
am I one, I have spent my life serving them. That little
one never thinks of herself. First she thinks of him—the
captain—then of me and 'Will this be too hard? Too much
trouble?' She even thinks of you."

"She does?" Vincent said.

"Certainly. She tries not to give you trouble. She is grateful for all you do. She says 'please' and 'thank you.' Anyone could tell she is not a lady. I do not know how to

stop her. But it is nice when people say please and thank you. It shows a good liver."

"Heart, you mean. My God!" Vincent said. "What with teaching her what knives and forks to use, what wines to drink, and teaching you the King's English, I sometimes think I'll go mad."

"Go mad? You mean more mad. That is not possible. All Englishmen are mad. But say no more about Mademoiselle. She is a good girl. I have bought her a wedding ring, not gold of course, to wear when he goes away. It will look better and give her confidence and also dreams. It is good for a young girl to dream."

"Dream my eye," Vincent said, banging the door as he left her.

Ha! Celeste thought. I fix him.

Vincent as a rule was as quiet in the house as a thief. But theirs was a friendly feud. She knew one day she would sleep with him. He had a certain charm, this Englishman. A *je ne sais quoi* that she had not met before in this Godforsaken land. It might be because he was a hussar. Her first lover had been a cuirassier. There was something to be said for the cavalry, though Vincent would have been shocked and astonished to hear himself compared to a French dragoon.

This ménage and way of life entailed further changes in Turnbull's life. Living either with his regiment or in Mayfair as a bachelor, he used hansoms and had never felt the need of private transport. Now he did and bought a hansom of his own and a fast, well-bred chestnut mare to go with it. Vincent had his way and found the equipage, the mare, and the coachman for him. The coachman wore a gray frock coat, gray trousers strapped under the instep, a gray top hat. His name was Spencer. He had, naturally, been in the 18th.

Fortunately lack of money never embarrassed Turnbull. Even living as he did, quite extravagantly, he found it impossible to spend his income. In those days the rich were really rich and the poor unbelievably poverty-stricken. No one even knew that there were social problems. The classes were still rigidly divided, though the aristocracy was being invaded by wealthy businessmen, manufacturers even marrying into county families. The era of the American heiress exchanging her wealth for a title had begun, and the cracks in the structure of society, though almost invisible as yet, were there under the glossy varnish of its exterior.

Turnbull soon found himself living entirely at the St. John's Wood house. At first he had gone there just for the night, but he had soon got tired of these nocturnal adventures. The first weekend after Elsie had settled in he stayed with her and on Monday he told Vincent to bring over everything he would need.

"Are we going to live there now, sir?" Vincent asked.

"Yes, we are. Have my letters readdressed and go over to Albany every couple of days to see that the place is kept clean."

"Yes, sir." It was turning out even better than he had dared to hope.

There might be some talk, but Turnbull did not care. He did not want to be bothered with social affairs now. The African business was nearing the crisis. He was more than ever worried about the attitude of the War Office, who still insisted it would be a short war, but were preparing an army corps and a division of cavalry to go out in case they were needed, though Lord Wolseley said that the troops stationed in South Africa would, in his opinion, be able to deal with any eventuality.

But Lord Wolseley, the commander in chief, once a great soldier, was in his dotage, though only sixty-six. His memory was so bad he would forget his secretary's name and even the memoranda he had written the day before. So there was no reason to value his opinion, though no one said this publicly.

Turnbull's other worry was still the boys. The two Van der Bergs and their mother—Elsa's mother—and his other friends in the Transvaal, those simple farmers who had been so hospitable to him when he was hunting on the veld.

He did not want to go out to dinner, did not want to have do discuss the situation with people who thought he must know everything that was going on because he was working at the War House.

Elsie was an immense relief. She took his mind off

things. He had not lived in a house run by a woman since his mother died, and had forgotten what it was like. Not that Vincent was not a good servant. But there was a difference. More flowers in the vases. Flowers in pots. Magazines and papers scattered about. A suspicion of perfume in every room and delightful near-disorder. Vincent, the soldier, dressed everything by the right. By God, he thought, his rooms had always looked as if the man used a tape measure to arrange things—as if he measured the spaces between them.

He was persuading Elsie to read magazines and books. In the evening she read aloud to him and he corrected her accent and explained the words she did not know. He bought her a dictionary and an atlas, the atlas because she did not know where Africa was and confused it with America. They both began with A.

By knocking out the partitions between the loose boxes in the stable he made three stalls capable of holding his two horses, if he wanted to bring them over from the jobmaster's near the Park, where they were boarded, as well as Daisy, the chestnut mare.

One of his horses was Ranger, the brown charger he had had in the Transvaal. An old chap now, fat and sedate, but lively enough when he felt the tan of the row under his hoofs. The other was Peter, a gray Irish hunter, on whom he had won several point-to-points, a big horse that stood 16.1 and was as quiet as a baby. Both these animals were more than horses to him. They were friends who had shared some of the great moments of his life. He had taken Elsie to see them several times and was amused to see how small she looked beside them. He had taught her how to give them sugar with her palm flat, the thumb pressed close to her hand.

"Won't they bite?" she said. "What big teeth they have." She sounded like Little Red Riding Hood and the wolf.

"They won't bite, darling. They want to be friends." This when Peter had blown into her face with wide nostrils.

It was Vincent who had suggested that the jobmaster put Ranger into a break and train him to harness.

"A private hansom is not the thing for Miss Elsie," he said, "when you go. I've got a buyer for it and the mare. A brougham, that's the thing for Miss Elsie, sir. Very smart and ladylike, with Corporal Spencer to drive it and a boy beside him we can dress up as a footman. He could help about the house and the garden, sir."

That was worth thinking about, and they might as well try the brown in harness. He was so quiet and intelligent it should not take him long to get used to it. It would be nice when he was in Africa to think of the horses with Elsie, of her feeding them sugar, carrots, and apples.

And now that he was here in a place with a garden, what about Queenie? The keeper at the court had charge of her with the other gun dogs—two setters and a clumber spaniel. The other dogs did not mind being left, but Queenie was always almost mad when he came, and was utterly despondent when he left. The others loved anyone who opened a gun case.

Elsie came into the room with a vase of white carnations.

"I arrange them nicely, don't I, John?" she said. At last she called him John. "Celeste taught me." She put them on the marble mantelpiece near the Empire clock, but not in the middle of the space between it and the edge, as Vincent would have done.

"Elsie," he said, "do you like dogs?"

"Dogs? I don't know anything about dogs."

"You've never had one?" Even now it was difficult for him to realize that there were women who'd never been near a horse or owned a dog.

"I've never had anything," she said. "Never before, I mean."

"Would you like to try, darling? I've got a bitch in the country I'd like to send for."

"Bitch," she said. "I didn't know that was a dog."

"A female dog. A lady dog."

"Could she have puppies?" Elsie clapped her hands. "I picked up a puppy once. It was lovely. Black and white, all fat and soft. It was lost," she said. "It tried to follow me so I ran away. They'd never have let me keep it." Tears came into her eyes. She was a funny girl.

"Of course she can have pups when she comes into season. Vincent will see to it."

"What's season, John?"

Now he had to explain the facts of life to Elsie. That

was queer too, considering. "Every few months a bitch comes into season. Then she'll take a dog. Mate," he said.

Elsie went into peals of laughter. "Oh," she said, "how funny that is. When you think of girls, I mean. Bitches wouldn't suit Mrs. Fitz, would they? Not that kind anyway—not dog bitches."

"Will you stop talking about Mrs. Fitzherbert," Turnbull said.

"Yes, John. But it's hard. You see, that has been so much of my life."

It was true. Her experiences of life were chiefly those of a brothel.

Seeing him annoyed, Elsie said, "But I'm learning. It all seems very far away now, as if it happened to another person."

"It did, Elsie. That wasn't you. Not the Elsie I know."

"Then how did you meet her, Captain?" she asked mischievously.

"Shut up," Turnbull said. "That's all over and done with. Come here and kiss me."

She was sitting in his lap when Celeste came to announce dinner. She had taken on the job of parlormaid herself when Turnbull had suggested getting another servant. She did not want another girl in the house. Not with Vincent. She had discovered that not only was he a dashing ex-sergeant of light cavalry, he was also a man with money in the bank. Now she would never go to bed with him. Not, at least, till they were married.

As they went in to dinner Turnbull said, "Then I can send for Queenie?"

"I'd love it. I'd love another bitch in the house," Elsie said as she sat down, swishing her skirts beneath her and looking up at him from under her lashes.

"Damn you," he said, "you just do things to infuriate me."

"I know," Elsie said, "but only when we are alone. I'll be careful, I promise. I'll forget everything. I really will. But I couldn't help it. It was so funny. Till now I thought bitches were nasty girls, not nice dogs."

CHAPTER 11

A LONG GOOD-BY

TURNBULL ran up to the cavalry barracks at Colchester as often as he could. Each time, he had seen his colonel and tried to get himself recalled to active duty. The applications were put in and invariably refused.

"It's no good, old boy," Sir Charles said. "The War House won't let you go."

"And you'll go without me."

"I doubt it, John. I have an idea you'll be there before us."

"A staff job?"

"Of course. A red cap band with gold on it and all the girls after you." He laughed. "The pack in full cry, my boy, and every earth stopped."

"I'm a regimental soldier," Turnbull said. "I belong here."

"You were and you did. We miss you, but haven't a hope of getting you back. Not yet, at least. But we'll go on trying. Give it a bang every few months. If we lose some senior officers we'll have a good case. If I'm knocked out, for instance, you could be second-in-command."

"And my squadron?" Turnbull had said.

"Jackson's got it, and he'll keep it. He's all right. A bit slow perhaps, but he's all right."

And that was that. A couple of glasses of sherry, some gossip with his friends, luncheon—steak and kidney pie with cold grouse a second choice, roly-poly pudding with treacle sauce, a spoonful of ripe Stilton, a pint of beer— and he was off again.

That was the way it had been each time he went up. But this time it would be different. This was the last time. He was on his final leave and packing up to go. This was good-by.

He was met at the station by the colonel's dogcart. A very smart, black, high, two-wheeled vehicle that would hold four—one with the driver and two others with their

123

backs to the two in front. Generally there was only one person on the back seat, a groom, or a boy footman, dressed like a man in a top hat, long-skirted coat, white leathers, and boots, who was called a "tiger." And very smart he had looked, too, standing at the head of a tall horse till he started off, and then running behind and jumping up on the tailboard and into his place back to back with the coachman, his arms folded on his chest. Their top hats were cockaded of course, their uniforms dark rifleman green, because Colonel Sir Charles Eaton's wife's father had commanded the 50th Rifles and she wanted it that way. What Juliet Farraway, now Lady Eaton, wanted she usually got. So the uniform was rifleman green and the device on the silver buttons a lion couchant, the Eaton crest.

But all that had gone with the present emergency. No tiger, no coachman. A trooper in khaki, Jim Stanley, from his own chestnut squadron, was driving.

It was like Charles, he thought, to send one of his own men to meet him. The big brown horse between the shafts was nearly clean-bred and hated to wait. He also appeared to hate trains, and Stanley was having trouble with him as he put his foot on the dogcart step.

"Good morning, sir. Glad you came, sir. He's a handful, he is." He turned the brown and they went up the street at a spanking trot, the horse well into his bit, a Liverpool with the reins buckled into the center hole and pulling hard.

It was a curious feeling to be driving up these familiar streets for the last time. Curious to think of life, of England.

Everyone said the grouse shooting had been wonderful. The season was still on. In September the partridge shooting had begun very well too, with big and plentiful coveys. The pheasant shooting had been good too. It had been a good year for them. The keepers, raising pheasants under hens, had had few losses. The weather had been just right for them, with not too much rain or heavy dews. On every estate in England during the summer the weekend visitors had been taken to see "our young birds," the mottled pheasant chicks running in and out between the slats of the coops that held their foster mothers. On a big place there were sometimes hundreds of coops and thousands of young birds.

It had been a good year all around, as far as game birds went, that is. Human affairs had gone less well. But good as the shooting was there was scarcely an officer today with a shotgun in his hand. They were all back with their regiments.

There had been no cubbing in September. There would be little fox hunting for the officers of Her Majesty's Army this year. The sweet music of the hounds would be unheard by them. There would be the cries, the sound of hunting horns, the shout of "Foradaway," but that would be later, in Africa, in the pursuit, not of sly Reynard, but of the Boers.

Pink coat, red coat, scarlet soldiers or members of a hunt. How alike they really were. Replace a hunting crop with a saber and you had a soldier in a uniform not very different from that of a cavalryman of the line. Change his top hat. Bash it down and tie it in the middle so that it looked like a kind of mortarboard and you had a lancer's cap. Tie a plume to it and you had something approaching a hussar's busby. And the men were the same, the hunters and the soldiers, for most of the hunters were, or had been, soldiers and most of the soldiers hunted.

This was England in the autumn of 1899 in the fall of the leaf. Some trees were already naked, others were gold or russet brown. Only the conifers, the rhododendrons, and the gorse were still green. And the grass, for this was England.

In Africa it was spring. In Australia too. Everywhere down under below the equator—the mythical belt that holds the world's belly in its place—the country was in bud.

The army would sail from a peaceful winter into a summer war. A kind of topsy-turvydom like war itself, in which the lives of the young and best were thrown away and the least useful preserved from danger.

The barracks seethed as equipment poured in, as reservists came back to the colors, as khaki was issued and fitted. Remounts were being broken to cavalry drill, and the grindstones sang with the scream of sharpening sabers.

A squadron was doing close-order drill on the square. Infantry drill. Rifle exercises with carbines. Turnbull had never seen the like of it before—British cavalry with fire-arms.

Nor had he ever seen Regimental Sergeant Major Ellis drill men. He took parades. He shouted markers out.

"Where the hell's that band? Mr. Benson, sir"—to a cornet—"would it be too much trouble for you to keep that horse in line? Spoils the look of things, sir. Looks as if you didn't know no better." And that young officer never had his horse out of position again.

But this was different. Ellis was giving orders. He was on foot, dismounted. He was purple in the face with rage.

"Now," he shouted, "again! By the right QUICK maarsh. ABOUT—T'n. ABOUT—T'n. ABOUT—T'n. HAALT. ORDEEER ARMSS. SLEOOP Armss. PREE-SNT armss. OORDER armss. STAND at eees."

"Now," he said. "Now I'm going to tell you something. You're not recruits. If you was I wouldn't feel the way I do. Sick, that's what I feel. You makes me sick at my stummick. I could throw up right here on the parade ground." He was flicking his whip in the air, swishing it like a sword. "It takes a lot to make a regimental ser-geant major throw up on a parade ground, but by Christ if it could be done you could do it."

He now looked as if he was going to burst with rage.

"God damn you! Do you think I like it? Marching around here with popguns like bloody infantrymen. Me hauled out of me office, hock deep in papers, because the drill sergeants can't handle you. Sulking, they says. Dumb . . . insolent . . . idle . . . the bloody lot. So I've got to do it. Me. On foot—dismounted. But you'll do it, by Christ! We'll all do it. If the Queen wants to give her light cavalry popguns as if they was dragoons that's her business. If she says to me, Her Majesty does, 'Regimental Sergeant Major Ellis, we'll use carbines in the future,' then we'll bloody well use carbines. Now that's over, and we'll have no more bloody nonsense in the Second. AT-shon. SLEoop-armss. Diis-miss."

The men broke away. They looked smart in their khaki, in helmets, cord riding breeches with leather strappings inside the knees and puttees fastened at the bottom, the tapes over the tops of their boots. Steel spurs shining.

Smart, proud. And Turnbull realized once again that there could be no courage without pride, and no pride without discipline. The history of the regiment. The spit and polish, the hours of close-order drill, all served their purpose—the welding of a number of individuals into a single unit.

The smart soldier in his walking-out clothes, his pillbox on the side of his head, his whip under his arm, his spurs jingling on the pavement, was the brave soldier. The smart soldier and the brave were one man, inseparably joined by their training, the *esprit de corps* that made these men a band of brothers who, even if at times they detested one another, were bound together by their pride in the regiment.

There were people who questioned all this, who said, "What's this got to do with fighting?" Well, it had a lot to do with fighting. It would prevent men from breaking if things went wrong. It could hold them with a mixture of pride and shame. Pride in a regiment that had never been defeated, never deflected from its objective no matter how heavy their loss. And shame that made any other course impossible.

Regimental Sergeant Major Ellis came up to him and saluted.

Turnbull acknowledged the salute. "Morning, Sergeant Major," he said. "Bit of a surprise to see the regiment with handguns."

"Yes, sir, it is. Looks like the beginning of the end. The end of us, that is. Which would be a pity, sir. The cavalry's a pretty thing . . ."

The sergeant major was a well-read man—more so than some of the officers possibly—but not on parade. There he dropped back into its own vernacular. You could not curse troops in an educated manner.

"You may be right," Turnbull said. "You know I was in the Transvaal."

"Yes, sir, I remember when you got extra leave. There was a young lady, was there not?"

"Yes, and she died. I was very depressed for a while. But I got to know the Boers. I know how they will fight. They'll just use their horses for transport. They'll shoot at us when we are on the move, force us to deploy, and then they'll hop on their ponies and ride away."

"We could catch them, sir."

"Yes, if our horses were in the condition they are to-day. But our horses aren't used to living in the open, and you never found out at Wynberg how hot and cold the Transvaal can be. And remember, Sergeant Major, those Boer ponies carry nothing. Just a man, a saddle, a rifle, some ammunition, a blanket, and an overcoat, two or three pounds of dry meat and bread. That's all.

"Their ponies live on grass, live on the veld, without corn, and can go seventy miles in twelve hours. More if they have to. The smaller commandos won't even use wagons. No wheeled transport to worry about or defend. Their meat's alive, cattle on the hoof driven with their spare horses.

"Well, I must say good-by," Turnbull said, holding out his hand.

"Wish you were coming with us, sir," Ellis said as he saluted, and turned sharply about.

The trumpet sounded:

> Come to the cook house door, boys,
> Come to the cook house door.
> The officers' wives have pudding pies,
> And the soldiers' wives have skilly.
> And the soldiers' wives have skilly.

Then came the officers' luncheon call. By God, he thought, how I'm going to miss it. How I miss it now. How lovely the call of a trumpet was. Not sharp and harsh like a bugle. A trumpet had a terrible sound, a thin, screaming wail that pulled your heart up from your belly to choke your throat. The last winged notes of the "Last Post" on a trumpet, for instance, hanging like stars in the silence of the night, dying slowly as if the sounds had been alive, and were falling dew-soft upon the waiting earth.

He went into the anteroom and was greeted by his friends. Jackson came up to him, a senior lieutenant and acting captain who no doubt would soon be confirmed in rank. A good chap. A bit slow, as the colonel had said, but a good chap and an old friend.

"I'm sorry you're not coming with us, John. But I'll do my best with the squadron."

Turnbull laughed. "I love 'em," he said, "but it's a bad color. Remember the general inspection soon after you joined us? When Prescott commanded the squadron. How well they looked, pretty as a picture till the day before the general came. You'd think they got stage fright. The lot of them came out in a muck sweat and must have lost ten pounds in a night. I wish we could have weighed them. But you'll find them like that, Jackie. In fact, you must know it by now. There's a cycle with chestnuts. You build them up, and then when they reach a certain point they drop right down for no reason at all—just nerves."

"Like redheaded girls," Jackson said. "Very hot-tempered and excitable. Hard to keep in condition, I've been told."

"You'd better try one," Turnbull said. "You might learn something about horses from her. You know," he said, "I sometimes think we learn about horses from women, and about women from horses."

They smiled at each other and raised the pale amontillado in their sherry glasses.

The anteroom, which had been Turnbull's home for so long, was still the same. The same portraits of past colonels, the same battle pictures, the same heads. The big ovis ammon an officer called Harris had shot in 1855 in the Himalayas. It was said to be a record. An ibex from Turkey. A Rocky Mountain goat, a gaur, a Cape buffalo, a moose, a wapiti, a pair of chamois. All good heads, records or near records, presented by the officers who had shot them. There were the silver cups the regiment had won racing, at pigsticking, polo . . . in their glass-fronted cupboard. There were weapons—pigsticking lances, sabers, spears, trophies—each with a story.

The big, dark red leather armchairs, the old Turkey carpet, the heavy mahogany furniture, all just the same as he remembered it when he first came into the mess as a cornet of horse. All just as his father, who had once commanded the regiment, would have remembered it. He looked up at his father's portrait and wondered what the old boy would have made of Elsie.

After luncheon the colonel said, "I've arranged to have your batman seconded. He'll go back to London with you."

"Biglow?" Turnbull said.

"Yes, I thought you'd like it and he asked me if it could be arranged."

"Thanks, Charles. Nothing could please me better."

They shook hands. There were more good-bys.

"Good-by, John. Good-by, old chap. Don't finish it before we get there."

And then he was off, with Jim Stanley driving him and Biglow in the back seat.

The last time he had said good-by to anyone was in South Africa, to the Van der Bergs. To Catalina and Elsa's brothers. Leaving Boetie had hurt him particularly. He had grown so fond of the boy. He wondered if Pasha, the pony he had given him, was still alive. There was no reason why he should not be. Basutos were very tough.

It occurred to him that there were many kinds of good-by. Good-by when one would meet again tomorrow was meaningless. Next week or next year was still meaningless if there was no tie of affection.

But a *long good-by* was almost, but not quite, *adieu*—to God. Did you then commend your friend to God? Say we shall meet again after death? Adieu was forever. What he called in his mind a long good-by was for a long time, a time so long that when people met again they might have changed their hearts, or their minds, so that there might no longer be room for what they had once shared. With the Van der Bergs he had been sure it was adieu, though he had not said it. He had been convinced he would never return to a place where he had suffered such extremes of pain and joy.

But he was going back and there would be no joy in it this time. None at all. Only sorrow.

With Elsie, too, it would be a long good-by. Neither he nor anyone else knew how long it would be before they met again. Those who said that if there were war it would all be over by Christmas were wrong. Nor could he guess if she would change in his absence—develop in some new direction, away from him. Or that he would feel the same toward her. He doubted it. Men changed. Time changed men. In war, time was accelerated and men changed even faster.

It was not going to be easy to say good-by to Elsie.

But it was not being as hard as he had expected. Elsie had known it was coming. She was being very brave, even gay, as she helped him to pack.

He was glad to have his old batman, Trooper Biglow, William, Benjamin, No. 71475, a man of thirty with seven years' service and a clean crime sheet. Their desire to be together had been mutual.

Biglow had said, "Nice to be back with you, sir. Like old times, isn't it?"

"Not quite, Biglow. We're on our own this time."

"We'll make it, sir," Biglow said as he climbed into the back seat of the colonel's dogcart.

When the London train came in, they parted, Turnbull going into a first-class carriage and Biglow into a third. No officer ever traveled third, even in mufti.

A small, temporary good-by had been said to the regiment. Now for the long good-by to Elsie, his little light of love. He was not looking forward to it.

In the train Turnbull thought of the men he had said good-by to—au revoir, because he was pretty sure they would soon embark for South Africa. He thought of the cavalry, the service that was his life. The Tins, Tin Bellies —1st and 2nd Life Guards in their red tunics and white horsetailed helmets, and the blues, all on big black horses with white leathers and high jack boots. They had fought dressed like that at Waterloo. In the Crimea and even in the first Boer war, only twenty years ago, the British had worn scarlet.

He thought of the dragoon guards, the dragoons, the heavy cavalry, and then of the light cavalry, the 2nd, 3rd, 4th, 6th, 7th, 8th, 10th, 13th, 14th, 15th, 18th, 19th, and 20th Hussars. The 5th, 9th, 12th, 16th, 17th, and 21st Lancers. The light cavalry that were the eyes of the army. If the sergeant major was right, and he might well be, their function would remain even as mounted infantry. But the cause of the heavies was lost. They were the last reserve shock weapon. The tremendous weight of big men and heavy horses flung like a hammer at troops that had begun to waver. Their time would never come again.

Light cavalry was mounted on horses with some blood. Hunter types that were fast and could jump. The heavy cavalry had commoner, bigger, cold-blooded horses— light vaners, almost cart horses, with hairy heels. It was funny how that expression was used for people to cover lack of breeding. Vincent, with his contempt of the heavy cavalry, amused him. He did not even think much of the Grays, the crack 2nd Dragoons—the whole scarlet-clad bearskinned regiment that was mounted on gray or white horses.

It was curious that a foal was never born white. They started life a rusty black that turned to dapple gray and, with age, to white. But in army parlance there was no such thing as a white horse. They were all called grays. He thought of horse colors: chestnuts from almost red to dark liver with self-colored or paler manes and tails; bays, a rich brown with black manes and tails, some with black points, that is, black legs and faces, and some without; of browns defined by having paler touches on their legs and faces. A black horse was a brown if it had so much as a brown tinge to its nose. He thought of white marks—socks, stockings, a star, a blaze, a race, a snip. Every horse in the army had its description entered, its height, color, sex, age, and a registered number burned into its hoof.

The other colors, strawberry and blue roans, duns, iron grays that did not fit into the cavalry went to the mounted officers of the infantry. The only exceptions were the cream, pie, and skewbald horses of some cavalry bands, and grays for the trumpeters.

The function of the light cavalry was to protect and screen the force advancing behind them. They came into contact with enemy light cavalry performing the same mission and fought them in small skirmishes where a whole troop was seldom engaged.

They were also used in pursuit to turn a retreat into a rout; to lance and cut down fleeing men. The action at Balaclava had been unusual. A mass charge by a brigade of light cavalry was very rare.

He thought of the difference between British and French cavalry. The British, both light and heavy, charged all out *ventre à terre*—fox-hunter style—the fastest horses and bravest men reaching their objective first and generally dying first.

The French heavy cavalry, Napoleon's cuirassiers for example, came on in solid waves, riding knee to knee and stirrup to stirrup. First at a walk, then at a trot, then at a hard canter, the whole earth shaking beneath the weight of their horses. They came on, striking the infantry as a long balk of timber might, pushing them over, sabering them, and trampling them under their horses' hoofs. Wave after wave of heavy horsemen like the waves of the sea had been flung at the British squares at Waterloo, scarlet hedgehogs prickly with bayonet spines. The first rank kneeling, each rank firing volleys on command, each covering those who were reloading with a curtain of protective lead.

No square had been broken. The flower of Napoleon's cavalry lay dead, a struggling mass of dead and wounded men and horses before them. As the waves of cavalry broke around them they received further volleys in their backs from the rear side of the square as they rode past.

He wondered what the impact of two ranks riding boot to boot at a cantering speed of say ten miles an hour was.

What a formidable thing for an infantryman with only a muzzle-loading gun to face. What iron discipline, what trust in his comrades he must have to pour in his powder, tamp it, ram in his bullet, putting all his attention on the gun in his hand, not daring to look up in case he made a mistake as the ground he stood on shook under the hoofs of the charging horses.

Then to hold his fire till the order to fire came. To stand firm, their guns empty, with only their bayonets to protect them from the steel-cuirassed men, helmeted, their horsetails flying. Their sabers raised, the horses' nostrils flaring red, their eyes glazed with fright, enormous, a few feet from their own.

In a square only one man had to falter and a gap was made into which a single cuirassier could force his horse. Even if he died there, the square was broken. It could never re-form, and its members, rock-strong together in formation, could be sabered, slaughtered like sheep.

In the army only three things mattered: discipline, love—love of comrades and the regiment that must never be disgraced—and pride, the pride that was born of discipline and love.

But the Boers were going to be something different, something new. They had no discipline, but their love of their land was fanatical, and each man was an army alone. This was what he had tried to tell them at the War Office.

This was what they had refused to believe. . . . His mind went on searching for subjects as the train ran smoothly back to London. . . .

The one thing he did not want to think about was parting from Elsie.

CHAPTER 12

THE PRESENT

FOR SOME TIME Elsie had been collecting combings from the captain's pair of silver-mounted brushes. The man had told her that he needed quite a lot to select from. "We can only use the best, miss."

"Of course," she said. But the captain did not lose much of his bonnie brown hair, as she called it to herself. Then there was the design to choose, from a book of sample drawings. Some were very fanciful. She chose two lovers' knots suitably entwined in a heart-shaped locket.

"It's much easier if they are dead," Mr. Brown said. "We just come along and clip what we want. Many's the hair watch chain I've made," he said, "for some poor widower. It's a nice thought, I think, very nice, miss. Every time he looks at his watch he strokes her hair like."

"That is nice," Elsie said. If she died she would like the captain to have a watch chain made of her hair. It was, as he said, a beautiful idea.

"When I die you might make one," she said rather doubtfully.

"Oh, miss, that isn't what I meant at all. But I'll have it ready for you in ten days. Yes, miss, in ten days. If you can bring me one more lot—some good ones. You couldn't snip a few, I suppose, miss?" he suggested as he bowed her out of his little shop.

She would wear it on a long gold chain to hang between her breasts. Now she had to get something for him. She sent for Vincent.

"Vincent, I want to give the master something to take with him. Something he'll use all the time. He's got

brushes . . . a watch . . . I don't know. You tell me what
to get."

"I don't know either, Miss Elsie, but I have an idea.
Why not another set of razors and a strop? You could
keep his here, miss, and give him some new ones."

"What a good idea, Vincent. You can take me to get
them tomorrow morning. Where shall we go?"

"To Asprey's in Bond Street, of course, miss," he said.
There were only certain shops for certain things, as far
as Vincent was concerned. Wilkinson for swords. Swaine
and Adney for whips. Tautz for breeches. Peel's for boots.
Locks for hats. Hawkes for uniforms . . .

"You won't tell him, will you, Vincent? It's to be a surprise"

"I'll not tell him. And, Miss Elsie, I'll only put them in
at the last minute, with a note from you in the case, so
he'll not know till he's out at sea and needs a shave. That's
what I'll do. And I'll extract our set at the last minute.
I'm going to the train with him, of course. What about
you, miss?"

"I'll stay here. There'll be a lot of people he knows there.
Friends, ladies, and so on. I don't want to make him
ashamed."

"You're a good kid, miss," Vincent said, giving his master's mistress a light pat behind. "I think he's lucky, the
captain is. Lucky in the two of us."

Vincent had promised to keep the set of razors and
the strop secret. But that was all. He had other news for
the captain.

"Captain, sir," he said one morning when they were
alone, "do you know what Miss Elsie is doing?"

"I don't want to hear any scandal from you or anyone
else," Turnbull said. "What Miss Elsie does is her own
business."

"Yes, sir," Vincent said, "but I thought you'd be interested in knowing that she's collecting the combings from
your hairbrushes."

"She's what?"

"Collecting your combings, sir. She's shown them to me.
Quite a handful by now."

"What for?"

"To make herself a locket—heart-shaped, it is. I've seen

it, sir. She's going to take your hair and have it platted
into some kind of design, she says, and wear it on a chain
round her neck when you go. 'Then some of him'll be here
with me.' That's what she says. Do you know, sir, if you
will pardon my saying so, I think we've got a good girl
there."

But now No. 7 was in an uproar. Elsie, dry-eyed, flitted
about helpless as a kitten. Celeste was in tears. She was
half in love with *le capitaine,* which was her normal condition if she found herself in the company of any personable man for more than a couple of hours.

Only Vincent and Biglow, who were old friends, were
profitably employed with their master's pile of luggage.
The two black uniform cases, dappled with dark red and
marked with Captain Turnbull's name and regiment, were
already locked. There were, besides these, two long, coffin-
like metal trunks, a big canvas kit bag, a rolled heavy
canvas Wolseley valise—a sleeping bag that contained his
blankets and pillow, a heavy leather suitcase for use on the
ship, a hunting saddle packed in canvas, his camp kit—a
folding cot, a folding table, chair, and a combination
green canvas bath and basin.

Biglow was taking them down to Southampton in advance and was to meet Turnbull on the *Dunnottar Castle.*

There was one more day to spend, and Turnbull decided
to take Elsie to the zoo. He was a fellow of the Zoological
Society. "Mind if I come too, sir?" Vincent said.

"Mind, Vincent? I'm delighted."

Vincent was going to miss the captain. He was annoyed
to find he liked him so much. Lovable, that's what he was,
damn him, and so easy to fiddle that it was like taking
chocolate from a baby. What annoyed Vincent was that
if he had not liked him so much he could have made a lot
more out of him.

He had asked out of a sudden impulse if he could go
with them. He had not been to Regent's Park since he was
a nipper, and—this was not quite an afterthought—he was
still worried about Miss Elsie. There was something in
the wind. His soldier's instinct warned him. He'd seen a
man about in the street the other day he had not liked
the look of, a navvy with a pick on his shoulder. He had

been quite near him, and his hands had been white and looked soft. His fingernails were clean. As he passed No. 7 he had stopped and stared at the house.

"We'll take the stick," he said to himself. He meant his sword stick.

In the lion house Elsie began to cry. Her feet hurt. She didn't like the smell of the big cats and was suddenly convinced that her beloved captain would be eaten by a lion. They looked so ferocious. Having discovered, or rather been shown in an atlas, where Africa was, she had read up about it. The book had said a lot about lions and how ferocious they were, and nothing about the Boers at all. Lions were the real danger.

"Oh," she sobbed, "you'll be careful, won't you, John? You won't go out at night, will you? That's when they're worst."

How had Elsie got the idea that the Boers were more dangerous at night? "What's going to hurt me at night?" he said.

Elsie pointed a kid-gloved hand at a black-maned lion that lay asleep in his cage. "Lions," she said. "They eat people. I couldn't bear it if you were eaten." Her tears started anew.

Turnbull wanted to laugh and to kiss her, but he could not hurt her feelings by laughing at her. Nor could he kiss her in public, so he compromised by patting her— surreptitiously, he hoped—on her behind, an unsatisfactory gesture to both because of her whalebone stays. What a sweet, loving, stupid little thing she was.

The three of them had lunch in the members' enclosure, and he calmed Elsie with his stories about Africa, told her how he had spent two weeks trying to get a lion and had never got near one, though he had seen the spoor.

Vincent talked about tigers. He had been on a tiger hunt in India. He had been there as batman to Lord Lucwell. He had sat behind his master in a howdah on an elephant. "We shot two, Miss Elsie," he said.

Elsie now wanted to go for a ride on an elephant, and they did, the three of them, grownups among a lot of children. A captain of hussars, his valet, and a very pretty girl.

And pretty she was. Pretty as a picture to those who
saw her up there in an autumn costume of dark plum
cloth that fitted as tight as a skin except at the back,
where the skirt was bunched into the suspicion of a bustle.
She had on a purple bonnet trimmed with dark, shiny
red cherries that were filled with cotton wool. She knew,
because she had opened one to see. She had on high
black kid button boots with two-inch heels, black gloves,
and carried a black patent leather reticule. Her dark hair
fell in ringlets on either side of her heart-shaped face.
Her high bust was pushed higher by her stays. Around
her neck she wore a long black-green cock-feather boa.
Her stockings were gun-metal-colored silk.

In a miserable kind of way Elsie was very happy. Here
she was perched on an elephant trudging around Regent's
Park with Mr. Vincent and the master. She was satisfied
now that he would not be eaten by lions, but tomorrow, by this time, he would be gone. The linchpin
of her life knocked out. Like a wheel on its axle she
would continue to turn, but if anything went wrong there
would be nothing to hold her back in place.

Of course there would be Mr. Vincent and Celeste and
Ellen. Also Millie and Charlie the boy, and Queenie, all
new additions to No. 7. Queenie and she got on in an
amazing way, almost as if they could read each other's
thoughts. She had never known a dog's kissing tongue
was so soft, its nose so cold, or its eyes so tender and
beautiful. Queenie had come just at the right time and
she belonged to the master too.

Elsie was smiling softly at the trees that were level with
her eyes, as if they were people, when Turnbull said:

"If anything should happen, Elsie, you are not to
worry."

"What could happen?" she asked.

"I might get hurt, darling—killed," he said.

"You said there were only a few lions."

"It's a war, darling. I mean the Boers. They'll shoot at
us."

She supposed he was right. But she had put the idea of
war out of her head. One thing at a time was enough.
His leaving her was enough for now. Only half listening,
she heard him say, "I've been to see my lawyer. You will
be well provided for—five thousand a year of your own."

She bit her lip and clenched her hands together. I mustn't cry, she thought. I mustn't spoil our last afternoon together.

At last the moment arrived that Elsie had been waiting for in expectation, because the thought excited her, and in fear, because of what it meant. The captain was going to put on his uniform. She had looked at it often enough, touched the long-skirted barathea cavalry jacket with its scarlet neck tabs, the chain epaulets; the beige whipcord breeches, the top boots polished and boned by his man till they shone like fresh horse chestnuts.

He put on his shirt, pulled up his breeches, laced them over the calves, and with the boot hooks in his strong hands drew on the boots,

"The spurs," she said. Kneeling down, she fitted them on his heels and buckled the straps over the instep. He buttoned his jacket and she handed him the belt, to which was attached a long cavalry saber. The right epaulet had to be unbuttoned to take the cross strap that prevented the belt from sagging under the weight of the weapon.

"Put on the cap," Elsie said. The pretty cap with the red band and gold crown of the General Staff above its gold-edged peak.

Elsie knew no history. She was unaware that women for hundreds of years had armed their men for war. Knights in armor cap-a-pie watched by their ladies. Boer women at this moment, six thousand miles away, handing their rifles to their farmer husbands.

There has always been an attraction in a uniform, something that excites women as they watch a man changing, turning from the civilian they know into a stranger —a warrior, assuming a new virility.

They dined at home, falsely gay with champagne, Vincent serving them solicitously, Celeste tearful in the background, Ellen running panting up the stairs in her apron, her face red from the fire's heat, to see if everything was all right.

The night was terrible. A night of endless, exhausting love, as if they must wring out their passion like a cloth—and tears. But Elsie managed one thing. While Turnbull slept she had stuffed her crepe-de-Chine night-

dress, rolled into a tight little ball, into his dressing case.
She wished she could see his face when he found it.

Before breakfast, after the cup of tea Vincent brought
to the bedroom, he was gone. Only his man accompanied
him. Vincent had decided against leaving his mistress.

At last Elsie was alone, her own mistress for the first
time in her life, and another house in England was
masterless.

PART THREE

LOVE AND WAR

> *"There is a time to love and a time to hate."*
>
> ECCLESIASTES 3:8

[*South Africa and England—October to December 1899—Summer*]

CHAPTER 13

THE WAGONS COME

IN AFRICA the war was for the moment pretty static. The Boers had invested Ladysmith completely. There were Boers on every hill and *kopje*. The men who should have swept the British like dust before a broom into the sea and taken Durban settled down to wait for the town to surrender. Ten thousand horsemen lay idle, watching the enemy build up their defenses.

Seeing that they were likely to remain here for some time, the Boers began to build shelters and make themselves comfortable. There were no parades, no drills, except for an occasional fatigue party to the railway to fetch supplies. This inaction killed their fighting spirit and many of the burghers gave themselves leave and went home. Others arrived, and from day to day not even the generals knew the exact strength of the force under their command.

There was some long-range sniping at the English. There were visits to neighboring farms to see what luxuries could be scrounged—a chicken here, a suckling pig there, some milk or eggs, begged or stolen. In a couple of weeks tents were served out and Moolman's squad settled in. So far they had been lucky. Only Bothma had been hit and his wound was already healed.

Now at last, stationary and comfortably housed, they really began to get to know each other as they rode over the veld or sat talking by their fire.

The hardships of war did not affect Moolman. They were less arduous than many of his hunting expeditions. Also, the food was better, and he had the companionship of men he liked. Every day he grew fonder of the two boys he had taken under his wing. Patriotism was only a word to him. Like most Boers, he was not fighting for honor or some obscure commercial interest. He was fighting for his land, for his right to be a free burgher, and out of hatred of the English.

Fifteen of Moolman's forty years had been spent on the veld with only sky for a ceiling. He was uneasy in a house. Because of his experience he was a better forager than most, and able to make the best of even the greatest discomfort.

"Yes, Boetie," he said one night as they all sat talking, "when it is raining there is always some place where it is raining a little less. In the lee of a bush or behind a rock. In every situation there is always the knowledge that things might be worse, and often something to be learned. In war it is important to know what not to do."

It was typical of Moolman that he carried a receptacle —half cup, half basin—that had once been white enamel, tied to his saddle by a *voorslag* threaded through a hole in its edge to a dee on his saddle. He used it for everything—cooking, drinking, washing. "Why," he said, "should a man need more than one dish, or more than a sheath knife and a spoon to eat with?" With him everything was cut to the bone. His equipment was as good and as spare as his body.

"Always look for the strange," he told them, "for something which should not be there. A dark spot, a moving branch, the flick of an ear, the flash of light on a horn."

O'Brien remained depressed at having fought his brothers in the fusiliers. Upset at having fought them and upset that any Irishman should fight as a soldier of the Queen. But there were a lot of Irish regiments, and though most of them were not in South Africa, there were many Irishmen scattered in British regiments right through the army. It puzzled him. Even the Irish love of a scrap did not seem enough to justify it. At night he still had nightmares at the horror of it, of having killed men of his own kind.

Beyers tried to console him with tales of his young wife's beauty.

The Groenplaas Kerels, as they had been called at first in the Pretoria Commando, were now known as "Moolman's Men."

"Of course we have not yet come very far or fought very much," Moolman said. "But too much luck always frightens me. It is dangerous to be too happy or content." He thought of how happy he had been once. That was real happiness. Luck, fate, call it what you will, had led him to the very pinnacle of content and then thrown him into the abyss of despair.

"To be safe there must be some ill fortune," he said. "Some thorns in the bed of roses."

With the commandos settled, the women who had got news of it began to come in wagons with their families, to cook, wash, mend, and take care of their men. Some men had even gone home to fetch their wives.

The laagers became homelike, with children and dogs playing among the wagons, with women standing at the cooking fires, with washing hanging on the line. Women's voices were heard, girls' laughter, the shouts of unheeding children, the barking of dogs, the crow of an occasional cock. Some of the women had brought their poultry slung in crates under the wagon beds. A few had brought milk cows. There was a lull in the war. People were almost in a holiday spirit, dancing and singing in the evenings. Surely the English would surrender soon and it would all be over and they could go home.

A few days after Moolman's talk about the dangers of good luck and happiness, when Boetie was riding over the veld to exercise his pony and continue training it to follow without being led and come at a whisle, he came across Jan Beyers, his dog beside him, sitting on an ant-hill staring into space. He dismounted.

"Why are you by yourself, Jan?" He said.

"I am not fit company today. I worry about her," he said. "I fear some terrible thing has taken place. I do not know, before God I do not know, if I can stand it. Never was a man's heart so sore, Boetie. To ride off and leave a girl alone upon the veld like that, with only an old man to take care of her. Man," he said, "we are not six months married yet."

"Yes," Boetie said. "It must be terrible."

"She is only eighteen and lovely. Man, as lovely as a lily blooming in the moonlight."

Boetie liked Jan Beyers. He was a brave man, a fine fighter. It made him sad to see him heartbroken.

"I may go," Beyers said. "Many have ridden home to

see their families and farms. But if we all did that, what would happen? I spoke to Moolman and he said, 'Follow your heart.' But my heart is in two places. That is why I am here, *jong*. It is best to suffer alone."

"You have been alone long enough," Boetie said. "Let us ride back together."

When they got back they found that Bothma had gone. Without a word he had saddled his horse and slipped away. Things were slack and he was going to profit by it to go home. *Huis toe* was the Dutch for it, for going home. More and more burghers were giving themselves leave, while others were turning up out of the blue, encouraged by what seemed victory—men who had so far evaded the call-up. Every Boer of military age, over eighteen, even if he had a wooden leg, had been called up. But the landdrosts had raised only about two thirds of the country's strength when mobilization took place. Dependent on the popular vote for their jobs, they did not enforce penalties on those who claimed exemption for one reason or another.

There were others, men who had been so far away hunting in the bushveld that they had only just heard of the war. These were prime fighters who lived by gun and saddle.

Then there was the town scum, rounded up and more or less driven to war. These reinforcements swelled the Boer numbers but added nothing to their strength. They came from the slum quarters of Pretoria, where they had drifted when they lost their cattle in the great rinderpest epidemic of '96 and, debased by town life, they had sunk into almost total apathy, the breeding of children their only activity.

It took Bothma ten days to get to Groenplaas. Nothing had happened there. Time had stood still. But time was a variable. He had not been away long but in that time he had been wounded in battle, and his adventures and hardships had been such that to him it seemed a lifetime. He was astonished and somewhat shocked to find so little changed at home, and after a week of near idleness he decided to leave. He had chased up the Kaffirs a little, but knew that as soon as he left they would relapse into idleness. He had repaired a plow, had the wagon axles greased, and that was about all. He had played with his children, telling them stories of the war. He had slept with his wife. And now it was time to go.

No one had seemed particularly glad to see him. Jacoba, who had been so passionate at their parting—it was partly the thought of her love-making that had drawn him back —had been quite cold. His return, after what seemed only a few days to her, was an anticlimax, and his wound, a flesh one in the arm, was already scabless, just a red mark on the white skin; nothing at all heroic. Catalina at the big house merely asked for news of her sons and said, "When are you going back?"

The Bible was certainly right. Both a hero and a prophet were without honor in their own country. But it was Jacoba who had amazed him most. She was not the woman he had left. She did not even seem to believe some of his stories.

He returned even more slowly than he had gone, aware now that it had been a mistake to go home. It had weakened his resolution. No good could come of this war. It served no purpose. He was even beginning to think that an English administration might have been an improvement on what they had. He believed in progress.

What, after all, was freedom? Was it freedom to be dragged from your home to fight in a war in which you no longer had any belief? The sooner it ended, the better for all concerned.

At the farms where he slept he found the women still eager for war, confident of victory, and sure that a negotiated peace was near. It had happened in '80. It would happen again. They wanted only two things—victory and their men back. Both seemed increasingly unlikely.

When he reached the commando, he found that things had not changed much. No one appeared to have missed him. Boetie asked him how his mother was and Servas questioned him about the farm and crops. How were the mealies looking? How many cows had calved?

Shortly after Bothma's return Boetie, out on the veld, saw a horseman approaching. There was something strange about him. He wore Boer clothes, but they did not look right. Boetie rode into the fold of a hill and waited. Moolman had said, "Always look for something strange, something unusual. It might be a British spy." Then suddenly he realized what was wrong. The rider was a woman in man's clothes that were too big for her. He rode forward.

The girl pulled up her horse, a handsome gray. He took his hat off and said, "What are you doing here, miss? This is a battlefield."

"I seek a man, *jong*. I seek my man. He is with the Pretoria Commando. I am told it lies this way."

"I belong to it," Boetie said. "And who is your man?"

Her blue eyes lit up. "God has sent you to me," she said. "*Ja*, God be thanked. He is well? He is unhurt?"

"What is his name?" Boetie asked. She was just a girl and no beauty at that.

"Jan Beyers of Boskop."

"Well, he was right," Boetie said. "You are indeed a beauty. That is what Jan says of you. 'My wife is a beauty.'" It was a lie, but it would make her happy to know that Jan said that of her.

"Then he is here?"

"He is here, not three miles away."

"And well?"

"He is well, but he pines. I have never seen a man so sore of heart."

"He need pine no more. I have come to him. We will fight side by side as we would have lived." She leaned forward from her saddle, and put her hand on Boetie's thigh.

There were other women whose men were fighting with the commandos, but they were not young. It would be strange to have a girl like this in the corporalship.

"I will not be a nuisance to you. I can fight," she said. "Just look." Before he could express his surprise, she had raised her rifle and put two bullets into a rock a hundred yards away, her gray standing steady beneath her. "My father taught me. I was with him till he was killed."

"How was he killed?"

"He was speared by savages. I shot one and got away on Bloubooi." She patted her horse's neck. "Now we have nothing. The cattle have gone, the house was in flames as I rode away."

"Come, then," Boetie said.

Beyers recognized the horse before his wife as he ran forward, followed by his dog.

"Hetta, Hetta," he cried as he lifted her down and took her in his arms. His face had changed, lighting up with the inward fire of his joy. The gray horse stood quiet. Boetie sat in his saddle staring at the scene. So this was love. To Jan this ugly girl was beautiful . . . It was for her he had pined.

Pasha and the gray horse breathed, snorting, into each other's faces as the Beyerses, both crying now, clung to each other.

Moolman rode up on his buckskin.

"Magtig, what goes on here, Boetie?"

"It's Jan's wife," Boetie said. "They kiss."

"I have eyes," Moolman said.

The Beyerses broke away and turned to him.

"It is Hetta, my wife. This is our leader," he said to the girl, "Moolman."

She bobbed her head and held out her hand. "I have come to join you," she said.

Jan looked astonished. So it was not just a visit. "The farm?" he said. "Your father cannot manage it alone."

"There is no farm, no cattle, no house, and I have no father now."

"What happened?"

"Kaffirs," she said. "With the men away they raided."

"My God!" Moolman said. "Again it happens." He patted the girl's cheek. *"Mevrou,"* he said, "fifteen years ago it happened to me, and I lost all—"

Because of that, because she had nothing and no place to go, she joined the corporalship. Moolman saw to that.

They had a girl with them now, a good girl, a good wife to Beyers, who cooked and washed for them all.

That night Jan Beyers sang happy songs as the ugly girl, almost beautiful in the firelight, sat beaming at her man—with his dog Rand lying between them.

CHAPTER 14

THE CAPE OF GOOD HOPE

EVERY DAY when Turnbull used his new razors, one for each day, and his new strop, he thought of Elsie. She had known he would. She had said so in the note he had found in the blue-velvet-lined mahogany case. In an unformed, childish hand she had written: "Please think of your Elsie when you shave." He did. It made shaving more enjoyable.

How she would laugh when he wrote and told her that on the day they landed when he wanted to look his best he had cut himself. No doubt Vincent would laugh too. Queenie would look up at them wagging her tail. He liked to think of them all at home, for that was what No. 7 had become. Distance and three weeks at sea had crystallized his emotions. He had given up worrying. Time enough for that later on. For the moment No. 7 Acacia Road was his home and Elsie was its mistress and his love.

It was the nightdress that had done it. She must have got up in the night, crept out of bed, terrified of waking him, to pack it in his dressing case. He thought of her naked, her eyes full of tears, rolling it up and stuffing it in at the bottom so that it would not be found till he settled in on board. He thought of her mind, of what he thought she was thinking. She was trying to give him a piece of herself. A nightdress was a kind of skin, a second skin that she had worn and taken off for his delight. Crepe de Chine so pale a pink that it was almost white. He remembered buying it in the Burlington Arcade. The woman who had sold it to him had said, "It's so fine, sir, that you can pull it through a wedding ring." She had known very well that men did not buy nightdresses like that for ladies who wore wedding rings. But there it was, a crumpled fragment like the petal of a flower that smelled of her, of her tuberose perfume, of her body.

Biglow had found it. His face a parade-ground mask, he had said, "Madam must have thought it would come in

150

handy, sir," as he smoothed it and laid it out beside his master's blue- and white-striped silk pajamas. Biglow never called her Miss Elsie. She was Madam to him. But he thought a lot of her. "Good for the captain, she is," was what he had told Vincent and Vincent had told Turnbull. Vincent was a great carrier of good news. The bad he kept to himself.

While Biglow occupied himself with the rest of the luggage, Turnbull folded the nightdress up and put it in the drawer of his bedside table.

The voyage had seemed interminable. There was a break at Madeira where the *Dunnottar Castle* dropped her anchor for a few hours and he was able to send a cable to Elsie. There was the mild excitement of passing a ship homeward bound that had hung a blackboard over the side with a message saying: "BOERS DEFEATED. THREE BATTLES. PENN SYMONS KILLED."

This prompted General Buller to say at mess that night that he hoped it would all be over before they got there.

That was about all that happened on the voyage. There were some schools of flying fish skittering out of the water, and an albatross followed the ship for a while after they had left St. Helena. He knew some of the cavalry officers on the staff, having met them on maneuvers or at the Cavalry Club. But both 127 Piccadilly and 7 Acacia Road seemed very far away. He made friends with Winston Churchill, a young war correspondent who had been a lancer and was going out for the *Morning Post*. And Philip Ketteringham, a captain in the 60th Rifles. But he was bored with ship life and delighted to hear that Table Mountain was almost in sight.

He went on deck but had to wait a couple of hours before he could see it. He thought of the other times he had seen it. The first when the regiment had been stationed at Wynberg. The second when he sailed away, leaving his heart behind him. Now his heart was in England.

And there it was—a dark oblong on the horizon that grew slowly bigger.

He wondered how long it would be before they got to the fighting.

At the Cape of Good Hope, Mr. and Mrs. Edward de Lange were going to meet the *Dunnottar Castle*. It was a two-hour drive from Morningstar, the farm in Wynberg, to the Cape Town docks. A beautiful drive through some of the most beautiful country in the world, past Groote Schuur, Cecil Rhodes's home, where he had planted hundreds of hydrangeas that were in full, pink, balloonlike flower in the sweet soil, past vistas of Table Bay, past flowers and shrubs, past pine trees and the great oaks and fine homes of Newlands. Everywhere beside the road there were arum lilies, as the English called them, wild here and looking in the distance as if some immense picnic party had left papers scattered on the veld. To the Dutch they were pig flowers, *varkblomme*, because pigs dug them up, being inordinately fond of their tuberous roots.

They drove on, downhill, into the town, Cape Town, nestling at the foot of Table Mountain and creeping up its flanks.

The De Langes had a town house in Long Street that they used when Parliament was in session. Edward was a Member, a descendant of one of the few old Dutch families that had thrown their lot in with the English and had become Anglicized by blood and tradition. The others were the Van Bredas, the Van der Byls, and the Cloetes.

Anna de Lange had been happily married for ten years and had two young girls—Eva aged seven, and Lina, who was nine. So far there had been no matrimonial disagreements. Though she had no love for England, Anna spoke English perfectly and had many English friends. She had been too young to be affected by the first Boer war. She and her husband had felt the same about the raid in '96, a disastrous and shocking event, engineered by Rhodes, that had ruined the mutual trust of Boer and Briton.

But this was different. Now she and Edward were on different sides of the fence. Educated at Rugby and Oxford, half English through his mother, the daughter of a British general, he took their side and was contemptuous of Paul Kruger, the Boers, and all they stood for. Then there was her sister Dora in Pretoria. They had been very close as children and wrote to each other every week. If there were war the Transvaal would be enemy country. My country, she thought. There would be no letters and she would be cut off from her sister and the Willows, the house where they had both been born.

That they were going to meet Sir Redvers Buller and his staff was not her wish. She had merely agreed to accompany her husband. The great ship was almost in now. Men were shouting, lines were being thrown, lines to which hawsers as thick as a man's arm were tied, fat ropes like snakes that were wound around the stumpy iron bollards. The decks were alive with khaki, thousands of men all the color of manure.

In the saloon the officers were grouped behind a short, fat man. They all had red, like fresh blood, on their caps and collars. They wore their caps, many of them gold-edged. The fat general had more gold than the others. His face was red, flushed with drink, but sad. He seemed to her to look bewildered. The table behind him held bottles of champagne, some opened, and glasses—wide-mouthed, fragile-stemmed champagne glasses. What a lot of glass and china must get broken in a storm at sea.

The staff officers, with the exception of two ADCs, were not young. They were in their thirties or forties, mustached erect, well set up and confident in their brown top boots, spurs, and Sam Browne belts to which swords were attached by brass-buckled frogs. The swords had silver hilts and leather sword knots. The scabbards were covered with leather. Many of the officers wore medals. The dark blue and green of the Indian frontier, the blue and white of the Egyptian campaign, the yellow and black of the Matabele rebellion, medals that, if you knew them, were a history of their wearers' war experiences.

The general had a whole row of medals. Nearest to the buttons of his tunic, in the place of honor, was the plain, plum-colored ribbon of the Victoria Cross, the greatest of them all, presented more often than not post-humously to the wives of the recipients who had been killed in action. Very few of these brave men lived to have this bronze Maltese cross pinned to their breasts by the Queen.

The sun coming through the portholes illuminated the scene. The brass buttons shone like gold, the guards of the swords and the spurs flashed silver, the red tabs of the staff bled more profusely.

Anna liked the look of one man. He stood away from the others as if he did not really belong among them. A captain from his stars—of thirty-five or so. The regimental badges worn on his collar were two crossed swords with a horse's head between them. He stood erect as the others but seemed sad. There must be good men among them, she thought. Perhaps this was one. His eyes were blue, his bristly mustache dark brown, and he had cut himself shaving. Was it that that endeared him to her? Did it make him human, remove him from the neat, shining automatons about him? Or was this just the woman in her? The incredible, stupid, tender woman in whom a wound, even a shaving cut, brought out some ancient instinct of succor? Perhaps it was not possible to hate a man, even an English soldier, who could cut himself. She felt herself smiling.

Still smiling at her thoughts, she found herself shaking hands with Sir Redvers Buller. *Magtig,* she thought, for the smile seemed glued to her face, I hope he does not think I am welcoming him.

Champagne corks popped. White-coated stewards went around with glasses on silver salvers. There were more civilians in the saloon now, English from the Cape come to greet the general. She nodded at those she knew.

She found the blue-eyed captain at her side. He smiled at her and said, "Since there is no one to introduce us, may I introduce myself? My name is Turnbull, Captain John Turnbull of the Second Hussars."

She held out her hand and said, "How do you do."

He went on, "I think I have seen you before, though I have never met you. You are Mrs. De Lange of Morningstar. I used to ride over your place and have hunted jackal with your husband's hounds."

"The Second," she said. So that was why the badge seemed familiar. "You were stationed in Wynberg a few years ago."

"That's right," he said, "and very happy I was. But I am not glad to be back. I have too many friends in the Transvaal. This is a miserable business," he blurted out suddenly after a pause, "but a soldier goes where he is sent."

"It is not the Transvaal yet, Captain Turnbill," she

said. "It is still the South African Republic. It was my home before I was married. I was born in Pretoria."

"Pretoria," he said. "Church Street, the square . . ."

"You know it?" she said.

"I know it well."

"I have a sister there—Mrs. van Reenan. She has two daughters. I have two girls too. If you are a farmer females are good," she said. "Heifer calves. But with people it is not the same. Men want sons. It is their name. They do not want it to die. But girls are nice too. Do you have a girl, Captain Turnbull?" It never occurred to her that a man of his age would not be married.

Without thinking Turnbull said, "Oh yes."

"What is her name?"

"Elsie." My God, what was he thinking of?

"How old is she?"

"Twenty-two."

"Then she will soon be getting married, I suppose. At twenty-two a girl should be married, Captain. She needs a man. Is she attractive?" He must be older than he looked to have a girl of twenty-two.

Turnbull was beginning to enjoy himself. In for a penny —in for a pound. "Lovely," he said. "She is very dark with big brown eyes."

"You sound as if you love her, Captain. It is nice for a girl to have a father who loves her, but hard on her later sometimes."

"I hope so," he said.

Before she could continue her inquiries, her husband had taken her arm. "We must go," he said.

"Good-by, Captain Turnbull," she said. She had not even had time to introduce Edward to him.

On the drive home her husband said, "I told the general if he was short of quarters we would put up a couple of officers. It's a bit far out of course, but it's near the camp."

"No, Edward," Anna said. "That is too much. Not in my house. Not the enemy. Can't you understand what I feel?" She put her gloved hand on his arm.

"Edward," she said, "this is going to be hard for us, you on one side and I on the other. But we have our love and the girls and the years we have spent together, living in one house, sleeping in one bed. But we must be

patient with each other and careful." She hesitated a minute and then said, "in this war"—how she hated the word,
how all women must hate it; particularly those with sons
—"in this war what will be a victory for you will be a
disaster for me, and vice versa. We must remember that
until it is over. God help us." She began to cry.

"I'll send a man to the general with a letter, darling,"
her husband said. "It is your house. You must choose
your guests."

She stopped crying. An idea had occurred to her.

"No, Edward," she said, "you must not do that. We'll
have them."

"To please me?"

"Perhaps," she said, smiling up at him through her
tears. But it was not that. Not that at all. With staff
officers in the house she might get valuable information.
If she were friendly she might be able to get letters
through to her sister, who could pass it on.

The great deception was begun.

CHAPTER 15

DIANA

THE GENERAL and his party were cheered through Adderley Street as they drove up to the Mount Nelson Hotel.
But things were not quite as bright as they had seemed
at sea. There were no British victories. Boer successes were
bringing volunteers from Europe. Hollanders and Frenchmen, Irish and Germans were streaming into the country.
The Cape Dutch, who were British subjects, were crossing
the Orange by the hundred to join their compatriots to
the north. There were pictures of British prisoners being
marched through the streets of Pretoria, and the very day
after their arrival President Steyn renounced his pledge
of non-invasion and the Free State Commandos crossed
the Orange River into the Cape Midlands.

Turnbull was thinking of his conversation with Mrs.
De Lange and the turn it had taken. Did he have a girl?

Was she pretty? At twenty-two she was old enough to be married. My God, he thought, that'll make her laugh when I write about it. All except the married part. He did not think she would marry anyone else, and for him to marry her himself was unthinkable—almost.

With nothing much to do till the general took the field, Turnbull was walking on the lawn of the hotel garden when he heard his name called by a woman, and turned to see Diana Darnley, an old friend, someone indeed who had at one time been rather more than a friend.

"My dear," he said, striding toward her, "what are you doing here?"

"Fishing in troubled water, John, while Darnley's at the front. I couldn't bear to let him come all this way alone. He might get into mischief. But with me here if he gets a little leave there'll be no excuse, will there?"

"I should think not. Not with you at hand."

She laughed up at him, her hand on his arm. "Would you like to guess a number?" she said. Then, answering herself, she went on: "I know you wouldn't. You never liked guessing games, so I'll tell you." She swept an almost invisible curtsy. "The magic number is 301." Then she turned, twirling her lace-edged parasol, and walked slowly past the fountain, up the steps to the terrace, and sat down at a table in the shade of a tree where two young officers, in red tabs that looked like those of ADCs, joined her at once.

How well he knew her. How well he had known her. She hadn't changed her man-hungry ways. She was what this new chap Freud, who wrote about these things, called a nymphomaniac. That her reputation was perfect was due only to her discretion. Major Charles Darnley, of the 22nd Lancers, was ten years older than she. He would come into money and a title one day, and Diana had no intention of losing either by being careless or stupid. She had never lost anything in her life. The daughter of a parson in the Shires who had kept three hunters, she had been brought up among horses and grooms. Educated by governesses and her father, she had always managed to get what she wanted and do what she wanted.

She had learned about men from the grooms but had never been in any danger from them. Virginity in the 1880s was not something to be lightheartedly lost in a hayloft. She just played with the grooms, teased them, and learned about men from them. The rest, the real fun, had had to wait till she was married. Always gay and playful, no one could believe ill of her. Least of all her husband, to whom she submitted her manifold charms with a mixture of modesty and roguery, tricking him into attentions, teasing him as she had teased the grooms but not running away from him as she had from them. How could a man believe that so loving a wife had such an endless store of the gifts she thrust upon him that there was enough for all comers? If they were the right sort of men and came singly. She never had two lovers at once. She was a faithful mistress and a safe one. She never talked. Most women found it impossible to keep the fact that they had a lover secret from their friends. That was one of the reasons they had lovers—to boast of them.

Turnbull knew he would go to her room. She had known he would come. They had seen it at once in each other's eyes. For a moment he was furious with Elsie. It was all her fault. Before Elsie, before he had lived with her, a woman now and then had been all he required. Even the affair with Diana had been very episodic. Elsie was always beautiful, always charming, always willing. So now, with the habit of women and three weeks on shipboard without one, he was going to sleep with Diana again—just because she was there. Pretty, dainty little Di, who was as hard as nails. He remembered her saying once, "Men want women, don't they? They need them. Even if they are married they don't get enough and go to tarts and pay them." He'd said, "Yes." "Well," she went on, "I'm like a man. I'm a woman that needs men, needs more than one man can give me. I want them and I pay them." He had looked at her curiously. "I pay them with my body. Does that make things clear?" It had. The liaison had lasted three years, lasted until the regiment went to South Africa and he had met Elsa. Now it was going to begin again.

Thanks to Elsie, damn her. There was one consolation, though. It could not last this time. They would be going up country in two or three days.

Diana was twenty-six. She had been married when she was seventeen. In nine years she had changed very little.

Nothing affected her feelings. Her affairs were meaningless emotionally. They flattered her vanity, the intrigue amused her, and the act satisfied her physically.

She was a real English beauty—rose, white, and gold. She stood five feet without shoes and weighed seven stone. She had tiny feet and hands, beautiful insteps and ankles. Her waist when laced up was fifteen inches around. Without stays it was eighteen. Her blue eyes were large, innocent as a kitten's, and set wide apart under long lashes. No one in the wide world could have looked sweeter. It was impossible to believe that butter would ever melt in so gentle a mouth.

She saw Turnbull twice later that day. She smiled at him and nodded gently, indicating acquaintanceship but no more. She never spoke to her lovers, never went out with them, never did more, if she met one by accident, than discuss the weather and pass on.

"Know her?" Ketteringham, who was with Turnbull, asked.

"I met Mrs. Darnley some years ago at home. Nodding acquaintance. But she is a pretty woman, isn't she?"

"I know Darnley," Ketteringham said. "A nice chap. In the Twenty-second. Got a D.S.O. the other day. But older than she is—a lot older. You'd think a girl like that would kick over the traces, but there's never been a word of talk about her."

Turnbull dined with Ketteringham rather than join the general and the rest of the staff in the private dining room upstairs. He had excused himself on the grounds of intelligence. "I may pick something up, sir," he'd said.

"By all means, my boy, by all means," Buller said.

The dining room was full, and everyone, including himself, was in full dress—tails, white tie, buttonhole, and all.

The women wore ball gowns. There was only a scattering of khaki, though all the men were soldiers recuperating from illness or were on staff. The air was fragrant with a dozen perfumes. The women were as brilliant as brightly colored birds. It was curious how war excited women. It brought out the worst in most of them. Some were officers' wives. Some were adventuresses. Some were here to have all the fun they could in this world of women-starved men. Few if any were doing anything to help the sick or wounded. Some of the amateur nurses who had come out to help and found themselves unable to stand the gaff had returned to the Cape, where they posed as Florence Nightingales.

"Clever of her to come out," Ketteringham said when they saw the Honorable Mrs. Beecher across the room. She had been divorced.

"She had bad luck and I must say I admire her in a way. There are a lot worse than she. They just haven't been found out," Turnbull said, thinking of Diana.

"A bit blatant, old boy, though. Bad taste, I mean," Ketteringham said.

"It was the only way she could get a divorce from Beecher. He had no choice when she lived openly with Frank Hartley, and then for him to get killed in the National."

"It's a dangerous race and a sort of coincidence that it happened at Beecher's Brook. I mean, every time someone says her name or she says it herself it must ring some kind of bell. But she carries it well, doesn't she?"

"Lord Tortly took it badly, I hear. She's his only daughter—apple of his eye and all that. Refuses to see her now."

"Kitty Rogers is here too," Ketteringham said. "She's staying at the Queens at Sea Point. Came out here three years ago, directly after her divorce, and is doing very well, I hear. She went to Johannesburg and only came back when the trouble started. By jove," he said, "I've never seen such diamonds. She'd got one the size of a walnut. Flaunts them, too. But I'm not surprised. She's a looker and a looker who's a lady and doesn't mind who she takes on in South Africa, as long as he's rich, can do very well."

"I've never understood it," Turnbull said. "With that kind of man, I mean."

"Millionaires must have a charm of their own," Ketteringham said. "And what's a woman to do if she's got nothing?"

The men went on gossiping, but Turnbull's mind was not on what they were saying. He was watching Diana at a table for six. She was the only woman. Even in a room full of lovely women she stood out. Her dress was heavy white satin cut low over the shoulders to the soft swelling of her breasts. She wore the Darnley pearls. They were famous. She had not taken off her long gloves but wore them with the hands tucked into the wrists. The fine kid, molded into her arms, gave them a greater significance. On one wrist over the glove she wore a diamond bracelet. He could see her rings flash from where he sat, but she never looked his way.

After dinner he joined a party in the cardroom and played whist till eleven. In his room he wrote a letter to Elsie and read a detective story by Conan Doyle in the *Strand Magazine*.

In her room Diana Darnley was waiting. She had waited so often for so many men. She enjoyed it. She liked getting ready for love. She liked the anticipation.

She was wearing a very thin lawn nightdress with a lace yoke. Over that she had a peignoir of lace—ruffle after ruffle of it, so that she seemed to be embedded in a garment of gossamer white foam that rippled like water when she moved. She had white mules decorated with marabou on her feet.

On the dressing table a single lamp with a pink shade gave the room and the woman a rosy glow. By her double bed on the night table were her Bible and prayer book.

She was very careful never to miss church on Sunday, at Christmas, or at Easter. She gave generously to all charities. Her aim was to create a picture of unsullied conventional virtue, the best defense against gossip. No one she knew would ever believe any scandal about her.

She took a French novel in a yellow paper cover from a drawer and settled down near the light to read. She had been well educated and read French perfectly. She knew what a pretty picture she made. She was intensely happy, as content as a purring cat, as contented now with the delight of anticipation as she would be later with that of satiation. The hour or so that lay between the two she enjoyed. It flattered her to have such power over a man. She enjoyed her body and felt it a waste not to use it to give pleasure, to both others and herself.

There was an aura of perfume about her. Her bath had been scented. She loved to soak in hot perfumed water. Then came the talcum powder, scented too, and the dabs of lilac perfume here and there—behind the ears, between the breasts, under the unshaved arms, on the flat

smoothness of her belly. Always after her bath she stood
naked, admiring her body—silk-smooth ivory tipped with
gold. This was the most beautiful thing in the world.
This was what she worshiped. That others should worship
it too seemed only right.

Though the book was in her hand she was not reading.
She was lost in dreams. Not of Turnbull—one did not
have to dream of reality—but of Wanthope. Brigadier
General Lord Wanthope, with a big house in Grosvenor
Square, a deer forest in Scotland, a shoot and hunting
box in Ireland, and a county seat in the Shires—Warwick-
shire, where he was honorary master of the Pulker, said
to be one of the best packs of hounds in England. When
he retired he would be master, of course. That was understood.

She still loved horses and hunting. When she was a girl
it had been wonderful. Going out, with her father's second horseman to take care of her when he could be
spared. Half servant, half lover. He was assistant stud
groom at the Haras de Bondel in France now. She wondered if he ever thought of her—he must of course—and
how he got on with French women. It was he who had
told her to stick to horsemen, men who hunted, rode
steeplechases, played polo—the cavalry. "Miss Diana,"
he'd said, "men who are good with horses are good with
women. They have good hands." She often thought of it
and had sometimes almost laughed at the most inopportune moments.

It was Henry Wanthope who had recommended Charlie
for the D.S.O. Not at her request, of course. But she'd
led up to it slowly, day after day. That was at Aldershot
before the war, but with war a near certainty. She'd said
it would make Charlie so happy if he got a chance to dis-
tinguish himself. All he needed was a chance.

Well, he'd been given the chance. She'd known it would
work. Henry felt guilty about her. He thought he was the
first, that he was responsible for her downfall, so, though
he certainly never put it into words or even thoughts,
when the chance came to reward the man he had
cuckolded he gave it to him—gave him the chance to risk
his life and get the reward if he came through.

Charlie was a brave man, even a reckless man, but she
had encouraged him.

"Oh, Charlie, it would make me so happy if you got something."

"Got what?" he'd said.

"I don't know. Mentioned in dispatches—a decoration. Not a V.C. of course, that's too big a risk . . ."

Seeds in men's hearts were sown as a gardener sows seeds in a flower bed. You sowed the seeds and one day with a bit of luck you picked the flowers.

Diana had seen Kitty Rogers and Audrey Beecher and had cut them both. She hated fools, because they were dangerous. She hated these two women even more, because they were not fools.

Audrey had dared to run away openly with the man she loved, and, if Frank had not been killed, would probably have been quite happy living with him in the South of France or Italy. She could not have gone on living in England. It would have been too humiliating. But it had taken courage. She had played her cards and lost the game, but it had been a near thing. Still, it was hard to think of staking one's life on happiness. On a dream. Kitty was a horse of a different color. In a way she envied Kitty. She did what she liked and didn't give a damn. She had a dozen friends, all of whom knew each other. It was a kind of syndicate. They even had a joke about it at the Rand Club. They said, "It takes a dozen millionaires to take care of one Kitty Rogers. None of us could afford it alone." And it might not be just a matter of money. Perhaps a dozen flabby old men . . .

But this was certainly the place for a divorced woman. People were very tolerant here. Everything at home was very fixed, very stratified—socially, morally, financially, and religiously. There were definite rules for all behavior and precedents for everything. But here . . . Here it was different.

Turnbull often wondered if he had been a fool about Elsie. He was no Sir Galahad. Looked at from six thousand miles away in its true perspective, that is what he had done: Taken a little harlot out of a house of ill fame and made her his mistress. Acted like a boy, thinking he had found that mythical creature—mythical as a griffin or a unicorn—a tart with a heart of gold. Brothel, bordello, cat house, whorehouse, knocking shop. There were hundreds of them, with thousands of girls, in every big city in the world. From luxurious and expensive dens of iniquity like Mrs. Fitz's to places that catered to workmen. Except in the most unusual cases with the most unusual women, as they aged and lost their looks or became diseased, the girls' course was downward. Few ever reached the top. That was where the most attractive began, but all or almost all reached the bottom. That was what he had saved Elsie from, but was it worth it? Was she worth it?

The pendulum of his emotions swung this way and that. One minute he had hit the jackpot, finding a perfect girl whom he could trust with his life. The next, like a bloody fool, he had saddled himself with a parasitical little tart who would bleed him to death if he didn't get rid of her.

Shaving was the worst time—when he used her razors, all seven of them engraved with a day of the week. The good-by to Elsie had been touching. She had not wanted to come to the boat or even the train.

"I want to stay here and cry all by myself," she'd said.

Every day, as she got used to security and comfort, she seemed to get lovelier and harder to leave. Vincent would take care of her. He was sure of that. And make a pretty penny doing it, too.

Turnbull had a bath and decided to shave again. He picked up his new razor strop.

"It's something you'll use," she'd said in the letter he had just received—it must have come out on the boat with him, "and every day you'll think of me. And I'll think of you going 'slap-slap' up and down with your razor."

Well, darling, he thought as he stropped, here I am, shaving for another woman and thinking of you. He laughed. There's a catch in this somewhere. When he had done he put on a dark blue silk dressing gown and went into the passage. How lucky they were on the same floor.

He did not knock on Diana's door. He scratched it softly with his fingernail to warn her, paused, and turned the door handle slowly.

The scene was beautifully set. The roselike woman in the rosy glow of a single shaded light. Every detail had been thought out, even the way she got up in one graceful movement and slid, apparently bonelessly, into his arms. That had always been her charm for him. And now his thoughts of Elsie had thrown him back into Diana's clutches. He took her hands and kissed them.

"You were so long, John. I thought you were never coming." Actually the time had passed very quickly with *Les Amours de Lili.* She had only just had time to pop it into a drawer as he opened the door.

He picked her up and carried her to the bed.

"Lock the door, John," she said, "and be quick."

It was almost light when Turnbull left her room. "I want a book," he said. "Look better if I have a book."

"I haven't got a book," Diana said. She wanted to get rid of him now that she no longer needed him. She would not need him again till night. The peace he had given her would carry her till then. She certainly wasn't going to give him *Lili.* She wanted to go on reading it now. She did not want to sleep. She wanted to appreciate fully the glow that pervaded her. It was not happiness. It was not mental. It did nothing to her heart. It was the same feeling that made a cat purr, one of immense content. She would read now, have breakfast in bed, and sleep till lunch. She was already planning her day. What she would do, what she would wear, whom she would see, while her desire was stilled.

Turnbull looked around for a book. Later he could not imagine why. He had felt that it would be better for a man to come out of a woman's room at four in the morning with a book, even if it was a Bible, for that was what he had picked up, than without one. Nevertheless that was what he did, and, Bible in hand, returned down the passage to his own room. In ten minutes he was asleep, and dreaming of Elsie, damn her. Even in his dream, which he knew was a dream, he damned her for complicating his life.

At six-thirty an Indian waiter woke him, bringing his early-morning tea. As he sipped it, he went over yesterday, last night, over Diana, his mind roving over her like hands. Then on an impulse he picked up the Bible. It came open at the second Book of Samuel. There was a four-leaf clover, brown with age, pressed in it here as a marker. He wondered who had been with her when they found it. What had they been doing? Making love on the grass? She would not do that now. She was too sophisticated. Now she wanted beds, perfumed sheets, and rose-shaded lights. But then . . . ? Then, as a girl perhaps. Hotter and less careful. He wondered.

His eye fell on the word "Uriah . . . Uriah the Hittite . . . the forefront of the hottest battle."

By jove, he thought, what a war story. Those thousands of years ago a king who had wanted a woman had sent her husband into the forefront of the battle and got him killed. Suppose a general did that today? Why not? He could easily enough. Suppose it was that stupid, courageous Charlie . . . ?

He had heard of its happening before. His father had told him, "Don't get a reputation for too much bravery, John. If you do they'll always expect you to be brave. You'll come to expect it of yourself. I mean more than brave, John. I mean that a man can reach a stage where, if he does not expose himself recklessly, he is ashamed."

He looked at the Bible again, at 2 Samuel 11, Verse 15: "And he wrote in the letter saying, 'Set ye Uriah in the forefront of the hottest battle, and retire ye from him, that he may be smitten and die.'"

And the sequel. Verse 24: "'And the shooters shot from off the wall and some of the king's servants be dead, among them thy servant Uriah the Hittite is dead also.'"

Turnbull paraphrased the last line:

"'. . . and among the Queen's servants Charles Darnley is dead also.'"

He wondered if such a thing could really happen. The idea was so horrible that he could not understand his even thinking of it. The dried clover leaf and the Bible's opening as it had were just accidents. Darnley was not a close friend and he did not feel he was doing anything particularly wrong sleeping with his wife: In view of what she was it had to be somebody. But there was something about Diana that frightened him. Something hard, utterly selfish, despite the soft, clinging body that she used to such effect. He knew he was being used by her, that she had taken advantage of him in some "Eve in the Garden way." If she had left him alone, it would never have happened. But she knew men and their needs that coincided with her own. There was no love in it, not even the imitation of love. There was only mutual satisfaction. Every night disgusted him. Yet still he went back to her room, enslaved by her beauty, his mind full of Elsie, his little love, at home.

But the affair with Diana helped to ease his nerves. Making love to her took the edge off his fears. Things were not going at all well for the British.

On November 15 an armored train was captured by the Boers. This had been a very simple operation. Every few days an armored train, a homemade job of iron plate and vertical railway ties, puffed out of Estcourt and up the line a few miles to have a look at the Tugela. Some hidden Boers, waiting till the train had passed, rolled a few big rocks onto the line. When the train came back, they fired at it with a field gun, a pompom, and their rifles.

Their haul was two men killed, twenty-two wounded, and a subaltern, with fifty-three NCOs and men of the Dublin Fusiliers and the British war correspondent for the *Morning Post* taken prisoner.

He was depressed at the way things were going, and the capture of his shipboard friend did nothing to cheer him. One did not have to be a strategist to know that the army corps should never have been split up or that the G.O.C. should control all his forces and not just one isolated section of it.

This train incident created a great sensation, was described in English papers as "the great armored train disaster." Churchill's fellow correspondents wrote most sympathetically about him and, not knowing whether he was alive or dead, eulogized him in a near obituary manner, praising his courage and his English, of which at twenty-four he was already a master. Churchill in November 1899 was in the news instead of writing it. If he's alive he'll like that, Turnbull thought. His dream was a political life, and good publicity like this might help him secure a seat in Parliament.

The plan for conducting the war that had finally been agreed upon with Lord Wolseley was a converging drive on Bloemfontein from Cape Town, East London, and Port Elizabeth. Having captured the capital of the Free State, the army corps that was now on its way would proceed to Pretoria, the capital of the Transvaal, take it, and the war would be over with both capitals in British hands.

But instead of sticking to this plan Buller divided his forces and set about trying to relieve the pressure on the besieged towns of Mafeking, Ladysmith, and Kimberley. Half his army corps was sent to take up a defensive position south of the Tugela.

Another portion of it was sent under General Lord Methuen to relieve Kimberley while Generals Clery, Gatacre, and French were to hold the Orange River front. It was these arrangements that kept them all in Cape Town, and it was not till late November that Buller and his staff reached Pietermaritzburg, where he took over the command of the Natal front himself, thus creating a position in which the commander in chief, instead of being in a central situation, was isolated on the right flank of a four-hundred-mile front.

The day after they left Cape Town there was a small, inconclusive action at Willow Grange against a force commanded by Colonel Walter Kitchener, Lord Kitchener's brother, which was remarkable only for the fact that for the first time British officers went into action carrying rifles and with only modified badges of rank, thus making themselves less conspicuous to the Boer marksmen.

But three days after Buller's arrival Lord Methuen was defeated at the junction of the Riet and Modder rivers, twenty-four miles south of Kimberley.

His force consisted of 7700 infantry, two batteries of R.F.A., four companies of engineers, 360 marines and sailors with four twelve-pounder guns. The infantry included the Guards Brigade and among the cavalry were detachments of 9th Lancers, New South Wales Lancers, and Rimington's Guides.

The Boers were commanded by Jacob Prinsloo and Adriaan de la Rey. They had previously fought two small engagements with Methuen at Belmont and Graspan. In both the Boers had fought in their classic fashion, holding the tops of ridges and *kopjes*. In both they had been shelled out of their positions.

De la Rey, a natural soldier, now decided to dig trenches in front of the Riet River with his guns hidden on the far side. The British walked into his trap and lost 71 killed, 389 wounded, and 18 missing. Cronje, who ar-

rived later, was in command, but the trenches and forward position were De la Rey's idea—something new in
warfare. This action was claimed as a British victory
though the total Boer loss was only 150, among whom
was Cronje's son, who died of his wounds.

But at the end of it, Methuen had not achieved his
purpose—the relief of Kimberely—and the Boer force, almost intact, still lay between him and his objective.

None of the news was cheering. Things were going even
worse than Turnbull had thought they would, but there
was no pleasure in saying, "I told you so."

General Headquarters was in the wrong position. A
commander in chief should not be stuck on a flank like
this. And, though horses and mules were pouring into
South Africa from Britain, the United States, Hungary, the
Argentine, Canada, and Australia, Turnbull was upset
both as a cavalryman and horse lover that General French
should have been made to take his remounts straight off
the ship and, still in their heavy winter coats, into action
in the burning heat of the northern Cape. Without a period
of acclimatization the wastage would be enormous.

Both Elsie and Diana seemed very far away, not merely
in distance but in time. It was impossible to believe that
only a fortnight ago he had been sleeping with Diana.

CHAPTER 16

ALONE

It took Elsie some days to recover from Turnbull's departure. Her world had collapsed. The cable from Madeira
contained two words: "LOVE JOHN." She kept it down
the front of her bodice with the hair locket that had fortunately been finished in time. She did not know what
she would have done without it. At the end of a week the
telegram was almost illegible, so she made a little silk
sachet like an envelope for it. At night it went under her
pillow. For another ten days she remained dazed. Turnbull's going had not made a gap in her life—he had been
her whole life. It was now all gap. But slowly she began

to get annoyed at herself. This was not the way the 2nd behaved. She thought of herself as a hussar now. He had talked about them so much. Other women were suffering too.

She called Vincent and reverted to her past, to the vixen who, taken advantage of by force since childhood, had, when she could, turned with tiny snapping fangs.

"Vincent," she said, "I'm sick of the bloody lot of you. 'Do you want this, Miss Elsie? Do you want that, Miss Elsie?' Cushions at my back, a cup of tea every five minutes, sherry at eleven, a footstool under my feet. I'm not a bloody baby."

"No, miss," Vincent said. Had blood, the kid had. Getting hot under the collar. He was proud of her.

"We're going to do something, Vincent. We're not going to mope any more. He wouldn't like it."

"No, miss."

"But what the hell will we do?"

There it was, in his lap again. "I've no idea, Miss Elsie," he said, "but we might . . ."

"Might what? Don't stand there like a stuck pig."

Might what indeed? He'd have to think quickly. "There's something the captain would like, miss. You might knit him something. A scarf, say."

"Of all the bloody silly things I ever heard!" Then she felt ashamed. "You know, Vincent," she said, "I'm sorry I lost my temper. That's the trouble. I'm no lady. But I'll have a go at it."

"Half-bred, miss, from what you told me that first day."

She laughed. That was the first time she had laughed since he left.

"But I tell you what I'll do first, Vincent. I'll go and have my hair done. Done real nice at a court hairdresser's. Think they'll let me in Bruton Street?"

"You look all right. Just keep your mouth shut and for Christ's sake don't swear, miss."

That was how she went to André's—court hairdresser. When she walked in a tall, slim, dark man in a cutaway came up and said, "And what can we do for you, madame?"

"My hair," she said.

"Yes, madame." Not a lady but pretty. He could do something with her and business was business.

"Wash? Curl? Set?" he inquired.

"The lot," she said. Then she forgot what Vincent had told her and said, "I've never been in a place like this before. I just want you to make me look pretty."

"Madame," he said. She liked that. She was wearing the rolled-gold wedding ring Celeste had given her. "Madame, you are pretty but in this establishment we gild the lily. Madame," he repeated, "you are pretty but we will make you beautiful. I'll do you myself." This was because she was an original. It would be a change.

By the time it was over, Monsieur André—he really was French—knew a great deal about her. Her friend had gone to the war. She could not bring herself to say husband in spite of the ring. She was twenty-two. It was apparent that she did not know how to do anything except one thing. She had a black dog, a female bitch. She had brought the word out hesitantly. It was the first time she had used it in cold blood. A house in St. John's Wood with a full staff. A carriage. That he knew. It was waiting for her outside. Altogether an interesting young lady. She appealed to his Gallic chivalry. They understood these things better in France. There a mistress of this type, very chic, *soignée,* kept by a rich and distinguished man, had an assured position in society. Here—he shrugged his shoulders. But of one thing he was sure. This captain of hussars, her friend, must be missing her, particularly in the evening.

"Voilà!" he said. "Madame, it is done. Get up and look at yourself in the mirror. I have kept my word. You are no longer pretty—you are beautiful."

Elsie stared entranced into the glass and clapped her hands. "Is that me? Really me?" The girl who looked back at her was lovely. The dark hair shone like a newly blacked kitchen stove. Ringlets curled to perfection danced over her ears. Piled up and swept back in tiers of curls, the coiffure was more Empire than fashionable Victorian, but Monsieur André, the tonsorial artist, had not been able to resist the temptation. After all, this was not a society woman, not one of those sheep who desired to resemble each other like fashionable peas in an expensive pod.

"It is an original style, madame, a creation, if I say so myself."

"It is lovely," she said, and then, to his delight and astonishment, and the shocked gasp of the girls in the shop, she stood on tiptoe and kissed his cheek. That was the only way she knew of expressing gratitude, of saying, "Thank you." It was a beautiful and graceful gesture, the gesture of a happy child, and she was little more. From that instant Monsieur André was her slave.

Her eyes, which had been bright with excitement, clouded, misted with near tears.

"If only he could see me," she said.

"He will, Madame, and as Madame gets older she will become more beautiful. In three months, six months, a year, ten years always more beautiful. And now," he said, "if Madame will be good enough to follow me . . ." He led the way to his office, past the white-smocked girls who stood gaping.

He indicated a chair. "Madame will permit an impertinence?" he said.

"Of course," Elsie replied.

"The clothes," he said. "Madame has not been well advised." He wrote an address on a slip of paper and under it wrote, *"Faites votre mieux"* and signed it, *"André."*

"When she has dressed you, madame, there will be a no more beautiful woman in London."

The visit to the hairdresser had been a success. Life was quite simple if you went out to meet it. She did not know that it was simple for all beautiful women if they were rich. The transformation had astonished her.

The next month was passed fitting clothes and shopping. Madame Valéry was enchanted. Elsie was enchanted. Celeste, who always accompanied her, was enchanted. Fitting followed fitting. Dress followed dress. Lace-trimmed lingerie foamed in waves about her feet as Celeste undressed her.

"If Monsieur le Capitaine could only see Mademoiselle he would become *fou*—mad," she said, *"véritablement fou.* It is terrible to see such beauty wasted on the eyes of a simple maid like me."

At last, unable to stand this waste any longer, when

Elsie stood in her corset and a petticoat trimmed with
Brussels lace, she called Vincent in to see.

"*Viens,* Vincent," she cried. "Come and see this miracle
of beauty."

Quite unself-consciously Elsie pirouetted on her toes,
the petticoat flying up around her long silken legs.

"Lovely," he said. "Lovely. But you know, miss, it's not
right to show yourself to a man like that."

"Vincent," Elsie said, "I can't behave well all the time.
Not with my friends."

She was learning about horses and carriages from Vincent. When he took her in the park he showed her vic-
torias, barouches, broughams, dogcarts, governess carts,
breaks, coaches. He taught her the colors of horses, the
names of different breeds of dogs. The jobbing gardener
told her the names of flowers. She sent for catalogues
with pictures. She bought flowers for the little greenhouse.

Soon . . soon . . . any day now, a letter would come

It came six weeks to a day after he had left. It was a
lovely letter, an anxious letter. How was she? Was she
happy? Was she eating well? How was the staff? How
was Queenie?

By now he'd know it all, the ship bringing his letter
probably having passed the outgoing vessel with twenty
of hers on board. She kissed it and stuffed it down the
front of her bodice. Then she laughed. How many could
she keep down there? She fished it out and put it in a
little rosewood box with silver mountings. She would keep
all his letters in the box tied with pink silk ribbons.

The letters came regularly now each week. He had left
Cape Town. He had met friends at the Mount Nelson
Hotel. There were quite a few ladies in South Africa,
some that he knew. . . .

If she were married to him she could be there. But
she was not married. If only I could get out, she thought,
and then put the idea behind her. It was too absurd.

Elsie had been shopping at the Army and Navy Co-
operative Stores, where the captain had opened an account for her. This store sold only to officers of the
army, navy, and their dependents.

Vincent as usual was with her. They were standing in

Victoria Street waiting for the carriage when she saw a familiar figure.

"Alice," she cried, running forward. "Alice, what are you doing here and why have you got your bag?" She had a heavy carpetbag in her hand that was weighing her down.

"Elsie—oh, Elsie, you do look grand." Alice stared at her in astonishment. "So it came off," she said. "We often talked about you but we never knew. Are you happy?"

"I was till he went away."

"He deserted you?"

"No, dear, he went to the war. But you, what are you doing here?"

"Going to the station. I'm going home and never coming back. I can get work there at the hall. Oh, Elsie, I'm so frightened."

The carriage drew up by the curb. Charles had seen them. "Get in, Alice. Take the bag, Vincent. You're coming home with me for the night. I want to hear everything."

"A carriage," Alice said.

"Yes, dear, and a house. Everything. I fell on my feet."

"Oh, Elsie, how lovely."

They got into the carriage. Alice ran her hand over the dark blue leather upholstery and began to cry. "I'm so frightened. I'm so frightened," she sobbed.

"Where's Betty?" Elsie asked.

"Gone," Alice said. "Gone since yesterday. But her clothes is all there. Everything. And her money box. Something's happened to Betty," she said. "I knows it. They caught her listening. She used to listen at the door. Curious, she was, and they've caught her. That's why I ran. Never even waited for me wages. I just put on me 'at, packed me bag and ran. They'd've stopped me if they could but I was in the street when Bill came after me. Oh, oh, oh," she cried, "what will I do . . . ?"

"Go home like you said," Elsie said.

"But Betty. What's happened to our Betty? She was so sweet and pretty. We was such friends. We shared everything. Sometimes we slept in the same bed. When I was homesick. So good and pretty. So good and pretty," she said again and again.

"That's the girl that tipped you off, Miss Elsie, isn't it? That Betty," Vincent said.

"Yes, Betty told me what was going on."

"Looks bad," Vincent said. "If they caught her at something like that they'd kill her—or worse."

"Worse?" Elsie said.

"Yes, miss. They could take her to a house—a bad one, a cheap one—and work her to death. Or break her so her own people wouldn't know her. Till she don't even know herself, don't even know who she was or where she's from. I've heard of it, miss."

"My God!" Elsie said. "Bloody murderers."

Alice went on crying slowly, a dirty handkerchief crammed into her mouth.

When they got to the house, Elsie took her to the little sitting room and told Vincent to bring some tea.

"I'll bring the brandy, too, miss," he said. "A bit of medical comfort, as we used to call it in the Eighteenth. Do her good," he said as he went out.

Slowly, bit by bit, Elsie got the story. Alice was hysterical part of the time.

"Oh," she said, "we never should have gone to a place like that. Never. But the money was so good and the tips and the excitement and all those 'andsome men running in and out. That was what Betty liked. The 'andsome men and the tips. They'd pinch her bottom and give her a quid. They never pinched me, Miss Elsie. Not much to pinch. I'm not pretty like her. . . . It ain't safe to be so pretty if you're common. Look where it got you, Miss Elsie, and the other girls. You was lucky and you was brave or you might be there yet. . . .

"On Thursday night Betty was not there," Alice said. "I had the whole floor to do all by myself and did I have to run. But everyone was nice and patient. I thought she might be ill up in our room. But I hadn't time to go and see. But when I got there it was empty. The bed hadn't been slept in. So I went to see *'er,* woke *'er* up, I did. I said to the madam, 'Where's Betty?' There *She* was, 'er 'air in paper curlers, and she says she don't know. Then she says she'd gone.'

" 'Gone,' I says. Fancy going without taking anything. Not even her clothes. Not her china money box . . .

shaped like a pig, it is. Not saying good-by to me wot
loved her and slept in 'er bed. But I didn't say nothing. I
was too scared. I just went upstairs, packed me bag, put
on me 'at and ran out. I was just out of the door when
that Bill tried to grab me.

"Oh, Miss Elsie," she said, "we servants wasn't supposed
to know nothing. But we all did. We knew about the
room. He took you there, didn't he, Miss Elsie? I mean
that's when he beat you black and blue."

Vincent was right. Terrible things could happen. They
always tried to pretend they didn't, but they did, and
Betty was so pretty. Just the kind Mrs. Fitz would like
to get her hands on. And once they'd broken a girl in
she was finished, no pride any more, nothing left in her
but fear. As obedient as a whipped dog. In a way she'd
been lucky starting as a kid, sort of growing into it. But
when they got a big girl like the ones Mrs. Fitz got at
the servants' agency, they broke them. They didn't talk
afterward. She'd seen some of them, just for a minute
like, but Mrs. Fitz never kept them long. All the regular
girls were like her, used to it. But a big girl, a good girl,
would fight. She'd heard there were men who liked them
like that, who'd pay a lot for it. And then there was Bill,
who got his greens whenever he wanted them. He liked
whipping girls and breaking the new ones in.

"I'm glad you're out of it, Alice. We'll drive you to
Victoria tomorrow and put you on the train," Elsie said.

Queenie put her front paws on Alice's chair and licked
her tear-stained face. Alice kissed her nose and threw her
arms around her. There was a lot of comfort to be found
in a dog. Elsie had discovered that for herself.

She'd forgotten it all till Alice brought it back. It was
only three months, but they seemed like three years, like
a lifetime. Her new life was all she could remember now.
She seemed to have spent all her life in this dear little
house, taken care of by Vincent and surrounded by servants who were her friends. But the past caught up with
you. It was like the tail of a kite. No matter how high
you flew it was always there behind you if you looked
around.

Something was starting at No. 20. Some new train of
events. First her running away. Then Betty's disappearance.
And now Alice frightened out of her life.

She'd talked to Betty quite a lot. She knew she had a dad and two brothers in London—all big men. Betty had been so proud of them. Every Sunday she had gone home to take care of them. To mend their socks and sew on buttons and things like that. What would they do when Sunday came and their pretty little sister did not come home? They'd do something, she was sure.

When she and Vincent got back from seeing off a still-tearful Alice, she found Millie, the tweenie, waiting for her with a book in her hand.

A tweenie was a between maid, an odd-job maid, usually quite young, who did all the work the other, grown-up servants found too heavy or unpleasant to do. The house-maid made the beds and the tweenie emptied the chamber pots and slops. The tweenie carried the hot water up-stairs. The tweenie fetched coal for the fires and cleaned the grates, polished the front-door brass, and, kneeling on a sack, Bath-bricked the white steps of the house each day.

"May I speak to you, miss?" Millie said.

"Of course you can."

Millie held up her book. It was a child's reader. There were pictures of farm animals in color on the cover. "I picked it up," she said. "It was lying in the gutter. That wasn't stealing, was it?"

"Of course it wasn't stealing. What do you want it for?"

"Oh, Miss Elsie," she said, "I was wondering if you'd teach me to read."

"I'll teach you," Elsie said.

"Oh, thank you, miss." Millie seized her hand and kissed it. "You're good," she said, "that's what you are. We all say you're real good." Then, covering her face with her apron, she ran down the stairs to the basement, where she belonged.

It was a funny world. Me, good? Elsie thought. Me, a little tart that's dropped on me feet and living like a bloody princess. But if good was being filled with love for everyone, perhaps she was good. Until three months ago she'd loved nobody. It had all been bottled up inside her, fizzing and bubbling like champagne. Now she was pouring it out as if it was wine and everyone about her a glass. And she was knitting. A khaki muffler. It was just about done. She hoped he would get it for Christmas. Vincent had been right again. Knitting was nice. She liked the click of the steel needles. Ellen had taught her. Socks next, she said. Socks? Well, Ellen would have to turn the heel for her, but she liked the idea of it. The captain had such pretty feet.

CHAPTER 17

THE HELOTS' REST

THE WAR in South Africa was static. Ladysmith, with General White, Kimberley, with Kekewich and Mr. Rhodes, and Mafeking, with Baden-Powell were all besieged, surrounded by Boers who appeared to have no greater eagerness to take these towns by storm than the contained troops had of breaking out.

The British forces under Bulldog Buller had so far not been able to relieve any of them.

Cut off from supplies, the besieged were far from comfortable, everything being in short supply, and the defenders suffered more physical hardship than actual danger. Eggs were ten shillings a dozen and then rose to forty-eight shillings. Cigarettes were a shilling each and many officers were smoking dry tea leaves. Most of the horses and mules had been turned loose for want of forage and those not captured by the Boers were now rounded up, slaughtered for food, and turned into such delicacies as a soup paste called chervil, sausages, meat rolls, and jelly. As there was no wheat flour, bread was made from mealie meal and gluten extracted from laundry starch.

Malnutrition and disease were the real enemies. In Ladysmith there were two thousand enteric and dysentery patients in the three-hundred-bed hospital.

The town was shelled by the Boers in a desultory fashion. The guns were given names: Long Tom, Fiddling Jenny, Puffing Billy, and Silent Susan, so named because the shell arrived before the report was heard. The damage caused by gunfire was negligible. A fortnight's casualties consisted of one white civilian, two natives, one horse, and two mules.

The Boers never fired before breakfast, knocked off for lunch, and stopped for the day at teatime. There was no fighting on Sunday, the one exception being a dozen shells dropped on a polo field where some British officers broke the Sabbath by indulging in a few chukkers. The Boers were not going to have the Sabbath broken by anyone—friend or foe.

It was a most curious war. In Kimberley, for instance, a Boer medical officer came into the town under a flag of truce to buy chloroform for his wounded. On Christmas Day the Free Staters fraternized with the British troops from the opposing trenches and they all went swimming together.

Even Diana Darnley, who took no interest in the war, was aware of this curious situation. She was, however, surprised when at two one morning there was a knock on her door. She woke with a start. Who could it be?

"Who is it?" she said.

"It's me. Charlie."

Good God! Charlie. Her husband. Suppose, just suppose, it had been last night, or if Sean had been with her again. She had half expected him.

"Darling," she said as she sprang out of bed, not even waiting to put on a dressing gown before she unlocked the bedroom door.

She flung herself into his arms. His buttons hurt her breasts. His belt buckle bit into her stomach as she buried her face in his neck. The perfume of her hair was in his nostrils. She knew her Charlie. He would not wait to undress.

It was only after breakfast, which they had in their room, that she got the story. Charlie was not a great talker. He did not have to be. He usually left the talking to her. But now he talked. After love, after a few hours' sleep, after two eggs, three rashers of bacon, four pieces of toast—two with butter and two with marmalade—two cups of coffee, he felt splendid and talkative. There was so much to tell this beautiful, loving wife of his. He knew other men found things different. Their wives did not fling themselves into their arms. Did not . . . did not do any of the things Di did. Ladies did not act like that. Ladies were not supposed to enjoy love. Only to put up with it.

Diana lit a cigarette. She took it from a gold case.

"So you smoke now," he said.

"Only in my room, Charlie. I'm so nervous worrying over you." She laughed lightly and came to perch on his knee. "With you away at the war. The worry, Charlie, never knowing how you are. If you're well. If you've been hurt. Oh, Charlie." She turned her face into his neck and began to cry. She felt his arm go around her and his hand cup her breast. "Again, Charlie," she whispered. "Again. It's been so long."

Twenty minutes later she heard the story.

Wanthope had brought him down from the front to look into something. "There's been too much delay with the stores coming up," Charlie said. "There's a snag somewhere. I've got to find it. Nice of him to choose me, wasn't it, Di?" he said. "He knew you were here. I never told him but he knew. Knows everything, Wanthope does."

"I wonder how he found out?" Diana said, her blue eyes as round as saucers.

How did he know indeed? Who knew better? Three or four others knew as well. But none better. The peacetime rule of one man at a time was out now. Life was too short. How long had she got? She'd soon be thirty and after that how long was there? Of course it was risky. But Wanthope was not too bright, and he was so vain that he thought any woman he was interested in would never look at anyone else. And as for Charlie, all you had to do was to make love to him. Make love every time he came near you. And what an original idea that was. Something completely original for a woman of her class with her own husband.

"He could have brought down anyone but he chose me. Very decent of him," Charlie went on. "He brought John Turnbull, too."

"Turnbull? Captain Turnbull?"

"You know him?"

"We've met. He was here for a few days with Buller before he left. What's he doing down here?"

"Horses, Di. He speaks Dutch and Wanthope wants

him to see if he can buy some remounts from the farmers in the back veld."

Diana laughed. Four of them, here at once. Charlie, John, Wanthope, and Sean, the handsome young lancer. "Oh dear," she said, "I do hope we don't get involved socially. I want you to myself, all by myself. Here, alone. Just the two of us."

That night Charlie gave his wife more news.

"You know what he said, Di?"

"Who said?"

"Wanthope."

She was lying on her side in her chemise. This position showed her small waist, the beautiful rounded curve of her hips, and her long, slim legs. Her long fair hair was down and loose, her eyes veiled, wide, dull, almost unfocused.

"What did he say, darling?"

"He said he'd give me my chance. The next chance that came."

"Oh, my darling," she said, holding out her arms. "How wonderful! But do be careful. Surely a D.S.O.'s enough?"

Wanthope, on the second day at the hotel, asked Charlie if he thought his wife would like to ask him to tea.

"I'm sure she would," Charlie said.

"You'd better ask her," Wanthope said.

"The general wants me to ask him to tea?" Diana said. "You mean he wants to meet me? I wonder why?"

"I suppose I've said how wonderful you were."

"How nice you are, Charlie. Not many women have husbands like you. Of course I'd like to meet my husband's general. If I can charm him he might be nicer to you." She laughed softly.

"What a pretty laugh you have, Di. You know, sometimes I seem to hear it in the night. That's strange," he said. "Lying alone in a camp bed in a tent on the veld. You sound so happy and amused, the way you do sometimes when we make love."

"Like this, Charlie?" She laughed into his face, her eyes dark, almost mauve with desire.

They sat at a table on the terrace waiting, talking

desultorily. Then she saw him. Because they had come down on army business they were all in uniform. General Wanthope looked splendid, bemedaled, booted, and spurred.

"Isn't that the general, Charlie?" she asked.

"Yes, that's him. How clever you are to recognize him at once." Charles stood up.

"Here we are, sir.

"Diana, General Wanthope. My wife, sir."

"Ah," General Wanthope said, bending over the gloved hand she extended, allowing it to droop gracefully from the wrist.

"So you are Diana," he said. "Forgive me, Mrs. Darnley, but I've heard so much about you."

"Do sit down, General. Order tea, Charles. Sandwiches, General?"

"Yes, please."

"And you, Charles . . . ?"

An Indian waiter, white-clad, with a scarlet sash and white cotton gloves, brought the tea.

"Milk and sugar, General?" Diana asked.

"Yes, please."

My God, Diana thought, we both ought to be on the stage.

She loved to pour tea. It was an art. Little girls began to learn as soon as they were strong enough to lift a teapot. Little girls in short frocks and lace-frilled drawers that showed. Some who were talented learned to be ladies very young.

Diana wore a white *broderie anglaise* dress with a high boned collar that made her hold her firm little chin a little higher than usual. She had a floppy hat of the same material fastened with two pearl-topped hatpins to the rolls of her heavy hair. She had her string of pearls around her neck; she wore long white suède gloves. Below her dress was a fan of white, lace-trimmed petticoats from which her feet, in their white suède shoes, peeped modest as mice. The orchestra played softly in the background. Beautifully dressed people moved about the terrace, the women in white or light-colored dresses. They all wore big hats. The men, mostly soldiers in mufti, were in white flannel trousers and wore navy jackets or blazers. Conspicuous among the soldiers were the mining magnates, refugees from the Rand and Kimberley, the stout, cigar-smoking men who had given the Mount Nelson its new name—"The Helots' Rest."

"What's a helot?" Diana asked.

"A helot means a slave or serf. In Sparta the helots were the lowest class of the population. But Milner did not mean it that way in his dispatch. He meant that the British in Johannesburg were enslaved by the Boers because they had no vote, Mrs. Darnley."

"Well, here they are the lowest and the richest," Diana said, laughing.

"What a witty wife you have, Charles," the general said.

Charles said, "I'm glad you think so, sir. She's certainly a good talker. Keeps people amused. That's more than I can do," he said. "I'm stuck unless it's horses, huntin' and shootin'," he said.

"He has another subject, General," Diana said.

"What's that?"

"Ladies. At least one lady. He's very good at amusing her." She made herself blush. This was a very valuable trick. It was accomplished by projecting a series of pornographic thoughts pictorially on the screen of her mind. She could cry when she wanted to, too. She had often thought, particularly at times like this, that she would have liked to go on the stage, except that actresses were not socially acceptable. Why, if a soldier married an actress he had to send in his papers—resign the Queen's commission.

But how well things were going. How well the tea party had begun. She had sat there with Charles waiting, looking sweet and beautiful. A modest wife sitting with her husband on the terrace of this lovely new hotel. She knew people were thinking what a lucky man he was.

And he was. And so were the others.

Starting with her father's second horseman—it seemed quite fair to count him—there had been a lot of lucky men. She smiled sweetly at her husband and dimpled. God had really been very good to her.

At last the tea was over.

"A great pleasure, Mrs. Darnley," the general said, taking her hand, now ungloved, and bending over it again. "I can only tell you that I envy Charles in one way for having so lovely a wife, and am sorry for him in another for having to leave her. We leave early tomorrow, Charles," he said.

When the general left them they strolled in the garden. They looked at the young palms that had been planted on each side of the drive. They walked under the trees—oaks, gums, Norfolk pines. These trees were old. They had been here when this was a farm; later it belonged to the Admiralty.

Diana tore some white bark from an Australian paper tree and shredded it between her fingers. The game with Wanthope had excited her. They looked at the goldfish in the fountain pool. They listened to the canaries singing as if their hearts would break in the big aviary by the curved windows of the dining room. Diana picked a scarlet hibiscus and pushed it into her hair above her ear.

"Do you know what that means, Charles, when a girl does that in the South Seas?"

"No, darling," he said.

"Then I'll show you, Charles." She paused a minute to gain her breath. She looked entrancing under her small, lace-edged parasol. "Charles," she said, "it's our last night for God knows how long. Let's dine upstairs in our dressing gowns."

"All right," he said. Charles was not an articulate man. But there was a queer thing about Diana. When she felt like that, when she did not build up to it, when it was an immediate desire flooding her, she always called him Charles, never Charlie. So that was what the flower meant. That was what they did in the South Seas. Over an ear, what? he thought. He grew red in the face and laughed.

That night Diana let him brush her hair. It was the only part of her toilet he was capable of assisting her with, and only that because he was so fussy about his horses' tails that he often groomed them, pulled them, and banged them himself. He was not the kind of man who could lace stays or put a satin garter on a silk-clad leg.

Her hair reached to below her waist and he brushed it beautifully, with long, sure strokes. That was something she would miss.

The big bed was rumpled and for once she did not care what the waiter who wheeled in the dinner with its bottle of bubbly in a silver ice bucket thought. Quite the contrary. A woman who did that in the daylight . . . Well, nothing could be a greater indication of her love for her husband. Like the French, she thought, from five to seven. Perhaps they were right. One did enjoy one's dinner more.

The hibiscus blossom was turning black on her dressing table. She wondered if one could use scarlet hibiscus flowers to rub on one's lips as one used geraniums. No lady used rouge of any kind.

She rolled her hair into a great knot. She knew this was a beautiful pose in a naked woman. When she raised her arms to her head, her breasts were tightened and pulled upward. She glanced over her bare shoulder at Charles. He was watching her.

From a drawer she took a little book of *papier poudré* papers. They were quite thin, like a cigarette paper, bound in a black cover. She tore out a sheet and rubbed her face with it. This was as near as a woman of fashion came to using powder. When she had done she put on a dressing gown of Brussels lace over faint salmon-pink satin, tied the girdle, and put on her mules. She was again ready for anything—for the waiter with the dinner wagon or for Charles again when the waiter had gone.

It was light when Charlie dressed. He looked out of the window at the oaks in full green voluptuous foliage. Beyond them was Table Bay, which would soon be full of the troopships now on the sea coming from everywhere. Ships from India, with the white regiments stationed there. No Indian troops were being used. This was a white man's war. Ships from England, from Canada, from Australia, and from America—the United States and the Argentine —with remounts. At five in the morning everything was quiet. Only the doves cooed. A pair of them landed on the white wooden rail of the balcony. The cock blew up his chest till he almost burst, and began his bowing courtship.

Charles finished dressing. He was in no great hurry. They were having breakfast in the dining room at six and leaving at seven.

He looked at his wife. How lovely she was, her fair hair spread out on the pillow around her face like a golden halo. He wondered when he'd brush it again. The long lashes over her cheeks, her full lips not quite closed over her teeth. Her lovely breasts moving slightly up and down in deep breath of sleep. She was one of the few women he had ever heard of who made love naked. What a scandal there would be if anyone ever heard of it. Though of course no one would believe the story. Altogether too incredible. He tiptoed out of the room with a slight clink of spurs,

Turnbull had started breakfast. "Hullo, Charlie," he said. "Enjoy yourself?"

"Nice time, John. Makes a change, doesn't it?"

Well, John thought, what the eye doesn't see the heart doesn't grieve about. And in the end, which was best if you looked at it in an unconventional manner? A woman from whom you get no pleasure but was faithful, or a woman who was wonderful to love who occasionally shared her charms with other men? "Damned if I know," he said aloud.

"Know what?" Charles asked.

"Nothing, Charles. Push over the marmalade." They stood up as the general came in.

"Good morning, sir."

"Morning," he said, sitting down.

"Bacon and eggs. Sausages. Liver and bacon. Kipper. Kedgeree, haddock, boiled eggs," the waiter said.

The general ordered liver and bacon and coffee.

"Might as well have coffee. That's something no soldier ever learns to make," he said. "Get me any horses, John?"

"I picked up a few, sir. About twenty. But I know where to get more if I had the time. I got good ones, real Boer ponies. Two tripplers. All about fifteen hands. Short-coupled, good bone. The usual dash of Spanish and Arab blood. But it wasn't easy, sir."

"Why not?" the general said, with his mouth full.

"Well, sir, British staff officers aren't exactly popular down here. And even if they like you they daren't show it, because of their neighbors. Daren't sell horses, either, but I got over that one.

"You see, sir, there's a lot of trouble here. The few that

are content to be British subjects are regarded by the others, who are in the majority, as traitors. In fact, everyone seems to be a traitor to someone."

"That's what I wanted to know, John. That's why I brought you down here. The temper of the people more than the horses. Will they rebel if they get a leader?"

"If they see a good chance of success and if they get a good leader.

"But the horses, sir," John went on. "I didn't buy them. I just listed them. Owner, description, and so on. And arranged with a dealer to buy them for us on the open market."

"They'll run them up, John."

"Of course, sir. But not too much. And they'll be cheaper in the end than the remounts we're buying from the Argentine. They'll live. They're used to the country."

"And what about you, Charlie?" the general said. "Got things fixed up?"

"Yes, sir. It only took about a couple of hours."

"I thought it wouldn't take long," General Wanthope said. "But I had an idea you might like to see your wife. You're the only one of my officers with a wife over here."

"Thank you, sir," Charles said. "Very good of you, sir. I'm most grateful."

"It won't be long before we see some more action," Wanthope said. "With what Buller's got now we ought to be in Ladysmith in a week or so."

There was so much coming and going at the Mount Nelson, so many general officers and their staffs, so much luggage, so many doors opening and closing, so many carriages, cabs, and saddle horses on the drive that no one noticed Wanthope's party leave, and no one cared except Diana, who was relieved to find her husband gone, and the young lancer, who, having seen them drive off from his window, was so happy that he sang more loudly than ever in his bath.

CHAPTER 18

DENTWHISTLE

THOMAS DENTWHISTLE, also known as Tommy the Cosh and Slasher, was an important member of Mr. Samuel Tupper's organization. It was he who was sent to No. 20 when Mrs. Fitz sent for help.

Mrs. Fitz and he were old friends and quite often he dropped in for a friendly visit. His "Just passing this way and dropped in to see if you would give me a cup of tea or a glass of port"—according to what time of day —usually ended in his having a little something else on the house. "Of course, any of them that aren't busy, Mr. Dentwhistle, if you are in the mood to be entertained." To the girls he was just a regular customer, one of the few civilians. A man who took what he wanted quickly, silently, and never gave nobody sixpence.

And there he sat in her den, his rather high black bowler and black kid gloves on the table beside him. Eyes blank as gray shoe buttons stared at his hostess out of a face as featureless as a dumpling. But a dumpling made of putty-colored stone on which vestigial features had been impressed. A vague pinching up to make a nose. A knife slit for a mouth. His hair was grizzled and cropped short like that of a criminal, a sailor, or a servant, and he had been all three. His white collar was very high, coming up to his ears, which were his only beautiful feature, being small, faunlike, and rosy pink. He wore a black tie with a black pearl pin and a gray frock coat buttoned high with no waistcoat showing.

He sat with his knees together, his feet together, his hands together on his knees, utterly still—a figure cast in lead—listening to Mrs. Fitz as she began the story of the recent misadventures that had taken place in her house.

There was one very curious thing about Mr. Dentwhistle that might not have been immediately apparent to anyone entering the room where they sat. At a time when almost everyone of any pretensions carried a cane he was without one.

"Well," Mrs. Fitz said, "he was quite right. There was a spy in the house. She let the cat out of the bag and I've caught her, Mr. Dentwhistle."

"How?" His lips had not moved, nor his eyes flickered. He never blinked, no more than a cod frozen amid the ice and green parsley sprigs on a fishmonger's white marble slab.

"First," Mrs. Fitz said, "I put some letters in a drawer in my desk that I generally leave locked. I stuck those letters ever so slightly together, just in one tiny place, with gum. Then I left the drawer open a little and tied a hair, one of my own, Mr. Dentwhistle, from the knob of the lower drawer to the bottom of the upper, fastening it there with a piece of black sticking plaster. The top drawer could not be pulled open without breaking the hair. The letters could not be handled without the gum lifting the surface of the cream laid paper."

"And?" Mr. Dentwhistle said.

"And then I went downstairs, told Betty to hurry up and do the room as I was expecting to entertain some friends, and went out. When I came back the drawer was closed but it had been pulled out. The hair was broken and the letters had been touched."

Mr. Dentwhistle said, "Ah."

"Still," Mrs. Fitz continued, "I didn't wish to be unjust, so I set another trap. I got out my little case of tools and I drilled a very small hole in the door so that I would put my eye to it and see if anyone was looking in through the keyhole."

"Why couldn't you just have opened the door and looked, Mrs. Fitzherbert?"

"And have them know I knew and run for it? What can you be thinking of?"

"That's what I was thinking of," he said.

For a moment Mrs. Fitz paused, thinking of the man's duplicity. Fancy him trying to catch me out, an old hand like me. Then she thought of her little case of tools. How seldom she used them now. They had belonged to Harold. He was the second man she had lived with, chosen to live with, that is, and not had forced upon her. He was a burglar. One night he made a good haul. Three hundred

and fifty quid. They had hidden it under the plank in
the floor. Then she had got him drunk, packed his tools
in her own carpet bag, wrapped up in her clothes, stuffed
three hundred pounds down the front of her bodice—
"between me tits" was the way she thought of it—and
had turned Harold in. Gone to the coppers. "Get 'im,"
she'd said at the station. "God's truth I'm scared of 'im.
Look"—she'd opened her bag and shown her clothes—
"I'm clearing out. Going back to my ma. You'll find
the money he stole under the floor boards. A fortune, it
is," she said. "Fifty bloody quid."

Her ma was in a pauper's grave, but in a sense she was
going to her ma, as we all are all the time. But that three
hundred quid had started her off. She'd bought some
young girls from their mothers and guardians, taken a
house, cleaned them up, trained them, and been on her
way. She owed Harold a lot and they were a splendid set
of tools. He had taught her how to use them, too. Quite
sentimental about them, she was.

"And then?" Mr. Dentwhistle said.

"Then I sent for her. I said would she please call Bill.
When Bill came I called her again and told her to bring
some port. The kind you like, Mr. Dentwhistle. I knew
there wasn't any in the cupboard, so I gave her the key
to the cellar and told her to bring up a new bottle. Bill
went down after her as I had instructed him to do.

"I'd had plans for that young lady ever since I'd set
eyes on her. A real beauty, Mr. Dentwhistle. A high-step-
per and a redhead at that, as you know because you have
remarked on her yourself."

"I hesitate to advise someone with your professional
experience, Mrs. Fitzherbert, but I believe it's best to leave
redheads alone. For those that want reds it's easy enough
to dye them."

"That shows what you know, Mr. Dentwhistle," Mrs.
Fitz said. "And what could you know on the outside?"
Her professional integrity was at stake. "Why," she went
on, "you're just a procurer. You try and palm off a dyed
one on a man that likes redheads. He'd know it in a minute, Mr. Dentwhistle. They smell different. So put that in
your pipe and smoke it."

She sniffed loudly and went on:

"What happened now, Mr. Dentwhistle, is because of

that very thing. Bill didn't just beat her and have her the way he's supposed to do with the new ones to the trade. He went mad for her. Fought him off, she did, the little fool, and he beat her to a pulp. Unrecognizable she is. A big loss, too, because I had great plans for her. You'd be surprised, Mr. Dentwhistle, the men I've had in this very room, sitting in that very chair you're sitting on, talking about that redhead just because she was a redhead—some of the richest men in England, too."

"May I ask why you did nothing about this before? Why you had to wait till she betrayed your confidence and told this girl Elsie of your plans for her future abroad?"

"I'll tell you why, Mr. Dentwhistle. Betty has a father and two brothers, all big men, who're fond of her."

"If they are fond of her why did they let her work in a place like this?"

"There's nothing wrong with this place. The money is good and the tips is good, and the food is good, and it's interesting. She saw a bit of life here, more than she would in some damn respectable private house as a cook-general or a housemaid. And stop 'er? How could they stop 'er? God damn it, Mr. Dentwhistle, she was a real redhead, not a dyed one. Don't you know you can't never stop 'em. And that's why I sent for help so urgent-like." Mrs. Fitz's English was slipping a little now.

"But what is so urgent, Mrs. Fitz? I mean, why today rather than tomorrow?"

"Because tomorrow is Sunday and when she don't come they'll come here to find her. And they mustn't find her."

"And where is she, Mrs. Fitzherbert? Downstairs? And what are your ideas on the subject?"

"It's up to you, Mr. Dentwhistle. Her looks are gone but her body will recover with a bit of luck. She has a pretty figure. It's up to you. Is it easier to dispose of a live body or a dead one? She's got to be got out of the way, one way or another, tonight."

"The answer is export, Mrs. Fitz. It's a nice shape, a white skin they want. I'll be round with the doctor and the ambulance. A little rest in the country, Mrs. Fitzherbert, and then a sea voyage. She should spend the winter in Egypt, I think. A most salubrious climate. At least I've found it so, though rather hot in the summer. And now what of the other young lady? Elsie, I believe her name is."

Mrs. Fitz, her mind relieved about Betty, now exploded with rage. "That little tart," she said. "I picked her up out of the gutter, dressed her, fed her, taught her. Do you know," she said, "that when I took over this house I wanted to build it up? Make it the best house in England. Do you know what I did? I got a young Cantab, they come from Cambridge, you know, to live here for a year. Gave him the run of the house to educate my young ladies. Reading, writing, arithmetic, and so on. The three R's, geography, and history. Do you know something? When I took over this place all you could say was that the girls were clean, young, and pretty. Young and pretty because they were thrown out when they stopped being. Clean because we had a doctor to them every week and the class of client we have is generally very careful where he goes. But stupid. Mr. Dentwhistle, all these pretty young ladies could do was lie down on their backs.

"Who won the Derby? Who won the Grand National? Who was Dizzy? Never heard of Disraeli or Gladstone or William the Conqueror. Never heard of the Franco-Prussian War. Bismarck? The Kaiser? No idea of the British Army. Their clients, mind you. They thought the Twelfth were Hussars, thought the Dragoon Guards were Household Cavalry. Confused Australia and America because both began with a H. Yes," she said, "we had some real little Cockneys then, but corkers. Sharp as needles that made the officers laugh. But when the Cantab left they knew something. Not much, but enough, and he'd taught them to read the Pink 'Un—*The Sporting Times*. That was about their mark. But that was about all the officers read. It nearly killed the Cantab, that year did, what with teaching twelve such stupid girls and them being so grateful. Well, Elsie was one of them. Educated by me own Cantab. And then runs away."

"Yes, this girl Elsie," Mr. Dentwhistle said. "Shall we discuss her for a moment? I appear to have a busy night before me."

"I want her back, Mr. Dentwhistle. I want to take the hide off her back. Do it myself. That I do, and rub salt into the blood."

"Dear Lady," Mr. Dentwhistle said, "these thoughts do you great credit. An eye for an eye, a tooth for a tooth. Then, even beyond justice is the pleasure of revenge, the exercise of sadism that comes so natural to the fair sex, as does the acceptance, the almost willing acceptance, of pain. In most women these two are almost always compounded in a greater or lesser degree. If women were not masochists how do you think you could hold your girls, who half like their degradation? Who can be sure they do what they do only because they must. I often doubt it. And you, who were one of them once . . ."

Mrs. Fitzherbert held up her hands in horror. "Mr. Dentwhistle," she said, "how can you?"

"I know it all, Mrs. Fitzherbert. I know about the three hundred pounds you stole from your burglar pimp. I know about the children you bought and prostituted, so do not interrupt me. We are in the same line of business and there is no need for hypocrisy between us. I have no virtues. I have no feelings. I have no interest other than money and power. There is a relationship between knowledge, which is power, and money, vulgarly known as blackmail. That is why I like knowledge, Mrs. Fitz. That is power, that is money. Money, gold, I like. Indeed it is my God because gold is everything. Sometimes I tip out a bag of gold and arrange it in little piles.

"Five sovereigns will buy a night with a beautiful girl, a wonderful dinner with the finest of wines, a day's hunting on a hired horse, a weekend in the country, a rare book, a reasonable painting, *bibelots* of various kinds, a small jewel, a box of superb cigars. That little heap is none of these things, but it is all these things. It represents them all. While I have it I can enjoy them vicariously, knowing that all I need do is to push them one by one into my sovereign case"—he pulled it out of his pocket as if to demonstrate—"and go out and enjoy any of them.

"I make bigger heaps—heaps in groups. Ten. Ten groups of a hundred—a thousand pounds. For a thousand pounds I can buy a girl, or a race horse, or a house, or a small yacht. Everything is implicit in money. As long as it is not spent you have everything. But to return to Miss Elsie, as she is called in her household. You see I have investigated her—if you did get her and you whipped her back raw you would be destroying not merely the skin of a pretty back, but money. Think of it that way. Would you sooner have your fun or your money? The reason I am rich, Mrs. Fitzherbert, and I am though I may not look it, is that I have always preferred money to fun. In fact my only amusement has been making money.

"I will now describe to you the very pleasant situation in which Miss Elsie finds herself at Number Seven Acacia Road. She has three menservants if you include the young groom, who is little more than a boy, and three maidservants. Her maid, the cook, and a young girl—a tweenie—who helps them both. A staff of six and a charming house. Abduction is impossible. Not only is she well protected but she has become well known in the area for her free spending and her charities. The hue and cry would be too great. So the loss of her person must be written off. It is no use crying over spilt milk, Mrs. Fitz, no use at all. But there is another aspect to this situation. That of retribution or punishment. I have been instructed to punish her, since recovery is impossible. If one girl gets away with such an act of insubordination and ingratitude, others might be tempted to follow suit, discipline would be undermined, and the whole structure of the organization destroyed."

"What are you going to do to her, Mr. Dentwhistle?"

"I am going to visit her personally quite soon, dressed as a messenger from a flower shop. I shall bring a large box of flowers. The door will be opened by Celeste, the lady's maid who also acts as parlormaid. If I do this at about eleven in the morning it is unlikely that Vincent, that is, the captain's man, will be in. He usually goes for a short constitutional at that time.

"I shall therefore insist on seeing the lady of the house. 'These flowers,' I shall say, 'are being delivered on Captain Turnbull's orders and his instructions are that they must be given to Miss Elsie Smith in person.' I will give them to her. She will hand them over to the maid when I present her my receipt book to be signed. Like this—"

He rose and bent over Mrs. Fitzherbert, giving her a notebook and a pencil. As she looked down to write, an open razor flashed out from under the book. A streak of light shot past her face and was gone before she had time to scream.

"I shall cut her, Mrs. Fitzherbert. Miss Elsie will be punished by the loss of her nose.

"Well, Mrs. Fitzherbert," Dentwhistle said, "I will go and make the arrangements. There is a lot to do, and it's funny how these things always happen at the weekend."

He looked at his watch, a gold half hunter, on a gold chain on his vest that only showed when he unbuttoned his coat. Mrs. Fitz, white under her rouge, shaken, still trembling, watched him fascinated—a rabbit to his snake.

"Four o'clock, Mrs. Fitzherbert," he said. "I am a man of regular habits. I did not really need to look at my watch. I seldom need to but I like to verify my concept of time, to check it, as it were. You'd be surprised," he said, "sometimes I've been right and my watch has been wrong. But that was in the old days—when I did not have such a good watch. This one is a Waltham, a gift from a grateful client. I did not cut him. He was so pleased he gave me this gold timepiece. But what I was about to say when I disgressed was that at this time—at four of the afternoon—I am accustomed to take my tea. See to it, please. With hot crumpets and plenty of butter."

It was five when he had finished. "I see you are getting nervous, Mrs. Fitzherbert. But there is plenty of time. More haste, less speed is Tommy Dentwhistle's motto. And his favorite story is that of the tortoise and the hare. But ladies are always impatient. So I will detail my plan.

"One." He began to tick off his fingers. "The ambulance is nearby and always ready. It can be here in half an hour. Two, if the good doctor is drunk, as is possible since it is Saturday, I shall impersonate him. I shall merely take his silk hat. It is fortunate that we both have the same size head—six and three-quarters—his black bag, and stethoscope.

"So, madam, if you will have the patient ready at six precisely your good man William and I will carry her out on the stretcher. And, leaving William behind as the faithful guard of your establishment, I will take the young lady out to the rest home we have in the country—we should arrive at Rose Cottage about midnight—rouse the housekeeper, and put the patient comfortably to bed.

"The sea voyage may be a little harder to arrange. We may have to wait until the self-inflicted damage to her face, so common among lunatics, is healed. And then there is the matter of the ship and what area would suit her best. I am inclined to think, as I said before, that the Near East, my dear lady, is better than South America.

"She has a beautiful body, you tell me, with, I assume, the white skin that goes with her auburn coloration. Yes, with a face which—from what you tell me—will not regain its pristine beauty—I think the East. With a pretty white body, a yashmak covering the lower part of her face, and her eyes darkened with kohl, we should do well with her in Cairo, Mrs. Fitzherbert. I am convinced she will be happy there. Very happy and comfortable."

He picked up his hat and gloves and then said, "I know you have long been curious about one of my habits, Mrs. Fitzherbert—the reason I never carry a cane. Now you have joined the select few who know. A cane inhibits me, madam. A cane is not easily mated to a razor."

Without appearing to move Dentwhistle flashed the open razor before Mrs. Fitzherbert's face again, and, leaving her white and trembling, slipped out of the room like a ferret.

That'll teach the old bag, he thought as he called a hansom by whistling loudly between his fingers.

A man of parts, Mr. Dentwhistle was—a most capable chap.

Mr. Dentwhistle's mother had been a lady of Spanish extraction, and only moderate virtue, resident in Gibraltar. That was where he had been born. His father had been a private soldier, Archie Dentwhistle, of the 1st Gordon Highlanders, then stationed at the Rock. His childhood memories were of Barbary apes, swinging kilts, and skirling pipes. Also of sunshine, mules, steep hills, shady patios and the blueness of the Med., which only much later he found out was the sea.

When the Highlanders went home, his mother followed, being a British subject, under the illusion that England and Scotland were one country and that her Archie was bound to be stationed within easy distance of London, where their pleasant association could continue, unchanged except by the exigencies of the northern climate.

When her geographical error became apparent, Mada-

lena Sorina settled down in Shoreditch and entered with
notable success the only profession open to one of her
talents. The boy, neglected at home, took to the streets,
where even as a small child the combination of his
mother's Spanish fire and his father's belligerence soon
made him the leader of a gang whose oldest member
was only nine. Discipline and organization seemed to be
bred in him. Perhaps Tommy Dentwhistle's father had
been a general—and why not?

Age and size, he realized, were not everything. At
eight you were small. To gain in size and weight was
just a matter of arithmetic, of adding numbers to the
gang, and for a while this gang of babies was the terror
of Shoreditch. A couple of them would annoy a respec-
table-looking citizen till he gave one of them a cuff. The
child would then let out a terrific cry, a scream of terror,
and forty children—boys and girls—would pour out of
every street and every tenement upon the brute who had
struck a child. Pour out and pour over him. In a specially
taught drill the larger boys would surround the victim,
driving their heads into his body and kicking his shins,
as smaller children climbed onto his back and beat the
man's head with their tiny fists. When they had him
down they kicked him, stomped him, and stripped him
even of his clothes.

As the kids grew older they branched out, becoming
more ambitious. This was particularly true of Tommy,
who had become so ambitious that the police were hot on
his trail. To evade them, he joined Her Majesty's Navy.
For seven years he sailed the seven seas, visiting every
continent and almost every great harbor in the world.
Either they were British or his ship put in to show the
flag and exchange compliments with the authorities, none
of whom dared be anything but friendly in those days of
gunboat diplomacy.

It was the navy that had made him the man he was. It
was here, by hard work and devotion to duty, he had
learned a dozen useful arts. He was not only a good
sailor, an A.B. who could tie knots, sail a boat, paint,
calk, row, signal both Morse and semaphore. Oh no, he
had also learned bookkeeping with the paymaster,
cooking in the galley, and waiting in the officer's ward-
room. He had been a yeoman. He could be a valet, press

clothes, wash, iron, even starch and finish collars. He got into the engine room and learned something about steam engines. He was from the first a perpetual volunteer for any job that was not his own. His messmates thought him a fool till they found out what he'd picked up. One officer even taught him the elements of navigation. Dentwhistle could take a sight. From the master-at-arms he learned to take a rifle apart and put it together again.

But this was not all. His rough childhood had made him realize that a man should be able to defend himself if attacked, and when he got shore leave, instead of seeking drink and women, he looked for some instruction in the local art of self-defense. He learned judo, karate, and the Indo-Chinese method of kicking a man in the face. His little trouble in England with the police had been due to an accident he had with a blackjack. It was not his own. He had borrowed it from a friend and, as it was a few ounces heavier than the one he was accustomed to, the man he had struck had died. It was his first accident, but it had seemed both wise and patriotic to slip away and join the navy. He was considered an expert with a blackjack by his peers, who had given him the nickname of "The Cosh." Tommy the Cosh. It was not bad to have such fame so young. He was only eighteen, which had made him all the more embarrassed by what had happened. After all, he was no beginner.

He had, however, a great piece of luck in Sydney, where he learned to use a sandbag. This is a much more delicate instrument than a blackjack. A man can be knocked down, knocked unconscious, and even killed without the skin being broken. He had become such an expert that he could tap a lady on the back of the neck and put her out for an hour so neatly that when she came to she only had a headache.

His next piece of luck was in Jamaica, in Kingston, where he met a big buck, six feet two at least and a good fifteen stone, flashing a razor in a bar. He liked the way he did it. The neatness and the style of it.

Half an hour later he was beside him. "My name is Dentwhistle," he said. "Tommy Dentwhistle, A.B., of H.M.S. *Thunderbolt*."

The big black man stared down at him. "What do you want, white man?"

Dentwhistle was afraid of nobody. "Something you've got, black man," he said. "And I'll pay for it."

"What've I got, white man?"

"A razor."

"My razor ain't for sale, white man. That's for cutting, it's not for shaving. Don't you know Niggers got no beard? We uses razor for cutting. I cut men. I cut women. Everybody knows. Want someone cut they comes to me. Backus is my name. Yes sir, they comes to Backus. I'm an American, I am," he said. "My father was a slave an' his daddy was a Congo king. But I'm a king right here though the white folks don't know it. What's a king?" he asked. "A man who gets what he wants. That's me. Food, women, clothes, drink—and I don't pay for nothin'. That's a king."

"Do you like money, King?" Dentwhistle asked.

"How much?"

"A fiver. Five pounds. That's what I'll give you. A pound at a time for five lessons in cutting."

"You're on," the king said, wrapping his great hand around his. "Come on. Come home with me and I'll learn you."

And learn him he did. That was how later, after he had been honorably discharged from the navy, he became known as Slasher.

When he left the service he was twenty-five years old, hard in mind and body and skilled in many ways. His most useful skills in civil life were his talent for various kinds of self-defense and a wonderful head for figures. This was almost extrasensory. He could cast up a column of pounds, shillings, and pence and write down the result without further calculation, without turning the pence into shillings or the shillings into pounds.

He spent a day in Portsmouth considering the future and then made up his mind about how to put his major gifts to their greatest use. He first went up to London. In London he found two men he thought might suit him. They were pugs, third-class fighters who were aging and would have to look for other work before long. They were neither of them punch drunk, nor were they sots. One was named Jim Craven. It was a queer name for a fighter, Dentwhistle thought, but the man was uneducated and did not know what it meant. The other man was known as Billie the Buster or Buster. He seemed to have no other name. Both were heavyweights and overweight, and both willing to take on any job that did not mean hard work.

Being more or less insensible to pain, they did not mind taking any amount of punishment in the ring. But the public was tired of them. They just took it. They did not fight back any more.

"I'll give you a job," Dentwhistle said. "Good pay and a commission."

"What's the job?"

"I'll tell you later."

"When later?"

"When we've been to my place and had a talk."

Dentwhistle's place was a loft over a warehouse. He got it for nothing. All he had to do was to keep an eye on the crates stored on the ground floor. At one end of the room from hooks he had screwed into two rafters hung his hammock. Some nails driven into the wall acted as clothes pegs. His sea chest was a seat. A big empty crate was his table. On another crate he had a white enamel washbasin and a big brown water pitcher with a spout like a watering can. There were three other crates for seats should he feel like entertaining guests. The rest of the loft was empty.

"Sit down," he said. "Now I think, and this is just a guess, that this job will pay two quid a week and another three at least in commissions if we work at it."

"What's the job?"

"I'll tell you later. First I want to know if that kind of money interests you. Or can you do better than that?"

"You know bloody well we can't," they said together. "And now what's the job?"

"Before we talk about the job there's one more thing."

"What thing?"

"I want to fight you."

"You're mad," the Buster said. "We're pugs. We could mash you to pulp with one 'and tied be'ind our backs."

"Yes," Dentwhistle said. "That is what you think. And as long as you cherish that illusion I'll never be the boss. So I'm going to thrash you. If you want the job, then fight. What's to stop you if you can beat me so easily?" He stripped off his coat.

"Have it your way, guvnor," Buster said, "but you're asking for it, that's what you are." He took off his jacket and waistcoat. His great muscles bulged under his shirt as he rolled up his sleeves.

"This way," said Dentwhistle. "I don't want to smash my house furnishings." He laughed.

Buster stood crouched in the prize fighter's stance, his left leading, his right across his upper chest, guarding his face.

Dentwhistle, looking very small, stood opposite him, both hands up with half-open fingers as though he was expecting to catch something.

Buster feinted with his left and then drove a terrific right at Dentwhistle's chin. The right arm and right foot came forward together; the whole weight of his body was behind the blow.

The fist never made contact with Dentwhistle. It went on, and the Buster's body followed it, flew through the air over Dentwhistle's shoulder, and landed with a crash on the dusty floor. Dentwhistle brushed his hands against each other.

"Want any more?" he asked.

"That's not boxing," the Buster said.

"I didn't say box. I said fight. I don't fight for fun. If I'd wanted to I could have pulled your arm out of its socket and it would have hung there useless forever. Or I could have smashed it. Do you want another try?"

"No damn fear," Buster said. "Let Jim have a go."

"Want to, Jim?" Dentwhistle asked.

"I'll have a go."

He had hardly had time to face Dentwhistle before it was over. Dentwhistle spun on his left heel, leaned over to the rear, and back, and kicked Jim Craven under the ear. He went down as if he was poleaxed.

"Chuck some water over him, Buster," Dentwhistle said. "When he comes to we'll talk."

"Now," he said when they were settled, "am I the boss? Is that clear? Do you understand that though I'm smaller and lighter than you I can, because of certain tricks I have learned in foreign parts, break you into little pieces if I feel like it. Kill you. Is that clear?"

"That's right, guvnor," they said, "you've won."

"Very well," he said. "Here's a fiver each. I want you

here at ten o'clock tomorrow wearing blue serge suits, black bowlers, and collars and ties."

"Yes," they said. "But the job?"

"You'll see tomorrow."

The next day Dentwhistle, with his goons behind him, marched into a bookmaker's office. "What do you want?" a frightened clerk said.

"The boss. Get him." The young man ran to a frosted-glass door.

Before he reached it a fat, red-faced man in a loud black and white check suit appeared.

"And what do you blokes want?" he asked. "Want to lay a bet?"

"No," Dentwhistle said. "We've come to help you. You've got some bad debts—welshers. Every bookie has. We'll collect for you and go fifty-fifty."

"I'll think it over," the bookie said.

"We've no time to waste," Dentwhistle said. He turned to Buster. "Buster, throw that chair through the window. Jim, tear up the ledger."

"Stop! Stop! Yes, I've got some bad debts."

"Now you're talking sense," Dentwhistle said. "Give me the list."

He had one ready. Most bookies do. They look at it if they feel too happy.

"Now," Dentwhistle said, "put a ring round those you think will pay up in time. That'll be about half of them probably."

"About half," the bookie said.

"Well, we won't touch them. Just the others, the ones you know won't pay. You don't grudge us fifty per cent of that, do you?"

"I certainly don't."

"Then it's a deal, Mr. Buxton. That's the way I like to do business. In a deal both sides must be satisfied." And with the list in his pocket, followed by his gorillas, Dentwhistle went out.

It was his success as a collector of bad debts and the excellence of his organizing abilities that led Mr. Samuel Tupper to send for him. By this time he was known as Slasher. He'd only had to cut two of Mr. Buxton's clients before the others found the money somehow.

CHAPTER 19

THE BROTHERS

ON SATURDAY, Joe Norly said, "I don't 'old with it. Not with our Betty's working in a knocking shop no matter what the brass is, and I'm going to tell her so when she comes 'ome tomorrow." He was an immense man who lifted a bag of coal as if it was a small parcel.

His two sons, equally large men, said, "Nor we don't neither."

"I saw 'er," their father said, "near 'ere in Knights-bridge."

"Who? Betty?" Tom asked.

"No, the madam wot runs the kip."

"What was she doin' down 'ere?"

"Nothing good, I'd say. Had a girl with her. Pretty as a pitcher. Didn't look like a tart, she didn't. I'll talk to Betty again when she comes 'ome," their father said.

"Ambitious, that's wot she is," Henry said. He was a bit slower than his brother. "Talks like a toff now, she does, learnt it there."

"Do you mean them tarts talks proper?" Joe asked.

"Learns it from the men. That's wot I think," Henry said, "an' she learns easy, does our Betty. Wants to be a lady."

"Lady my foot," Joe said. "She's common, we're all common, and so is most people. But I'll talk to 'er. By God," he said, "I'll take a bloody strap to 'er."

"If you does it's the last we'll see of 'er, Dad," Tom said. "An' wot'll we do then?" He looked around the room. Since their mother's death three years ago they had only had Betty to look after the place. When she went into service, there had been no one except a neighboring slattern who mucked the place out as if it was a stable, which was why, when Mrs. Fitz took Betty on, she had demanded a full day off a week. Something quite unheard of in those days. She had only succeeded because of her appearance, which Mrs. Fitz knew would appeal

to her clients. So she was given Sunday, a slack day in
the business.

The Norlys lived at the bottom of Yeoman's Row, a
cul-de-sac opening into Knightsbridge. It began well, with
a series of Regency and Georgian houses, and degenerated, as the distance from Knightsbridge increased, into
a slum. Their rooms were over the stables where Royal,
the big black Shire, and the coal cart were kept.

Joe Norly loaded up coal and little bundles of split
kindling wood every morning at the yard and sold it to
his customers in the vicinity. Betty was the apple of his
eye, the girl being the dead spit of her mother when he
married her. Rare enough at all times, but particularly so
in those brutal and wife-beating days, theirs had been a
good and loving marriage. Joe did not drink. Not more
than a couple of pints of bitter a day. He saved money,
and his cart and horse were his own. He was very fond
of his black and kept him fat and well groomed, spending
a long time every evening washing and combing the long
white feathers on his legs, his mane, forelock, and tail.
Like so many powerful men he and his sons were quiet
and good-natured, as well they might be, for few had the
temerity to cross them. Someone had told him that these
great heavy-feathered English work horses had once carried knights in full armor, against their peers in France.
Now, known as Shires, they had once been called the
English War Horse or the Great Horse of England. He
could well believe this, for no one could fail to see the
splendor of such a beast, a cart horse now, but of a
breed that had once carried kings.

Tom, who had been turning things over in his mind,
said, "Where'd you see 'er, Dad? That madam?"

"Know the agency, Tom? About halfway between 'ere
and the old Brompton Road on the other side, that's
where I saw her."

"I'm going to tell the nippers," Tom said. "They can
keep an eye open there. Might as well do nothin' there
as 'ere." He got on well with the kids that ran wild in the
row. He'd say, "Somefin's up, kids, down there. Somefin'
I'd like to know about. So keep your peepers open and
there'll be a copper or two in it."

A big English copper penny was quite a sum to the nippers. They could buy a big bun for it, or four small farthing buns.

From that day on Mr. Tupper was bothered by urchins when he got out of his carriage. "Give us a penny, guvnor . . . a copper . . ." He wondered why he had never noticed them before

But that began a few days later.

By lunchtime, when Betty had not come, the men became uneasy, moving around their two rooms like big bulls in a pen.

Joe had platted red ribbons into Royal's mane and tail to please her. She loved to pet and talk to the big black horse.

They had everything ready for her to fix their lunch. It was a kind of treat. Each Sunday the four of them would talk it over and decide what she would make the following week. Today it was to have been fried liver and bubble and squeak—a mixture of cooked potatoes and cabbage fried up together.

"Wot about something to eat, Dad?" Tom said. "Shall I fix it up?"

"I've no 'eart to eat," Joe said. "Something's wrong. I know something's gone wrong. I feel it 'ere." He put his hand on his chest.

"I'll brew up a pot of tea," Henry said.

They had tea and thick slices of bread and butter. They did not dare go out in case they missed her. They did not talk. They had nothing to say. They smoked. They rumbled a bit, growling under their breath.

At four o'clock it was nearly dark and still she had not come.

Joe got up from his armchair, knocked his pipe on the edge of the iron cookstove, and said, "We're going up there, boys. Come on."

They went at once. They had on their Sunday clothes. Blue serge suits with bright handkerchiefs knotted at their throats, cloth caps on their heads, and black boots that smelled of homemade blacking that was a mixture of soot and vinegar.

"Walk across the park?" Tom said.

"No, we'll take a growler," Joe said.

They picked up a four-wheeler at the hackney cab stand and drove off, silent, preoccupied, not thinking really but feeling emotions they could not put into words. Three big, inarticulate men. Honest, sober workers who, though slow to anger, felt it working up and taking hold of them as the old cab horse jogged along.

Neither of the boys had ever been in a cab before. Joe had on his wedding day with Betty's mother. He'd taken her on his lap in the privacy of this little room on wheels. He'd pulled down the curtains of the window and had held her, kissing her and holding her, while she said, "Don't rumple me, Joe. Don't rumple me. Can't you wait?" Of course he'd waited. Women wore so many clothes. But he'd rumpled her and he'd loved her.

Like as two peas the two women in his life were. Redheads, quick-tempered and loving. By God, he thought, if anything's happened to that girl. He gashed his fist into the palm of his hand with a noise the cabby heard on the box. A rum go, he thought. Three big workingmen in his cab and no luggage. Generally the only reason people took cabs was luggage—no room for it in a hansom.

At No. 20 they lumbered out of the cab and paid it off.

"No, don't wait," Joe said. "We just wanted to get 'ere clean and not all sweated up."

The three stood in a row looking at the big brown mahogany door.

"Ring, Dad," Tom said.

Joe rang and then on impulse raised the heavy brass knocker and smashed it down with a blow that sent it nearly through the door.

As it was Sunday, Bill opened the door. What drunken young pup had used the knocker? Everyone knew the house was closed Sundays. Even girls had to rest sometime.

He got a surprise when he opened the door and three enormous men stood looking at him.

"Yes?" he said. "This is the wrong 'ouse and the servant's entrance is in the basement."

Joe brushed him aside and came in, flanked by his sons.

"Now," he said, "where is she?"

"Where's who?"

"Our Betty."

"I don't know," Bill said. "She's left."

"Left, has she?" Tom said.

"Yes."

"When?"

"Last night." And that was God's truth—left on a stretcher with the doctor in attendance.

"Get the madam," Joe said.

"She's resting."

"Get her, d'you hear, or we'll come and look for her."

Bill went upstairs. The men looked around the hall, at the thick carpet, at the paintings on the wall, two almost life-sized bathing nudes. Harem scenes with half-draped yashmaked girls in the background.

"So this is it?" Joe said. "Where she worked. An 'igh class knocking shop. Who'd a thought it? It's worse nor what I thought. Aye," he said, "much worse."

Mrs. Fitz came down slowly, with dignity, making an entrance to what she feared was going to be an unpleasant scene.

"You came about Betty?" she said. "You are . . ."

"I'm her father. Them's her brothers and where is she?"

"I wish I knew," Mrs. Fitz said. "We were all so fond of her. She was here on Friday and yesterday she was gone."

"Gone, eh?" Joe said. "And where would she go but 'ome? Waited for her all day, we did. With liver and bacon and bubble and squeak all ready to 'er 'and. Gone, eh? And you don't know where, eh?"

Tom said, "Take us up to her room."

"I don't know," Mrs. Fitz said. "I mean . . ."

The two brothers stepped forward. "Do you want us to look for ourselves?" Tom had his hand on the stair banister.

"I'll take you to her room," Mrs. Fitz said.

What a good thing she'd had her stays on and her hair done. It had only taken her a minute to slip on her dressing gown. It was made for emergencies and looked almost like a dress. She panted up the stairs in front of them, pausing to catch her breath at the landings.

Girls' heads popped out of the doors. A fair head with its long hair down, a brown head with its hair piled high and tied with a ribbon.

"That's them," Tom said.

"Aye," his father said, "young 'arlots."

When they came to the room under the eaves where Betty and Alice slept, Mrs. Fitz threw open the door.

"That's her bed," she said. "You can see it's not been slept in."

"Aye," Joe said, "and that's 'er money box." He picked up the red china pig. "I gave it to 'er." He threw it on the floor. It smashed. Golden sovereigns and half sovereigns rolled out, ran over the bare boards, and settled in a scattered pattern.

"Pick 'em up, Tom," he said.

"And do you think my girl'd leave twenty bloody quid like that even if they was the wages of sin?" Joe said.

"She was a good girl," Mrs. Fitz said. "No one ever laid a hand on her. I saw to that."

"But they gave her money, didn't they, them toffs, for cleaning up after they 'ad lay their whores? And she dressed 'em. I know what she did. She told me." Tom had put the money in his pocket and opened a cupboard.

"There's her clothes," he said, "all of 'em except her uniform. She go out naked?" he asked.

"I have no idea," Mrs. Fitz said. "She just disappeared."

"Left her clothes, her money, her hairbrush, her comb and went out naked. Now tell us the truth, ma'am." Joe had her by the arms and was shaking her.

Mrs. Fitz's hair was coming down. He was hurting her. She was frightened.

"I don't know," she said. "I don't know," she gasped, almost sobbing.

Tom got an idea. "Who sleeps there?" he said, pointing to the other bed.

"Alice," Mrs. Fitz said, and then clapped her hand to her mouth. Alice had cleared out and there was no trace of her. She'd taken everything with her. She could have said no one, but that wouldn't have been any good either. They knew about Alice. Betty would have told them.

"Bring 'er up," Joe said. "I'll talk to 'er."

"She's gone," Mrs. Fitz said. "Just took her things and left."

"So she took her things and our Betty didn't?" Henry said.

"Yes, that's right."

"Something fishy 'ere, Dad," Tom said. "Something downright fishy."

"We'll be back," Joe said. "If she don't turn up in a couple of days we'll go to the police." He turned on Mrs. Fitz and shook his finger in her face. "We ain't frightened of coppers. Never been inside any of us. We got friends as is coppers." And with that they left and walked home through the park.

On Monday, when they had finished work at the Garden, the skilled, heavy work of carrying baskets of fruit and vegetable on their heads—they could both carry fifteen empties piled up like a column on top of their caps— Tom said, "We're going back, 'Enry."

"Back?"

"We'll 'ang about a bit, 'ave a bite to eat and go back to Betty's place. We're going to talk to that big bastard wot let us in."

"Get nothing out of 'im," Henry said.

"I think so, 'Enry. Oh yes, I think so."

This time they only rang the bell. A girl in a smart uniform opened the door and tried to close it, but they pushed their way in.

"We won't 'urt you, dear, but we wants our sister."

"Your sister?"

"Betty," Tom said.

There were some opera cloaks and hats on the hall table and the sound of girls laughing. Business had begun.

Leaving the maid gaping, the two men went into the drawing room. There were three men in full evening dress in the room and one in a smoking jacket and black tie. They were flirting with six pretty girls, in their teens and early twenties. The man in the black tie had a small blond girl on his knee. In a corner a big musical box was playing. Three of the men were smoking cigars. The girls were dressed in off-the-shoulder dinner gowns cut so low that their nipples showed.

Tom's eyes popped. So this was how it was done. Seeing them, two workingmen, unwashed and still dirty from the Garden, the girls screamed and clung to their escorts. They were not at all frightened. Men were all the same, rich or poor. But it was a good excuse to scream and work up some excitement.

The men shook the girls off and came toward the brothers. A tall, sandy-haired man with bristly mustache said, "What the hell are you doing here? Get out."

"Don't try anything, mister," Henry said. "We're just looking for our sister."

One of the girls said, "Betty?"

"Know her?" Tom said.

"Course I know her. She used to dress me. But she's gone."

Hearing the girls scream, Bill had rushed upstairs. He was hardly into the room when the brothers seized him—one on each arm.

"You're the chap we wants," Tom said. "We was just going downstairs to look for you. That's where you live, ain't it?"

They marched him out.

They went down a passage and through a swing door covered with green baize that gave onto a stone staircase that led to the basement. The gloom was not brightened and only partially illuminated by a single fishtail gas burner. It burned in a half circle of yellow flame edged at the bottom with blue.

"Where is it?" Tom said, giving Bill's wrist a twist.

"Straight on," Bill said. These big bastards. If he'd been ten years younger—if he hadn't drunk so much—if . . . if . . . But they had him, God damn them. Tears of rage formed in his bloodshot eyes.

Tom kicked open the door. Bill's room was small, almost square, and smelled like the den of an animal—of sweat and urine, with human overtones of sour beer and tobacco. There was a grubby bed against the wall, covered with rumpled gray blankets—he used no sheets—and a filthy cushion for a pillow.

Tom closed the door. "Let 'im go, 'Enry," he said.

"Now, you're going to talk, you son of a bitch," he said.

Free now, Bill straightened up and flexed his muscles. What had he to be afraid of? He was a pug, wasn't he? A pro. Christ, he'd fought bigger men than these and if only he could get to the bed. There was a cosh under the pillow. With a cosh . . .

Tom was sizing him up. "No funny business," he said.

"Don't try to pick anything up. An' it's no bloody good blowin' yourself up like a bloody turkey cock. You're not a fighting man any more. You're no pug. You're soft. Soft. Fat with beer, booze, and women. Either of us could take you on alone, so don't try nothing with the two of us together.

"Now where's me sister?"

"I don't know. No bloody idea where that little tart is."

Henry hit him on the point of the jaw before he could get his hands up.

"We'll tie him," Tom said, taking the red handkerchief from around his neck. They tied his hands behind him and his feet together.

"Now we'll take a look round," Tom said. "Take it slow and thorough, 'Enry. We're in no 'urry. No 'urry at all. Wot we do with 'im depends on wot we finds. There's something fishy in this 'ere place and it's down 'ere somewhere. I'll bet my bottom dollar it is."

With Bill's eyes following them savagely they began their search. There was a table and on it a comb and dirty hairbrush, a looking-glass, a bottle of brilliantine, and a pint mug still half full of beer.

"Interrupted his boozing," Henry said.

There was a drawer in the table, empty but for a cosh. There seemed to be nothing but clothes in the rickety deal cupboard.

"Don't close it, 'Enry," Tom said. "Chuck everything out on the floor."

When they'd got the clothes out, they found a whip hanging on a nail in the back. It was oiled and clean— the only well kept thing they had found so far.

Tom swished it through the air.

"Nice whip," he said. "Jockey's. We may try it later on. Aye," he said, "we should get a peep out of him with that." There was nothing else in the room except for an enamel chamber pot under the bed.

"See if the knots are tight, 'Enry," Tom said. "We're going to leave him and take a look round."

They found the wine cellar. It was locked, but they could see through the slatted door. There was nothing but coal in the coal cellar.

There was only one door left. It was fastened by two large bolts. They moved easily and showed traces of grease.

No glimmer of light came from outside. Tom struck a match.

"Christ!" he said, and lit the gas, another fishtail set close into the wall.

For a moment the two men were too shocked to speak. There was a bed in the room with a dirty mattress on it. At either end of it were two straps. Tom felt them. They were soft and pliable. The bed was bolted to the stone floor. On the wall opposite the bed was a ring bolt masoned in the wall six feet from the floor.

Henry pulled the mattress off the bed. In the better light beneath the gas they could see bloodstains on the ticking.

They took them in, took in their meaning, but that wasn't what held them. There, caught in the angle-iron edge of the bed, was a fragment of lace. There was no mistaking it. Betty had been tied down and whipped here. They had traced her this far. They had a lead at last.

Tom picked up the fragment and unraveled it a little. Handmade and no mistake. No mistake that it was hers. It was lace their mother had made. Yards and yards of it were left when she died. Old Joe wouldn't sell it, and Betty used it to trim her underclothes. There was plenty of it still at home.

"We can't tell Dad," Henry said. "He would kill him."

"No, we won't tell Dad," Tom said. "And we won't kill him. We'll do worse."

He took the fragment gently between his great fingers as if it was the petal of a flower. He wasn't angry. He was ice cold. He didn't know himself. "Me sister," he said, "me bloody little sister . . ."

They walked over to Bill on the bed together, in step, their hobnailed boots loud as horses' hoofs.

Tom held the fragment up before Bill's eyes, an inch from his nose. "You've 'ad it, Bill," he said. "Whether we kill you or not depends on you. Now talk!"

"I don't know nothing. I don't know what you got in your 'and."

"And that room?" Tom said. "Is that where you whips 'em?"

"Only sometimes," Bill said. "Just when the madam says so."

"And have them?"

Henry brought the jockey's whalebone-centered cutting whip down on his face. He screamed.

"And have them?" Tom asked again.

"Sometimes," Bill gasped, "just to break 'em in. When they're new like."

Henry spat and raised his whip again.

"No," Tom said, "not his face. We don't want to 'urt 'im yet. 'E's got to talk first. Now talk, you bastard. Talk fast. Where is she?"

"I don't know."

"'It 'is legs," Tom said. "We need 'is face for talking." The whip whirled down once more.

Bill writhed away from it as Henry hit him again. The pillow fell on the floor and Tom picked up the other cosh.

"Now where is she?" he asked.

"They took her. The doctor did. On a stretcher."

"What doctor? What hospital did they take her to?"

"He's not a doctor. He just looks like one and they took 'er to the country to 'is 'ouse in Slough. It's a cottage like, all on its own, away from everything."

"And then?" Tom said.

"They'll ship 'er out like they always do."

"Aye," Tom said. "Now this cottage? You been there?"

"Yes."

"Then where is it?"

"A mile before you gets to the first 'ouse on the London road. There's a road leading to the left. That's where the cottage is. Rose Cottage, they calls it. It's the only one."

"'It 'im again, 'Enry. Give 'im a dozen."

The whip went up and down with all Henry's strength behind it. It cut through Bill's clothes. Bill's screams turned into sobs. He was half fainting.

"Chuck that beer in 'is face, 'Enry."

Henry emptied the mug into his eyes.

"Now," Tom said, "do you want some more?"

"It's the truth," Bill moaned, "it's God's bloody truth."

"Let 'im go, 'Enry. Let 'im loose."

Free, Bill struggled up and sat on the edge of the bed.

"Get up," Tom said. "Now we're going to give it to you, 'ammer you into a pulp. And when you're down we'll kick the bloody balls off you."

That's how they left him—a screaming eunuch on the stone floor.

CHAPTER 20

ROSE COTTAGE

BEFORE the two brothers went into the house, they washed their heavy boots at the stable tap. They had not spoken on the way home.

"And now what'll we do?" said Henry.

"Fetch 'er tomorrow. And we need some brass and a bit of shuteye. Put on our best clothes. And mind, 'Enry, not a word to the guvnor. Not a bloody word. We've been at the market all day, see. Same as bloody usual. Just late, that's all."

Their father sat in his chair, his head sunk in his hands, brooding. On his lap was a heap of lace. When they came in he raised it. It ran out over his gnarled hands and between his fingers in a white waterfall. "She loved it, the kid did," he said. "Remember 'ow she used to take it to sew on her clothes. Pretty things, that's wot she loved. Mary," he said. "Mary," now confusing the two of them, wife and daughter. "Me two little chestnuts," he'd called them. "Me chestnuts."

His sons said nothing.

"Leave 'im alone, 'Enry," Tom said. "I'll brew up some tea. Then we'll 'ave supper—sausage and mash."

"I can't eat," Henry said. "Christ, man, 'ow can you eat?"

"You eat, 'Enry boy. You're going to need your strength." Tom put the sausages in the pan, pricking them with a fork, while Henry mashed the potatoes.

Their father had drunk the tea they gave him. But when his supper was ready—all dished up—he refused it. Before he turned in he stood by the door of the bedroom and looked back at them.

"Find 'er, boys," he said. "I'm too old. Old Joe's too old. By God," he said, "I'm an old man now, with both me girls gone. . . . An' see to Royal. I forgot 'im. Just fancy that. Forgot me 'orse."

The boys went down to Royal. He looked around and

214

whinnied when he saw them. He had not been watered or fed for the night. He cocked his ears at Henry as he led him out to the water trough, his hoofs loud on the cobbles. He knew something was up. He dipped his big head into the trough and raised it to blow his love and water in Henry's face.

While the horse was out, Tom mucked out the stable, filled the rack with hay, and put an extra ration of oats into the manger.

The men stood on each side of the big horse, watched him eat. Tom slapped his neck and said, "She loved 'im, our Betty did."

"Aye," Henry said.

In the morning the two men went to the station early in their blue suits. At nine-ten they got a train to Slough. At ten o'clock they were there.

They called a porter.

"Where's a good jobmaster 'ere, mate?" Tom said. "We wants to 'ire a trap."

"White's is as good as any, chum," the man said, "as good as any and more honest than most. 'E's in the 'Igh Street about 'alf a mile down on the left."

They found Mr. White, a thickset, clean-shaven man in boots and breeches, a tweed hacking jacket, and a bowler.

" 'Orse?" he said. "I got plenty, and traps, too."

A quarter of an hour later they drove off behind a good bay mare with the ribbons in Tom's hands. It took them a while to get out of the town on the London Road. Then the little houses thinned out and stopped abruptly.

"It must be a mile from here," Tom said. "A mile and on the right."

The road was good macadam. The mare's hoofs rang cheerfully as she trotted out, well into her bit and collar. A nice little tit. Fresh, game, and good-tempered. They had a nose bag with her lunch in the back and some sandwiches they had made at home for themselves.

"It may take some time," Tom had said, "so we might as well be ready." They had brought some other things, too. A bag of tools and each a heavy blackthorn that was almost a club.

The mare, trotting all out and boring a little, was doing ten miles an hour. She was almost past the turn before

Tom saw it and swung her around onto the dirt road. "A four-wheel cart was 'ere yesterday," he said, looking down at the road. "It come and it went." He gave the mare her head and then they saw it. A thatched cottage rather bigger than most of its kind and covered with creepers. Roses that were over and almost leafless now except for an odd shrunken, late blossom here and there.

"Like a bloody Christmas card," Tom said. "Safe that way, too. No one'd think anything could 'appen 'ere."

They tied the mare to the gatepost, took out her bit, and slid the strap of the nose bag over her head.

Tom took the tools. They both had their sticks.

"I'll take the front," Tom said, "and you stand ready at the back in case I bolt them."

Tom knocked on the door with his stick. There was no response. He hit it harder. Nothing happened. Then he dumped the tools out of his bag and picked up a cold chisel and a hammer. He drove the chisel in beside the lock, between the door and the jamb. Then he put in the crowbar, gave it a heave, and the door was open. The lock sprang and landed on the bare floor inside with a bang.

There seemed to be only four rooms. They all gave off a central passage about five feet wide. The first room was a parlor. Comfortable, smelling of smoke and sherry with recent occupation, a cozy, carpeted room, with black horsehair-covered furniture and six stuffed birds sitting on a branch under a glass bell on the mantelpiece. On the walls were samplers. The one nearest to him read, "God Is Love," in blue cross-stitch on a white ground. It had a plain oak frame. The only picture was a lithograph of the Queen.

The door on the left opened into a bedroom, a man's from the shaving gear on the washstand, and comfortable, too. There was a closed roll-top desk. It wouldn't take long to open with the bar when they had searched the house. If that bastard had given them a wrong steer they'd be for it. Burglary. Breaking and entering and God knows what else. But he wasn't through yet. The next room on the left was a woman's bedroom. It smelled sour and unclean. Only one room to go now. He opened the back door.

"Kitchen's out 'ere," Henry said, pointing to a lean-to.

"Nothing in there, but there's some stuff in the meat safe an' the milk's still fresh. Think they got wind of us?"

"Don't know," Tom said. "There's only one room left. If she's not in there they can put us inside—breaking and entering."

This door was locked.

Tom sprang it with the crowbar. The room was dark, airless, and smelled bad. The windows were closed and covered with heavy curtains that kept out all light.

Henry caught hold of them and tore them down, curtain rod and all. It was barred.

"No, don't," someone cried. "No more, please. Don't. I'll do it."

"Jesus," Tom cried, "it's 'er." It had taken him a second to recognize his sister and get used to the light.

The girl on the bed was naked. The dirty coarse brown blanket that had covered her was on the bare floor beside her. Her body was covered with welts and bruises, her hands strapped to the rails of the bed behind her head. Only her hair was the same. Her long, liver-chestnut hair all matted and snarled. The girl they looked at had no face. In its place was a bloody pulp that had no eyes. The lips were swollen into a kind of pomegranate. There was nothing in the room but a slop pail in the corner, a canvas folding stretcher leaning against the wall, and a grubby white straight jacket hanging on a nail behind the door.

"Water," the girl muttered, "water."

"Get some water, 'Enry," Tom said. "I'll get blankets." He tore them off the bed in the front room and covered his sister. Henry gave her water, holding her up, a sip at a time.

The trap was six feet long from dashboard to tailboard if it was let down on its chains.

"The stretcher," Tom said. They opened it up and carried the girl out of the room, one at the head and one at the feet. She kept crying, "No, no. Don't take me on board." She did not know her brothers.

"Stay with 'er," Tom said, and went back into the man's bedroom. He smashed the roll-top, picked a sheet off the floor, and dropped the contents of the desk into it. He broke open the drawers and tipped them into the heap.

He looked around the room to see if there was anything else. Just another straight jacket. He took that, too.

Now they carried their sister into the garden, took the nose bag off the mare, and put back her bit.

They lifted the stretcher and ran it in over the tailboard. It fitted all right. Tom took the reins. "Untie 'er, 'Enry," he said, "and pass up the sheet." He tied the four corners, stowed it in the trap beside the stretcher, and climbed up.

"Where are we going, Tom?"

"To the police. Get her into 'ospital."

"By God," Henry said, "I'd like to meet that chap."

"We'll do the same to 'im, we will," Henry said.

"We'll do the same," Tom said, and spat into the road over the spinning wheel.

"Dentwhistle," the girl moaned in delirium, "Mr. Dentwhistle is the doctor."

"Rose Cottage?" the police sergeant said. "Why that's Dr. Brown's place. It's a sort of 'ome for loonies. Many's the drink I've 'ad with 'im."

"Then you know 'im?"

"Of course I know 'im. A London man. Specializes in loonies. Girls mostly. 'E told me 'e 'ad quite a name for getting 'em well. 'Completely cured,' that's what 'e said. Takes 'em on a sea voyage. 'Does wonders,'" Sergeant Carr said.

"'Ave a look at this lot." Tom dumped the sheet on the floor of the charge office and undid the knots.

"Where'd you get it?"

"Rose Cottage," Henry said. "That's where we got it. Out of 'is desk."

"I'll 'ave to 'old you," the sergeant said. "Burglary, breaking and entering, the bloody lot."

"'Old and be damned," Tom said, "but get that girl into 'ospital first."

"I've sent for the ambulance," the sergeant said. He picked an account book out of the heap.

"Accounts," he said. "My God! They was selling girls like groceries. It's 'ard to believe." Then he said, "'Ow am I to explain all this? That's what I want to know. You're not police, you've got no warrant. A couple of bloody burglars, that's wot you are."

"All right, then, you 'old us. We just went for our sister, chum, and we got 'er. There's laws, ain't there, about abduction, about white-slave traffic, about stealing good girls and selling them to knocking shops in foreign parts? Ain't you ever 'eard of 'em? Don't you know the bloody law?"

"Not in Slough, mate," the policeman said. "Quiet country place, this is. No murders, no rapes, no nothing. Just a chicken pinched now an' again. But I won't 'old you. Just give me your names and addresses so we can find you if we wants you.

"Christ," he said, running his hands through his hair, "a pretty kettle of fish. An' that Dr. Brown. Who'd 'ave thought it?"

A two-horse ambulance drew up. A doctor in a white coat came in. The two men with him had the stretcher down on the road.

"Beaten up," the doctor said. "We shan't know how bad she is for a few days."

Some passers-by, drawn by the sight of the ambulance and stretcher, stood looking down at the girl's face. A cheaply dressed young woman with a fat boy holding onto her hand said, "Ain't dead, is she? You beat 'er?" she said to Tom.

Tom bent down and ripped the blanket off his sister. There she lay naked, bruised, and whipped in the morning sunlight.

"Look at that," he said. "Look what happens to girls in Slough. That's me sister," he said, "that's our sister Betty. Wot's left of 'er." The doctor covered the girl again.

The woman with the fat boy said, "You didn't ought to do that, not in front of a child."

"I want to see, Ma," the boy said, his eyes popping. His mother slapped his face. He began to howl. Then she kissed him. "The nasty man," she said. "What a dirty thing to do in front of a kid."

By this time the stretcher was in the ambulance.

"Wot'll we do, Doctor?" Tom said.

"Telephone to me. I'm Dr. Charles Strong. I'll take care of her." He patted Tom's shoulder. "In a couple of days you can come and see her."

"We'll come," Tom said. "We'll come with our dad."

He was now occupied with another problem. How did one telephone? He had never used one.

CHAPTER 21

THE HAIRDRESSER

ELSIE now went to the hairdresser every week, accompanied by Celeste, who enjoyed talking to Monsieur André, because he was French—it was a relief to talk her native tongue again—and because he was a man.

Her hair was not the only reason for Elsie's going, either; not only had André become a friend and adviser, but she could see well-bred and well-dressed women there and watch them as if they were caged animals in a zoo. She was learning to look like them, act like them, and talk like them. It became a kind of hobby for her, a form of dramatic art. She acted out parts in her drawing room with Vincent and Celeste, part audience and part Thespian, taking minor roles. It filled in time, and, what with her gardening and teaching Millie to read and do arithmetic, time was passing fast. They were doing well, too. She was only a few jumps ahead of Millie and in spite of the captain's writing to say that this was a case of the blind leading the blind he'd be surprised one day, the captain would, to find her quite a lady, and educated, too.

"I must say," she said to herself one day, "that ladies when they are alone say some very queer things." They said exactly the same things Mrs. Fitz's girls had said. They just used different words and different voices, that was all. But it was funny that so many married ladies who had only one man, or were supposed to have only one man, had much the same ideas about men as the little tarts at No. 20. Of course, and this was a new idea, they were the same men. She even recognized some of the names. She began to laugh so hard that Monsieur André, who was working on her hair, had to stop. Her laughter was so infectious that he laughed too, and some of the women she could see from where she sat were smiling.

Smile on the other side of their faces, she thought, if they knew what the joke was. That they would.

"What was the joke, madame?" Madame, he called her now, and she had got used to it. Madame Smith, Mrs. Smith. She had replaced the rolled-gold wedding ring with a real one and had bought herself a nice engagement ring —four emeralds and four diamonds set alternately in a plain gold band. It was, Monsieur André said, in very good taste. He had helped her choose it.

In early December, listening to two women talk, Elsie heard more than gossip. She got a bit of information that was to change her life. She had not seen them before, but they were both young and good-looking. They were talking about the hospital Lady Finch-Haddley was taking out to South Africa. One woman was fair and the other fairer still. Later she must ask André if he'd had anything to do with it.

The fair one said, "I'd thought of going till I found out what she expected me to do."

"What did she expect, Muriel?" That was the very fair one with the touched-up hair. She was sure of it now.

"Work, darling. Scrub, and things like that. Like a servant, and—imagine it, nurse common soldiers. How could she expect a lady to do that?"

"Well, she's a lady all right, darling, but she's plain. I'll tell you something. I think I'd sooner not be a lady if I was plain. I mean if I could choose plain and a lady or pretty and common. I'd choose pretty."

"I'm sure I don't know," Muriel said, "but I know I wouldn't go all that way if I couldn't nurse officers. Young officers who weren't too ill. Not too ill anyway to . . ."

"Of course, darling, that's what we all feel. We would do our duty, be patriotic and everything, but there are limits. I suppose your husband's gone too, dear," she said.

"Oh yes, darling. There's hardly a decent-looking man in London any more. That's why I wanted to go. If it had been possible, which it isn't, not with that woman, anyway."

"Well," the other woman said—Elsie never found out her name—"she'll have a fine time getting girls to go out as servants. I don't suppose she'll get anyone unless she takes lower-class people."

They went out together with a rustle of petticoats, a "Good-by, Monsieur André," and a wave of perfume.

Monsieur André had never known Elsie to sit so still; she even went on sitting still when he had done.

When Elsie had her coat and hat on she sent Celeste home in the carriage and went to speak to Monsieur André.

"André," she said, "do you know Lady Finch-Haddley's address? I have a message for her about her hospital." The papers were full of it and she was one of his customers.

"I'll look it up," he said. A few minutes later he gave it to her. It was in Wilton Crescent.

She picked up a passing hansom and a few minutes later was climbing the steps of the house. She rang the bell, looking calm enough outside but all of a twitter inside. This was the kind of house the captain was used to visiting, but she'd never even been up the steps of one before.

A butler opened the door. He held a silver tray in his hand which he proffered for a visiting card.

Elsie tumbled to it at once. "I forgot my cards," she said. "I am Mrs. Elsie Smith and I want to see Lady Finch-Haddley."

"Lady Finch-Haddley is not at home, madam," he said, adding in his mind so clearly that Elsie could almost hear the words, "Not to the likes of you, anyway."

"It's about the hospital," she said. "I know she's in town so as it's urgent I'll just wait."

She knew the type. This was another Vincent. They were all trained one way and if you did anything they weren't used to they were foxed, utterly baffled.

Picking up her skirts, being careful to show the lace frill of her petticoats, in a black-gloved hand, she swept past him and sat down on a big gilt red-velvet-upholstered armchair—it was rather like a throne—and looked about her. She had never seen furniture like this, so big, so grand. Shiny black wood things, with gold handles and legs. Great china vases as high as a child. The carpet was thick, buff-colored, with a design of dull red roses. And the pictures! In front of her was a colossal, fat semi-draped nude with a little, quite naked boy beside her reclining on a cloud. She felt happier at once. Here was something she was used to. It only proved what she had come to believe—that all women were much the same, all more or less alike, though some were more so than others. That this feeling of democratic comfort had been induced by her big Rubens might have surprised both Lady Finch-Haddley, when she swept in from the morning room, and the butler.

"What's going on, Homer?" she said. Then she saw Elsie. "And who is this?"

Elsie rose very gracefully the way she'd been taught at No. 20.

"A young person, My Lady. She says—"

"I can see that for myself, Homer, and she can say it to me now that I am here." She turned to Elsie, looking at her through her lorgnette. A pair of glasses stuck on a stick. Just fancy that, Elsie thought.

"And what can I do for you, young lady?"

"It's the hospital, Your Ladyship," Elsie said.

"Oh, something to do with the hospital? Then we had better sit down. Homer, bring sherry and some biscuits into the morning room."

Lady Finch-Haddley was a plain, rather horse-faced and horsy woman of forty-five. She was a widow, her husband, Colonel Sir Francis Finch-Haddley of the Coldstream Guards having been killed in the hunting fields some ten years before. He had been a man of immense wealth.

Lady Finch-Haddley bred hunters—most of them except the stud stock were in the army now—and Irish wolfhounds. She had discovered the ragged remnants of this noble breed in various parts of Ireland. None of them purebred, but all recognizable from the drawings and descriptions of earlier times. By judicious crossings with Scottish staghounds and Danish boarhounds, or great Danes, and careful line breeding, she had reproduced an animal that became extinct as a pure breed in the seventeenth century, not long after the last wolf in Ireland was killed. Lonely, rather bored, capable, and very rich—she saw the war as an opportunity for turning a dream, begun as a child by reading about Florence Nightingale in the Crimean War, into reality. She would finance, form, and direct a field hospital staffed by girls and women of the upper class and take it out to South Africa.

Then her difficulties began. She had sufficient influence to get all the necessary permits. She had no difficulty in buying the stores—tents, beds, sheets, blankets, and medical supplies. But the nurses were another story. Very few of the women she spoke to, though they rode hard to hounds and could dance all night, felt strong enough to undertake the arduous and tedious work required in a hospital.

They would come if they could nurse convalescent officers and provided they were accompanied by a staff of domestics who would do the rough and dirty work. Private soldiers and noncommissioned officers—the "other ranks," as they were called—they wanted no part of.

She had four licensed nurses lined up to act as sisters. She had a young surgeon who wanted practice, and then, finding she could get no further with girls, she had decided to drop her social sights.

By the time Elsie turned up she was ready to take anyone who looked healthy and seemed willing. She had so far collected two parsons' daughters, country girls, ladies but not socially inclined, who were really interested in helping sick and wounded men, one officer's wife whose husband had been killed in the first weeks of fighting, and three upper-middle-class girls, daughters of shopkeepers and clerks whose motives appeared mixed, but who seemed capable and willing to work. She needed a dozen more. Was that what this young person, as Homer called her, had come to see her about? Anyway, they would soon see. She was certainly a pretty little tit.

"Sit down, my dear," she said, "and tell me what I can do for you."

"I want to be a nurse and go to Africa," Elsie said.

"Nursing is very hard and dirty work, my dear," Lady Finch-Haddley said. "Servants' work. I have had a lot of ladies say they wanted to join and then back out when they found how hard it would be and that I was not going to run a hospital for officers. The F.H.F.H.— the Finch-Haddley Field Hospital—is for other ranks. NCOs and private soldiers."

"Troopers?" Elsie said. "Cavalry?"

"Of course, my dear. Troopers too. But why do you ask?"

"I like horse soldiers," Elsie said.

"Well, that's something, anyway, but what about the work?"

"I can work, Your Ladyship," Elsie said. "I'm not a lady."

"You certainly look like one."

And she did, almost. She looked like what they were beginning to call new ladies—*nouveau riche*—and from the way she dressed she certainly wasn't poor.

"You say you can work and are willing. But some of it's dirty work, unpleasant. Bedpans, blood, wounds, and so on." Lady Finch-Haddley waved her hands in a way that she thought expressed all this—a kind of wool-winding gesture.

"And there's something else," she went on. She looked at Elsie's hands. Her rings were covered by her gloves. "Are you afraid of men? Naked men, I mean? You'll have to bathe them and so on. They don't look like babies, you know."

"I love babies," Elsie said.

"Everyone loves babies. But men. Do you think you could manage that part?"

"Oh yes," Elsie said, "I think I could."

"And by the way," Lady Finch-Haddley said, "what is your name?"

"It's Mrs. Smith. Elsie Smith. But I'm not married." She felt her wedding ring and engagement ring through her glove with her right hand. "I'm a kept woman," she said.

"Indeed," Lady Finch-Haddley said. "Then why exactly do you want to go to South Africa?"

"He's there," Elsie said. "The captain. I won't tell you who he is but he's in the cavalry."

"And he's been good to you?" Really, the things one came across in wartime. A girl like that in my house, sitting in my morning room.

"Oh yes," Elsie said, "I love him and I've got nothing to do now. Just the house he gave me and the servants. They are all so nice. Vincent, that's the captain's man, and my French maid are teaching me to be a lady so I'll surprise the captain when he gets back."

"But you want to go out there?"

"Not to see him. I don't think he'd like it. Not in public like. In a little house it's different."

"A love nest." Lady Finch-Haddley sniffed.

Elsie smiled at her. "That's what the captain calls it, Your Ladyship, 'our love nest.' "

"Don't call me Your Ladyship, Mrs. Smith, call me Lady Finch-Haddley."

"All right," Elsie said. "But don't call me Mrs. Smith. I'm not Mrs. Smith, not really. It's just play-acting while he's away. I'm Elsie Smith—Elsie," she said.

A brave little thing, standing up to me like that, thought Lady Finch-Haddley. Not many of 'em had the guts to, not even the well-bred 'uns.

She said, "All right, Elsie. But you look so young. Do you think your father will let you go?" Being kept in London was one thing, and going to war another.

"I've got no dad, Your Ladyship. An' I've seen naked men. An' my captain's at the war an' I'm sick of doing nothing." She got up, sweeping her long skirts around her ankles. "But I suppose it's no good. I knew you wouldn't have me, but I thought I'd try. I was a fool to come. It was just one of those bloody women talking at the hairdressers' and laughing and saying you wanted girls wot would work and it wasn't for them—not bloody likely. That's why I came. I wanted to help but you'd not touch the likes of me with a bloody barge pole, not a girl that's kept." Her brown eyes burned with anger and she swept over the carpet in full sail for the door.

"Stop!" Lady Finch-Haddley snapped. Elsie stopped. "Come here, Elsie, and sit down beside me. Damned if I don't like you," she said. "I'd like to have you with me."

"Oh," Elsie said. She flung her arms around her and gave her a kiss. Lady Finch-Haddley was speechless. This girl was going to be a problem. The lower classes were so demonstrative and affectionate. But she liked the girl. Couldn't help it.

"I'll work hard," Elsie said. "I'll do what you say and give no trouble."

"Girls as pretty as you are always give trouble. Born to it, you are." Elsie wondered how she had guessed. "But there's one thing, my girl. You're just Miss Elsie Smith and don't tell anyone else what you told me. Leave me your address and I'll let you know when we sail. It will be in about eight weeks, I think."

"That's lovely," Elsie said. "It'll give me time to finish with Millie."

"Who's Millie?" Lady Finch-Haddley asked.

"My tweenie, one of my maids. The little one. She's just sixteen."

"Yes, my dear, but what are you finishing with her?"

"I'm teaching her to read," Elsie said.

Lady Finch-Haddley went into peals of laughter as the butler came into the room. It was years since he'd heard Her Ladyship laugh. What had he missed? Anyway, he'd made the young person wait. Sherry and biscuits certainly, but not at once for young persons.

The two women sipped the sherry. Elsie didn't like it. It was too dry. But she drank it and nibbled a water biscuit. Then she rose and held out her hand. "Good-by, Lady Finch-Haddley," she said, "and thank you very much."

"Thank you, Elsie. I wish I had a dozen more like you." And she did.

It certainly was a topsy-turvy world, but she had not laughed like that for years.

When Elsie got home she looked around the drawing room. How pretty it was. The captain, as she still called him, had said it was no use spoiling a ship for a ha'porth of tar. She wasn't sure what he meant except that he'd spent a lot of money on it and chosen everything himself.

She rang the bell.

Vincent came in. "Miss Elsie," he said, "you rang?"

"Yes, Vincent, I have something to tell you. It's rather a lot so you had better sit down."

He sat on the edge of a pale blue brocaded chair.

"I am leaving here, Vincent."

So it had come. It always did in the end. Once they'd gone that way. Couldn't do without a man. Got somebody else to keep her, no doubt. Always the same with these flighty ones that showed the whites of their eyes. He wondered how he'd break it to the captain.

"Who is it, Miss Elsie? Do I know him?"

She laughed. "It's not a he, Vincent, it's a her. Lady Finch-Haddley. I'm going to South Africa with her hospital."

"South Africa?"

"Yes, I'll be doing some good and I'll be near him. I may see him—the captain," she added.

"You love him, miss." Vincent was almost shocked. That a woman like this could love a man.

"I love him," she said. "He is my life."

"Yes, miss."

"But I'm going, Vincent. And you can't stop me." She jumped up and kissed him. She was so happy she wanted to kiss everyone. In three months she'd be near the captain. In the same country over the sea.

CHAPTER 22

SLASHER

WEDNESDAY, November 13, was a dark day for Mrs. Samuel Tupper. For the first time in sixteen years of marriage her husband had eaten no breakfast. Not even one egg, and he usually had two. He had not tried to eat it. Had not even taken off the top by tapping it on the side with his knife all around and taking it off in a neat little cap like a trepanning surgeon.

"Aren't you going to eat anything, Tupper?" she said.

"No," he said, "and don't worry me, Edith."

"Well, have some more tea." She filled his cup.

The children sat still as they had been taught to do, wide-eyed mutes who spoke only when spoken to.

Mr. Tupper, the small, neat, rather clerical-looking, clean-shaven man, was, beneath his outward calm, boiling with rage.

All this work. All these years of building up a splendid business, jeopardized by two Covent Garden louts who had all but killed William, a faithful though stupid servant, stolen a parcel from Rose Cottage, wrecked the place, and—and this was what really infuriated him—not only made it useless by informing the police of its true purpose, but started a ball rolling, a snowball that might increase in size as it went on, and end God knew where, even here in Dulwich. And Edith was surprised that he was off his feed.

They would probably find Ellen wihhout difficulty, and where would he find her equal as a housekeeper for the new Rose Cottage he was already planning? She had worked in an asylum and knew the patter. She could deal with anyone who asked awkward questions, and had done so many times, to the silly fools who tried to come to the help of a screaming girl in a straight jacket being forced into a cab or carried out on a stretcher. She had had the background he wanted. Her reputation for discipline in the asylum had been excellent and she had been sacked only because of her affection for the bottle. Gin had been her downfall. But he had put the fear of God into her and she was a reformed character. Then she had run a baby farm with such success that the law had got after her. He had found her working as a charwoman and picked her out of the gutter.

But she would lead them to the doctor, a vain, stupid man, a weekend drunkard, and from there the scent would lead to Dentwhistle, his alter ego.

"Drink your tea while it's hot, Tupper," his wife said.

He sipped at the cup, not because he wanted tea or to please her, but to keep her quiet.

He would have to see Dentwhistle at once. They'd put their heads together. The whole operation might have to be made over, and in the meanwhile they'd lose money.

But when Mr. Tupper got to the office and sent for Dentwhistle, he was not to be found. He was told that Mr. Dentwhistle had gone out.

The reason Mr. Dentwhistle was not to be found was that he felt the time had come to deal with Elsie. His orders had been to attend to her when convenient. This seemed a good time, with the other girl safe in Ellen's hands at Rose Cottage and nothing of particular importance in view until he had arranged her passage, and it was no use even considering that until the wounds on her face were healed. That was the worst of men like Bill. They were so impulsive.

Mr. Dentwhistle had passed No. 7 Acacia Road on several occasions. Once he dressed as a navvy, a working-

man with a pick over his shoulder, once as a businessman in a black cutaway and a top hat, once as a grocer's
delivery boy with a bicycle and a basket. He had paced
the distance to the two cross streets. Forty paces to Oak
Street and sixty to Ashley Road.

Now he came as a florist's man with a long box of white
chrysanthemums. They had large feathery heads and were
suitably funereal, suitable to the death of Miss Elsie's
beauty. At the corner of both Ashley Road and Oak
Street he had a hansom with a good horse between the
shafts waiting for him, paid in advance. "I may come
running," he said. "The moment I jump in, drive off
fast for Hampstead."

He went through the gate in the low wall of No. 7, over
the flags, past the iris now heavy with seed pods, their
swordlike leaves still green and sharp, up the six whitened
steps to the apple-green door with its shiny brass knob,
knocker, and letter box, and the shiny bellpull set like
an acorn in the brass saucer of its escutcheon.

He pulled the knob. He felt the drag of the wires as
they ran through the tubes masoned into the wall, and
heard the jingle of the bell in the basement.

The green door was opened by the French maid. A
pretty piece—white-capped, aproned, her dark eyes curious about any personable man, even a florist's delivery
man.

"Yes?" she said.

"This Miss Elsie Smith's house?" he asked.

"It is." Her eyes became even more friendly now that
he was legitimate.

"I have a package for her," he said. "Flowers."

"I will take them, monsieur."

"No, miss," he said. "They must be signed for by the
lady herself. My instructions are to put them into her
own hands." He raised the box as if to check the label.
"They are from Captain Turnbull," he said, "with the
compliments of . . ."

"That is different," the girl said, turning her back
to him. A pretty back. He wondered on what beds it had
lain and with whom. If he had not been engaged in a
more serious business he could have placed her very
well. She was a popular type—dark, flashing, and full-
fleshed without being fat.

He followed her into the hall. She left him to find her mistress. He looked at the front door and checked the lock. He had only to turn the handle to open it. The green door was solid mahogany and painted only on the outside.

He heard the tap of high heels. Miss Elsie was coming. When he saw her he realized her value as merchandise, saw the reason for Mrs. Fitz's anger at the loss of such a little money-maker.

Her dark hair was piled on her head, her brown eyes seemed enormous due to the dark shadows below them. She was dressed in a pink frock sprigged with small moss roses. She had beautiful arms and a waist that, confined in stays, was no more than fifteen inches. Her mouth was a fresh pink, the lips moist, her teeth small and regular when she smiled at him. What a piece! What a piece of goods, and what a shame to spoil it. Waste, that's what it was.

"You have some flowers for me, I hear. From Captain Turnbull," she added.

It really seemed a shame to do what he was going to do.

"Yes, miss," he said, and he raised the white cardboard box to give it to her. The maid who stood beside her took it from his hands as he had foreseen.

"Will you be good enough to sign my delivery book?" he said, and held it out with a pencil. As she bent forward to take it he changed it from his right hand to his left, bringing the right up with the folded razor between thumb and forefinger and flicking it open as he raised it to strike.

Only then, when it was too late, did he notice the big black dog at her side. Before his hand was high enough to strike the dog had leaped at his throat, jumping silently without a growl. Queenie's teeth met on his jugular. He fell beneath her with a scream, blood spurting from between his fingers, just as Vincent, feeling something was amiss, ran into the hall and dragged the bitch off him.

"A towel, Celeste," he shouted, but by the time she came with it the florist's delivery man was dead and the carpet soaked with blood. The open razor lay where it had fallen and his mistress was flat on her back in a faint.

It looked like a battle with two corpses. The flower box had broken open. The great, fat, white chrysanthemums lay scattered, one of them stained with dark arterial blood almost on the face of the man who had brought them. Queenie, her long hackles erect in a black fringe, stood growling between the prostrate man and her mistress.

The getaway hansoms waited in vain. How well it had all been planned. If he was pursued he had one waiting in either direction. Everything had been foreseen—everything but the dog. As he died beneath her teeth perhaps he wondered how he had missed it. The one weak link in the chain of his forethought that had broken.

So they're still after her, Vincent thought. He was under no delusions as to who was behind this attack. His agile mind was now occupied in thinking of how to protect her name from scandal. Her name, the captain's, and his own. Nothing must get into the papers. And look at the mess—the blood.

"Get her to bed," he said to Celeste. She picked her mistress up as if she was a child.

Ellen and Millie, the tweenie, now arrived from the basement.

Ellen said, "Jesus, Mary," and followed Celeste into the bedroom. Millie came forward, saw the blood and the dead man, and fainted.

Women, Vincent thought. Where the hell were the men—Charlie and the boy? Queenie was scratching and whimpering at the bedroom door.

Leaving the bodies on the carpet, Vincent went through the French window of the drawing room into the garden and called Charlie.

"Come here, Charlie, and look sharp, and bring the boy."

"Coming," Charlie shouted.

Vincent waited for him.

"It's a mess, Charlie," he said. He turned to the boy, "And don't you faint too. We've got to get this man cleaned up before I get the police.

"We'll make up a yarn. They'll say we should have left it, but you can't leave a mess like that, not in a house like this.

"Get a bucket of water, boy—two buckets. And the stable broom."

By the time he got back Millie was sitting up and gasping. Vincent had poured half a tumbler of brandy down her throat.

"It burns, Mr. Vincent," she said. "It's like poison."

"That's because you're a kid," he said. He snatched the glass from her, filled it, took a couple of gulps and handed it to Charlie.

"Wot about me?" the boy said. "I feels faint too."

Charlie gave him the dregs.

"Now wash the floor, clean the place up," Vincent said as he left to go to his pantry. He was back in a few minutes with a tall vase full of water in which he arranged the chrysanthemums. The bloody one he rinsed in the stable bucket. "Good as new," he said as he put it in with the others. "Never know which one it was. That you wouldn't, would you, Charlie?" He gave a laugh. "Like being in the Eighteenth again, Charlie," he said. "Another bloody war."

Vincent liked a bit of excitement, "some goings on," as he called it, and Miss Elsie would be safe for a bit after this. Must have been one of their top men to have planned it so well. And soon she'd be safe on the water. He had plans in his head for that, too. What he'd do after she'd left. Great plans.

The sergeant who accompanied Vincent back to the scene of the serious accident, as Vincent had put it, said, "And what exactly occurred?"

"There's a body," Vincent said, "a corpse. A cadaver bleeding like a stuck pig in our front hall."

"Dead?"

"Dead as mutton."

"What happened, Mr. Vincent?"

"Queenie killed him."

"Who's Queenie?" Was this one of those interesting crimes of passion? the sergeant wondered.

"Queenie's our flat-coat, our retriever bitch. She was protecting me. This chap comes with flowers. I opens the door and he goes for me with a razor. The bitch is there beside me. She jumps for his throat and cuts his jugular, neat as a whistle, and there you are. What a bloody mess on the carpet. Light-colored it is."

"You touched nothing, I hope, Mr. Vincent?"

"Touched nothing? With all those girls in the house screaming and fainting when they saw the blood, dropping like ninepins. They came running when they heard the fracas. Of course we cleaned it up. The men and I. Washed up the blood and shoved him in a corner with a horse blanket over him, a night blanket of course."

"You should never do that, Mr. Vincent. A body should be left till the police come."

"Not in our house. But I'll remember next time, Sergeant. Mind you, I was excited. Chap doesn't go for you with a razor every day, and if it hadn't been for Queenie I'd be dead. But he brought some nice flowers, white chrysanthemums. I'll show them to you—and the box, the florist's box."

"The razor?" the sergeant said.

"On the carpet beside the corpse."

When they got to No. 7, Charles was standing at the open door staring down the street waiting for them.

"Not much evidence of a crime left 'ere," the sergeant said.

"Crime. What's the crime? I open the door, a chap with a razor goes for me"—Vincent winked at Charlie—"and our dog gets him. What's the crime? Accident if you like."

"That the body?" the sergeant said.

"Take his rug off, Charlie," Vincent said, as if it was a horse.

The sergeant bent over Dentwhistle's bloodless face.

"My God!" he said. "It's Slasher. We've wanted 'im for years but never been able to nail 'im. Clever he was."

Vincent put the razor into his hand. It was still open, the open blade bent right back against the handle.

"Done a lot of harm with this here, he has, Mr. Vincent. And don't worry, there'll be no trouble about Slasher."

"We don't want it in the papers," Vincent said.

"I'll send for him. Have him out in an hour. Trouble? Why should we have trouble if Slasher's found dead in the street? Many had cause enough to kill him."

CHAPTER 23

THE HITTITE

IN THE BOER CAMP more and more visitors arrived from Pretoria to join in the social life and watch the big guns shell Ladysmith. Discipline, always vestigial, ceased to exist. It was not war, it was a picnic. But the veld near all the invested towns was being grazed out by thousands of horses. Forage was impossible to obtain and the ponies lost so much condition that in Cronje's force of eight thousand burghers at Kimberley more than two thousand found themselves dismounted. This was entirely due to the Boers remaining stationary instead of conducting the war of movement for which they were so ideally equipped.

Boetie was enjoying himself, but Moolman was depressed by inaction. He was not used to staying so long in one place. As the corporalship saw it, the news, most of it rumor, was not bad. The British commander in chief, General Buller, was massing troops for the relief of Ladysmith south of the Tugela. He was said to have forty thousand men and a great number of guns. But fifteen thousand Boers were holding the north bank of the river from a point below the Colenso Bridge to Spion Kop, many miles upstream. So with this force between the commando and the British there was no need for immediate anxiety. As to the troops in Ladysmith, there seemed very little likelihood that they would break out, as they were suffering great food shortages and were unfit to fight.

But on December 19 the situation changed. During the night a detachment of British climbed Lombaard's Kop and destroyed the Creusot Long Tom there. The Boers could ill afford to lose any of their big guns. And this was the end of their peace. A day later half the Pretoria men were ordered south to reinforce the north bank of the Tugela.

They rode south in a loosely extended formation, Servas

and Boetie on either side of Moolman, the Beyerses, man
and wife, knee to knee beside them. Nel, O'Brien, Prinsloo,
and Bothma brought up the rear of their party. It took
them three hours to get out of the overgrazed area onto
good veld. Here the grass was green, and the mimosa
trees in full, golden, sweet-perfumed flower, with the
bees busy among them.

"You should not be here, Hetta," Beyers said. "Before
God, you should not be here."

"Where should I be, Jan? Would you rather I lay dead
at home? What is left to me but you?"

"*Ja,* my heart," he said, "you are right. All we have
is each other and I want no more." He put his hand on
her thigh. "It is only that I am afraid of your being
hurt. War is no place for a woman."

"Nor for a man, Jan. But a wife's place is at her husband's side."

They rode on in silence, each filled with anxiety about
the other.

By nightfall they reached the Boer trenches on the
Tugela and found the burghers already there quite nervous.

"*Jong,*" a big black-bearded man said to Boetie, "we
do not like it here, cooped up in narrow trenches like
snakes in a ditch. Our horses are miles away. And who
is leading us? Louis Botha, a farmer like ourselves,
against the English commandant general himself, a man
who has been at war since childhood."

The trenches were well concealed, camouflaged, though
the word did not exist then. Botha was convinced that by
secrecy, that by hiding his position so carefully, he could
compensate for the numerical weakness of his force of
eight thousand Boers against Buller's eighteen thousand.
The forty thousand English had been a latrine rumor.

The burghers were less convinced and demands for
sick leave poured into headquarters. They were not
dealt with in the usual free and easy manner. The sick
were given purges that immobilized them and the run on
the medical units was halted.

These narrow trenches, the first ever used, had been
invented by De la Rey as the only possible defense
against shrapnel. They had already been proved almost a hundred per cent effective, but the Boers on the

Tugela did not know it. They had never fought pinned down before. Their tradition was to occupy a position on a *kopje* or a range of hills with their ponies in safety behind them, and when things became too hot to abandon their posts and ride away.

Ten miles or so south of where Boetie was talking to the black-bearded Boer, Turnbull was watching General Buller as he sat at a table, his maps in front of him. He had just finished a bottle of champagne.

His face was puffy from lack of sleep, his mouth slack with indecision. "The bloody stuff's warm," he said. He had already made up his mind three times and changed his plans three times.

The relief of Ladysmith had become an obsession. Roberts was at sea, on his way to take over his command. He must have one success. Roberts had cabled him to stay on the defensive. Jealousy, Buller thought. He wanted all the glory. He signaled to White in Ladysmith: "I doubt Lord Robert's forecast's coming off and I think I had better play my hand alone."

He had to take Ladysmith and take it by himself, without help. He must round off a career that hitherto, till this damn South African command, had been glorious. Victoria Cross, commander in chief, Bulldog Buller, the idol of the common soldier.

The first plan had been to cross the Tugela and march through the hills to Ladysmith. Then he decided to bypass the Boers, for, though Botha had only eight thousand men to his eighteen thousand, he decided that their entrenched position was impregnable. He telegraphed to this effect to the War Office in London and said that he was going to march upstream around it. His telegram had just gone off when he got news of Methuen's defeat at Magersfontein, and changed his plan again. He would attack the impregnable position on the Tugela after all.

For three days he bombarded the Boers and then called his senior officers and told them of his revised plan. The orders issued that night read: "The enemy is entrenched on the kopjes north of Colenso Bridge. . . . It is the intention of the general officer commanding to force the passage of the Tugela. . . ."

It was at this juncture that Wanthope, Turnbull, and

Darnley returned from Cape Town. Hearing they had reported, Buller sent for Turnbull. He was supposed to be an expert on Africa, one of the few besides himself who knew the country at all.

"You wanted me, sir?" Turnbull said, saluting.

"I do. You know these bloody Boers," he said. "What would you do if you were me?"

"I'm a captain of hussars, sir. Strategy is not my strong point."

"I'm not asking about strategy, Turnbull. I just want to know where the hell the Boers are."

This had been worrying Turnbull too. Suppose they were not in the hills that they had been shelling or suppose the shelling had been ineffective. This idea of an artillery preparation for an assault was new. It looked splendid with the lyddite bursting shrapnel in yellow and black clouds, and the heavy guns sending up great tornadoes of earth. But how much good it did no one knew yet.

"Suppose you were a Boer?" Buller said.

"I'm not sure if I'd stay in the hills, sir."

"Well?" Buller asked. "What should I do?"

"I'd send out a mounted patrol, sir, to feel them out and make certain." Good God, Turnbull thought, this was elementary. Why had it not been done?

"I'll do that, Turnbull. Please be good enough to ask General Wanthope to come over here."

Turnbull rode over to the cavalry lines.

"General Buller's compliments, sir. He would like to see you."

They rode back together.

He could understand that Diana might have an interest in General Lord Wanthope. Apart from being a peer and one of the richest men in England, he was a magnificent-looking man, six feet one, fifty years of age but with the figure and carriage of a man of thirty. He'd been on the General Staff a long time, seconded from his regiment, the 10th Dragoons—the Royal Blacks—and always wore their badge, a golden eagle with half-open wings, on each side of his scarlet collar tabs.

When they reached Buller, Turnbull went to the mess tent for a cup of tea. For the moment there was nothing to do.

It was quite by accident that an hour later he happened to be outside and saw a detachment of lancers, about half a troop, with an officer in command, riding north toward the Boers.

Good Lord, he thought, lancers, the steel points of their lances glittering like silver in the hot sun of afternoon. And it was on his advice that Buller had acted. He'd said, "A reconnaissance, sir. A mounted detachment to go forward and feel them out." But he'd meant M.I.—mounted infantry, not lancers.

Calling for his horse, he galloped to a little hill where he could get a good view of the patrol. With his glasses they seemed so near that he could touch them. He'd been right. Charlie was leading them. He'd recognized the horse, a bright chestnut with three white stockings and a blaze.

Nothing was done all afternoon. Nothing could be done till the patrol returned. The army stood by, waiting.

Moolman saw the cavalry first. He could hardly believe his eyes. A dozen lancers, their lances' heads glittering like silver, led by an officer on a chestnut horse, were riding toward them.

"Come on," he shouted. "They must not reach our position. They must not find that our trenches are hidden on the flats. We'll take them on the far side of the river."

He led Boetie, Servas, the two Beyers, and the rest of his group into the open.

"They'll think we are a patrol," he said as he headed into the water. It was shallow here and the stream was slow, not even up to their shoulders. Holding their rifles over their heads, they reached the south bank and deployed, taking what cover they could behind thornbushes and ant heaps. The English, who did not seem to have seen them, came on, riding on at a walk.

"We'll wait till they are a hundred yards away before we fire," Moolman said, "and I'll shoot first."

They waited. Boetie was trembling. This was terrible, this cold-blooded business. It was hunting, not war. It was like lying near a waterhole waiting for unsuspecting buck to come and drink. But these buck were men.

He opened his bolt and slid a cartridge into the breech. It slid in beautifully, silently riding the greased and polished mechanism. The brass cartridge case armed with death crept like a snake into its hole as the bolt came forward to seal it. They were five hundred yards away.

"Wait for me to fire," Moolman said again, "and when you shoot, shoot carefully. None of them must get through. I'll take the officer on the chestnut."

They seemed to wait for hours. The English halted and looked about them. The officer swept the terrain with his glasses. If he had done it sooner, Boetie thought, he would have seen us and stopped.

He had no wish to kill these men. In spite of the battle at Elandslaagte and the hatred of most Boers for the cavalry, he could not bring himself into this mood. His friend the captain was a hussar. Boetie could not hate yet. In action he was all right, carried forward by the excitement of his own fears, but this was different.

Moolman shouted, "Now!" fired, and missed.

The officer drew his sword and Boetie saw it flash as he shouted, "Charge!"

The points of the lances fell. The horses began to gallop. The Boers fired, not rapidly, but deliberate, sighted shots. Saddle after saddle was emptied till only two men were left—the officer and another—and still these madmen rode on, accompanied by three riderless horses. Now the trooper's horse went down. The officer dismounted, the reins of his chestnut over his arm, and got the man into his saddle. The Boers held their fire. You could not shoot so brave a man. The officer mounted behind the trooper and swung the horse around. There was a single shot, the last one fired. The officer slipped from the saddle and the man galloped on alone, a horse with an empty saddle and flapping reins running beside him.

"I do not like to miss," Moolman said, opening his bolt and blowing down the barrel.

Boetie's knees were so weak he could not get up. Finding himself in this position, he began to pray.

The others went on to help the wounded and shoot the incapacitated horses. There were four men wounded. They did what they could for them, bound up their wounds, gave them water, and left them with their dead. Most of the dead had been shot in the face and chest as they lay along their horses' necks with outstretched lances.

Moolman said one strange thing as he stood over the

officer, the officer he had shot. "A brave man," he said. "It was a pity to do it but I cannot afford to miss. To shoot, the eyes, the heart, and the hand must be one. To miss is to weaken the heart, and to bring doubt to the hand, so that afterwards more misses are probable."

A strange, hard man, Boetie thought. A man who had been fashioned by life, turned by it, as though life was a lathe, making some men one way and others another. I wonder what I shall be like when I grow up, he thought. He knew he was a boy no longer, yet not quite a man, but manhood was being thrust upon him.

The action at the Tugela had begun. The first round, slight as it was, had gone to the Boers. The burghers waded the river again, returning to their trenches elated, all but Boetie, wondering how they were going to dry their clothes.

At six a shout went up from the cavalry lines, a cry, as a wild-eyed, riderless horse, the stirrups flapping, its saddle almost off, galloped among the tents, followed closely by a wounded man on a chestnut nearly black with sweat. It had three white stockings and a blaze. Charlie's horse, Turnbull thought. But it was not Charlie. It was a trooper. He pulled the horse up onto its quarters in a rear at headquarters.

"Christ!" he gasped. "They got us. I'm the only one wot got away," and fell from the saddle.

The horse near foundered, stood still, head down, curded with sweat that, red with dust, looked like blood, its barrel going like a bellows as it gasped for breath. Its knees trembled. Its nostrils were wide and red as it blew out and sucked in great gulps of air. Turnbull went up to it and gently pulled its ears. "Jack," he said. The horse looked at him with wild eyes and pushed its nose into his belly. Jack knew him. He undid the girths, dropped the saddle on the ground in front of the general's tent, and led the horse away himself.

"If he lives I'll keep him," he said. "Diana won't say no to that." Horses meant a lot to Turnbull.

So he had done it, he thought. That splendid-looking man had murdered Charlie, had played David to Charlie's Uriah, while Bathsheba waited in Cape Town. He had murdered Charlie as surely as if he'd shot him in the heart.

Did mankind change at all? Were the same crimes repeated over and over again through all history? ". . . Set ye Uriah in the forefront of the hottest battle." He thought of his father's words about courage, of how a brave man might become reckless and continually challenge fate, trying to possess danger, clasp it to his arms like a woman, becoming ashamed if he let a chance to prove his courage slip. Like a man who had to have every woman he saw. Charlie had it, a kind of madness that Diana had encouraged in their nights of love.

After mess, and a very silent meal it had been, with Buller drinking even more than usual, a Major Tower, in the 22nd Lancers, came up to John.

"Turnbull," he said, "I don't know you very well but I'd like a word with you."

"Certainly," John said.

"We'll go outside if you don't mind."

It was a beautiful, still, warm, star-filled night, almost luminous with their light.

"I trust you will not take offense, Turnbull, at what I'm going to say, but I can't help it if you do. It's about Wanthope. You've been with him a lot. But steer clear of him."

"I was a friend of Charlie's too," John said.

"Charlie was more than a friend to me," Tower said. "We joined the Twenty-second within a week of each other. And they were our boys, by God. Ten of our boys dead for nothing.

"But it's not only that," Tower went on. "I'm not squeamish, you know, but my brother's in the Blacks, and they won't have him back. That's why he went to the staff. There was a young trumpeter, a good-looking boy of seventeen, who hanged himself in barracks ten years ago. Of course nothing could be proved but the colonel suggested the staff to Wanthope."

"Boys?" John said.

"Boys and young girls. Children, really, when he can get them."

Now something came back to Turnbull, something Elsie had said about a big man that even Mrs. Fitz would not have back in the place. A big man with horses on his collar. He must have been there in uniform, something most unusual in London, but he might have been on his way to Aldershot on maneuvers.

"He hurts girls," Elsie had said, "marks them so people ask questions."

"Thanks," John said. "I'm much obliged."

"I just thought I'd tell you, Turnbull. Steer clear of him. He's a bad lot. Good night."

"Good night," John said.

Tower walked off into the darkness, his spur rowels clinking.

Now he had the picture, Turnbull thought. That accounted for Diana. That explained what she had let slip out. He'd always wondered what it was. That was why Wanthope had never married. With what he had—title, riches, looks—you'd think every mother in England would have been chucking her daughter at him for the last thirty years. But they knew too much about him. So what was left? A woman like Diana. She was beautiful, she was well bred—her grandmother had been a Gore of Ackland —and she was still young enough to breed.

By God, he thought, if she only knew. She'd not get the house in London, she'd not be a great hostess—Lady Wanthope of Grosvenor Square. She'd find herself put out to grass, like a brood mare, at that dreary place in Ulster.

She was a small woman but wide-hipped. She'd refused to have children with Charlie, he'd heard, because of her figure. Of course Charlie had not known that. He just thought it was bad luck, not that she had some trick to prevent her taking.

Well, she'd not trick Wanthope. He'd breed her every year. He wanted heirs.

Turnbull was almost sorry for Diana. If Wanthope had tricked her into thinking she could manage him, she was going to be hoist with her own petard.

This time Greek had indeed met Greek. He saw it all. But Charlie. Poor, dear, brave, stupid old Charlie. What a bloody shame it was. He rubbed a tear from his eye. A lot of midges tonight, he thought. Being near the river— always a lot of mosquitoes and midges near water. But what a shame it was. Everyone had loved Charlie except his wife. And she'd not get Jack back. She was the kind

of woman who would sell him to anyone, even to a
knacker. And he wasn't going to pay for him, either.

In his tent by the light of a hurricane lantern General
Wanthope was writing to Diana. He wrote:

Dear Mrs. Darnley:
I have bad news for you. Your husband, Major Charles
Darnley of the 19th Lancers, was killed in action today coming
upon a party of Boers while on reconnaissance. He led his men
in a charge in the best tradition of the cavalry but ran into an
ambush. He saved the life of one trooper whose horse was hit.
He dismounted and put him onto his own charger and
mounted behind him. This is how he was shot. The man, the
only one to return, told the story of your husband's heroism.
I have put him in for the Victoria Cross, which is, as you
know, the highest decoration and greatest honour that can be
accorded to a British soldier, officer or man.
This letter is more unusually difficult to write since I had
the pleasure of making your acquaintance. Charles, as you
know, was a great personal friend. He volunteered for this
dangerous mission. I tried to dissuade him, thinking of you,
saying that a younger and unmarried officer should go. There
were several who wanted to, but Charles was eager for more
honour and glory, possibly to lay the laurel leaves at your
feet. These are things we shall never know. I can only repeat
my regret at having lost a friend and the 19th and the cavalry
a most gallant officer, though this is as nothing to the loss
you have sustained. If the manner of his death, the splendour
of his courage, the fact that his name will be added to the already long and famous list of heroes in his regiment can be
of any comfort to you in your bereavement, you certainly
have this knowledge and with it all the sympathy that one
man, even a general officer, can give to the wife of another.
If at any time I can be of assistance to you in any way,
though our meeting at the Mount Nelson was so brief, please
call on me and consider me a friend.
                                    Yours sincerely,
                                    Henry Wanthope
                                    G.O.C. Cavalry

The general put down his pen and listened to the guns
that had begun to batter the Boer position. Nothing could
stand up to that kind of fire.

PART FOUR

THE TURN OF THE TIDE

*Tides turn, ebb and flow. There is no
end to them nor the seasons . . .*

ANON.

*[South Africa and England—December 1899—
March 1900—Summer and Fall]*

CHAPTER 24

VICTORY

ONCE they got used to the shells screaming over their heads, the two-day bombardment of the hills by the British made the Boers uneasy but no more than that. Botha told them to sit tight. Only by concealing their position could they expect to withstand an attack from such a superior force as that which opposed them.

A comforting message had come from Cronje at Magersfontein, assuring them that the new explosive lyddite, despite the noise it made and its black, greenish-yellow smoke, was harmless as long as they stayed in their trenches. This was particularly true, since they were not being shelled at all. The British thought they were in the hills to their rear. But it kept them in their trenches, down and well under cover.

The two forces were about four miles apart. Every tent on the British side was visible to the Boers, while the British saw no sign of the enemy. Buller, looking at the hills his guns were battering, was convinced the Boers had withdrawn and that the party that had decimated his lancers was just a patrol, perhaps even the tail end of a Boer guard doing some investigation on its own. He was sure they had gone.

Turnbull remained doubtful. Because you did not see any Boers it did not mean they weren't there. There was something else that worried him. Buller had deceived General White, telling him that the attack could not be launched till the seventeenth. This meant that, instead of the Boers being attacked by the thirteen-thousand be-sieged Ladysmith troops in the rear while Buller with his eighteen-thousand attacked them frontally, they would have only a single force to deal with and their line of retreat was clear and unimpeded.

Buller had decided on this deception of his own general

because Ladysmith was riddled with spies. But what, after all, would it have mattered if the information had come out? It might even have made the Boers jumpy. But the result of it was that on the morning of the fifteenth White, waking to the grumble of distant gunfire and having no orders, stayed where he was, though he could have broken out easily, there being only six thousand Boers left investing the town. The others had gone to reinforce Botha on the Tugela or had given themselves leave.

The day dawned cloudless as usual, with the usual promise of intense December heat, as Buller's columns moved over the veld toward the river. At five-thirty the heavy guns, drawn by trains of sixteen oxen, rumbled into position behind the advancing infantry and opened up on the Colenso *kopjes* where it was assumed some Boers might still be lurking.

Clouds of red dust and the black and yellow fumes of the exploding shells obscured the hills from view. Columns of smoke and of earth were sent up by the exploding shells. There was no sign of a Boer. Not a rifle shot. No man could live through a bombardment like that.

The plan of attack was simple and suicidal.

One brigade was to assault the Boer center and another the Boer right, until the river had been forced. They would then link up and a mounted brigade would push through to seize Hlangwane, a hill on the Boers' flank, from which to enfilade their position if they were still there. This force had two brigades in general support.

The artillery consisted of twelve field and six naval guns manned by some five hundred field-artillery men, horse gunners, and bluejackets of the Royal Navy. They were under the command of Colonel C. J. Long of Omdurman fame. His orders were to rely on the long-range naval guns until the infantry, under Major General Hildyard, was well forward, and then follow with his horse-drawn artillery—the fifteen- and twelve-pounders. This was standard procedure. Guns must always be behind the infantry.

Long, however, had evolved a new theory. He thought that the guns should be pushed forward into the enemy's face, where they could destroy him at point-blank range and pulverize him in retreat, catching him in a box of bursting shells. So, in spite of Hildyard's orders, he pushed on till he was a full mile ahead of the infantry.

All this Turnbull and the rest of Buller's staff saw through their glasses. The twin worms of the brigades advancing, deploying, changing into ants that were hardly visible in their khaki against the veld, and then by God the gun teams went on alone, as if they were going to charge the Boers all by themselves. Long must have gone mad.

He had sent scouts forward to screen his guns. They ranged through the scrub on the near bank of the river and must have come on what the vultures had left of the lancer patrol's horses.

Two batteries of field artillery were within two hundred yards of the river to the right of the village of Colenso before they halted for action—that is to say, before the drivers swung their teams around so that the guns would be left with their muzzles facing the enemy, and the horses, unhooked from the limbers, could gallop off to safety. It was an astonishing sight. Quite unbelievable . . .

From their hidden trenches the Boers watched the British with amazement. The Lord God had indeed delivered the Philistines into their hands.

The gunners were so close that Boetie, who was on the left of the Boer line with the Pretoria reinforcements, could hear the English order action front, even the snorting of the horses and rattle of the trace chains. He saw Moolman lay his cheek along his rifle stock. He did not mean the gun teams to get away. Without horses the guns were theirs—immobilized.

It was his shot that broke the silence. The driver of the lead pair of one team was flung from his saddle as the horse went down. Moolman had shot through the man's leg to get the horse as well.

At the crack of his shot a hail of bullets swept over the gunners as they struggled to unhitch the horses, cut the dead from their traces, and get the rest under cover in a donga a quarter of a mile away.

Then the Boer artillery and machine guns opened up. The oxen pulling the naval guns were hit and smashed free of their yokes as the native drivers ran for their lives, while the bluejackets tried to bring their guns into action by manhandling their tracks and cover the field guns that now lay stranded on the open veld.

The field gunners fought on, firing at an unseen enemy. Half an hour after the action had begun, officers and men lay wounded and dead by the hundred. Long, wounded to the death, still refused to retreat. "Abandon be damned!" he shouted. "We never abandon guns." Carried to a ditch already full of wounded, he went on crying in his delirium, "My gunners are splendid. My gunners are splendid."

The ammunition in the limbers was nearly finished. The reserve ammunition was in wagons three miles to the rear. At 7 A.M. the survivors received orders to retreat and the batteries were left, their muzzles still facing the enemy, but silent, manned by the dead.

The artillery tradition that guns were never abandoned dated from days when guns were hand-forged rarities, often named and engraved with coats of arms—objects of almost mystic reverence. They were like flags—battle standards—eagles. The morale effect of their loss was enormous.

Once again the British had been trapped, had walked right into an enemy they could not see and whose position was still unknown. It had happened to the Guards at the Modder, to the Highlanders at Magersfontein, and now to the gunners at Colenso.

Buller, unaware that he had lost his guns on the right, had not pushed forward the attack in the center as a diversion. Instead, he gave his attention to the left. The brigade in action here, made up of Irish regiments, was commanded by Arthur FitzRoy Hart, a veteran from Aldershot remarkable for immensely long mustaches waxed to needle points, and the reputation of being a very smart and up-to-date soldier. He believed that it was absurd to space men out in extended order and that nothing could stop a resolute attack by men advancing shoulder to shoulder. This was correct if they ever reached their objective.

By now the cavalry patrols had got some idea of what was going on and, having seen the Boer trenches on the other side of the Tugela, warned the general of his danger.

But FitzRoy Hart, not one to be stopped by a cavalry warning, pushed on with a native guide to show him the way to the ford.

In spite of the fact that there had been British troops in the immediate vicinity for years, no one had bothered to map the area. But even if there are no maps there is always some kind of road or track leading to a ford. No one appeared to notice that the veld was virgin. The native guide, probably in the pay of the Boers, or possibly because he did not like white men of any kind, and was delighted to see them kill each other, or even out of pure childish mischief, led the British into a U-turn of the Tugela, into a peninsula surrounded on three sides by water and entrenched Boers. Having done this, he ran away.

The Boers opened a furious fire on this second God-sent target. Completely encircled except for about a sixty-degree arc in their rear, whipped by aimed rapid fire from some of the best shots in the world, the men began to deploy and take cover. Hart stopped them and drove them forward in mass formation. An officer, in the lead, finding no drift, no track leading to the river, and no guide, turned the brigade back.

But Hart ordered the men on again even deeper into the loop and, calling for reinforcements, added still more troops to this tight-packed bloody target of humanity milling around and around in a corral of death, neither seeing their enemy nor even knowing exactly where he was.

In forty minutes four hundred of them were down, but they would not yield while Hart, still unhurt himself, led them. It was only when Buller rode down and personally ordered a withdrawal that the Irish left the field, grumbling and unwilling. Once more brave men had been led into disaster by a fool.

This retirement of the Irish on the left almost coincided with the loss of the guns in the center, and the whole British line was falling back except for a mounted force commanded by Baillie Hamilton, who led his men into a mealie land where, leaving their horses concealed in the crop, they crept up under continual fire from the Boers toward Hlangwane. The possession of this hill would make the whole Boer postition untenable. It was the key to the Tugela.

Finding himself unable to proceed further without help, Hamilton sent for reinforcements from the nearest supporting brigade. This was refused, as the commander had just received orders from Buller not to commit his force.

The position now was roughly as follows:

In the center there were twelve deserted guns neatly drawn up in line. Behind them Hildyard's brigade was regrouping and moving into position to attack. Buller, still unaware of this disastrous loss until a staff officer galloped up with the news, then thought all the guns had gone, including the six long-range naval guns.

This loss, with Hart's defeat, made him give up any idea of winning the engagement. But he must get the guns back. They represented half his artillery and without them. he had no hope of relieving Ladysmith.

Hildyard advanced on Colenso to protect the stranded guns. His men in extended order, covered by the fire of the naval guns, took the village and had the Boers on the far bank on the run—retreating to their trenches on the hillside three miles away. Then just as the naval guns were trained on the fleeing Boers, someone shouted, "Don't fire. They're our chaps," and the opportunity was lost.

On the left Hart's exhausted Irishmen were bathing in a small tributary of the Tugela while they licked their wounds and counted their missing.

Buller was unaware of Baillie Hamilton's difficulties. Strongly supported, his action might have changed the course of the battle, but Buller's mind was on his guns, and as soon as Hildyard's brigade had them covered from the village he ordered them to be rescued.

Captain Schofield, one of Buller's ADCs, was ordered to collect a party of men to limber the guns and bring them back. His call for volunteers was answered by Corporal Nurse, two limber teams of the 66th Battery, and two officers. Captain Congreve of the Rifle Brigade, and Lieutenant The Honorable Frederick Roberts, the only son of the field marshal.

The two teams of six horses and three drivers each galloped across the open, their limbers bouncing behind them. An officer rode beside each. Young Roberts, laugh-

ing and switching his stick like a jockey's whip, charged
into the Boers' fire and was hit by three bullets. Congreve was hit too. But Schofield, Nurse, and the drivers
succeeded in reaching the guns, limbering them up, and
with a mixture of courage and good luck got two of them
away without another man or horse being touched, though
six bullets went through Schofield's clothes.

In spite of his wounds Congreve and Major Babtie of
the Royal Medical Corps crawled across the fire-swept
ground to bring Fred Roberts into the donga where the
surviving gunners had taken refuge. It was here that
young Roberts died.

The next attempt to save the guns was made by Captain
Reed, but he gave up when he had lost seven men out of
thirteen and thirteen horses out of twenty-two. Buller had
got two guns back. The rest stood as they had before, the
earlier dead now supplemented by the new.

Though neither of them knew it, Turnbull and the Van
der Bergs were nearer together than they had been since
Elsa's funeral. Only the Tugela lay between them. He was
with Buller and a dozen other staff officers, gallopers, and
orderlies, watching the battle from close enough to be
under fire.

The staff did not consider that anything was gained by
this unnecessary exposure, but it endeared the general
to his men. It was his habit, his concept of the way a V.C.
should behave.

Shells were bursting near the group. The horses were
restless. The officers sat them grim-faced, trying to pretend it was a play, that the wounded were not hurt, and
that the dead would get up when the curtain went down.
Only two of them had seen action before.

Buller turned in the saddle and smiled. "Getting hot,
hey?" he said. Cool as a cucumber. That was what it was
to be an old hand, Turnbull thought. A moment later
the staff surgeon was struck by a direct hit from a pompom that mashed both man and horse into a bloody pulp
not five yards away. Turnbull turned white, nearly vomiting as he dismounted and ran to help a man whom he
knew to be dead, blown half to pieces, on a kind of
soldier's reflex. His horse, already jumpy, jibbed and reared

at the reek of blood, nearly jerking the reins out of his hand.

"He's gone, poor chap, we can't help him," Buller said as he led his party away from the body.

There was another shellburst, this time fifty yards away, but a fragment of spent casing hit Buller in the side, almost throwing him off his horse. But he remained unmoved and continued eating his luncheon sandwiches as he watched the battle being lost and five Victoria Crosses and eighteen Distinguished Conduct medals being won before his eyes. But courage was not enough.

In that desperate hour, exhausted by long hours in the saddle under a broiling sun, by seeing young Roberts wounded, the gun rescue attempts fail, and his own honest and honorable career in jeopardy, Buller's spirit broke. He was no longer the dashing leader of irregular cavalry that had won the Cross twenty-odd years ago. He was a man of sixty, soft from good living, weak and irresolute, and now at his last gasp.

All was not lost had the ability to think not left him. Hildyard had to some extent restored the position in the center. Under covering fire of the naval twelve-pounders, his infantry had advanced by making short rushes across the open veld, taking cover, when they rested, behind anthills as hard as stone that dotted the veld.

They had fired over the walls and through the windows of the houses in the village of Colenso, driving the Boers out of their forward trenches on the far side of the river. This was the target the bluejackets had not fired at, believing they were their own people.

Hildyard's men were entrenched now and covering the lost guns, which could easily have been fetched under cover of darkness when the teams would have been in no danger.

But Buller had lost his nerve. He neither waited for darkness to recover his guns nor blew them up. He left them standing there, breech-blocks intact—a splendid Christmas gift for the Boers.

The battle was over without the Boer position ever being seriously attacked. Half of Buller's force had not been engaged.

Toward noon the retirement was begun. By two-thirty

the army was back in camp. The failure was complete. The Tugela had not been crossed and Buller was not a yard nearer Ladysmith.

This was the end of Black Week, as it came to be called, with another casualty list that again filled several columns of *The Times*. It contained 1130 names. In this action 7 officers and 136 men had been killed, 47 officers and 700 men wounded, and 20 officers and 220 men had been taken prisoner or were reported missing.

The particular feature of interest in the battle of Colenso was that the Boers had been invisible. General Lyttelton, in action with a brigade on the left flank, said he never saw a Boer all day. He described the action as "one of the most unfortunate battles in which a British army has ever been engaged. In none has there been a more deplorable tactical display. There was no proper reconnoitering of the ground. No certain information of any ford at which the river could be crossed. No artillery preparation. No proper target. . . ."

Buller had marched out of Chieveley with a force of 21,000 men: 16,000 infantry, 4000 cavalry and mounted infantry, and a strong body of artillery that included naval guns. It was the biggest force any British general had led in the field since the Battle of Alma in the Crimea.

Among the noncombatants of this army was a small volunteer unit of Indian stretcher-bearers. One of them was the young lawyer from Durban who a half-dozen years before had organized the Natal Indian Congress party. His name was Gandhi. A "body snatcher" in army parlance, one of the men who carried the wounded to dressing stations.

The battle was over when Servas was hit. There was a single shot. Some disgruntled soldier firing off a last round into the blue just for the hell of it got him in the shoulder, spinning him around and knocking him down.

Moolman was onto him in a minute, tearing off his shirt and clapping a field dressing on the wound. "It went through, thank God!" he said to Beotie, who, his face white with fear, was watching him. "It missed the bone."

"Damn it!" Servas said. "It was finished. Fancy being wounded after a battle."

"You'll get a rest, anyway," Moolman said as he helped him up and led him toward the dressing station. Boetie followed them, carrying his brother's rifle.

Next day Buller was granted an armistice to collect and bury his dead. Without waiting for instructions from England or consulting his own senior officers, he heliographed a quite incredible message to White: "As it appears certain that I cannot relieve Ladysmith for another month, and even then only by means of protracted siege operations . . . you will burn your ciphers, destroy your guns, fire away your ammunition, and make the best terms you can with the general of the besieging forces, after giving me time to fortify myself on the Tugela."

At midnight, as soon as the armistice ended, Buller struck his camp and moved slowly down the line, leaving Ladysmith to its fate. Before he moved he sent another message, this time to the War Office: "Regret to report another reverse."

This dispatch reached London on Friday. This was the last straw. The greatest and best-equipped army ever to leave England had been checkmated by a lot of farmers. The three besieged towns appeared doomed to the indignity of surrender, and ten guns had been lost. Imagine that—ten British guns!

But there was more than this. There would be international repercussions now that Britain's weakness and ineptitude were exposed.

"Today," Louis Botha wired to the Volksraad, "the God of our fathers has given us a great victory."

God had given the Boers ten field guns with six hundred rounds of ammunition. Their losses were forty against Buller's 1130.

Buller's attempt on the Tugela at Colenso took place on December 15, the eve of the day, still sacred to the Boer nation, that commemorated their fathers' victory more than sixty years before over Dingaan, the treacherous Zulu chief, which broke his power. Sixty years before, a tributary of this same river, the Tugela, had run with Zulu blood.

This annual celebration, coincident with their victory over the English, was taken as a sign and a testament. The following days were set aside for solemn thanksgiving. The Boers were not as surprised as the rest of the world. They had expected victory and were saying "Thank You" to God for His help—a kind of grace after a meal of battle.

There was mail for Turnbull at the base camp—four letters from Elsie and a parcel—a Christmas parcel, *with much love*. A khaki muffler six feet long and eighteen inches wide. *I made it all by myself except the first six rows. More love, Your Elsie.*

My Elsie, he thought. The thermometer in the mess tent registered ninety-eight degrees. Just the temperature of blood. He was still shaken by what he had seen, still unused to the wounded and the dead, and the date, too—the anniversary of Elsa's death. Elsa and Elsie . . .

CHAPTER 25

BLACK WEEK

LONDON, between the tenth and sixteenth of December, was bitterly cold, with some snow flurries and pea-soup fogs, as though the weather too had been affected by the war news.

Unable to wait till she got home, where the newspaper would be waiting, Lady Finch-Haddley, on December 16, 1899, at precisely three in the afternoon bought the first newspaper of her life from a man in the street. This important event took place on the corner of Bond Street and Piccadilly. Important not merely to Lady Finch-Haddley but to the women of England. Never till now, till this week, which Mr. H. H. Asquith described at a Tyneside Liberal meeting as "the week closing tonight has been in some respects one of the blackest weeks within the memory of living men among us. . ." had a well-bred woman bought a paper from a newsseller in the street. Now they were all doing it.

Black Week had begun when General Sir William Gatacre, in the Cape Colony, decided to attack the Boers and Cape rebels at Stormberg Junction. Hearing that the railway pass through the hills was strongly held, he attacked the Kissieberg, a small range of hills whose end formed one side of the pass. The wheels of the wagons and guns were muffled by rough covers of oxhide, and although there was no chance of action before dawn, the troops were ordered to fix bayonets, which meant that these already tired men had to carry their rifles at the slope to avoid sticking each other in the bottom.

When the moon went down the force churned about in the darkness as they followed the guides, and by accident alone Gatacre found himself almost but not quite where he wanted to be twenty-four hours after he had left his base. He had reached the position by following the western base of the range and got to the pass that separated it from an isolated *kopje* which he mistook for his objective.

The Boers on the heights of the Kissieberg, having their predawn cup of coffee, saw the British below them and opened fire.

Gatacre ordered the *kopje* occupied. His men flung themselves at the slopes, attacking the cliffs, which were too steep to climb except at certain points—chimney-like faults widely separated from each other. The few men who found them reached the top and were fighting desperately to establish a foothold, when they were swept away by the fire of their own guns, the gunners being confused by the rising sun, which shone in their eyes. The discouraged and exhausted men fell back. Gatacre saw his infantry retiring, but was unable to stem their flow to the rear. They were too tired to mount a second attack, so, making the best of a bad job, he marched them back to Molteno.

A Boer commando now attacked them from the west while they were still under fire from the Boers on the Kissieberg in the east. For a while the British field guns were in action, trail to trail, firing both east and west at the same time.

The infantry, really exhausted by this time, lost its morale and degenerated into an undisciplined mob, a dead duck to the Boers had they exploited it to the full. As it was, Gatacre got away with only ninety casualties. At least that was what he thought till he discovered that by some oversight six hundred men had been left behind on the slopes of the Kissieberg. These men, who had not been told of the retreat, had surrendered when they found themselves alone.

News of this disaster reached London on December 11, a Monday.

On the very day of Gatacre's defeat Lord Methuen left the Modder River on his final bid to relieve Kimberley. Convinced of success, he heliographed to the besieged town that he was on his way.

The Magersfontein hills are the watershed of this portion of the Modder. They rise slowly into the low range that runs parallel to the river, Magersfontein itself, on Methuen's right, rising two hundred feet out of the plain, overtopping all the rest. The Boers had been observed digging in on its slopes by cavalry patrols.

Methuen could not go around the hills to the west, as there was no water. If he went east he would have to force a loop of the river that was well defended. His only course was straight ahead. Once he had the Magersfontein heights, Kimberley would be in his hands.

He decided on a night march and an attack at dawn. There should be no problems in the short five-mile trek across open country. The Highlanders, regarded to be among the finest fighting regiments in the army, were selected to spearhead the assault.

Methuen's first move took place on the morning of December 10. He sent the Highlanders out in a demonstration that was supposed to draw the Boer fire and disclose their position. But the Boers never fired a shot and the Highlanders, their kilts swaying, pipes skirling, marched back again.

Now the gunners took over and for a couple of hours they plastered the hills. At midnight the troops moved off with the Black Watch in the van. Before they had gone very far, the light rain had turned into a driving storm, its blackness lit by flashes of lightning. In the distance

on the horizon above the hills in front of them the Highlanders could see the beams of the Kimberley searchlights. Only the hills stood between them and the relief
of the Diamond City, but their advance was slowed up by
mud. The dry sand of yesterday had turned into a glutin-
ous paste.

To keep in formation, the troops now marched shoulder
to shoulder in ninety-six successive lines—an immense
rectangle containing four thousand men boxed in by
ropes held by guides on either flank. This formation was
called "mass of quarter columns," each company being
drawn upon two lines, and all moving close on each
other's heels.

To extend would waste time and, once extended, the
men would move more slowly. So they continued their
advance, still in ninety-six lines for another seven hundred yards, when a line of thick bush held them up, and
it was only at 4 A.M., with Magersfontein about half a
a mile ahead, that they finally got the order to deploy.

The men were bunched together. The rear lines had
closed in on the leading troops, who were moving outward to either flank, when suddenly they were blasted by
a wall of fire. Thousands of rifles were firing into them
from point-blank range. Not from the hills where they
had expected the Boers to be, but from under the very
feet of the Black Watch. Within minutes hundreds lay
dead or wounded, and the survivors, the flower of the
army, the Highland Brigade, were in flight. First dozens
and then scores of Highlanders rose from the ground and
ran for it.

As usual, when a battle was over, there was an armistice and the ambulances began to move over the silent
battlefield. British doctors and stretcher-bearers who went
to help the wounded the Boers had picked up were guided
through the lines blindfolded.

Before evening Methun's men were back in their camp
on the Modder. A thousand-odd men had been killed,
wounded, or were missing, seven hundred of them Highlanders. Some regiments had lost 60 per cent of their
officers. The Highlanders were bitter. Their beloved brigadier had been killed. They had "been led into a butcher's
shop and bloody well left there."

On Monday, London had received news of Gatacre's misfortune at Stormberg. Now on Thursday came the news of Methuen's losses, with three thousand of England's finest troops defeated in action. But all was not lost. They still had Sir Redvers Buller, the commander in chief, who, with a great army at his back, was moving forward to relieve Ladysmith in Natal.

Then came the news of Colenso, the third disaster of the week, the final straw that broke the back of the camel called complacency. Complacency became impossible when the British commander in chief, with the finest army England had ever sent overseas, had been disastrously defeated.

This was the news that Lady Finch-Haddley read, that Vincent read aloud to Miss Elsie and Celeste. It was unbelievable. Horrible!

"Those poor Highlanders," Elsie said. *The Times* special correspondent described how the Highlanders who had not run away lay prone, their dark kilts and gleaming mess tins conspicuous againt the drab gray-green of the veld, an easy mark for the Boers. Their faces in the ground, the tender backs of their knees raw with blisters from the burning summer sun. They had had no food. Their water bottles were empty, most of them having given all their water to wounded comrades.

It was the backs of their knees that worried Elsie. That was the focal point of disaster to her. And poor Bob's only son had been killed at Colenso. What a name to give a place.

It is probable that the impact of Black Week on England has never been equaled. There had never been anything like it before or since. Not even the disaster of Dunkirk.

The total casualties of Black Week were three thousand. In World War I, Passchendaele alone cost the British four hundred thousand men. In World War II, Dunkirk left England defenseless. Yet neither appears to have produced the emotion of Black Week.

For eight hundred years England had been isolated from the Continent, secure, certain of her power. Remote wars against savages with their trifling losses had not prepared the English public for this holocaust. In the Indian Mutiny reinforcements had brought immediate victory. In the Crimea, England had powerful allies.

Here were defeats, unknown since the American Revolution, of an army more than double the size that either Marlborough or Wellington had led to victory in Europe. Now, shown in her weakness, England found how much she was loathed, as she stood isolated, like a wounded lion, surrounded by jackals. England was hated for her prosperity, for the way she had lorded it over everyone as a nation, and for the arrogant behavior of English tourists abroad. Hated for her self-sufficiency, phrasemongery, and hypocrisy.

Britain's rival powers were delighted at the exposure of such weakness, while the British became more patriotic then ever, hysterically and sentimentally patriotic.

The story of how each Victoria Cross was won was discussed in every pub. There were pictures of war heroes in every shop. Wounded soldiers were acclaimed.

John Dunne, the fourteen-year-old bugler who was wounded at Colenso, was a star turn. He was met by a vast crowd at Portsmouth, cheered through the streets, and taken to Osborne, where the Queen presented him with a new bugle to replace the one he had lost in action.

Then there was the fox terrier that had searched the battlefield till it found its dead master, and lain down beside him. This news story was meat and drink for English dog lovers.

And Lord Roberts, V.C., Bobs to the people, had lost his only son. Cronje had seen his son mortally wounded, but that was different. He was an enemy.

CHAPTER 26

CHRISTMAS

BOTH the Boers and Britons had thought the war would be over by Christmas. But at Christmas, the day that marks the birth of the Christ Child, these two Christian nations were still at war.

The Boer gunners at Ladysmith fired their own version

of Christmas puddings into the town from their guns. Messrs. Lyons sent ten thousand Christmas puddings to the troops in the field and every soldier received the Queen's gift, a small flat tin of chocolates with her picture in color on it. Thousands of Balaclava helmets and woolen scarves knitted by the ladies of England arrived for men dripping with the sweat of summer. Turnbull's had just been an early one.

It was on Christmas Eve that Winston Churchill escaped from the State Model School at Pretoria. He had been captured carrying a pistol and was accused of being a combatant. War correspondents were supposed to be unarmed. Churchill had watched his guards out of the window of the privy and escaped over the wall when they were not looking. The Boers, who had been very happy about his capture, for as they said, "We do not capture the son of a lord every day," offered a reward of twenty-five pounds for his recovery. But he was not caught and after a number of adventures found his way to Delagoa Bay and finally reached England in a blaze of publicity. He later made enough money recounting these adventures on an American lecture tour to allow him to stand for Parliament at Oldham.

The Boers refrained from any action on Christmas Day. The British amused themselves with hurdle races and tugs of war, gymkhanas and impromptu military tournaments, while the Boers spent their time digging trenches, undisturbed by British shellfire.

"It will soon be over now," Boetie said, for like everyone in the Boer camp he was elated by their victories.

"I don't think it will be like it was last time," Moolman said. "It is more serious than Amajuba, where we killed Colley. This time they are really commited. They have so many troops here and more on the way that they dare not let go."

Though they did not know it, Lord Roberts had already been at sea two days.

But Moolman's words did not check their optimism. This was the beginning of the end. The English would get tired of it soon and go home.

Beyers sat by his wife playing his concertina softly as she leaned against him. He was playing to her, to his

beloved, trying to squeeze out a message he had no
words to express. But neither needed words. They were
not even there as they stared with glazed eyes into the
dying fire. Their dog snuffled between them. All they
wanted was to be together. That they were together even
in war seemed better to them than to be separated in
peace. In the trench at Colenso they had fought side by
side. Hetta had been accepted by the group as one of
them, a comrade who was also a woman.

Boetie wondered how he had ever thought Hetta ugly.
Or was it that love changed people's faces? Still thinking
of this, wondering at this great mystery of which he as
yet knew nothing, Boetie rolled himself in the cocoon of
his blanket and went to sleep.

Moolman was watching the Beyers couple too, and saw
himself as a young man again filled with love and hope,
sitting, walking, eating, and sleeping beside his own young
wife. Time after time, generation after generation, men
followed in each other's spoor. Love was a kind of track.
Yes, he saw it that way. First each alone, the young man
and the girl—alone and lonely. Then they met and their
tracks merged as they went on together. Then more tracks
joined them, the spoors of little children with dragging
feet that grew into more boys and girls who mated and
started off on their own.

Moolman thought of his own past. His dead, and
his heart that had died by the ashes of his home and the
terrible remains of those who had loved him and counted
upon his protection. He had not been there when he was
needed. He had betrayed them. Sometimes he woke in the
night from a nightmare in which he heard his wife scream
his name, his sons' cry of "Pa, Pa," bleating like lambs
as the Kaffirs tossed them and caught them on their spears.
At least they died fast, those little men. But she hadn't.
What had they not done to her? How many sweaty, naked,
wild-eyed savages had taken her? Cutting off her breasts,
ramming the butt end of a kerrie into her and leaving her,
her home in flames, to the waiting vultures. Since that day
many Kaffirs had died beneath his gun. He was sorry about
the British officer of lancers he had killed. But it was a
habit now. Yes, he thought, since that day when my
heart shriveled and I lost my soul, I have been a killer
of beasts and men. Those had been wild days and he

had been a reckless fool to settle and try to farm so far away. But the Beyers girl had had the same experience, much nearer to civilization. How lucky she was to have escaped, covered by her father, the old man who had gone down fighting a solitary rear-guard action.

His mind roved like a dog over the action they had just fought. Their own little battle by the river, and the big battle that had followed it. What good fortune they had had so far. Only Servas had been hit and he was in no danger. Bothma's scratch did not count. But it was too good to last. There was no cause for optimism. The English were not going to give up and become the laughing-stock of all the world. The Boers' only hope was a change of government in England. If the Liberals came in there might be peace. And with these thoughts he too rolled himself up to sleep in the glow of the fire beneath the bright stars of Africa that he knew so well.

All the world slept now. The Boers and the British. All but the sentries, the patrols, and the jackals and hyenas that sought the rotting dead. All but the little, big-eared steenboks that nibbled away the night, the termites, and the dung beetles rolling the balls of manure that were the nurseries of their young. Big, strong, almost circular beetles, cousins of the sacred green scarabs of the north. And the owls hunting on silent wings.

Next day, skirting the main battlefield, Moolman and Boetie went down to the Tulgela, to the site of their own little battle, and rode their horses through the river to the southern, English bank. There lay its remains. Lancers' broken weapons, decomposing horses over which the vultures crawled like gray, giant lice, croaking, fighting with open beaks, twisting bare pink necks and immense outstretched striking wings. As they came near, the birds ran off lumbering, flapping their wings, desperate with fear till at last they got the air beneath them and rose, suddenly majestic, into the air, up and up into the silent blue of it to swing in idle circles on the currents rising from the hot ground as they waited for this interruption to their feast to end. Some people believed vultures to be immortal. No one had ever found a dead one, or so it was said. Nor was superstition far out, for vultures live half a century or more.

The ground about each dead horse was bare of grass, trampled into dust, ringed with the white chalk of vulture excrement, and dusted with gray-brown feathers torn from the quarreling birds.

Moolman spat on the ground. The smell of death was new to Boetie. The almost sickly-sweet stink of putrescence. Later he would learn that dead men smelled different from dead horses. That dead mules and cattle had still other recognizable odors. But this was the knowledge of old soldiers, not of young ones.

"I brought you here," Moolman said, "to see what we have done. This is our work. Had they been able they would have done the same to us. *Ja*, this is the aftermath of war. The harvest. Men born of women, once children, here lie dead. Those horses"—he pointed—"their remains, were once foals running on the green veld of England with their dams. Now food for *aasvoëls*. A strange thought that those English horses should now fly in our sky. I brought you," he went on, "to see horror, to make you hard. It is in my heart that the path before us will be long and terrible. Therefore, while I may, I will teach you what I know, and before God the lessons that I have learned have not been easy."

Boetie knew he was thinking of his ravished wife, his boys, his farm, his cattle, and his hopes.

Boetie knew this man well now. His resourcefulness, his courage, and his bitterness. Moolman had been right to bring them. To fight, to shoot, was one thing. To see the results a few days later another. The experience was now complete. But he wanted a memento of it. He wanted to force himself into an act that would burn this day into his heart. To the right of them twenty yards away lay a horse whose rider he had killed. He had killed the horse, too. Near the horse was a broken lance. From this horse and this one alone the party that had come to pick up the dead under a white flag of truce had omitted to remove the headstall. All the other saddlery had been salvaged. He wanted the broken lance head and the horse's bit.

Throwing the reins over his pony's head as he dismounted, he ran to the carcass, undid the brass buckle of the throat lash, and, seizing the top of the bridle between the ears, dragged it off as the flies that covered what was left of the dead beast rose in his face. Now for the lance. A moment later he was back in the saddle with Moolman laughing at him.

"*Ja*," Moolman said, "the horns of a buffalo, the tusks of an elephant, the spear of a Kaffir, the bridle of an Englishman. Men do not change. When we kill we want something from the dead—a proof—a talisman."

Then the English saw them and burst two shells over but short of them. They exploded with loud bangs that set the horses plunging. The fumes burned their throats as they breathed them in. The shrapnel pattered like hail in front of them, sending up little puffs of dust.

"*Huistoe!* Homeward," Moolman shouted as if the laager was a home, and they swung their horses into the river, splashed through it, and galloped up the slope on the far side.

Boetie, laughing wildly, was a boy again. He leaned over his pony's neck; the broken lance head extended beyond Pasha's mousy nose. He was a British lancer. The reins lay loose on the pony's withers, his rifle was in his left hand. As he laughed tears poured down his dusty face. Half child, half man, torn between the instinctive pride of a young warrior and the horror of what he had seen. Dead men and horses he had seen before, but then he had been in action or exhausted and used up after it. This time he had been fresh. It was different to see it on a lovely summer day when you were not tired.

Oom Paul had killed his first man when he was fourteen, but that had been a Kaffir. He, Louis van der Berg, had killed white men in battles not three months after his sixteenth birthday. I will be Boetie no more, he thought. That is for children. I am Louis van der Berg, a man.

When they reached camp he turned in his saddle to Moolman. "Moolman," he said, "I am Louis now. We left Boetie down by the river."

"*Ja*, Louis," Moolman said. "It is time to grow up. That is why I took you there."

While they had been away new orders had come in. Piet Joubert was becoming impatient. Since Ladysmith would not surrender, they would take it by storm. Four hundred of the Pretoria Commando were to create a diversion at the red fort to hold the enemy's attention while the main force of Free Staters attacked Wagon Hill. It was now January 6, 1900.

Among the Pretoria troops were new arrivals. A number of poor whites from the town, gutless dregs forced into service who refused to move. By their defection the force was reduced from four hundred to two hundred. But there was no time for talk. So, leaving them hangdog and sullen, the rest, which included Moolman's lot, moved off over the plain toward the earthwork.

As dawn broke the English saw them and opened such hot fire that they were brought to a halt. The field kornets hesitated to give orders to advance again, not certain that the men would follow them.

At this moment of hesitation a man in police uniform whom Boetie had never seen before, a splendid figure of a man—one of the President's own bodyguards who had been visiting the camp and volunteered to join the commando, sprang forward, shouting, "Follow me!" Startled into action, a number of the boldest ran forward again in spite of the fire.

The fort was built on a stony outcrop and for the four hundred yards that separated them from it there was no cover except the embankment of the Harrismith railway line. Reaching it with only one casualty, the Boers, short of breath from their charge, flung themselves down to rest instead of ramming the charge home, though they were so close they could see the muzzles, like black snouts, of the defenders' rifles poking through the loopholes.

Once down, the Boers snuggled into the hard earth as if it was their mothers' bosom.

Moolman cried, "Come on!" and, followed by Boetie, ran to some boulders twenty yards away and hid behind them. They lay there firing into the loopholes, waiting for the order to advance that never came. But suddenly, with a shout, the big policeman, followed by fifteen men, leaped onto the railway line and charged the fort.

"Charge!" Moolman shouted. Boetie and some others rose, but before they had advanced more than a few yards a volley flamed from the fort, bringing the other attackers down in a struggling heap, all but the policeman, who ran on alone.

"Down!" Moolman cried. They took cover but were

able to see the policeman try to climb the wall of the fort. Bayonets were driven at him but parried by his rifle. He reached the top, was silhouetted against the sky for an instant, and fell dead from a pistol shot in his belly.

Six of his party were dead. The others lay trying to bandage their wounds without showing themselves to the enemy.

There was no hope of success now. Moolman led the boys back, crawling one at a time over the embankment to where the rest of the attacking force still lay under cover. It was eight o'clock and the day was warming up.

They could hear the sound of a violent battle coming from Wagon Hill, the key whose possession would end the siege. The Free Staters were attacking. Guns of all calibers were firing. They could see shells bursting in the air and clouds of dust rising from the ground. Thousands of rifles were rattling, sharp, staccato, cracking like whips while they lay helpless in the ever-increasing heat of the sun, pinned down by fire from the fort. As the sun rose the wounded moaned and cried for water. Moolman and some other marksmen put an occasional shot into a loophole of the fort but apart from that there was nothing to do but wait for darkness. The state of the wounded grew worse as the heat increased. Everyone was thirsty, but the wounded were in agony, crazy for water. Since nothing could be done, Moolman told them to pretend they did not hear their cries.

The heat grew more and more intense, the air thick, heavy, with an almost palpable texture. Then the sky darkened, becoming lead-colored. The lead turned to livid navy blue, with black clouds racing on a wind high in the heavens, and then as if the bottom had been knocked out of a great reservoir, hail and rain fell in torrents, in such a deluge that the fort was blocked from view.

"Now is the time," Moolman shouted, and led a final charge toward the fort through the driving rain. Only Boetie and Nel followed him. They reached the wall without a shot being fired, screened by the pouring rain. But, seeing they were alone, they turned back to find the rest of the Boers gone, leaving their dead and wounded.

In camp their tents were down and their possessions washed away. No fires could be lit. Moolman raged at the loss of a God-sent opportunity. "In the rain we could have got them," he said. But how many knew as he did that lions hunt best on the wildest nights.

This was a sad and uncomfortable night, sitting cold, shivering, fireless, and hungry, knowing that their wounded still lay untended. The news came in later that the Free Staters, despite their courage and the loss of three hundred men, had failed to take Wagon Hill. This added to their depression. It looked as if Moolman was right after all. There was no cause for optimism.

In Adderley Street in Cape Town, Diana was shopping for mourning. She knew she would look well in black and was mildly amused at the way everyone commented on her courage.

"A real soldier's wife," they said. They supposed she would go home.

"No," she said, "with my husband killed I cannot desert. I'm going to do something to help." She shrugged her beautiful shoulders as if she was thinking of what she could do.

"You know he's been recommended for a Victoria Cross?" she said, her eyes filling with tears.

How brave she was.

A credit to England.

In London, Lady Finch-Haddley, depressed by the war news, came to a decision. For years now she had spent Christmas alone—Christmas with all the trimmings: turkey, chestnut stuffing, mince pies, and plum pudding served flaming in brandy, champagne and liqueurs—all by herself in her big dining room, with the table set for twenty people—the absent and the dead.

Her table was always set for two, Finch's place laid as it had been in his lifetime. This was not a matter of sentiment, Isobel Finch-Haddley was not sentimental. It had begun as a kind of macabre joke. He would like it up there if he was looking down at her. Just as he liked her hunters and her Irish wolfhounds. His humor had suited her own, sardonic, ironic, cynical, but very human. A cynic he defined as a man who did his best, expected the worst, and was glad if things turned out better than he expected. "In that way, Isobel," he said, "I never suffer any disappointments." She wondered what he would have made of Elsie. Liked her, she thought. Yes, the old boy would have liked her. "Nice pet you have there, Isobel. Nice little thing to have on your knee. Amusing, too."

Amusing. There were so few amusing people now, so few at least for her. She did not want to entertain for its own sake. Did not want people to come to her house because her food was good, her wines superb, her cook one of the best in London. She wanted friends about her. She still had a few. But many were dead, others had gone to live in the country, as she had herself, but the exigencies of war and the hospital idea had made her open the Wilton Crescent house again. Other friends had just dropped out of her life, filtered away by the sieve of time. She bored them. She was out of touch with the social life of Mayfair and Belgravia. But if she raised a finger, if she took the trouble to write a few notes, call on a few people, they would all be back—the whole trencher-fed pack of them. But she did not want them. I'll have the girl, she thought. She'd ask Elsie to take Christmas dinner with her. The girl intrigued her. She was too good to leave in the hands of her captain's apparently excellent manservant, and a French maid of dubious morals.

To Lady Finch-Haddley everything French was suspect, a very popular fear born of the French Revolution and that man Napoleon. Of course things had changed since then. Napoleon III, the pale reflection of Bonaparte, had come and gone. His lovely wife, the Empress Eugénie, was living quietly in Richmond. Her son had been killed fighting with the British in the Zulu War. But a vestigial suspicion of the French remained, now chiefly canalized into a fear of the women of France. Loose, the lot of them, with no sense of decency or morals. It was doubtful even in her prejudiced mind if adultery was more common in France than in England. But here at least it was not blatant, and if men kept mistresses they did so discreetly and did not flaunt their amours in public.

By God, she thought, that captain must have fun with Elsie. That was the way Finch would have seen it. And this time, the first time for years, she was going to have fun at Christmas herself.

She rang the bell. When the butler came in she said, "There will be two for Christmas."

"Yes, My Lady."

"And I want it done properly. A Christmas tree, crackers, paper hats—the lot."

"Yes, My Lady. Would Your Ladyship consider it impertinent if I asked who we are going to have?"

"Miss Elsie, of course."

"Of course, Your Ladyship."

"You approve, I hope?" Lady Finch-Haddley did not give a damn whether her butler approved or not, but she was curious to see what he would say.

"As this is the festive season, Your Ladyship, and as I have been in Your Ladyship's service so long I would like to tell you what we say in the servants' hall."

"What do you say?"

"We say, 'God bless Elsie,' Your Ladyship. For though I cannot approve of all she does, she has brought sunshine into this great house."

Elsie was in despair. Lady Finch-Haddley had asked her to Christmas dinner. Now it would all come out. Not just the captain. She knew about that. That was nothing.

"No, no," she sobbed. "I couldn't do that. I can't come."

"Why?" Lady Finch-Haddley said. "You have nowhere else to go, have you? You're all alone?"

"Oh, I'm alone, but that's not it. I couldn't eat here. I know how to eat," she said defiantly through her tears. "I'm not afraid of that. Vincent taught me. Knives, forks, spoons, everything," she went on vaguely, "but it's not that. It's . . . it's . . ." Her sobs began again and redoubled. "I'm a whore, Lady Finch-Haddley. I was in a house. He took me from a house and I've no business here at all."

Lady Finch-Haddley had no idea what a house was, and only the vaguest notions about whores. They were biblical in a way, she supposed. Harlots. Daughter of the horseleech, and so on.

"I was in a house," Elsie said again.

"Of course, dear. That's nothing to get excited about. Everyone lives in a house." Sometimes this girl was peculiar—almost unstable. She supposed she was trying to say she had lived in a slum. Well, she knew that already,

and she had done wonders with herself. She only re-
lapsed occasionally. What with her ridiculous captain,
whom she seemed to think was God, and his admirable
manservant, all of them training her as if she was a dog
or a horse.

"You don't understand," Elsie sobbed. "A house with
other girls." At times like this she almost wished she was
back there. At least you knew where you were. And the
girls had been pretty and nice enough, though she never
knew any of them very well. They did not meet or talk
much. The maids, Betty and Alice, had been her best
friends. The girls were busy at night, slept in the day,
and ate without much conversation. She pulled herself
together and said:

"A whorehouse."

Lady Finch-Haddley began to understand.

"You mean a brothel?" What an interesting life Elsie
had led.

"Is that what they are called?" Elsie said, surprised.
"I never knew what that word meant. Anyway, you see
why I can't come, why I should not be here at all."

Lady Finch-Haddley was still not quite clear about
the matter, but no doubt she would find everything out
in time. Elsie was not very good at keeping things to
herself.

In the end she succeeded in comforting the weeping
girl and Elsie had Christmas dinner at Wilton Crescent;
turkey, mince pies, Christmas pudding, the lot. A real
blowout.

She was glad Vincent had taught her to eat nicely.
They had champagne, which Elsie had always heard called
fizz, bubbly, or a bottle of the widow.

They drank to absent friends. The dead were in Lady
Finch-Haddley's mind. The captain was in Elsie's, though
Alice and Betty and even Mrs. Fitz were hovering in the
background.

At Buller's headquarters in Natal the mood was far
from festive. It is difficult to celebrate defeat. Roberts
was on the water on his way to take over, and as usual
the general used champagne and brandy as a solvent to
his depression.

Turnbull wondered where Elsie was tonight. He knew

she was thinking of him and wondered what it would have been like to spend Christmas with her.

When they drank to absent friends it was to Charlie he drank. And he said it aloud, "Uriah the Hittite, poor devil."

"What did you say?" Ketteringham, who was beside him, asked.

"Nothing, old boy, nothing at all."

An ADC, being the junior officer present, stood up when the port had gone around, and said, "The Queen, God bless her."

Everyone stood and toasted Her Majesty, Queen of the United Kingdom of Great Britain and Ireland, the Dominions Overseas, Defender of the Faith, and Empress of India. The Queen, whose commission they all held. They stood up with the scrape of chairs pushed back and a rattle of spurs. They raised their ruby, blood-colored glasses so that the light shone through the Iberian wine and drank to the health of the Queen and the confusion of her enemies—the farmers of South Africa.

. . . The Queen, God bless her!

In the Bay of Biscay, sitting at the captain's table on the *Dunnottar Castle*, Field Marshal Lord Roberts, on his way to pick up Major General Lord Kitchener at Gibraltar, was going through the same ceremonies.

So was every officer in every mess from Scotland to Hong Kong, from Gibraltar to Cairo, from Khartoum to Singapore. Every officer in every mess all over the great empire upon which the sun never set. For as it set in one place—as the Jack came down to the sound of a bugle in the dusk—it rose and the Jack went up in another.

In South Africa the common soldiers untied the red, white, and blue ribbons from the Queen's box of chocolates, looked at the old girl's picture and guzzled thousands of plum puddings, by courtesy of Messrs. Lyons, at once an advertisement and a patriotic gesture.

CHAPTER 27

BOBS

On December 22, 1899, a small man with white hair and bright blue eyes, very neatly dressed in deep mourning, had embarked on the *Dunnottar Castle* as she lay in the Southampton docks.

There were no flags, no crowds, no bands to see Field Marshal Lord Frederick Sleigh Roberts, the new commander in chief of the South African Expeditionary Force off on the same ship that only three months before had carried Sir Redvers Buller, the man he was going to replace, to the seat of war.

At the end of November, before Black Week, Lord Roberts, then commander in chief of Ireland, had written most pessimistically to Lord Lansdowne, the Secretary of War.

"A serious reverse would endanger the Empire and one seems possible in spite of the fact that the Force in the field now is . . . more than double what Marlborough had . . . or Wellington had. . . ." and offered to take over command himself, when "I shall hope with God's help to end the war in a satisfactory manner."

Lord Lansdowne had been Viceroy of India during Roberts' command there and was his friend. He discussed the letter with Lord Salisbury, the Prime Minister, who, at sixty-nine, thought Roberts, at sixty-seven, too old for the exigencies of war. "Besides," he said, "Buller might well achieve a brilliant success on the Tugela within the next few days."

But the next few days brought Black Week, and after some discussion with Lord Wolseley it was agreed that Roberts was to succeed Buller, provided he had Lord Kitchener, the idol of the public after his conquest of the Sudan, as chief of staff.

As to his age, Roberts informed the Cabinet that they "need have no misgivings about my physical vigor. For years I have led a most active and abstemious life, waiting for this day."

Roberts was, like so many great soldiers, an Irishman —a picturesque and romantic figure. Small, neat, bellicose, and at the same time gentle, with an immense regard for the needs of the private soldier, whose admiration for "Little Bobs" was boundless. Both British and Indian troops would have followed him anywhere. His reputation was built on his personal gallantry, and his great flank march in Afghanistan from Kabul to Kandahar was regarded as one of the British Army's greatest exploits since the Napoleonic Wars. Roberts had been the first British general to realize the importance of accurate rifle fire.

Kitchener accepted the offer to join Roberts with a telegram of a single word: "Delighted," from Khartoum. A telegram was sent to Roberts in Dublin. He came to London at once and accepted the command at 10 Downing Street. In the afternoon of that same day his old friend Lord Lansdowne broke the news of his only son's death in action while trying to rescue the guns at Colenso.

A few days later when Roberts went to take leave of the Queen she wrote in her diary, "He knelt and kissed my hand. I said how much I felt for him. He could only answer, 'I cannot speak of *that* but I can of anything else. . . .' "

There is only one other case in the annals of the British Army of both a father and son earning the Victoria Cross. So Roberts was something rather special. A general, a hero, pulled out of near retirement at his own request to do a particular job that he felt himself capable of accomplishing with the help of God and the soldiers under his command.

Kitchener was the last addition to Roberts' small staff, which consisted of his military secretary, Neville Chamberlain, a billiard player who was said to have invented snooker, and Colonel G. F. R. Henderson as his intelligence officer, the biographer of Stonewall Jackson and the author of *The Science of War*.

This was the first time in British military history that decisions were reached by a number of experts, and this group assembled on board ship was the infant that finally grew into the General Staff.

At Southampton, Gibraltar, and again at Madeira, Roberts cabled to Buller, telling him to remain on the

defensive, but on reaching Cape Town he found a wire
waiting for him to say that he was starting on a new
campaign to relieve Ladysmith.

Apart from this the situation was stabilized. Sixteen
groups of Boers and Britons lay sweating in an apparently
unbreakable clinch.

Kitchener was an extraordinary man. Only Captain
Maxwell, his ADC, loved him. There was no one who
did not fear him, and he seemed quite satisfied with this
situation.

Lord Esher, the Secretary of the Office of Works, wrote,
"Kitchener is not attractive. None of the men who served
with him were attached to him. I should doubt anyone
loving him. It is the coarseness of his fibre, which appears
in his face to a marked degree. . . ."

But Kitchener did not seek love. He wanted fear and
admiration, and this was the man who, boarding the
cruiser *Isis* at Alexandria, reached Gibraltar on December
26, 1899, where he transferred to the *Dunnottar Castle*
with Lord Roberts on board. They reached Cape Town
on January 10, with a new plan of campaign that they
had worked out on the voyage.

They were a strange pair. The big, heavily mustached
misogynist—he would have no married white officers in
the Egyptian Army—hard, furiously ambitious, and in-
tolerant. And Bobs, the small, bandbox-neat soldier who
was the idol of the army. Lord Roberts, warmhearted,
genial, and kindly, was suffering deeply from the loss of
his only son.

Kitchener was forty-nine and Roberts sixty-seven. Kitchener's relative youth was responsible for his appoint-
ment. Lord Salisbury could be persuaded to give Roberts
command of the British forces only if Kitchener accompanied him. This accounted for Lord Roberts of Kandahar
and Lord Kitchener of Khartoum being teamed up together—two soldiers utterly different in character and appearance, who nevertheless were able to work together
without strain.

Both had seen much action. Neither had ever been defeated, but neither had fought white men. They had fought
only inadequately armed savages with vastly superior
weapons.

They were a strangely assorted pair. The long and the

short of it. Roberts stood five feet five to Kitchener of Khartoum's six feet two. The old and the young. The loved and the hated. The Indian native troops adored Roberts. The Sudanese and Egyptians had mutinied against Kitchener.

The Boers' hope for peace through a collapse of the British will for war, a change of government, the surrender of the besieged towns, or the intervention of a foreign power—Germany or the United States—had failed. The initiative had slipped from their hands. England was determined on swift, unambiguous victory. But Buller, who had sailed on the same ship as the new commanders hardly more than two months before, had been equally sure of victory.

They landed in Cape Town on January 10 and left on February 6. On Roberts' last night in Cape Town he dined with Rudyard Kipling at the Mount Nelson Hotel. Kipling was in South Africa to see how Tommy Atkins was faring and to distribute gifts from the "Absent-minded beggar" fund that he had founded. Among the gifts were pajamas for the nurses at Wynberg, where all nighties were discarded, and another step forward in the emancipation of the fair sex was taken.

The next evening Roberts and Kitchener drove in a closed carriage from Sir Alfred Milner's house to Salt River Station, where they boarded the northbound mail. Their departure was secret, and by avoiding the Cape Town terminus no one knew that they had left for the front, and the curtain began to come down on the first act of this great drama. But it was going to be a two-act play, though nobody in the cast or audience guessed it yet.

It was still too soon to stand up and sing "God Save the Queen."

CHAPTER 28

A LATCHKEY

ELSIE was popping in and out of Wilton Crescent quite often now. Lady Finch-Haddley she regarded as a kind of cross between a mother, an aunt, and a madam. She had hated her mother and never known her aunts if she had any, but had a romantic concept of what an aunt would be like—wise, strong, rather like an old tree in whose shadow you could sit in comfort and security.

It was a great relief to have someone besides the captain know all about her and still not despise her. Lady Finch-Haddley was even quite ready to discuss No. 20 with her, and sometimes brought up the subject of prostitution, a new word to Elsie, all on her own. She really did seem interested in what she called fallen women.

"Some falls, some is pushed, and some just lays down all by themselves," Elsie said.

"Not 'is pushed,' dear. Are."

"Are pushed," Elsie said.

"And lie down, not 'lays' down."

"Lie down," Elsie said. She did not mind being corrected. It was for the captain, so that he would not be ashamed of her when he came back.

One day, for no particular reason except an ill-defined curiosity, Elsie said, "Do you know Lord Fenton, Lady Finch-Haddley?"

"Of course I know him."

"Do you think I look like him?"

"Look like him? Why should you, my dear?" She was really getting fond of this extraordinary girl.

"He's my dad," Elsie said.

"Your dad? Your father, Elsie? Are you sure?"

"Yes," Elsie said. "My ma told me and she ought to know."

"But how?"

"The ordinary way," Elsie said. "She was a servant at the hall and he had her. Lots of gentlemen do in the country, you know. They get bored just hunting and shooting."

"They're married," Lady Finch-Haddley said.

"Oh, that! That's no fun. Just breeding heirs. That's why they go to houses like Mrs. Fitz's place."

"Elsie!" Lady Finch-Haddley said. "Where in God's name did you get that from?"

"The captain, I think. Or Vincent. It wouldn't be Celeste."

"And why did you tell me about it? Fenton, I mean."

"I wanted you to know that even if I wasn't a lady I wasn't common, either. I'm half-bred," Elsie said proudly.

Lady Finch-Haddley couldn't keep a straight face. She put down her cup and began to laugh. The only things that made her laugh were this girl's remarks. By God, she thought, Finch would have loved this little tit. This big, horse-faced woman had loved her husband and never got over his loss.

"Vincent says," Elsie continued, "that half-breds make good chargers, chasers, too. A blood horse and a light van mare you know."

"Vincent's taught you about horses?" Lady Finch-Haddley said.

"Oh yes. I know them all," Elsie said. "Blood horses, three-quarter-breds, half-breds. Hunters. Hacks. Arabs. Anglo-Arabs. Cobs. Then the heavies: Shires, Percherons, Punches, Clydesdales. Then there's driving horses: Cleveland bays, Hackneys, Yorkshire Coach horses. And colors. I know colors, too. Bay, chestnut, brown, black, gray, cream, dun, strawberry roan, blue roan."

"What's a piebald?" Lady Finch-Haddley interrupted.

"Black and white," Elsie said, "and a skewbald is brown and white."

Elsie was flushed and breathless. "Was it all right?" she asked.

Lady Finch-Haddley leaned over and kissed her cheek. I'm getting quite common myself, she thought. It's catching.

By this time everyone in Wilton Crescent, from Lady Finch-Haddley to the scullery maid, had given up about Elsie. Mr. Homer, the butler, had long since told Her Ladyship he could not keep that young person in her place.

"You might as well give in, Homer," she said. "I gave her a latchkey today."

"You what! Your Ladyship?"

"Gave her a latchkey. Save the servants a lot of running up and down stairs since she's here every five minutes."

"That's it, Your Ladyship," Homer said, "up and down stairs all the time. Miss Elsie has no business downstairs."

"She loves young girls. Did you know she has taught one of her girls to read? And I believe, please regard this as confidential—" Lady Finch-Haddley paused and looked at her butler.

"Of course, Your Ladyship."

"I believe that Miss Elsie had an unhappy childhood." What an understatement that was. The rest of the business had come this morning when she had said, "Elsie, you ought to have a latchkey of your own."

Oh, there had been quite a scene. A repetition of the one before Christmas but with more details. Very common indeed. Elsie had cried on her bosom. That was the correct term, she believed, and she had cried into Elsie's new hairdo and enjoyed it, too. She had almost wished she was a man, a hussar, Elsie's captain, for instance, when she held her in her arms.

"I can't," Elsie cried. "Oh, I can't."

"I know, dear," she said. "You were in a house, you were a . . ."

"No, no," Elsie said, "it's more than that. They tried to cut me."

"Cut you?"

Then she had become nearly hysterical.

"They was going to sell me to America and he saved me, he did, and then only last week they sent someone with a razor to cut me and Queenie killed him, and there's blood on the captain's new carpet. I don't know how to tell him. He did everything so nice in that little house. Vincent had it washed before the police came, but it still shows and he sent me to bed and said that man tried to cut him, so as to keep it out of the papers, but I'm still afraid. It's to teach us not to run away," she sobbed. "If a girl runs away and they can't get her back they cuts her with a razor, and they tried to steal me back, too, but Mr. Vincent was there with his little stick that's got a sword inside and he saved me. Oh, oh, what shall I do? Suppose something happened here and I disgraced you . . ."

Now at last it was all out. She had not mentioned the attack before or the kidnap attempt at Albany. She had been too upset and ashamed.

"I was saying, Homer," Lady Finch-Haddley went on, "Miss Elsie has had a very unusual childhood, but she's willing to learn and has a nice nature."

"That's it, Your Ladyship, and very unsettling it is."

"She's not quite a lady," Lady Finch-Haddley said. "Just half-bred, you might say. But I am glad you all like her. I find her invaluable, not merely her cheerful company, but in a therapeutic manner."

"I know she makes Your Ladyship laugh. That first day . . ."

"When you took so long with the sherry and biscuits."

"I'm sorry, Your Ladyship, but that's the day I began to like her. You see, we have not heard Your Ladyship laugh since the Master passed away."

When Homer had gone Lady Finch-Haddley sat back. Therapeutic was the word. If I meet Turnbull in Africa, I'm going to tell him something, she thought. Elsie had let out his name. I'll say: "If ever you want to marry that girl I'll give the wedding in my house, and half London will be there or they'll know the reason why."

That's what she'd say. Her bright blue eyes flashed angrily about her own empty drawing room.

It was three days before Elsie dared use her latchkey, and when she did, opening the door as quietly as a thief, she let out a scream. The Slasher affair had done her nerves no good. But this, this she simply could not believe. It was like a nightmare.

There in the middle of the Aubusson rug, under the picture of the lovely fat naked lady and little boy, was an animal, an enormous shaggy beast as big as a child's pony. When she let out another yell, the first seemed to have paralyzed it, it came toward her, its yellow eyes on hers, its long tail wagging.

"Jesus," she said, "you're a dog," and held out her hand. "A Queenie," she said, "a bloody great Queenie."

Homer, who had been resting—Lady Finch-Haddley was out—came into the hall.

"I thought I heard a scream," he said. "Gelert didn't hurt you, did he?"

"Oh no," Elsie said, kneeling in front of the dog and throwing her arms around him. "I just didn't know what he was. I came in and saw him. That's when I yelled. Then he wagged his tail and I knew. You see, Homer," she said, "dogs is the only animals that wags their tails to show they're happy. That's what the captain told me once. So it must be true."

"It's true, Miss Elsie, and would you like me to bring up some tea?"

"Oh no," she said, "and have it all alone? I'll come down and have tea with you."

What the hell could you do with a girl like that?

"Delighted, I'm sure," Homer said, and he was, in an unhappy kind of way.

Lady Finch-Haddley was glad she had sent for Gelert. Her kennelman said he was pining. Imagine a great brute like that pining. "Come here," she said. The dog rose slowly, came to her, and stared into her eyes, which were level with his own as she sat.

"Frightened our Elsie, did you?" she said, patting his head. "Well, I'm not surprised. Do you know what Gelert is, Elsie?"

"What is he, Lady Finch-Haddley?"

"He's an Irish wolfhound. I told you I bred them in the country."

"I forgot," Elsie said. "But where are the wolves?"

"There are no wolves even in Ireland now."

"Then he's just for fun?"

"A pet, Elsie, that's what he is."

"I always thought pets were small," she said. "The captain used to say I was a pet, but he's bigger than me. What does he weigh?" She looked at the dog.

"Two hundred pounds."

"What's that in stones?" Elsie said. "I can't divide by fourteen. It's two figures. The captain was just beginning to teach me long division when he left."

"He taught you? And you teach Millie?"

"That's right," Elsie said, "sort of passing it on. But Vincent's teaching me arithmetic now."

My God what a girl. Sitting down with her butler and letting him teach her arithmetic. Absolutely no sense of position. No authority and everyone in her household doing exactly what they liked, but all of them taking care of her as if she was a prize pup.

"I'm going to take Gelert with me," she said. "He might as well be eaten by a lion as pine away in England." She too thought Africa was filled with lions.

The dog wagged his tail slowly to and fro. As long as she was with him, as long as she talked to him, he did not care what went on or where he went.

Lady Finch-Haddley began to laugh quietly to herself about the Rubens that Elsie called, "the lovely fat naked lady in the hall." Only today she had told her that it made Wilton Crescent seem quite homelike. It appeared that there had been nudes in the hall of that place—the house.

How strange that a girl should still think of a brothel as a kind of home. Her own little house, the love nest, she still regarded as too good to be true. Just a place her captain let her live in. How touching those phrases were—"the captain," "my captain." There was nothing else in this girl's life.

She was fascinated by Elsie. Hundreds and hundreds of men, and she feels like the captain's bride, trying to learn things she thinks will please him. A girl with no advantages whatsoever who was making something of herself.

Elsie's story had started an interest in prostitution. She was making inquiries here and there and finding out some curious things. She did not believe in good works, missionaries for the blacks, and so on, but cruelty she abominated. The world was a strange place. Perhaps, she thought, those who had ill-treated Elsie might one day regreat what they had done. If I got really interested, she thought, with my money, the people I know, and the strings I can pull . . . I could do something, especially with Elsie knowing the ropes. Once the war was finished and the hospital was done with . . .

Life was not over yet. The war had given her one interest and had brought her Elsie, who had given her another. . . .

Elsie got up to go. She knew Lady Finch-Haddley was lost in some dream of the past or thinking of the hospital. She said, "I had better go home," but she didn't go. She stood there pulling her gloves on and off.

"Well, what is it, Elsie?" Lady Finch-Haddley asked. "Either sit down or go home."

"I've got something to show you," Elsie said. "Something nice. If you've got time?"

"What have you got?" Lady Finch-Haddley asked.

Elsie was really like a child with a toy. As soon as she got something new she had to show it. She was so natural, so disarming. The girl was such a paradox. A belly full of the fruit of knowledge on the one hand and near infantile innocence on the other. With people she liked she had the trust of a child or a puppy. What happened to children and puppies? When did they lose their smiling trust and stop wagging their tails? Was it with puberty? Was it earlier? She often wished she and Finch had had a child, a girl preferably. A boy was lost too soon. At seven or eight he went to boarding school and that soon stopped his tail wagging. But with a girl, well, with a girl it would have been interesting to see what happened. She smiled and said:

"Well, what is it? And stop fiddling with that chain. First the gloves and now the chain."

"It's on the chain," Elsie said, undoing it. "Look." She put the locket, still warm from her breasts, into Lady Finch-Haddley's hand. "It's 'is 'air," she said, "the captain's hair. I saved it."

"Good God!" Lady Finch-Haddley said. "He's not dead. They generally make these things up . . ."

"He's away," Elsie said, "and I've got a bit of him here hot against my heart. It's a lover's knot, you know —combings," she said, "I got them off his hairbrushes. He doesn't know I took them. And he's got something of mine, too, that he doesn't know about—didn't when he left, anyhow." Elsie stared at Lady Finch-Haddley with wide saucer eyes, her full, kissable lips slightly apart.

Lady Finch-Haddley knew this conversational gambit of Elsie's. This was her cue. This was the way Elsie's previous companions must have talked, in a kind of perpetual guessing game. "Guess what? . . . No, not that . . . I give up . . . Now tell me . . ."

"What?" Lady Finch-Haddley said.

"A nightdress," Elsie said, "a silk one." She paused and

then went on dramatically, "A dirty one that smelled like me."

"How nice, Elsie," Lady Finch-Haddley said. "How very nice," watching her drop the locket into the secret valley that was its home. Then she laughed. A captain of hussars sailing with the commander in chief of Her Majesty's Army in the field with his mistress's dirty nightie folded in with his striped pajamas.

"They are striped, aren't they Elsie?"

"What are?"

"His pajamas."

"Blue and white," Elsie said. "They are all blue and white."

"Blue for a boy."

"Yes," Elsie said, her eyes misting over. "Blue for a boy and I wouldn't care about us not being married. Not at all I wouldn't."

In her circles marriage and children did not always go together. Elsie was really quite an education. A liberal education. She was a girl who grasped the essentials of a situation and let the rest go by. It was the river that counted to Elsie, not the banks it flowed between or the driftwood of convention that floated on its surface. Young, pretty, and soft as Elsie was, Lady Finch-Haddley was sure that there were few occasions she would be incapable of meeting. And they would begin soon—the occasions. Everything was just about ready. Even the girls—a mixed lot, but they seemed willing to work. The last hurdle had been jumped today. Space on a ship for them all with their equipment. They were nearly ready to sail, and she had forgotten to tell Elsie.

"We sail next month, Elsie," she said, and Elsie burst into tears.

CHAPTER 29

THE QUICK AND THE DEAD

AFTER their victory the Boers rested around Ladysmith, still expecting peace negotiations to begin at any moment. The setback at Wagon Hill and the red fort were forgotten.

Then the Pretoria Commando was sent to Zululand to create a diversion. They rode through its lovely rolling hills, dotted with circular cattle kraals and beehive huts, without the help of guides. The Zulus preferred the British to the Boers and gave them no help. Nor could they find any trace of the British force they were supposed to engage.

But Boetie, riding with Moolman, though he missed his brother, enjoyed the peace of this country and drank in its quiet as though it was wine. It was wonderful to hear no shots and ride in peace over the veld, the long grass brushing their stirrup irons. To camp, sitting quietly over their cooking fires and sleep soft and un-afraid.

Moolman was not worried about Servas. He had found his feet. He had done what he could for him. He had taught him not to fear his fear, saying only a fool is never afraid. He had taught him all the tricks an old soldier can teach a young one, and now he was on his own recuperating on the staff in Pretoria.

Boetie was different. Half child, half man, still filled with ideals, wide-eyed, virgin. His hands had touched no woman's flesh save the forgotten fountains of his mother's breast. But a man lay latent there, in the yolk of him. He loved the boy's fearful courage, his timid bravery, his tentative feeling for the Africa that was Moolman's very life. Not every Boer knew that the veld was more than grass and rock and mountain. That *Ons Land* meant more than Our Land, that it had something to do with God. As though this were another firmament beneath one's feet, as though there were stars down here too. The wild flowers perhaps, and that the moon, reflected in a vlei, was no reflection but another moon. Boetie had the soul of a hunter who, as he hunts, killing God's creatures, is yet seeking God. What bird is more revolting than the *aasvoël*, the vulture? Yet, on high circling wings as it watches the earth for death, a man looking up can see great mystery there. He is conscious of death, of his own littleness, and of God.

Often when on the veld Moolman had thought, What if I die here on the tusk of an elephant, the horn of a buck,

by a Kaffir spear, or of fever? What of it? It will not
be death, for there I will be high in the sky sailing on
vulture's wings. There I will be in the bush with the
hyenas and the jackals. There I will be deep in the
earth among the ants.

Dead, alone on the veld, a man did not leave it. He
was merely spread out upon it, over it, below it.

Once, miles from anywhere near a great cream-of-
tartar tree, the soft bole of its trunk thirty feet through
its pulpy heart, he had found the skull of a man, the remains of his rusted gun beside him. No more than that.
The lesser bones had gone. But the skull, polished and
bleached by time and sun, lay there on grass grazed
smooth as a lawn by buck.

That was the way to die. Alone, like a dog. Like an
animal. With no gawking crowd to witness the indignities
of death, with no coins upon the eyes, no sagging jaw
supported by a rag. No winding sheet, no tears, no
mourning but the cooing of the doves. That was a hunter's
death. The gate that would lead him back to those who
had preceded him into the spirit world. Now, since it
was so long since they had left him, his family was not
alone. A great company had joined them, for among
his friends there were, even at his age, because of the
way of his life, more dead than quick.

Perhaps too his dogs would be there, his horses and
some favorite oxen. Who knew what would be there, or
where "there" was? Or if it existed. But in his own
time every man would one day find the answer.

That was the tragedy of war—that men found the answer before they had asked the question. That was why
young men die so hard. They had not lived. They had
not seen the sunrise in a woman's arms, tossed their
young sons into the air, or watched them suck their
mother's milk. They had not plowed their lands, sown
or reaped their crops.

This was what he wished for Boetie, his new son. His
son reborn. Not happiness, but life, the full unbearable
beauty of it, and a woman who would one day help him
bear it. No man was strong enough to bear beauty quite
alone. The slow heron over the evening vlei. The wild
cry of a flying crane. The fishing saddle-bill. A pride of

lions walking in the dusk. The corkscrew curl of the kudu's horn. Elephants. Sea cows.

The endless beauty of it. The sweet perfume of ancient thorns abuzz with bees. Trees that took five years to grow an inch. There were trees that he had slept beside as a young man which in twenty years had not changed at all.

He thought of winter dawns in the high country. Miles and miles of empty country dipped in silver. Hoarfrost on every grass blade, on every leaf, on every tiny branch, every sharp spiked thorn a silver needle. And strung between the trees and bush, great spider webs, wheels of spun silver. All changing as the sun came up, melting to its heat.

And the animals, the buck that had survived the terrors of the night coming out of hiding to warm their bodies, standing on the east of every bush as if they worshiped the rising sun, before they took their small devious paths through dew-drenched grass to water. This was his Africa, the Africa of the Boers, even of those whose eyes and hearts were blind to it.

The cities, the riches, and the mines were for Outlanders, the strangers ignorant of all but gold.

But this peace was too good to last and was broken by a messenger—a man on a sweating horse—the usual harbinger of disaster. They must return at once.

They rode all night, passing men running unashamedly away from the scene of action. The bold and the cowardly passing each other in the darkness without greetings, each scornful of the other.

Reaching their objective at daybreak, they found things even worse than they had expected. The Boer trenches on the north bank of the river had been evacuated, and even burghers who had stood fast were discouraged and losing hope. Instead of suing for peace the British were redoubling their war effort.

At Chieveley and other bases down the line Buller had collected some 30,000 men. He left 7000 to guard his stores and pushed on with the remaining 23,000. This time he was going to make a job of it.

There had been much heavy rain. The troops marched through mud up to the horses' hocks. Some wagons could not be unstuck even by the use of eight oxen. Mules drowned in the mud. By nightfall the whole force was strung out knee- and axle-deep in mud.

And Buller, established in his new headquarters, spent several days collecting a fortnight's supply of provisions.

Churchill reported that this delay gave the Boers time to make new dispositions and wrote in his dispatch, "It is poor economy to let a soldier live well for three days in order to kill him on the fourth."

Dundonald's mounted troops were sent to occupy Spearman's Heights. From here the scene was imposing. On the horizon to his left were the jagged peaks of the Drakensberg. The source of the stream that began at the Upper Tugela and later, by the time it reached Colenso twenty miles away to the right, was called the Lower Tugela.

The river here was easily fordable. A small range of hills lay beyond it, dominated by a larger hill, almost a mountain, known as Spion Kop.

Ladysmith lay only twenty miles away to the north. From the top of Spearman's its heliograph could be seen flashing. Buller flashed back. Here was the obvious route. He was on his way once more.

The Boers at Colenso numbered no more than two thousand.

But the baggage, the rations, and all the endless impedimenta without which no British officer could fight took four days to arrive. By that time the Boers had doubled their strength and were ready for them.

Buller then changed his plans. He decided to cross the river at Trichard's Drift, go around the back of Spion Kop and across the plain to Ladysmith with the main part of his army, leaving a strong contingent as a containing force at Spearman's.

But instead of leading the troops himself Buller handed over the command of the attacking force to General Warren.

Turnbull, at Buller's side, was utterly at a loss to account for this curious arrangement. Warren was not a good general. He had only his divisional staff to deal with, a large force that would be spread out over miles of country. He had a reputation for bad temper. He was in addition an engineer unaccustomed to handling troops of the line.

The British movements were obvious to the Boers and reinforcements had been sent for—the Zululand contingent among them. Volunteers were called for to go to the Tugela, where Buller had moved twenty-five miles upstream and was preparing to mount a large-scale attack on Spion Kop.

Fifty men of the Pretoria Commando, including Moolman's section, stepped forward and within an hour they were off. They crossed the Klip River after dark and reached the rear of the *kop* before a dawn that roared with gunfire.

They rested their horses and cooked a breakfast of mealie porridge and coffee. Then they were ordered to dig in on a ridge a mile away, and, being issued picks and shovels, they moved off with their horses.

When the trenches were dug Boetie and Moolman walked across the hills toward the sound of rifle fire to see what was going on. The noise got louder as they approached. At last the Boer line could be seen stretching out along the top of the next hill. Mushrooms of black smoke and earth hung suspended above them as the shells fired from the other side of the Tugela burst on their position.

"Let's join them," Moolman said, and they moved on to the Boer lines. From here they could see the silver ribbon of the Tugela wind its way down the valley below. The far side was alive with British troops, both foot and horse, while from the woods behind them the flashes of the English guns were clearly visible.

During the night the English had forded the river and established several bridgeheads on the north bank, following some of the ridges that ran up from the river. The Boers they had pushed back had re-entrenched themselves on the crest of the heights and were firing at the enemy who lay only a few hundred yards away.

The men Boetie and Moolman had joined were Free Staters, the Transvaalers being on their left flank downstream. There were about twelve thousand burghers lined out along the hills here, Spion Kop forming a pivot that was the key to the position.

The Boers were firing only when a hit was certain, to save ammunition. Their guns, for the same reason, remained silent.

Boetie had never been exposed to such a concentrated bombardment and only because of Moolman did he remain steady. Howitzer shells came lobbing down and men all around them were being blown to pieces. Rifle bullet wounds were bad enough, but this was a terrible experience. Men literally blown apart, turned into great chunks of raw meat, limbs and even rifles being thrown into the air by the force of the explosions. Such a bombardment must mean an attack, but it never came.

Boetie and Moolman remained in the firing line till dark, when they returned, with much relief, to their own commando.

It rained during the night and Boetie slept fitfully, still disturbed by the sights he had seen. At three everyone was awakened by the sound of rifle fire from Spion Kop. Later it died down and the Boers slept once more in spite of the rain that continued.

At dawn the sound of gunfire increased. While the men breakfasted, spent bullets whined over their heads. Their meal was disturbed by a man galloping up with the news that the British had taken Spion Kop in the night.

If the *kop* went, the whole Tugela line would collapse, and they were ordered to saddle up, fill their bandoleers from the supply wagon, and follow the guide. They rode through a hail of howitzer shells, randomly fired over the hill in front of them, to the base of Spion Kop. Here stood hundreds of saddled horses in long rows. Above the horses a thousand Boers were climbing the hill, many falling wounded or dead from the close-range fire of the British established on its summit. The dead lay scattered on the steep slope as if they had been thrown there haphazardly by some giant hand. Like corn flung out to poultry. They lay in groups. They lay alone. The wounded were trying to dress their wounds and crawling back to the security of the horse lines in dead ground.

As they watched, some Boers reached the crest and were met by British soldiers with fixed bayonets. They flashed like heliograph signals in the sun. The hand-to-hand fighting continued in silhouette on the skyline, and then the Boers seemed to drive the British back and disappeared from view.

Leaving their horses with the others, the Pretoria men moved up to reinforce the attackers, climbing over the dead and dying men scattered thickly on the slope, which here, on the north side of the *kop*, was not particularly steep or hard to scale. Reaching the top, they found the Boers were holding only its rocky fringe, the kind of stone girdle that so often edges the hilltops of Africa. The British held the rest of it and were dug in behind a wall of loose stones only twenty yards away. The fire from here was so terrible that no further advance was possible. Moolman's party flung themselves down among the dead and opened fire. The English were near enough for a stone to be tossed into their line from the Boer position. Volley after volley came from Lee-Metfords in the stone *schans* twenty yards away. More Boers were killed. Prinsloo, at Boetie's side, was hit between the eyes and died like an animal, twitching and kicking his heels in the reflex of instantaneous death. The Boer wounded were groaning, some screaming with pain. Only the dead were still. Boetie fired till the barrel of his rifle grew too hot to hold, but without knowing the results of his shots or those of the other Boers. They only knew what they were suffering, but had no idea of what was happening to the English behind the *schans*. Some bullets unquestionably were going in the interstices of the loose-packed stones; others, striking the rocks, sent up splinters that must inflict wounds of some kind.

At last the Boer guns began to give them support, firing over their heads. Never was the scream of shells more welcome, and the British fire slackened. It was now about nine and the heat of the sun was increasing. By midday the vertical rays beat down upon them as they lay without food or water. The section would have broken but for Moolman's encouragement and abuse.

No reinforcements reached them. They felt they had been deserted, for, looking down into the valley behind them, they could see horsemen riding away to the laagers in the rear. This was the only movement—a trickle of desertion to the rear and a savage deadlock in the two lines of men who opposed each other on the hilltop. Both sides held their ground and the close-range, point-blank fire went on without cease, hour after hour.

Next to Boetie was a German officer, a volunteer by the name of Von Brausewitz, who had been disgraced because in some Berlin café brawl he had spitted a civilian with his sword. Broken from his regiment, he had joined the Boers and sought death on every possible occasion. Now, in spite of Moolman's curses, he stood up several times to fire, and each time was missed by the hail of bullets that he drew. Then he must have decided to end it once and for all. Without even his rifle in his hand he stood to light a cigarette and puffed at it as if he was on a street at home. A bullet hit him in the head and he fell, lying only a few feet from the muzzle of Boetie's rifle.

The Boers lay still waiting for a target, the glimpse of a British helmet or an extended hand. Exhausted, hungry, thirsty, they still held on as grimly as dogs to a wounded buck. All about them the dead were black as Kaffirs, covered with a thick fur of flies attracted by their wounds, drinking blood and laying their white oval eggs in the open wounds.

As it became too dark to see, the firing slowed up, and a silence even more terrible replaced the noise of gunfire, broken only by the cries of the wounded as they called for help and water.

The English were crying out too. Their plight seemed to be as bad as that of the Boers, though this was small comfort to them. Boetie could even hear what they said.

"Give us a hand with Jack, mate . . . Water, for Christ's sake . . . Nobby's dead, poor bugger . . . Copped it in the belly. Where's the officers? . . . All dead, the bloody lot of them. . . ."

Moolman had moved during the action. Boetie, alone with the dead and wounded, felt his nerve going. He was trembling. In the darkness he seemed to see men advancing, saw bayonets sharp as spears against the sky, and, unable to bear it any longer, he slipped away. He could not be expected to hold Spion Kop all by himself. Not a boy like me, he thought. He had fought all day. Done all he could. And now he was off to find such of his friends as remained alive. He moved through the darkness till checked by a challenge: *"Wie's daar?"* Boers, thank

God. A moment later he found himself with Moolman, Nel, and the two Beyers.

They remained where they were till nearly midnight. Then they gave up and slipped down the mountain they had scaled the previous dawn. In the dark they fell over the soft bodies of the dead and reached the bottom with their hands sticky with Boer blood—the blood of brave men spilled like wine in the attack.

Most of the horses in the horse lines were gone, but their own and those of the dead and wounded were still where they had been left at daybreak, their barrels sunk in for lack of water.

At once they made for a spring that lay nearby, and found some of the worst hit, those too bad to be moved far, in charge of an old man who was doing what he could for them by the light of a stable lantern.

No one knew the exact position. It seemed that the Boers had failed to take the *kop* and that as soon as it was light the Tugela line would be enfiladed, rolled up, and the British, having broken through, would be on their way to the relief of Ladysmith, and all these deaths, these wounds, this blood, would have been for nothing.

Moolman told them to forage for food, taking it from the saddlebags on the horses of the dead, and join the Carolina wagon laager that was the nearest to them. The Carolina men, who had been hardest hit of all, were loading their wagons and getting ready to trek. They had no intention of being outflanked by the British as they moved north to relieve the town. Since Elandslaagte the Boers' fear of being charged by cavalry was overwhelming. There was fright amounting almost to panic among them. Many were wounded. All had lost friends and relations.

Then, just as the lead wagon began to roll, there was the sound of a wildly galloping horse coming toward them.

Someone roared, "Halt! Pull up those wagons! What are you—men?" Boetie could not see his face. "Are you Boers or women? Do you want to be caught moving and helpless? Do you want the cavalry to hit you as you trek?" Then the man rode on, moving into the night, shouting, rallying the men, telling them the shame that would be theirs if they left the line. This man, the word went around, was Louis Botha, the new commandant general of the forces who had replaced old Piet Joubert, who was ill.

Botha succeeded in checking the retreat and the men who had trickled away from the battlefield came shame-facedly back. Theirs was not the only commando Botha had turned. He rode all night from laager to laager, ex-horting, encouraging, threatening, and by the force of his will averted complete disaster.

Moolman's men returned with the Carolina burghers to the foot of Spion Kop, leading their tired horses. They lay down and slept beside them, till wakened by the heavy dew and the cold of dawn.

With the first light they looked up at the hill above them and saw no movement. Then suddenly two Boers appeared against the skyline, holding their rifles above their heads and waving their hats. The British for no apparent reason had conceded Spion Kop and had gone.

Leaving their horses, the Carolina men and Moolman's party climbed the hill again. Not a shot was fired at them from the British *schanses*.

They climbed over the low wall and found the English dead in the trenches, lying in swaths, some piled three deep, one upon the other. Hundreds of dead lay in this small strip of rocky veld where the Boer guns had torn them to pieces. The havoc was unbelievable, shocking, and terrible. Broken men mixed with smashed rifles, torn equipment, and scattered, empty cans of rations, bully beef, Maconochie . . .

Again Boetie was struck by the mess, the muddle, the devastation. Men and earth mixed up together, with blood-soaked bandages, scattered paper, the remains of news-papers, letters from home, and here and there a photo-graph torn by shellfire or trampled into the mire—a girl smiling, a young wife holding a child, an older woman who was some boy's mother.

Turning from the bloody and sickening sight, the Boers looked down toward the river and saw the British in full retreat. Boetie felt Moolman's arm go around his shoul-ders. He was trembling like a frightened horse with emo-tion. Long clouds of dust rose from the retreating con-voys.

Buller's second attempt to cross the Tugela had failed.

Soon the English doctors and stretcher-bearers arrived to bury their dead and carry off the wounded. The dead in the trenches were buried where they lay in a long mass grave, buried in each other's arms the way they had died, lying this way and that like broken dolls oozing sawdust that was blood.

The Boers carried their own dead down the hill in blankets, loaded them in the commando wagons, and rode off behind the shattered remains of their friends, the riderless horses of the dead trotting with empty saddles beside them. But at least these men had not died for nothing, because now the British were certain to make peace, having found the Boers to be invincible.

Buller could have resumed the battle, but he was sick of Spion Kop, Spy Hill, as the Boers called it, since from its heights the whole of the surrounding country could be seen. He decided to wait a few days and try some other plan. He supervised the retreat over the Tugela personally, having resumed command of his forces. That he had not lost a pound of his stores was his boast. He had merely lost 374 men killed or dead of wounds, 1055 wounded, and 311 missing or prisoner. This was the price he had paid for handing over the command to Warren. But the troops still loved their "Bulldog" and cheered when he thanked them next day on a great parade for all they had done and the courage they had displayed.

Meanwhile the staff officers observed the Boer positions and mapped them as far as was possible.

Turnbull through his glasses saw a slim blonde girl in a white dress and carrying a red parasol walking about among the trenches on Spion Kop, where only a few days ago so many men had died. Did she want to see where her father, husband, brother, or lover had fallen? Did she want never to forget this spot? To fix it in her mind forever? With her still on his mind he went on with the plans for the new attack that was to take place, this time at Vaalkrantz by way of a pontoon bridge that Buller would throw across the Tugela while he made a feint in another direction. When they were done and it was light enough to see, Turnbull rode over the pontoons without a shot being fired at him. But the general refused to advance until his bombardment of the hills was completed. But even with this delay the attack succeeded and by 4 P.M. Vaalkrantz was taken.

Then, suddenly afraid of another big casualty list, Buller changed his mind once more and ordered a withdrawal. He wired to Lord Roberts that to get through the gap he had already almost forced might cost three thousand men. "Do you think the relief of Ladysmith is worth the risk? It is the only possible way to relieve White. If I give up this chance I know no other."

Roberts, whose advice to stay on the defensive had been ignored, felt he could not allow another engagement to go off at half cock and wired back:

"Ladysmith must be relieved even at the loss you anticipate. Let your troops know that the Empire is in your hands . . ."

But even these orders were not enough for Buller. He hesitated for hours.

By now Louis Botha had arrived and drove the Boers to action. When the grass in front of Vaalkrantz was set ablaze by bursting shells, the Boers charged over the smoldering veld under cover of the smoke, almost overrunning the British line, and were checked only by a counterattack.

More British troops arrived to strengthen the line, but Buller remained irresolute and finally telegraphed to Roberts that "the engagement would uselessly waste life," and he would "try something else." Four hundred casualties had already been incurred to no purpose.

The next three days were spent marching the troops and their six hundred wagonloads of stores back to camp at Chieveley, and Buller wired to Roberts that he was going to make a "desperate dash" for Ladysmith.

This time, once across the Tugela, the British began to advance up the valley and continued until the fire of the Boers brought them to a halt. In spite of this, Buller continued to pour more men, guns, and baggage over the river till there was an immense pile-up of useless matériel behind the immobilized troops.

Buller now had twenty-five thousand troops strung out like a long necklace for miles, with no room to concentrate for a break-through. The regiments were mixed up, and his artillery too crowded to be effective. But the men on the hill still clung there without food or water, under continuous fire from the Boers, amid the stink of their rotting dead, who lay grotesquely among the rocks of the steep hillsides, like discarded garbage, head down, head up, a rolling body caught and held by a single rock, bent around it like a hairpin; hanging on, listening to the moans and screams of their wounded, to whom they could offer no help.

Once again the Boers had held the British. Word was passed along the line that Buller had asked for an armistice to collect his wounded and bury the dead. The rumor proved correct and it was not long before the doctors and stretcher-bearers were going about their bloody work and the troops of both sides merged into a great mixed group as if they had been the spectators instead of the participants of some frightful game, and now that it was over were meeting on the field where it had been played to discuss its finer points.

They exchanged tobacco and patted each other consolingly on the shoulder. Brother Boer was not such a bad chap. . . . These English boys were not to blame. It was the Government, Chamberlain, the Queen . . . The few Boers who spoke English were surrounded by groups of Tommies. An old burgher, hearing Boetie speak English, dragged him off to where General Littelton was standing.

"Tell him," the burgher said, "that we have all been having a rough time."

Boetie translated.

The general said, "I suppose so, but to us of course it is nothing. This is what we are paid for. This is the life we always lead."

"Great God!" the old Boer said when the words were explained to him. Translation had not been enough. The life of a professional soldier was inconceivable to a home-loving cattle farmer.

But in spite of having held the British up, the Boers were uneasy and hundreds of men were leaving the new line that had been formed in the rear of Hlangwane. They were drifting toward the wagon laagers, holding meetings, and in general showing signs of demoralization. The stiffness had gone out of them, their fighting spirit weakened to near-nonexistence by their disappointments.

What good had their victories been? For what had all
this blood been lost? For what purpose had so many
good men died?

Things were so bad that Botha had to establish a new
line still farther to the rear, where Moolman's men took
up a position on a ridge with their horses in dead ground
close behind them. For a time there was no action.

By 10 A.M. next day the British engineers had completed another pontoon bridge with a signboard marked,
"To Ladysmith." The troops swarmed over it and the new
attack began. The roar of Buller's massed artillery made
the ground tremble. The whole Boer position seemed to
be erupting showers of earth and flame. Under a curtain
of bursting shells the British infantry advanced with fixed
bayonets, invisible to the Boers crouched in the trenches
till the barrage of gunfire ceased and they were almost
on them.

"Meet them!" Moolman shouted, climbing out of the
trench, his voice loud in the uncanny silence. Boetie stood
at his side. Next to him were the two Beyerses, man and
wife. Then came Nel and Bothma. On Moolman's left
was O'Brien the Irishman.

The English came on, their bayoneted rifles at the high
port. Many fell, dropping under the fire the Boers poured
into them, but they were not checked. Boetie brought two
down with two shots, missed another, and went on firing.
He heard a cry and saw Jan Beyers go down. Hetta knelt
beside him for an instant. Then, seeing he was dead, she
stood over his body, her legs apart, and poured shot after
shot into the advancing troops. Before God that girl could
shoot. Her long fair hair was down, streaming behind her
in the breeze that had sprung up and blew the dust and
smoke reeking of hot cordite into their faces.

A bugle call rang out. An officer shouted, "Charge!"
raising his arm. Moolman brought him down with a shot
in the breast. The English, still closer now just below the
crest of the ridge, were for an instant invisible. Then
their bayonets and helmets appeared and the fighting became hand to hand. Moolman parried a thrust, drove his
Mauser barrel into his opponent's belly, and fired. As the
man fell he seized his Lee-Metford and fought bayonet to
bayonet with the man who followed him. Hetta Beyers, her
yellow mane flying, was holding her rifle by the barrel

and laying about her. Boetie, who had dropped back a pace to push another clip of cartridges into his magazine, saw her smash the skull of an English soldier who had lost his helmet. Her eyes blazing, screaming with fury, she flung herself onto another man and went down with a bayonet thrust in her side.

The British troops were shouting, "Come on, you bastards . . . We've got 'em now!" Some growled like dogs, cursed, panted. They looked like devils, their faces streaked with dirt and sweat, their helmets lost or awry. The first wave faltered, weakened by their losses, and fell back below the ridge top. But behind them the plain was alive with men. Line after line of Englishmen, the leading men with their bayonets fixed and rifles at the high port. The others came on carrying guns at the trail. Checking their first rush was all the Boers had been able to do.

"To the horses," Moolman shouted, dropping the English rifle with its dripping bayonet and picking up his own. Following him, they turned and ran, jumping onto their ponies and galloping off as the next line of British scaled the hill, leaped the trench they had just abandoned, and fired at the backs of the retreating Boers.

The bullets whistled past their ears. Neither man nor horse was hit. But Moolman's party had ceased to exist. The Beyerses dead, together as they had been in life. Nel and the Irishman were dead. Bothma was plastered with blood from a wound in the head. Even Rand, the Beyerses' little white dog, had died in the battle.

From behind them, mixed with the sound of rifle shots, came the shouts and the cheers of the British. A gap had been blasted in the line, through which wherever they looked the British poured, and beyond them, as far as the horizon, Boer horsemen, guns, and wagons were in full retreat.

Riding north at a slow canter, Moolman led them to the main laager in the rear, where their depression was further deepened by the latest news. They had known that Ladysmith would be relieved. But it now appeared that the British cavalry under French were entering Kimberley and, worst of all, that General Cronje had surrendered at Paardeberg with four thousand men.

The prospects that had seemed so bright early in the month had proved to be a mirage at its end.

That night it rained. There was such a storm as was seldom seen even in South Africa. The rain came down like a waterspout as the thunder rolled. They were soaked to the skin, miserable at the outcome of this long battle that had been fought in installments. The lightning illuminated the thousands of Boers fleeing the battlefield, on foot, on horseback, or riding on mule and ox wagons. Mountain paths became streams, dry sluits ran like rivers. Horses, cattle, and men caught in the rushing water were drowned and hurled to destruction in the freak waterfalls that leaped like wild beasts over the cliffs. Unpursued, they fled as if the devil himself were after them.

Even Moolman was caught in the infection of panic and led his party through the ruck as if he was charging through an enemy, sliding, slithering, climbing, and forcing their horses to get into the van, knowing this was their only hope of getting away if the English pursued them.

Boetie rode numb with cold and horror. He could not get his mind off Hetta Beyers, standing over her man and going down beneath a bayonet thrust. And Jonas too was missing. They had lost him somewhere.

At last, after months of blundering, Buller, by using his whole army at one time, in one place, had taken the heights of the Tugela in six hours.

He heliographed to White in Ladysmith, "Everything progressing favourably," but did nothing to destroy the fleeing Boers against whom even God seemed to have turned that night.

But Buller had no thought of pursuit or even of advancing. His next signal to Ladysmith was, "Have thoroughly beaten the enemy. Believe them to be in full retreat. Have sent my cavalry to ascertain which way they have gone." This, when a child could have followed the spoor of this routed force.

A patrol of Dundonald's cavalry approached Ladysmith in the late afternoon and was challenged. "Who goes there?" the sentry shouted. "Ladysmith relief column," was the reply.

Men issued from their shelters, their faces streaming with tears. As the cavalry rode into the town everyone remarked on their fat horses and the plump figures of the men. General White and his chief of staff, General Sir Archibald Hunter, and Colonel Ian Hamilton rode forward to greet the relieving column. The troops shouted at seeing the officers; the garrison and townspeople took up their cheers. Cheer followed cheer. Hats took to the air like birds.

White thanked his garrison.

"Thank God," he said, "that we have kept the flag flying."

The crowds stood bareheaded as they sang "God Save the Queen," and then broke up to see if they could cadge a bit of bread or a cigarette from the troopers who had relieved them.

The siege, which had lasted 118 days, was over and the total casualties of the British since Buller had first set out to its relief totaled more than the entire Boer force that had opposed him. But old Joubert had been right to fear Buller's persistence. He was like the famous bulldog whose master cut off all his legs as it hung to a bull's nose, for a wager he would never let go.

And now, though General White led his half-starved garrison in pursuit of the Boers and had to turn back after five miles, owing to their exhaustion, Buller refused to use his fresh troops to follow them, and was even displeased with White's attempt to do so when he arrived in Ladysmith ahead of his army to look the town over. Instead, he returned to his headquarters and spent a couple of days organizing a formal entry. It was made with pomp and ceremony, with flags and bands. The mayor made a welcoming speech. Buller made a speech of thanks to his troops while the Boers scuttled away to safety over the veld.

Had the British pursued them with a battery of horse artillery and a squadron or two of cavalry, the bulk of the Boer guns and transports would have fallen into their hands. At every storm-flooded spruit there were fierce quarrels among the teamsters. Wagon wheels got locked, draft animals, both oxen and mules, became unmanageable. Every commando was confused. No one even knew where they were going. A single salvo of shrapnel would have done the trick. But it was never fired. And when daylight came the weather cleared, the tangle was slowly straightened out, and the Boers fled on, putting what distance they could between themselves and the British, who, instead of pounding at their heels, were celebrating the relief of the obscure little town that they had brought back into the British fold.

CHAPTER 30

LONDON NEWS

ENGLAND had recovered from Black Week. Bobs and K of K had arrived in South Africa. There were now 180,000 British troops in the country, a total that far outnumbered the entire Boer population if every woman and child were included.

News—war news—was something new, partly because there had been no wars since the Indian Mutiny and the Crimea, and partly because the entire population was now literate. Literacy can never be confused with education though it must precede it, and this new mass public was supplied with the kind of meals it could digest. The gutter press was born. Another new phenomenon was the telegraph. News was now received within hours and this immediacy gave it a reality unknown before. Afrikaans words like *trek, kop, donga, dorp,* and *drift*—hill, gully, village, and ford—used by the war correspondents, brought the African veld into the parlors of Brixton and the pubs of Highgate.

Then, just when everything was going nicely again, the news of Spion Kop broke.

News vendors in the streets, cashing in on disaster, shouted, " 'orrible slaughter at Spion Kop . . . desperate fighting . . . 'undreds killed . . ."

The British public, slow to anger, patient as it was, now got into an ugly mood. After Black Week the wave of patriotism that had run over the country, sweeping men, on the tide of their emotions, like dust into the pan of the army, now went sour and turned on the Government. Things that had been kept dark began to leak out —about war profiteers, about no maps, moldy forage, and defective ammunition. . . .

The Government trembled like a tree in a storm. Even its own adherents asked questions in the House, as the opposition, all-out opponents of the war, redoubled their efforts to bring it to a close. A "Stop the War" party was organized. Lloyd George, the Welsh lawyer M.P., became even more vociferous. A pamphlet "Shall I Slay My Brother?" by W. T. Stead, was widely distributed abroad. The fall of the Salisbury-Chamberlain cabinet was predicted.

From Cape Town, Milner cabled that the lifeline of the Boers through Delagoa Bay must be cut. Old Kruger had been pretty smart, for a Bible-reading peasant, to know that in order to exist his republic must have its own access to the sea.

But there were some diplomatic problems involved. England had forgotten to ratify an agreement with Portugal in the seventies which would have given her military passage and some control over Portuguese East Africa. Milner wanted to blockade Lourenço Marques, but the international situation was too delicate for this. Instead, British warships searched all ships proceeding to Mozambique for war matériel. These losses prevented European firms from sending more munitions to the Boers, and English agents bought up all nonwar material they could lay their hands on, to the vast profit of the local merchants.

The Portuguese, however, did co-operate with Britain in charging volunteers arriving to help the Boers very heavily for their passports.

Not that any of this was a great help at this juncture, and the opposition tabled a motion to bring down the Government, charging "Want of knowledge, foresight and judgment. . . ." and Stead published another pamphlet, "Are We Right?"

But Chamberlain, handsome, suave, an orchid in his buttonhole, an actor and orator, pulled the Government's chestnuts out of the fire of attack with a masterly speech.

"We have been too eager for peace," he said, "though where we got that idea it is difficult to see," and then went on with what would appear to be irrelevant figures and remarks about the empire, and succeeded, by personality alone, in explaining the British defeats in the field as "finding the weak spots in our armor in order to rectify them." This is the art of the politician—to make black seem white, to explain that the real picture is the negative and the positive only an optical illusion.

The empire was his baby, as it had been Disraeli's. He admitted errors, saying all men were fallible. Then, without real relevance but with immense effect, he flung the stone of a statistic into the still, waiting pool of Jingo Imperial Patriotism.

He said the number of colonials now helping the mother country exceeded Wellington's total forces at Waterloo and almost equaled in numbers the men sent to the Crimea.

Waterloo kept bobbing up. Lord Roberts had earlier referred to the same figures in a different way. The battle was won on the playing fields of Eton. That was according to the Duke of Wellington. But Waterloo was still a magic mood-bringing word in England and he went on about the colonials:

". . . and these peoples shortly—very shortly as time is measured in history—about to become great and populous nations, now for the first time claim their share in the duties and responsibilities as well as the privileges of Empire. . . . You are the trustees: they look to you as holding the leadership of your race. . . . We are finding out the weak spots in our armour and trying to remedy them; we are finding out the infinite potential resources of the Empire; and we are advancing steadily, if slowly, to the realization of that great federation of our race which will inevitably make for peace and liberty and justice."

Verdomde Kamerlane, as the Boers called him, had pulled it off again. On the division the Government received 352 votes, the Opposition 139, in spite of Lloyd George's dynamic attacks. But this little Welshman had now left obscurity behind him. The spotlight was not going to leave him till he died.

Some of the points he made were sharply barbed. In attacking a statement of Chamberlain, who had spoken of the Transvaal as "the country we created," Lloyd George replied, "In the beginning Joseph Chamberlain created heaven and earth—including the Transvaal . . ."

His most bitter attacks were against the Rand mineowners. "Look," he said, "it is simply a matter of pounds, shillings, and pence. And they, the Uitlanders who have caused all the trouble, are leaving other people to get them out of it, while they lounge in Cape Town hotels such as the Mount Nelson, often called 'The Helots' Rest,' the Queens and the Grand. . . ."

Lloyd George said, and he was probably right, that, given time, the moderate Boers would have ousted Kruger, and then he dramatically cried, "Where are those moderates now? Now they are in the field." He answered his own question. "They are Boer generals now: Joubert, Schalk Burger, Lukas Meyer, Louis Botha, De la Rey, and even President Steyn."

England worshiped Mammon and served God and the Queen. Her heroes were J. B. Robinson with his gold, Carnegie with his steel, Rockefeller with his oil, Pierpont Morgan with his railroads, and, above all, Cecil Rhodes with his diamonds, the man who, till the fiasco of the Jameson Raid, had seemed to have half Africa in his pocket. His dream of a railway from the Cape to Cairo fired the imagination of everyone, from peer to cabdriver.

Against this drive to empire was set the Little Englander pro-Boer sentiment of the Liberals. It was about as effective as a water pistol. England wanted a government that was conservative, strong, and stable. The Liberals were none of these things. The feeling of the country was imperialist and all classes joined in the fight to silence Labour and reduce the Liberals to impotence. The man on the white horse was Joseph Chamberlain, who, with an orchid still in his buttonhole, was the Colonial Minister.

In Cape Town, Diana Darnley, to whom the war meant very little beyond the company of men, was looking at the letter in her hand. She had just taken it out of a drawer to read it once more.

She was smiling to herself. Men were quite extraordinary. Turnbull must really like that little tart.

The letter was from Fanny Hantock, Lady Hantock of Hawley in Sussex. It began:

Dear Di,

"I wonder if in South Africa you have run across a Captain Turnbull of the 2nd. I hear he is keeping a girl he got out of a brothel in an establishment in St. John's

Wood. I got this from my French maid, Marie, whom you will remember, and whose information is usually accurate. She got it from this woman's maid, another French girl called Celeste. These girls meet as you know and exchange gossip of all kinds, but this seems authentic and Marie is astonished at the scale of the establishment. A butler, maid, cook, scullery maid, coachman, a boy, and God knows what else. *Ce capitaine*, as she puts it, appears to be very rich and ought to be worth some attention if he is personable.

"By the way, forgive me for not commiserating with your great loss, but I always knew how you felt about Charles, so really think you are well out of something you should, with your looks, never have got into. Still, an attractive widow with no children and some fortune—the relict of a V.C.—should have no great difficulties. But for God's sake, if you can't be good, which I doubt, knowing your temperament as I know my own, please try to be careful. For the likes of us, dearie, men are an unfortunate necessity, but we must never let them know it. How I wish I was with you. I may manage it yet, if I can find some hospital unit I can join where they do not expect me to work. The dear Duchess is, I think, about to raise the kind of unit that would appeal to me, and even to you. It is to deal with our convalescent officers only. After all, they have to go somewhere, have to be taken care of by someone, and the uniforms are very fetching—pale gray with gray suède shoes and gray silk stockings, and gray does suit us both.

"England is quite denuded of men and we are alone here—roses that there is no one to pluck or even smell. My dear, I often envy you. Alone, free, and not too badly off, in a world of handsome officers starved for what you are so well equipped to give them. I will amplify that into what we both are etc. etc. with dots and asterisks in the fashion of our best lady novelists. . . ."

The letter went driveling on, page after page of it. But Fanny was a pretty thing, hot as they came, but very careful. Modest to the point of prissiness, with downcast eyes and restrained movements and who, if she got the chance and was sure she was safe, would fling herself upon a man like a small panther; desperate for fear of detection, she demanded satisfaction in the shortest possible time. This was not surprising, as her husband, Sir James, was a man of sixty-five, worn out by his debaucheries years before he had married her out of the schoolroom. Not that there was any vice in Fanny. She was a good girl who would have made the right man a good wife. James Hantock had not even been able to get an heir with her and her two children were by other men, something he knew but glossed over, with brags of his own potency. Diana was pretty sure he had thrown her into the arms of the fathers of these children, guests in his house, in order to get the heirs he needed to carry on his ancient name.

Once again it occurred to her that pedigrees were nonsense unless traced through the female line. Only a woman knew the father of her children and the only pedigrees worth a damn were those of blood horses because the mares were always watched. Turks and Arabs might know their sons, but this was seldom certain outside of the Orient.

But just fancy John Turnbull being such a fool. Being taken in by a little whore, tricked by her into setting her up. Why she'd bet a thousand to one that the moment his back was turned she had betrayed him. Common women were not to be trusted, particularly those with that kind of experience. No one knew better than she did that a girl accustomed to men had to have them. Elsie apparently was her name. And who had ever heard of a girl called Elsie who was not a servant?

It was absurd that her pulling John's leg about this *faux pas* of his should have caused a quarrel. She lit a cigarette and walked up and down her bedroom, irritable and quite unable to sleep. That was what war did to men; it brutalized them. They lost their niceness.

She wondered what Wanthope was doing and when she would see him. There were things that were more important than what she called *ces minutes d'amour*. There were money, a title, and a position in society that would make her the envy of all her friends. She stubbed out her cigarette and went to bed as the sky over the trees in the garden paled in the coming dawn.

On her table was a copy of *The Illustrated London News,* with a drawing by Caton-Woodville, its caption

—"An Ancient Custom of War—Saluting the Wounded."
An officer was saluting, the men standing at the present
as the stretchers were carried by.

In the northern Cape men were dying, the new dead
scarce cold in their graves. Jackals, sniffing blood, trotted
over silent battlefields in the dawn that Diana had been
looking at out of the window of her hotel.

Later, as the sun came up, the air warmed and the
vultures that had been sunning themselves rose from the
trees with lazy wings and swam upward, ever upward,
till out of sight of man they circled, watching for death
below.

CHAPTER 31

KIMBERLEY

TURNBULL had been transferred to Roberts' staff at Colonel Henderson's request. A man who knew the Transvaal
and could speak Dutch was invaluable.

Returning to the Mount Nelson, he worked with the
rest on the details of the new plan of attack. The nights
he had spent with the widowed Diana, hating himself
and hating her, so much so that he broke with her in a
scene that was made no less bitter by the fact that the
words they exchanged were whispered, and he was delighted to entrain for the front. But how in God's name
had the Elsie story come out? What had really infuriated
him was the way she had made it sound—cheap.

The British camps dotted along the Western Railway
were filled with men and materials of war. Ramdam was
the first objective, and the last water. The Riet River
would have to be crossed before they reached the Modder.

Like a python uncoiling to strike, the army moved off.
French left his tents standing to deceive any Boers who
might be watching, and reached the Riet with both men
and horses exhausted by a long march in the grueling
heat and a brush with De Wet's commando.

An English cavalry horse carried about twenty stone
(two hundred eighty pounds). The weight was made up
by the trooper, saddlery, saber, carbine, an extra bandoleer of ammunition worn around the horse's neck, nose
bag, heel rope, two spare shoes in a leather frog, a blanket,
saddlecloth, a rolled blanket, and cavalry cloak. The
horses were large, unaccustomed to heat, and required
at least five pounds of oats a day to be fit for work.
As there were no oats or other supplies, French rested
his cavalry, waiting for the wagon train to come up and
hoping to make an early start over the twenty-five miles
of waterless veld that separated him from the Modder.
But, owing to the usual mix-up, the transport columns
did not get away till next day, by which time Roberts
had arrived with Turnbull and the rest of his staff.

They watched French's six thousand horsemen move off
into the burning near-desert scrub with their ammunition
wagons, medical units, forty-two guns, and a cable cart
that unwound its spool of wire behind them.

De Wet, hidden in a nearby hill, also observed the start
and sent a mounted messenger to Cronje with the news,
his own telegraph having been cut.

As French approached the Modder he swung half left
and confused the Boers by making them think he intended
to cross the river at a ford on the right, where they prepared to resist him.

The pace was killing. The horses had no water. Those
pulling the guns and vehicles suffered the most. To add to
their troubles, the veld was set alight by a match dropped
by a trooper and the telegraph wire that led back to
Roberts was burned.

At last, when the green banks of the river came into
sight, French wheeled and charged for the other drift,
putting the Boers there to flight and capturing their supplies. The British crossed, occupied defensive positions on
the *kopjes*, and led their horses down to the muddy water
for a desperately needed drink. Five hundred horses were
either dead or foundered.

French had succeeded in the first part of his mission.
Behind him the army was stretched out like a sagging
string as it marched through clouds of dust, with sand up
to the axles of the transport wagons. To get the naval

guns across the Modder, four hundred men were needed as well as double spans of oxen.

Though his objective was Kimberley, French could not leave the Modder till enough infantry came up to hold it. But in spite of a forced march of twenty-four miles in twenty-four hours, the lead division did not reach the river for two days.

Cronje now for the first time realized his danger. In spite of the distance from rail, not only cavalry but infantry as well were marching around his flank not ten miles away. He did not abandon his carefully thought-out defense works, being reluctant to leave them or trek with the great convoy of wagons and civilians, women and children who had flocked to his laagers. He withdrew his head laager to the north of Jacobsdal, leaving the wounded there, his own and the captured British, in the care of the German doctors, and confronted French with a skeleton force of four hundred burghers.

As soon as the infantry were entrenched on the Modder, French set out for the twenty-mile ride into Kimberley.

The British were immediately shelled by the two guns Cronje had sent with his men. They were soon silenced by French's horse artillery thirteen-pounders. The Boers remained spread out along the ridges that dominated a valley two miles long. It narrowed at the far end into a bottleneck surmounted by another low ridge. If he broke through, French would have Kimberley in his hands.

The cavalry general made up his mind and with the 6th Infantry Division behind him as spectators ordered the last great charge in the history of war. The 9th and 16th Lancers were the first into the valley, charging in the true Light Brigade Balaclava tradition. Guns to the right of them, guns to the left of them, into the valley of death rode the six thousand. They galloped forward; twenty-four thousand steel-shod hoofs sent up great clouds of dust into which the Boers poured their fire. Wave after wave of horsemen followed, their red and white pennants flying, lances poised, sabers bare, flashing silver through the cloud of dust. Behind them the horse gunners were firing over their heads, the scream of their shells adding to the noise of the Boers' rifles, the shouts of the charging horsemen, and the thunder of pounding hoofs.

The extended formation of the light cavalry and the dust made good marksmanship impossible. All the Boers, and watching British infantry, could see was an occasional riderless horse galloping on the fringe of the dust cloud. Only when they reached the ridge in closer formation, now compressed by the topography of the land, riding almost knee to knee, did the Boers really see what they were up against—thousands of wild-eyed, sweating, shouting troopers armed with flashing steel and almost bolting horses were upon them. They broke at once and ran, to fall, hacked beneath the hussars' sabers or spitted on the lancers' silver lance heads.

The terror of the cavalry at Elandslaagte had not been forgotten and the knowledge of what this break-through meant to their line spread panic like a contagion among the Boers, each carrying it, as if it were the plague, wherever he went.

The sword of a cavalryman was used in two ways—with the blade, to hack and cut, or with the point, using it like a lance, the trooper leaning forward with his arm stretched out and the weapon's point beyond his charger's nose. With both lance and saber used in this fashion it was the momentum—the horse's speed—that drove the steel into the flesh and, once engaged, the right hand, holding the sword or lance, was allowed to swing back and the same momentum that had driven it in, the speed of the galloping horse, pulled it out as the trooper swept past his victim, leaving him on the ground behind.

Away to Cronje's left Methuen had unleased a bombardment on the Magersfontein range and was occupying the Boer main force, which, having got news of the cavalry charge, was melting away like butter in the sun.

French was through. Kimberley lay before him. But he was not able to advance. The besieged town could not believe that relief had come at last, and thought it was a Boer trick. It was some hours before he could persuade the defenders of the town that the mass of horsemen they saw on the horizon was their own.

It was not till late in the afternoon that the first patrol, made up of Australian irregular horse, rode in to be welcomed by the inhabitants, who ran cheering from all sides.

The situation at Kimberley had been a queer one. Kekewich had been in command of the town, but Cecil Rhodes, who regarded himself as the owner and creator of the Diamond City, fought him all the way.

When Kekewich rode out to meet French, he took a wrong turn, missed him, and returned to find Rhodes entertaining him at his own house, where he refused to allow Kekewich to meet his rescuer for more than a few minutes, and shouted, "This is my house . . . You shan't see French . . . Get out! . . . "

It was late evening when French had ridden in. A squat figure with an awkward seat on a horse for a cavalryman, a dragoon, and an Irishman at that. He rode quietly, his face the impassive mask that was the accepted military fashion of the day. But he had pulled it off. Kimberley was relieved at last and he had done it.

That was the news he flashed to London.

"Kimberley has been relieved."

The four-month siege, which had cost fifteen hundred lives among both white people and natives from wounds and disease, was over.

In the cavalry charge the British suffered only nineteen casualties, two killed and seventeen wounded.

The forward march of Roberts' army began with the crossing of the Riet and Modder rivers. Not at their confluence, but where they were separated by twenty-five miles of bare, burned-up plain. Cronje had not opposed this movement, having no idea that he would be attacked from his left flank till French seized the drifts on the Riet and Modder.

But the British now had a serious setback unknown to French. Behind him some of the infantry had wheeled toward Jacobsdal and had occupied it after some fighting.

Still farther back behind the infantry came the transport column of a hundred seventy wagons. The leading sections of this great "supply bank" were just crossing the Riet, covered by a small escort, when De Wet appeared out of nowhere with a thousand men at his back As soon as the British saw him, the draft oxen were driven under the riverbank for shelter and a breastwork was built of oat sacks, biscuit cases, and boxes of bully beef. For a time the escort held the Boers off. Then they tried to get the oxen into safety. The Boers shelled them and they stampeded, together with their native drivers. Sixteen hundred oxen were lost and the wagons of food and forage that were desperately needed immobilized at the drift.

Speed was essential to Roberts if Bloemfontein, the capital of the Free State, were to be reached. He sent for his Service Corps commander and asked what stores they had left. Only half rations, was the answer.

The old general, still neat as a pin, paced up and down for a few minutes, then said, "I'll do it. I think the men will do it for me." This was Bobs talking, the man for whom the troops would do anything. Wagons were commandeered, Red Cross vehicles stripped of their insignia, and the hauling of supplies from the nearest point on the railway to Jacobsdal was begun.

Roberts' greatest fear was that Cronje would attack his long and defenseless line of communication. But he need not have worried. Cronje was a broken man. Gripped by a complete paralysis of will, he sat in his tent reading his Bible in utter dejection, while his wife stroked his head. Boer after Boer came in to plead action, begging him to move before the British pincers closed.

Hours passed before he decided what to do. French was to the north of him; Methuen was to the south. The west was open but a desert, bare of grazing and without water, to which he could not commit his women and children. The east was the only hope.

By midnight he was moving. Five thousand men, many with their families, four hundred wagons, and several thousand loose horses and cattle.

The fog of war now enveloped both armies. Roberts was uncertain of Cronje's position. Cronje, unaware of Roberts' intentions, got a fair distance away and formed a laager near the river.

French, who knew nothing about Cronje's breakthrough, was trying to round up the Boers who had been besieging Kimberley. He went after them but was forced back by lack of water for his again exhausted horses. All he could do was to turn his guns onto the Boers, but a dust storm sprang up and under its cover the Boers slipped away.

The relief of Kimberley had been an achievement, but the Boer force that had invested it had not been beaten or even engaged. It was still intact.

For Roberts everything depended on speed. Cronje must be caught, and he ordered French to head him off and pin him down till the infantry could catch up.

But the cavalry was in a desperate state. They had been in continuous action for six days, fighting over country that was all but waterless. Many of the horses had been in poor condition when the action began, being remounts that were not fully recovered from their sea trip from the Argentine or Australia. Many had been overloaded, and many of the men, little more than recruits themselves, were poor horse masters. An officer wrote, "I had a horse parade and there were only twenty-eight horses that could raise a trot. A week ago I commanded the best mounted regiment in the British Army."

As a result, when Roberts' orders reached French, only twelve hundred sound horses could be found in all the cavalry to attempt this thirty-mile dash over the veld. French rested his horses for a few hours and then set off with two batteries of field guns, to cut off a force of five thousand desperate Boers fighting for their lives, their freedom, and the women and children they had in their convoy.

In addition, though French did not know it, Ferreira, with a force several hundred stronger than his own, lay across his path.

Meanwhile Cronje plodded on toward the rising sun. He did not hurry. He did not know that the British infantry was making forced marches through the night in his pursuit. He thought he had only to keep moving to outdistance all pursuit.

Then at noon, after passing a hill on the north bank of the Modder known as Paardeberg, he began to cross it to reach the Bloemfontein road. The leading wagons were on their way down a slope toward the ford. His men and their families were resting under the shade trees on the bank and preparing to eat their midday meal. No scene could have been more peaceful. The English were a long way behind. Bloemfontein and safety lay only a few days' march away.

Suddenly the quiet was shattered by a salvo of bursting

shells. Hundreds of men, women, and children ran to take cover under the bank. Oxen bolted, wagons were upset.

But Cronje sent out no patrols, no scouts. No one even attempted to discover the size of the force that was attacking them. Cronje and his five thousand men were paralyzed by this surprise. They did not even collect their oxen or get their wagons over the river.

French was attacking them. His twelve hundred horses were now really finished, and his position desperate. The Boers outnumbered him four to one. He was safe only as long as they did not attack or Ferreira's force did not come up and take him in the rear.

For hours he searched the horizon. Hot hour succeeded hot hour, but he saw no sign of the dust he sought in the west. Then at last he saw it. Kitchener had driven his infantry in a march of thirty miles in twenty-four hours, much of it through scorching heat. The men were exhausted, beat, their lips cracked, their mouths parched. They had only had their iron emergency rations to eat, but they had arrived. Cronje was cornered.

As darkness fell Kitchener, his two ADCs, and Captain John Turnbull lay down to sleep. Tomorrow was going to be a busy day.

But sleep would not come to Turnbull. He was too tired, too exhausted by the march. He had led his horse a great part of the way, partly to save him and partly out of shame. How could he ride when the exhausted infantry, laden with rifles, packs, ammunition, water bottles, side arms, and entrenching tools, slogged through the sand? They staggered as if drunk. Their eyes were almost closed, bloodshot with glare, glazed with lack of sleep. Some fell asleep between one step and another, and came down. Men helped their comrades, taking their arms, carrying their rifles. He had seen one man with three rifles. Their endurance was unbelievable. A halt of ten minutes in the hour was all they had. Then they were driven on. "Fall in . . . Stand up . . . Get up there . . ." the color sergeants shouted. Men of iron.

He had marched beside Kitchener. Kitchener had not dismounted. He rode up and down the column driving the men, forcing the pace. Now he knew what a forced march was.

Then there was French's charge. What a sight that had been. How lucky he was to have been with the 6th Division and seen it. How he had longed to join it. It had been a cavalryman's dream, a mass charge of light cavalry and the 2nd had missed it.

But that was not all. There were women in it. His Elsa seemed very close, perhaps because of her brothers, who might be fighting here. And Elsie, and that bitch Diana. How shocking it was that a woman should have such power over men. A Circe.

The girl in white with the red parasol on Spion Kop . . . he could not get her out of his head; and the story he had got from one of the doctors about a Boer girl in man's clothes having been killed by a bayonet thrust in the last phase of the battle at Spion Kop. Pregnant, too, the doctor said. . . .

It was not easy to sleep with so much on his mind.

In the Boer laager the commandants were urging Cronje to break out before the British could surround him. But he refused. Too many of his men were dismounted, having lost their horses through scarcity of feed. A break-through would mean abandoning the wagons that were the private property, almost the only capital, of the burghers. He sent to Bloemfontein for help. Ferreira had fifteen hundred men to the north and De Wet was closing in with as many from the south. They would stand and fight.

One aspect of the situation had occurred to no one. Lord Roberts had caught a cold and was laid up in Jacobsdal. Lord Kitchener was in command. This was going to make a big difference to everyone, Boer and Briton alike.

CHAPTER 32

BURIED TREASURE

AT GROENPLAAS, Catalina van der Berg was sitting on the stoep staring at nothing with her sons' letters on her lap. They were good boys and wrote when they could. They had been in action again. They were well. Servas had been wounded, but it was nothing to worry about. Their horses were well. As if she gave a damn about the horses. Her sons had been exposed to fire. They had fought in victorious battles, but she was without pride in their achievements, only sad. Sadder than ever now, because the new commanders Roberts and Kitchener had arrived in Africa. They were much more able men than Buller.

Klaas was before her. She had not seen him come.

"There is more news from the Baasies?" he said. "They are well?"

"They are well, Klaas, from their last letters, and their horses are well, but my heart is sore. Baas Prinsloo has been killed and others of their section." How was she going to break the news to Martha?

"My heart is sore also, *mevrou*," Klaas said. "The witch doctor has thrown the bones again and here is his advice. These are his words: 'When the enemy approaches drive the cattle out of the kraals, hide them in the bush so that when the storm passes something will be left.' And this is how I interpret his words. It is in my heart that the old Baas left the *mevrou* some gold."

"*Ja,* Klaas, I have five hundred golden sovereigns."

"*Mevrou,* I have a plan. If the storm comes let us hide the oxen. Let us bury the gold beneath the great stone in the hearth."

"That is the first place anyone would look."

"*Ja,* but this his how we will do it. I alone will dig. We will dig deep and bury the gold in a small box. We will then cover that with soil which we shall wet and tamp down. Then we will put in an iron box I have found that I will lock and break open with a crowbar. This we will bury with untamped soil so that if they come it will look as if the money was already taken.

"You can say you did it, spent the gold, and threw the box back into the hole. For who would think that there would be two boxes? Also we must be careful not to mix the soil, for deep where we plant the real box is the sub-soil that is yellow, whereas the top is red. Is this not a good plan? For should the worst occur the oxen will be safe in their lower kraal and the one that is found will be empty."

"I will think about it," Catalina said.

"I will come tonight when it is dark and the servants sleep. I will bring a buck sail on which to put the earth, a pick, a spade, a bucket for water and the box, which I have already broken open. The other box in which we will put the gold is in the Baas's office beneath his desk." Without another word he left her.

Catalina did not go to bed. She sat up thinking of what Klaas had said. She did not even know if he had seen the old witch doctor. The ways of a native mind were devious. What she did know was that, doctor or no doctor, Klaas thought the tide was turning against the Boers. These simple Africans had a certain prescience about great events. They got news that no one else received, passed mouth to mouth across vast distances, gossiped about what they had seen and heard, and with amazing ability fitted it all into a composite pattern, a patchwork design that was often near the truth.

She thought of the day Klaas had brought the witch doctor to her. It had been before the war began, less than a year ago, but now it seemed a lifetime. An old, very dirty man, dressed in castoff European clothes. His face had been wrinkled, shriveled like an old shoe that has been thrown out on the veld, but his eyes were bright as wet brown stones, cold as the eyes of a cobra.

Before she had said a word, he said, "The lady wishes to know the future." It had been a winter day, very cold and bright.

"I do," she said. "I will pay you well."

"The lady is sure?" he said, opening the little rawhide bag he carried. "I can only tell the truth," he said. "If you are to die tomorrow I will tell you."

"Tell me," she said.

Taking up the bones in his hand and breathing life into them, he had cast them into the dirt at her feet. He stared at them for a full minute. Then he looked up at her. "The lady is sure?" he asked.

"I am sure, Doctor."

He looked at the bones again and closed his eyes. "I see sorrow," he said. "*Ja*, like the shadow of a vulture's wings over you and the land. I see horses. Many horses.

I hear guns. I see blood and smoke and fire and death. Many men will die, and beasts too. At the end nothing will be the same." He had waved his hand at the house and the stables, embracing everything in his gesture.

Looking back now, she was not surprised at what he had said. No one needed bones to foretell the future of the republic, and a Kaffir witch doctor knew everything. House servants told him what they heard. There was a grapevine—she wondered now why she had told Klaas she would see him. But there was no doubt that things were going badly for the Boers. Every day, even as she sat here, ships were on the sea bringing reinforcements—from England, from India, from Canada, from Australia and New Zealand. The thought of these colonial troops frightened her, for they too were farmers, men of the veld, though a different veld.

It was evident that if Klaas did not actually expect the worst he was preparing for it. Petrus must have foreseen some such eventuality, for he had always kept five hundred pounds in gold ready for an emergency and had told her many times it was not to be touched except in the direst need.

She seemed to feel him at her side, a warm ghost. The ghost of her dead love, of the man who had made a woman of her and given her his sons. Sons of their father, indeed, who would, if they lived, become men as fine as he. She thought he seemed satisfied with what she had done, satisfied that she had done her best with the fine material he had left her—these two fruits of her womb. Perhaps he watched over them too. Perhaps this man Moolman of whom they wrote had been sent by their father, by God, to replace him.

She found herself crying softly but without unhappiness. The tears just came oozing out of her eyes as the sap might ooze out of a tree trunk, bringing relief to a tension that had become unbearable.

Her mind was now a blank, leafing through the past as if it was a book of pictures. Page after page of happiness that had never died, living always in her heart, living on, even growing as if it was a plant, sending out searching rootlets, hairs into the earth of the distant past. The hours went by as she relived the happy, carefree days of her girlhood, of Petrus's courtship, of their marriage, of their love. It was all so clear, as if it was yesterday, not lost over the horizon of the years, but here, fresh and fragrant. His burning eyes, his hands so tender upon her young flesh. His voice muted with passion. Oh Petrus, she thought, oh Petrus, how lucky I am to have known such a man as you. In her mind she used "known" in both its senses—the usual one and that of the Bible in which a man who loves a woman knows her, has knowledge of her and she of him. The secret knowledge of the flesh, which, by the sacrament of marriage, is joined to a spiritual knowledge whereby the two who are one flesh become also of one mind and spirit. Many women, married though they might be, had never had this. And it was this that had held her widowed, almost again virgin in her mind, as she lived out the lonely days that were far from lonely in her heart and memory.

She thought about love. The love of man and the love of animals. A girl living on a farm knew about the brutal, terrible love of animals. She had been six when she first saw a stallion grasp a mare's neck with his teeth and serve her. In her mind she could still hear the mare's hoofs as she kicked against the stallion's chest. She had been white. He had been dark brown, almost black. It had all been very symbolic somehow, and never forgotten. Even as she watched she had known that she had seen all this before, with bulls and cows, too. But never so close, never involved in it as a person. What fools people were not to know that a child of six was a person. What a greater fool she had been not to know that a boy of sixteen was a man.

But the big brown horse had gone on, undeterred by the kicks, like a man when a girl has slapped his face. If she did not want him she would never let him get near enough to be slapped. That was the price of a kiss. She remembered how she had slapped Petrus and how he had laughed at her and pulled her to him.

The horse had gone on, half beside the mare, half upon her back, his teeth gripping her neck just above the withers. His mane and tail were flying, his ears laid back, his nostrils a flaming red, his eyes showing a rim of white, and then the mare stood still for him. Right there in front of her. The great dark horse upon the white mare, thrusting at her, his forelegs grasping her, his crest raised, his loins arched. For her, for the child watching, the world stood still. This was a moment of revelation, the biggest in her life so far. Even now she doubted if she had ever seen anything greater or more magnificent than these two horses, blowing, stamping, sweating, above her; silhouetted, out of focus, against the bright African sky. They were so close she could watch the belly of the mare expand and contract as she breathed, and gasped, sagging under the stallion's weight. She could see his near foreleg almost at eye level—the horn of his hoof, the little ring of white hairs on his coronet, spilling over onto it. The great knees, forearms, chest, and the terrifying snorting, bare-toothed, eye-blazing head. She could see the stallion tushes—the canines. His eye—enormous, glazed, at once blank and furious. The long forelock dangling, the mane, the white star on his forehead, and the immense pulling and driving thrust of his loins. The toes of his hind feet cutting into the soil, almost hidden in it. His black tail a whirling flag.

The stamping of the hoofs, the snorts, the foaming saliva dripping from the stallion's lips, the blood on the white mare's neck where he had bitten her, and held her to love. The smell of horse sweat. All this in her nose, her eyes, her ears. All running right through her, from her bare feet upward as the ground shook beneath the impact of this tremendous act. For laugh as one will, call it what one will, this is an act of God, an act of creation, and never more so than when it is performed by a black blood horse and a snow-white mare within five yards of a girl of six.

She knew they could have killed her. She knew they did not see her. These horses lost themselves, became invisible, unexisting, when so engaged. No longer horses, as lions, buck, dogs, and men cease at these times to be what they are, becoming mechanisms, engaged in forging the future, shooting their arrows of sperm into the womb of time.

There they were, trampling, sweating, swaying, still enormous against the sky, till they broke apart, the horse coming down on his forelegs with a thud, almost falling with the exhaustion of his effort. The white mare slipping from between the elbows of his forelegs and running lightly on springing pasterns, like a deer, her white tail flying.

The stallion recovered, stood foursquare, his legs ex-

tended, the head on his crested neck raised high to neigh—
to give his stallion scream of triumph and of challenge.
Then with a snort he had trotted off, following the mare.

A moment later they were grazing, heads down, side by
side, their long tails, white and black, flicking the flies
from their quarters.

That was what it was like, this act of love. How well she
remembered it as a woman. The rising excitement, like a
little wind that rustles, raises, and turns up the leaves of
the trees as though they were skirts. The storm that bends
them till they must break, but they don't break, and then
the calm. The utter stillness, when everything is as it was
before, only more so, for now there are no underlying possibilities. For a while there can be no more storms . . . for
a little while . . .

Of course she had known none of this as a child. She
had only felt it. The great event had been etched on the
copper of her soul. Only later, much later, had her own
life supplied the ink, little by little, till at last the picture
had been complete. It seemed to get more complete as
time went on, and more details were added, till this event,
this stallion and mare act, seemed to embody all life, all
its spirit, or at least its drive. Had she been younger, it
would have meant nothing, she would have run away,
frightened at the noise, at the thunder of pursuing hoofs.
Older, she might have turned away, having learned that
such things were not nice to watch. It was true that birth
was not nice, nor love in this aspect, nor death, nor life
itself. Very little was nice in life and that little utterly without value.

Never, it seemed to her, had she thought more deeply
about that day, that day more than forty years ago. She
only thought about it now to turn her heart and mind away
from Boetie, from the memory of his back, and the brown
quarters and black tail of the bay pony that Captain
Turnbull had given him. Her boys riding away with guns
in their hands. Her baby with a real gun, not a toy.

It would be good if I could really cry, she thought.
But she could not. She had cried for her husband. I was
a girl then, she thought, at least a young woman and full
of water. A young, loving woman is soft and moist, like
a ripe fruit that bleeds its juice if you squeeze it—an

apricot, she thought. And now I am like *mebos,* an apricot
sun-dried and salted. She should have put some *mebos*
in her boys' saddlebags. How could she have forgotten?
What a time to think of it—months after they had gone.

How wonderful it would be, she thought, to be young
and full of water, of juice, and be able to cry properly,
to let go in gasping sobs and perhaps to feel life move in
you again. It was terrible to feel no passion. Even her
sorrow was not a passion. A passion is a storm that passes.
This was too deep. She was like a dry leaf falling,
twisting down from the tree caught in the wind of
disaster. There was no hope in her, only sorrow for
herself, her sons, her land, her old President. "Pray
for me," Oom Paul had said. She would pray. She would
pray for all the world, even for the English.

Her dreams and memories were broken by Klaas's soft
knock at her window. She went to the kitchen door to
let him in and lit the stable lantern that stood on the
shelf ready for use if it was needed in the night. She
turned the wick down to a candle glimmer and led the
old man into the sitting room. He made three trips to
bring in all he needed. Everything had been piled by the
back door before he knocked. A pick, a shovel, a buck sail,
a crowbar, a bucket, two short round sections of log to
use as rollers when they moved the great hearthstone, and
the iron box that he had broken open.

First he spread the buck sail, then, using one of the
logs as a fulcrum, prized up the stone and slipped the
other log beneath it. Working from the back, he raised
the stone again and held it while Catalina inserted the
second roller. The stone was now moved forward, away
from the hearth where it had lain since Petrus's father
had built the house.

Then Klaas began to dig. He was stripped to the waist,
his body black, invisible in the light of the tiny flame
except for the sweat that shone like molten gold as it
ran down his lean flanks.

There was four feet of good red topsoil. Then came the
yellow, gravelly subsoil. He went down six feet. He was
filling the bucket with earth and Catalina was drawing it
up on the riem he had worn around his waist. She piled

it carefully in a separate heap. He went down eight feet—two feet more.

"The gold," he said, and Catalina brought her husband's small steel safe. Standing on top of it, Klaas took her hand and she dragged him out. He shoveled in two feet of the subsoil.

"Water next," he said. They poured buckets of water into the grave in which the gold was buried. Her husband had put the gold into that safe with his hands, the hands that had loved her. It was as if a part of him were being interred.

Dropping back into the pit, Klaas tramped the wet soil down and then rammed it with a log Catalina brought from the heap of firewood in the yard.

The broken ironbound box was now put in, and the rest of the subsoil packed around it. The red soil followed the yellow and was tramped down. The hearthstone was rolled back. The soil left over was now carried out by Klaas, bucket by bucket. When the buck sail and other gear were removed, Catalina swept up the floor of her sitting room.

"*Mevrou,*" Klaas said, "wife of my master, we can do no more. The oxen are safe in their hidden kraal. The trap is laid. The decoy prepared." With that he knelt and kissed her hand. "The Baas was a good baas," he said, "and I who loved him am a good servant who has never betrayed his trust."

Jan Bothma was one of the many who had left the war. He was tired of it. The war was lost and there was no point in continuing to fight. Besides, he had been wounded again, very slightly, it is true, but no one would have thought it to look at the bloody bandage about his head. But a nicked ear bleeds very freely and he had made the most of it.

He had reached Pretoria in the early morning, given his horse a good feed, slept all day, and, the moon being full, had decided to ride to Groenplaas by night. He rode over the old familiar road thinking how good it would be to get back. Fighting was for boys like Servas and Boetie, or that hunter Moolman, the hunter of savages who had become a savage himself. He thought of the

Beyers girl fighting like a wildcat after Jan had gone down, bayoneted. Nel and O'Brien had been killed and he himself had been severely wounded. *Magtig*, how he had bled. It was a wonder he had survived. I am a lucky man, he thought. Another inch and the bullet would have been in my skull.

When he got to the Groenplaas turnoff he struck a match to look at his big nickel watch. It was 3 A.M. He was looking forward to surprising his wife. He glanced at the big house, a lighter patch in the dark trees that surrounded it.

But why was there a glimmer of light from the *voorkamer*? He tied his horse to a branch. He stood well, but so near home the temptation might be too much for him. Rifle in hand—there might be burglars—he crept forward till he reached the walls. Wagter, the big watchdog, growled but, recognizing his scent, did not bark. He came up to put his nose into his hand. So it was not burglars. He looked into the room cautiously, his face shaded by his hands.

Before God what was going on here? There was the old Basuto Klaas digging in the fireplace. The great hearthstone was out, mounted on two logs as rollers. There was a pile of earth on a buck sail and an iron box stood open near it, with the Mevrou van der Berg bending over in front of it.

Gold, he thought. They are burying gold. It amazed him that she would trust that old Basuto rather than a man like himself. Of course he had not been there when her plan was made. She had not even known he was coming. But if he had been there it would have been the same. A Basuto who had been with the Baas when he was killed, who might indeed have killed the Baas himself. He ignored completely Petrus van der Berg's white companion. What Jan Bothma did not want to believe did not exist. He was never confused by facts.

He walked back to his horse slowly. Gold. What a magic word. With gold he could buy a place of his own, be a baas, a master, not a bywoner. He had never in the near forty years of his life even thought of a place of his own. The gap between his present position and that of an independent farmer had been too great. But here was a bridge. Here under his hand was a golden bridge to the gap. He must make a plan. There was plenty of time. What a good thing he had come back. What a good thing he had been wounded. The ways of God were certainly very strange.

CHAPTER 33

THE INTERPRETER

AFTER his wound had been dressed at the main laager, it had been decided to send Servas to Pretoria, where the President was in need of educated English-speaking men for his Intelligence Service. He got there just in time to see the message the President wired to Louis Botha, the new commandant general. It began:

"It seems to me as if your faith and that of your "burghers has been replaced by unbelief. . . ."

It was a long telegram, but it arrived too late, and even if the Boers had had time to halt and read the Bible as he counseled, "Victory is in the hand of the Lord alone and not with the multitude of horses and chariots. . . ." it could have had no effect.

Servas spent his time in Pretoria dictating translations of such English news, dispatches, and newspapers as fell into the Boer hands. Many did, and much of the news was false, the work of Roberts' chief of intelligence, Colonel Henderson, an artist at laying a trail of false information. He sent misleading telegrams to British generals "in clear" for the benefit of the spies who would pass them on to the Boers, and then countermanded the orders in code. He gave secret, off-the-record news to unreliable correspondents, news that was bogus, under the oath of secrecy, knowing they would be unable to resist such a scoop. And as usual in war, there were double spies. True information had to be sifted from the false, the false due to error alone, and human fallibility, from that given out by the enemy with intent to deceive.

Servas, who had been interviewed by the President when he came from the front, found him kindly to such as he, a fighting burgher, but bitter about the cowards, shocked at the lack of faith in God and eventual victory that was spreading through the commandos like a disease. He sat at his desk, his crepe-bound top hat resting on his great brassbound Bible. Adamant, rock solid, savagely blinking his bloodshot eyes. Rock, buffalo, lion, bull. All these came to Servas's mind as he stood first on one foot, then on the other, before this old man, this uncle and father of his people—Oom Paul the Voortrekker.

"Your home is near here, *jong*," the President said. He had a remarkable memory for names and faces. "You are the son of Petrus van der Berg, my godson, whose father was my childhood friend. *Ja*," he said, "those were great days, with all Africa in front of us and the English far behind. But once more they have caught up with us." He banged the table with a gnarled fist that, thumbless, looked like a knobby root. For an instant he had forgotten the boy. Then he turned to him and said, "Your mother was here before the war began. I told her to pray. She is a good woman but a fool to think that the world is round.

"Go and see her, boy. Take a horse from here, and ride over for a few days and let her nurse your wound."

Servas took a quiet gray and rode home with his arm in a sling, a young wounded hero. Older by years in the five months that had passed since he had ridden out with his brother to the wars. He thought of how they had met Moolman on the road. He thought of his mother and his home. What a black month this had been. Ladysmith and Kimberley relieved, and Cronje taken with all his men.

If the English had had a Black Week in December, they had made up for it now. The tide had really turned and the future seemed even darker than the present, with the British getting stronger as the Boers weakened. He thought of what the President had said about men going home on leave. They were entitled to do so, but many chose moments that were inopportune.

At Groenplaas nothing was changed but nothing was the same. As Servas rode into his home he noticed at once that, as he had aged in war, so had the place. It looked the way a man looks who has neglected himself—unshaven, dirty, his hair unbrushed. The life had gone out of the farm.

He sat his horse, looking at the garden, the yards

and building, astonished that deterioration should be so fast. But it had been neglected for a whole summer, a whole growing season, and only the worst of the weeds had been scoffed out.

He saw his mother in the distance but made no move toward her, watching her as if she were a stranger. She moved more slowly, her back was less erect.

It was Wagter the Boer hound that saw him first. He was walking beside his mother. He stopped, raised a front paw, and sniffed the air, then turned, and in a wild gallop made for his master. That was when Catalina first saw her elder son, sitting still as a statue, his arm in a sling, on a gray horse she had never seen before. Where was General? Was he dead? Where in God's name was Boetie? Had he come to tell her he was dead? Was that why he sat so still, staring at her?

She went toward him quickly.

"Boetie?" she said. "Where is Boetie?"

"With the commando, Ma," Servas said, dismounting and putting his good arm around his mother as he kissed her.

How hard and thin he was. All the puppy flesh of young manhood had gone. This was an adult, a man who had seen war, had killed men, and was ready to make one.

"Your wound?" she said.

"It is nothing, and will soon be healed."

"And General?" The black, the son of her husband's horse and therefore a part of him, seemed suddenly very important. If General was well nothing could be wrong.

"Boetie has him, Ma." It was true he had left him with Boetie but that was before the great retreat.

Klaas came running up and clasped him in his arms. "Baasie," he said, "my Baasie." His eyes were full of tears.

Anticipating what he would say next, Servas said, "Baas Boetie is well. He is with the commando."

Klaas led the gray away and Servas entered the house with his mother. It seemed strange and unfamiliar. Perhaps he had grown unaccustomed to houses, to being under a roof. Or perhaps Groenplaas really had changed—perhaps a house, like a woman, needed a man.

There was no dirt here. His mother was too good a housewife for that. But a dying man could be clean and tidy with the shadow of death showing only in the dullness of his eyes. The windows of Groenplaas were shiny, clean, but an invisible shadow lay upon them. Never, even after battle with his friends lying dead, had Servas felt a greater depression. He wished he had not come home. He wished he could go out tonight and sleep rolled in his blanket, his head on his saddle beneath the familiar stars. But he knew he must stay with his mother and cheer her if he could. But there was so little he could say.

His mother picked up the burden of his silence with a basket of woman talk, of small things. Of calves born, of turkeys raised, of peafowl chicks, of the lands and the crops. They had, in spite of everything, a fair crop of standing mealies that they would reap in the fall.

She told him how Bothma had returned and was still bandaged from the terrible head wound he had sustained.

"Wound?" Servas said, laughing. "He was never wounded. All he had was a nick in the ear. It must have healed long ago. Before God, a girl child has a bigger wound when her ears are pierced for rings. I heard this from Boetie, who sent me a letter with the commando news—poor Prinsloo dead, the Beyerses, Nel, and the Irishman. All dead, with Bothma acting the hero."

A peacock gave its wild, eerie scream. Out of the window Servas watched it strutting, its great tail a jeweled fan in the sunlight. Groenplaas was the only place he had ever heard of that had peafowl. His father had given the first pair to his mother as a present soon after they were married. Now one way and another they must have thirty.

That night Catalina washed and bandaged the wound in her son's shoulder. Strange thoughts went through her mind. Of Christ, the man being bandaged. Of Mary Magdalene, of Mary Mother of God, of Servas as a baby being changed. There was some strange affinity between a woman and bandages of fine linen, going back perhaps to the not so long ago when women wove their own from the flax they grew. Women had some strange affinity for wounds, for blood. All their nubile lives they were concerned with it. Each month, each birth. And the blood of men wounded in battle.

The hurt was nothing. A flesh wound that was near healed, but she thought of what it might have been.

Servas rode over the farm. Nothing serious was wrong, but nothing was quite right. He saw Bothma and gave him the news of the commandos.

"I will be back, *meneer*," he said, reverting to the by-woner once more, "once my wound is healed." He touched the bandage that went round and round his head, binding it so that it looked like a big dirty egg.

"Naturally," Servas said, "but you must not hurry. A head wound is serious and must be fully healed before you ride again."

"I know that," Bothma said. "It is my only consolation. What is the good of going back to be a burden on my comrades?"

Later in the evening, as he walked among the violets under the great white-trunked gums, Jacoba Bothma came to him. She was still a handsome woman, more so now than usual, her blue eyes aflame with anger.

"*Meneer*," she said, "it is not I who hold him here. Since I first saw what he calls his wound I have told him to go back. He is no longer my man, though I carry his child in my belly. How was I to know that the man who looked like a bull was nothing but a Kaffir cur? Even my children are ashamed, but they will come out all right, *meneer*, for I have good blood. We also, like Meneer, were *voortrekkers*. But it is in my heart that Frikkie will run away to take his father's place. If he does, *meneer*, and I do not know how to hold him, I have told him to find you. You are the Baas and you must teach him to be a man."

The next day Servas kissed his mother and rode away, his saddlebags full of food she had cooked for him, and *mebos*—sun-dried, sweet, salted apricots. This time she had remembered. A woman gives food to her sons and her body to her man. For Catalina there was only food to give now. A widow's life was all kitchen and no bed.

She watched one ride away where three had ridden before—her two sons and their servant. Her heart cried out for her Boetie, her baby. But he might have changed too. This man who rode away today was as strange to her as the horse he rode. One day if they were ever together again she would have to get to know him. Servas loved her, she knew, but it was the love of a stranger, the hand of a stranger on her waist, the kiss of a stranger on

her cheek. That was what a few months of war could
do to a boy.

At his cottage Bothma had just chopped off the head of
another chicken to get fresh blood for his bandages. He
was now shameless in front of his family. They would never
tell what they had seen, never acknowledge that their
father was a coward. But how could he go back when there
was so much gold nearby? Their hearts would change.
They would bless him yet when they found he had made
their fortune. He owed it to them, to his family, to remain.

CHAPTER 34

NO LADY

A DISCIPLE of Freud might have been puzzled by Elsie,
or, on the other hand, he might have fitted her into some
special category of infantilism, of a nature so primitive
that it was incapable of suffering trauma. It is of course
possible that in the depths of her unconscious some debauched serpent of sexuality swam in the cesspit of her
past. But none of this was apparent on the surface of the
girl's life or in her dreams, which, even when they were
of love, were of a most romantic nature in which her desires were always fulfilled, amid a background of palms,
ferns, roses, singing birds, music, conservatories, playful
kittens, and little naked boys with wings and bows like
the one in the hall at Wilton Crescent.

In Elsie the term "willful forgetting" was exemplified to
its very highest degree. And what she did remember was
always the best of however bad a lot. In fact, looking
back, her life seemed to have been one of continual improvements, culminating in that "Home away from Home"
No. 20. She had been happy there. The girls were nice.
The food good, the rooms comfortable, and the clients
lacking in real vice. Mrs. Fitz and the final drama with
the South American man with the hairy back, Bill's beating and its sequel were all more than blotted out by the
perfection of her life with the captain. A real fairy prince
if ever there was one. Horse and all.

Elsie had no idea of human motivation. She merely responded to kindness when it came her way, avoided pain, and lived from day to day, just filling in time at first, waiting for her captain to come back, and now, looking forward to going to South Africa because she would be nearer to him and was bored with doing nothing in London. Except for the staff of servants at No. 7, Monsieur André, Lady Finch-Haddley, and the servants at Wilton Crescent, she had no friends and knew nobody. She read a great deal now, books that Vincent got from Mudie's Lending Library for her. Mrs. Humphry Ward was her favorite author. She also liked Marie Corelli and stories about Sherlock Holmes. She made Millie read them aloud to her.

She wrote to Turnbull every day and posted what amounted to a diary once a week. She heard from him fairly often, twice a month so far, and with Vincent's help marked where he was on a large-scale map remarkable for its inaccuracy that she had pinned up with thumbtacks on the dining-room wall.

She took walks with Vincent and Queenie, with Celeste and Queenie, Charles and Queenie, and the boy, as they still called Jimmie, and Queenie. But her life had no reality. She was happiest with Lady F.-H., as she called her, whom she regarded with a mixture of admiration, awe, and love. By now she realized there were many kinds of love. Her love for Lady F.-H., for the captain, for Queenie, for Vincent, Celeste, Millie, and the others were all different. The same, but different the way a golden sovereign was different from two half sovereigns, eight half crowns from ten florins or twenty shillings or forty sixpences—all were worth a pound, but each looked different and felt different in your hand.

She visited the stables every day with carrots, apples, lumps of sugar, and was welcomed with snorts, neighs, and stamping hoofs. She was quite unafraid of horses and went into the stalls to pet and handle them, much to Celeste's annoyance, because she often came back stinking of horses—"*Madame pue de cheval*"—and with spots on her dress where they had nuzzled her.

It may have been this interest in horses that made Vincent—after all he had started it with his lessons in breeds and colors—make to her a suggestion when they were out walking one morning.

"I've thought of something, Miss Elsie," he said. "If you are going to South Africa."

"What have you thought of?"

"I'm going to teach you to ride. You like horses, you have a way with them, and I've got it fixed up. A friend of mine runs a manège [he called it manage] and we can use it if we go early. Six o'clock, he says. And we'll have it to ourselves for an hour."

"I'd like that, Vincent."

"Yes, miss, but there's something else. I can't teach you sidesaddle. You"—he hesitated to bring the word out—"you've got to wear breeches, Miss Elsie."

"And what's wrong with that?"

Vincent was appalled that she could not see what was wrong.

"Nobody does, Miss Elsie. Not in all England."

"Then I'll be the first."

"You will. And there's another reason, Miss Elsie. A lady cannot get on or off a horse alone. Suppose you was in a tight corner, miss. If you could only ride sidesaddle and there was no one to put you up you might as well not be able to ride at all."

"We'll get some breeches made, Vincent." She clapped her hands with delight. "We'll go to Savile Row tomorrow."

"You can't do that, miss. You'd have to be measured by a man."

"Why not?" She thought it would be rather fun. She had pretty legs.

"Your . . . your legs, miss. What you wear. Things . . ." he said vaguely, not caring to name them "No, no," he said. "Celeste will do it. She'll write it all down, and I'll spin a yarn about a friend of the captain's, a young boy in Africa, wanting them."

This seemed a splendid idea to Vincent until the cutter looked at the measurements.

"Waist seventeen? You sure that's right?"

"That's right."

"Thighs, calves, length from the crotch to the ankle . . . Funny boy you've got here, Mr. Vincent."

"All right," he said, "you've got me. It's a girl. She wants to dress up in jodhpurs as a joke."

"Not very decent if you'll permit me to say so, but that's your affair. I'll tell you something though, Mr. Vincent. No label. No Tautz label in ladies' breeches. We couldn't have that."

Ten days later the jodhpurs were delivered. And Elsie retired with Celeste to her room to put them on, while Vincent waited, more excited than he would have believed possible, to see them. The shoes had been easy. He had just drawn a line around her foot on a bit of paper.

He could hear the two girls laughing behind the closed door, but at last it opened. And he saw what looked like a very beautiful, long-legged, dark-haired boy in buff jodhpurs, brown shoes, and a white silk shirt. Celeste had pulled Elsie's hair back, platted it, and folded it up against itself, tying it in place with a wide black silk moire ribbon.

Vincent was embarrassed but was not going to show it. The Master should see her like this, he thought. Then he thought, How shocked the Master would be. All he said was, "You'll do, Miss Elsie. You've got the legs to grip a horse."

Next morning the lessons began. Charlie drove her down in the carriage. She wore a long coat that reached to the ground so that her breeches would not show and scandalize the neighbors.

At the manège she took off her coat and Vincent showed her how to mount the quiet old roan mare that was used for beginners, and how to hold the reins. Three days later she was able to canter slowly around the ring with her mare on a leading rein and Vincent, looking very erect and soldierly on a big chestnut horse, beside her.

She took to riding like a duck to water. She was young, she was fearless, she loved horses, trusted Vincent, and did exactly what he told her. The exercise did her good. She went to Hatchard's and with Vincent at her side bought a number of books on horses, horses' training, riding, and hunting. Here was something she could really learn. Not like arithmetic or geography. This was interesting and useful, and Charles, somewhat jealous of Vincent, hired a dogcart and taught her to drive.

It was some time before she dared tell Lady Finch-Haddley about it.

"Learning to ride, are you?" she said. "Who's teaching you, my dear?"

"Vincent is."

"And what does he know about it?"

"He was in the Eighteenth," Elsie said.

"I know, dear, but they don't ride sidesaddle in the cavalry."

"And nor do I," Elsie said.

"What did you say, Elsie?"

"I said I don't ride sidesaddle. I ride astride like a man."

Lady Finch-Haddley was flabbergasted. Then she said, "My God, I always said a girl could do it. We did it as children—bareback—so why did we have to stop later on? Do you know what they said? They said the inside of a woman's thighs were round, not flat like a man's, and they could never grip a horse. Ever fall off?" she asked.

"Not yet, but I expect I shall one day. Vincent says, 'Just tuck your chin into your chest, land on your shoulder, and roll over.' Doesn't sound hard, does it?"

"If a horse falls sidesaddle," Lady Finch-Haddley said, "you don't come clear. You fall with him. It's much more dangerous." She paused and then she said, "Can I come and watch you?"

"Of course," Elsie said, and next day, much to Vincent's consternation, Her Ladyship was there, and before she left had given so much advice and so many orders that Wortly, the owner and Vincent's friend, said, "You'd think she owned the bloody place, wouldn't you? But she knows horses, that old girl does. And so she ought to, come to think of it. She looks rather like one herself."

A month later, at the end of February, when the forsythia was a yellow flame in the park and the grass carpeted with purple, yellow, and white crocuses, the Finch-Haddley Field Hospital, fully equipped, fully staffed, and accompanied by an Irish wolfhound and a flat-coat bitch, sailed from Southhampton on the *Norham Castle*, a big ship of twenty thousand tons.

Vincent was left in charge of the staff at No. 7, with instructions from Elsie that full wages were to be paid and no one was to be sacked. She wanted everything to be just the same when she came back.

"I want to think of it that way, Vincent," she said, "when I'm over there, all that way over the sea with the savages and lions."

The farewells had been tearful and emotional. She had kissed everyone, including Vincent. Everyone had kissed her, including Vincent in a very respectful manner.

Millie had of course wept buckets because she could not both go with Elsie and stay with the other servants at No. 7. She cried all the way to the station while Queenie licked her face.

Lady Finch-Haddley had said she must not go down in the carriage or have Vincent see to her luggage. "We want no talk, my dear. You come in a growler with Millie, who is your maid, and your dog."

It suddenly occurred to Elsie that now, for the first time in her life, there was no one to tell her what to do and that she was responsible not only for herself but for Millie and Queenie too. They didn't want to go to Africa. They just wanted to be with her. It's me that's lugging them off, she thought, and I'll have to look after them.

When the initial fright of responsibility wore off, she thought she might like looking after people. It was a bit like the plants in her little greenhouse. You gave them water and manure and you kept them warm.

By this time they were at Victoria and she told a porter to see to their luggage, while Millie and the dog stared at her, their eyes full of respect, admiration, and love. They knew she was going to take care of them.

In London, Tupper had continued to prosper. War was good for his business. Passions were loosed like dogs and, as always in war, the spirit of licentiousness and debauchery that is present in any great city rose on the tide of patriotism and was given free rein on the grounds of boys being boys and that masculine activity of all kinds should be encouraged at times like this. And what could make a country more worth fighting for than its brothels and its whores?

The export side had gone well too. There were so many ships going to odd places to fetch remounts that several new and profitable markets had been found. Who would

ever have thought of Australia, South Africa, or the
United States before the war?

Dentwhistle had been a great loss. A man of his caliber
and experience was always hard to replace. But no one
was indispensable, and an adequate substitute had been
found. The Rose Cottage incident had worried Mr. Tupper for a while, but thanks to some hints dropped in the
right quarters by Mrs. Fitz the affair had been hushed
up. Certain of her clients in the Government had been
told about the possibility of a scandal in Slough in which
their names might easily appear.

As Mrs. Fitz said: "My dear sir . . . my dear Lord . . .
what could I do under oath in court? The stories," she
said, "were greatly exaggerated." A great deal of nonsense
was talked about the abduction of girls and what the
papers, always sensational, had taken to calling the "white-
slave trade." Of course no one knew better than her distinguished clients at No. 20 that her girls were a happy
lot and always only too pleased to oblige their honorable
friends. But what wouldn't the yellow press make of it?
It might give the liberals just the weapon they needed to
bring the war to an end and disgrace England, discredit
England in the eyes of the world. . . .

Mrs. Fitz, with her mittened hands neatly folded in her
lap, would nod her head wisely. Her dyed auburn curls
would dance as she smiled at whomever she was taking
into her confidence, and in the month that followed the
incident she talked to a lot of very distinguished people
indeed.

There was, of course, a certain amount of bitterness
left in Mr. Tupper's heart. Two girls had got away. His
best man had been found dead—murdered, yet apparently killed by a dog. Rose Cottage, when he put it up for
sale, had not fetched a good price, and Mrs. Fitz had
made the most outrageous demands with which he had
had to comply before he could enlist her help. That she,
an old employee, a woman whose fortune he had made,
should behave like this was a bitter blow to his belief in
personal gratitude and the general probity of mankind.

But he was not a man to cry over spilled milk and,
once his initial rage was spent, he simply made himself
forget the whole thing.

One thing had occurred over the last year or so that

had disturbed him at first but that he later dismissed from his mind as being of no importance. This was the appearance of street urchins, not only in Knightsbridge but even here in the near-country of suburban Dulwich. They were always popping up, here, there, and everywhere, with their caps in their hands, whining, "Give us a copper, guvnor. Give a pore orphan boy a copper, mister."

He supposed the story of his generosity when they first started bothering him had got about. It just showed how dangerous generosity could be. But he was used to them now and even carried a few loose pennies to throw them. One had nearly been run over trying to retrieve a copper from under the hoofs of a carriage and pair. He always threw the money into the road. He liked to watch them dash in and out of the traffic. Little bastards, make them nippy on their feet if it didn't kill them. Then he chided himself for the expression. That was not the way a church-warden spoke or even thought. That was the old Tupper on the way up, not the Mr. Tupper who had arrived.

Things in Yeoman's Row had been going very well since they had got Betty back. Old Joe sat watching her hour after hour. Her disappearance had been too much for him. He had never been the same again. Tom now drove Royal around with the coal and Henry went to the Garden alone. But they were happy and comfortable. The place was clean and neat and the food the best they'd ever eaten. And in spite of the state she had been in when they found her, Betty had recovered most of her looks. Her tiny tip-tilted nose had been too small to break. Her cut and swollen lips had healed and there had been no internal injuries to her lovely body. On Sundays the boys took her out. They took her to Hampstead Heath, to Kensington Gardens, to Kew. During the week if she went out to shop, old Joe with a blackthorn cudgel accompanied her. By God, they all just wished someone would try something, that they did.

For a while they were sure the police were going to take some action. So was the doctor who had taken care of her and become their friend. It was he who said, "This business is being hushed up. There must be some important people in it somewhere."

"Justice!" Tom said. "By God, there's one kind for the rich and another for the likes of us. If that had happened

to the honorable Miss Rich Bitch instead of Betty Norly
there'd have been hell to pay. Questions in the House
. . . That's what there would have been."

But if the law was doing nothing they were doing quite
a lot. The Row boys had found out where Tupper lived
and who he was. They had ridden on the back axle of his
carriage. They had run for miles beside it. Once they
knew the route he took, they had relays waiting for him.
In Dulwich they had found other children ready for a
lark, especially if there was money in it, and Tom Norly
was generous. Coppers always and tanners sometimes.
And the old man, Tupper—the guvnor, as they called him
—always gave them something if they persisted long
enough.

There was now no doubt about the relationship of the
agency, Mrs. Fitz's house, and Tupper's villa in Dulwich.
None at all. The brothers had also found out about the
fruit export and import business. Only partially educated,
but no fools, they began to get the pattern, to put two
and two together and build the structure up into a picture that was pretty near the truth. Betty added details that
tied their suppositions together, and a plan began to form
in their minds, born of an idea given to them by Betty.

"I'm going back," she said one day. "I'm going to answer one of the advertisements put in by the agency for
general servants and housemaids."

"No you're not, my girl," Tom said.

"They don't know me there," Betty said. "I'll answer
and apply and they'll tell me to come back and Mrs. Fitz
will see me. They'll tell her at once, send someone over
perhaps. They don't get girls like me every day." She looked
down at herself appreciatively as if her pretty body had
not given her trouble enough already.

"And . . ." Tom said.

"And we'll have it out," Betty said. "I'll scratch her
bloody eyes out. No I won't," she said. "I'll act surprised.
Say I thought it was a regular servants' agency. Then I'll
say I don't care. If she wants me I'll go to her. I'll say
after what happened to me at the cottage I don't care.
She'll say what about you. What about your brothers?
And I'll say they threw me out when they found I wasn't
a good girl any more."

"You're not to say that, Bets."

"I'll say it," she said, "and she'll believe me because that's the way they think. They think when a dozen men have had a girl one after the other she's finished, broken, and they can do what they like with her. They think she won't go home, if she has a home, and most of them don't, and if she did her folks would throw her out."

"My God!" Tom said. "To think of it!"

"It's going on, Tom," Betty said. "That's why I want to do it. It's going on this very minute here in London. Quite near us perhaps."

"And then?" Tom said.

"Then she'll take me to the cab they always have waiting. I'll have my basket and a bag with all my things. And that's where you come in. As we get into the cab you get in too and then we tell her what she's got to do."

"What's that?"

"Give us a letter that you'll take to Tupper. We're going there, Tom, to Tupper in Dulwich. We'll drive there in a growler and you'll go in with the letter from Mrs. Fitz. While Henry and I sit in the growler waiting. Then you'll call us in. He's never seen you, you know, and he'll think you're a couple of her roughs."

"And then?" Tom said.

"Then," Betty said, "then you hurt him. Oh Tom," she sobbed, "hurt him, hurt him bad."

That was the plan.

A few days later Mrs. Fitz was astonished to get a note brought over by a boy telling her to come over in the morning. It was marked "Urgent."

"I have a very good maid here," Mrs. Humphries said. "She's staying the night and I told her I had a lady whom I was sure she would suit and that she would be over tomorrow."

At ten next morning Mrs. Fitz was at the agency. Mrs. Humphries was all of a flutter when she was shown in.

"My dear," she said, "I've never seen anything better than this. Beautiful," she said, "beautiful. A real redhead. She says she's twenty-three. A lovely figure and lots of style."

"Bring her in."

Mrs. Fitz arranged herself in her most respectable manner, her dark skirt spread out, her gloved hands folded in her lap. She was wearing a black bonnet and no powder or paint. Her dyed hair was hidden. She looked like the middle-class housewife she was impersonating, a woman in search of a domestic servant with good references. She had forgotten to ask Mrs. Humphries what the girl's name was or if she had relatives. That was the worst trouble. Most girls had relatives—all the pretty ones seemed to. One often had to take the second or even third best because there were people who would ask questions if the girls disappeared.

When Betty came in Mrs. Fitz gasped.

"What are you doing here?" she said.

"And what are you doing here, Mrs. Fitz?" Betty replied.

"Looking for a maid."

"For what kind of work?" Betty said. "Bedroom work?"

"Now, Betty," Mrs. Fitz said, "there's no need to be like that." She was as pretty as ever. Fancy having recovered from the beating poor Bill had given her. If she could get her back . . . If there were no strings . . . If it wasn't for those two damn brothers—murderers, that's what they were, bloody murderers. But she was a real knockout. Better than she had ever been.

"Well," Betty said, "I was nearly killed, wasn't I? Think I liked it?"

"You shouldn't have fought him. It's no good fighting a man. You get it anyway and a hiding as well."

The girl was acting very nervous, twisting her handkerchief in her white-cotton-gloved hands.

"What is it, Betty?" she asked. "Why are you here?"

"I need a job," Betty said. "I don't seem able to keep a job. It's the men," she said. "It's as if they knew, could smell it or something. As soon as their wives are out . . . You've no idea, Mrs. Fitz."

Now was her chance to ask about the brothers. "What about your brothers? Why don't you go home?"

"Oh, them," Betty said. "They chucked me out when they found out. Out on me ear. Said no whore was a sister of theirs, that's what they said."

"So you'd come back to Number 20 and work there? Upstairs, I mean, with the other girls? You'd do well, you know. The gentlemen were always asking about you before. But you'd be willing now?"

"Willing? I'd be willing. After the common trash, the louts, and for nothing, too. Gentlemen would be a change."

"When could you come?"

"Now," Betty said. "I've got me basket." She got up.

"Come along then, my dear. I've got a cab waiting," Mrs. Fitz said. "We'll go home and have a nice cup of tea and I'll introduce you to the other young ladies. All new since you were there. Nice girls. Pretty too, but not as pretty as you, dear. We'll get top price for you, all right. But we can talk business later, can't we?"

"Yes," Betty said, "there's plenty of time for business," as she followed Mrs. Fitz across the wide pavement and down the steps to the road where the cab was waiting.

Mrs. Fitz got in. The cabby put Betty's basket and bag on the roof. Betty got in, and then the door on the road side opened and the brothers got in.

"Not a word, you old bitch," Tom said. "Just one peep out of you and you'll get hurt. We've squared the driver so don't think he'll help, and if you shout we'll fix you.

"But you won't shout, will you?" he said. "We don't want any more inquiries from the police, do we, Mrs. Fitz? Not after Rose Cottage. London isn't Slough. Not by a long shot." He knocked on the cab behind the box with his blackthorn. "Drive on," he said. "Drive on to Number 20 like you always do. You see," he said to Mrs. Fitz, "we know it all. We know the racket. We know about the agency and the house next door and the import and export fruit business, and about Mr. Tupper and his 'ouse in Dulwich. Nice 'ouse it is, too. A wife and two kids. 'Ow do you think 'e'd like to 'ave 'is daughter broken in at Number 20? She's too ugly, of course, to be much of an earner. But there's other 'ouses, cheaper 'ouses for them as is not so fussy or can't afford to be.

"Christ, you old bitch," he said, "we're coming in with you and we may tear the place apart or we may not. Just depends. Just depends," he said.

"When we gets there you're going to give us a letter to Tupper. You're going to say 'I'm sending that girl Betty Norly to you with two of my men. They brought her to me and I can't keep her. You'll 'ave to send 'er on somewhere. They'll take her wherever you say.'

"That's what you'll write, you old 'arridan." Tom lifted

his stick and brought the ferrule down hard on Mrs. Fitz's toe. She screamed.

"Shut up!" Tom said. "That's just a taste. Do you know what we'll do if you're a bother? Fix you so you'll never walk again. That's what we'll do.

"You think you know about toughs and roughs and 'ard men because of all the bad 'uns you know. But let me tell you, Mrs. Fitz, there ain't nothing as 'ard as a good man when 'e's angry. Nothing as 'ard as men like us after what you done to our Betty.

"So you think it over," he said, "think it over." He raised his stick up to his chin again, ready to bring it down once more.

"No!" Mrs. Fitz cried. "No! I'll do what you want."

"You do it," he said, "and there'll be no bother. The letter, some sandwiches and beer, a little talk with the girls to see none of 'em's there unwilling, and we're off to Tupper."

"What'll you do to him?" Mrs. Fitz said. To do something to Tupper was like doing something to God.

"Fix him," Tom said. "We'll fix the bastard."

"Like Bill?" It was impossible to believe they'd to that to a gentleman like Mr. Tupper.

"We may," Henry said. It was the first thing he'd said. "If he's got any."

At No. 20 they got out.

"You wait," Tom said to the cabby. "Put 'is nose bag on and wait. We'll send you a sandwich and some beer."

They went in and up to Mrs. Fitz's cozy den. How happy she had always been in this room, away from it all, the green baize door closed and bolted. A nice fire, a cup of tea, crumpets dripping with butter, a glass of port. She looked at the sporting prints on the wall. Hunters jumping timber. Gentlemen in pink coats falling off their horses. There were things on the mantelpiece—nice things. A silver carriage clock, a bit of rock from South Africa that had gold in it—a streak right across it—two china cats. Presents from friends, from gentlemen she'd been able to please in some special way. She looked at the red-plush-covered sofa, at the antimacassars she'd crocheted herself. Somehow she had the feeling that all this was going to end soon, that there'd be changes in her life.

"Ring the bell, Betty," Tom said. "We want sandwiches

and beer. Now you go over there and write." He took Mrs. Fitz by the shoulder. "Write," he said, "and no bloody nonsense."

A maid came in.

"Tell her what we want, Mrs. Fitzherbert," Tom said, "and don't forget the cabby. Now I'm going to look at the girls."

"You can't," Mrs. Fitz said. "They're not up. It's not business hours."

"And I'm not here on business," Tom said. "Come on, Betty, you show me the way. Watch her, Henry," Tom said, pointing to Mrs. Fitz. "Any nonsense, knock her down."

They went down the passage on the first floor and then up to the second, banging on the doors.

"Come out, girls, we've got something to say to you," Betty said. "Come on, just as you are."

And they came—a dozen of them—with their hair down, in mobcaps, in dressing gowns, in skirts and petticoats with a silk shawl thrown over them.

Betty said, "I was here once. I know what it's all about. Any of you want to get out? Any of you being held here?"

All the girls were talking at once, laughing and pinching each other. What a joke, and what a fine big man. "Who's he?" they asked.

"My brother," Betty answered.

"Like any of us?" a big blond girl said, going up to him. "No money," she said. "Just for love, ducks. You look nice and common for a change. Wot about it, girls?"

"If 'e wants it 'e can 'ave it," came the chorus.

"Then you're all right here?" Betty said.

"We're all right now, my girl, but we wasn't once," the blonde said. "This is all we're good for now."

"Come on, Betty," Tom said. "We'll be off."

"Come back, you big bugger," the blonde said. "Come back any time. We likes the looks of you."

The girls rocked with hysterical laughter. What a joke. What a hell of a joke, offering to get them out. Where to? Out onto the street without a bloody roof over their heads when they were well off here, in the best bloody bawdyhouse in the West End of London.

Henry met them with the letter in his hand and they drove off toward Dulwich.

Brenthurst, Mr. Tupper's villa, was a neat, yellow-brick, three-story house with a slate roof. A drive led up to the front steps past shrubbery of variegated laurels, rhododendrons, flowering currants, and hawthorns. Behind the shrubs were some bigger trees—copper beeches, sycamores, and chestnuts. The drive was circular, embracing in its gravel arms a green lawn in whose center stood a weeping ash.

The iron tires of the growler crunched on the gravel.

Tom got out and pulled the shiny brass knob of the doorbell.

A neat maid, white-capped and aproned, came to the door. Nothing fast or pretty here, oh dear no, Tom thought.

"Mr. Tupper?" he said.

"Who is it?" the girl asked.

"Say it's the gentleman from Mrs. Fitz," he said.

"Gentlemen?" The girl suddenly became quite impudent. "All right," she said, "I'll tell him. You wait here."

She was back in a few minutes looking quite surprised.

"He'll see you," she said. "This way . . ." She led him through the hall and flung open a door.

"The gentleman," she said, announcing him. "Gentleman indeed," she whispered in his ear as he passed her.

Tupper was seated at his desk, a neat, slim, clean-shaven man with thin gray hair that thickened into a kind of badger pad over each ear. He had no eyebrows. His eyes were gray and wide-spaced, his mouth large and lipless. He looked, Tom thought, rather like a dogfish he had seen a man catch once on the pier at Brighton.

"Well?" Mr. Tupper said. His voice was soft but quite expressionless.

"Here," Tom said, handing him the letter.

"Here what?" Mr. Tupper said.

"Here, Tupper," Tom said.

A vein that had not been apparent before began to throb on Mr. Tupper's temple.

"Hasn't Mrs. Fitzherbert taught you manners, my man? When you speak to your betters you call them sir. Understand?"

"When I speak to them I do, Tupper," Tom said.

Mr. Tupper got up and moved to the bell. "I'll have you shown out," he said, "and any trouble from you I'll call the police."

"I shouldn't, Tupper," Tom said, sitting down and taking out his pipe. "We don't want no police when I come here with a present from old Ma Fitz."

Mr. Tupper sat down again at his desk and opened the letter.

"She should never have done this, never. It's most awkward. Most inconvenient."

"I'll go get her," Tom said. He went out down the hall and opened the front door.

"Come on," he said.

Henry helped his sister out of the cab. Tom led the way to the study. Once inside he closed the door.

" 'Ere she is," he said. "A beauty, isn't she? Why don't you keep 'er for yourself, Tupper?"

"How dare you speak to me like that!" Tupper said, but there was something in it. He'd forgotten what it was like, what it had been like in the old days with the pick of the crop at his disposal. . . . But he had to get rid of her now. Put her somewhere. This was the girl that had given so much trouble, the one who had tipped off that girl—the girl the South American had wanted—who had cost him the loss of Rose Cottage and Bill's services. It was she who had been responsible for the whole Slough scandal and the way Mrs. Fitzherbert had been able to blackmail him. And she was lovely, lovely, a delicious bit of stuff that was worth a fortune. But he'd have her first. Keep her somewhere. What a fool he'd been all this time just thinking of the money side. But then he'd seen men in the business go down that way. Go woman mad. Kill themselves at it. But not me, he thought. And it wouldn't harm her. A woman was not a postage stamp that could be used only once. A sort of smile appeared on his face, like the grin of a shark. The eyes remained cold, gray, expressionless, dead as the eyes of a fish on a fishmonger's slab, but the thin lips turned upward a little at the corners and gave a glimpse of his large, yellowish teeth.

"You got a place?" he said.

"We've got a place," Tom said.

"Then keep her till you hear from me. Give me the address. I'll have something fixed up in a day or two," he said. "But be careful. This girl's got two brothers big as you are, from what I hear. Nearly killed one of my best men."

"We kicked the bloody balls off him," Tom said.

"You . . . you . . ." Tupper's face turned white.

"They're my brothers," Betty said. "They've come to get you." Tupper opened his mouth.

"Don't scream, Tupper. You don't want a scandal 'ere too, do you? 'Ere in Dulwich with a wife and two kids and churchwarden and all?

"We know all about you, Tupper. You know the kids, the nippers that's been following you? We put 'em onto you, we did.

"We found out about this 'ouse and the agency and the other 'ouse and the fruit import and export and the other 'ouses. The bloody lot. An' we got our friend the doctor what attended to our Betty to write it all down nice and proper on a writing machine. And do you know where we sent it, Tupper? We sent it where it can't be 'ushed up. That's what our friend said. Not even by the King 'imself. We sent it to the Inland Revenue Department, that's where we sent it, because the doctor said, 'I'll bet 'e's not been paying 'is taxes, that's what I'll bet.' And soon the gentlemen will be 'ere, Tupper, and there, Tupper, and everywhere, and then you'll be in the jug where you belong.

"But first we're going to 'urt you, Tupper. That's what our Betty said. ''Urt 'im bad, Tom, for all the girls 'e's 'urted. All the girls 'e's 'urted. All the girls 'e's lived on.' A pimp and a whoremaster, Tupper."

"No," Tupper said. "I'll pay you. I'll give—"

"Money!" Tom said. "Money you've made out of girls on their backs. Do you think we'd take it?"

Betty had turned the key in the study door and stood with her back against it. What were they going to do to him, those big, wonderful, terrible brothers of hers? Sometimes she was afraid of them. Especially when they were quiet. They'd been very quiet ever since they had found her. Slow, quiet, hardly swearing, and then swearing soft.

She could see they had planned it. Because they hardly spoke.

Tom said, "Now 'Enry."

Henry went behind Tupper, forced open his mouth, stuffed a sock in it, and held his left hand behind his chair. Henry came around the desk quite slowly, took Tupper's right wrist, held it on the mahogany-top table, and then, pulling a ball-and-peen hammer from his pocket, smashed it down a dozen times, so hard, so fast, that it sounded almost like a single blow.

Tupper had fallen fainting from his chair.

"The sock," Tom said. Henry pulled it out of Tupper's mouth and put it in his pocket.

" 'E'll touch no more girls," Henry said, "and 'e'll write no more letters, and 'e'll not say a bloody word, either."

They turned away. Henry unlocked the door of the study. They went out to the growler with Betty supported between them. Fainted, the girl had.

When they got to a pub they went in for a drink. The lot of them, Betty, cabby, and all, to drink to it, to Tupper's end, they said.

"Aye," the cabby said, "Tupper's end," as he raised his tankard. Who the hell Tupper was he didn't know or care, but he'd drink to anything so long as the drink was free.

CHAPTER 35

THE END OF A LAAGER

KITCHENER thought Cronje had ten thousand men, and he knew there were other Boer forces in the offing. He had fifteen thousand and decided to attack at once. More British troops were on the way but could not arrive till late afternoon, and after their long march would not be fit for use till rested.

Daylight showed the Modder twisting sinuously between banks two hundred to three hundred yards apart. The Boer wagons were straggling along the north bank. The women and children were near the water, partly concealed by bush and trees. Trenches had been constructed above the riverbanks to cover their central laager. The ground on both sides of the river rose in a gentle slope with the laager in the center of a saucer through which the river ran like a deep crack.

Kitchener did not reconnoiter the position, thinking it a waste of time, but flung in his men, expecting to overwhelm the Boers with their first rush. The attack began at

7 A.M. and as he watched the leading troops deploy he said exultantly, "We'll be in the laager by ten-thirty."

His killer instinct was aroused by the damage his guns were doing. Boer ammunition wagons were blowing up. Other wagons were on fire, the whole Boer position was being pulverized, smashed into nothingness.

The regimental officers would have preferred to surround the laager and reduce it by attrition, thus saving much life—that of their own men and the Boers. There were too many women and children among them for any but the hardiest to enjoy the sight before their eyes.

After an hour's desperate fighting the most advanced troops reached the bank but were too exhausted to cross the river in the face of the fire that met them. Kitchener wanted the bend of the river cleared so that he could advance along both banks toward the central laager. To accomplish this, he threw in the Highland Brigade, as the mounted infantry and infantry attacked from upstream, but they could not advance because Boer reinforcements arriving from Bloemfontein were attacking their rear.

A Cameron piper leaped into the water, found a safe crossing, and set his pipes skirling as he marched up and down under cover of the bank, his kilt swaying as he piped the Seaforths and the Black Watch across. But even the famous Highlanders were impotent against the hail of lead that met them.

In the river bed amid the exploding shells, the burning wagons, the bellowing oxen, and the screaming children, General Cronje sat holding his wife's hand and trying to comfort her. There was nothing he could do. They had to stick it out till rescue came from De Wet, from Ferreira, from Bloemfontein. Help, he knew, was on its way. How much or how successful it would be he had no idea. All he could do now was to wait, to comfort his wife, the mother of his sons, and pray to his God.

So well hidden were the Boer defenses that a Scots Horse gunner said, "Mon, we could sight these bloody guns better with ear trumpets." But see or not see, the guns continued to fire, bursting shrapnel over the laager and plastering the river with high explosive and shrapnel. In this first few hours all the thousands of Boer livestock were killed, and only twenty horses left alive.

By ten-thirty, the time that Kitchener had allotted to

taking the laager, nothing had been achieved except heavy casualties and the knowledge that with their stock and wagons destroyed the Boers could not get away.

The attack having withered, Kitchener, undeterred by his losses, flung more troops, as if they were stones, into this boiling pot of battle.

Hanley's mounted infantry were digging in. A message was sent to Kitchener that they could advance no farther. His men had had no rest after a terrible twenty-four-hour march and had not even had time to eat before being engaged.

But nothing, least of all considerations of flesh and blood, was going to stop Lord Kitchener of Khartoum, who had never lost a battle. He knew the enemy's losses must be comparable to his own, but he had men to expend and they did not. He now decided to throw in everything and attack both upstream and along the northern bank, where his main objective, the laager, lay. He replied to Hanley's message about his exhausted men in a curious way:

"The time has now come for a final effort. All troops have been warned that the laager must be rushed at all costs. Try to carry the infantry with you but if they cannot go the M.I. should do it. Gallop up if necessary and fire into the laager."

This was the command of a madman. There was no braver man than Hanley in the army, but this was the order of a man blinded by blood lust. Yet the orders, suicidal as they were, were clear.

On various pretexts he sent his staff away. One of them had a blood horse that still seemed fairly fresh. He borrowed it and with a small group of his M.I. he advanced upon the Boer position. Then, driving his spurs into his race horse's flanks, he galloped away from his men alone, outdistancing them by five hundred yards, riding full tilt at the Boer defenses, to fall riddled with bullets inside the lines.

And still the battle raged. The Cornwall Light Infantry charged with fixed bayonets. The Welsh and Essex attacked along the ground that Hanley had covered in his last ride.

De Wet and Ferreira now joined up with the Bloemfontein men to create another diversion. Cronje's burghers, encouraged by this help, threw back the Cornwalls, and as evening fell the exhausted troops laid down their rifles and slept beside them. Knowing the British to be desperate for water, the Boers, in spite of the shelling they had sustained and their own casualties, allowed them to get it from the river without firing a single shot.

The net result of this action was a stalemate. The Boers had lost their livestock and their transport. The British had suffered thirteen hundred casualties. There was great suffering in the laager, for the Boers had left all their doctors in Jacobsdal and the women had to do the best they could for the wounded.

Cronje's officers again urged him to break out. He could have done it, but he refused. All he did was to shorten his own line. It was only his iron will that held the Boers together.

Kitchener had had his first lesson in fighting white men. It would not be his last. But he was unmoved by his losses and wrote to a lady in England:

"I hope the authorities will keep their hair on, and if they want a victim to sacrifice I am always at their disposal. War means risks and you cannot play the game and always win."

In other words, those once used by Napoleon, it was impossible to make an omelet without breaking eggs, even if the eggs were men and the omelet blood.

This was the end of the first day of the attack on Cronje's laager and the Boer men, women, and children within it. It was February 18.

Next day Kitchener prepared for another onslaught on the contracted target that the Boers, who had pulled in their horns during the night, offered him. But his commanders, being commanders of men, not of machines, and having lost enough yesterday to no purpose, appealed to Lord Roberts for a decision.

The old general had recovered and, upset at the report of the battle, left Jacobsdal and reached Paardeberg by 10 A.M. in the mule-drawn wagon that was his field headquarters.

Cronje sent a messenger with a request for a twenty-four-hour armistice so that the dead could be buried and the wounded attended to. Roberts, afraid that the time would be spent by the Boers in strengthening their defenses and resting their tired men, refused, and demanded Cronje's surrender.

Cronje answered with these words:

"Since you are so unmerciful as not to accord the time asked for, nothing remains for me to do. You do as you wish."

Turnbull being at another part of the line, a man whose Dutch was far from fluent mistranslated the message as meaning that Cronje would surrender, and as the British troops moved toward the laager to occupy it they were driven back by a storm of rapid fire.

Roberts sent a message back to Cronje to ask him what he meant.

"I will never surrender," the Boer general replied. "If you wish to bombard, fire away."

Although he outnumbered the Boers by six to one and surrounded them completely, Roberts was still not certain of success. No one except Kitchener wanted to attack again. The price of an assault would be tremendous. The hospital service was already overworked with the casualties of the day before. A siege was the only other choice, but a siege presented grave dangers. At any moment the Boers might get more reinforcements and, if his lines of communication were cut, Roberts might find himself stranded in the middle of nowhere to bleed and starve to death.

But some of the Boers who should have come, the force that had besieged Kimberley and eluded French, had no belly for the fight and asked their old commander in chief, General Joubert, for further instructions. He answered:

"How is this possible? Are there not instructions enough from the banks of the Modder River, whence for so many days already General Cronje has been calling in his agony 'Come relieve me'? What other instructions can now be given or demanded than, with one voice and with one mouth, 'Burghers of South Africa, go and help deliver your General from the might of the tyrant'? . . . Relieve Cronje, cost what it will . . . wavering and doubt, unbelief and mistrust, will not only bring sorrow on your South Africa and the whole Afrikaans people, but destroy our whole national existence. Therefore, trust firmly in God and He shall give you strength. Relieve Cronje."

There was no further action that day, though the British guns continued to shell the laager. So ended the second day.

On the third day there was some threat from the Boers in the south. They were moving toward the railway that was Roberts' lifeline. He dealt with them and continued his shelling, though more carefully now as he was getting short of ammunition.

His aim was to prevent the Boers from concentrating for a breakout by smashing the shelter they had made for their food and remaining livestock. De Wet was a worry. What was he going to do? He was not a man who did nothing.

Roberts now sent some infantry to occupy a line between Kitchener's *kop* and the river, while French with his cavalry attempted to drive De Wet into the trap the infantry had prepared.

But De Wet was not going to be encircled. At a wild gallop he led his commando down the one valley French had left unguarded and got clean away.

This was another of the exploits that were to make De Wet famous, a legendary, almost phantom figure, appearing out of nowhere and disappearing into space.

De Wet fell in with the Natal reinforcements at Poplar Grove. This village had become a rallying point for the rescuers.

Roberts now learned that Cronje had women and children with him—Kitchener had left that out of his reports —and offered them safe-conduct to his own lines, an offer that Cronje turned down. Roberts also offered doctors and medical supplies.

Cronje said, "If they come they must stay."

Roberts refused this. Cronje then suggested a neutral hospital and Roberts refused to agree.

But things in the laager were bad. They were being pounded by fifty pieces of artillery ranging from great 4.7 naval guns to the twelve-pounders of the horse gunners. They were also under continual machine-gun fire from the British, who at some points were only six hundred yards away. They could not move out of their trenches. The air was thick with dust and the green, poisonous fumes of exploding lyddite.

But that was not all. It was February, one of the hottest

months of the year. The Boers were surrounded by thousands of rotting carcasses, the cattle and horses killed by shellfire, whose stench could be smelled miles away. Then on top of this each Boer, safe enough in his trench as long as he stayed there, had to squat day after day in the growing heap of his own fly-covered excrement. Dead animals almost blocked the Modder, infecting the water so badly that the British troops called their drinking water dead-horse soup.

An engineer on a captive balloon, the first time the air was ever used for observation in war, made sketches of the Boer lines and also directed the artillery fire.

De Wet had now four thousand men at Poplar Grove and was getting ready to strike. His intention was to cut a slice out of the British cake, a corridor down which Cronje could make his escape as De Wet fought a rear-guard action to protect him.

But the relief did not come off. The Boers who were not picked men skulked behind rocks and would not close with the British. Owing to cloudy weather the heliograph was no good and as he did not know what was going on, Cronje did not counterattack in their support, and De Wet rode back to Poplar Grove.

In the afternoon there was a storm and the Modder came down in spate. This cleaned up the river, washing some of the dead horses and cattle away, but added to the Boers' discomfort by half filling the trenches with flood-water, leaving them standing up to their knees in sewage. This was very hard on the wounded, and Cronje agreed to release all British prisoners if he could send with them an equal number of his own most serious casualties.

On the seventh day of the siege it rained all day. Nothing happened except that Danie Theron volunteered—since in this weather the heliograph was still useless—to get a message through to Cronje. Waiting till dark, he rode up to the British lines, crawled past their outposts in the pouring rain, swam the swollen river, and reached the general.

De Wet's proposal was a break-through. The Boers now had stood eight days of hell and were desperate. But the river had risen eight feet and they could get out only by building a bridge. But mixed with desperation was the apathy of exhaustion, of horror piled on horror till the mind no longer took it in. Their trenches were water-logged. Their helpless wounded cried and wept. Their wives and children were sick. They were near starving, living on a ration of half a biscuit and a chunk of rotting trek ox a day. They felt their countrymen had abandoned them, and endlessly shells continued to explode in the polluted air.

Everyone on both sides knew the climax was at hand. In Pretoria there was an all-night vigil of prayer in every church.

The Boer bridge was started, but even if it were built the Boers felt a breakout was bound to fail. What about their women and children? What about horses? Almost all were dead and the few left unfit for use.

But Cronje shouted all opposition down. "Tomorrow is Majuba Day," he said. "Our sacred anniversary of the first Boer War when we defeated the British and killed their General Colley."

He was certain that even if human rescue did not come God would smite the enemy Himself. But in the afternoon there were more surprises. First, some pom-poms poured a stream of tiny shells into the camp. This was the first time the British had used them, though the Boers had had them since the outbreak of war.

Secondly, something much worse, a siege train of four howitzers arrived and began to drop a plunging fire of 120-pound shells into the camp, shells that exploded in clouds of smoke "that looked like rows of magic trees springing suddenly to life." The howitzer fire destroyed the bridge that had just been finished, and while the whole earth shook with the fury of this new bombardment, the British advanced to within two hundred yards of the Boer trenches.

This was the ninth day of the battle and the Boers knew the end had come. Their sufferings had been for nothing. The dead had died for nothing. And for them all—for this great force of four thousand Boers—the war was over. Soon, as prisoners separated from their wives and chil-dren, from their beloved land, they would be sent over the sea that they had never seen to Bermuda, St. Helena, and Ceylon—islands they had never heard of.

At six-thirty on the tenth day, on Majuba Day, the white flags went up on sixteen-foot bamboo whipstocks and group after group of exhausted men began to leave the laager. Cronje could not halt them, but sat with bowed head watching his burghers go. At eight he sent a message to Lord Roberts surrendering and throwing his men "on the mercy of Her Britannic Majesty."

The bugles blew cease-fire, and for the first time in ten days there was no sound over the Muddy River. The battle of Paardeberg was over.

Roberts sent one of his generals to escort Cronje to the British lines where he had formed a hollow square of Highlanders about his headquarters wagon and waited, walking up and down in front of it, to meet him. A very neat little soldier in khaki, booted and spurred, a forage cap on his gray hair and no badge of rank save the jeweled Kandahar presentation sword that hung from the frog of his Sam Browne belt.

As Cronje rode into the square on a starving gray horse, the Highlanders presented arms to this, the strangest general they had ever seen. Bowed over his saddle, looking cold and beaten, was an old bearded man in a slouch hat, a green overcoat, frieze trousers, and homemade veldschoenen thrust into rusted stirrups.

Roberts held out his hand. "I am glad to see you. You made a gallant defense, sir," he said.

The old Boer did not answer, and the two generals had breakfast together under a tree where the final arrangements, the obsequies of a great force, were at last agreed to.

Turnbull, talking to a Boer commandant, asked him what they had thought of Hanley's charge. He said, "We did not know what to think of this lone horseman rushing at us. We did not want to shoot a man so blatantly inviting death and so defenseless. But we were afraid that he was running berserk or would suddenly wheel away to give information about us. We had no choice. We shot him."

"Do you know why he did what he did?" Turnbull asked.

"No. Was he mad?" the Boer said, lighting his pipe.

"No, Commandant, only madly brave. He was ordered to lead his mounted infantry at a gallop against you. The order was given to him and he obeyed it. But obeyed it alone."

"*Magtig*," the Boer said. "That would have been certain death for all."

"Greater love hath no man than to lay down his life for his friends," Turnbull said.

The Boer smiled and said, "Is it not strange, Captain, that we, both white and both Christian, should be at war?" With that, still puffing at his pipe, he turned away and rejoined his men.

Four thousand prisoners were assembled on the river-bank, their rifles piled in a great stack as if they were hay and not the harvest of war. One hundred fifty wounded were brought in. No more than that, so good had been their trenches.

The British troops were astonished when they saw the prisoners stumbling by. Bearded civilians, unkempt and filthy, dressed in near rags, carrying their belongings in gaudy blankets or bright knotted handkerchiefs. Many of them had umbrellas up to keep off the sun. Some wore galoshes. With them were their women and children, also veterans of the siege.

Were these the men that had held off the flower of the British Army for so long? Not only here but elsewhere. The men who had defeated Methuen, Buller, Gatacre . . . ? It was hard to believe, but it was true, and no one knew it better than the British soldiers who had fought at Paardeberg.

PART FIVE

THE CAPTAINS

*". . . The thunder of the
Captains and the shouting . . ."*
JOB 39:25

[*April to July 1900—Winter*]

CHAPTER 36

THE MANY FACES OF LOVE

WHEN dawn broke Boetie and Moolman halted. The plain was an astonishing sight. As far as they could see in all directions the Boers were retreating. Boers, wagons, loose stock were all moving north like migrating game, away from danger. Luckily the big guns had got away by rail. But this scene, in which they were also actors, was disaster. Not only had the British broken through and relieved Ladysmith. They had weakened the Boer will to resist.

"Huis toe!" was their cry. "To hell with it! Let us go home."

The night had been terrible, with thunderstorms and drenching showers of icy rain. Shivering men stood grouped beside their shivering horses, or rode forward slumped in their saddles, their rifles slung on their backs.

No one could experience a high-veld storm without being aware of God. Not a gentle, loving Jesus, not a Savior, but the terrible God of the Jews of the Old Testament, Jahweh—Jehovah.

A storm began in the late afternoon when the heat became oppressive, blanket-heavy in the still air that produced no calm. Men were nervous and irritable in that electrically surcharged atmosphere. The horses' ears twitched, cattle ceased grazing and even chewing the cud. They stood listless with switching tails.

Great white, anvil-shaped thunderheads grew mountainous against a sapphire sky that seemed to stand like a backdrop a long way to their rear. The clouds' edges were sharp and clear as if cut out of thin metal with a knife.

Then the clouds darkened, becoming leaden. The sky behind them turned to navy blue, to indigo. Along the horizon there was a low bar of red dust carried by a wind that picked up soil and light rubbish—fallen grass, mealie trash, leaves, and branches—as if it was a hand that swept it forward in its grasp.

But here it was silent, the air still. There was no sound. All nature seemed to be waiting. Then the wind struck them with a whirlwind of red dust. In an instant the temperature dropped thirty degrees and the black sheet of the sky was torn by the purple jags of lightning as if it was paper. The electricity in the earth sprang up to meet the stroke with a smell of sulphur. The wind, by now, had passed on. There was only the lightning, and the rolls and claps of thunder that accompanied it. So far the storm was dry and the more dangerous for that. Free, unchained by the conducting power of rain, the lightning struck blow after blow at iron-filled *kopjes* till they seemed alive with fire.

Then the rain came. First in separate drops as big as pennies, then in sheets, in squalls, that were followed by hail whose icy stones were sometimes big enough to kill sheep and penetrate light-gauge corrugated iron.

Dismounted, shivering, their teeth chattering, the Boers held their horses' heads, trying to soothe their fear, while they waited for the storm to pass. And pass it did. In an hour it was gone and the sky summer bright once more, leaving no trace but the dripping trees and the soaking grass. Veld paths ran like streams. Sluits became rivers, rivers were savage seas of liquid mud as the topsoil of Africa was swept toward the ocean.

The Boers remounted. Their dripping horses had changed color and were almost black with wet. The men were so wet that they did not even notice their soaking saddles. They rode on hoping to get out of the track of the storm, the swath it had cut across the veld, to find dry wood, build fires, and dry their clothes and blankets.

Even when the sun rose and its heat drew steam from the soaked men and horses, the scene remained dismal in its lack of order, in its fluidity. Men and beasts all drifted along the lines of least resistance; wagon drivers shouted and quarreled as they jockeyed for position at every drift and spruit. The wheels of the gun limbers and transports became locked. For a while there seemed to be no end to the confusion. But at last some kind of natural order took place. The strong pushed forward and left more room for the weak, who at last succeeded in extricating themselves.

Moolman collected a small party about him and formed a rear guard whose purpose was more to encourage the laggards than protect them from an enemy who did not attack.

The great base at Elandslaagte was reached after dark. Here they met General Botha and Lukas Meyer, trying to check the retreat and bring some order into the confusion. They even threatened to shoot the horses of the Boers escorting the wagons. But the tide swept on. All that remained now was to destroy the vast supplies at the base, the railhead for the whole Boer operation in Natal. Boetie and Moolman helped to set fire to this pyre of the Boer hopes in the east. Stores of food, clothing, medical supplies, case after piled case, small wooden mountains, neatly named and labeled, were set alight, took fire slowly at first, and then went off, roaring on the wind that had sprung up. Once the blaze took hold everyone ran back as the ammunition began to explode with loud firecracker bangs. Scarlet and yellow tongues of flame shot into the air, illuminating the clouds of smoke. Bullets sang and whined through the air as the cartridges popped harmlessly, unchambered, and fell in a hail of lead over the veld.

There was something terrible about this destruction. Irrevocable and against all instinct. Blankets, oil, paints, biltong, rawhide riems, boots, saddles, all gave the pall of smoke their sickening flavor. This was a testament of British victory, a pillar of flame, by night visible for fifty miles, that was by morning, when they were far away, a pillar of smoke rising arrow straight in the now windless African sky.

The tears in Boetie's bloodshot eyes were not all due to the smoke. This was a terrible thing to have done, to have seen, and to have been one of those who put a match to so many hopes for freedom. He was not fully hardened yet.

Moolman looked at him and laughed. "Don't cry, boy," he said. "These are only things. There was no love in them. Money bought them. Money can buy more. Cry when you see homes go up, women ravished, and stock killed. This is nothing. Come," he said, "don't sit there and stare." He lifted his bridle hand, set his heels into his horse, and cantered on, with Boetie riding behind him.

Moolman was right. It was a question of values. The difference between a boy and a man was this knowledge —part of it anyway. Women—girls—came into it too. Since he had watched the Beyerses together, a great curiosity and yearning for love had come over him. Once, quite by accident, he had come across them making love in a clump of bush in the afternoon. There was no privacy by the campfires at night, which they were too shy to leave for so obvious a purpose. He had been struck by the strangeness of it. He had never thought of it before, not consciously at least. A man and woman drawn together like animals to create their kind, and yet not like animals at all. For with animals when it was over it was done with and forgotten. But not with people. He would never forget their expression. Their tenderness as they sat hand in hand by the fire that night. Perhaps when she died fighting over the body of her man Hetta had been with child. Perhaps he had glimpsed the beginning of it, of this great man-woman mystery. He felt his face harden as he thought of a man's life and all that lay before him. Love, a girl, a child, children, a home, lands, and stock. The manifold joys, sorrows, and responsibilities that he one day, if he lived, must bear. But with whom? Somewhere in the world, in Africa, there was a girl now living as unaware as he of her destiny. When would they meet? Where?

Moolman had known all this and lost it. He was a survivor of life's storms, a man beyond pain now but also, in a way, beyond love. Marked by the tempest, his face granite, his dark eyes like black stones, the man was untouchable. Nothing could move him. Not pain, not fear, not discomfort. He had ceased to believe in God, though, and this was a paradox. He sought death because he believed in heaven and hoped to find his wife and children there. Or, and this was another possibility, perhaps he just wanted extinction—to be snuffed out like a candle so that he would feel no more pain. Boetie knew that much of this hardness was a mask, that the man was banked like a fire with the ashes of his will, by his great pretense that nothing mattered. He knew, too, that he, Boetie, had done something to him, stirred up the embers of love in this strange, hard man who, though he never said so, now loved him like a son.

In Moolman he too had found the father he had lost. So both of them, man and boy, had by the strange alchemy of war formed a bond of blood as strong as the blood of marriage, for it was in blood that men were conceived and born. What difference that this was the blood of men—the many they had seen die, their friends and the men that they had killed—rather than that of a woman? For the blood was spilled in Africa, the mother of their race, the land for which they fought. And she, this motherland, was sorely hurt, though how sorely they did not yet fully know. But the fire at Elandslaagte was a great wound in her side.

As they rode Boetie thought of this other mystery. A man's love for his homeland. Not just his own bit of it. Not just his farm, his lands, but the whole of it. The wide veld, the rugged mountains, the great skies. The whole vastness of it that was their heritage, the land of their fathers, that their fathers had wrested from the wilderness, taming it with gun and plow, tending it, reaping it. They themselves as much a part of it as the red soil, as the swirling dust devils, as the bush and the trees. This was something no man could explain. He could only feel it with every beat of his heart, with every pulse of it. This was another face of love. How many faces did it have? Did Moolman know? Did any man ever know? For a land, for a woman, for a home, for a child, a dog, a horse, for inanimate things—for his rifle and his tools. For a thorn in full yellow, perfumed flower, for a flying bee laden with honey. How many and varied were the faces of love?

Perhaps it was better to be a boy and wonder than a man who knew. Perhaps the sharp edge of it was blunted by experience. Perhaps he had something that Moolman had lost, though he too must have had it once. There was a kind of poetry in this ignorance, this innocence. The tree of knowledge was there before him. One day he would pick its beautiful and bitter fruits, but there was no hurry. If he lived there would be time and to spare to savor it. If he died it would not matter. At the moment, this moment, apart from the disaster of the Boer failure in Natal, he was content enough. He was well, he had a good horse under him, a rifle in his hand, and the days of his life and Africa lay before him, spread like a great carpet beneath his feet. He leaned forward and patted Pasha's neck, thankful that neither of them had been hurt.

A man lived on many levels. The level of now—the good horse, the warm sun, the knowledge that he had escaped death many times, the strange arrogance of the survivor in battle, and on another, political level—an abstract level of right, wrong, and freedom for which, without logical cause, a man—and in this sense he was a man—was ready to sacrifice the reality of his life, to spill his blood, to die if need be, just to prove that he was alive, sentient, and aware that there was more in life than mere comfort and security. It was written that the first shall be last and the last first, so that perhaps in the end those who sought to save themselves would lose more than their lives. They would lose their souls.

The war was still to Boetie a great and dangerous adventure. He was fighting for the freedom of his land but could not hate the English. Turnbull, the English captain he had loved. He thought of him in full uniform at Elsa's funeral. He thought of him when he tended Pasha, the pony he had given him. The English, as such, were separate in his mind from the enemy, though the enemy were English. He was still too young to hate and had not yet sufficient cause.

They rode slowly now and swung due east toward Bloemfontein. De Wet was there somewhere between the Free State capital and Kimberley, preparing to make another stand.

When the war news reached Pretoria, Kruger, with some of his staff, Servas among them, set off for Bloemfontein to confer with President Steyn. It was essential to hold the town, and the longer Roberts could be kept away the greater their chance of success. Cut off from the central railway and far removed from the Western line, the English line of communications would become more precarious every day.

The forces at the Boers' disposal were: De la Rey with a thousand Zarps (South African Police) and more men on the way from Colesberg. De Wet, at Poplar Grove, had six thousand men entrenched and ready to bar Roberts' advance from Paardeberg, and when the rest of the reinforcements arrived from Natal and the Cape, the two presidents hoped to have a force of twelve thousand men ready for action.

Still this was a serious crisis and the presidents decided to make a new peace overture and addressed a proposal to the British Government stating, "In the sight of the Tribune of God all forces should withdraw behind their own frontiers and the two republics be given full independence."

While these negotiations were going on, the problem of preventing the burghers from surrendering had also to be dealt with. Traveling in his four-horse Cape cart with an escort of mounted police, Kruger set out for Poplar Grove to try to instill some fighting spirit into De Wet's dispirited men, who were far from eager to go on with the war.

The President had hardly entered De Wet's tent when the rattle of musketry broke out. Servas, who was waiting outside, ran in. "Quick," he said, "the English are here."

Fortunately the horses had not been outspanned, and a moment later the President was in the Cape cart with the horses going at full gallop toward Bloemfontein, the two-wheeled cart rocking behind them and Servas on a police horse riding beside him. At Abraham's Kraal, a farm fourteen miles west of Poplar Grove, they met De la Rey with his thousand policemen on his way to reinforce De Wet. But they were immediately enveloped in the dust clouds of retreating burghers and wagons, few of whom could be persuaded to stand and make a fight for it, in spite of Kruger's threats, and his orders to the police to fire on the retreating Boers. No shot was fired and the flight continued. Kruger looked broken. His features became leaden. Life seemed to leave him. He raised his stick threateningly at the men who galloped past and scarcely looked his way. At last a few of the bolder men were persuaded to halt and try, under De la Rey's leadership, to stave Roberts off while the defense of Bloemfontein was prepared.

This was the Boer picture. A handful of men—De la Rey with fifteen hundred police and oddments facing ten thousand British in an effort to hold them off until the defenses of Bloemfontein were ready. He succeeded in so doing till evening, but at six-thirty the British infantry under an artillery barrage got close enough to charge in strength. The Boers fought till the last moment, some were too late to reach their ponies, and three hundred casualties were suffered.

Roberts' plan was to advance in three columns, ten miles apart, that were to converge in four days on the central railway line south of Bloemfontein. But suddenly he changed his mind, having heard that strong Boer reinforcements were coming from the north. Everything depended on the rapid capture of Bloemfontein. He had to have supplies if his army were not to starve. So he changed his objective and told French to ride hell for leather for Brand Kop, a hill four miles south of the capital; its capture would place the town at his mercy and outflank the Boers.

At 1 P.M. in the full heat of the day French set out, and the Boers fled. Roberts sent a prisoner into Bloemfontein promising to protect all life and property if his entry were unopposed. The English and moderate Boer inhabitants who were against the war welcomed this news. The others, the die-hards, inspanned and trekked north under cover of night. President Steyn went by train, leaving only a weak rear guard, and some of Theron's scouts in disguise to act as spies. Steyn only just got away. The train pulled out as a cavalry patrol cut the line.

The first Englishmen in Bloemfontein were three journalists who said with some justification that never before had a capital city been taken by newspapermen. Exercising the persuasiveness of their profession, they got the mayor to drive out and meet Lord Roberts with the keys of the town, and on March 13 Roberts, with his staff and foreign military attachés, rode in at the head of the cavalry division.

The weary, tattered troops pulled themselves erect in their saddles as with brightening eyes they saw civilization again, a town with streets, brightly dressed women, children, and flower-filled gardens.

The streets of this enemy capital were decorated. Some in the crowds even cheered the exhausted men and stumbling horses. Here was another paradox of this curious civil war in which the emotions fluctuated, seesawing between cordiality and hatred.

How near both sides had been to total victory now became apparent. When Roberts rode into Bloemfontein he only had five days' supplies left. If the Boers could have held him up for five days, the whole British force would have starved. When they entered the town their forage was finished and the men's rations all but gone. They had a three-month supply of everything, but it was five hundred miles away, on the far side of the Orange River, whose bridges had been blown up by the Boers. It was only by seizing the food in the town that disaster was avoided, missed by a hairsbreadth.

The British missed their chance when they failed to capture Kruger. That this happened was due less to the fog of war than to a personal grudge.

At the beginning of the action Lord Roberts had spoken to his commanding officers. He said:

"I have asked you to meet me here this afternoon in order to communicate to you the proposed plan of operations for tomorrow. The enemy, as you know, occupy a strong but somewhat extended position in our immediate front. The object is, of course, to block the road to Bloemfontein, and as far as the information we can procure goes, it is apparently the only place between here and Bloemfontein where our progress could be checked. It is difficult to calculate the exact strength of the enemy, but allowing that the troops withdrawn from Colesberg, Stormberg, and Natal have joined, it seems scarcely possible that it can number more than fourteen thousand, at the outside, with perhaps twenty guns. To meet this number, we have thirty thousand men and one hundred sixteen guns. . . ."

French was to ride around the Boers' right, take them in the rear, and pin them down for the infantry and cut off their retreat.

But French, the dashing cavalry leader, rode slowly. True, his horses were in low condition, but his heart was not in the operation. There had been trouble between him and Roberts.

At Paardeberg, after the losses at Waterval, where most of his transport had been captured, Lord Roberts had cut the rations of both men and horses. The men were cut from five biscuits to two per day and the horses' oats reduced from five to three pounds.

The supply officer reported to Roberts that French's horses were getting more than their share and the general was reprimanded for disobeying orders. The error was that of the supply officer, who had based his calculations on the horses reported fit for action. It had not occurred to him that sick horses had to eat too.

French was furious. He felt his horses had already been abused, and now was so dilatory that he allowed the Boers, including President Steyn, to escape the net that should have trapped them.

When the British rode into Bloemfontein some people cheered and others put on dark mourning clothes. Boer girls flaunted orange and white ribbons of the Free State on their hats or wore them around their waists. But a few days later everyone turned out to listen to the army bands when they played the latest London dance tunes in the evening.

Parliament House was commandeered as a hospital. The offices of the *Friend* were taken over to publish an army newspaper, and Kipling joined the staff to write sketches and poems. One of his most famous lines was "Spare the solitary horseman on the skyline. He is bound to be a Britisher."

But it was not all beer and skittles for the British. Some of the birds that had been on the wing since Paardeberg came home to roost. Old Cronje might still have the laugh on the British—a bitter, sardonic laugh— for within a week Roberts had 1000 men in hospital. By the end of April, when he marched north, he left 4500 men in hospital. More sick had been sent to the Cape and thousands were dead. Out of 200,000 British troops in Africa 15,000 were hospitalized, 75 out of every 1000. And this did not include the dead.

Instead of being able to push on into the Transvaal after a week's rest, Roberts was held up for seven.

Once again God had smitten the Philistines, and the Boers, who needed rest too, had time to regroup.

It was Cronje's dead oxen and horses that had decimated the British. It was the polluted river at Paardeberg that fathered the outbreak of enteric among the near-starved and exhausted troops.

In Bloemfontein, in the overcrowded tents, the disease ran away and amok. The medical equipment was short, and unskilled doctors failed to diagnose the illness. There were too few nurses and doctors. The Bloemfontein Club was used as a hospital by Dr. Conan Doyle, who took charge of it.

At Paardeberg it had been impossible to prevent the troops drinking the water of the Modder, fouled by the rotting carcasses of Cronje's stock. In that terrible heat the British soldiers, sweated dry, had to replenish the water in their systems. So they drank and filled their water bottles with this liquid poison. It was useless to tell them to boil it. Even the officers drank it, saying that if they knew it was full of cholera and enteric still they had to have it. They had it and many died of it, in a kind of posthumous revenge, as if Cronje's poor dumb slaughtered beasts had turned, more savage than lions, on their destroyers.

Now the apocalyptic horseman of disease was riding high. More people—men, women, and children, soldiers and civilians, Boer and Briton, black and white alike— were to die of sickness than by shells and bullets. Roberts' wife and daughter had joined him in Bloemfontein and helped to nurse the sick, who were dying at the rate of fifty a day.

Over the residency floated a little silken Union Jack with a shamrock in the corner. It had been made by Lady Roberts and was run up on March 13, with due pomp and ceremony. Bloemfontein, the "Spring of Flowers," now was British. One day the flag would come down, but the British dead are still there. And if love had many faces, so had death.

CHAPTER 37

THE NURSE

THE *Norham Castle* was loaded to the scuppers with troops, army matériel, and equipment. Lady Finch-Haddley, her doctors, nurses, and girls were the only civilians aboard.

The voyage, uneventful enough, was a tremendous adventure to Elsie and the other girls, none of whom had
ever been to sea before except for two of them who had
been to France. But even for them the great liner was a
strange and wonderful world and bore no relation to the
paddle-wheel cross-channel steamers of their European
experience. Lady Finch-Haddley had a cabin to herself.
The four nurses shared a cabin. The two doctors were
squeezed in with some officer replacements, and the sixteen girls bunked eight to a cabin. Only three of them
who had been to boarding school had ever slept with anyone but their mothers, and their modesty amused Elsie.
It took her all her time not to tell them about Mrs. Fitz.
Neither she nor Millie was seasick, but most of the others
suffered terribly and thought they were going to die.

Elsie, sitting in Lady Finch-Haddley's cabin, asked her if
she thought they were all pregnant.

"Of course not, dear."

"But suppose. Just suppose they were and we landed
with fourteen pregnant girls and the papers got hold of
it." She had learned to read newspapers with some attention and saw the dramatic headlines in her mind. Not
being sick herself, she saw only one reason for the endless vomiting of the others.

Naturally the girls, once they were up and about again,
were surrounded by young officers. Elsie in particular, as
she was the prettiest and had been up and about ever
since they sailed. This was a curious experience for her.
She had never met or even seen men as people before.
Their charm and chivalry surprised her. Their politeness.
Getting up when she came near them. Their offers of rugs,
deck chairs, chocolate, books. Their conversation, which,
much to her surprise, she was able to follow. They danced
with her. They held her hand. Several kissed her and suggested more intimate meetings, all of which she parried
with the greatest skill while still holding their affection.
This admiration, so different from the masculine attention
to which she had been accustomed, went to her head a
little, making her gayer and happier. Her admirers little
guessed its real cause. Each hour was bringing her nearer
to her captain. Apart from him she was utterly without
desire, apparently sexless, an untouched virgin. But one

man, a Captain Rees Owen of the Welsh Fusiliers, she
became very fond of.

"If you could get rid of that damn girl for a few minutes there's something I'd like to say to you," he said one
morning.

It was very hard to get rid of Millie. In this floating
world Elsie was her only security. She clung as close as a
leech.

"When?" Elsie asked.

"Tonight, Miss Smith. Say at ten, on the boat deck."

"I'll be there, Captain Owen," Elsie said.

"Alone?"

"Yes, alone. You don't mind Queenie, do you?"

"No, I don't mind the dog."

At ten Elsie met him. He took her hand and kissed it.
Then he pulled her toward him and kissed her on the
mouth, his lips gently soft but urgent.

They were off Cape Verde, the sea was smooth, oily
with great low swells over which the white moon burned a
silver track. A warm breeze from West Africa blew over
them, loosing strands of Elsie's hair.

"I love you," Owen whispered. "Will you marry me?"

"Marry you?" Elsie could not keep the astonishment
out of her voice.

"Yes, darling, will you be my wife?"

This was something she had never expected. Anything
else, but not this. It just showed how far she had come.
How pleased John would be. A nice man, a gentleman,
an officer, wanting to make her his wife. The captain,
Vincent, Celeste, Monsieur André would all be proud of
her when they heard about it.

"Don't say no, Elsie. Not now. Take time to think it
over. I'm not a poor man. I could give you a nice home."

Not nicer than No. 7, our love nest, she thought. Not
nicer than that.

He kissed her again. Her eyes, her ears, her neck, her
mouth, more fiercely this time.

How nice it was to feel a man's lips on hers again, a
mustache that was even more bristly than the captain's in
her nostrils. She felt herself melting in his arms, her
body softening as if it was wax, fitting itself into his. A
female sculpture into the hot matrix of the male, bent,
pliable, exact. For an instant she wanted him, wanted a

man. It had been so long, more than four months, to a
lovely body unaccustomed to such starvation.

Men. What was there she did not know about men?
What experience had she not had? In her mind was the
composite body of man, all of it. Not the captain, not
Owen, just man. The feel of him. The pulsing weight of
him upon her. The seeking hands. The mouth. The smell
of cigars, of whiskey, of hair tonic, and clean sweat. The
hard, rippling muscles of a man's back under her hands.
The flat belly. The powerful thighs. The curly hair of his
body. The light of his eyes bright with his want, glazed
like those of an animal, quite expressionless in its satisfaction. For a moment, pressed against Owen, she was
not Elsie. She was woman, young nubile, and alone, being
forced by something much stronger than herself into an
ancient fulfillment in which blood, utterly divorced from
heart or mind, called to blood, pulse cried to pulse, on
this warm, tropic, moonlit night. The training of a whole
lifetime was against resistance. Acquiescence to masculine
desire had been whipped into her childish flesh. *No* was
an unknown word in her vocabulary of sex. For her a
man's wants, his desires, his lusts, all demanded satisfaction. He was the appetite, she the meal, trained to be consumed. But this was new too. Never till the captain had
she ever wanted a man. She had always been taken. Now
with Owen the feeling swept over her like a wave again.
She knew that if they had been alone in a room, in private,
he would have had her. This was the difference between
bought love and free. A free woman wanted to give herself, a bought one was taken.

She knew suddenly that she was like Queenie, in heat,
desirous for no reason except that desire was natural for
all female things. For a dog or a mare, for all animals
at certain stated, calculable intervals. For a woman at any
time, given the proper stimulus. She did not think this
in words—there had been no opportunity to formulate
such ideas before—but knew it with a kind of sudden
vision, a sense of all creation, of life, and her own place
in it as a woman.

As if he felt her weakening Owen's hand roved over
her body. She broke away. She was not angry. He had
done nothing except to pay her the compliment of a proposal. What had followed was a runaway affair for which

she as much as he was responsible. A man's hands followed his thoughts. They were the penultimate instruments of love.

"Don't go, Elsie," Owen said. "I love you and I want to marry you."

Calm now, she said, "Don't you think some things should wait till after marriage, Captain Owen? I mean if I do agree?"

"I'm sorry, my dear."

"I'm sorry too," Elsie said, going to the rail, leaning over it to look at the stars. How bright they were. In a couple of days when they crossed the line she would be in the Southern Hemisphere and here, when she looked at the stars above her, they would be the ones that he would also see.

Desire was still there, as urgent as ever, but it was for him. I'll have to wait, she thought. I'll have to wait a long time, but it will be worth it.

"Good night, Captain Owen," she said, going down the companionway to the salon to write to the captain. My captain, she thought, her eyes moist with tears at the thought of what she had so nearly done.

Table Mountain, with Cape Town nestling at its foot, its white tablecloth of cloud tumbling over its side, was like a vision of the Holy Grail to Elsie, the grandest, most magnificent thing she had ever seen. But she had never seen a mountain before, never even seen the country till she went by train from London to Southampton. And that was her first train ride.

Table Mountain seemed to her like an enormous plug that closed Africa. There it was at the bottom of the continent. Her future and her captain lay behind it. There lay the war and behind it what Rhodes called the "Hinterland and My North."

By this time Elsie knew quite a lot about Africa, about Cecil Rhodes and Paul Kruger, the Uitlanders, the gold mines and the diamonds, the wild Kaffirs, the Zulus who had been defeated by the British only twenty years ago. She had been a willing pupil with willing teachers and, though much of her knowledge was garbled and inaccurate, she had a general idea of what was going on, though no one had really been able to explain what the war was about because these simple soldiers did not know.

Lady Finch-Haddley boarded out her staff, doctors, nurses, and girls, and took Elsie and Millie to the Mount Nelson with her, fully aware of the jealousy that this step would cause but afraid to have anyone as pretty and as ignorant as Elsie on her own in the town. There was no knowing what she might do or say. On the ship the girls had been too seasick or too preoccupied with the officers who followed them about to have much time for gossip. But here, with the girls going about like a covey of partridges in the turnips, anything might happen. For Elsie was completely inexperienced in ordinary life, which to her was a kind of Alice in Wonderland existence. She knew nothing about shops, about prices, about buses, trains, or railways, and would have given herself away in the first twenty-four hours. Once people began to talk there would be no end to it, and if any of them angered her Elsie would, as likely as not, confound them with the truth and a flow of language that would curl their hair.

So it was, "You come with me, my girl."

"And Millie? What about Millie and Queenie?"

"They'll have to come too, I suppose."

And that was the way it went. There was no room at the Mount Nelson. None at all. But when Lady Finch-Haddley stormed the hill, charged in full sail into the manager's office, and informed him that either there would be two rooms at once or she'd buy the place from the Union Castle Company and fire him, the rooms were found.

The next few days were spent clearing the hospital equipment and getting it loaded into flatcars for De Aar, which was where the hospital was going to be set up.

Lady Finch-Haddley found numerous friends at the hotel. A general or two and many officers who were the sons of people she had known in her social days. Among them there were plenty who were only too pleased to take Elsie sight-seeing, with Millie and Queenie tagging along.

They went to Wynberg, to Chapman's Peak, to Woodstock, to Stellenbosch. Elsie, who had never seen wild flowers before, came home with armfuls, enraptured by the country.

"The whole thing's just one bloody great park," she said to Lady Finch-Haddley.

"Try not to swear, Elsie."

"I try. It's just when I get excited."

"I know, dear, but you are a very excitable girl."

And now something to get excited about did happen. Queenie had an affair with an Airedale belonging to General Forrestier Walker, commander of the Cape area, on the front lawn of the Mount Nelson among the pepper trees just below the fountain.

If anyone had missed hearing about the field hospital before, they heard about it now. About Nurse Smith's flat-coat and the general's Airedale. There was even a cartoon in the Cape *Times* of a dog with an Airedale front and a retriever behind looking at a rat and saying, "Shall I kill it or carry it home?"

At the time Elsie was desperate, thinking the Airedale was going to hurt Queenie and astonished that she did not defend herself. Millie, who knew about dogs, being a country girl, pulled her apron and her skirt with it over her head. This was her solution to most problems. If you stayed covered up long enough and did not suffocate, they disappeared. Lady Finch-Haddley went into peals of ribald laughter. The crowd, and of course there was a crowd, was amused, disgusted, or just pretended nothing was going on. Well-bred ladies did not cover their faces with their skirts. They just acted as though they were covered.

By the time Lady Finch-Haddley consoled Elsie and explained what was happening, and Millie had taken a couple of peeps out of a corner of her apron, a bright eye appearing like that of a mouse peeping out of its hole, and, discovering she was standing in her petticoat, had readjusted her blue uniform dress, it was over, and Queenie, her face all smiles, her pink tongue hanging out and her tail wagging, was making her way over to her mistress.

"We'll have to shut her up now," Lady Finch-Haddley said, "though it's rather like locking the stable when the horse has gone."

"Shut her up?" Elsie was indignant. "Why," she said, "that great big brute of a dog—"

"It's just so that we don't have every dog in Cape Town in the Mount Nelson garden, Elsie."

"You mean they'd all come? Do they tell each other how nice she is?"

Elsie found herself taking a new notion of Queenie, and it seemed simpler to Lady Finch-Haddley to say yes. After all, why not? Perhaps animals did tell each other things.

"We'll have pups now," Elsie said, suddenly delighted. "How long does it take?"

"Sixty-two days."

Elsie began counting on her fingers. Puppies. How lovely that would be.

But before a week was over they were on their way north, with the sick and wounded coming in before the tents were up. They came in canvas-covered ambulances marked with a red cross, in springless mule trollies and ox wagons. The stretchers were laid in lines in the sun to await attention. There were four hospital tents, an operating tent, a tent for stores, the nurses' bell tents, a marquee mess tent, and a cookhouse to be put up before the men could even be got under cover. The beds had to be broken out of their crates, sheets and mattresses found, beds made, surgical equipment and stores to be set up. But, astonishingly enough, under Lady Finch-Haddley's direction and with the aid of the soldiers and natives put at her disposal, the F.H.F.H. was in some kind of order before dark. By midnight under the flame of the acetylene and hurricane lamps the patients were in bed, fed, and the worst of the dirt cleaned off them. Elsie found herself directing the other girls. Unaccustomed to blood, dirt, and smells, half of them were in tears. They washed dysentery patients stuck into their clothes with excremental discharges, and stripped stuck and bloody bandages from the wounded, who winced but seldom cried out, though some wept quietly with relief and exhaustion. Death, which had seemed so near a few hours ago, now was being held back, by the weeping girls who attended them. There were Boers among the casualties. Several wounded, bearded, sunburned men, their faces as brown as mahogany, who watched these enemy women with cold and bitter eyes.

Lady Finch-Haddley went from tent to tent. Erect, furious at every delay.

"What did I tell you, silly creatures?" she said. "Work, dirt, stink, and blood. And you've got it. And by God, don't act so coy. There's nothing wrong with a naked man. Treat 'em like big babies with bearded faces and body hair. Flat on their backs they can't hurt you, you silly crying little bitches. You'll all see a man naked when you're married anyway. You're just seeing one sooner now. And remember, girls, some woman loves the lot of 'em—a mother, a wife, a sweetheart. They'd do it for your man. You do it for theirs."

There was nothing new to Elsie in men in one way, but everything in another. It was difficult to believe that these men who lay like patient children were fighters in their virile prime, masters of women and makers of children. This was the third phase of her experience of men. In the first she had been their slave. In the second, from Turnbull to Owen, she had been something to love and cherish, and now, here before her, was a third facet of manhood. Grown men as helpless and grateful as children brought out a feeling of motherhood in her that she had not known existed. At last she had found something she could do well. To her each man was her captain, on each, even on the sullen Boers, her hands were tender.

Soiled bandages lying on the ground like bloody snakes snatched at the girls' ankles. The hospital-trained sisters were almost as much at a loss as the girls themselves. There were no floors to the tents. The wooden sectional floor boards had not arrived with the rest of the gear. Under the beds were tussocks of grass, between them the veld was churned to dust. There were not enough enamel cups for water and they were passed most unhygienically from bed to bed by trembling girls, shattered by this first experience of reality. What about charts, about diagnosis, about temperatures? Where was the routine by which the nurses had lived their civilian lives? Intimidating though they might be to the girls in their starched efficiency, Lady F.-H. frightened the life out of them. They had never been spoken to like this before.

"If you don't like it you can bloody well get out," she said. "I'll nurse them myself with these little bitches once they've got over their squeams and nerves. You don't need thermometers to see they're ill. But none of 'em are going to die while I'm here to see they don't. Hear that, boys?" she said. "I've handled worse than you. I'll tell you what's worse—that's a pack of foxhounds with distemper."

A feeble laugh went up from the men. "An old Tartar, by God. A one, that's what she is. But a good one."

"You silly bastards," she said. "You're not dead. You're alive and you're going to stay alive, and in a month or so most of you'll be trying to pinch my girls' bottoms. But I won't have it. When a man's well enough to pinch a girl's bottom he's cured. But you can think about it. Think about what you'll do when you're up and about. Think about girls, pray to God, eat what you're given, do what you're told, and we'll send you out of here on your feet."

By the end of the first week the floor boards had arrived, every bed had a chart hanging at its foot. Temperatures were taken twice daily and the nurses had forgiven the "old hag," as they called Lady Finch-Haddley, who, without any right to the title, never having nursed anything but foxhounds and horses, called herself the Matron.

Elsie was a born nurse. She was the one the worst cases asked for. One boy, a hussar, she saved by never leaving him, sleeping on the floor boards beside his bed in spite of the nurses' orders. They appealed to Lady F.-H. She shouted them down. "He needs her," she said. "He's afraid. He's just a baby, only seventeen, and he's frightened alone."

"Alone with all those other men!"

"A boy like that's alone without a woman, Sister. It was a woman that brought him into the world and he's gone back to that time now. As long as he thinks Elsie is his mother she'll save him."

And Elsie did, by love alone, spoon-feeding him, holding his hand, and kissing his cheeks.

The men all knew what she'd done. They no longer called her nurse. She was Miss Elsie to them—"our Elsie" when they were alone.

By God, Lady Finch-Haddley thought, I was right about my little half-bred. I'd never have believed an old stick like Fenton could get a filly like that. Old Fenton in the Treasury, an ex-cabinet minister, dry as his own wastepaper. Life was really very interesting.

All the girl had needed was a chance. Me and that captain of hers, Lady Finch-Haddley thought, naturally putting herself first and leaving out Vincent.

Millie was doing well too, but took orders from no one

but Lady F.-H. herself or Miss Elsie. She turned savagely on any nurse who told her what to do. "I belong to Miss Elsie," she said. "She brought us 'ere, me and Queenie, an' she tells us wot to do."

Queenie was another worry to the nurses. A field hospital was no place for a flat-coat retriever bitch so heavily in pup that she could only waddle after her mistress. But here again Lady F.-H. won her battle. "The men like the dog," she said, "and she likes them." This was true. But Queenie had favorites, the young hussar in particular. She sat for hours staring into his face and wagging and thumping her tail on the wooden floor.

Elsie was delighted with the idea of pups. She'd keep them all and pop them into the beds of the loneliest patients when finally they arrived.

Elsie had her own ideas about nursing, based on the principle that happiness was more important than hygiene. She had already proved it to her own satisfaction. Happy men got well.

By now the nurses had pretty well given up about *that girl*. Elsie could handle the other girls far better than they could. She did more than her share of work. The men adored her. The nurses had never seen a girl so good with men before and felt it must be some inborn talent.

"You'd think," Sister Agnes said, "that she'd been with strange men all her life."

Elsie lost herself in work. She had never really worked before and enjoyed using her muscles and brains. She liked to organize, to think of what would please each individual man. She could not think of them as cases. They were men and men had always been her life. In a curious inverted fashion she repaid the brutalities she had suffered with kindnesses that brought inexplicable tears to the eyes of her patients. She succeeded in making them ashamed by showing them this other side of the female penny. Women were much more than the instruments of pleasure some of them had thought them to be. Women had a hidden strength that they could give to men. As a woman relieved a man from the intolerable burden of his lust, so she relieved him of his fears and anxieties when he lay helpless. Each had been helpless before, an infant in his mother's arms. The situation now repeated

itself with an interval of years and experience between
the two. He had known women, had slept with women.
In a way these girls were the women he had lain with and
loved. Perhaps in a way they were his mother. There was
a vague incestuous feeling, a curious ambivalence. Part
of it was so right—that a woman should tend him because
he was as helpless as a child. Part of it was wrong—that
he, a grown man, should be handled by marriageable girls
as if he were a baby.

Only with Elsie was there no feeling of this, because
Elsie loved them all, but was not there at all—only her
love, an abstract thing, and her clever hands were there.
Elsie was far away, hiding in the arms of her captain,
who did not even know she was here in Africa.

But she got news of him; an occasional trooper from the
2nd who knew some gossip, a man from GHQ with dysentery who had actually seen him.

"Funny thing, Nurse," he said, "he's got a little black
mare he calls Miss Elsie." She nearly burst into tears at
this bit of news.

Then orders came and they had to move from De Aar
to Bloemfontein. What a business that was, sending the
wounded down the line, packing up, trekking over the
veld in wagons for days—a forced march to meet the
emergency of sickness that was decimating the men who
had fought at Paardeberg.

Bloemfontein. Roberts' headquarters. There she would
be within a mile or two of Turnbull. How was she going
to resist the temptation? What could he be thinking of
her, with no letters, no news? She had left with Vincent a
dozen letters to send that said nothing, but they would
all have gone by now. And besides, they were not the usual
day-by-day, hour-by-hour reports that he was used to. He
might be thinking anything. She knew what he would be
thinking. He'll think, she thought, that I'm not faithful to
him, that I don't love him, that I've gone to another man.
Why shouldn't he think that with a girl like me? So with
this in her mind she cried herself to sleep in her wagon bed
every night.

The Boers had cut the railway line in so many places
that everything Roberts needed had to come over the veld
in convoys, and the interest of being a part of this curious

procession prevented Elsie from being too moody during the day. She had never seen oxen before, never seen the endless plains of Africa that reminded her of the sea.

The line of great wagons rolled and rocked over the veld, remounts and cattle for slaughter churned up clouds of dust on either side of them. The drivers' whip claps sounded like pistol shots when they screamed in high-pitched voices to their oxen.

And about them a cavalry guard moved in a screen of scouts, advance guard, flank and rear guards.

Elsie wondered if any of them were 2nd Hussars, but felt too shy to ask.

When the F.H.F.H. reached Bloemfontein, the condition of the troops was beyond belief. Hundreds of men in the last stages of typhoid were lying on ground sheets—they had no beds—with only a blanket to cover them. There was no milk, few medicines, no mattresses or pillows, no nurses to help them, only untrained orderlies who seldom washed their hands even after handling the slop pails. In some tents ten sick and dying men lay so close together that there was no room to step between them. Flies in black clusters covered the faces of men too weak to brush them off.

A doctor, one of the few, almost dead himself from overwork, said, "If you have antiseptics you have no water. If you have water it is insufficient and so bad that all you can do with it is to boil it, filter it, and chuck it away." He burst into laughter. "That's what you do, Lady Finch-Haddley. That's what you do," he said.

"You do," she said, "but I don't."

Nothing, it seemed to Elsie, could get the old girl down. No hardship, no stink, and there was plenty of it—vomit, excreta, stale sweat, urine, rotting scraps of food—or flies. Small flies, big fat bluebottles, shiny metallic green ones. Everything was covered with a fur of flies. One got into Elsie's mouth and she spat it out. Got to keep your bloody kisser shut here, she thought. But work—Christ, there was work for them all here—women's work. The taking care of men in one way or another had always been her life. But this way was a change, for now she was strong and they were weak.

CHAPTER 38

THE SWEEPINGS

IN AFRICA both the British and the Boers were resting. The Boers were licking their wounds and making new plans. The British lying doggo, waiting for the supplies that would enable them to refit before the bitter, high-veld winter began.

The fall of Bloemfontein, the Orange Free State capital, had a profound effect in England. Confidence was restored. The great powers ceased pulling the British lion's tail. When they found that lions as well as worms could turn.

Milner had to cable home to stop the stream of tourists arriving with every ship on the tours of the battlefields that Thomas Cook was offering. And the old Queen made two public drives through the streets of London to give the crowds an outlet for their patriotic fervor. It did them good to cheer.

Peace proposals made by both Steyn and Kruger were contemptuously turned down. The Queen of the Netherlands asked the Kaiser to support collective action on the Boers' behalf, but he avoided the issue, saying that, unless the United States took the initiative, God's instrument for punishing injustice with relentless severity might well be the German fleet that he was now building in preparation for *Der Tag*, certain that God would be *"mit uns"* when the time came. But in the meantime the Boers, as far as he was concerned, could stew in their own juice, and after all the Queen of England was his grandmother.

Roberts, the Boer bird almost in his grasp, issued a proclamation on March 15 offering amnesty to all Boers willing to lay down their arms and go home. Eight thousand Free Staters accepted the offer, took an oath of neutrality, handed in their rifles, and went home.

The fate of the Cape rebels, technically British subjects, still remained in doubt. But clement treatment seemed certain.

If Roberts had been able to push on now, at once, the war would have been over in a month. But he could not push on without horses or supplies. Only a third of French's horses were fit for use. Ten thousand horses a month were being brought into South African ports, and another five thousand were being obtained locally— bought from the Basutos, commandeered, captured, or caught wild on the veld. And still there were never enough, so great was the mortality. The remount department was incompetent, composed of officers unfit for regular service. To relieve pressure on the railway, horses were driven in herds over the veld before they were acclimatized and had either grown or cast their coats. Horses from England, sleek in summer coats, arrived in the African winter. And those that left England with heavy winter coats were put to work in temperatures that often topped a hundred degrees. Many of the troopers and mounted infantry were poor riders, and the horses were unequal to the strain that was put on them.

This was the horse picture and, apart from the railroad and the slow, plodding oxen, horses and mules were the only form of transport. In the Boer War men either rode horses or marched on foot.

While Roberts was held up in Bloemfontein, Chief Justice Gregorowski led a deputation of lawyers to President Kruger, urging him to stop the war. Oom Paul replied in biblical terms, quoting the Revelations: " 'The beast,' " he said, " 'would war with the Church and seem to overcome it, but in the end God will intercede.' " The English were of course the beast.

Old General Joubert now died of old age and a broken heart. His saddled horse followed the gun carriage that bore his coffin. All the consular officials in Pretoria followed the procession. Lord Roberts sent condolences, saying that the dead commandant general's personal gallantry was surpassed only by his humane conduct and chivalrous bearing. . . .

The British could well do Joubert honor, for had he acted more decisively at the outbreak of war its course might well have been different. Piet Joubert, the man who had refused to take God's hand when He only gave him a finger, was now out of it. It was at his own wish, when he first fell sick, that the command had passed to

Louis Botha, a man in his full powers and a born soldier.

The Boer leaders were now younger and at the same time more experienced: Botha, Hertzog, Smuts, De Wet, and such old warriors as Christiaan de la Rey.

As Kruger's will and health failed it was Steyn to whom the Boers looked—a big, powerful, steadfast man, cultured, fully aware of the strength of the British Empire but ready to defy it in the name of God, justice, and freedom.

The Free State Government had moved to Kroonstad, and new plans were made. Families were banned from the convoys. Women were forbidden to fight. All transport was to be cut to an absolute minimum. Foreign volunteers were encouraged and were put under the command of the Count de Villebois-Mareuil, a colorful French officer who had once led the Foreign Legion.

Given time to recover themselves, and learning through their spies of the exhaustion of Roberts' men and horses, the Boers rallied. They still had two great hopes. The foreign nations might intervene, or Britain's will to continue a war of which many of her people disapproved might wane, and a negotiated peace with honor still be achieved.

This was the position when Christiaan de Wet and his brother Piet rode northwest, their destination unknown to any of the two thousand horsemen who accompanied them, Moolman and Boetie among them.

It was curiously exciting to ride into the unknown under a leader like Christiaan de Wet, with his reputation of unbroken victory. They rode west for a day and then, having thrown any possible spies off the scent, went south toward Sannah's Post, where Bloemfontein's waterworks were situated. The scouts reported that they were held by only two hundred men, and De Wet informed his troops that he was going to take the place and cut off the town's water.

That night, March 30–31, Piet de Wet set off with sixteen hundred men to drive the garrison toward the four hundred his brother Christiaan had hidden below the banks of the Modder.

Moolman, lying beside Boetie by the river, told him that these were the tactics of a pride of lions. The roaring male driving the game toward the waiting lioness—in this case Christiaan.

But while this operation was in progress a British cavalry brigadier—General Broadwood—with two thousand men and a train of supply wagons reached the waterworks.

Christiaan now found himself confronting two thousand men with only four hundred, and if his brother and Olivier, who was also in action, did not come up in time, he might find himself trapped. So, characteristically, he decided to take a chance and attack.

Broadwood's men were resting, assuming everything to be quiet and that they were in no danger. Piet now arrived and dropped some shells into their bivouac. Thinking they were outnumbered, the British inspanned and began to cross the spruit.

Not a sound came from Christiaan's men, not a shot. The lead wagons were allowed to cross. Then Christiaan himself went into the river bed and directed the terrified drivers to either flank like a policeman—one to the left, one to the right, and so on.

Two gunner officers, thinking this was the usual mix-up that occurred crossing any drift, thus went straight on and were taken by De Wet, who at gunpoint ordered them to dismount and told them they were prisoners. One officer broke away and shouted, waving to the following gun teams, "Files about . . . Gallop!"

This was the first sign of an engagement, which up till now had been conducted in utter silence. The Boers opened rapid fire on the escaping battery and the standing horses of the captured guns before they could get away.

Boetie had not fired a shot. He just lay staring open-mouthed at this fantastic scene. The captured wagons in the sluit, the dead gun horses and the wounded kicking in their traces. The escaping battery. Beside him Moolman was firing cool, calculated shots.

"Shoot, God damn it!" he shouted. "Shoot the horses!"

Automatically Boetie fired, hitting a wheel horse through the shoulder and bringing it down. It was almost worse to shoot a horse than a man. . . . Again he was overcome by his feelings. Not a shot had been fired at them, and it occurred to him again that he could fight only when he was frightened. He had to be shot at first. But now that he had begun, his rifle became alive in his hands and he brought down a driver who was trying to cut out a wounded horse. The guns, now seventy yards away, unlimbered and opened fire at point-blank range, but the Boers were too well entrenched for much harm to be done. A British officer had his stick knocked out of his hand by a bullet, stooped to pick it up, and was killed. Volunteers ran forward to try to manhandle the guns away. Once again, as at Colenso, every effort was made to save the guns. The prestige of the guns remained. But at last Broadwood disengaged himself. He had lost six hundred men, eighty of his ninety wagons, and seven of his twelve guns. But this was not the most serious part of the British loss. Their water was cut off, and water for a whole town had to be brought up by the railroad, already strained to the breaking point. This water shortage caused a further increase in the enteric epidemic, and before the end of April two thousand more people in Boemfontein were dead.

The job done, both De Wets rode off with Olivier and, hearing that Dewetsdorp, a village named after their father, was being held by four hundred English under Gatacre, they attacked and defeated them.

All over the country the Boers took new heart, and many who had taken the oath of neutrality changed their minds and rejoined their commandos.

Roberts was shaken. The Boers were far from beaten as he had thought. In a week they had captured almost a thousand men, an enormous booty of guns and supplies, and, worst of all, had cut off his water.

Nor was this all. To upset his calculations further were the Boers who had taken the oath and had gone back to battle. It was as if the dead he had written off had come to life again. The arithmetic had gone wrong. That which had been subtracted now had to be added in again.

De Wet's impassioned pleas had been too much for the Boers. Their oaths had been given under duress. They had thought themselves defeated, but with the De Wets still in the saddle, adorned with victory, they could not hold back.

As to their rifles—the ones they had handed in were elephant guns, muzzle-loaders, ancient pieces that were of no value. Their own weapons they had buried, for without arms they would have been helpless against wild beasts or natives.

De Wet was a man, a leader; under him they would serve again and win. Boetie was as elated as the others. This was war indeed. High adventure. Fast riding and fighting, behind a leader who knew his business, a man with brains and a will of iron—loved by no one, followed by all.

But Christiaan de Wet, like Sir John French, like every other man, had his Achilles' heel, his weaknesses and his prejudices, his loves and his hates.

The greatest of these was his hatred for the Colonials. Brabant's Colonial Division was made up very largely of South African volunteers fighting their brothers for a wage. "The Judas Boers," with their thirty pieces of silver, whom he called the "sweepings"—the scum of Africa. Brabant's men were occupying the village of Wepener. Collecting a force of six thousand burghers, De Wet decided to attack them, not out of any military exigency but out of hatred alone.

Wepener lay on the border of Basutoland, and here on April 9 the astonished natives watched the white men fight against each other.

Dalgety, one of Brabant's colonels, had his men ready, well entrenched among the hills outside the town. Behind them the mountains of Basutoland towered in cathedral cliffs and pinnacles, sharp-edged against the lowering sky.

De Wet got into action at once and almost at once the rain began. Only Christiaan could have held his men. Soaked to the skin, their teeth chattering, they lay firing their rifles at anything that moved. At 2 A.M., the rain still pouring, De Wet, a sjambok in hand, flogging the more dilatory of his burghers, led an attack right up to the British trenches, where it was repelled by a bayonet charge.

This was a new experience for Boetie. Blinded by rain, running through the mud into a hail of bullets, and finally finding himself face to face with dark forms barely distinguishable as men except for the flash of their grinning teeth and the shining whites of their eyes. He parried the sharp points of the lunging bayonets with sidewipes of his rifle that almost paralyzed his arm. Slipping in the mud, and the slip may have saved his life, Boetie drove the muzzle of his Mauser into a traitor's belly. He felt its softness as it gave to his thrust, and fired. Blood up now,

he had no further consciousness of fear, only of a fighting rage. All around him were the flashes of rifles, the
sound of explosions, the crack and whistle of bullets, the
bang of rifle striking rifle, even the opening and closing
of bolts. There were no men. Only the forms of men, half
visible like devils in the bitter driving rain. His fingers
were so cold he could hardly feel them, almost frozen to
his gun. He fought on till Moolman at his side pulled him
back.

"We can't do it!" he shouted. "They are too strong."
And together with the other Boers they fell back, leaving
their dead and wounded behind them. Still they did not
give up, but fought on for four days in the rain, their only
consolation being that the plight of the defenders was as
bad if not worse than their own, for their trenches, below
the runoff of the hills, were flooded and any man who
moved out of them was doomed.

Moolman's life seemed charmed, like those of so many
who seek death but do not court it. As long as he was
near him Boetie felt safe, as if this older man was some
kind of talisman.

So there they lay surrounding in a half circle the British Colonial troops in whose rear were the foothills and
mountains of a foreign state—the territory of Basutoland.

Lord Roberts, getting reports of the action, heliographed for permission for them to retire into Basutoland.
But even this was impossible, as their horses were all dead,
killed by the Boers' fire. The discomfort of the flooded
trenches was almost unbearable. The men only got food,
and cold at that, after dark when the ration parties came
up to carry off the wounded and the dead. Their one hope
was the approach of the relief columns that were said to
be on their way. They must hold out until they came.

In a way this action of De Wet's was a godsend for
Roberts. At last he had De Wet pinned down and hoped
to destroy him, to catch him in the triple net of the columns he had flung in his direction. With De Wet out of
the way he could continue his march north without
danger to his line of communications. But De Wet was
not Cronje or Joubert. As the relieving troops approached,
he sent small picked forces to hold them up, continued
his attack on Wepener, got his own transport wagons away,

and held up the British by a skillful rear-guard action. It was not until April 25, after sixteen days of siege, that the first relief column entered the village, only a few hours after the last Boers had got clear away.

Yet this was not the end. Ian Hamilton had been sent to recapture Sannah's Post and restore the city's water supply. This he did, and continued on, hoping to cut off De Wet at Thaba N'chu, but when he got there he found the Boers to be safely laagered on the other side of the mountain. French now joined him and they hoped by attacking from both sides to take De Wet in a pincer movement, but the Boer defense was so vigorous and French's horses in such poor condition (he lost two hundred in a sixty-mile ride) that the attack was called off and De Wet, slippery as an eel, was out of the net again.

The Boers were exhausted but also exhilarated. Theirs had been a notable achievement. They felt themselves real veterans now, a picked body, the very bone and muscle of resistance from which all the useless fat had been whittled away. This was the beginning of the hard core, the very pulse of the Boer heart. They trusted Christiaan de Wet. For the first time in the history of their nation, a commando had been disciplined. There was no more of the democratic nonsense now that had lost other battles. De Wet ordered and they obeyed. He had even reduced Commandant Vilonel to the ranks for disobeying orders and bringing more transport than the new regulations permitted. These were no longer mounted farmers who all thought themselves to be generals, but soldiers—a body of irregular horsemen whose fighting qualities had never been equaled before, nor since surpassed.

"By God," Boetie said, "that was something!" The cold, the fighting on foot, the lack of hot food, and no ponies nearby to escape on.

Moolman laughed. "We are alive," he said, "and in war, as long as one is still living things could always be worse."

It was now May 1. May Day. Winter was at hand in Africa. In England the hedgerows were in bloom with dog roses and scented honeysuckle. In the daytime the cuckoo called, and when the cuckoo slept the nightingale began. War and peace. Winter and summer were six thousand miles—a hemisphere—apart. Snow tipped the peaks of the Drakensberg and south winds, born in Antarctica, began to sweep the high veld, the great plains of the Transvaal that lay a full mile above the sea.

Strange tales of war, fact, fancy, or latrine rumor, percolated through the commandos, seeping down from above, rising from the very veld by a kind of capillary action.

There was the story of Count de Villebois-Mareuil's death. He had set out with a hundred fifty Frenchmen to blow up the bridge across the Modder that the British had repaired, but deflected his course to attack the village of Boshof, where he was caught by Methuen, who sent 750 mounted men and a battery of guns to take him. Most of the Count's men escaped, but with a small party of hardy men he went on fighting till the British were less than a hundred yards away when he fell, wounded to the death.

So this great soldier, gentleman, adventurer, and knight-errant escaped from the era of chivalry, died facing the enemy in the cause of freedom, his boots still on his feet, and was buried by Lord Methuen with full military honors. "The Last Post," a firing party, the lot. And another little drama of this strange war was played out, as the volley crashed into the still air of Africa and the bugles wept their lament for the brave dead.

Another event dealing with a foreign volunteer was the death of the Russian Colonel Maximoff, who, with a hundred-odd men, surprised a party of Gordon Highlanders and ordered them to surrender. Their leader, Captain Towse, told his men to take cover and fired his pistol point blank at the Russian. Both men fell wounded. Towse held out till help arrived, but he lost his eyesight and was later decorated with the V.C., the medal pinned onto his breast by the Queen herself in London.

But now, at last, the long rest at Bloemfontein was over. Roberts was ready to close in for the kill. The capture of Pretoria, which would end the war. With both capitals in British hands the Boers must inevitably give in, having nothing left to fight for. But Roberts was wrong. His was a European, an urban point of view. To the Boer farmers, towns, even capitals, meant little. There was still plenty of Africa to fight for, plenty of room on the veld to maneuver. They were now going to play with space, juggling it like a ball, operating in a country that they knew, living off the land without any lines of communication. Both time and distance were on their side. The more Roberts extended himself the more vulnerable he became. And the longer they held out the more chance there was of something happening that would favor their cause.

But Roberts, marching north to victory, did not know this. He did not know Africa or the Boers.

The news that Mafeking had fallen reached London at 9:30 P.M. on Friday, May 18. The siege of seven months was over, and all England was in an uproar.

The couple who had come to make love at No. 7 never even finished their dinner, and a hansom was called. Vincent, Celeste, and the cook piled into a growler. "West End!" Vincent shouted as they set off at a canter, the cabby cracking his whip, but they did not get very far. The streets were filled with streams of people that poured into the main thoroughfares, singing, shouting, cheering. They sang "Rule Britannia," "Soldiers of the Queen," "Rule Britannia" again. "The Absent-minded Beggar." "God Save the Queen." A flood of people going one way met a flood of people going the other. From the Mansion House to Piccadilly, from Regent Street to Park Lane the mass of humanity, welded by song and sweat into a vast river, flowed and eddied. Brass bands appeared from nowhere, people danced when they found room. London had gone mad and the verb "to maffick" was born.

It was daylight when Vincent and his party got home. He had bought all the papers. The story of the siege and Baden-Powell, its hero, filled the papers. This little frontier town had made the headlines in a big way and given a new word to the English language—the village that the Baralong tribesmen called the place of stones, so poor was the soil. A featureless, undulating landscape, half desert, almost treeless—trees were so rare that they were landmarks. A shallow, sluggish stream, the Molopo, ran through it, invisible, unexpected except where the bush, low scrub here, followed its tortuous course like a dirty, olive ribbon spread over the red, dusty veld. Four thousand feet above sea level the nights were cold, but the daytime heat was intense. Bone dry except after summer storms, when a flooded spate turned the river into a torrent. All quickly come and quickly gone, like a gambler's gold. A tin-roofed shanty town decorated with the only trees that could stand the savage climate and the poor soil—blue gums and feathery pepper trees hung with tiny scarlet berries. Trees that looked like weeping willows at first sight and recalled them nostalgically to those who came from the more temperate and well-watered regions where they grow.

The houses numbered three hundred. The white inhabitants—mixed Boer and English—twelve hundred. The Baralong, five thousand. This was the capital of Bechuanaland, with a resident commissioner for native affairs, a resident magistrate, a jail and courthouse, three hotels, two schools, several chapels and churches, a convent and a Masonic hall.

Mafeking was on the old "Missionary Road," opened up by Moffat and Livingstone, who were followed by Cecil Rhodes's pioneers as they struck north over the Limpopo. This country, Bechuanaland, was the link that joined Rhodesia to the Cape. It also cut the Transvaal off from the Atlantic Ocean and their German friends in the west. For years the Boers had pressed on the Bechuanas, even establishing two absurd little republics of Stellaland and Goshen that lasted a year or two within their territory.

Mafeking had also an emotional connotation among the Boers. It evoked the name of Dr. Jameson. This had been his headquarters during the raid, and they were determined that "not one stone of the village should be left upon another." Mafeking must cease to exist.

The Boers had reason for their optimism. They had beaten the English in '81. The Kaiser, twirling his mustache and rattling his saber, had sent a telegram congratulating the President on his rout of "the Jameson criminals" in '96. France still smarted under the humiliation of Fashoda. Russia was sympathetic and waiting her chance to fall on Turkey and India. Foreign intervention and the ruin of England had seemed certain.

The siege had lasted two hundred seventeen days. Twenty thousand Boer shells had been fired into Mafeking.

Fifteen hundred British and colonial fighting men had held nearly fifteen thousand Boers at bay for all this time by a series of bluffs and ruses, by mine fields that contained only buried boxes of sand, by dummy men, dummy guns, and unmanned fortifications, by a portable searchlight constructed out of a biscuit tin illuminated by carbide from a supply that a salesman had brought into the town hoping to get people to use this new gas instead of kerosene lamps for illumination.

Against them the Boers employed a six-inch gun, enormous for those days, firing a ninety-four-pound projectile, and a number of lighter Krupp and Creusot guns, and one-pounder Vickers-Maxims. Some interesting letters were exchanged between Colonel Baden-Powell and General Cronje after the Boers had failed to take Mafeking by storm.

Cronje wrote:

Honoured Sir: Since it appears to me that there is no other chance of taking Mafeking than by means of a bombardment, I have to adopt that course with regret. I have to allow you forty-eight hours to prepare your people, black and white. You have to see that noncombatants leave Mafeking before the expiration of that time. If you do not comply with this I will not be answerable for the result. . . .

The time allowed to you I reckon from Saturday 21st, at 6 A.M., till Monday morning, the 23rd, at the same hour.

Baden-Powell replied to Cronje in the following terms, which sound curious to our ears, accustomed as we have become to the massacre of civilians and destruction of property:

Sir: I am sorry that you have to confess yourself unable to take Mafeking without bombarding it. But this course you are quite at liberty to take if you imagine it will help you. At the same time I would remind you that the present war is of one government against another—not of people against people. Now you purpose to inflict damage upon private property and a peaceful town, and possibly to injure women and children under the excuse of war. . . .

I am much obliged to you for giving warning to the noncombatants to move away from Mafeking; but they do not propose to avail themselves of it. In return for your courtesy I wish to warn your people that I have had the ground at a distance around Mafeking prepared with dynamite defence mines. Some of these are self-acting; the others are fired from observation points. I am loath to make use of them except when special reasons of defence may demand it. . . .

The British armament consisted of seven Maxims with only sixty thousand rounds of ammunition, and a Hotchkiss one-pounder, a two-inch Nordenfeldt firing a three-quarter-pound shell, and four seven-pound muzzle-loaders, dating, quite unbelievably, from 1820. Only 576 men were equipped with Lee-Enfields. The balance of the garrison had obsolete Martini-Henry single-loaders.

Later, two more muzzle-loading cannon were in action. The first was a homemade howitzer whose barrel was a steel tube that had been a steam pipe, strengthened with a jacket of iron railings that had been bent into rings and shrunk onto it, mounted on the chassis of a threshing machine with broad, iron-tired wheels. The second was even more curious. An officer, riding out one day, had come across a gatepost, half buried in the sand, that looked like an old cannon. It was dug up, cleaned, and turned out to be a bronze sixteen-pounder ship's gun dated 1770, but bearing no royal cipher that would have proved its naval origin. It was therefore believed to have come from a privateer wrecked on the coast, since it was known that one of the tribes migrating north to Bechuanaland had carried a gun with them, finally abandoning it when they ran out of powder at Mafeking, the place of stones. Named Lord Nelson to commemorate its naval career, it was soon in action and to everyone's surprise had a range of three thousand yards, and at the first shot sent its ball bouncing into the Boer laager at which it had been aimed.

All this, the initiative and the defense against such great odds, was due to the British commander, Colonel Robert Stephenson Smyth Baden-Powell, a man of forty-one, a 13th Hussar who had served in India, Malta, Afghanistan, the Gold Coast, and Egypt. He had served in

Africa at the Cape, Natal, and Zululand, had ridden eight hundred miles alone on a scouting mission, pretending he was a newspaperman, through the Transvaal and Free State. In 1896 he had fought the Matabele in Rhodesia, where he and the great American scout Fred Burnham became friends. In India he had commanded the 5th Dragoon guards with great success, and it was in India that, to interest young soldiers, he started a course in scouting. Carrying this idea further in Mafeking, he organized all the boys into a Cadet Corps of messenger boys. They were the actual forerunners of the great world-wide Boy Scout movement.

Baden-Powell issued stamps, printed money, set up a factory for processing horse meat. There was no more grazing for them, so, as an Irish officer said, "We killed the horses to save their lives."

When a horse was killed, the mane and tail were cut off and sent to the hospital for stuffing mattresses and pillows. The shoes went to the foundry for making shells. The skin, after having the hair scalded off, was boiled with the head and feet for many hours, chopped up small, and . . . served out as "brawn."

The flesh taken from the bones was minced in a great mincing machine and the bowels used as skins into which the meat was crammed to form the sausage ration.

The bones were first boiled into a soup, and then pounded into powder that was added to the flour.

Another addition to the diet of the besieged population was sowens, made from the husks of forage oats. They were soaked for forty-eight hours, the scum removed for chicken feed, and the residue boiled up into a paste resembling that used by paper hangers—a mess that was filling and just edible with the addition of salt and other flavorings. A form of blancmange made with the *poudre de riz* stocked by hairdressers was tried but did not prove to be a culinary success.

The rations dwindled to a theoretical half pound of horse brawn and a quarter pound of vegetables per day. A pound of flour, stretched with bone meal, was issued each day with a quart of sowens. Swarms of locusts, usually a curse, were welcomed, and were served curried. There was plenty of curry powder.

"Vincent, put the paper down."

"Locusts," he said. "Fancy eating locusts."

"*Sauterelles,*" Celeste said. "*Mon Dieu,* what next? But in Paris in the siege they ate rats. My father told me. *Civet de rat.*"

"Well, he was French," Vincent said. "They'll eat anything. Frogs, snails. These were English people—civilized . . ."

"So I am *barbare* . . . a barbarian me . . . French, who were civilized a thousand years before you, when you ran naked in little pants of blue paint and ate people. Me, a barbarian! What next, I ask myself."

"All right," Vincent said, "you are civilized, you are beautiful."

"That's better," Celeste said. "My God, I am tired." Tired. No wonder. Everyone was tired.

What a night it had been. Whistles blowing everywhere for hansoms, traffic jammed from West End to East End, from the Bank to Park Lane, well-dressed men climbing lampposts. Buses, their two white horses standing patient in their harness, became islands in a seething sea of shouting, singing people. They sang "Pop Goes the Weasel," "Dook's Son, Cook's Son, Son of a Bloody Earl." They sang music-hall ditties. Bareheaded, they sang "God Save the Queen." They sang hymns—"Onward, Christian Soldiers." They chanted psalms. They cheered the Queen. They shouted, "Bravo Baden-Powell!" "Well done Mafeking." "Hurrah! Hurrah!"

This miserable little dorp, a shanty town of one-story brick houses with tin roofs, might have been a great capital for the fuss that was made of its relief. Mafeking was nothing, Mafeking was everything—a symbol. Though a symbol of what no one quite knew.

Vincent pulled Celeste into his lap and kissed her. She was a good girl. Just his cup of tea.

"Men," she said, "they are the same. It is only one thing they want."

"Not just men, Ducks," he said. "The women come here on their own, don't they? It's about the same, half and half, like beer. But they make more fuss about it and want more for it. Want to have their cake and eat it too. . . ." Vincent thought about Miss Elsie and the captain. He wondered if he'd been at Mafeking. Where was

Miss Elsie? And Queenie? Who in the world had ever heard of a flat-coat bitch killing a man? He'd bet she had had pups by now if he could find someone to bet with, because Miss Elsie'd never stop her. Not she, with her good heart.

It would be a day or two before business settled down again. People were too excited even for love.

Vincent began a story in the *Strand* magazine about a detective called Sherlock Holmes, by Arthur Conan Doyle, a doctor who was serving in South Africa. He liked his stories. But he was unable to concentrate on this one. Things in South Africa were not as good as they looked. No matter how many people shouted and sang.

The captain's letters had not been encouraging, nor had Miss Elsie's. And he had a lot of other things to think about. The captain did not know Miss Elsie was in Africa. She posted her letters back to London and he stamped them and sent them on. They took about three months to make the round trip, and he could not imagine what he found to say.

The captain never wrote to him directly about her. How could he? He just said, "I hope you're taking good care of Miss Elsie," and things like that. To which he replied that he was . . . But that was not the whole of it. There were worse things, though in looking back it was difficult to see quite how it all started or even who began it. It was probably his wife's fault—the girl who had run away with a dragoon who was a publican and had got fatter and fatter till she died of it. Her heart being incapable of dealing with the soft mass of rosy flesh she had become. The prettily rounded girl he had married— and what, after all, were curves but adipose tissue?—had gone from the high condition he had described to the stoutness of a matron and beyond that to a slug-like grossness. Her high-stepping beauty had come back to Vincent's mind when he got the letter.

"Dear Sergeant Vincent," it began, "I am sorry to inform you that Audrey is dead and buried last Tuesday, the 15th ult., her passing much regretted by all and by me your humble servant more than anybody. I cannot say I ever liked you or that from what she said you ever made her happy, but as one member of Her Majesty's cavalry to another I felt I should inform you of my great loss. She was a splendid woman." Vincent pondered the phrase. The kind of woman a dragoon would like, massive as a Flemish mare. It was extraordinary how women changed, with age, with good food, no work, and lots of beer. Audrey had always liked beer.

He had got no further with the letter. Celeste snatched it out of his hand and he never saw it again. He often wondered how it had ended.

"So—Monsieur Vincent is *veuve*. And now nothing stands in the way of his mad passion but a few words and *un bout de papier*. So get your 'at, *mon cher—chéri* —and we will proceed to the *mairie tout de suite*."

The passion was true. Vincent in his maturity, he was forty-one, had been teased into near madness by this French girl, the maid he had obtained for his master's mistress. She was a delectable creature. Slim but rounded, fiery, with a quick mind, neat fingers, and a wonderful head for figures. He got his hat and they went to the registrar's office together. A week later Vincent, duly spliced, was accorded the privileges that he had so long desired and that Celeste, chaste for too long, was eager to share now that the *bout de papier*—her marriage lines —was safely locked in her tin trunk.

The witnesses were Ellen, who cried with happiness, and the boy, now promoted to coachman, as Charlie had gone back to the colors.

It had all begun so simply. Bored with idleness, Celeste had started making lace-trimmed lingerie and hats that she sold through a kind of lady's-maid underground at a handsome profit. She next decided to branch out and turn No. 7 into a small but very select shop. Other maids with time on their hands made more lingerie. Ladies came to see her hats and bought them. And then, one day a lady came, a very pretty lady, with a wedding ring on her hand, accompanied by a man so solicitous that he could not have been her husband.

A day later he returned alone. She saw him in the drawing room.

"Madame Celeste," he said, "if you will allow me to speak in confidence about a matter of some delicacy, I should be most grateful."

"But of course, *monsieur,*" she said.

"Then let us begin this way," he said, putting two folded five-pound notes into her hand.

"My name," he went on, "is of no importance. Perhaps you could call me Mr. Ten. Two fives make ten." He was obviously a man of humor.

"Monsieur Dix," she said, "pray continue."

"You have here, madame," he said, "a house that is staffed but empty. Your master and mistress are both in Africa. So here is what I am going to suggest. That for a certain sum, the exact amount to be arrived at later, you will permit me and my friend to come here occasionally for tea. There are unfortunately few places where a gentleman can converse with a lady who is not his wife without danger of scandal or interruption. I trust I make myself clear, madame."

"But absolutely, Monsieur Dix. For a certain sum, not yet specified, Monsieur would like to entertain a lady to tea in this establishment. If it would not derange Monsieur, for convenience and to ensure complete privacy, would Monsieur mind if tea was served in the bedroom?"

"That would be very nice, madame. Cozy, as we say in English."

"Also, since this house has an entrance through the garden, Monsieur might find it more convenient to come in that way. The garden has a certain charm. The flowers are beautiful for London, in summer only, naturally, and it is surrounded by a high wall.

"There will be no charge. How could there be for so slight an accommodation? Are we not Christians bound by God and nature to assist each other when confronted by problems? But of course Madame cannot go away empty-handed. She will buy one of my confections. A hat, a little lingerie. Both being completely handmade and original, I charge very highly for them. Would Monsieur consider fifty guineas too much? Half in advance naturally."

It was in this charming manner that No. 7 knew love again. First that of Vincent and Celeste. Then that of Monsieur Dix and his blond paramour. Then others, many others. Never more than one couple a day. But among certain ladies of fashion a Celeste hat was a kind of trademark, a cupid footprint sewed into the lining of a bonnet.

The word spread through valets and maids, and, not surprisingly, many of the gentlemen were officers of cavalry. Either waiting to go to South Africa, or returning, incapacitated by wounds or illness, from the scene of action.

Even the brougham came in handy. Who could suspect so discreet a vehicle?

Vincent was not one to spoil a ship for a hap'orth of tar. The meals Ellen cooked were gastronomic miracles, the wines he served of unsurpassed vintage. The flower-filled house was beautifully kept by a new French house-maid introduced by Celeste, a plain but honest peasant woman whose Norman cupidity made her blind, and whose lack of English ensured her silence. Even French people could not understand her.

The savings of this admirable couple rose to astronomical heights, and they began to invest money in house property, most of it in the slums where the rents were high and the upkeep negligible.

Vincent had begun to put on weight. Marriage suited him, and as he was a man of property a certain rotundity emphasized his affluence.

His master still paid the rent and wages, but these were put into a special bank account in Captain Turnbull's name, for Vincent was an honest man.

Eventually, when he hoped to be braver, he planned to tell his master what he had done and buy his lease, which still had twenty years to run. He would also take over the furniture at the full purchase price, and naturally he would take care of the horses, which he loved almost as much as his master, till the captain wanted them. If the running cost of No. 7 were enormous, so were the profits.

But it wasn't all beer and skittles and it was getting harder and harder to write to the captain about a mistress who wasn't there. It must all look very fishy, and he'd bet the captain thought there was another man in the offing. And suppose he asked him? What then? To lie well, you had to start young, like a conjurer, to keep all these balls in the air.

CHAPTER 39

PRETORIA

THE DAY was beautiful, crisp, calm, one of those bright blue, early autumn days that bring the Transvaaler's heart into his mouth and tears into his eyes. The poplars were candles of yellow gold. The Lucerne seemed greener because the veld was brown. The chrysanthemums burned their dark red and pink flames in the garden beds. Purple bougainvillaea poured over whitewashed walls and the bright red flaming stars of the poinsettias turned their faces to the sun. God was in His heaven.

The war was over, and the British were marching into Pretoria to take over the capital.

"They are coming, Mother," Renata said. "The khakis are coming, the rooineks." She stamped her foot.

"The war is over," Louisa said. "We have fought hard, but we are beaten by the greatest empire the world has ever seen. We need have no shame." She could not understand her sister. At first it had been she who had felt the war. She who had been the patriotic one. Renata had been too upset by the horror of war to feel its excitement, nor did she miss the men. But slowly, as the tide turned and disaster overtook the Boers, her outlook had changed, and now when it was over she seemed unable to face the facts. She looked at her sister as if she had gone mad.

"What on earth are you doing, Renata?" Renata had her wide-brimmed straw hat on her knee, and was tying a *vierkleur* ribbon around the brim

"Doing? I am decorating my hat, and then I am going to see the British come in. I want to see what manner of men they are. I want to see their horses and guns, and I am wearing the ribbon so that no one will imagine that I am there to welcome them." She put the hat on. The green, red, white, and blue ribbon of the South African Republic hung in a streamer down her back. "I shall take my bicycle," she said, and walked out of the room.

Louisa and her mother watched her ride down the drive, the wide *vierkleur* ribbon flying like a flag behind her.

"Why did you let her go, Mother?" Louisa asked, biting her lip. "She will make trouble for us all."

"It is over, Louisa," Dora van Reenan said, but her voice sounded uncertain even to her own ears. She knew her people. The generals had made peace. But every Boer thought himself a general and each was a law unto himself. They might well refuse to give up.

She thought of her sister, Mrs. de Lange, at the Cape, who had been sending her news of British reinforcements arriving, other gossip and rumors that might be of value to the Boers which she obtained from the British staff officers quartered in her house. Her guests had no idea that her sympathies lay with her own people. The information she sent had been given to the Boer intelligence officers. The English seemed to think that with both capitals in their hands the war was over. But the peace had not been signed.

Renata was right and Louisa wrong. As they were Boer women, it was their duty to help their country as long as a single burgher remained to fight.

As she neared Government Square, Renata noticed a change in the behavior of the Kaffirs. They seethed over the pavements, forcing the white people onto the road. They were free at last. The British liberators had arrived. The Boer regulations that had imposed a curfew and kept them off the sidewalks had been canceled. Freedom had come overnight.

Renata heard a band playing, and in the distance the wild skirl of the pipes, which she had heard described. Now they were coming. It was unbelievable that they were really here: the martial music, the mounted officers, the flash of the sun on the brass instruments, and the bare steel of the bayonets were a fact. An endless snake, like a khaki python, four men wide, wound past her. Then came some cavalry, also four abreast, with their lance butts in little buckets on their stirrups, and held with leather loops over their right forearms, the red and white pennants dripping like blood and snow from the lance heads.

The Englishmen were sunburned, red as lobsters. They did not go brown like the Boers. That's why we call them rooineks—rednecks—Renata thought. Their obvious exhaustion did not move her. The more exhausted they were the better. Their red faces were plastered with red dust. Coat after coat of it lay on their skins, and through it, running down each side of their noses, were deep furrows cut by their running sweat. Their eyelashes were thick with dust, each hair coated till it looked as thick as the lead in a pencil. Their eyebrows were solid bars of dust. Their faces, smeared here and there by their hands, looked as if they were plastered with dry blood.

Renata was astonished at the size and condition of the cavalry and gun horses. The savage, bare-kneed Highland troops appalled her. These were the devils in skirts she had heard about, who fought to the music, the wild screeching of their pipes. Their skirts, as she called them, swung as they marched, dark beneath their khaki aprons. She had never imagined men like the Guards, rank after rank of them, not one under six feet and looking taller in their helmets, marching like automatons. Never an inch out of line, their bayoneted rifles sloped at the same precise angle. The solid tramp of their booted feet had a rhythm of its own. Light infantry passed her with their bugle badges, marching with a short, sharp step, their rifles at the trail.

The idea of disciplined troops, of soldiers, was new to Renata and all Boers. There was something shocking and undemocratic about it to her. These were mindless men. Brave enough but incapable of original thought or action. They fought where they were told. They made nothing, created nothing. They had no farms, no lands, no homes. They were like dogs, obedient to the orders they received from their officers, and the officers were no better.

Men . . . men . . . an endless river of exhausted, sunburned men. Many were lame, some wore bandages. A command was given. The snake halted, shivered, and flattened itself as the men lay down in the road. Some pulled food from their haversacks. Others made no attempt to eat but lay like hounds exhausted by the chase, and slept.

The air was filled with the smell of dust, of man and horse sweat, of dirty, unwashed men in filthy clothes. So this was what we fought, Renata thought. This monster. No matter what you did to it, no matter how much of it you destroyed, it could always replenish itself and replace its parts from the great empire upon which the sun never was supposed to set.

She knew that it could never be beaten. She knew, too, suddenly, as if God had revealed it to her, that this monster could not win, either. Not completely. Not forever. These men did not live here. It was not their Africa. "It's our land," she said to herself. "They are here today, but tomorrow they will be gone—like a nightmare that is over." As if it was a sign from heaven, clouds covered the sun and the blue day was gone.

A soldier eating some bully beef at her feet looked up and said, "Thank God it's over."

"Over, Tommy," she said, "over? The real war has not even begun."

The man's blue bloodshot eyes opened in astonishment. "How do you know, miss?" he said. "The peace is signed."

"I feel it," Renata said. "*Ja*, I feel it in my heart."

The troops stood up and marched on. More bands played. At three o'clock the Union Jack was hoisted on the government buildings. How strange it looked, with its red and white crosses on a blue ground. How strange it looks against our sky, Renata thought. It was eighteen years since it had flown there. Put up by Shepstone in 1877 and taken down after the English defeat at Amajuba, all before she was born. She knew the dates. She had learned them at school. The square was lined with cheering troops who held their hats on the muzzles of their raised rifles as they shouted.

Boetie had not expected to be caught by the British in Pretoria. Their rapid advance had been a surprise to everyone. He had no horse or rifle and was to all intents and purposes a civilian. Of course he could take the oath of allegiance to the Queen, or of neutrality, and go home. But the idea only passed through his mind as the shadow of a cloud passes over a water-filled pan, blotting out its brilliance for a moment and then leaving it clear as before. In the meantime he might as well watch the British march into the town. He would be safe enough among the crowds that lined the streets and something might be learned from the experience. Moolman had taught him that. "Watch everything, Boetie," he had said. "Learn everything." But his

heart was sore from the loss of his brave pony. Pasha
had foundered outside Johannesburg and he had had to
shoot him. That was a hard thing to do. To kill a friend.
He had shot other horses. Pasha had felt no pain. What
pain there was was in his own heart. So much had gone
with the little horse. A bond to his home, to his mother, to
Elsa, and to her captain, who had given Pasha to him.
Well, he had betrayed him, as in the end most animals
were betrayed by men. There had been a terrible moment
before he pulled the trigger when it seemed to him that
the pony knew what he was going to do. The muzzle of
the rifle was only an inch away from the star on Pasha's
forehead. It was in just the right place—a bull's-eye for
death—at the point where the diagonals drawn from eye
to ear crossed. He had pressed the trigger and Pasha
had gone down, his hoofs kicking the dust convulsively in
the reflex of death.

General, too, was gone, with Moolman riding him after
his buckskin had been killed. A bullet had passed behind
Moolman's legs, going through both flaps of the saddle, but
General, wounded to the death, had galloped another
thousand yards before falling in a crumpled heap. They
had got rid of the English by then, given them the slip,
and that was what had foundered Pasha. The double
burden had been too much for a pony.

Then later he had lost Moolman in a skirmish. He had
seen him catch and mount a loose English troop horse and
gallop away.

Boetie felt someone was watching him. There were
many spies, *hands-uppers,* who were willing to betray their
own side. He knew he looked suspicious, dirty and unkempt, though he had done the best he could to improve
his appearance when he reached town. Raising his hat,
he shouted, "Hurrah! Hurrah!" as a blaring British band
came past him. He was surprised to feel the wheel of
a bicycle pushed into him behind the knees, causing him
to stagger, and he heard a girl's voice hiss in Dutch, "And
you call yourself a man! Why aren't you out fighting them?
Instead of standing here to cheer and gape like a woman?
If I was a man . . ."

He turned to look at the girl. What a shrew! But that
was what the country needed. Enough women like this
and we'll still win, he thought.

She was fair, with golden eyes. Around her hat she wore a *vierkleur* ribbon.

"Shut up," he whispered. "Do you want me caught?"

"What are you going to do?" Renata asked.

"Hide if I can find a place and then get back to the others; to De Wet if I can find him in the north. I have served under him before."

"Do you know Pretoria?"

"I live near here, at Groenplaas, twenty miles away. I am Louis van der Berg. Groenplaas is my home."

"I have heard of it," Renata said. "You must come to us." Louisa would make a fuss, but she could deal with Louisa. Her mother, she was sure, would agree. "We will hide you. Go to Sunnyside and find our place—the Willows. Everyone knows it. But be careful. I will see you there." With that she mounted her bicycle and rode away, the bright ribbons of the Transvaal floating like a flag of defiance behind her.

When she got home her house was surrounded by British troops. They were camping everywhere. It looked permanent. They were pitching tents. Hundreds of them were springing up like dirty white mushrooms, wherever she looked. And she had told the boy she had met to come here!

Boetie had no difficulty in finding Sunnyside but was astonished to see it surrounded by British troops, apparently settled down there for good, eating their supper outside the tents.

As he watched two soldiers came toward him. Military police, judging from their arm bands. It was no use running away. He stood still, apparently unperturbed, waiting for them.

"Hey you," the bigger one said, "what the hell are you doing here?"

"What's the good of asking him, Jack? These bastards don't talk English."

Boetie smiled at him. "This bastard does," he said.

"Good God!" the big man said, "and good English, too. and what, may I ask, are you doing here? You're a Dutchman, aren't you?"

"Working for you," Boetie said. "Looking for spies and traitors."

"Got any papers?"

"Am I likely to have papers? What would the Boers do if they caught one of their own men with English papers? And I don't write anything down, either. It's all in here." He tapped his head with his knuckles.

"Spy, eh? Well, get on with it, chum." The two men turned and walked away in step, their nailed boots ringing on the quiet road.

That had been a close one, Boetie thought, his knees trembling. He waited till the Englishmen were out of sight, and then stepped through a fence into a garden. When it was dark he would go to the Willows. There would be no guards around a Boer house and he was expected. He lay down behind a bush, shivering with cold and the reaction of fear. His mind occupied itself with the girl. He did not even know her name, but his pulse beat faster at the thought of her. She was beautiful. How wonderful to see her again. Also wonderful to be warm and eat in a house. He thought of his mother, of his room at home only twenty miles away. He could march it in six hours easily. But having got there, even if he got there, he would still have to get away and to shelter him would bring danger upon his mother. But so it would on these people, these strangers. But there was more safety here. There were more people about, and besides, where was the fugitive better off than in the heart of the enemy camp? He was no longer a soldier. He was a fugitive, a hunted man, unless he chose to sign an oath of neutrality or loyalty to the English Queen. He was prepared to do neither as long as a single burgher was left fighting.

The sky grew darker and one by one the bright stars came out, pricking the night, twinkling ice cold in the firmament above him. There were still sounds coming from the British camp—shouts, orders, songs. He would have to wait till all was quiet. It got colder and colder and he could not keep his teeth from chattering.

He thought of the night not so long ago when they had camped by a group of thorns and a small pan that still held water. As they lay in their blankets they could hear the glassy crackle of forming ice as it spread over the surface of the pan. This had been the beginning of winter. It had set in early and very hard.

The night had been bitterly cold but still, windless, and

bright with stars. Every blade of grass a white dagger. The old twisted thorns were silvered as if each tortured trunk, each tiny branch, each spine, had been individually Christmas-wrapped. Between the trees great cobwebs were spun, tying them into parcels with silver cart-wheel strands. A cold, starlit world, white against a night sky that was a deep blue, almost but not quite black.

The blankets of the sleeping men had been white fur. The tethered horses, no longer bay, brown, or roan, were white—silver statues, breathing smoke like dragons, standing over the black patches where they had staled.

The campfire had glowed like a red eye, a jewel in the darkness, the gray ash illumined by the slowly burning wood.

Unable to sleep, he had put more dead branches upon it. They sizzled like cooking meat as the hoarfrost melted, and then they caught and burned up in a yellow flame that turned the silvery night into flickering gold, and threw the horses' shadows like skins on the ground beside them.

He had got up to pet Pasha and clean his Lee-Enfield, wiping it down with an oily rag. "Tame your horse, and keep your rifle clean," Moolman had said. "In war these are your only friends."

He had given the pony a tiny crust of dry mealie pap. The others had nickered and pulled toward him, but he had none to spare for them and little enough for himself. "Little and often," Moolman had said. "It is not the amount you give a horse, but how often you give it that counts. Ten handfuls an hour apart are better than one bellyful. What he covets is attention. Feed him tidbits, talk to him, touch him. Breathe into his nostrils and pull his ears. Speak his name over and over."

When he lay down again he had seen his footprints. Their double line black, on the white carpet on the veld, which tomorrow's sun would burn away. It had seemed symbolic to him somehow. Symbolic of war, pain, sorrow. Perhaps with time all these too might be burned away. Lost and forgotten. Poor Pasha, he thought. Poor brave little horse. Tears came into his eyes as he lay shivering in the shadows.

He thought of the girl again. He wondered what her name was. Soon, in another hour or so, he would be able to ask her.

The men about the gates of the Willows looked at Renata with interest, delighted to see a pretty girl again. A sentry tried to stop her.

"Halt?" she said. "What for? I live here." He let her pass on down the drive.

On the stoep her mother stood with a pistol in her hand facing two British staff officers. Louisa stood behind her.

"Just for the night," she heard one say. "We should be no trouble. It's cold at night in a tent."

"Yes," her mother said. "It is cold. And it is cold for our men out on the veld, too. So why should I give you beds in my house? You who have driven them from their homes. Except by force you will never billet your-selves on me."

"I'm sorry," the Englishman said.

"Sorry for what? Your attack? Your occupation of our land? Or—because you will sleep cold? Please go," she said.

They saluted and turned about to see Renata watching them.

"My other daughter," Dora van Reenan said. "Come in, Renata." The women went into the drawing room to-gether. "We will have coffee, girls. There is much to be decided now that they are here."

"Yes," Renata said, putting down her cup. "We have a guest coming, a young Boer who wishes to escape and get back to De Wet."

"Here?" Louisa screamed. "You're mad! Do you want to destroy us?"

"How was I to know the place was surrounded? His name is Louis van der Berg of Groenplaas."

"And he is coming here?" her mother asked.

"Yes, if he is not caught on the way. But I do not think he will be caught."

"Where did you meet him?" Louisa asked.

"In Government Square, watching the English. He stood beside me. I said, 'Why are you not fighting?' 'I want to be,' he said, 'but I have no horse and threw away my rifle when I saw I could not outdistance the English on foot.' 'And now?' I asked. 'Now I must hide, rest for a day or two and then find my way to a commando. My people are with De Wet.' So I said, 'Come to us, to the

Willows at Sunnyside,' so we must be ready for him."

"You fool!" Louisa said.

"We shall be ready," her mother said. "We shall turn no burgher away from here no matter what the risk."

"And have the English upon us?" Louisa had tears of frustration in her eyes. "We are beaten. Beaten." She stamped her foot. "And the sooner it is all over the better. These are the victors."

"And to the victors go the spoils, I suppose, Louisa," her sister said, now equally angry. "The girls perhaps? Before God I believe you will fraternize with them, talk with them, dance, ride, play games with them. Is that what is in your mind already? Within a few hours of their arrival?"

"They are men," Louisa said, as she went out, slamming the door behind her.

"What's the matter with her, Mama?" Renata asked.

"Men," her mother said. "She misses men and their admiration more than you."

"I miss men too. All my friends have gone to war. Just as hers have. But I will have no English friends. I hate them all."

"You have not seen them the way she has. You saw them tired and dirty. Two very handsome young men were here this morning. She gave them coffee on the stoep."

"Magtig," Renata said, "a Judas. A Judas in our home."

"A girl, my child."

"Am I not then a girl?"

"Ja, you are a girl, but of a different sort. You do not have Louisa's vanity. She basks in admiration like a lizard in the sun. And you," her mother said, "you, my poor dear, have the steadfast heart and iron will that makes it impossible to accept defeat."

"I accept nothing, Mama. Do you accept defeat?"

"No, Renata. But in a storm it is the tree that bends to the wind that survives. I am bending now, but I will spring back. I have plans. Nothing to tell you yet, but they are there in the back of my mind. I have an idea. A petticoat commando. A drawing-room war, fought with silk taffeta and furbelows. And now—what about your young man?"

"He is not my young man. He is just a Boer boy who needs help."

"He is a young man. Only you have seen him, so for the moment, Renata, he is your young man. And this may account, to some extent at least, for your sister's anger.

"Anyway, we must stay awake to see if he comes when it is dark and all is quiet. Only a fool would try to approach now. We will keep the dog inside and you, with a heavy coat on, will stay on the stoep till dawn."

But Renata did not have to wait till dawn. At a quarter to twelve she saw him slipping from the shadow of one shrub to another and went toward him.

"So you have come."

"*Ja*, I have come, but I was nearly taken."

"How did you escape?"

"I said I was a spy working for them. I spoke good English and they believed me."

"Come," Renata said, taking his hand. "We will go in the back way."

Her hand was warm and soft in his. In the starlight she was beautiful. Her honey-colored hair looked very pale. He could look down on the top of her head and see the parting white as milk.

"What is your name?" he asked.

"Renata. Renata van Reenan. My father was killed with the Pretoria Commando at Spion Kop."

"I met him," Boetie said. "We lost many good men there. Renata is a beautiful name." He paused and said her name again—"Renata."

She had never heard it said like that before, so softly, so gently. The sound of it passed over her like a warm breeze, like the wings of a bird that came to rest on her heart. Involuntarily her clasp of his hand tightened, and he pressed back.

"It is wonderful to find a friend, Renata," he said. "I have never had a friend who was a girl before."

By then they were in the house.

"This is Louis van der Berg, Mama," Renata said to her mother, who was waiting. "And here is my sister Louisa," she added.

Boetie took Mrs. van Reenan's hand. "You are sure, *mevrou?*" he said. "You know the risk you are taking."

"I am sure, Louis. Come this way." And she led him upstairs to one of the guest rooms. Renata's sister had not spoken beyond greeting him. She watched him go with big dark eyes.

"I hope you will be comfortable," Mrs. Van Reenan said.

"I shall be comfortable, *mevrou*."

"Renata will bring you food."

"Thank you," he said, smiling. "I am very hungry. I have not eaten since yesterday."

The girl had gone out of the room to the kitchen.

Dora van Reenan was turning down the bed.

"Do not do that. I will sleep on the floor. I am too dirty for a bed, and if anyone came looking for me they would see it had been slept in. If anyone comes I will get out of the window, drop to the ground, and hide in the garden."

"Do what you like, my son. You are at home here. This is a Boer house." She went out of the room as Renata came in with food on a tray—cold meat, bread, and a big jug of milk thick with cream.

"Eat, Louis," she said. In those few minutes in the kitchen it had come upon her, struck her like a blow in the belly. She had never known that her heart lay so low in her body. She was in love with this boy she had found lost like a dog in a hostile crowd. The boy who said she was his friend, who had never had a friend who was a girl before.

In her imagination she felt his hard young hand in hers again. The hand of a boy who had killed men—the enemies of her land. She watched him eat. At first carefully trying to control his manners, then wolfing his food ravenously, a starving boy. She watched him like a mother. For food, from her own milk to her child, to the feeding of strangers, was a woman's function.

When he had done, Boetie wiped his mouth on his wrist. They both laughed.

"Commando manners," he said, and they laughed again. How easy it was to laugh with him.

"I'll go now," Renata said. "Sleep well, Louis. Good night."

"Good night, Renata," Boetie said, taking her hand. Their hands seemed glued together as though the veins and sinews were one. As though the blood in the veins of one flowed into the blood in the veins of the other, as though their sinews were one, binding them together the one to the other, the boy to the girl. Their eyes, in the half-dark of the candlelit room, were joined too by a gaze that held them fast, as if each sought to drown in the eyes of the other, in the pool of their darkness.

So, with the magnet of as yet unacknowledged love, they were drawn to each other, coming closer and closer till their faces all but met. The smell of Renata's hair was in Boetie's nostrils. The smell of soap, of woman. The smell of sweat and war, of man and horse and burned powder, the reek of dirt overwhelmed Renata. This boy was filthy, feral. He smelled more like an animal than a man. He had no beard, just a down like the fluff on a young pigeon's breast on his face, but his eyes burned into her and his breath was sweet. Nearer and nearer his face came till it was against hers, his hard lips on her soft ones, his hard chest against her breasts, his hard arms about her. Her hand felt the muscles of his back, the matted hair of his head. And suddenly she knew she had no further problems, no further worries. The past was over, the future beginning. She had found her man. Loosing his grasp, she ran from the room. She could stand no more today, no more tonight. She must be alone. Alone with her love. Alone in her mind with the stranger who had come into her life and taken it for his own. Her mother was right about her being steadfast. This was forever.

When she left him, Boetie was breathing fast. So this was love, this incredible, beautiful pain. This splendid agony of mind and body. Till now, though he was nearly seventeen, he had never known he had a body. Now he was aware of little else.

He knew that this moment they had had together would never come again. That tomorrow, or really today, since dawn was breaking—they would be shy with each other. That later the shyness would break down, melt like ice in the sun of their meetings, and that love would grow like a tree. But this, the bursting of its seed, could never happen again. The young tree, its first fragile leaves open, could never again return to the security of the ground. The adventure of real life had begun. This was what the

Beyerses, dead side by side in battle, had had, what Moolman had had in the north before his tragedy. Much that had been hidden from him before was now apparent in this new and painful happiness.

CHAPTER 40

MISS BUTTERFINGERS

WHEN Renata went into Boetie's room in the morning with his coffee, she found him sitting on the floor reading his small New Testament.

"Good morning, Louis," she said. "Why are you sitting on the floor?"

He laughed. How wonderful it was to see her again. The few hours since they had said good night seemed like days. Her eyes were downcast, their long pale gold lashes lay over the apricot of her cheeks. That was what her cheeks were like—cream-colored, almost tan, but red blushed, ripe with life.

"I'm too dirty to sit on a chair. Besides, I'm used to the ground. I like it. You know," he said, "out in the veld it is strange, when we sit on the ground. Africa is like our mother's breast. The ground is what we fight for. *Ons Land,* Renata, our sacred soil. Much of it is hard and stony. Poor land, but ours. Won by our fathers' blood."

She looked at him. Those wonderful sherry-colored, gold-flecked eyes met his.

"You understand," she said. *"Ja,* Louis, you understand. If I was a man I should be there."

"We have women fighting," he said. "We had a woman with us. Hetta Beyers, who was killed with her man. A big, strong, ugly girl made beautiful by her love, and more beautiful by anger in the battle. Her blue eyes flashed like fire."

Renata clasped her hands and stared at this strange young man who was hers. She had never realized how dangerous men were. This boy had killed. Nothing would ever tame him. Not she. Not anyone. No one would change his heart. He would die first. She did not want him tamed.

Real men were like bulls; they could only be slaughtered or cut. Dangerous, too, was his power to hurt. Not that such as he would ever lift a hand against a woman. But her heart—a man with the whip of his tongue could hurt a woman's heart. Or by neglect. Or negligence. And she alone had the power to soften him. That was the strange and terrible power of a woman. By putting out her hand she could check him as one checks a horse with a bit, and the bit was love, his love of her.

They were in each other's power. That was what love was. Power to make or destroy. Young as they were, almost children, forced into maturity by war, the weapon of love had been put into their untried hands. The man, to be softened, directed, and cared for, the woman, to be protected and controlled. The strong and the weak. Each strong and each weak in different ways, together hand in hand, body to body, and heart to heart they could hold the world at bay.

"You should hear Moolman," Boetie said. "It is he who taught me to love Africa. He is a hunter. He has told me of the north where the wild beasts still roam in thousands, and the veld is as God made it, untouched by ax or plow."

"You were reading the Bible," she said.

"*Ja,* it's a New Testament my ma gave me." He held it out. "Just see how dirty it is. But I do not care," he said. "It is God's earth upon it. It is Africa." He stood very straight and slim before her. "A bath," he said, "or water to wash."

"You shall have it."

"When I am clean I shall kiss you."

Renata looked down and then directly at him. "*Ja,*" she said, "we have not long."

"You feel that too?" he said.

"Yes, Louis. Something very wonderful has taken place between us, something for which we should thank God."

"It was fast," he said.

"*Ja,*" she said, "it was fast like lightning, but it has struck." With that she left him.

Half an hour later Adam, the houseboy, came in with hot water and a flat tin bath.

"Can I wash the Baas' clothes?" Adam said.

"What shall I wear?"

"The old Baas' clothes. The Baas who is dead—killed by the English. I will ask the Nooie?"

"They must be dried secretly," Boetie said.

"I will wash my own clothes too." The man laughed. *"Magtig,"* he said, "the clothes are ragged enough to belong to a Kaffir."

"I have nothing to give you. I have no money. Not a tickey," Boetie said.

"The Baas has made my young nooie happy."

"So you know?"

"All Kaffirs are not fools, Baasie. I knew at once by her step. She walks like a young buck, dainty but firm. I know by her back, by the light in her eyes. These are enough."

Boetie bathed and went back to his Bible. Peace was to be found in its pages. It brought his mother close to him. His mother and his home. This little leather-bound book was his only link now that Pasha and even his saddlery were gone. Servas must have escaped with the President. Jonas was lost, adrift somewhere. How utterly alone he would have been if God had not sent this girl like an angel from heaven to care for him.

Adam emptied the bath water, took away the bath, and swept the room. There was now no trace of its occupation.

It was good to be really clean again. He had not been clean for months, having only bathed in streams and often soapless since he had left home.

Adam brought the clothes, those of his dead master. They were too big, but they were clean.

At twelve Renata brought his lunch and sat to watch him eat. Now he ate more carefully. His great hunger was gone.

When he had finished he came over to her and took her in his arms. "How old are you, my heart?"

"Sixteen," she said.

"I am not yet seventeen in years, but old, very old, in other ways. A year ago I was a child. Now I am almost a man."

"I am a woman," Renata said. "I could bear a child."

"Ja, my heart, when this is over we shall have them,

you and I, and live at Groenplaas with my mother and
Servas my brother. There will be enough for all. It is a
good farm."

"I will go where you say, Louis, for that is a woman's
duty."

"Where you are will be my home, Renata. Is indeed
already my home, for in your hands you hold my heart,
my very life." He took her hands in his.

"I must go," Renata said. "I cannot bear to be with
you too long, nor away from you, either. I will bring
more food this evening. More food and a good sleep
will put you right, Louis."

It would put him right but he would never be the same
again. For now he was a man, having seen both war and
love. The final experience of it, his possession of Renata,
was only a matter of time—a certainty, separated from
him only by days or months of war. With Renata and his
mother in his mind he lay down. She would replace
Elsa in his mother's heart. Yes, he thought, I will bring
my ma a beautiful daughter. Then, lying down with his
head on his hat, he slept on the floor beside the bed.

It was Mevrou van Reenan who woke him.

"Quickly," she said. "Come with me. Ask nothing.
Just come."

Accustomed to sudden alarm, Boetie followed her
downstairs.

Renata was doing her hair when her mother opened
the door of her bedroom. "What . . ." she said.

"Quick," her mother said. Adam came in with the flat
tin bath. Sixpence, the pickanin, followed with hot
water and towels.

"Get undressed."

"I've finished," Renata said. "I'm just doing my hair."

"Hurry, you fool. The English are going to search the
house. Take down your hair, undress."

"What is it?" Renata gasped, letting down her long,
honey-colored hair. She could see Louis standing in her
father's clothes behind her mother.

"Come in, Louis," Dora van Reenan said. "Get under
the bed."

Boetie came sheepishly into the room. "I'm sorry," he
said, "I—"

"Hurry! My God," Mrs. van Reenan said, "if they catch you, they'll shoot you as a spy. Get under that bed. Undress, Renata, take off your frock. Throw it down. Now, when they knock on the door, say you are having a bath. They think he is here, and are going to search the house. Come in, Louis. Hurry! Get under the bed."

Shoot him—shoot her Louis, Renata thought as she slipped out of her dress. In her petticoat and camisole she lifted the valance of the bed. "You're not to look, Louis."

"I won't look, Renata, and I'm sorry."

"I'm not sorry." And she was not sorry. Here was something she could do for the republic. Save a fighting boy. Something she could do for her lover—save his life. He had told them he was a spy.

If her mother told her to have a bath, she was going to have one, do the thing properly. She knew her mother only meant her to be half dressed. But if she were half dressed they might still come in. Naked it would be impossible, even for an Englishman.

"They'll shoot me," Boetie said.

"They won't get you." Renata was undoing her corset. She could hear the men talking, opening and shutting doors.

She stepped naked into the bath. There was a knock on the door. She had only just been in time.

"Come in," she cried. The door opened. A staff captain with red tabs, two troopers behind him, came in.

"My God!" he said, turning back. "Get out!" he shouted to the gaping men as he closed the door.

"I'm sorry," he said through the door.

"I should think so," Renata said, "bursting into a girl's room like that."

"Why did you say we could come in?"

"I thought you were my mother."

"You've seen no one, I suppose. We are looking for a spy."

"Mr. Captain, I am a Boer girl. What is a spy to you is a hero to me. But do you think I allow even heroes to see me in my bath?"

"No, I'm sorry. Please accept my apologies."

"Wait," Renata said. "In a quarter of an hour I shall be dressed. Then you can apologize properly. Indeed," she added, "I'm not sure that you should not propose to me, for what you have seen no man has yet seen, and no man will see again until he is my husband." How she hated these people. These invaders of her country, and now even of her home. But she knew she could disarm them. Play-act with them, trick them if she had to.

"I will wait," the man said.

Renata began to laugh. The young officer on the other side of the door laughed too. When she heard him go she got out of the bath, still naked, and rushed to the door to lock it.

"He's gone, Louis," she whispered, lifting the valance.

"Magtig," Boetie said, "put something on."

"Don't you think I'm pretty, Louis?"

"You'll marry me when this is over?"

"Ja, Louis. How could I help it and remain a virtuous girl? There is nothing left for you to see. Do you know something? I do not think you closed your eyes."

"How could I? I had to keep my eyes on the Englishmen. They would not have taken me alive."

"And me?" Renata said.

"You were in the way and you are beautiful. More beautiful than I had imagined possible."

In the drawing room Dora van Reenan was still talking to an English captain, a good-looking man who seemed nice enough.

"Of course," she said, "search by all means. How could I stop you, anyway? But what exactly are you looking for?"

"A spy. We think he's hidden here. He was seen in the vicinity yesterday. He said he was working for us."

"A Judas Boer," Mrs. van Reenan said contemptuously.

"That is what we thought, but the Intelligence have no record of him."

"Well, I know nothing of it. No one is hidden here. If he was, I should know."

"Of course. But he could have got in without your knowing."

Mrs. van Reenan shrugged her shoulders. "Very well, search. Nothing is locked. But how anyone could get here with your people all around the house as thick as vultures on a carcass, I am at a loss to understand."

"It's a pity you won't give up and end this unfair struggle. You have the admiration of the world but it cannot go on."

"Why not? We still have the De Wets. Look at what Piet's just done." This was a sore point with the British. Only a few days before the fall of Pretoria, Piet de Wet had caught a force of five hundred Imperial Light Horse near Lindley and, reinforced by General Prinsloo, had forced them to surrender.

"How did you know that, Mrs. van Reenan?"

"Everybody knows. You do not know Africa. If an English sparrow falls, we hear of it." She looked upward as if such news came from the Lord.

"Do you also know what happened in Potchefstroom, where the Royal Scots hoisted the flag that was hauled down here in eighty-one?" he asked. "Some of our people buried it in a coffin with a paper that read 'In memory of the British flag in the Transvaal which departed this life on August 2, 1881, aged 4 years.' Colonel Gilden, commanding the regiment, dug it up, took it to Scotland, and gave it to the regiment when they sailed for South Africa."

"I did not know the story," Mrs. van Reenan said. "But it has given me an idea. We too will bury our flags, and like the Lord our Savior, one day they will rise again." She smiled brightly at the officer. How she disliked these sleek, smooth, well-dressed men with their bright buttons and clean boots. Their full bellies and fat staff horses, smug with the weight of an empire behind them! "I trust you will enjoy your stay in South Africa. We have splendid shooting here." And she smiled again.

"I respect your views, Mrs. van Reenan, but we are only doing our duty."

"Yes," she said, "and we are only protecting our homes. You remind me of the man who, having wounded a sable, called it a treacherous beast because it charged. But do have some tea. War is one thing, hospitality another. My husband would never have allowed you to leave without refreshment. Of course he was killed at Spion Kop." Sweeping her skirts to one side, she sank gracefully onto a low chair. "Sit down, Captain," she said, "and let us converse. There are still many subjects that are not controversial. The weather, for instance. I assume you are aware that we have no winter rains in the Transvaal. It is wonderful for picnics and war."

She could hear the other officer and the two men with him tramping about the house. They were upstairs now. Louis had been clever not to disturb the bed.

"There are the stables and outhouses," she said. "You might as well be thorough."

The Englishman said, "I had better introduce myself. I am Captain Turnbull of the Second Hussars." Then, to her astonishment, he spoke in Dutch. "I do not like this war. I have been very happy in Africa. And sad, too. For I was to marry a Boer girl. She died."

"So that's how you learned Dutch?"

"Yes," he said, "and from the farmers in the back veld when I was hunting. I have been as far north as the Limpopo and into the Matabele country."

"Please sit down, Captain." Dora van Reenan had been astonished to hear herself ask an Englishman to sit in her house. But . . . but, the plan was taking shape. Make a friend—a false friend—of this man. He could be the opening wedge.

"I think I met your sister in Cape Town when I landed with General Buller—a Mrs. de Lange."

"My sister Anna . . ."

"Of Morningstar in Wynberg? Is she not your sister?"

"Yes, she is my dear sister."

Renata came into the room, cool and neat.

"My daughter, Renata," Dora van Reenan said.

The captain bowed.

"And where is the other officer?" she asked.

"Still searching," her mother said. "I told them to be thorough."

"I want to see him, Mama."

"May I ask why?"

"Why? Why because he came into my room when I was in my bath and he must apologize."

"Why did you not lock the door?" her mother said.

"When do we lock doors in this house of women? I thought it was you."

Her mother, meeting her eyes, almost laughed.

"Terrible," the captain said. "Terrible!"

"*Ja*, Meneer Captain. I am a young girl. It gave me a shock."

Louisa came in and put her arm around her sister's waist. She was still furious with her. All this trouble was Renata's fault and she had not even seen this boy. But she knew they made a pretty picture—two young Boer girls standing side by side, one dark and one fair.

"My other daughter, Louisa."

"How do you do," the captain said.

Louisa smiled shyly and looked down. These Englishmen were not as bad as they had been painted. Clean in new uniforms and shining boots. She liked the jingle of his spurs as he went to the door and shouted.

"Johnson! Give Captain Johnson my compliments," he said to the trooper in the passage, "and ask him to come here."

"He's gone, sir. When we'd been through the stables, he went back."

"The coward!" Renata said, and began to laugh.

"What's the joke?" Louisa asked.

"Joke, Louisa? There's no joke. He burst into my room while I was in my bath."

Turnbull thought she must have been a pretty sight. They were both good-looking girls who would one day become lovely women. But he liked the dark one best. In a way she reminded him of Elsie. They must have got their looks from their mother.

Already, after only twenty-four hours, half the people at headquarters were talking about the three of them. Soon they would be buzzing around the Willows like flies at a honeypot. There was lots of honey here. He wondered if anyone would get it.

Adam came in with the tea. The conversation continued, partly in Dutch and partly in English.

Dora van Reenan, in black as usual, said, looking at her daughters, "The girls are all I have now. My husband is dead, buried where he fell on the veld."

"*Mevrou*," Captain Turnbull said, "this war is terrible. It is terrible to fight one's friends. There is one in particular who would have been my brother-in-law and must now be old enough to fight. I gave him a bay pony."

"What is his name?" Dora van Reenan asked.

"Boetie. Boetie van der Berg of Groenplaas."

Renata's saucer slipped from her hand and the cup of tea was shattered on the red granolithic floor. "Oh!" she said, recovering at once. "How could I be so careless?"

"Butterfingers," her mother said. "Little Miss Butterfingers."

Turnbull smiled at the girl. What must it feel like to have enemies in your home? Such a pretty little thing, too. There had been girls like her at Paardeberg. He could not help thinking about the Boers, about what Cronje's laager had suffered. It was unbelievable to have British guns shelling a position where there were women and children.

He was also worried about Elsie. Her letters had been so short and odd. Quite different. If something was wrong surely Vincent would have told him, but there had been nothing in his letters. But he might not dare. If the news were really bad he might be afraid to tell it. Suppose— and this was the experience of other men who had kept girls—suppose she had gone off with another man? Well, if she had, she had. It was probably absurd to expect a girl like her to remain faithful for even a few months. He'd asked for it, and he'd got it.

There had been something queer about her letters ever since Christmas and even before that. She seemed to be concealing something. He supposed that, still feeling some gratitude toward him, she found it difficult to write, did not know what to say or how to break the news. The letters had just petered out, getting weaker, as it were, more and more watered down.

He thought of cabling Vincent and then decided against it. A man could hardly cable to his valet for information about his mistress. The best thing to do was to forget her. It had been nice while it lasted. Wonderful, in fact, and now it was over.

He looked at the boy mopping up the spilled tea and picking up the pieces of the broken cup. The saucer had not broken.

He said, "The saucer did not break."

Dora van Reenan said, "They often don't, do they? That is why one always has so many odd saucers."

Turnbull said, "Yes, I suppose so," and got up to go.

The women rose to see him off, standing grouped almost defensively. Turnbull bowed. They gave a kind of half-derisive curtsy. The door closed behind him.

He had gone at last. The house was unoccupied. Now they must plan. Quickly.

As the Van Reenans made plans for their guest's escape, great affairs beyond the knowledge of small people were taking place. A few miles away the Boer generals were meeting at a whisky distillery, part of Sammy Marks' Model Farm, to discuss the possibility of peace. The meeting opened with a prayer, the odor of sanctity mixing with the fumes of alcohol. Marks, a Russian-Jewish financier, a friend of President Kruger's, was convinced that the continuance of the war was futile. He had given freely to both sides, everyone was his friend, and as such no better middle-of-the-road mediator could have been found.

Botha was depressed. Defeat stared him in the face. All the Boer leaders were there, all believed the end of the war was near, but none dared acknowledge it. De la Rey denounced the Government, and even threatened to set up a republic of his own. Faced with such opinions, with such a diversity of ideas, such disagreements, surrender seemed the only course. But none of them could stomach it. This was today. By tomorrow something might happen. God, the God of their fathers, might intervene. Schalk Burger pleaded for delay. And while they delayed, certain events were taking place in Pretoria.

Lord Roberts, at Mrs. Botha's suggestion, wrote the Boer commander a letter very correctly in the third person stating:

Field-Marshal Lord Roberts presents his compliments to Commandant-General Botha and begs to inform him that he has had the great pleasure of receiving a visit from Mrs. Botha, from whom he learns that the Commandant-General would like to have an interview with Lord Roberts.

Botha, unused to this mode of address, replied:

From your unsigned letter . . . it appears as if I had expressed a wish to have a personal interview with your Excellency. This, however, is wrong.

and he had the honor to be Lord Roberts' obedient servant Louis Botha, Commandant-General.

This was June 7. In the twenty-four hours since seeing his wife, Botha had changed his mind. He was no longer ready to surrender. God, using De Wet as his instrument, had come to the rescue of the Boers, his chosen people. God, as they had hoped and prayed, had intervened.

Christiaan de Wet had attacked the garrisons along the line north of Kroonstad and had split his force into three units with such success that they had captured seven hundred prisoners and destroyed more than half a million pounds' worth of stores. He blew up a bridge that had just been rebuilt by the engineers, destroyed the railway line for several miles, and cut all communication with Bloemfontein.

The Boers' hopes soared again. There was no further thought of surrender.

An inexplicable mystique now enveloped the Boer mind. De Wet's success was in fact no great victory, but it had come at a critical moment and was taken as a sign from God. And a new battle was begun, the players on both sides arranging their men as if it was a game of chess, around Diamond Hill and Pienaar's Post. It was an indecisive action that both sides claimed they won.

This was the last pitched battle of the war, the end of its first phase, but by no means the end of hostilities; rather, in fact, the beginning of a totally new war, a guerrilla war much more suited to the temperament of the freedom-loving Boers than the disciplined British who opposed them.

June 7 can therefore be taken as the end of one thing and the beginning of another, much more terrible affair, in which brutality on one side and hatred on the other appeared for the first time. The British, completely exasperated, resorted to desperate measures, described by Lloyd George in England as measures of barbarism; while the Boers, loath to behave in kind, fought on, their hearts filled with bitterness.

There were no fixed lines, no positions held by the Boers. Everything was fluid, and Moolman had little difficulty in getting through to De Wet on his English charger.

CHAPTER 41

A WOMAN'S CLOTHES

THE SCHEME for Boetie's escape from the Willows was simple. Disguised as a girl, he was to be driven by Adam to the edge of town in a Cape cart. Once there, he would slip away, cast aside his lady's garments, and seek the nearest commando.

The plan as devised by Dora van Reenan had the merit of simplicity and as happens with most simple plans absurd difficulties began to develop at once. The first was Boetie's beard that was not a beard at all, merely a golden fluff like that on the breast of a squab. But he was proud of it. For months he had fertilized it with any fat he could find, Moolman having told him that fat would encourage its growth.

"It's got to come off," Dora van Reenan said. "Without it you'll make quite a pretty girl."

This was the last straw. Boetie, now deeply involved with Renata, wanted more beard, not less. He did not want to be a pretty girl.

"No, *mevrou,*" he said, "I could not do that. How, without a beard, would anyone know I was a man?"

"There are other ways, Louis, though perhaps not quite so obvious." Dora van Reenan, an earthy woman, was irritated by this boy's stupidity. Did he think Renata would like him less without his fluff?

Boetie, profoundly shocked by this remark, blushed and was silent. This was not a subject for argument. Then he came up with another idea. "I do not know how to shave," he said. "I have never shaved. I have no razor."

"Then I will shave you." And, covering his face with a lather of soap, Dora van Reenan stripped it clean. "Yes," she said, when she had done, running her hand over his cheek, "the bottom of a baby could be no smoother." The girls, who had been watching the operation, laughed.

Next came the question of clothes. Renata would have given him everything she had, but she was too small, so

430

he had to wear Louisa's things, and she grudged him every garment, particularly her stays. They were hard to get and both pairs had been specially made for her. But in the end she gave in to her mother too.

The girls were sent out of the room while Dora dressed Boetie, and that was not easy either. Losing his trousers and replacing them with Louisa's lace-edged drawers seemed the final indignity to Boetie. No beard. No pants. Stays girthed about him so that he felt like a saddled horse. Then a petticoat, also lace-edged. A skirt, a bodice with a high boned collar, a little fur-edged jacket, a bonnet like a coal scuttle covered with flowers that would conceal the shortness of his hair—it was tied with wide ribbons under his chin—crocheted mittens on his hands, and he was ready to face the world. First the girls—he was to dine downstairs—and then later, tomorrow, the enemy.

His real dangers were his voice and his feet. It was decided to let down the hem of his black skirt still further so that it touched the ground.

"Take small steps," Louisa said, "like this." She minced across the room to show him what she meant.

Later, alone with him, her mother and Renata having left the dining room, Louisa came close to him. "You love Renata," she said. "She has told me. But it is my clothes you are wearing and I want them back. Give them to Adam if you can. I'd like to wear clothes that have been worn by a man."

She was very close to him, nearly as tall as he on her high heels, her breath in his face, her hair against his cheek, her mouth soft and moist within an inch of his. "Kiss me," she said. "Kiss me quickly. If only I had gone down to see the English come in, it would have been me instead of her you had met and loved. I could give you more," she said. "I have more to give than that little cold, blond-fish sister of mine." At that moment she felt this to be true. She wanted him to kiss her, wanted his body against her own, his arms about her.

Boetie recoiled. "I can't," he said. "I can't." But he felt his desire. This was something quite different from what Renata had offered him.

Louisa gave him nothing; she only demanded that he should take. She knew she would always be like this,

knew that a woman who gave nothing but allowed everything to be taken held the power in her hands, and this
boy who said he belonged to her sister appealed to her
strangely in his woman's clothes. Her clothes—her stockings, her corset, her drawers about his legs, her skirt over
his belly and his hips, her purple bodice and fur-edged
jacket. All he wore of Renata's was a bonnet garnished
with a salad of pink roses.

Unable to resist the impulse, Louisa put a hand behind
Boetie's neck and pulled his face down to hers. For a
moment he resisted, then, in the intoxication of her near-
ness, of her soft lips, of her perfume, of her lithe body
pressed into his own, fitting it as a mask fits a face, he
gave way. His arms went around her waist. She bent
backward from him, drawing his face after hers with
the honey of her kiss. A moment later she broke away
laughing.

"So," she said, "you belong to Renata! Are you sure,
Louis? Are you quite sure?"

He wasn't at all sure. He was only sure that he was in
love with both girls now. He did not know that he was
just a young man, the prey of his own natural lust.

"Let me straighten your bonnet, Louis," Louisa said,
standing in front of him to adjust the ribbons as Renata
and her mother came back into the room.

"Good night, I'm going to bed now," Louisa said, and
walked slowly out, her slim hips swaying.

"Are you all right, Louis?" Renata asked. "You look
funny."

"I'm all right," he said. "It is just that I am afraid."

"Don't worry," Mrs. van Reenan said. "You look like a
pretty girl that's just been kissed under the mistletoe. If
you meet any troops that will be your only danger.
They may want to make love to you." She looked at her
daughter. "I'll leave you but don't stay too long. Louis
must get some rest since he leaves early tomorrow."

When her mother had gone Boetie took Renata in his
arms with a strange urgency. He felt awful. Here he was
in love with both girls. Inflamed by one, he courted the
other with a passion he had not known before, to which,
much to his surprise, Renata responded with great ardor,
mingling tears and laughter with her kisses and embrace.
A monkey's wedding day of love—that was how the

Dutch described a day of alternate bright sunshine and showers.

When Boetie got to his room he found a taffeta petticoat on his bed with a note saying, "Wear this as well. Two petticoats may be better than one. Louisa." What did she mean? What did she want? Was this what being grown up meant? He was glad he was going back to war. It would at least get him out of this new dilemma.

In her own room Louisa was smiling as she stared into the mirror and brushed her hair. With hardly any effort at all she had taken this Boer clodhopper from her sister, had sent him crazy for something neither he nor anyone else would get till she was ready to give it. It would be to a rich man, a man a good bit older than herself. She had no belief in love, not at least on her part, though men moved her in a certain way. Even Louis had done that. In his arms heat had flooded her body, weakened it, but not her mind. All the time she had known how she looked and the effect she was creating. Love was not for her. Certainly not with a young man. She knew what she was cut out for—an old man's darling, an expensive toy who, seeming so light and frivolous, would always know just what she was doing and how far she could go.

Still, it was amusing to think of her clothes on that boy. Of his body in the borrowed linen. And there had been some pleasure in the roughness, the near brutality of his embrace. It was fun to rouse the beast, greater fun still to tame it. With these thoughts in her mind she turned on her side and slept.

In the morning Renata brought Boetie his breakfast, and left him laughing, saying her mother would soon be in to help him dress. He had as usual slept in his clothes on the floor ready to escape, but the room had an oddly nuptial look with a complete set of young lady's clothes laid out on the bed. A moment later Renata burst in again to fling herself into Boetie's arms.

"I am afraid, Louis, I am so afraid," she sobbed. "Suppose they catch you?"

"They won't," he said, hoping he was right and still bewildered at everything that had taken place in the last few weeks. He missed his brother; he did not know where Moolman was, or even if he was alive. He wanted to go home and see his mother but did not dare. He loved this small crying girl. He could hardly describe even to himself what he felt for her sister, the wild excitement he had felt with her. Having lost everything, even his horse, he had found himself accepted in a few hours by this family, which, made manless by the war, had taken him to its heart. Dora van Reenan seemed to regard him as a son, as Moolman did. Everyone seemed to want to adopt him as if he was a stray dog, and stray indeed he was, detached from both home and commando.

But how odd it was that he should fit into this niche, filling the empty hearts of two people as different as the hunter Moolman and this woman, who was so different from any he had ever met before. A rich townswoman who read books, knew the world, and thought like a man. He would ask her to go and see his mother. She could drive over with Renata. She could say he was well, that he loved and missed her. That he was still her Boetie. Then there was the shock of having seen Turnbull, the English captain, mounted on a chestnut race horse behind the English generals. He had seen him clearly and wondered what would happen if he were recognized. Renata had put it out of his mind but now the scene came back to him, the full horror and significance of it. The dear flag coming down the halyard, fluttering like a wounded bird. The Jack going up bravely as a victorious falcon. The generals, the big man and the small, both cast in the bronze of khaki, impassive, as they watched that endless array of troops go by. These were the men he had fought. But spruced up, even exhausted as they were, they looked different. He had seen what disciplined troops were, and seen their menace. And this was only the spearhead of a far greater force, the tip of a vast pyramid of power, only the very point of the blade that was being driven so relentlessly into his land. But they would fight on. *Ja*, before God, they would fight till they were all dead, the lot of them, if they must.

He thought of Johannesburg as he had passed through it—deserted, empty of life—of his ride in the crowded train filled with refugees and rascals. Of Pretoria, his home town, faithless, filled with cowards and hands-uppers, some so shameless as to cheer the invaders. The sound of the bands, of martial music still rang in his ears. The brazen trumps of power. The shouting of the captains, the snort of the war horses. That was in the Book of Job. How little things had changed.

He sat to read his little Testament again as he waited for his hostess. If ever a boy needed God's help it was he. Alone, destitute, going forth unarmed, in woman's garb, to meet an army. He was on his knees when Dora van Reenan walked into his room.

A strange picture met her eyes. A kneeling boy caught in a bar of the sun praying with a dirty little leather-bound Bible in his hand. Tears came into her eyes, tears of anxiety for the boy that Renata loved, tears of rage that such things should be. She stood still, waiting for him to finish, to make his peace with God, for he might well need God's help on this adventure. Outside she heard the horses being put into the Cape cart. Old horses, all that were left to them. Beasts that had not been worth while commandeering. Boetie looked up, saw her, and scrambled to his feet.

"Mevrou"—he forced a smile—"Good morning, *mevrou*," he said.

"Good morning, Louis. They are putting in the horses. I have come to help you dress." She smiled at him. "Don't be shy," she said. "I have seen men before. It's just like putting on a fancy dress for a dance."

When it was done, the bonnet tied, she said, "If you hide your feet no one will know. Now we will put your clothes into this bag." She held a red and green carpetbag open for him as he stuffed in his things.

"Taking them off will be easy," Dora said; "easier than putting them on. The stay laces will have to be cut. There are no other problems." Then she kissed him gently as a mother, sadly as a woman sending yet another man off to war. How many women? How many men? Even the English over the sea. There, too, men had left homes never to return. This one she prayed would come back for his own sake and her daughter's.

Downstairs the girls were waiting to say good-by. He kissed them both, his sisters now, his lovers too. Louisa decorously on the cheeks. "Come back," she whispered. Renata differently, drawing life from her lips, sucking up her love as a thirsty horse sucks water from a trough.

"Good-by," he said. "Good-by. *Tot siens*—till I see you—and may it be soon."

Mrs. van Reenan kissed him again and he climbed into the cart beside old Adam, his carpetbag between his feet. It was strange not to be holding the reins himself, stranger still for one used to good horse flesh to be driving behind these two old unmatched crocks. In a minute he would face the first hurdle. The sentries at the gate.

They never even looked up.

Now they were in the road, the horses' heads facing the north, the north that was still free.

They drove for an hour, slowly klip-klopping along. They passed some marching infantry. A detachment of cavalry clattered by at a dusty trot. Out of the town they pulled up. Adam outspanned the horses, tied them to the wheel of the Cape cart, and prepared a fire. The setup looked natural enough—a Boer girl and her servant cooking a meal off the road. The carpetbag indicated that she was on her way somewhere.

When they had eaten, Boetie left Adam, taking the bag with him. Behind a clump of bush he changed and, packing Louisa's things, still fragrant with her scent, left them and slipped off up a small dry donga, a tributary of Pienaar's River that ran only in the summer rains. Here he lay waiting for dark. He heard Adam inspan, saw him come for the bag and drive away with a rattle of harness, the crossbar banging against the pole of the cart.

Now he was really alone, with the enemy both behind and in front of him, but at least he was no longer disguised as a woman, no longer likely to be shot as a spy. Even more than his aloneness he felt the lack of a horse and a rifle. He felt naked without them. His vision on foot was restricted. His speed dependent on his own ability to run, his hope of defending himself negligible. All he had was his sheath knife. Already cold, as night fell it became colder. The very stars seemed to distill an icy temperature that fell like a cold blanket from the indigo sky, covering everything, silencing everything, giving promise of a winter that would be harder than usual, particularly for those who would have to face it homeless and without warmth or cover.

Then a hunting jackal called, a high, slavering cry, half bark, half scream. A homelike sound to Boetie—and he got up. It was time to move. When he had gone ten miles he saw fires and realized that they were troops, English unquestionably, camped in front of him. Proceeding carefully on his hands and knees, he crept nearer, and nearer still. He could hear the men talking, see their faces illumined by the fire. They sat with their rifles beside them. This was a picket of some kind. There would be sentries farther out and he had, by good fortune, passed the main body of sleeping men. They were cavalry. Their puttees were fastened over their boots, not under the knee. They had on spurs and wore bandoleers about their chests.

"The buggers are about done now, Bill," a mustached man wearing a sergeant's stripes said. "This is about the bloody end of it and I'm not sorry."

"Sorry? Christ!" a dark-faced man answered him. "A thousand bloody miles of bugger all we've come. How big is this bloody place? An' wot's it all about? Towns, they call 'em. Bloody villages. Not a proper pub nor a girl. Right savage bitches they are . . . vixens. Spit in your eye before you've laid a 'and on 'em . . ."

"That's right," another man said. "That's right, mate, and I miss me greens. I'm a man as 'as to 'ave 'em."

"Well you're in the wrong bloody place unless you like 'em black," the sergeant said.

"Black . . . No bloody fear. No 'air on their 'eads and they stinks. . . . Lousy as cuckoos . . . I got me own lice, thanks, says I to a black bitch wot comes up to me. Man, you could see 'em moving in 'er woolly 'air. Like sheep they are . . . Sheep's wool. An' wot's a woman with no 'air I ask you that? Jesus, like a boy with tits, that's wot a 'airless woman's like. . . ."

The talk went on about women, about beer, about food . . . A good steak and kidney pie with a pint of bitter . . . stout . . . a nice 'am . . . a joint of beef done just right— all bloody in the middle—with Yorkshire pudding . . .

"Makes a man dribble just to think of it . . . An' wot price a bath? Soap . . . 'Ot water and all an' the missus to scrub your back. . . ."

Cavalry or mounted infantry. There must be horses nearby. Boetie lay listening and then he heard it. The stamp of a hoof and the rattle of a chain. To his right. The horse lines were not likely to be well guarded, perhaps not even guarded at all. He crept off, moving like a snake through the grass. He must not frighten the horses. He tested the air and swung away so as to reach them upwind. At last he saw them outlined, black against the night sky. His mind was made up. He was going to steal a horse and chance being fired at. It was hard to hit a moving man in the dark. There would be no chance to pick one. Nor could he take a horse at the end of the picket line. He'd have to crawl in among them. Fortunately he was facing their heads. Going still more slowly, he advanced. Now he could see their cocked ears. They knew something was moving but did not know what. He snorted through his nose and moved nearer. A horse with a blaze snorted softly back at him. He snorted again. The horse extended his nose. Boetie snorted, and moved till his face was touching that of the horse. Then he lay breathing into its nostrils as his hand found the rope to which they were all tied. He found the halter rope and undid the knot. His hand was on the horse's cheek now. He got up, stroked its neck, and pulled its ears. It had a long mane, thank God. Now for the most difficult part of the job. Drawing his knife, he cut the horses on either side loose. Then he slashed the picket rope and seized his horse's mane and jumped onto its back with a wild Boer yell of "Charge!" The horses, scared out of their sleep, plunged and reared. The two loose horses broke away, galloping beside him as he rode into the night. The picket rope cut in two was pulled this way and that as the maddened horses jerked at it. Some wild shots were fired, but he was away free, barebacked, on a horse that seemed fresh, willing to go, and easy to control with the headrope used as a neck rein. If there were English pickets here, there must be Boers in front. He could only hope they would not shoot him, for he was conducting what would seem to them a new war maneuver, a cavalry charge in the dark. All around him the horses that had broken away, twenty at least, were galloping wildly in his company, north toward what must be the Boer lines.

"I come. I am alone," he kept shouting in Dutch to the empty night, as his horse jumped bushes, slipped, staggered over loose stones, slid down a donga on its quarters and up the other side with a prodigious scrabbling leap. Now he was among Boers. There was a high shot that cracked like a whip over his head and a cry of *"Wie's daar?"*

"Van der Berg—a burgher," he shouted. "I have escaped with some horses."

"Horses!" the cry went up. The horses, blown now and once again with men, slowed up and were seized.

Boetie slid from his own horse and stood beside it fondling it and stroking its neck.

"Come to the corporal," a big Boer said, taking his arm. "Where are you from?"

"Pretoria," Boetie said.

"You came through the lines, *jong?*"

"*Ja.* I stole a horse."

"*Magtig,* did you not know there is a battle going on?"

"How was I to know?" Boetie said. "I came to seek a commando, ran into some English, stole a horse, cut the others loose and rode on. Where is Pretoria Commando?" he asked. "And do you know a man called Moolman? He is my friend."

"My name is Harman," the big man said, "Hermanus Harman, and I know Dirk Moolman. He is a corporal now under De Wet. I will take you to him."

Leading his horse, Boetie went with Harman. "I must have a saddle, a bridle, and a gun," he said.

"You shall have them," Harman said. Then he shouted, "Moolman! Corporal Moolman! Here is a boy who says he is your friend."

A moment later Boetie was in Moolman's arms.

"My boy," he said, "my boy . . . *Magtig, jong,* I was worried about you."

"And I about you," Boetie said. With Moolman he was safe. Nothing could happen to him as long as he was with Moolman. This was June 7, the second day of the battle of Diamond Hill, which had been begun while Boetie was learning to be a girl at the Willows.

In two crowded days Boetie had known love for the first time and war again. He had been shot at by both British and Boers, stolen a dozen horses, and was back safe with Moolman and his commando. Love . . . Before God, he knew he could have had both girls, had the time and opportunity offered. The one with a kind of laughing, savage bestiality in which he took all and got nothing, and the other softly with the full beauty of fulfillment.

He knew, too, in his heart that he wanted them, wanted either or both, wanted to be a man before he died. For the first time he felt death near, the air of its wingbeat was upon him, the sound of it like the leather wingbeats of a bat in a darkened room.

In Pretoria, Louisa was going through the clothes in the carpetbag, fitting new laces through the eyelets of her stays and folding the drawers away—trophies of an inconclusive engagement. Renata was crying in her room. Dora van Reenan was thoughtful, sad, and anxious. News of the battle Botha was fighting had reached the town. Where was the boy Louis? How had he fared? She knew no more than what Adam had told her, that he had seen him get safely away. . . .

Wait, watch, pray. What else was there for women to do? There was more, and she—they were going to do it. Renata out of love, Louisa for the excitement of the game.

If Louis got through he would arrange it. He was to go to Botha, whom she knew, and inform him that she was getting what information she could about the British for the Boer forces, and would forward any news he sent her to Europe—Holland and England—through sources at the Cape.

If he had got through, there would soon be news. The Willows was going to be a clearinghouse. No place could be safer, set as it was within a few hundred yards of the British GHQ house. A headquarters of Boer Intelligence surrounded on all sides by British troops. What place could be less suspect?

The scene was now set for a great drama. The actors were ready in the wings. The stage was bare—sinister—waiting for the overture of gunfire to begin.

North of Bloemfontein there was much activity, and De Wet, driven off by Methuen, came back in his inimitable manner and attacked a train south of Kroonstad. More Boers who had given up the war and gone home dug up their buried rifles, saddled their ponies, and returned to the field.

Roberts, convinced that attacks on the railways could be executed only by the Boers receiving inside information, issued a proclamation stating that persons in the vicinity of an attack would be made prisoners and have their houses burned. He followed this with a second proclamation. Residents on the railway line might be held as hostages to guarantee the safety of a train. Neither proclamation had the slightest effect. Rather the contrary. Methuen, on orders from Roberts, burned De Wet's farm to the ground. This did not improve De Wet's mood and he continued to harass the British with even greater vigor.

The eastern Free Staters paid no attention to the annexation of their country. Annexation was just a word to them. Rundle, in command of the British in this area, was under continual attack by Boers who, when pursued, simply disappeared behind a smoke screen of burning grass. Now the veld was dry. The tall coarse grass needed only a single match to set it flaring and roaring away. North of Rundle, Lindley was being besieged and the scattered commandos were concentrated around the town. As usual they failed to take it. Quarrels among the leaders ensued, and one of them, Piet de Wet, surrendered to the British out of pique. When Christiaan got the news he swore to shoot his brother down like a dog if he ever ran across him.

The Boers were driven away from Lindley and found themselves penned in against the mountains by sixteen thousand British troops under Clements. The mountains— the Wittebergen and Roodebergen—form a horseshoe seventy-five miles in diameter, pierced by four passes. If the British could hold the passes the total strength of the Free State, some nine thousand burghers, their president and leaders included, would be bottled up.

But the Boers knew what they were doing. They had come into this great amphitheater to rest and to refit as best they might, and though the passes could be used by the British to keep them in they could also be used by the Boers to keep the British out. They were, after all, doors that opened two ways and could be bolted from either side.

This great mountain cup the Boers called the Brandwater Basin, after the river that had its source here, was no cozy dell. Dominated by the jagged, snow-capped peaks of the Drakensberg, sliced by the knives of erosion, a hundred kloofs and gullies pierced the foothills. Darkness came early and light late, the great mountains cutting off the sun's rays as it rose and sank. The basin had a sinister quality in spite of the good grazing, good crops, and the streams of water, always a rarity in South Africa, that ran down every valley.

Owing to the gloom of the overpowering mountain scenery, and unaccustomed idleness, quarrels began to develop among the Boers. Perhaps they had been unwise to come here. Perhaps they should have gone north to join Botha and De la Rey in the Transvaal. Perhaps this . . . perhaps that . . .

If they stayed here long enough Roberts would concentrate on the exits and hold them trapped forever. They decided to leave, split into four groups. De Wet was to go first. He left on the very day that the British were preparing to seal the exits.

Moolman and Boetie rode side by side on their English horses through the pass that wound its secret way among the mountains. Black cliffs rose on either side of them. Beyond them high in the sky was a single star. The only sound was the shuffle of the horses' feet, the creak of saddlery, the sound of a falling stone and once the bark of a baboon, one of the hundreds that slept in caves and crevices on the berg.

Boetie was glad to be out of it. He had not liked the feeling of being penned in. He was a high-veld boy and not at home in mountain country. He rode carefully with a tight rein, keeping his horse's head well up and checking its stumbles. A good enough beast but common, an Argentine with great hoofs like soup plates, a change from his beloved mountain-bred Basuto pony. Pasha gone. General gone. Witbooi gone. Moolman's buckskin gone. These horses had been a part of his life. They left a gap in it almost as large as the men who had been killed, and the woman. Hetta. From Hetta his mind leaped to Renata, the girl who had saved him, the first girl he had ever really met. Certainly the first he had seen naked. The soft, rounded beauty of her body came back to him as he rode through the night. His love. His life. How strange it was that a man should feel like this. . . . Now there were more stars pricking the sky. The handkerchief of deep night blue between the cliffs had become a blanket. They were coming out of the port, the pass in the mountains, like a string pulled through a great stone keyhole.

The order came down the line to canter. De Wet wanted to be well away by dawn.

So good was De Wet's discipline, so afraid of his wrath were his men, that he had moved his twenty-six hundred horsemen, four hundred wagons, and five guns out of the basin, passing within a mile of the British without their knowing he had gone.

But the next parties did not leave the basin as scheduled on the following night. Instead they argued about who should command what, while the British moved toward the four main passes and climbed the outlying heights that dominated the Boer position, heights that, such was their contempt for the British, the Boers had neglected to invest. When dawn broke late over the dark mass of the berg, the Boers found themselves under fire from which there was no protection. Only one exit was left to them, the so-called Golden Gate, thirty miles away over a wicked and tortuous road. Believing this exit impossible of use, the British were not holding it in strength.

Now democracy reared its head. Since no Boer of equal rank was senior to another, they sat arguing all night as to whether Marthinus Prinsloo or Paul Roux should lead them out of the trap. There was much to recommend both. Prinsloo was an old man with a long white beard and therefore experienced. Paul Roux was a parson and would therefore have God behind him. In the end, old age won. But by the time they got to the Golden Gate the British were massed there. In the dark the Scots Guards broke through. By dawn the veld was full of British troops. There was a man behind every tuft of grass and every rock, and the Boers were forced to surrender. The place where this happened was aptly named—Verliesfontein—the "Spring of Bereavement."

On that day the Boer forces lost 4500 men with all their guns, horses, and transport. In the week that followed the British took 3000 more head of cattle, 4000 sheep, and 6000 good horses. They also destroyed 2,000,000 rounds of small-arms ammunition.

This was a bigger haul even than the Paardeberg surrender—a bitter blow to the Boers. But they were not beaten yet. Not by a long shot.

De Wet, the very keystone of Boer resistance, had got away with 2600 men and the President.

Perhaps the best way to understand these Boer-British actions is to see the Boers as quicksilver—as the quicksilver of a broken thermometer on a bare table—the table is Africa—and the British small blocks of wood being used to try to pick up the mercury. As soon as they got near enough to close on it, it broke into pieces or a hundred pieces, only to coalesce again later.

The Boers never waited to fight a pitched battle. They waited to be attacked and ran away, or swung in a great circle to fall on the British lines of communication; lines that led like long worms from every railhead to every force in the field.

The British lines of communication were the weak link in their chain of attack, and what a link it was, with more than a thousand miles of railway line to be guarded. Every yard of it vulnerable with stores at every railhead dump. And great convoys of lumbering wagons winding their way over the veld. The wagons were the prime prey of the Boers, who, by attacking them, not only deprived the British of their needs but also supplied their own.

After the Boer defeat at the Brandwater Basin the war took a new turn.

The British were blockading Lourenço Marques which was the Boers' only source of supply from the outer world, that is to say, their friends—Germany, France, and Holland. And the Delagoa Bay–Pretoria railway line became the main British objective. President Kruger, with the bullion that was the Boer war chest, was at Machodorp, near the Portuguese East African frontier. If they could get him and his gold the war would be over.

A great attack was planned but failed, for Botha, warned of it through spies, was ready and turned it back. He then broke up his forces, forming separate independent commandos operating as far as possible in the vicinity of their own homes. This improved the morale of the men, gave them a chance to refit, and meant that they were fighting in country that they knew as well as the palms of their own hands. And the western Transvaal, which was supposed to be pacified, suddenly burst into flame again, with seven thousand Boers in the field under De la Rey and Jan Smuts, the young state attorney general.

This was the news that Moolman was told to take to Pretoria. The details of the Brandwater Basin disaster and De Wet's dispositions. The generals out of touch with each other communicated via the central Boer Intelligence in Pretoria right under the noses of the British.

"I am taking a dispatch to Mevrou van Reenan, Boetie," Moolman said, when he came back from seeing De Wet. "Have you a message for her?"

"Mevrou van Reenan? She is in this?" Boetie said.

"She is part of the organization—one of its founders."

Boetie was horrified by the risks she was taking. Suppose she was caught. What would happen to Renata?

"Of course I'll write," he said. "When do you leave?"

"Tonight. I'll go by night. I have got a disguise all fixed up. I'll be an old Kaffir. I'll ride as far as I can and then abandon my horse."

"But you? Why you?"

"Because I am a hunter and a scout. Because I talk English and two Kaffir tongues. But I got a surprise when De Wet said I was to go to the Van Reenans' house, the Willows, in Sunnyside. He should have sent you." Moolman laughed. "Now give me the directions."

Boetie drew him a plan.

"And afterward?" Boetie said. "When you have delivered your dispatch?"

"If they do not shoot me I shall find my way back. Don't worry, boy. Don't worry."

Moolman smiled at him. It was good to have someone to worry about him, to care whether he came back or not. He hoped he would get a look at the girl.

CHAPTER 42

THE GIRLS

DORA VAN REENAN looked down at the old blanket-clad Kaffir cringing in the red dust of the garden path before her. They were well screened here by fruit trees—peaches, plums, pears, bare now, freed from the richness of their summer harvest. She cut some twigs with her clippers.

The Kaffir put two small folded pieces of paper near her right foot. "Let the clippers fall," he said.

She let them go and picked up the papers when she stooped.

"It is from De Wet," he said. "The other is from Boetie." Then he whined, "A shilling, give an old Kaffir a shilling."

"You are all the same. Beggars, the lot of you," Mrs. van Reenan said, and, fishing in her reticule, gave him a coin. She went on snipping peach trees, pruning the long shots back.

"In one way or another I will come when I can," Moolman said.

"How are things in the field?"

"Better in some places than others. With Delagoa Bay closed to us now we have to live on the English convoys. We must capture all we use. Clothes, blankets, ammunition, rifles, food, forage, horses, everything."

"And the farms? Is it true about the farms?"

"Not a farm is standing, *mevrou*. Not a head of stock is left alive in all our land. The plight of the women and children is pitiable. They take them in, herd them like cattle into trucks. Some escape to join us. Some starve, some are murdered or worse, by Kaffirs. It is all in there. With De Wet's report of his actions and dispositions."

"It's no good sitting there," Dora van Reenan said. "You'll get no more from me today." She turned her back on him and continued her work. When she looked around he was gone.

Moolman slipped away through a gap in the garden fence. An old hobbling Kaffir of no interest to anyone. He hung about for a while, begging, scrounging in heaps of rubbish, and then drifted gradually to the north, where he would get past the outposts with as little difficulty as he had got in. Reeling a little as if drunk, singing to himself, and playing the Kaffir piano in his hand. This spying business was a nice change. He enjoyed the gamble, the high stake of playing his life unarmed and alone among the enemy. He had been chosen for the job because of his knowledge of English and his ability to disguise himself as a Kaffir and speak their tongue, a Swazi-Shangaan of the Portuguese border. He had seen a lot and learned a lot. His worst fears had been confirmed about the English strength. And he had also got a glimpse of Boetie's maid, Renata, and her dark sister. They had not seen him.

This news of the concentration camps and the burning of the farms must reach England. When they knew the truth, public opinion might change. The great powers might exercise moral pressure. There was still a chance of peace while the Boers were undefeated.

But the girls would really have to help and Dora would have to let Captain Carter court her. The pity of it was that she liked him and it would be difficult to take advantage of him. At first she had thought he was interested only in Louisa. He had brought her presents, taken her riding and driving. But now she knew it was she he came to see. Louisa had only been an excuse. And the classic situation of a mother and daughter being involved with the same man, and an enemy at that, had arisen here in this tiny capital of a defeated state.

She had no idea of how it had begun. Turnbull had brought him around. Then he had begun to come on his own. Ostensibly seeking Louisa's company, but she had felt his eyes on her and slowly realized what was in his mind. Known and responded to it in a way that made her ashamed. Captain Carter attracted her as no man ever had before.

But what was worse was that Louisa knew it, and a curious, silent, hidden rivalry had sprung up between them. Louisia did not love Morgan Carter. She loved only herself. But here her dearest possession, her vanity, had been attacked. Louisa's vanity was not her Achilles' heel. It was the frame on which her total personality was hung, like a dress on a peg. Her strengths and her weaknesses were identical. Thin-skinned with youth, beauty her only weapon, she was at once furious and afraid to find it buckling in her hand.

Dora van Reenan thought of her daughters. How different they were! Louisa was tall, dark, with flashing eyes; Renata was small, slim, honey-fair, with eyes that were almost a golden yellow. In temperament, too, they were utterly different. Louisa was quick-tempered, active, but apt to lose interest in things if they did not go well at once. Renata was slow to be aroused, but patient and determined to carry her every project through to the end.

Their reactions to the war had been different, too. Louisa's indignation and fury had burned itself out in the first few months, and when the British had occupied Pretoria, she had not welcomed them, but had soon forgotten they were English, the enemy, these facts being lost in the greater one of their being men, their coming bringing to an end the tedium of the past year. For Renata even the handsomest young officer was invisible, a faceless perambulating uniform that touched no chord in her being.

And now she must manage the girls, drive this ill-matched pair as if they were a team of horses. Make Renata see that she must be friendlier. Make Louisa control the vivacity in which she blurted out everything that came into her head.

The girls came into the room together. She tried to see them with a man's eyes. Particularly the eyes of a young man who had been suffering the hardships of a campaign and seen no young women for months. In such terms they were delectable, ripe as peaches to the hand of the plucker, trembling, ready to fall at the first touch. How strange it was to be thinking of her own daughters as if she was a procuress. Thinking of their lustrous hair, long lashes, their wide eyes, young, firm breasts, hard bellies, and soft thighs; at the prettiness of their ankles as they came walking toward her, their skirts swinging. She could see from their flushed faces that they were angry with each other. There was nothing new about that, either.

"Those men," Renata said. "Those damned Englishmen! One of them tried to touch me." She looked down and swept the imaginary defilement from her skirt. "Do they think we are horses, Mama?" she cried. "To be patted as we go by?"

"You little silly," Louisa said. "What harm could he do you?"

"To be touched by an Englishman is harm. I am a Boer maid, with a father dead. Their hands," she said, and shivered. "Imagine their hands upon you."

"Sit down, both of you," their mother said.

They looked at her in astonishment.

"Sit, I said."

They sat as primly as little girls, their hands in their

laps, staring up at her. This was a mood they did not know.

Of course this might not be the time, Dora van Reenan thought. But when was the time? When did one say things such as she was going to say?

"You love your mother, don't you?"

"Of course we do," they said together.

"Then you have got to do something for her, both of you—and stop quarreling."

"What must we do?" Louisa asked.

"First, you must swear by the Bible that you will never speak of this." She went to the table and put the Bible on the sofa between them.

"Lay your hands on the Bible and swear," she said.

"We swear," the girls said.

"Very well, then, here is what we must do. Remember, it is for our country. It is honorable."

"*Ja,*" the girls said.

"A man has been here," their mother said.

"What man?" Louisa said, her eyes brightening.

"Moolman, the hunter, Louis's friend. He came in disguise. He came in rags, his face stained—as an old lame Kaffir."

"Did he have a letter for me?" Renata asked.

"I'll give it to you in a minute."

"And?" Louisa had lost interest. Moolman was over forty.

"We are organizing a service so that we can get news from the commandos to the Cape and Europe."

"Where will you get the news?" Renata asked. She had a great admiration for Moolman, who was Boetie's friend.

"Yes, where will you get it, Mama?" Louisa was interested again.

"News of the commandos from Moolman and the English from you. And you will get it from your officer friends. And you, too, Miss Renata." She turned on her younger daughter. "You understand? You will be friends with them. You will get information."

"I must speak to them, smile at them, let them take my hand!"

"Before God, child, if it is necessary, you must let them kiss you. It is for our land."

"Me!" Renata jumped to her feet and stamped her foot.

"Me! No better than a whore like my sister!"

With a quick movement her mother was at her side, slapping her face. "I told you to sit down and listen," she said, "and listen well. If it came to that and was important enough, the answer is yes, even that. Even if you have to lie with one of them. This is all a woman can do. The men give their lives, so why should a maiden fear the blood of her maidenhead?" She began to cry. "My God, that it should come to this. That I should tell you this. But your father died for his country, and *ja,* if you must, you must sacrifice yourselves." She cheered up suddenly and smiled as she wiped the tears from her face. "But it won't come to that. You are too good, too clever. And much as I hate them, they are gentlemen. They will respect you."

Renata spat on the floor.

"Wipe that up, and control yourself. And you, Louisa, remember to keep that pretty mouth of yours shut. Use your ears instead."

Renata put her handkerchief back in her pocket and pointed to her sister. "Look at her mouth," she said, "just look at her lips, as wet and pink as fruit from kissing."

"Stop it, I say," her mother said, "or I shall whip you like a child. Stop playing and make up your minds to act as Boer girls."

"As spies. Harlots and spies. *Ja, ja,*" Renata cried, "mistresses to this scum from across the sea that have overrun us like locusts, like Isaac, except that we are girls whom you would sacrifice."

"It will be fun," Louisa said. "It will give us something to do."

"Just see that you do it, then," their mother said, "and don't betray your trust, for the lives of brave men will lie in your hands."

Renata put out her hands in front of her to look at them, as if she saw small, brave men cupped in them like eggs.

"Now leave me," their mother said.

The girls went out of the room, Renata reluctantly—she wanted her letter, Louisa with an impertinent switch of skirts.

What had she said to her daughters? Had she said more

than she meant? Lie with them if you must. This to her own daughters, who had never known a man. Was this to be her alibi? Was this what had been in her mind when she spoke? Was this Englishman what she had always desired in her heart? She knew now, with the greatest clarity of mind, that her husband had meant nothing to her. His departure had scarcely left a gap in her life, had hardly changed a thought or habit. She knew that if Morgan Carter wanted her she was his. She knew she had lied to her daughters, and would be heartbroken, no matter what information they obtained, if they accepted her word, her more than tacit permission to misconduct. The price would be too high. She had been thinking of herself and her own hidden desire and hope.

It broke down to Carter. She wanted him herself and was jealous of Louisa. Renata was safe. She had made no secret of her love for Boetie. Late one night she had crept into her room, sat on the floor beside her bed, and confided her hopes to her mother. Her hopes and her love. She was a one-man girl. Nor, except for his youth, could she find the match in any way unsuitable. A fine boy who would grow into a fine man. A brave fighter, according to Moolman, who seemed to regard him as a son, a half owner of a good farm only twenty miles away. One day she would drive out and visit his mother, Mevrou Catalina van der Berg, another widow like herself but a real one from what she had heard. A beautiful woman who for years had kept all men at arm's length.

And I, she thought, after only a few months . . . So if the outward situation was the same the reality was different. As different as two identical walnuts, one of which held a rich kernel crumpled with memories and the other a dry husk of shriveled and unfulfilled hopes.

Renata had said, "I love him, Mama. We love each other. He is my heart, my life."

"You have not . . . ?" She could not then bring herself to say the words.

"No. No. We have been close, Mama, kissed, and he has touched my body since it will one day be his. But no more. We can wait for that." Then she had sprung up and said, "But I am glad he saw me naked. Glad, glad, because now I shall be forever in his eyes. Forever before him, as Eve was before Adam—naked and unashamed.

I only felt shame when the Englishman came in like the snake into Eden. *Ja*, then and only then did I try to cover my nakedness. But not for Louis. If I am beautiful the knowledge of my beauty belongs to him."

As unself-consciously as a child she had dropped her nightdress to her feet and stood like the golden pistil of an arum, rising out of the white kid flask of its bloom. Raising her hands above her head, she said, "Am I beautiful, Mama? Am I?"

"*Ja*, you are beautiful." And she was—breath-takingly so. In her youth, in her splendid uncaring that went beyond all modesty. She had then stooped, pulled on her long nightdress, and run from the room.

If Louisa had done that, her mother thought when Renata had gone, the act would have been prurient, filled with mock modesty, coquettishness, and false shyness. Each movement would have been calculated to excite. That was what was so remarkable in such an utterly inexperienced girl. It had existed since her earliest toddling years. Somehow, even when she was only four or five, she had always given an impression of femininity. No man she had put up her face to for a kiss or onto whose lap she had climbed could fail to feel the latent sensuality of this child who was already woman.

She knew she was being unfair to Louisa, regarding her as a rival, and why could this not be just another trick? Why could a man not first court the daughter, switch to the mother as a blind to make the girl jealous, and then, taking advantage of her emotion, allow the girl to triumph over her mother by her acquiescence?

Tortured by her thoughts, by a passion she was now ready to acknowledge, by remorse, by jealousy, by fear for young Louis, on whom Renata's happiness depended, by fear for Moolman, the courageous spy who took his life in his hands for the cause of his country, worried about the letter that must be sent to Oom Paul—the President—in Holland, terror of involving her sister Anna at the Cape, regret at her impulse to force her girls at any and all cost into espionage, she tossed and turned in bed. It was hours before she fell asleep.

In her room Renata was reading Boetie's letter for the seventh time. She had read it six times and put it in a drawer with her handkerchiefs. Then, unable to resist the impulse, convinced she might have missed something, though it was only a page long, she got it out again.

She had never seen his handwriting before. Her first letter from him. Her first love letter. Her boy, her man, the father of the children she would one day bear.

She stared at the crumpled paper, at the smeared pencil script in her hand, stared as if in some magic manner, by staring hard enough, she could materialize him, see him there before her, feel his arms around her, his kisses on her open lips.

In the field

My heart, my heart,

With the help of God and my friend whom may God protect this message of my love may reach you in a few days, for we are not far distant. Night and day I think of you, of your gentle beauty. You are always with me by the campfires in the night, even in battle you are at my side. I am well. My new horse that I took from the English is well. We are in good heart and confident, if not of victory, at least of a satisfactory peace and our freedom regained. Without this, ours is blood lost, and the flower of our nation will have died in vain. So pray for us. Go and see my mother, for she will love you, and give her my love. Tell her all I have told you and what is between us. One day, I know the opportunity will come, I shall get back to the Willows. Almost every night someone slips through the British lines. Both in and out. So do not be surprised to see me. The time will come when I can wait no longer to clasp you to my bosom, heart to heart.

A thousand embraces and kisses, Renata my love. *Tot siens,* till I see you.

Your Louis.

What a letter for a girl to get. She wondered if any girl had ever received one like it. Perhaps every girl thought that of her first love letter from a soldier away at war. How many thousands had been written? To how many thousands of girls in all the wars of history?

If only she could have answered it, poured out the gold of her love as if it was money on paper, wrapping it up in a parcel of tenderness and passion. If only . . . How many onlys, how many ifs there were. But if there had been no war there would have been no Louis. Someone else perhaps, even certainly, but not Louis. That there could have been someone else seemed inconceivable to her as she lay on her bed and wept. What did he mean, the horse he had taken from the English? What risks had he run?

Until she got to know some British officers, which had not taken long, Louisa had never realized that there were bachelors in the world who were not boys.

Boers all married in their teens or very early twenties. A widower remarried quickly. So these young and youngish men who were heartfree were a new and exciting phenomenon to her. They opened up a new world—one in which men could live without women because they had good servants, both male and female. In Africa a man had to marry. He could not run a farm or even a house alone. Even the most competent Kaffirs were incapable of cooking, cleaning, or doing laundry without constant supervision.

Though she would certainly have acknowledged it to no one, Louisa much preferred having the English camped around the house to having a Boer force. This was not a question of patriotism or the lack of it, but of glamour. The Boers, dull, bearded, and not overclean, could not compare with these smart, well-dressed officers and men. Everything they had shone—the buttons, cap badges, belt buckles, rifle butts, spurs, boots, and leggings.

All the English troops were clean and well turned out, but those near the Willows, which was in the headquarters area, gleamed like newly minted sovereigns.

Louisa was standing on the stoep tapping her riding boot with a thin whip of polished rhino horn. Captain Carter was coming to take her for a ride. She laughed now at her indignation when she had heard that a lot of ladies' sidesaddles had been captured from the British at Dundee. She thought, How furious I was at their impertinence, imagining that Boer girls would go riding with them. And now just look at me.

It was really funny, and it just showed how one could change, could grow up. Although it was less than a year ago. She had been a child then, and was a woman now.

To be a woman, to be courted by a man like Morgan Carter and others, was most enjoyable. She spent a lot of time at her mother's long mirror, looking less at herself than at what they would see. She disassociated herself

from her own reflection, stood back from it to examine
herself objectively, as if she was a man. It was no use just
admiring yourself, though that was pleasant enough. You
had to see what a man saw. See with a man's eyes. Think
with a man's desire. There must be titillation without vul-
garity. There must be suggestions of lace that hid more
lace, of perfume whose place of origin was elusive. An
ankle, the glimpse of a calf, the swell of a breast as an
evening dress slipped off a shoulder. All this she knew
by some instinct, had known since childhood, but until
now had had no audience, no appreciation.

She was wearing a navy riding habit that she held high
in her left hand, showing a smart black spurred boot.
Under the apron that covered them were black riding
breeches. She had on a tight white jacket, a white stock,
and a black tricorne hat that had come from Paris and
was a present from her aunt Anna at the Cape. She had
black gauntlet gloves on her hands.

While she waited so impatiently she watched her mother
pruning the fruit trees in the garden.

Her mother astonished her. Not only by her change of
attitude about the English, deceitful as it was, but by a
new youthfulness in her step and a brightness of eye she
had never seen there before.

She seemed to enjoy this spying business. Intrigue certainly came natural to women. It was their answer to the
physical strength of men. Even Renata, prude that she
was, liked her secret romance with Louis van der Berg,
though what she could see in a boy so little older than she
was herself was hard to imagine. Louisa liked mature
men who knew about women, how to please and talk to
them. Men like Captain Carter, in fact. Just look how
clever he was, wasting his time with Mama so that she
would think he was interested in her. As if a man could
be interested in a woman of her age.

Of course she must have been a very pretty woman
once, but that time had passed. That was why a girl had
to make such haste. How little time she had—ten or fifteen
years at most. Less if she married a poor man and had a
lot of children. Much less. But she was not going to marry
a poor man.

It was her intention to marry a British officer. Carter, if
she could. If not, someone else. She had several alterna-

tives. She had no intention of remaining in South Africa.
London and Paris called her. Shops. Streets she had read
about—Bond Street, the Rue de Rivoli . . .

She heard horses. Captain Carter, looking very smart
on his black charger, was leading a gray mare with a sidesaddle on the off side of his horse. He saluted, dismounted
by throwing his leg over the black's neck, and said, "This
is the gray mare I told you about, Louisa. A pretty thing,
I think, don't you? And used to a lady."

It was not every horse that would take a sidesaddle or
stand the skirt of a habit flapping against its belly. They
had to be trained to it. Bringing the mare around to the
near side of his horse, Captain Carter cupped his hand
to take Louisa's foot. As she stepped onto it he gave a
slight heave that shot her into the saddle with her right leg
over the straight pommel, her left leg over the curved one
below it, her booted foot resting in the safety stirrup.
There was nothing quite so safe or so dangerous as a sidesaddle. Nothing could shake the rider loose unless a
girth broke. The danger was a horse falling, because there
was no chance of coming clear, and the woman and the
horse came down together. But a pretty girl who was a
good rider looked her very best mounted, and on a horse
Louisa's lovely figure, straight back, and small waist
showed to perfection. This was one reason she liked riding
so much.

She wore her long hair tied with a wide black ribbon,
It reached the small of her back.

Captain Carter mounted and they rode at a walk down
the drive and out into the road, turning north toward
Wonderboom, which was their objective—the great group
of parasite figs which, having killed their host, stood in
a circle around the spot where it had died.

The officers of the HQ staff called Louisa the Black
Rose and Renata the Lily. They had a joke about it. Where
is there a Lily with thorns and the Rose without them?
The answer of course was at the Willows.

Since the British had moved into Pretoria a great deal
had happened at the Willows. Dora van Reenan had established communication with her sister at Morningstar,
who forwarded what she sent her to a Meneer Ryk in Holland, who passed it on to the President. She was also get-

ting and sending news to De Wet and the commandos in the field.

Socially she had done well, too, as soon as her mind had been made up to make friends with the enemy. Both Captain Turnbull and Captain Carter were frequent visitors to the house, dropping in for tea and inviting her and the girls to concerts, dances, and other entertainments. Young officers on the staff with very little to do called on the girls and were well received by them. Even by Renata, who felt that she might be helping Boetie by her espionage.

So it was with some surprise that one morning she received an official visit from a Major Larson, accompanied by a subaltern and two troopers, all mounted, clattering into her yard. They dismounted and, leaving the troopers to hold their horses, came clinking up the steps onto the stoep.

She went to meet them.

The officers saluted. Major Larson, whom she had met on several occasions, said, "Mrs. van Reenan?"

"I am Mrs. van Reenan, as you well know." What a fool the man was.

"This is an official inquiry," Larson said. "May we go inside?"

"If it is official we shall remain outside. My home is for my friends, even if they are enemies. But do sit down." She pointed to the chairs among the potted plants that lined the stoep.

"And now what is all this about, may I ask?"

"Do you know a man called Hans Cordau?"

"Of course we know him. Everyone knows him."

"May I ask when you saw him last, Mrs. van Reenan?"

"Last. I have not seen him, nor do I want to, since you came to Pretoria and he took the oath of allegiance to your queen. We are loyal Boers, Major Larson. As a people we hate you. Do you understand that?" she said angrily. "Hate you!"

"Then you know nothing of the plot?"

"Plot? What plot?"

"You were on the list," he said, producing a slip of paper. "You were among those who were said to know Cordau well."

"We did know him well. He was my husband's friend.

But my husband is dead in the field, and we know no traitors. An open enemy is better than a traitor."

"Very well, *mevrou,* I'll take your word for it."

"Thank you, Major. But now, having come so far, please inform me about the plot."

"The plot," he said. "Good God!" He was relaxed now that this painful duty was over. "The plot was to set half Pretoria alight and in the confusion kidnap Lord Roberts and murder most of his staff."

"What a pity you found out," Mrs. van Reenan said, turning her back on him and going into the house.

So Cordau was a loyal burgher after all and had only taken the oath to be able to plan better. They would shoot him, that was certain. How she had misjudged the man. What mistakes it was possible to make. . . .

And this was only the beginning. When the girls came in they had more stories to tell. Thousands of Boer women and children were going to be turned out of Pretoria and Johannesburg and sent back to the Boer lines on the grounds that they supplied information to the enemy—their husbands and fathers—and consumed food that was needed for the occupation forces.

Four days later Cordau, condemned by court-martial to death, was shot. He refused to be tied, walked quietly to the chair in which he was to sit, asked to be blindfolded, and waited with folded arms for death.

CHAPTER 43

THE CAPE OF GOOD HOPE

EDWARD DE LANGE at Morningstar was delighted at the way his wife was entertaining the British. Two officers, Major Morley of the Grenadiers and Captain Gordon of the Seaforths, were billeted on them. In the summer there had been garden parties and tennis parties, teas and dinners. Now that the winter with its rain and storms had begun there was the jackal-hunting, with hunt breakfasts, a hunt ball, point-to-points and gymkhanas that were arranged for the fine spells of sharp, clear weather that came between the storms.

Anna, to whom he grudged nothing, looked even handsomer than usual in her new clothes. Shipments came from London and Paris by almost every mail for the Adderley Street shops. There was a good market in Cape Town, with the backwash of the war, the wounded and convalescent officers, the mining magnates of the Rand, the profiteers of various kinds, and the lovely women who had sprung from nowhere to minister to their wants.

It was impossible to entertain as the De Langes did at Morningstar without Anna's learning a great deal of what was going on. It was hardly necessary to ask a single question. She merely listened to snatches of conversation; strolled, before it became too cold, along the frontage of the house beneath the old oaks, past the great pots of hydrangea, with officers only too willing to tell a pretty woman, so obviously loyal, of their experiences, hopes, and expectations of what was to come.

The news went back to her sister in letters concealed in the luggage or on the persons of Boer sympathizers going north. She wrote openly, too, gossiping letters filled with rumors and stories for the delectation of the censors who cut them out.

In the beginning the plan of the two women had been to establish a *modus operandi* that could be used if the situation deteriorated still further, as obviously it might. This was a sort of dry run, a rehearsal for the real thing. But Anna was collecting English friends and making valuable contacts at the Cape just as Dora was in Pretoria.

General Forrestier Walker, in command of the city and the Cape area, was often at Morningstar. So were some of his staff. There were semiofficial lunches in the big dining room of the Mount Nelson Hotel. At one of them Mrs. Edward de Lange was introduced to Mrs. Charles Darnley, the widow of the lancer hero. There in all their glory she saw the wives of other officers, the bejeweled mistresses of the mine magnates, the full glitter of the great and half-worlds deployed for war and revelry in its spoils. It was shocking for her to see, even though she hated them so much, this lack of patriotism among so many of the English women. They appeared to think of nothing but their own appearance and the impression they made on those who watched them sweep by. But this was the stage she had chosen. This was the table from which the crumbs she sought fell with such profusion. The greatest difficulty was the deception she had to practice on her husband. Edward often told her things that she should not have known and she passed them on, torn between love of her country and hatred of herself for her betrayal of her husband. But she must betray someone, either her husband or her people, painful though it was.

Wanthope was back in Cape Town, seconded to the Remount Service, much to his disgust. His unpopularity had caught up with him again, and if the Blacks had not wanted him back, neither did the General Staff wish to keep him. He had quarreled with John French, a man for whom he had contempt as a mere commoner. So here he was back, handsomer than ever, bemedaled, with jingling spur chains and rowels, almost but not quite ignoring Diana and seducing other women who were only too ready to submit, needing only the opportunity, well aware of the splendid gifts that followed acquiescence to so rich a man. What did a few torn clothes and bruises matter when the salve was diamonds?

Diana, still certain of him, aware that he must have women and told that he avoided her only to prevent scandal, consoled herself with her usual discretion and without reproach from him.

"You're a pretty woman, Di," he said, "and you'd better have fun while you can."

She was both hurt and astonished at this lack of jealousy in so violent a man, but took him at his word, flirting outrageously with the men she did not sleep with, and practically cutting by day the men who came to her room at night.

Life in Cape Town went on much as usual except for its increased gaiety. Every hotel, the Queens, the Grand, the Mount Nelson, the smaller places, and boardinghouses were all full. The hospital in Wynberg was full too, but no one worried very much about that.

Money flowed like the champagne that Wanthope drank from the tiny satin slipper of his newest friend, the young grass widow of a horse gunner who at the moment was chasing De la Rey in the Transvaal.

No two cities could have been more widely divergent in attitude than Cape Town and Pretoria. Much more than a thousand miles of veld separated them. Cape Town, the base of a victorious army, its head, as it were, was the mouth through which supplies reached Pretoria, the occupied capital that could be thought of as the tail. The end of the line. For it was the tail of this strange beast that had to fight. It was changing slowly into a double-ended monster with one head that ate and the other that bit. New teeth were being fitted every day, but still the middle of the animal, dachshund-long, was subjected almost defenseless to the kicks of the Boers.

It was soon after, when Roberts saw that he could no longer hope to pacify the Boers with his methods of consideration and humanity, that Dora van Reenan and Renata drove over to Groenplaas. They had bags with them, being sure they would be asked to spend the night, the two old horses being incapable of making the return journey without food and a rest.

The drive took them seven hours. They went no faster than a man could walk, jogging along at three miles an hour and outspanning to have lunch, watering and feeding the horses on the way.

Renata was very nervous. The woman she was going to see would be her mother-in-law. Louis was devoted to her.

"Will she like me, Mama?" she asked. "Suppose she does not like me? Suppose she says we are too young?" Suppose, suppose, suppose. It was all suppose or silence for the whole twenty dusty miles.

In between her fear and suppositions Renata looked at the veld. She had never been this way before. If they got married this would be her road home from Pretoria. This road would be the link between her old home and her new one. How many times had Louis traveled it? Every bush, every outcrop of rock must be familiar to him. She looked at them with loving eyes, giving them personality, saying as she passed a group of blue gums or a large rock, "Louis must know you well." They had seen Louis go by a thousand times, since he was a child. They had seen him ride out to war with his brother. They were waiting for him to come back.

Her gold-flecked eyes were hard as she stared down the

road, her full lips firm. She reached over to the watch that hung from a brooch on her mother's bosom and turned its blue enamel back to see its face. In half an hour they would be there, at Groenplaas, the place where Louis had been born and grown up.

Dora van Reenan had chosen today to drive over to Groenplaas because Renata had not been able to get over Cordau's execution and needed a change. There had been some doubt about leaving Louisa alone, but Adam was there and after all, as Louisa said, "What could happen to me here with half the British Army around me?"

"You are sure you do not want to come?"

"I am sure, Mama," she'd said. "It's not *my* mother-in-law you are going to meet. So please don't worry." And she wasn't worrying. Louisa could take care of herself. If she were attacked by the British Army, which seemed improbable, she was quite capable of dealing with them in one way or another. Dora van Reenan was rather upset to find that she had so little affection in her heart for her elder daughter. The girl took after her father, a man, she discovered now, after his death, she had never really liked.

Alone in Pretoria, Louisa went from room to room. This business was upsetting. Not so much the execution. She had met Cordau of course, but the big, stout, middle-aged man had not shown the slightest interest in her, though he was known to like young girls. No, that was not it. It was Helga le Roux who was the trouble. Helga was a friend of hers and had been more than a friend to Cordau. Proud of this hidden relationship and unable to keep a secret—what, after all, was the good of a secret if you kept it?—she let slip a hint or two of the kidnap plan last time they had been out together.

Without fully realizing it herself, power had been put into Louisa's hands. The power to change, to destroy. She had not thought of it that way. She did not think of it that way now. She had only known that if she did something, or said something, a train of events would be set in motion. She tried to tell herself now that all she had done was save half Pretoria from being burned. Not that she had betrayed a patriot to his death.

A word—no, a sentence had been enough when she was

out riding with Carter. Then the wheels had begun to turn, the whole mechanism of British counterespionage had been set in motion, and now Cordau was dead. A Boer hero had failed in his mission due to a bragging girl and her friend who, unable to resist being important, had given him away. But would Helga think of her? Would she remember? How many others girls had she told? Would Carter, careless perhaps in his cups, say it was she? Already it was known that Cordau had been betrayed by a woman. But with luck people would think of Helga, not of her.

Unable to think of anything to do, she decided to wash her hair. Her body, any part of it—skin, eyes, hair, toe- and fingernails—was her great distraction, what reading might be to other girls, and it was always here to hand. There was always something one could do to care for a beautiful body. Music—the piano, which she played by ear—was another interest. She liked it because it made her the center of attention and enabled her to show her beautiful hands.

Adam brought her hot water, two eggs, and a small basin. She broke the eggs, separating the yolks and using them on her hair to give it luster. She rinsed it in three waters. Then, twisting her ringlets around rolls of news-paper, fastening them with tape, she went out into the gar-den to dry her hair in the sun, first putting a soft mask of goatskin with eyeholes over her face to prevent its being burned. These masks had been used by South African girls since the Great Trek and even before it.

Calm now, sitting out of the wind in the warmth of the winter sun, Louisa basked like a lizard. If Helga did say anything, all she had to do was to deny it. It was her word against Helga's. And why should Helga have told her anything? What would be the point of it? And if worst came to worst she could say Helga had told her of a quarrel she had had with Hans Cordau, who had been unfaithful to her. It was not true but would stand up as a reason for her betrayal.

All she, Louisa, had done was to save a lot of harmless people from being burned out and incurred a debt of gratitude from the British Intelligence. The power was still in her slim, long-fingered hands. She had never had power before, other than the little she had had over her father and other men by the exercise of her childish femininity. This was different. This was real, and the fumes of it went to her head like wine.

She wondered if her mother suspected her. For a moment she was afraid and then calmed herself. Her mother would not give her away. She might beat her. The idea of the scene excited her—the recriminations. Her accusations of jealousy. Her saying, "You threw me at him, at the English, you, you . . ."

Mevrou van der Berg was surprised to see her visitors. She saw a Cape cart with two old horses, two women, and a boy in the back drive in. The two women, or at least a woman and a girl, got out. She went to meet them. The older, a still-pretty woman and evidently the mother, said, "I am Mevrou van Reenan. This is my daughter."

"Come in," Mrs. van der Berg said, and led them into the sitting room. "Sit down. I will send for coffee." She wondered why they had come.

"We are from Pretoria," Mrs. van Reenan said.

"A long and dusty drive." Long indeed, with two old horses like that.

"We have news of your son, *mevrou*. Your son Louis."

"Boetie, my Boetie, you have seen him?"

"He spent two days with us. We helped him to escape."

"And now? Where is he now?"

"With Botha or De Wet in the north."

"How is he, *mevrou*? Is he well? Has he grown?"

"Since I never saw him before I do not know if he has grown. But he is a big boy, *mevrou*. He must be six feet tall at least."

"Taller than his father, then, or his brother." Catalina clasped her hands together. "Tell me more, *mevrou*. Tell me everything. He is my baby."

"Mevrou," Dora van Reenan said, "your baby is no baby now. In fact that is in a way what we have come about. Louis said, 'Go and see my mother. Give her news of me, tell her I love her. And take Renata to her' "—she glanced at the girl—" 'and tell her she has a daughter again.' "

"A daughter." Catalina looked at Renata, a beautiful young Boer girl, rich as cream, ripe as a peach, modestly sitting with downcast eyes.

"Ja, mevrou, that is why I said your Boetie is no longer
a baby. A baby goes to war, blooms there if he does not
die, and returns a man. But Louis has become a man and,
as a man, desires a maid. This girl, my daughter, is his
choice. That is why we are here. I think, *mevrou,* neither
of us will lose anything. I gain a son and you a daughter."

"Elsa," Catalina said. "He told you about Elsa?"

"I think he told us everything. About Elsa, about you,
about his brother Servas, about Moolman his friend, and
the English captain who would have been his brother."

"It went fast," Catalina said. It was hard to think of
her baby courting a maid. Kissing this girl, touching her,
being one with her.

"It is war, *mevrou,* as we all well know. In war things
move fast becase there is so little time for love or happiness. *Ja,"* she went on, "as flowers bloom, flower and seed
in a week when it rains in the deserts of the Karroo because they have so little time, so too is it with maids and
men in war. This is the law of nature, perhaps even the
will of God. If there is a God."

Catalina looked up, startled. "You too?" she said. "You
have doubts?"

"I have doubts," Dora van Reenan said. "I am not certain one way or the other. I still pray. I pray for the
Boers. I pray for your Louis. But do not the English-
women pray to God too? Is he not the same God? Are not
both Boers and English Christian people? Can you answer
that, Mevrou van der Berg? Can you tell me?" Dora van
Reenan leaned forward, her elbows on her knees.

"Mevrou," Catalina said, "I believe but I do not understand. God first took my beloved husband, then my young
daughter in the very bud of her womanhood. Now my sons
are gone. Alive, thank God, but gone now. Tell me more of
Boetie. Servas, my other boy, came back, but there was a
curtain of time and experience between us. War seemed to
have made him hard. He almost quarreled with our bywoner who is back here wounded. He doubted his word.
He spent all his time on the lands, in the fields, and with
the livestock, not with me, his mother. He was wounded
too and I tended him. It is a terrible thing for a mother
to see her son's blood, to know that he is in danger, and
that men, other Christian men, are trying to kill him."

Suddenly she cried. Great sobs rocked her. She had not

cried so since Petrus died. These women with their news of Boetie had weakened her. And the girl, this sweet young thing Boetie wanted, brought Elsa back to her. A girl in the house. There had not been a girl in this room since Elsa died. There was something about a young girl in love, some emanation of virginity, almost a perfume like that of some rare scented flower. The girl—what was her name?—Renata, was kneeling at her feet. She said, "Don't cry. Louis loves you. I will love you if you will let me."

In a moment their arms were around each other and both were crying, with a new-found happiness.

"A daughter," Catalina said.

"*Ja*, a daughter if you want me . . ."

Dora van Reenan had left the room and gone out into the yard. This was a fine farm, Louis's mother a good woman.

An old Kaffir came up to her, his hat held in his hand.

"*Mevrou*," he said, "does the *mevrou* bring news of my baasie? Is the young lady his beloved?"

"Who are you and how do you know?"

"I am Klaas. The servant of the old baas who brought the young baasies up. *Ja*," he said, "they are my heart, my life."

She took his hand. "The Nooie is my daughter and the betrothed of Louis, your baasie."

"I am glad," the old man said. "The time has come for him to mate. Neither the birds of the air, the beasts of the field, nor man can live alone." He looked up at her, his eyes bright with tears. "He is a good boy," he said, "without evil in him, and will make a fine man, like his father whom I served."

Dora felt tears in her own eyes. What a place this was with everyone crying. She turned to find Renata at her side.

"We are staying the night," she said. "She likes me." And then she too burst into tears again.

Women, Dora thought. Women and their tears. We cry when we are sad. We cry when we are happy. Sometimes we even cry for no reason at all. Her own face was wet as she kissed her daughter.

They had supper. *Babotie* and rice, sweet potatoes and

pumpkin, followed by a milk tart and watermelon *konfyt*. They drank coffee made of burned wheat and acorns, and talked of Louis. His mother spoke of him as a child, of his exploits as a boy. Renata spoke of him as a man, a soldier at the war, a lover. Dora van Reenan said that when she went into his room she had found him reading his New Testament.

"I gave it to him for his sixteenth birthday," his mother said.

"He told us so. It was dirty, its leaves dog-eared, and he said it did not matter, the dirt was Africa. *Ja*, he said, 'that dust is our sacred earth for which we fight.' "

When the meal was over grace was said again. Then Catalina read a chapter from the Bible and they prayed for the success of the Boers, for the freedom of their country, for the dead, the sick, the wounded on both sides, and kissed one another good night.

In the morning Catalina took them to look at the kraals and stables, the livestock, the lands and fields. They looked at the neglected garden, at the tall, white-stemmed gums and beefwoods, at the violets now bloomless in their winter sleep.

Renata, lagging back, dreaming of her love, whose house this was, found a boy at her side, shockheaded, blue-eyed.

"I am Frikkie Bothma," he said, "and I am going to war."

"You are too young," Renata said, her eyes meeting his. A fine brave boy with the high cheekbones and flat face of his race. "You are only a boy."

"Sometimes," the boy said, "boys must be men. If their fathers cannot be." With that he turned away and a pup that had been waiting for him, afraid of strangers, joined him at heel.

They lunched on cold meat. Before they left, Catalina said, "There is one more thing I must show you." She took them into the stoep and showed them the great buffalo horns over the door.

"My husband," she said as if it was a portrait.

"He shot him?" Dora asked.

"*Ja*, he shot him and was killed by him. They died locked together. Both were male, *mevrou*. Sometimes I think of it. The terror of the maleness. The mad grandeur of it that drives them, man and beast, to their death.

But"—she paused—"but only such can breed men. Only such can breed sons like mine. For only the bold can be gentle and only the strong can afford weakness. That is why I have kept it there all these years, a testament for his sons. That, too, is Africa. *Ja,* the earth on Boetie's Bible, the blood on the buffalo's horns. And only we, you and I—mothers—and the girls who will be one—only we Afrikaners can understand this terrible land of ours."

The drive back did not take so long. The horses, well fed and rested, trotted gaily homeward toward their familiar stables. Renata dreamed of her love, of Groenplaas, of Louis's mother, who would one day be her own. Sixpence chattered about the wonders of the farm, the amount of food he had eaten, and the stories old Klaas had told him.

They got back to find Louisa beautiful and smiling on the stoep to greet them.

"You had a good trip, I hope," she said, "and without adventures?"

"Everything went very well," her mother said. "Groenplaas is a fine farm and Louis's mother is a nice woman."

"Then everything is settled?"

"Everything but the war, Louisa." How irritating the girl could be.

Renata had not said a word to her sister. She had been looking at the drive. Someone with a horse had been here recently. Louisa was not a girl to stay alone for long. She wondered which of her admirers it had been—Carter, Lance Bridgewater, or one of the others.

To Boetie, after serving under the beloved old Adriaan de la Rey, De Wet was a new experience. He frightened the life out of him.

Since escaping from Pretoria and being engaged in the battle of Diamond Hill there had been no respite. Boetie hardly knew where he had been—in the northwestern Free State, the Northern Transvaal, here, there, and everywhere, riding, fighting, retiring, advancing, saddling up and offsaddling. Now they were out of the Brandwater Basin, riding in a three-mile-long convoy of guns and wagons. De Wet had President Steyn with him, and no finer prize than these two men could have been asked for by the

British, who were coming after them in a wide net flung out from the south pinning them to the Vaal.

They had no cover. The moment they moved, great clouds of dust gave them away. A large proportion of the British were mounted, so it seemed hopeless for ox-drawn wagons even to attempt escape.

But De Wet sent his wagons to the nearest drift, got them over, and fought off the British till they were safely in the hills.

Kitchener, in command, thinking he was making for another drift to the north where he could cut back beyond the British flank into the Free State, sent a force to meet him there.

De Wet divided his convoy and sent one half toward the upstream drift. This confirmed the British view and more troops were sent there to reinforce those already waiting for the Boers. Then De Wet changed direction, leaving the British utterly at a loss. Their next information was that he was headed northeast, but this too was a feint. Once clear of the Vaal, De Wet headed for the Gatsrand Hills, crossing the railway and going east in the direction of Ventersdorp.

Here the British under Methuen were on his heels and he had to abandon some prisoners and wagons as he went north toward Olifantsnek, the pass through the Magaliesberg that led to Rustenburg.

By now the Boers were beaten, or would have been under any other leader.

Boetie was so sleepy he almost fell from the saddle of his stumbling horse. No sooner did they stop to water their beasts or rest them when there was a cry of *"Opzaal! Saddle up! The Khakis are here!"* And they were off again. Moolman, the man of iron, one after De Wet's own heart, drove them mercilessly, jeering at them, cursing them, mocking them as girls disguised as men. Trek, trek all day. Day after day. Terrible night marches through the mountains and always the English like bloodhounds on their trail. First east, then north. They changed direction every day as De Wet dodged about till even the stars in the heavens seemed confused.

At last Methuen was sure he had them. Hamilton was moving up to the pass they were going through, and would meet them on the other side. Caught in this mountain gut, unable to maneuver, the prize would soon be in his hands —De Wet and President Steyn.

But as he got to the pass an exhausted native runner reached him with the news that De Wet was through and clear away. Hamilton had not got there in time. The eel was out of the net again.

The mountains that should have been his grave were now his buckler. De Wet turned east, he turned north, and then Steyn went off with a small party to try to reach Kruger. De Wet now dispersed his commandos and with a small picked force turned on his tracks, and by the end of August he was back on the banks of the Vaal not far from where the hunt for him had begun. In six weeks he had trekked five hundred miles. He had had thirty thousand British troops after him. He had got the President of the Free State safely away. He was still free, his force dispersed and intact. He had achieved a feat that made military history. Alone, with an undisciplined force, by character, iron will, and a natural, inborn talent it was hard to credit.

Moolman's corporalship and Boetie were still with this great leader and unlovable man. Man and horse were skin and bone, their clothes in rags, their ammunition short. But their hearts were high and, like him or not, it was something to be able to say, "We rode with De Wet."

PART SIX

METHODS OF BARBARISM

*"It is manifest that the leniency
which has been extended to the
Burghers of the South African
Republic is not appreciated by
them. . . ."*

—ROBERTS

*[South Africa—July to December 1900—
Winter, Spring, and Summer]*

CHAPTER 44

AN OFFICER OF INTELLIGENCE

MORGAN CARTER of the 50th Rifles was a slim, dark, active man of thirty-seven, well off, with a place in Somerset, a bachelor sportsman of catholic tastes. He was handsome in a dashing way, with a good leg for a boot. That is to say, with rather small calves, so that his riding boots fitted to perfection without a gap below the knee. He was not a ladies' man but liked women and had little trouble in having his way with most of them when he took the trouble.

The Van Reenan girl's slip, if it was a slip, and his detection of the kidnap and murder plan had led to his majority. Never having been able to use his brains before, indeed unaware that he had any, he really enjoyed intelligence work and realized, with some amusement, that he was a born policeman. His varied knowledge of life and his natural acumen, coupled with much reading, had given him great insight into people and motives. But he was still puzzled about Louisa. Had she hated Cordau? He had had her investigated. She hardly knew the man, so he had not told her. She had therefore got the information somewhere else. Who would know such a secret? Only a woman. For some obscure reason men tended to discuss with their wives and mistresses things that should never be mentioned. The bed, nuptial or otherwise, seemed to act as a catalyst, dissolving all caution. It now boiled down to Helga, whom Louisa did see upon occasion, both of them being interested in music. Helga, unable, like so many women, to keep a secret, had told Louisa and Louisa had told him. Why? That was the question. She had gained nothing by it. Nothing at all. Nothing material, that is, only a possible satisfaction in a feeling of power and importance. Above all, women liked this feeling. They enjoyed being madonnas when they had

473

a child, they enjoyed being ill, having operations. Even in a murder trial the accused, if a woman, seemed to enjoy the drama of the moment. This must be it. Louisa was a real woman—her interests vanity, power, a sense of importance, and a love of intrigue for its own sake. She would do good or evil, scarcely aware of the difference as long as she caused something to happen. Excited by the war, she had wanted to play a game, any game, to be in it.

This was the key and he was going to turn it.

He found her attractive, too. Deliciously so. Though too young for him now that he had got to know her mother better, a beautiful widow much nearer his own age. But there would be trouble if Louisa found out, so the only thing to do was to court them both, keep them apart, and hope for the best.

He decided to ride over to the Willows at once, and called for his horse. He only hoped someone would be in, even the little blonde with the sherry-colored eyes, though she was not his cup of tea. Pretty enough, but a milk-and-water miss, without any of the dash that he admired.

When he got there he found them all in. Dora van Reenan asked him to stay to tea.

"How did you guess, Mrs. van Reenan?" he said. "Because I came at four o'clock?"

They all laughed. A beautiful group in that comfortable room. The mother, almost a girl herself, and two girls who were almost women.

"We have a cake, too," Dora van Reenan said. "Thanks to the generosity of our enemies." She looked up at him under long dark lashes. How she hated these invaders. But this man . . . Well, it was hard to hate so handsome and well behaved a man. She knew he was attracted by her and attraction bred attraction. It was difficult not to like those who admire you. But it was not liking she felt for Morgan Carter. It was much more than that.

The girls were gay. Louisa played the piano. At five-thirty Carter rose to say good-by.

"Thank you, Mrs. van Reenan," he said, "for bringing a little home life into the dull routine of a soldier's existence."

"It has not been so dull lately, has it?" she asked. "Tracking down our patriots and shooting them in cold

blood." She spoke savagely. She liked this man too much
. . . She must hurt him. She must make him hate her, before—before— Her mind hesitated to formulate the
words. Before I love him, she thought.

"I executed no one," Carter said, "and I'm sorry you
take it that way. I got wind of the plot and had to ferret
out the truth." He bowed.

"Louisa will see you out," Mrs. van Reenan said.

What luck! He had hoped to be able to see Louisa
alone. What he had to say would take only an instant.

In the hall he took Louisa's heart-shaped face in his
hands and looked into her big brown half-frightened
eyes.

"And how's my little spy today?" he said.

She broke away, spitting like a cat.

"Don't say that!" she said. "Suppose someone heard
you?"

"No one will hear, darling, as long as I get more information. But if I don't—well," he said, "what do you
think would happen to a beautiful Boer girl who gave
such a secret away?"

Louisa's lips trembled.

"Good-by, Miss van Reenan," Carter said quite loudly.
"I hope we shall see more of each other now."

Louisa did not go back to the drawing room. She went
upstairs to look at the pretty Miss Louisa van Reenan in
the mirror and wonder what would happen to her if she
were found out. Traitors had been killed before. Neither
her sex nor her looks would save her. How ungrateful
people were. Not one of those whose homes she had
saved from fire would stand up for her. Not one. What a
fool I was, she thought. What a fool to be so altruistic.
She only had two friends now—her mirror and Captain,
now Major, Carter. He owed her a lot. Even his lightning
promotion. She would do as he said. Her mother would
encourage her, for she would get information for the
Boers too. She would be important, valuable to everyone.
And how absurd it was for a woman of her mother's age
to make eyes like that at Carter. How utterly absurd.

She washed her face and combed her hair, singing
softly to herself.

Downstairs Dora van Reenan was wondering what had

passed between Carter and Louisa. Why had she run upstairs? Had he kissed her? Was she untidy? And what were
her own feelings? Was she really jealous of her own
daughter? And what was the good of thinking about
Major Carter after what she had just said to him? If only
that damn girl would come down, she would go upstairs
herself. But two of them could not be in their bedrooms
at once repairing their ravaged emotions at the same
time. She laughed at the idea. A woman's face and her
emotions were almost synonymous.

"What's funny, Mama?" Renata said.

"Women, my girl. Women and girls are funny. As
you'll find out one day. Or perhaps you won't. You're
such a serious little thing."

"Aren't you serious, Mama?"

"Do you know, I'm not sure, Renata. I used to think
I was, but now . . ." She shrugged her shoulders and
went to the door to call Louisa. After all, she was her
mother and it was her house.

When the girl came in she told her to rearrange the
flowers that someone seemed to have touched, and
went upstairs herself to look in her own mirror.

She knew quite well that that was what Louisa had
been doing—repairing the ravages of a kiss or a near kiss,
or, worse still, rearranging her face after the anger of a
platonic good-by. How well she knew this daughter of
hers, who had her own hot heart and her father's calculating mind. How well she knew women and their relationship to mirrors. How, when they were young, they
watched for the first signs of womanhood, of budding
breasts. How they sought their characters, staring into
their own eyes, wondering. What kind of girl am I? What
shall I become? Who will love me? Who will kiss that
mouth, those eyes, that neck, those breasts? Whose hand
will smooth my hair? Who and when? These thoughts
were not put into words by nice girls, but they were
there at the back of their minds, in the deep closets of
their personalities, hidden like love letters under the
light lingerie of summer. When they dressed, when
they undressed, when they bathed, when they ran their
hands over their smooth young bodies it was there, the
near thoughts, all there in a mixture of wonder and ignorance. What were a man's kisses like? How did his hands

feel? That was for a girl. But a woman knew. She knew. With her it was no wonder but memory, regret at the waste of it all with a man she had not loved, and desire . . .

She thought of Louis's mother at Groenplaas. How she had loved her husband. She thought of the farm graveyard, of the stone to his memory, and the fresh flowers. Fresh flowers every day, for all these years though his body lay in the bushveld.

Love, passion, lust, desire, how confused they were. Young men rutting, young girls in heat, all ignorant, quite unaware of nature's tricks. Wide-eyed as does, ripe as plums for passion that might end in true love or burn away, leaving only the ashes of disgust. How did one tell girls this? And how, even if they knew, would it help them? What about herself? She was in love with Carter. She wanted him, an enemy, as a man. As a man in her bed. So how did her knowledge help her? What good was knowledge when it was pitted against the power of the flesh.

A woman like Catalina van der Berg had been armored by her memories, but she . . . It was her memories, her knowledge of man, that undid her.

To her own surprise and that of her children she dressed for dinner that evening, wearing a gown cut low, with bare shoulders and a train.

Louisa was amazed at her mother's looks, at her self-possession. Calm, her great eyes dark-shadowed pools in her creamy face. She was a woman. Woman to Louisa's girl. That dark red, a crimson lake velvet, its shadows and folds almost black, suited her. Age did not enter into it. There was only a richness here—of womanhood, of texture, of the play of light upon shadow. Even if she had been dressed Louisa knew she could not match her mother, that she was eclipsed. Something had happened to her since teatime.

They had wine, as if it was a celebration. Perhaps it was. But they drank to Renata, to her boy at the war, and all absent friends.

CHAPTER 45

A RAILWAY CARRIAGE

THE CAPITAL of the South African Republic was now a railway carriage on the Delagoa Bay–Pretoria line. For a while it had been at Machadodorp. Then, because of Kruger's rheumatism, it was moved ten miles east to the warmer climate of Waterval Onder, in the low veld beyond the escarpment. The President was old and sick. His eyes, always painful, were now terribly inflamed. The heart went out of him when he looked at the long rows of railway carriages in which his officials made a pretense of carrying on the affairs of a country that no longer existed.

Hour after hour, day after day, his head bowed in his hands, he sat at a table in the railway station, looking at the large Bible that lay open before him. It was not even his own Bible. Not the one that had come up with his father and mother on the Great Trek from Colesberg in the Cape more than sixty years before. He had left that one with his wife in Pretoria, for in it were the records of the births of their children and their children's children. This was a borrowed book. Northing remained to him of his own but his clothes.

Servas, still with him, was still translating English documents and papers, still trying to put favorable constructions upon unfavorable news.

This was the man he watched day after day. An old man dying, spending his last days in the land that had given him birth and to which he had given his life. How many dead in his life: Maria, his first wife, old Joubert, Kock, burghers by the hundred—exiles by the thousand.

Horses, dogs, lions, Kaffirs, elephants. What memories revolved in the mind of this fierce old man. His Tante Sanna at home in Pretoria. The thunder of battle. The churned-up dust of galloping cattle herds, smells of wood smoke, of gunpowder; sounds of laughter, shouts, screams, the roars of wild beasts must all have been echoing in his head.

478

On October 19, 1900, a year and a few days after the outbreak of war, nine days after his seventy-fifth birthday, Stephanus Johannes Paulus Kruger left for Holland on the Dutch cruiser *Gelderland,* which the Queen had placed at his disposal.

When he had gone the government, now headed by Steyn and Schalk Burger, abandoned the railway carriages and took to the bush, with Servas still on the staff.

The English called them the Cape Cart Government. Always in flight, always pursued, they seldom spent more than a few days in one place.

England in October was beautiful. The fall of the leaf delayed by an Indian summer, the trees bronze and gold, standing like ornaments on the grass. God smiled down at a countryside as peaceful and quiet as Eden. London was gay, laughing with victory, for the war was over. There was no doubt about that. Bobs had said so and was coming home, his work done, to receive the honors that were his due from the great Queen he had served so well.

A few bands of Boers might still be roaming like bandits on the veld, fugitives in what had once been their country. But Kruger had run away. Both Boer capitals were in British hands and an area the size of France, rich with gold, diamonds, coal, copper, iron, and God alone knew what else, had been added to the empire, to the lands of the dear old Queen. It just showed how right Kipling had been when he wrote:

Walk wide o' the Widow at Windsor
    For 'alf o' Creation she owns:
We 'ave bought 'er the same with the sword an' the flame,
    An' we've salted it down with our bones. . . .
Hands off o' the sons of the Widow,
    Hands off o' the goods in 'er shop,
For the Kings must come down an' the Emperors frown
    When the Widow at Windsor says "Stop!" *

What fools the Boers had been to defy her. Salisbury could go to the country now, certain of victory in a general—the so-called khaki—election, though it was Joseph Chamberlain, the sleek, suave, monocled, and buttonholed

* "The Widow at Windsor," *Barrack-Room Ballads.*

Colonial Secretary who had insisted on it rather than he.

It was a dirty election. Much mud was slung. Chamberlain was accused of war profiteering. His opponents did not care about British prestige. They, to quote Kipling again, were those of whom he wrote:

> And what should they know of England who only England
> know?—
>   The poor little street-bred people that vapor and
>   fume and brag,
> They are lifting their heads in the stillness to yelp
>   at the English Flag.*

This was the voice of England's singing gamecock.

Lloyd George, Joe Chamberlain's great protagonist, risked his life at political meetings where he protested the continuance of the war. "I say," he said, "it is time to stop the slaughter in the African sand of brave soldiers on either side."

But no one paid any attention to him and the government majority was increased by six seats. Perhaps the most curious thing about this unique election was that the people loathed the government, blaming them for the ineptitude with which the war had been conducted. But, certain that a Liberal victory would mean political defeat in South Africa, they voted for the lesser evil.

This attitude made their tumultuous welcome of Lord Roberts on his return even stranger. For this hero had in fact performed miracles of ineptitude. Time after time this very lovable little man had thrown victory away. He had won no battles except the victory at Paardeberg, which was due to Kitchener's savagery and French's dash rather than Roberts' skill. All he had done was to drive the Boers before him as a housewife might sweep water over a linoleum-covered floor. They flowed on ahead of him and then when he had gone flowed back again.

He was cheered at Cape Town, met in London by the Prince of Wales, given the Order of the Garter by the Queen—the first general to receive it since Wellington—made an earl, voted a gift of a hundred thousand pounds by Parliament.

And while all this was going on the Boers were still un-

---

* "The English Flag," *Barrack-Room Ballads*.

conquered in Africa, possibly stronger, and certainly more resolute than ever.

But Roberts said there was nothing left to do in Africa except by police action, a mopping-up job of catching a few bands of guerrillas who were in fact little more than brigands. So certain was he of this that troops were being brought back from Africa by the shipload.

In actual fact Roberts' triumphal advance over the veld had been little more than a gigantic field day, and his losses due to sickness rather than to the shells and bullets of the enemy. He believed that with their towns gone, their railroads useless, their governments in flight, the Boers would give up. When this proved to be a mistaken idea he tried the strategy he had employed in Afghanistan, the burning of houses and crops. But the scheme that had worked so well against savage tribesmen failed against white men fighting to defend their homes.

Roberts' trouble was that he had no idea of what he was fighting. He was fighting a nation, and his methods welded it into a unity it had never known before. It could almost be said that Roberts created the Afrikaner people. Moreover, apart from trying to run the whole war himself, he was operating with weapons that were new to him and that he did not understand. As a gunner, he had fought in the Mutiny with muzzle-loading cannon. He still believed in the *arme blanche,* in cavalry charges. He was unused to modern, quick-firing rifles (particularly in the hands of the enemy), to machine guns and pompoms.

The Boers were not naked savages, nor were they the dumb peasant farmers they were assumed to be. They tapped telephones, they made their own ammunition, they even salvaged rifles that had been burned in pyres when prisoners were taken, and fitted them with new stocks.

It is difficult to understand why Roberts thought the war was over, since the enemy was still undefeated in the field. Perhaps he was still ambitious, and wanted the War Office, wanted to be commander in chief of the British Army, and hurried back while the post was still unfilled. He got it. And everyone was happy. Good old Bobs deserved this pretty plum. He had certainly trekked a long, long way over the veld to get it.

But as the winter winds swept over England and the

people ate their crumpets by the blazing fires of their hearths, spring came to Africa, and a new war was begun. Kitchener, eager to end it and to get to India—a man in a great hurry too—found this new and savage baby in his arms. That was his Christmas present from good old Bobs.

CHAPTER 46

THE HARD CORE

PARTICIPATING in a series of moves and countermoves, in small actions and small retreats, Moolman's corporalship, attached now to one commando and now to another as they coalesced and broke up again, found themselves at Bronkhorstspruit, the scene of the first battle in the War of Independence in 1880. And here, where Colonel Anstruthers' regiment had fallen into a Boer ambush and been cut up, they found Louis Botha, the commandant general, resting beside his saddle with a few pack horses and dispatch riders about him.

Boetie asked if he had received the message Mevrou van Reenan had told him to pass on once he was back among the Boers. Botha said yes. And he was grateful to her. A woman could be of great use in such circumstances, being much less suspect than a man, and he was particularly pleased that she had established contact with relatives at the Cape and friends in Holland. He congratulated Moolman for his cleverness in carrying dispatches in disguise and said that as there was a lull at the moment they might as well take a few days off and rest. Asking nothing better, they took over a deserted farmhouse and for a few days lay idle and watched General Botha, relatively secure here with plenty of routes of escape, put a new army together. He had three thousand men already and more were riding in every day.

Despairing of victory, thousands of Boers had given up and gone home. While commandos had melted away like snow in the sun of British victory. But those that had remained were the pick of Africa—the toughest, the boldest, the hard core of resistance, the backbone, the nerve and sinew of the republic. The others, the soft flesh, came and went as the tides of war veered. A small success and they were encouraged to return to the commandos. A small setback and they rode home again.

The first duty Moolman was called on to perform was to destroy or at least harass the railway line between Pretoria and Johannesburg. But it was too well protected to come within five miles of it.

A week later, as they offsaddled near a farm, they were spotted by a battery of British guns that dropped some shells over them. There was a huge weeping willow near a dam behind which five of the Boers took cover. A high-velocity shell hit the tree low down, passed through it, and exploded, not merely killing the men who were behind it, but scattering their mangled remains over thirty yards of veld. Later, when the guns had limbered up and gone, what was left of the bodies was scraped up with a shovel they found in the abandoned farm.

It was only by accident that Boetie had not been behind the tree. He had been running toward it, then, seeing there was no more room, had flung himself down in the grass.

Their next action was against a large force of British, an estimated thirty thousand men who were moving up on a fifteen-mile front over the Delagoa Bay railway line. This was the last outlet, the last window the Boers had left leading into the outer world. After five days' fighting, being pushed back all the time, Boetie found himself isolated once more, having lost touch with Moolman and the rest of the commando during a night action. But he was used to being lost now and simply rode north, knowing that sooner or later he would fall in with his own people. Before dark he met some Boers and was in action with them against a company of unsuspecting British infantry who came marching down a donga into their arms. A number were killed, but, owing to a cross fire from the survivors, the wounded could not be reached till after dark, by which time they had died of cold.

At dawn after this fight the Boers continued their retreat to Machadodorp, which only a few weeks ago had been the capital of the Transvaal, and was now deserted. From here only a single road crossed the mountains, and the commando found itself almost crowded off the track by fleeing farmers with their flocks, herds, and wagons loaded with women, children, and old men, all under fire from the British guns. The panic did not last long and by morning they were looking down at the low veld and out of the cold at last.

Below them the cliff fell in a granite curtain, the bush looking like a mossy carpet stretched to an infinite horizon, the green fading to the blue of distance. Here and there a giant tree, a baobab, jakkals-bessie or fig, stood out—a blob dropped on the carpet. Beyond the horizon was the coastal plain, a wilderness of tall reeds, marsh grass, lagoons, and mangrove swamps. Beyond that the sea, India, and the East.

Baboons lived in security on the cliff, inhabiting caves and climbing its face, as immune to vertigo as flies upon a wall. Feeling the presence of the men above, they barked. The old males with a deep, savage sound. The females in a higher, more hysterical key.

This was the wilds—as yet untamed, unknown except to a few hunters. A land held inviolate by its dangers. This was a country where death came quickly. The fever-trees, beautiful, with feather foliage and bark that had a green bloom like that of a grape, were believed to carry sickness. Certainly men who, seduced by their looks, camped near them got fever. But the trees grew only in moist ground near the water in which the mosquitoes bred. So, pragmatically correct as to location, the popular concept was wrong about the actual cause.

In the bush there were monkeys by the hundred, a prey to eagles, leopards, and pythons. Below this canopy of prickly bush, for in Africa there are few thornless trees, roamed the buck—eland, impala, kudu, sable, roan, waterbuck, reedbuck, wildebeeste, steenbok, oribi, duiker, buffalo, and zebra, wart hog, and bush pig. These were lion meat. Lower on the ground in the rustling grass were the smaller things—rats and mice and the snakes that ate them.

Elephants made key-shaped roads through bush: narrow on the ground since they set one foot on the spoor of another, and wide higher up where, for hundreds of years, they had pruned, by friction, the trees to fit their forms.

Rhinos grazed on low thornbushes. Hippos lay like giant pinkish rocks in the pools. Giraffes nibbled the young shoots of tall, flat-topped thorns, and everywhere were the scavengers. The vultures in the upper air. The hyenas and jackals in the scrub and the ants and beetles on the ground. All waiting for death, for sickness, their eyes sharp with hunger.

Packs of Cape hunting dogs—yellow, marked irregularly with black and white, their bat ears pricked—galloped over the veld in pursuit of anything they could kill and they could kill almost anything except an elephant.

Death and beauty walked here hand in hand. There was no waste, no blood spilled in vain, the dead of one thing giving life to another, so the balance of life, if it had been quality that could be weighed, would have been found constant; unchanging, since time began, for the land here, as elsewhere, before it was disturbed by man was always fully stocked.

But of all this immense activity there was little to be seen from the cliff top. Nothing, in fact. Even the baboons could only be heard, not seen, and down there in the bush there was seldom anything to see. For as a man advanced the animals fell back or stood still, frozen, invisible unless some sharp hunter's eye caught the flick of a fly-tortured ear or the glint of sun upon a horn among the trees.

In the low veld it was full spring. Many of the bushveld thorns were in perfumed flower and sang with bees, and the game in the open plains was plentiful—great herds of wildebeeste, some with russet calves at foot; zebra, impala, giraffe, all by the dozen, the hundred, the thousand. This was the Africa of the *voortrekkers*. They had seen it and it was no more. This was its last outpost, guarded by the tsetse and mosquito.

When they heard that a new force was being collected at Warmbad by General Beyers, Moolman led them there over the Waterberg, and here they stayed, resting, hunting for the pot, and occasionally going out on patrol as far as Pienaar's River, where the British had a camp. They lived on game and mealie meal. Beyers was a dark, moody man who insisted on daily religious services and even ordered the younger men to attend his Bible classes.

There was trouble when Moolman and his men refused to go to the compulsory services. Beyers threatened to throw them out of the commando, but in the end decided that the guns of these seasoned fighters might be of more value than their prayers.

Their next move was to Magaliesber, from whose heights they saw the smokestacks and dumps of the gold mines of the Rand once more. That evening Koos de la Rey rode in on his famous little white-faced pony and was greeted like a father.

A few days later they were in an action that ended in hand-to-hand fighting with bayonet thrusts, rifles being fired point blank into men's faces; the smell of blood, cordite, sweat, and dust, shouts, screams, the cries of the wounded all blending into a nightmare whole. The Boers won, but the ground over which they had charged was littered with dead and wounded.

The British fired a few last shots as they retired. Boetie hit one of the running men in the thigh and went over to him. He was bandaging himself with the first-aid pad that all British troops carried, but was quite friendly and cheerful, even showing Boetie a picture of his wife and children. What had he and this man against each other? What did this man want with the Transvaal except to get out of it?

The Boers were now attacked by a force of Yeomanry and threw them back. Boetie brought down another man and, going to see him, found that, much to his horror, half his head was blown off. By some accident he had reloaded his rifle with a clip of soft-nosed bullets he had found and kept in a separate pocket for shooting game. He unloaded his rifle and threw the rest of the cartridges away.

The British were really defeated, and the camp that had been De la Rey's objective was in their hands, and what a camp it was, a real department store. Never, since they had looted Dundee with its ladies' sidesaddles, had the Boers seen such plenty. Tea, coffee, sugar, marmalade, potted meat, sardines, salmon, chickens, biscuits, hams, flour, cans of butter, jam, bully beef, maconochie . . .

"Come on, boys," Moolman shouted as they ran into the

lines, "bust everything open and we'll have a belly full for a change."

They settled down, sitting on the crates or leaning against them, eating sardines and bully beef with their sheath knives. Boetie was spooning up Hartley's marmalade, wondering if a whole pot would make him sick, when General Beyers rode up in a fury.

"Get up! Get up!" he cried. "Get on your horses and follow the enemy!"

Moolman did not move. He held a sardine by the tail, dropped it into his mouth, and said:

"General, the dump was our objective. We shall fill our bellies and our saddlebags and set fire to the rest. We shall ride away on fresh horses. And as to the English, we have killed enough. What is the good of prisoners since we have no place to hold them? Have a sardine, General?" He held out the box.

Everyone laughed, and the feast continued. When they had eaten all they could, they picked fresh horses from the horse lines. Boetie took two—a chestnut gelding and a blue-roan mare. Both were small and short-coupled, far more useful on the veld than the bigger horses. He also took an officer's saddle and two saddlebags that he filled with tea, coffee, sugar, and salt and loaded more stuff on his pack horse.

The commando lived high for a few days on the looted food—a change from a diet of straight mealie meal and saltless meat. They had discarded their Mausers, ammunition being short, and all carried Lee-Metford or Enfield rifles. The chestnut Boetie had chosen had a white face like De la Rey's pony, and four white stockings. He called him Toll Free—Toll for short—as the Boers had a tradition in the old days that such animals were allowed through tollgates free. This idea many have come to Africa with the Huguenots from France, where a horse with white stockings was much favored. The English thought the opposite, and avoided like the plague a horse with more than three white legs.

The commando now moved to the Skurebergen north of Johannesburg and lay in hiding among the Tumbled Hills. While there the weather broke, the summer rains began pouring down, and Moolman, the old soldier, discovered a deserted farm where they were at least under cover and they lived well on straying sheep. It was here that they passed Christmas and welcomed in the new year—1901. Boetie, counting his age like that of a horse, was now rising eighteen.

Before long they were back in the Magaliesberg near the scene of their earlier action, and Boetie rode over to a farm where his friend Le Roux lay wounded. He was greeted by the boy's mother, whom the British had brought from Pretoria to look after the wounded the Boers had left behind. A surgeon visited them every day and British officers from the camp often rode over with fruit, cigarettes, and other luxuries.

Boetie did not stay long. There was always the possibility of a British patrol turning up in this no man's land between the lines.

Here was another example of humanity, of the strange relationship between fighting men, between combat soldiers who respected each other's courage.

And Boetie, as he rode away on his little roan, was more confused than ever.

CHAPTER 47

THE CHRISTMAS PICNIC

DORA VAN REENAN was alone. The girls had left the Willows early. Louisa and Renata and three others, a bevy of chattering young women, all, apparently at least, reconciled to such outings with enemy officers. They looked very pretty in their riding habits, bright-eyed, gay, excited by the company of men and the movement of the eager horses under them. The tossing heads, the swishing tails, the jingle of bits, the creak of saddlery as the men pushed up their habits to tighten girths and adjust leathers. There was something very thrilling in the feel of a man's hand so near their legs. On their legs, grasping a booted ankle to fit it back into an iron.

The Willows had been the rendezvous. Dora had given them all coffee. Lisa du Toit, Magda Brink, Helena van Breda and her own two had made up the girls. Captain

Turnbull, Major Carter, Lance Bridgewater, Gerald Fernley, and a boy whose name she did not catch were the men. They were going to ride into the bush toward Pienaar's River to see if they could see any game. There were some impala and other buck there and lots of monkeys. A Cape cart with lunch was meeting them and they would be back by evening. They were going to make a fire and have tea on the veld before returning. The situation was both delicate and interesting. Youth and sex on both sides neatly balanced against a war. A careless word could upset everything. In a flash the girls could cease to be pretty young companions. They would become Boers ranged against their English hosts—the invaders of their country. In this year and a half of occupation a kind of social truce had been established. Either the girls went out with British officers—riding, playing tennis, and dancing—or they did not go out at all. The British, seeing how touchy the girls were, steered well away from all controversial subjects and just flattered, teased, and flirted with their fair companions. In some cases they seemed to be quite serious in their courtship. There was very little doubt that Lance Bridgewater wanted to marry Louisa. But she was playing him off against Carter.

When the picnic party left in a swirl of khaki and riding habits, of prancing horses and switching tails, Dora van Reenan went back to her bedroom to lie down again. She had a racking headache and decided to spend the rest of the day in bed; with the girls away this was a wonderful chance to rest. She undressed, pulled the blinds down and tried to sleep. But sleep would not come. Her mind was too full of thoughts of the war, the girls, Louis van der Berg, Moolman, the President, Carter . . . He kept coming back to her mind. Carter and Louisa. Then her mind abandoned Louisa and was left with Carter. He dominated her thoughts in a way she would not have believed possible a few months ago. Just now she felt like a mother toward him, hoping Louisa would not hurt him, thinking of this man who was only a little older than she as if he were a child. That at least was what she tried to tell herself she felt as she thought of her daughter again and wondered what would happen if the occasion offered. Would Louisa draw back? She doubted it. Would Carter refuse to take advantage of her? That was more possible. But nothing was certain. She knew he would be sorry afterward, but afterward would be too late. She knew Louisa would regret nothing, that if she were found out she would taunt her with her own words—hoist her on her own petard. " 'Even lie with them if you must,' Mama. That is what you said. It is for Africa . . . As long as we get information . . . news that may save Boer lives . . . What, compared to a man's life, is the blood of a maidenhead?" Louisa would not fear to turn upon her if accused. Always reckless, hot-tempered, and hotheaded, and the war had keyed up these qualities still higher. Sometimes she hardly seemed to recognize her. More beautiful than ever, like a flower forced by the greenhouse of masculine admiration, she had an aura of near wickedness, as if she enjoyed what she did. Always naughty, flirtatious, coy, capricious, a coquette almost from infancy, the girl now burned like a flame under her outward natural girlish vivacity.

Still unable to rest, Dora went into the garden and sat in the dark pool of shade thrown by great willows, hidden by the weeping branches that fell in a green curtain over the water. Bright blue dragonflies shot like bullets into the hot sunshine, hung poised on shimmering wings, and darted back. Between the green saucer pads of the water lilies a fish rose at a fly and sank again beneath the silver rings it had created.

Under the trees there was only shade. It was no cooler. A storm was certain, but she doubted if the girls would return in time to avoid it. By four, she thought. There will be a storm by four.

Her headache was no better. The heavy air was charged with electricity. She had never felt more nervous or more highly strung. She knew it would last till the storm broke. Not only she but the whole world was bent like a bow, taut with the string of suspense. The birds were silent, even the trees and the shrubs in the garden seemed to be waiting for some event. Summer storms were usual enough. Sometimes they came almost daily. There had been one yesterday afternoon and they always frightened her. She had never got used to them in spite of having been born and brought up in the high veld. But the tension of the air seemed to presage some greater disturbance. Still ill at ease, Dora returned to the darkened house— even the closed shutters had failed to keep it cool—

and poured herself a cup of coffee from the pot that always stood ready on the back of the stove. It tasted bitter in her mouth. English coffee. At least coffee that would not have been available to her without "her English friends." That was how some people, loyal Boers whose men were in the field of prisoners, spoke to her now if they met her in the street. If they spoke at all, that is . . . your English friends . . . Some spoke, some went by with averted heads, some stared at and through her. They did the same with all the girls who went out with Englishmen. She thought it must be this as much as anything else that was driving Louisa to desperation. They were being treated as "hands-uppers," as traitors, as "Judas Boers," who were prepared to sell their country for a few paltry comforts and amusements. Coffee, tea, cans of salmon and sardines, sugar, bacon, needles, cotton. Yes, she thought, that is what they call us, we who have done more, so much more than they to help the President and our men.

She told Adam and Sixpence that she would eat no lunch. They could go to their quarters and rest. It was too hot to work.

When they had gone she went back to her room, took off her clothes, and lay naked on the bed. Even her skin seemed tight on her today. It felt as if it had shrunk into her flesh, compressing it, squeezing the nerves tight as springs. Sweat ran down her breast. It ran from her forehead into her eyes. But at last she slept.

The picnic party had gone well. Everyone was very gay. They had had a few short gallops. Couples had raced each other. But there was a kind of cat's cradle of hidden tension. The usual tension of young men and women, but different here. The men were conquerors. The girls, prizes of a sort, felt guilty at any pleasure they might have in the company of Englishmen when their own men were away fighting. They knew they were right as women, as girls ripe for love. But they were also Boers. But was this love? Any of it? Could such courtships end in marriage? Or was it just a dangerous game, a playing with fire? There was, too, a certain masochism, a certain enjoyment in being out with their masters, men who in earlier wars, in less civilized times, would have raped them and taken them at will—Boer Sabines. The Van Reenan girls were furious at being bracketed with the others who were the constant companions of the British officers. But what defenses had they? They could hardly say, "We are spies, and hate what we do." Moreover, Renata did not think Louisa hated what she did. Louisa had no interest whatsoever in the war. If she got information she got it by accident, and sometimes forgot to pass it on to their mother till it was too late.

The extraordinary heat was a still further excitant. The heat that sweat-darkened the armpits and backs of the girls' habits, the invisible sweat that ran down between their breasts over their bellies and down their thighs. Their heads sweated. Their faces, flushed with heat, were dusty, and smeared where the men had tried to wipe them clean with their silk handkerchiefs.

The horses were hot, crudded with white sweat that turned pink as the dust clung to it. Under their headstalls, along their cheeks, their nosebands, under their tails, and between their quarters they were rimed with a white frost of heat. The excitement of the horses competing with each other, tossing their heads, snapping, flicking their tails, added to the girls' unease. The animal life of the horses beneath them was communicated upward, not reaching their brains but soaking into their young bodies. Louisa's hair had come down in a gallop and hung like a black flag over her back. When she pulled up to knot it the other girls said, "Don't. Don't put it up. It's too hot to have it up. Let's all let our hair down." So they rode on, young women with their long hair down and floating behind them like little girls', giving them a look of both innocence and maturity which had profound effect on the men who followed them. For a man seldom saw a girl's hair down unless he had a sister. When he became engaged his fiancée might, if pressed, let it down for him to look at, but the gesture had overtones of special significance.

So that was the way they rode on this bright blue day, gold with heat, shimmering mirage, and sunshine. The trees and the veld full summer green, the dirt road red. The girls' long hair down, their mouths ripe as fruit for kisses, their eyes bright with laughter, their bodies calling for they knew not what, but calling the silent cry of

youth to youth, the cry of life, a demand for unknown
ecstasy as loud as the honeyflower calls to the butterfly, the candle to the moth.

Of all this, because of their training, habits, and the
morals of the time, nothing would come at all, except
that behind each, behind every girl and man, a head of
passion was backing up like water behind a dam that
might one day break or come to nothing and just seep
away.

Carter was riding beside Louisa. She really was a lovely
thing. There was something about these Boer girls, a freedom of thought and action, a courage fully equal to,
though different from, that of a man. She was riding his
little gray mare as usual. They got on well, those two,
and looked well together. Nicely matched. The dark-haired
girl and the dark-dappled mare with an almost black mane
and tail. So far they had talked of nothing. The weather.
The horses. The dance that was being prepared for New
Year's, and then suddenly Louisa said, "Let's race again,"
and set off at a full gallop, leaning forward, her reins
loose on the gray mare's neck. She knew Carter could beat
her but that he wouldn't. She knew he liked to chase her,
to watch her swaying in the saddle with flying hair. And
she, she loved being chased, loved the thunder of pursuing hoofs that would end when she slowed up and he
caught up with her, pulled alongside with his arm around
her waist, and pretended to drag her from the saddle as
she leaned toward him.

For Louisa these were all tricks, pretty feminine tricks
and wiles. Meaning nothing, meaning everything. A deadly
game. A childish amusement. When did the one begin
and the other end? She neither knew nor cared. It was
fun . . . fun. She loved the feel of the horse under her,
the feel of the saddle, the feel of her long hair pulling at
her scalp in the wind, the wind on her face. She loved
every minute of it—the feeling of extra life that the galloping horse and the rushing air gave to her. She was young,
she was pretty, she was as free as air. Honey to the bee,
milk to the cat, meat to the dog. She was Eve. She was
woman, all women, on the very edge, the very precipice
of experience. A fruit trembling on a bough, a flower
waiting for the hand that would pluck her for a buttonhole.

She was neither good nor bad, neither resisting nor acquiescent. She was nothing, just alive, floating in the currents of life as a bird is poised on the air currents that rise from the hot ground—a hawk, an eagle, a gull—neither seeking nor refusing. Just afloat like a cork on the waters of her budding femininity.

She tightened her reins. The gray mare slowed her pace. Carter thundered up to her, his hand went about her waist, reaching upward to her breast as he leaned over her legs. She felt the barrel of his bay against her. She leaned away, laughing and smiling into his eyes. This man would not betray her. The account was balanced—debit and credit. Matched to a silver tickey, to a penny. She need give no more. She could afford to give no less.

As they rode along slowly side by side now, waiting for the others to catch up, she said what had been on her mind as she galloped, "That was fun . . . I enjoyed it."

"So did I," Carter said, and he wondered if she knew what he had been thinking. He was sure she did, young girl though she was.

When they reached the great fig, the Wonder Tree, they dismounted and hobbled their horses. The lunch cart was waiting for them. Champagne, hock, siphons of soda, Melton Mowbray pie, cold chicken, cold ham, sweet cakes for the girls, and a Stilton for the men. All were disheveled, all hot, the girls excited by their little adventure with these uniformed men, away from their mothers' homes. Their parents had let them go because they could not have stopped them. Even Victorian authority failed under the pressure of such events as war, the scarcity of men, and the cooped-up feelings of their daughters that must break out or burst. Their hope of safety lay in numbers. The more of them there were the less could happen. Or so at least they hoped. But if nothing actually happend much could be begun. There was no room for subterfuge or great modesty. Certainly it could not be expected from the horses. The girls, sweat running over their bodies, their thighs sticky, gave up trying to be ladylike and mopped themselves with grubby handkerchiefs, as best they might. Tomboys, pretty hoydens, but nonetheless attractive to the girl-starved officers who were their escorts. They strolled off in couples, coming and going in a pattern like that of a dance. Some were always by the mess cart, some were always away.

Geoffrey Farrington, a young gunner friend of Louisa's on the staff, arrived late, too late for anything but the scraps for lunch and the dregs of the flat, now warm champagne—the ice had long since melted in the small portable icebox. And by now Carter was quite ready to leave Louisa to him and ride home. There was no doubt about a storm building up, and he saw no fun in getting soaked. He asked Renata to come back with him but she refused. She did not like the way he and her sister had behaved.

"No, I'll stay with the others," she said.

"There'll be a storm. You can feel it in the air."

"Perhaps, but if there is we are going to take shelter in the outsheds of the farm." She pointed to a house set in a group of gums. "It's all arranged," she went on. "So tell Mother not to worry if you go back. It's not much out of your way and she's a worrier."

Carter rode back at a slow canter. The storm broke as he gave his horse to Sixpence and went into the house without knocking. The drawing-room shutters were closed against the heat.

Dora van Reenan came into the room in a lacy dressing gown.

"I'm so glad you're back early," she said. "The storm . . ." She recoiled, clutching her breast. "You," she said. "What are you doing here?" She had been thinking of him all day and now here he was in front of her. "I thought it was the girls," she said.

"They sent me with a message. You are not to worry. They have arranged to take shelter at a farm."

The rain was coming down in torrents. His voice could hardly be heard as it poured down on the tin roof, cascading off the eaves in a solid curtain. There was a loud hissing crack, the room was illuminated with purple light as the lightning struck in the garden. The thunderclap, loud as cannon, came before the light had faded from the room.

Dora, always nervous in a bad storm, gave a gasping cry as Carter took her in his arms to soothe her.

He felt her body trembling, felt the softness of her flesh through the thin material. Her long hair was down her back, its perfume in his nostrils. Her lips, parted in fear, in surprise, at him, at herself, at this totally unforeseen situation, were close to his.

"I love you," he said. "I think I have loved you since I first saw you."

"Oh!" she gasped. "No! No!" But there was no resistance in her. The storm, the relief at its breaking, at things being out of her hands. There was not even anything to decide. Nature had decided, God, the heat, the storm, the girls' being away, even Renata, who had sent him with a message. If it had not been so hot she would not have been naked. If she had not expected the girls she would not have come into the room in her dressing gown. Even the dressing gown, her best, almost a bridal gown of white satin and lace. What in God's name had made her put it on? She had not worn it for years. She had thought she would try it on to see if it still fitted . . . Not just the dressing gown. Every circumstance had fitted like the bits of a picture puzzle.

CHAPTER 48

THE BIRTH OF HATE

At Olifantsfontein, General Botha informed the Boers of the new British plan. "Kitchener," he said, "is going to use the vast number of troops he has to sweep the country and drive us as if we were game into a trap. . . . For this purpose he is assembling fifty thousand men along the Johannesburg-Natal railway line."

Two days later, in the first light of dawn the skyline from east to west, as far as Boetie could see, was dotted with evenly spaced horsemen behind whom rose the dust of their guns and transport. The first great drive had begun.

The Boers retired, delaying the cavalry as long as possible and moving back as soon as they brought their guns into action. By midday the scene had changed. Behind the advancing British great pillars of rolling smoke rose into the summer sky. Every farm as they passed it was being put to the torch. This was unbelievable. Even as they saw it with their own eyes it remained incredible to the Boers that the civilized British, the greatest nation in the world, should act like raiding Kaffirs. Word spread that the women and children were being carted off to concentration camps. This the Boers were still less able to credit till a wild-eyed woman on a bay horse black with sweat rode past them, screaming, "My home . . . my home . . . my house . . . everything is gone. *Ja,* even my dog is dead . . ." and went on, still screaming.

So on a summer morning hate was born, a New Year's child, and Boetie, rising eighteen years, knew at last he was a man, for only a man can hate. In every Boer heart there was a new resolution. Shoot to kill . . . fight on till we die, for there is nothing left to lose but our lives, and nothing is left to live for if we live.

Turnbull, who was out with the General Staff on the drive, was appalled, utterly horrified at seeing peaceful Boer farmsteads go up in flames as the troops overran them. He had seen the orders, but printed orders were one thing—this was another. He had not believed they would be carried out. He had thought they were only a threat. Reprisals. Good God! Reprisals were not English. Thinking back, he was less sure. For a century or more the only wars the British had fought other than the Crimean, in which civilians had not been concerned, had been against natives: Afghans, Zulus, tribesmen on the Northwest frontier. And then there had been reprisals—villages shelled, huts set alight. But there had been a difference. The natives had mutilated the wounded and the dead, disemboweling them, castrating them. They had tortured their prisoners, and their huts, when destroyed, could be rebuilt in a matter of days. But these were white people, people like themselves. These were homes that had been painfully built over the years and filled with an accumulation of the years. Furniture, clothes, tools, books, pictures, family heirlooms, records. Little in the poorer farms of much intrinsic value, but dear to their possessors because of their scarcity. In the bigger places the value of the furnishings might well run into thousands of pounds.

He saw the first women and children being herded back to the railroad—distraught, some mute with despair, others hysterical, some crying, some cursing. Many carried babies in their arms, toddlers clung to their skirts. Big children carried smaller ones. Others, blind with tears, led each other by the hand. Some of the soldiers around them were laughing. So it had done this also. It was not only the Boers who were despoiled. The devil had been loosed in Tommy Atkins, too. The atavistic devils of rape and loot that lay latent in every man. It was for this Wellington had shot and hanged men in the Peninsula. He remembered his father talking of the Germans in the Franco-Prussian War, of the shooting of hostages, the destruction of homes believed to have hidden a franc-tireur—men who, though not in uniform, had tried to protect their land. Kitchener was conducting this operation as if it was a native war. Sitting his horse, Jack—he was his favorite now—Turnbull was frozen with horror at the sight of these bedraggled prisoners, civilians torn from their homes, at the sound of their laments and cries, at the curses of the old men—old Kaffir fighters, grandfathers, and great-grandfathers—the men who had tamed this land and broken it to the plow and had hoped to end their days by their own firesides.

Tears came into his eyes. That he, a British soldier, should live to see this day. If it had been possible in wartime he would have sent in his papers and resigned the Queen's commission. A number of officers had done that when ordered to Ireland, rather than be engaged there in a struggle not so different from this—another people fighting for their freedom in a desultory war that had lasted several hundred years.

A grand old man, his wrinkled face tanned to leather by the summers he had lived, his white beard reaching to his belt, strode by, erect, proud as a king. Seeing Turnbull so near, he shouted, *"Verdomde rooinek!* I have been burned out before. Twice I have seen children and cattle killed. But that was Kaffirs." He spat into the dust and strode on.

The little girl with long blond pigtails he had been leading broke back and, before Turnbull knew what was happening, he found a white kitten in his hand. "My pussycat," the little girl said. *"Meneer,* please save my pussycat," and she was gone, running after the old man she had left.

"Christ!" Turnbull said, now blind with tears. "Christ!"

There he was, a captain of hussars sitting a blood horse with a white kitten cuddled in his arms. The world had gone mad. Kitchener was mad. They could not know what they were doing. This was no way to end the war. He knew these people. He loved them. Brave, honest, charitable, hospitable, but obstinate to the death and capable of unrelenting hate. Now they would really fight. Violence and brutality could only beget further violence and brutality. Unable to stand this bloodless scene, more frightful in its implications than a battlefield, he turned and rode away, the kitten still in his arms.

An old man's hate. A child's trust and love. The kitten was a symbol of some kind, of something, he did not know what—of hope or peace, of a woman's instinct, even in so small a child, to save something.

As he rode back, he made up his mind. It was madness of course, but he was going to see Kitchener, Lord Kitchener of Khartoum, and tell him this was no way to win the war. It was his duty, even if he were cashiered for it. What he did not know then, what nobody yet knew, was that within a year one out of every five of the people he had seen herded away from their ruined homes would be dead.

Behind him the cavalry screen was advancing in extended order, followed by the guns and the transport wagons. Behind him the smoke of the burning farms billowed, brownish black, into a pale blue sky. Behind him over the horizon the Boers were retreating, fighting their interminable rear-guard action in their own inimitable manner, inflicting casualties and suffering a minimum of loss themselves as they held *kopje* and *rankie* till they became untenable, and then slipped away on their veld-raised ponies.

This war could go on forever now, with both sides so deeply committed by acts, described by Lloyd George as acts of barbarism, that neither could stop. The British had to justify themselves. The Boers had to have revenge.

When Turnbull handed over his horse, the face of the trooper who took his bridle was stony with controlled surprise. What the hell was this? The captain back already, dismounting with a bloody kitten held by the scruff of its neck.

In his quarters Turnbull told his batman to get him a
bath and give the kitten some milk. The man took the
kitten and petted it. Then he turned to his master and
said, "What shall we call her, sir?"

"Her?"

"Yes, sir. It's a she all right. Not that I ever saw a Tom
kitten or at least one that stayed a Tom."

"Call her, Biglow?" Turnbull said. "I don't know—how
about Pretoria?"

"Pretoria it is, sir." He put the kitten down and said,
"You wait, Pretoria my girl, I'll go to the mess and get
you some scoff. A spot of milk and a sardine. Wot about
that? 'Ow'd you like that?" The kitten purred, its tail in
the air as Biglow went for the bath water.

As to the drive, it failed. What hope had the heavy
British cavalry horses, accompanied by their unwieldy
transport, of rounding up the elusive and mobile Boers?
Then rain came to the Boers' aid, and the British convoys were bogged down up to their axles, and the foot
soldiers staggered through mud that was ankle deep and
sometimes even knee deep.

But the damage done to the country over which the
British had passed like locusts was incalculable. Houses
burned, crops ruined, all livestock driven off or killed in a
wide swath of destruction uncountenanced by any article of war.

And this was only the beginning.

Someone had to be told about this. Something had to be
done. Sitting in his green canvas bath, Turnbull made up
his mind.

It was not easy, even for an officer on the staff, to see
the commander in chief. Turnbull had hardly spoken to
him. His work of interviewing and interrogating prisoners
did not bring them into contact, and even that had been
largely taken over by loyal Dutch-speaking colonials—
Cape Boers who had chosen the British side. Of late he
had spent most of his time trying to correct and collate
the unbelievably inaccurate maps that had been issued to
the high command by the War Office.

He gave his name and rank to a young ADC, a shiny
bright boy officer whose father was a peer. After waiting

for an hour in the drawing room of the house that had been taken over as headquarters, the young man came back and said, "The commander in chief will see you now."

Turnbull followed the young officer, who opened the door for him. Kitchener looked enormous seated behind a desk loaded with papers. The walls of the room were covered with maps. Some of them he recognized as his own work.

"You asked to see me, Captain Turnbull?" Kitchener's gray eyes, as cold as ice, met his. He did not like to be disturbed. For an instant they stared at each other. Then Turnbull pulled himself together and said:

"I saw the advance this morning, sir, and the burning of the farms. I know these people, sir, and I thought—"

Kitchener's eyes took fire. "You thought," he said. "You dare to interrupt the commander in chief at his work to tell him you do not approve of his policy?"

"I thought it was my duty, sir."

"Your duty, Captain Turnbull, is to obey orders and not to criticize them." He paused and then said, "I have looked up your record. You certainly do know the Boers, since you were going to marry one of them. I can hardly call a British officer, especially a Second Hussar, a pro-Boer, but your attitude certainly suggests it. That is all, Captain Turnbull. You may go."

"Thank you, sir." Turnbull saluted again, turned on his heel, and went out, his spur rowels clinking.

So that was that. Well, to hell with it. He had done his best. He had salved his conscience and ruined his career. He was finished as a soldier now.

This opinion was confirmed when the orders came out that evening. Captain Turnbull was ordered to rejoin his regiment, the 2nd Royal Hussars, 2nd Cavalry Brigade.

He called Biglow. "We're off, my boy," he said. "The party's over."

The man said, "Yes, sir, I'll begin to pack up." His face was a question mark, but he said nothing else.

Turnbull decided to tell him before some cock-and-bull story got around the lines. Then he could say he knew all about it, that he'd had it straight from the horse's mouth.

"I went to see Lord Kitchener."

"Yes, sir," the man said, as if this was a daily occurrence.

"I was a bloody fool, Biglow. I went to tell him this farm-burning was a mistake. I saw it this morning. It was terrible, Biglow, terrible to see their homes go up like bonfires. And he didn't like it. Mine's 'to do or die, not to reason why . . .' So's yours, Biglow. Soldiers must not think. Mutiny, that's what it was. I think he'd have had me shot if he could have." This was a funny thing, too, to find himself discussing the commander in chief with a trooper. "And so we're going back to the regiment."

Biglow's face came alive. "I'm glad, sir," he said, "very glad."

"To be going back?"

"Yes, sir. We'll be better off there with our own mates, if you'll pardon me, sir, and I'm glad too you're against it."

"Against what?"

" 'Omes. This 'ere burning of their 'omes, sir. They're people like us, sir. That's wot we says. Soldiers is soldiers, but this fighting women and kids . . . Let the Colonials do it." Biglow, like most regular cavalrymen, hated the Colonial irregular horse.

Then he said, "We'll be going by road, sir?"

"By road," Turnbull said. So Biglow knew where the 2nd was. Secrecy was impossible in this army. Everyone knew everything, including the Boers.

At the door, as he was going out, Biglow turned and said, "We'll need a basket, sir."

"A basket?"

"For Pretoria, sir."

Two days later Turnbull reached the 2nd Cavalry Brigade. It had been a pleasant enough trek of quite a little caravan.

Turnbull rode in front on Jack, his batman and orderly behind him. The orderly led his two spare chargers —Jo, named after Chamberlain, a showy chestnut, and Miss Elsie, the little black mare. Then came a limber with their gear. The military precision of the detachment was somewhat marred by Pretoria's basket, fastened to Biglow's saddle, braced by the rifle in its bucket, to which it was also strapped, making the weapon useless, and by the four mongrels of various sizes and colors that his servants had collected at headquarters. One appeared to be part foxhound, another looked rather like a greyhound. The other two were terriers.

But it was wonderful to be back, with half-smiling troopers saluting him. A noncommissioned officer gave his fatigue party an eyes-right and came over when Turnbull called him, to shake hands.

"Nice to have you with us again, sir."

"Nice to be back, Corporal Farrar. Very nice indeed. Like coming home."

Turnbull glanced at the horses in the lines. They looked poor. But everything was shipshape. It always was in the 2nd. It was a regiment to be proud of.

There was a little dark red and yellow flag with a "2" in white on it to mark the HQ tent. Handing over his horse, Turnbull went in and saluted. Colonel Sir Charles Eaton looked well.

"Glad you're back, John."

"Returned to duty, sir."

"I know. I heard about it. You always were a bloody fool, John. You know, I suppose, your career is finished. A captain you are and a captain you'll remain."

"Yes, sir."

They both laughed.

"You'll take over your old squadron," the colonel said.

"Thank you. I'll leave you at it now, sir."

The colonel glanced at the papers the adjutant had just dumped in front of him.

"There's one more thing," the colonel looked up from the table. "Do you know any nurses, John?"

"Nurses? No, Charles." They were off the official basis now.

"Not a Nurse Smith at Bloemfontein? You were there, weren't you—with Roberts?"

"I was there, but I knew no girls." There had been that nurse he'd seen once who looked a bit like Elsie. But all dark girls looked a bit like Elsie. He saluted again and left the tent.

Well, know any girls or not, there was one in Bloemfontein who took an interest in him and the cavalry. "Horse soldiers," she called them. She'd saved one of the lads. Trooper Morris. Just a boy, down with enteric. Nursed him night and day, moved him into her quarters at night, they said. A hell of a row with the other girls. The old war horse who ran the hospital, Lady Finch-Haddley, had twisted their tails. Said they'd all sleep in a room with a man someday and might as well begin with sick boys. Something like that. At least that was the story he'd heard. Quite a Tartar apparently. But it was funny, the girl—this Nurse Smith—always asking about him. Anybody seen Captain Turnbull of the 2nd? Any news of him? And so on. Nurse Smith. "Miss Elsie," the boys called her. And hadn't he a little black mare by that name? There was something fishy about all this, but it would come out one day. Things always did in the 2nd.

There was quite a party in the mess as the word got around that Turnbull was back. By next day the loose threads had been picked up. A routine of parades, inspections of men, horses, horse lines, and rifles. The regiment was resting. They would be off again as soon as the horses were up to it.

Two days after Turnbull's return Colonel Sir Charles Eaton sat on a camp chair outside the tent he was using as an orderly room, glaring at the memo that had just been handed to him. "The bloody fools," he said. "The bloody fools!" The war itself was bad enough. But this!

"Orderly! Orderly!" he shouted. A trooper came smartly to attention with clicking spurs in front of him.

Fixing his gold-rimmed eyeglass more firmly in his left eye he said, "Give Captain Turnbull my compliments and ask him to come here."

The trooper, a red-faced country boy, said, "Sir," saluted, and went off.

The colonel resumed his scrutiny of the letter. A rocket. They had had the audacity to send him, the colonel of the 2nd, a rocket. After all we've done, he thought. One V.C., one D.S.O., four mentions in dispatches. Casualties. He thought of his dead and wounded, of the men who had died of fever, of typhus and dysentery, of the fine horses gone. Turnbull was one of the few of his old officers left to him. Thank God for an old friend at a time like this. And the other ranks. By God, when he looked at them on parade there was hardly one face in ten that he knew.

But the regiment went on. These boys were still hussars. It was still the Galloping 2nd—the "Gallopers," as they were sometimes called—and they had dared to write to him, to us, like this.

He looked at the memo again. General headquarters. He had nothing but contempt for the staff. They had tried to take the 2nd from him and make him a brigadier. They had attacked him when he had wanted to scrap some of the absurd equipment the cavalry had to carry, and again when he had suggested buying smaller, tougher horses. They still thought of cavalry charges. And now this, to fighting soldiers.

He had known it was going on. Kitchener's idea. It was what had brought Turnbull back. But that they should expect a regiment like his to do it. Colonial troops, perhaps, the Irish Light Horse, Lovat's Scouts, or dragoons. The dragoons had a history of rapine and debauchery.

"You sent for me, sir?" Turnbull said.

"I did. It appears we've got to do it. They say we have been remiss. They—" The colonel choked with anger.

"Do what, Charles?"

"Act like eighteenth-century dragoons, by God," he said. "Burn their bloody houses about these poor bastards' ears. Kill or drive off their stock and pick up the women and children and shove them into camps till it's over. Of course the Boers come home to rest, to refit, to see their wives and nippers. Of course every farmhouse is a base. But we're civilized men. Or I thought we were. We've deployed an empire against them and they've fought on. A handful of farmers, without pay, who have armed and mounted themselves."

Turnbull said, "Yes, sir. That's why I was returned to duty. Because I objected to it. I could have been court-martialed. Had you forgotten?"

"No," the colonel almost shouted. "No, Johnny, but *you*'ve got to do it."

"Me?"

"Who else? You know the country here."

How well he knew it, Turnbull thought. He'd ridden over a lot of it before the war. It had been strange to be back in the Transvaal after so long. Strange and terrible. It had ripped the guts out of him.

CHAPTER 49

THE MESSENGER

WHEN it was decided by General Botha to send a dispatch with more details about the destruction of farms and the disposition of his commandos to Pretoria, Dirk Moolman was chosen as the best man for the job because of his ability to assess the British forces that lay in front of the town, and his scouting skill. He would again go disguised as a native from the Limpopo, a Shangaan, since he spoke their language well. He rode off with Boetie and two others as escort, and then, leaving them to take back his horse, changed into suitable rags, stained his face and body with walnut juice, and meandered off toward the British lines. He passed several burned-out farmsteads and, seeing the British campfire, went up to it and begged for food.

He was given half a can of bully beef and two biscuits. He sat down a hundred yards away to eat and sleep. The situation, dangerous as it was, amused him. What fools the English were to think they would gain their ends this way. The bitterness of the tragedy struck him. After all, who knew more of such things than he? But the English would defeat their own ends. This would lengthen rather than shorten the war. Finding himself all alone among thousands of British troops gave him a strange elation. It was like hunting again, but this time he was the quarry. In essence he was a solitary man. It did not matter if he took risks. He had no one else to think of. And risk had been his life for so long. His life the stake in hunting and in war. A light breeze was blowing in his face, blowing toward the British troops he had just passed. A plan came into his mind.

It should not be difficult, not very, if he had a bit of luck. Putting out his little fire he moved south toward Pretoria and found what he had sought, a donga running almost parallel to the line of British advance. There was a half-moon that gave enough light for him to cut eight

506

clumps of dry grass and lay them flat on the donga's edge, about twenty yards apart. When he had done this he lit them, running from one to the other, and then ran on for a mile and hid in the bank where it had been undercut by the summer rains. Before he got there the veld was aflame. Caught in the hand of the wind, the long dry grass flared, leaped upward with sparks that flew a hundred yards before falling and catching again. Burning with thick clouds of smoke, for a lot of the grass was green, but there was enough old dry stuff to ignite it and keep the fire going. No one would look for him. No one would remember him. No one would have the sense to burn a backfire against the wind. Tonight the arsonists, the farm burners, would be caught in the flames themselves. Over the roar of the fire he heard screams and shouts. Ammunition was exploding. Smoke billowed upward to be lost in the night. The clouds glowed red as they reflected the fire below them—rose, pink, and orange, scarlet and yellow—as the flames leaped forward.

He stared for a while, well content with his work, and then moved on slowly, plodding like a Kaffir to whom time means nothing, so little that he does not even have a word for it.

By morning he was in Pretoria, begging his way. Just another Kaffir. Another drawn by curiosity, by the thought of pickings, by the magnet that draws all men, black or white, in war or peace, to the lights of the city.

By midday he was back at the Willows and, avoiding Adam in the stables, found Dora van Reenan by good fortune picking fruit in her garden.

"So you are back?" she said. "My God, can one never get rid of beggars?"

"It is your charity that brings them back, *mevrou*," Moolmna said. "A shilling. A shilling for a poor old man."

"A tickey is plenty. Too much. Why do you not work?"

Moolman, crouched in his filthy blanket, was scratching in the soil between his feet. "There is also a note from Boetie," he said. "There was no time to write much. Tell the little maid that he is well. . . . A shilling," he whined. "A shilling for an old Kaffir." He put a fallen peach on the spot where he had buried his dispatch, and slipped out of the garden.

Getting out of Pretoria was even easier than getting

in. Moolman simply walked past the pickets and the sentries, took note of the barbed-wire entanglements and new searchlights that were being erected, and trekked on over the deserted veld till he got onto the burn he had made two nights before. For miles the veld was black with patches of ash where odd trees that had flamed like torches in the dark, had burned down into gray heaps—little mounds, some of which still glowed. Overhead small hawks, black fork-tailed drongo shrikes, and bluejays hunted for burned and disabled insects and small animals. He came upon the remains of burned transport wagons and limbers with only their iron tires left intact. What a job he had done! Thousands of pounds' worth of war matériel had gone up in smoke. Some men had certainly perished too. The horses, cut loose, would probably have bolted and some of them might well be in Boer hands by now. People would think that the fire had begun with sparks from a burning farm and regard it as a judgment. Perhaps it was.

With this on his mind Moolman marched on until quite suddenly his old veldschoenen, the only shoes a Kaffir would have worn, gave out. The knife-sharp black stubble, the iron-hard, still-warm ground had worn out the thin leather of the soles. Soon his feet began to bleed and later to swell till he found it all but impossible to move. He could not go on. If he waited till darkness came it would at least be cool and his feet would have had time to rest. So with his head on his hat, after tightening his belt against his hunger, he lay down to sleep. He was still sleeping when a British patrol found him.

Instead of leaving him alone—what, after all, did a sleeping Kaffir amount to?—the sergeant in charge, a good Samaritan, dismounted and, seeing the state of his feet, pulled off his shoes to bandage them, only to find that under the dust and black ash this Kaffir's feet were white. They raised his shirt and here too white skin showed where friction and sweat had rubbed him clean.

This was a white man. A Boer. A spy. They took him in to be questioned.

The chances were that he would be shot. He must make up a story quickly and a good one at that. They had tied his legs under a spare horse that a trooper led by the reins. A story. How did one get a story? They passed near the ruins of a farm. Moolman shouted out and pointed. He spoke Dutch. No one was going to learn he understood English, so the men spoke freely in front of him. *"Plaas,"* he said, *"woonplek,"* and struggled to get free.

"Let's see what he does," a trooper said. "Let's let him go. If he runs we can plug him."

They got him down from his horse. In agony from his bleeding feet he ran toward the smoking ruins and began to poke about as if he was looking for something special. He found it. He had hoped he would. A family Bible under the rubble of what had once been a living room. Books were hard to burn. Feverishly he opened the flyleaf to find his new name. Herman van Niekerk, there it was. Born July 23, 1860. Near enough. He pointed it out to the man who had followed him. His wife's name was Maria. He said, "Maria." There were several children's names. He said, *"Seun . . . baba."* He made motions with his hand to show their respective heights. The youngest was less than a year old. Moolman cradled an imaginary baby in his arms. Then, carrying the Bible and wiping his eyes with his sleeve, he walked slowly back to his horse and waited for them to help him mount. What a bit of luck. What an escape. He had a story now. They would hold him certainly and send him over the sea, but they would not shoot him out of hand.

When Moolman left, Dora still continued to work in the garden and then sat down beneath the willows to rest. Nothing could have been less suspicious than her behavior. Peace. What peace there was here, a little island of it in a sea of military activity. Ever since she had heard of the farm burning, something in her had broken. This was a most frightful thing, and now she had the details.

Homes, some of them as well found as hers, reduced to ashes. Farms they called them, but farms were homes and more than homes. She saw the flames take in the window draperies, the thatch. The clouds of smoke, the roof trees falling in like broken backbones. A house, particularly a farmhouse, was a living thing, an entity of brick, stone, and wood. Each had a kind of soul, as if the happiness and sorrow each had known had become part of its very mortar.

This dispatch must get to the Cape at once and from there to the President in Holland. The news would change public opinion.

A woman she knew was leaving on the mail train in two days. It would be suitably hidden in case of search, and she would send it to her. A gift. There was no reason why one sister should not send another a gift.

Her eyes idly followed a dragonfly somewhat bigger than the others as it hunted. She considered the possibilities. At last she had it. A small silver manicure set in a leather case lined with blue velvet. She could raise the lining, put in the dispatch, and reseal it. She would enclose a note. She composed the letter in her mind:

Dear Anna,
Here is the silver manicure set that belonged to our mother that you said you had always wanted if I could find it. I was turning out an old trunk last week and came across it.

Not wishing to entrust it to the mail, that in these troubled times is often unreliable, I have asked my friend, Nella van Diglen, to take it to you.

She smiled. Anna would understand. Their mother had not had a manicure set. It had been a present from Anna when Louisa was born.

She thought of Carter. How careful they always were together, not even meeting each other's eyes. But it had been there. Each aware of the other, of the other's feeling. Each thinking of the lightning, the thunder and the rain, the orchestra of that wild hour.

His desire was answered by her own. Reason, the mind, was one thing. The weakness, or strength was a better word, of the flesh another. And this man whom she loved, desired, was an alien, an enemy. More than ever an enemy with this news. But these horrors were not his doing. Nor had the enmity of nations ever stood for long against the intimacy of individuals.

What nonsense words were. Good. Wicked. Sin. Fornication. Even adultery. They were all variables, utterly dependent upon time, place, and circumstance. She almost laughed. Time, place, and circumstance indeed! How they had all collaborated in her seduction. Mine, she thought. Was I seduced or was I the seducer? Between adults there could be no seduction. Her mind, torn between hot thoughts of love, of Carter's mouth on hers, of his hands upon her body, and a new horror at the turn the war had taken, she gathered her skirts about her, picked up her basket of peaches, and went into the house, to the drawing room still filled with the memories of love. Not even the bedroom, she thought, not even that, so quickly had the lightning struck.

Now for the manicure set and her own small part in this frightful game of war. Another pawn moving over the vast chessboard of the veld.

Louisa, naturally enough had heard the news, heard of Moolman's coming again disguised as a Kaffir and of her sister's love letter. Even without words she would have known Renata had heard from her boy lover. She was walking around in a daze, like a moon-struck calf, smiling, immune to all things, wrapped in the cocoon of her dreams.

She waited three days. That would give Moolman time to get away, and then, catching sight of Carter as he rode by, she waved to him. He came over to where she stood under the trees on the side of the street outside the gates. She had known he would come by, since his habits were so regular.

"Good morning, Miss van Reenan," he said. "How pretty you look."

"Prettier than usual?"

"I don't know, Louisa. I forget how you looked last time I saw you it was so long ago. But you must be prettier, or perhaps it is the dress."

She had on a rose-pink linen frock, wore no hat, and carried a red parasol that flushed her laughing face with reflected light.

"If you asked a pretty girl to go riding this evening she might go," Louisa said. "It might be interesting for you."

"I'll bring the gray around at five."

"Come earlier. Come to tea. I'm sure my mother would be delighted to see you."

What a minx, Carter thought. She knew nothing, but with the instinct of a woman guessed at something. He had seen her mother several times since the storm. They had been more than guarded. Their conversation had been banal. He wondered if they had been too careful.

He had seen Dora alone only once. Just long enough to tell her he loved her again and wanted to marry her. This to his own surprise. The words had been blurted out.

She had blushed and laughed, half happy, half disturbed. "A proposal," she said, "from a man on a horse in a crowded road," and had left him staring after her.

He wanted her. She would suit him. She had a lovely body and brains, too, an independent mind, something almost impossible to find in England today, particularly in a pretty woman. He wondered how much of his folly was due to the lack of feminine society. In his mind he placed her in London, at his home in the country, among his friends. She would not be out of place anywhere, nor would he be the first man to come back from the wars with a foreign woman, one of the enemy. His own great-grandfather had married a Frenchwoman he had met when the Allies were in Paris at the end of the Napoleonic Wars. There was also a physical attraction he had not known before. He felt it for the girl, too. Was it that he saw the girl in the mother? Or that the mother resembled the girl? A more mature version of her—the flower rather than the bud.

Louisa thought her mother looked strangely at her when she told Adam to bring another cup because she had asked Major Carter to tea. The look, and it was scarcely even that—no more than a flash of her dark eyes, a tiny tightening of her lips—meant what? Was she glad or sorry?

Her thoughts were interrupted by the arrival of the horses. Her mother had not even had time to comment on her wearing her riding habit. She had ordered the extra cup as she came into the drawing room, the skirt of her habit held high in her left hand. Carter's arrival, leading the gray mare, had occurred at the same moment.

The greetings had been formal, almost cold. A smoke screen of burning farmsteads lay between them. Between her mother and Carter. Now she was sure. Something had happened. If nothing had taken place her mother would have attacked him, brought the matter up, called him a barbarian. But when? Where? When had they been alone together? Never for an instant. Except when he had left them all at the picnic. They must have arranged it beforehand. No wonder their mother had been so eager for them to go. She laughed suddenly, almost choking on her cake. Her mother . . . A woman of that age . . . She gulped her tea and said, "Let's go if you are ready, Major. I certainly feel like a gallop."

Once they were out of town Carter pulled up to a walk. "Now," he said, "what's all this about?"

Louisa felt her heart beat more quickly. This was what she liked, this power. She had something he wanted. Something beyond her woman's body. Something that she held in her mind. This was real power. A woman's body a man could master. She was not strong enough to resist him. Nor, if she had been of a warm temperament, able to prevent herself melting in his arms and conforming to his desire, for, once aroused, she was a victim to her own. But the mind was different. Nothing could influence her mind. There she was cold, calculating. This was a combination that could lead the few women who possessed it to great success. There was nothing simulated about the passion of their bodies, but it was controlled, like a tap, by their minds. They could adjust it, turn it on full strength, reduce it to a trickle, or, with a swift turn of the hand, check it altogether.

"I have a bit of news," she said. "A Boer was here."

"Boers are here all the time, Louisa. It's very hard to stop people coming in and out of Pretoria."

"Spies?" she asked.

"Some are and some aren't."

"In disguise, Major Carter? Do they come disguised as Kaffirs with dispatches? His name is Moolman."

"He came to the Willows?" Carter asked, trying not to show his excitement. A Boer traitor had told them about Moolman. They had quite a file on him. He was said to be in the confidence of De la Rey and Botha.

"Of course not. How could he get there through all the troops? And what should three women do with dispatches? No, not the Willows. Somewhere else. And you cannot expect me to give away my friends. I just thought you would be interested."

"I am," Carter said. But she did not hear him. She had put a spur into the gray and had shot off at a gallop.

Louisa was not worried about giving Moolman away. He had had plenty of time to get clear.

Carter galloped after her.

They came back in the glow of the sunset.

"Have a good ride?" her mother asked when they pulled up at the house.

"Lovely," Louisa said, calling Adam to bring a bath as she ran upstairs.

She took off her habit and waited for Adam to bring the bath and the water. When he had poured it she sat down and gave him her legs one after the other to have her boots pulled off. One day, she thought, Morgan Carter will do that for me and more, too. Her mind was made up about him. She was going to teach her mother a lesson. She had asked for it. If it had not been for her mother she might have waited. There were other men. Younger, more amusing, but not so rich. Still, there had been no hurry before. She could have played about and still had him in the end, but now she felt a sudden urgency. She wished she knew what they were doing downstairs. She wished she knew more about love. More than just kissing. That was where a woman of her mother's age had an unfair advantage. And how disgusting it was—even to think about it. . . .

She rolled her hair tighter into a chignon at the top of her head and squeezed the big sponge with both hands over her back.

Renata was out, and Louisa had not been far wrong about what was going on in the drawing room.

Carter held Dora's hand in his. He stood near her. They were alone on the stage playing a curiously static love scene. Their thighs touched. In silence they looked into each other's eyes as if looking for some hidden truth. As if they could see the future there. As if they asked themselves if these were the eyes they would look into until they died. Quite still, they emanated a kind of latent action, the possibility of an explosion. Dora's breast rose and fell as she breathed. Carter's pulse beat faster. The girl had excited him. And he had had this woman. She was his. She wanted him, but he could not even kiss her here.

"I want you," he whispered into her ear. "I want to marry you."

Dora came to life. "Must you propose every time you see me?" she said. "And is this a good day? With the farm burning begun, the homes of the Transvaal burning like candles, and you smelling of horse sweat and hot for my daughter?" She swung away from him. "Do you think I don't know?" she said. "We are alike, she and I, alike in our appearance, in our voices. The only difference is that I am seventeen years older than Louisa and I do not have the temperament of a harlot."

There now, she had said it. It was out. She and her daughter were rivals for this man. But how stupid to let him know it.

"It's you I want to marry, Dora," he said. "She's a pretty thing but too young for me. Nice to ride with, nice to talk to, dance with. She's like a kitten, Dora, something to play with. Listen," he said, "if I asked you to ride with me, would you come?"

"I couldn't."

"Nor could you dance, not dance after dance with me. Nor play tennis, because you're a widow with daughters. So I take out one of the girls because she looks like you. Because it gives me an excuse to see you." Without caring now if Renata did walk in, he put his arm around Dora, pulled her to him, kissed her, and left. He did not even say good night.

Back at headquarters Carter telephoned to every picket, telling them to look for a spy disguised as a Kaffir.

But Moolman had asked his captors if he could wash his sore feet when they came to a spruit, and, once there, had bathed completely, watched by a trooper with a rifle.

"I felt so dirty," he said when he came back to the patrol. No Kaffir now, just a ragged Boer with a singed Bible in his hand. When he was admitted to hospital to have his feet dressed before he was sent to the prison camp, his name was registered as Herman van Niekerk.

No one on the periphery of Pretoria had heard of a man called Moolman disguised as a Kaffir. He had not been seen or taken prisoner. Moolman had disappeared.

Once again, for the thirtieth or fortieth time, in the secrecy of her room Renata looked at the scribbled lines: "I am well. I love you." What more was needed? What more could be needed in her whole life than that he should be well and love her?

CHAPTER 50

THE PROPHET

WITH Moolman away the corporalcy was taken over by Hans Swart, a small, overconfident man with whom Boetie did not get on. He led them into some unnecessary skirmishes and, refusing to retire in time, lost several men. One morning after they had trekked a few miles Boetie found he had left his saddlebags hung in a thorn where they had slept, and decided to go back for them. When he returned to find his people they were lost in the mist that had risen, filling the valleys with a blanket of cotton wool from which the tops of the *kopjes* rose like islands.

Convinced that Moolman was dead, probably shot as a spy, Boetie saw no reason to return to the commando, and decided to move off on his own and make for the Cape, where he had heard some new commandos were being formed. The Cape lay several hundred miles away to the south, but it promised new adventure and would get him away from Pretoria and his temptation to see Renata. If Moolman had come back he would have tried to. But if Moolman had been taken with the letters and dispatches the Willows would be watched, so the farther away he was, the better. Seeing new country was another draw. He wanted to see all this land, the whole of Africa, to cover it from end to end and make it his.

He had two good horses, biltong he had made from a kudu he had shot, salt, mealie meal, and a little bag of coffee from his English loot that he had saved for emergencies, two blankets, an English overcoat and rifle, and seventy rounds of ammunition.

Then disaster struck. Both horses came down simultaneously with horse sickness. When he got up in the morning their coats were steaming, a heavy foam, like soapsuds, oozed from their nostrils. They stood blowing and gasping for air, their legs trembling. Then they staggered, fell, struggled for a while, their legs kicking up the dust, and died, drowned, as their lungs filled with their own foamy discharge. Horse sickness killed thousands of horses every year in Africa. Some horses recovered and were then "salted," immune to the disease, and fetched high prices. But Boetie had never seen one die before.

His situation was now serious: alone, dismounted, and several hundred miles from where he wanted to go. He would have to abandon almost all his gear and press on on foot till he ran into some Boers. He made a pack of his saddle, using the stirrup leather as shoulder straps. He put his rations—biltong, mealie meal, salt, and the precious coffee—inside his overcoat, rolled the coat and blanket into a sort of long sausage that he lashed to the top of the saddle with strips of bark torn from a *vaalbos,* the small, flat-topped, gray-foliaged bushveld tree that the natives use for tying the cross of the roofs of their huts.

Clouds of dust warned him of a column of British troops, and he lay low, hiding, to watch them pass a mile away. A brigade of cavalry with their guns and transport.

A dark shadow swept over him, coming between him and the sun. A black patch moved over the veld in front of him as a vulture, gliding down on immense silver wings, landed beside his dead horses. That was the first. Within an hour there were a hundred, fighting, croaking, beating each other with their wings as they swarmed like lice over the carcasses.

Circling vultures, out of sight of man, but able themselves to see everything below them, patrolled the whole upper air. Each was watched by his circling neighbor so that when one fell, dropping from his place in the sky upon some dead or stricken beast, those next to him came down too, and those next to them in a chain reaction to any accident of wounds, death, or birth that left something helpless.

They would pick the eyes out of a living calf or a wounded man. Then they would tear at the soft-skinned parts, the inner belly, or the udder, and thus reach the entrails. They served a terrible purpose, these scavengers of the veld, and to Boetie seemed even more sinister than the hyenas and jackals that were the colleagues of their trade.

To Boetie, lying there watching and listening to the birds quarreling over what yesterday had been two good horses, came the sensation of awe and horror at the strange lack of waste in nature. Nothing was lost. Things were only changed. What had been a horse was now a bird. It would also be, when the vultures had gone, a hyena, a jackal, a crow, a rat, an ant. Horse or man. It was the same to the *aasvoëls*. In death man certainly lost his superiority.

By the time Boetie struck the old wagon pass over the Magaliesberg, he was in poor condition. His shoes had given out. He was exhausted, being unused to marching, much less to carrying a heavy load. But at last he saw men again—Boers grouped around a fire, cooking. Thirty men, all horseless, he soon found out, for the same cause as he. The sickness had struck hard.

The Boers were camped in the berg, hiding from the English who were active in the valleys below. For a week after Boetie joined them it rained. Their only shelter was the overhang of some big rocks on the mountainside. Their only food was biltong. There was no dry fuel to cook a hot meal.

By the time the rain ended the British had gone and the Boers made for an abandoned farm that still afforded some shelter, and near it found the remains of a burned-out British convoy. No wagon was intact. But the Boers decided they could build a vehicle by using a wheel from one and an axle from another, and before long a queer kind of wagon took shape under their skilled farmers' hands.

Some oxen were obtained from a herd of slaughter stock the Boer commandos were holding in reserve, and everyone set to work making ox yokes, skeys, and strops. The yokes were simple logs of wood, five feet long, four inches thick, and roughly shaped to the oxen's necks. They were pierced in four places—one hole on either side of the neck for each ox of the pair. Through these holes went the skeys—pieces of hard wood notched to take the leather strops or straps that passed under the ox's throat and were adjusted in the notches according to the size of the animal. The yokes were attached by a ring in the center of each to the trek chain that was fastened to the end of the wagon pole to which the two wheel oxen were inspanned.

When everything was completed the oxen were put in and the Boers, relieved of their saddlery and gear, set off to look for De la Rey.

They crossed a recent battlefield that was littered with the rotting bodies of mules and horses, each body crowned with vultures so full that they could not rise into the air. Vultures always run flapping, a few yards, before they can raise themselves off the ground, but these ran, terrified, flapping along the ground like chickens when approached, unable to get up. There were new graves and the usual garbage of war—bandages, equipment, broken limbers, crates, torn books and papers.

They went on through empty country that had once been prosperous farmland, now a devastated, unpeopled waste of trampled fields and black ruins.

At last they found De la Rey in laager at Tafelkop with a thousand mounted men and two hundred wagons filled with refugees—old men, women, and children— battle flotsam washed up into this comparative security.

With De la Rey was the prophet Van Rensberg, a wild-eyed, bearded, fanatical dreamer of dreams who believed himself possessed of strange powers. Boetie joined the crowd listening to him as he described a vision that had just come to him.

"I saw," he said, "a red bull and a black bull fighting. They charged. They retreated. They charged again, coming together with a thunder of hoofs and battering of skulls till at last the red bull, gored to the heart, sank down dead."

Van Rensberg stood, with eyes blazing, his hand stretched up to heaven. "The red bull is the English bull, and it is written that he will be defeated." Then suddenly he shouted and pointed, "See who comes!"

A horseman was galloping toward the laager. He pulled his horse to its haunches in front of De la Rey, who had been with them listening to Van Rensberg's prophecy. De la Rey tore open the letter the rider had brought him.

"Men," he said, "it is from General Botha. The proud enemy is humbled—his head is bowed—the English have proposed a peace conference."

A great sigh went up from the assembled men. Perhaps it was over. Perhaps the red bull was really down.

Van Rensberg, stroking his long beard, glared into the distant hills. Once again he had been right.

Boetie still had no horse. There were a lot of dismounted men at the laager—the party he had come with and many more besides, who spent their time as cattle guards while those with horses rode out on commando. There was nothing they could do but wait for a horse herd that was being driven up from the Free State and pray that it was not captured by the British on the way. A herd of half-wild horses was not easy to conceal.

As they sat around the fire one misty night, their peace was broken by the explosion of a shell and a bunch of De la Rey's mounted men galloped into the camp out of the fog. "The British!" they shouted. Shells burst all around them as the Boers ran for their oxen and inspanned them. Each wagon drove off on its own, making what speed it could, fanning out all over the veld. The fog held and the rain came to the Boers' aid. Boetie's crowd ran with their lightly loaded wagon. It carried only their saddlery, blankets, and cook pots. They could hear the English shouting through the mist. There were shots and cries, but they saw no one and once among the hills of the broken country to the north they were safe enough. It had not rained here, so they built a fire and finished the meal they had been eating when surprised. It had been brought along in a leather bag and was now decanted and warmed up. They sang a hymn to thank God for their escape, for sending the fog and the rain, and then lay down and slept.

In all this time, these months since he had met Renata, Boetie had lived in two worlds; one of immediacy, of reality, and the other of dreams. The two alternated, canceling each other out. In action, in firing at the enemy, in galloping off, in sweating on foot over the veld carrying his saddle and bridle, Renata, peace, his home, his mother, all seemed quite unreal. They belonged to a world that he could no longer realize as fact. A world he had read of or that someone had told him about.

Then at other times, sitting by the fire, resting in the lee of a rock, looking out over the vast and peaceful

plains of Africa or at the mountains that fringed the
horizon with their stark, stony lace, it was the war that
seemed impossible. It was absurd that he should be here
all these miles from anywhere with just a rifle for company. He listed the horses he had had so far. Pasha, the
English horses, the Boer horses taken from the English,
the remounts brought from the farms, and how he had
lost them. There were the Groenplaas horses—General
and Witbooi. Then there had been Soldat, Windvoel,
Pronk, Bles, Blausel, and others he had never even named.
Shot, bolted, stampeded in the night, foundered and abandoned, dead of horse sickness. He thought of the men,
his companions, that had changed so much with the ebb
and flow of war. Where was Servas now that the President
was in Europe? Was Moolman alive? Had Bothma recovered from his head wound? How was his mother? He
thought of the Beyerses. How often he thought of them,
of her in particular. Then Renata. She was always there,
the memory of her on his lips and hands. He would look
at them in surprise. And the other girl—Louisa. How had
she succeeded in doing what she had done? Setting him
on fire in an instant. She was like someone in the Bible,
some woman, some girl. He could not remember her
name. Was it Jezebel? Salome? He could not look it up,
as all he had was his New Testament.

But in all this reality there was no reality. He always
seemed to be outside of himself, looking at this boy,
this young burgher Louis Petrus van der Berg, doing this
and that. Fighting, eating, riding over the veld, sleeping.
Looking at him and criticizing him. Saying that was not
so bad. That was a silly thing to do. Well he's out of
that now. It was very disconcerting to be at once the
actor and the critic. But he knew it was good, for in
this way he was able to escape much hardship. When
he suffered, when he was cold and hungry and afraid,
it was not he—not Boetie. It was that other young man
whose reactions he observed with such profound interest,
as if he could learn from his experiences.

He thought of Moolman again. He thought of the time
they had cut the English telegraph line with no tools,
with nothing but their guns.

"We'll cut the line," Moolman had said.

"How?" he had asked.

"With our rifles, boy."

They had driven some twenty shots into each telegraph pole, after that he had scrambled up, about halfway, to tie a riem around them and a few pulls, allowing the poles to sway back and forth, had brought them down with a splintering crash.

The wires were soon cut and rolled, ready to carry away. The china insulators were smashed with the butt plates of their rifles and the poles set alight in several places. The line would eventually be repaired, but it would not be easy.

Then at last the horses came, a troop of three hundred unbroken mares. They were drawn for and picked by lot. Boetie drew No. 56, that is to say, he had the fifty-sixth choice, and the best were gone by then, or, not necessarily the best, merely the ones that looked the best. Always a good judge of horseflesh, Boetie now regarded himself as an expert, and picked a little short-coupled blue-roan mare. Roans and buckskins he regarded as the best and toughest horses. As Moolman had said, you never saw a bad roan.

All around him men were breaking their ponies, mounting them and being thrown by them before they were finally mastered. Kicking and squealing, bucking and rearing. But Boetie would have none of it. He tied up one of his mare's legs and spent a whole day handling her. He gave her no water till she would drink from a bucket. He rubbed her face with a sack tied to a stick till she no longer savaged it. He put his saddle on her and tightened the girths a little at a time, twenty times at least. Then he lay over her back and finally, her head tied close to the head of a tame horse, he mounted her. After a pig-jump or two he had no further trouble. He called her Star, partly because she had a small white star on her forehead, and partly because, as he was breaking her, a double-tailed meteor appeared in the sky whose streamers looked like a V, and the prophet Van Rensberg claimed it stood for *vrede*, meaning peace, though peace seemed no nearer and the meeting of Kitchener and Botha had borne no fruit.

For a month Boetie's party was engaged in desultory actions covering enormous areas, striking and retreating, sometimes going thirty hours with hardly a halt, riding, and then leading their horses to rest them. Changing horses, stopping only to eat and to allow the offsaddled horses to roll. Nothing rested a horse more than a roll in some sandy ground or in the ashes of an old fire.

Now, after an especially long trek, Boetie could feel Star failing. She faltered in her walk and stumbled. He dismounted to lead her, and then to his astonishment he saw she had begun to foal. As he watched her barrel began to heave and the white horn of her foal's hoofs started to protrude from between her thighs. He had had no idea she was in foal. She had shown no signs of it. The work she had done and the poor food had prevented her from making an udder. The foal was weak, but with a little help from him she got rid of it, and lay gasping on her side. Boetie did not know what to do. He was too near the English for comfort. But a horse was a horse. Without a horse he was certain to be captured. So he waited, stroking the mare's nose and pulling her ears gently, talking to her, and telling her what a brave girl she was. At last she raised her head, stood on her fore-legs, cocked her ears, and struggled up. The foal was dead. She sniffed it and paid it no more attention. Boetie put on her saddle again with slacked girths and led her on after the commando. The cold was bitter. Clouds of dust were being driven before a biting wind. Just before dark he caught up with five men, friends who were worried about him and had waited to see if he would catch up with them. They even had a spare horse.

CHAPTER 51

THE FINGER OF GOD

THE PRISONER roll call was at six in the evening. First there was the bugle call. Then the men collected on the red hard-baked parade ground. Not tidily, not fallen in, because the prisoners were Boers—farmers, free burghers —who had been captured as they fought for liberty.

Then came the young officer and the fat sergeant. To

the officer, the prisoners were rebels, an undisciplined lot who couldn't even form fours. He was Authority. He stood by the sergeant, who called the roll. The sergeant was the Voice. The Voice did not speak till the officer said, "Call the roll, Sergeant." Then he began. There were no A's, so he began with B.

"Basson!" he shouted.

A tall slouched man said, "*Ja.*"

The sergeant went on: "Brink, Byers, De Jongh, Duminy . . ."

The men said, "*Ja, ja . . .*"

Once they had answered they ceased to be there. Their bodies were there, but their attention—their minds and hearts—wandered. There was no need for more attention. They could go back to their dreams of their wives and children, of their homes and cattle, their dogs, their dead friends, the horses they had lost in war.

Moolman heard his name called. "Van Niekerk!"

"*Ja,*" he said. In his mind he smiled. Tomorrow, when they called, he would not be there. His plans were made. Tomorrow, when the roll was called, Hans Meyer would answer in his place.

He had it all figured out. There was a weak place in the wire. He looked at the sun. When it was high in the heavens and burning hot, he would slip through. The other prisoners would stage a fight in the far corner of the camp. In this heat no one paid much attention to things—not when the sun was so hot that the sentries burned their hands on their rifle barrels. These rooineks could not stand the heat. Of course he might be shot. But it was not likely. Anyway, in war there was always that chance; he refused to think of it. The next thing was a horse. That was planned too. For a month, ever since he had been taken, he had watched. He had missed nothing.

All morning Moolman waited. He had the hunter's ability to wait. He watched the sun crossing the burned immensity of the washed-out pale blue sky. He watched vultures circling above the camp. At midday he lined up to draw his rations with the others. He ate them calmly. It was nearly time now. He watched the sentries standing sleepily; he waited for the raised voices of the quarrel to start. He was still watching the vultures when it began.

He heard Du Toit shouting. He saw him hit Piet Swart.
He saw Piet fall with Du Toit on top of him. He saw
the others run up. The sentries, still lethargic, strolled toward the trouble.

The time had come. Moving quickly, he reached the
wire. It took him only a moment to cut the few remaining strands with the cutters he had stolen and creep
through. He was out. Now for the plan. The mistake
most people made was to try to get away too fast. Moving
slowly he drifted toward the quartermaster's store. This
was a big marquee. Another moment and he was inside.
Half an hour later he was curled up in the nest he had
made in a pile of crates. The worst was over.

If, as he hoped, his escape was not discovered until
the following morning, they'd figure he was clear away
and start after him. They wouldn't begin to look until
they were ten or twenty miles away from camp.

During the night he made a foray, collecting food from
the opened crates and stores on the shelves. He took
bully beef, condensed milk, and some herrings in tomato
sauce. Then he outfitted himself with a nice new British
uniform. It made him laugh to himself as he did it. Me,
Dirk Moolman a rooinek, he thought. But he could do it.
He could play the part. As soon as he had been captured,
he had borrowed shaving things and had taken off his
beard. The mustache he had left, and he spent much of
his time twisting it, twirling it and greasing it into points
till the ends stood out like a British sergeant major's.

From the very first he had studied their drill, watching
them and copying them. He knew how to salute. He
knew how to stand at attention, to stand at ease, to salute
mounted by turning his head smartly and dropping his
hand. His fellow prisoners thought he was mad when he
marched around the square straightening his shoulders
and saluting every NCO and officer he saw. *Ja*, mad, but
in a very sane way, he thought now. How to pass among
the British, that had been the question. Why, like a Britisher—then he would be invisible.

The morning roll call went off smoothly. So his absence had not been noticed. Next morning, though, when
they called the roll again and counted, they discovered
he was gone. He heard the bugles blowing, orders shouted,
men mounting and riding out. Let them look, he thought,

and went to sleep again very comfortably with his head on his old Boer clothes. He stayed hidden three more days. By now they would have given him up. He'd even heard the quartermaster say so as he sat in the store doing his paper work: "Got away, that's what he did."

This was all he needed. As soon as it was dark he crept out of the tent and walked smartly toward the horse lines. He even knew the horse he wanted—the colonel's little bay stallion. It was a Boer horse that had been captured and could live off the veld. He had a large buff O.H.M.S. envelope in his hand. He'd taken it from the quartermaster's office in the front of the store. He walked straight up to the sentry on the horse lines as if he was bringing a written order.

The sentry grounded his rifle to take the paper, and as he took it Moolman's hand closed on his throat. In a second he was gagged; in three minutes he was bound hand and foot and dragged into the forage. Moolman took a bridle from a hook, clapped a saddle onto the bay, led him out, and mounted. With the big envelope conspicuously held, he rode slowly out of the camp in the direction of headquarters, ten miles away. There was no one about except a sentry on outpost duty, who, seeing a cavalryman ride by in the moonlight, thought no more of it—an orderly taking a message, he thought, and not in any great hurry, either.

Once clear, Moolman began to canter, turning his horse northward. "*Ja*, my friend," he said, "you are a Boer horse again. A free horse, with less food but all Africa in which to *loop*, to run. Space instead of food." The stallion laid back his ears, flicking them to listen. He seemed glad to hear the Taal again.

Moolman laughed. To be free, to be riding over the veld again, to be riding toward the mountains. Once in the Waterberg, he was safe unless his own people shot him, thinking he was a British trooper.

He rode past gutted farmhouses. Their lifeless windows stared out of broken walls like the eye sockets in a dead man's skull. The work of the English, all of it, the cattle and horses taken, the houses burned, the women and children sent to camps to be secure against the restless Kaffirs. That was the story the British told. But till they had been turned out of their homes, till the Kaffirs had seen they could act with impunity, they had been in no danger. Boer women were unused to confinement behind wire. It had been done with kindness, they said, for their own security, as if one could burn a man's house and take his cattle kindly, as if one could abduct his family with gentleness.

He knew they had done it to break the heart of resistance, to remove these points of rest and succor for the tired Boers. It was war. *Ja,* it was war, but it was hard, and many women and children had died. Still, one of these ruined houses would give him shelter. He could hide there and rest, and graze his horse, knee-hobbled, in the night.

He figured he had ridden about sixty miles when he found a place he liked the look of, a burned-out house with a fine view in all directions. Here he could see who was coming and, if he had to run, could get a good start.

He dismounted and watered his horse at a little dam below a spring. Then he offsaddled and let the horse roll. When the horse had done, he picked up his saddle and led the animal through the front door of the ruin. Inside he found a fallen rafter and put it across the doorframe. "There, my boy," he said. "Now you'll live in a house like a man. Tonight you will graze on the veld, and tomorrow we'll be in the mountains."

He patted the horse's neck and went to explore the house, which was larger than it had seemed from a distance. The horse was in the *voorkamer*—the front hall. There was a doorway to a room on the left and one to the right. They would have been bedrooms. The one on the left had no door, and he went in. It held nothing but some charred remains of furniture and black, rotting, fallen thatch. The right-hand room had a door that fitted badly. He kicked it open and was astonished to see a woman lying on the floor with a child sitting up beside her—a little girl that was all eyes. The woman under the blankets propped herself up on her elbow.

"So, you are back. What do you want now? There is nothing more to take here and little left to burn. *Ja,*" she said savagely, "you can take us. But you will not get far with us. Leave us, leave us to die in our home place. Leave us so that our people, when they come back, will find our bones. Our man is dead," she said. "How will we stay alive without him?"

Moolman fell back. Then it came to him: she thought he was a British soldier. "Bring in the others," she said, "bring them all in to watch a Boer woman die."

"*Nee*," he said, "*nee, mevrou*, I am not English. I am a Boer who has escaped from the British. I am Dirk Moolman."

"Moolman," she said. "A Boer?"

"Yes. I have escaped. But you are starving," he said.

"*Ja*, we are starving. Bring us water. We can walk no longer. Before God," she said, "walk, we cannot even stand." She pointed to a tin cup. He took it to the spring. This was something. This was a devil of a thing. He looked at the mountains, a blue haze twenty miles to the north. No, not twenty. Now it was five hundred miles. He went back and gave water to the child. The woman was too weak even to hold the cup. "Tell me," he said.

"I will tell you," she said. "It was a month ago that they came. I saw them coming. They had assagais in their hands."

"Assagais?"

"*Ja*," she said, "long horse assagais."

"Ah," he said, "lances."

"Yes," she said, "their points glittered in the sun. I knew what they would do, so I took my child and some biltong and rusks, some blankets, and hid in the bush. They took my cattle and the horses. In three hours it was done. In three hours, *meneer*, the work of a lifetime went up in flames. Then we came back. My man had made the walls and ceiling on this room very thick. It was built to hold against the Kaffirs in the old days. I was his second wife. This was the first room of the house. Then, when things were more quiet, he built the other rooms."

"Yes," Moolman said.

"For a while we lived on what I had saved. There were a few chickens that escaped. I killed and ate the cats. Two pretty cats, *meneer*. I killed them when they came home, with a club. The door was burned, so I took one from the fowl *hock* and hung it here. Then we lived on water. *Meneer*, for days we have had nothing but water."

"I have no food," Moolman said. "I was traveling light.

They thought I was an orderly with a message, and so I carried nothing."

"You may have no food," she said, "but there is game here. There are buck."

"Can I catch buck with my hands?" he asked.

"There is a rifle," she said, "and ammunition hidden. I can shoot, but not buck. No, I cannot hunt. Fight, yes—I have fought Kaffirs with my man. A Kaffir comes toward you, but a buck runs away. I tried, *meneer*, but it was no good, so I saved the ammunition. It was in my heart that the Lord would send someone. A rooinek that I could kill, or a Boer who would save us. Had you come three days ago, before I grew so weak, *meneer*, you would be dead. I would have shot you dead as you stood in the door."

"Then it is the will of the Lord," Moolman said, "that I did not escape sooner. It would have been a pity if I had been killed. Where is the rifle?" he asked.

"Here beside me."

The woman rolled back the blankets.

He reached down for the gun. She pushed a bandoleer toward him.

"Clothes," he said. "I suppose there are no clothes."

"There are clothes. My man's clothes are hidden in a box in a cave in the *kloof*. You see," she said, "I wanted to make it clear that there was no man here, that I was alone. But then when they came, I was afraid. It is his Sunday suit."

"Now I can burn this uniform," Moolman said. "If I am caught dressed like this, and armed, they will shoot me."

"*Ja*," she said.

"It will give me much pleasure to burn it, but not the shirt and the boots."

"No," she said.

"I am going now," he said. "I shall come back with meat."

"The Lord protect you," she said.

He found the cave in the *kloof*. He found the box, changed, and shaved with the razor he found wrapped up in a piece of greasy paper. It made him laugh to think of himself clean-shaven and in her man's Sunday suit. It was a rusty black long-tailed coat, and there were also a top hat bound with crepe and black trousers that were very loose about the belly. He slung the bandolier around his shoulder. Dirk Moolman had vanished again or would have as soon as he burned the uniform.

Now for the meat. Less than a mile away, he saw a small herd of springbok. They were grazing quietly. Moving carefully, he got within three hundreds yard of them. Sitting down, resting his elbows on his knees, he took careful aim and fired. He brought a nice buck down. It did not take long to dress the meat. Now at least they had food. But they must not have too much, starving as they were. He made broth and fed them a few spoonfuls at a time. He kept the fire going and fed them every couple of hours.

Next day they were both stronger. The little girl, Sannie, was on her feet again, and her mother could sit up. His plight began to worry her. "You must go," she said. "We can manage now."

"How can I go on?" he said. "You have food only for two days. No, I will stay and hunt for you until you can travel. Then you will ride my horse with the child and I will get you into the mountains."

"It will take time," the woman said.

"It will take time," he said. "But we have time. In all the world, time and air and water are the only things that cost nothing. They are the gift of God."

"You are the gift of God, *meneer*," she said.

Melvina Brink was her name. She had gray eyes, blond hair, and was not more than twenty-five. The child resembled her. She was a tiny copy, in miniature, of her mother.

In a week he had them both up. He shot buck and picked wild spinach from the abandoned lands. He trapped small birds for variety and was satisfied with his patients' progress. In a few days they would be off. Once in the mountains, they would find other people. Women and children and old men living among the rocks like baboons, but free—freedom was what counted.

He went into the room where Melvina was cooking. She was well enough to do that now. The child was playing beside her. "Well," he said, "another day or so and I think we can be off."

"How long will it take us, do you think?"

"Two days," he said. "We should be able to do fifteen miles a day."

"And you?" she asked. "You will walk?"

"I will walk beside you and the child."

"You are a good man," she said. Then she said, "My man is dead."

"But you said when I came—"

"I said that because I did not wish to believe he was dead. Those were lies. *Ja,*" she said, "he was killed at Modder River. A fine man, he was, a brave man. That is why I wanted to stay. I could have managed, but now—"

"We will find people," he said vaguely.

She suddenly seemed beautiful to him. She had always seemed beautiful, with her big gray eyes and blond hair, but he had put the thought away from him till she had told him her husband was dead. A hunter had had to be free, to be able to move swiftly and to take great risks. Ivory hunting was no child's game. Besides, he had thought it was all over, that only memories remained for him, that no woman would ever look at a man like him. But now? Anyway, it was too soon to think of such things, yet the thought was in his mind. And he had grown to love the child. Besides, what could they do in the world alone?

He brought wood for the fire, and as he put it down the little girl ran in. "Men are coming. Men on horses!" she cried. Moolman went to the door. There were men, a detachment of British cavalry. They were so near that he could hear the rattle and clash of their equipment. He adjusted his top hat, smoothed down his tail coat, and went out to meet them.

A young officer, on a smart bay mare, rode forward. Very politely Moolman took off his hat, put his hand on his stomach, and bowed. "Sir," he said in English, "I never thought to welcome one of your race, but the times change, and I, being a man of perception, change with the times. In the house, in what is left of the house, after the improvements effected by your cavalry, lie a sick woman and a child. They need food. Bread, tea, and sugar. Perhaps you can spare her some?" He had seen this man before.

"You talk English well," the officer complimented him.

"Yes," Moolman said, "it was my good fortune to be well educated. Yes, *meneer*, I am a very lucky man." He thought of his escape and the fact that Melvina had been too sick to shoot him.

"I am going into the house," the officer said. "Corporal Brown, come with me. Bring two men." The corporal came with two troopers. They carried carbines in their hands.

"Enter," Moolman said. "We can offer you little hospitality, partly because you are enemies, but mostly because, as enemies, you have destroyed all this poor woman's possessions. But we have water—very fine, clear water with no trace of *brak*."

The officer said nothing.

Melvina met them, holding her child by the hand.

"The English are back again, *mevrou*," Moolman said.

"So I see. What do they want?"

"What does she say?" the officer said.

"She says, 'What do you want?'"

"We saw smoke," the officer said.

"Smoke to the British must be like honey to the bee," Moolman said.

"This area is supposed to be cleared."

"Yes, indeed. That is one word. Devastated is another."

The officer looked at the springbok hanging from a nail in the wall. He went up to it. "Shot," he said.

"Someone shot it," Moolman said. "I was lucky to find it before the *aasvoëls*."

"Yes," the officer said. "Someone shot it with that Mauser." He looked at the rifle Melvina was trying to hide. Then he looked at Moolman. "I've seen you before somewhere," he said. "Your eyes." He stared at him, looked him up and down. "Five seven," he went on, "slim, dark eyes, talks English well, mustache—but that could be quickly shaved. That's the description. By God, you're Van Niekerk!" He began to laugh. "Corporal Brown, arrest this man!

"You are the man who escaped! And to think it was only a fortnight ago I saw you in the prison camp."

"What discernment, *meneer!*"

"You escaped in a British uniform."

"Did I? I wonder where it is? If I did, I mean."

"If we find it, I'll shoot you," the young officer said. He was very fierce now, angry.

"Yes," Moolman said, "that is the rule of war."

The officer then said, "But why are you here? You have a horse—the one you stole. You should have been clear away."

"I stole no horse. I took back a Boer horse that the British had stolen. But as you say I should have been away, only unfortunately, or perhaps fortunately, when I got here I found this woman and her child on the point of death. I have been hunting for them. By tomorrow we should have been gone." He looked at the Waterberg again. How far the mountains had receded in the last hour. Not fifty miles now, not five hundred, five thousand at least. Distance had turned into time, into years—was lost.

"Is this true?" the officer asked.

"It is true."

"Corporal, call De Beer."

De Beer came. He was a Cape Boer, one of those who had gone with the English, a loyal man or a traitor, according to the point of view. "De Beer, question this woman," the officer said.

Melvina told her story.

"Is it true?" the officer asked.

"I think it is true. The stories tally, and she speaks no English," De Beer said.

"Van Niekerk," the officer said, "I do not like this business; many of us don't. We are soldiers. We do not like burning farms, deporting women and children, and stealing stock."

"It is possible that there are good Englishmen," Moolman said.

The officer ignored his remark. Sannie came and stood beside Moolman, clutching his leg in her arms.

"Come outside," the officer said.

Outside the officer said, "I suppose if I let you go you won't give me your word not to fight against us again?"

"No," Moolman said. Sannie had followed them out. He stroked her hair, fondling it the way a man fondles a dog's ears, or a horse's, pulling them gently.

"If this is found out I'll be court-martialed," the officer said.

"I understand."

"Very well. I cannot let you go, but you might manage to escape with the woman and the child. If you could steal a second horse, it would not be too difficult."

"I could do that."

"And if some rations were left out, you could steal them, too."

"Meneer," Moolman said, "I am an expert thief."

"Tonight," the officer said, "I will stable my horse in the house with yours and sleep here myself. I am very tired and shall sleep soundly. The men will camp by the kraal."

"It is a good plan, *meneer*. Can I go and tell the woman?"

He found her cooking some food the soldiers had given her. "Well," she said, "this is the end."

"No, Melvina, the beginning. Tonight we shall escape. It is arranged. I shall have horses."

"How?"

"The officer is going to let us escape."

"Why?"

"Why? Because he is a good young man and sees in this the finger of God. He is sick of destruction and perhaps wants to make up for some of the harm they have done."

"And then?" she asked. "We?"

He said, "One day we will come back here and I will help you rebuild what has been destroyed."

It was too soon to say more, to tell her of his old love and his dead sons. It was too soon to say that God had sent him to them, to replace what he had lost so long ago. So he said, "Are you willing, Melvina?"

"Ja, Dirk," she said. "In this I too see the finger of God, and who am I turn away when He points?"

"I will settle you safely," Moolman said, "and then come back to find my friends and finish up the war."

PART SEVEN

THE TRAITORS

> *"And Judas Iscariot which also betrayed Him . . ."*
>
> MARK 3:19

[*South Africa—January to December 1901—Summer*]

CHAPTER 52

THE WIFE OF JUDAS

THE TIDE had now definitely turned against the Boers. "Any fool," Jan Bothma said, "could see that."

"Ja," his wife said, "it turns when the cowards come home, pretending to be heroes. Return to fill their bellies with good food cooked by their women and fill their women's bellies with their coward's seed. Coward! Coward!" she screamed at him. "You have dared to do this to me! Me, who took you when you came home sick and bandaged only to find later that you were just nicked in the ear. Earmarked like a hog. I bore you one son while you were away"—she pointed to the cradle where little Flip lay sleeping—"and now I am full again but not proud of it. Ashamed of my belly, ashamed of my lust, of a love that is dead, of having taken a man with no more guts than a Kaffir cur, a lion that barks like a jackal, a vulture that tries to fly like an eagle.

"Don't come near me," she said, speaking softly as she raised a pan of boiling fat from the stove. "Don't try to touch me. From now on you sleep by yourself, cook for yourself, mend for yourself. You have no wife, Jan Bothma, no woman. And do not think you can overcome me, force me, beat me. A man must rest and if you touch me I shall kill you as you sleep, with a knife, blind you with hot water in your face, lame you. I could lame you now with boiling fat poured over your filthy feet!"

His son, standing by his mother, took on where she left off.

"Nor have you a son," Frikkie said. "Behold a fatherless boy. When they ask, 'Where is your father?' I shall say he is dead. Not in the war, oh no. Nothing honorable like that. He suddenly became a ghost, invisible. He is no longer to be seen."

"Stop!" Bothma cried. "You do not understand. But you will see. Before God you will see. We shall be rich. Masters, not bywoners any more. If you will just give me time."

But they had no time to give him. They drove him out, his wife with a pan of boiling fat, his son with his own rifle in his hand.

So be it, then. They had chosen. He would do what had long been in his mind. Saddling his horse, he rode off. To hell with them. To hell with all Boers, the proud fools who did not know they were beaten and still remained in the field, fighting this Goliath of empire as if David could do the trick again.

David! He spat over his horse's neck. Life was a matter of money, and he knew where money was. Idle money, buried like the talents in the Bible story. Every time he passed the big house he looked at the window where he had stood and watched it buried. Gold. Rich, yellow, smooth—he felt it in his hands, sovereigns running like water through his fingers. When he had gold his family would sing a different tune. They'd dance to his piping, to the jingle of sovereigns, the loveliest music in the world.

Since he had nowhere to come back to, he rode slowly, savoring the power of his knowledge, spending the money he had not yet got. A wagon, a fine span of oxen, a breeding herd, cows, bulls, some horses and sheep, a plow, tools—axes, hoes, bush picks, spades—for the Kaffirs he would employ.

What did he care about who ruled the country? All he wanted was a farm of his own and the peace that would create a stable market for his produce.

It was hot with the full heat of summer. Christmas was over.

It was Christmas that had brought all this trouble on. Jacoba had turned on him like a snake, asking him how he dared sit guzzling when the burghers in the field were all but starving. *Ja*, that was when it had begun. How extraordinary it was to have known so little about this woman, who had been almost a child when he had married her, and to find that for years he had been nourishing a viper in his bosom. It had come as a shock. He had foreseen trouble for some time but had hoped to

postpone it till he felt better, and had completely recovered from his frightful wound. Nick indeed! Did she
not understand the terrible psychological effect of such
a wound—the knowledge that death had passed so close?
The feel of the blood running over him, hot at first,
almost burning him, and then cold. Ice cold it had seemed.
The fear. Certainly he had been afraid. Everyone was
afraid of violent death. An ear, after all, was only a
fraction of an inch from the head.

Well, there was no further dilemma. He would not
have to tell her that he was sick of working like a Kaffir
for a pittance and a share of the crops he grew. Sick of
the danger of being picked up by a British patrol and
being accused of still participating in the war. He was
going to join the National Scouts, to sell his services—
those of a brave and accomplished soldier, to the English
for the sum of five shillings a day—a hundred fifty
shillings a month—seven pounds ten. More than he had
ever made farming, and certainly better than fighting for
the Boers for nothing at all, risking his neck, and finding
all his own food but meat. In a way the National Scouts
were doing the Boers a service by helping to bring the war
to an end. If one thought of Africa as a whole, in terms of
prosperity, instead of in this parochial, patriotic fashion,
no greater service could be paid to the country. Moreover,
the British were bound to reward such loyal service when
the war was over with a gratuity of cash or a gift of land.
Reward them anyway with something for the risks they
had run.

But there was some serious danger, too. Boers, when
they caught a Scout, shot him out of hand. Just put him
up against a wall and shot him dead. So a man who took
such risks could hardly be called a coward.

A "hands-upper," she had called him. Well, her insults
had driven him further than that, driven him into the
British forces, turned him into a Scout, into becoming
what they called a "Judas Boer."

Two hours after riding into town Bothma was uniformed and equipped by the British, of whose language
he knew very little beyond "yes" and "no," though he
understood it pretty well. But he had money jingling in
his pocket, good silver half crowns, a week's pay in advance, a Lee-Enfield in his hand, and five golden sover-

eigns for his horse. It belonged to the Van der Bergs at Groenplaas, but he wasn't going to mention that. After all, what were they but rebels now that he had taken an oath of allegiance to the Queen?

The formation of a corps of the National Scouts, a corps of traitors, the Boers called them, had been Lord Kitchener's idea. To hire men to fight their brothers was a policy he had employed with much success in the Sudan and elsewhere. It worked well. These men knew the habits and tactics of the enemy, since they were their own. It also saved British lives and money, money perhaps being more important than lives to Kitchener of Khartoum.

As a rule men who became Scouts went through several phases of degeneration. First they surrendered. Then they joined the British Army as mercenaries. Many thought that by surrendering they would help to bring the war to an end. They were men of peace, almost conscientious objectors, who had been mobilized half against their will and swept into the commandos by the commando law and the popular enthusiasm of the hour. Others were simply exhausted, tired of the war, utterly despondent and uncaring. They did not mind who won the war. All they wanted was for it to end.

But there were risks, too. The Boer secret service in Pretoria received lists from all over the country with the names of the Boers who had joined the Scouts, and if they were caught by the commandos they were executed and their fate publicized. But even with this deterrent, thousands of burghers had joined and were of enormous help to the British with their specialized knowledge of the country and the countrymen that they betrayed.

And it was with a detachment of Australian Frontier Horse, the A.F.H., or Cocky Boys, as they were called because they all wore the yellow crest of a white cockatoo in the pugarees of their slouch hats, that Bothma, in his new khaki uniform, well primed with drink, made friends. These were men of his own kidney—tough, rough farmers from Down Under, who feared neither man, God, nor Kitchener.

CHAPTER 53

GREEN NO MORE

JACOBA BOTHMA walked slowly to the big house. She had
come here as a girl, as Jan Bothma's bride. She had lived
here ever since, the wife of a bywoner, a share-cropping
foreman, happily enough. Loving her husband, bearing his
children and raising them, cooking, keeping house, at-
tending to the little kitchen garden, the orchard, and her
poultry.

She walked slowly because no one hurries to disclose
his shame. She stopped to watch a peacock courting, apparently enchanted with his own appearance, his great
bronze tail with its green eyes spread in a tremendous
fan. The little feather blobs on the top of his crest vibrated
as he rattled his stiff brown pinions along the ground of
the parade ground he had tramped quite flat and hard
as he swept up and down it, waiting for some coy female to arrive.

Jacoba had looked at the peacocks for years, but had
never really seen them before.

Still vaguely puzzled at the difference between looking
and seeing, thinking of peafowl, of anything rather than
what was really on her mind, she reached the house at
last and found Catalina van der Berg watering the plants
that stood in pots and tins on the stoep—ferns, ele-
phant-ears, climbing begonias, geraniums, lilies. Catalina
put down the can to greet her.

"Good morning, Jacoba," she said. "What a lovely day
it is." And it was—a clear, bright summer day, not yet
too hot. There was an almost sickly sweet perfume from
the orange and lemon trees near the house. There was
a hum of insects in the air—of bees, flies, and small
flying things. A beetle landed with a thud on the red
concrete between the women's feet and crawled into hiding behind the flowerpots.

Twisting her bare toes, wringing them like hands inside her rawhide shoes, Jacoba burst out, "It is my man.

He has gone! *Ja*, he has gone, *mevrou*, gone for good—the Judas bastard. Oh," she cried, "that it should come to this. That I should lie with a man for fifteen years, bear him children, and still not know his heart." Jacoba began to cry.

Catalina put her arms around her. She loved this girl. She had helped bring all her children into the world—the last one little Flip, only a few months ago.

"Tell me," she said, "tell me."

"Ja," Jacoba cried, pulling herself free, her eyes flashing, "he has sold us, my man has sold us. Betrayed us for thirty pieces of silver."

"Well," Catalina said, "we shall just have to get on without him."

"But me," Jacoba said, "alone with my children, fatherless?"

"As long as I live and my sons live you will not be alone. Come, my dear, we will drink coffee together."

"His wound, *mevrou*—it was nothing. Just a nick in the ear. Like one of the earmarks we put on a pig. He killed chickens—cut off their heads—to get fresh blood for his bandage. How is it possible, *mevrou*, for a man to do such things? A man!" She spat. "A eunuch to whom I have borne children. Is that not a miracle, *mevrou?*" She burst into hysterical laughter and ran off homeward, sobbing.

So Servas had been right about Bothma. First a coward, then a malingerer—and now a traitor, Catalina thought.

There had been no news of the boys for weeks. She opened the drawer that held their letters, the letters that had been in their hands and were now in hers. How near it made them seem, but how distant also. How tenuous the bonds of paper and pencil. A boy could write a letter and be dead before it reached his mother. He could be killed even as he wrote. Servas was still with the Government. He was safe for the present, anyway. But, she realized this now, and also the unfairness of it, that it was Boetie she had always loved the best. If he had changed the way Servas had, she did not know what she would do. There had been a strange glitter in Servas's eyes that she could not understand.

She sat looking at her sons' letters. It was some days since Jacoba had come with her news. Quiet, quite ordinary days. Outside on the bare, hard red earth between the house and the blue gums two shiny starlings, iridescent, metallic bronze and blue in the sunshine, their eyes blood-red, sought scraps and insects. On a low branch a jackie hangman, a black and white shrike, as predatory as an eagle, watched for tiny insect game to eat or impale, still living, on the sharp spikes of the thornbush that was his larder.

In the big trees hundreds of doves cooed, made love and nested, but the muted, unceasing sound was so much a part of Groenplaas that Catalina no longer heard them, though the sound had been one of her first impressions of the place. The doves. Never before had she heard so many doves. Their cooing had been like the sound of running water.

Bothma, having enlisted in the Scouts and having been outfitted, was given a week's leave to settle his affairs. His affairs had been mainly those of the bottle with his new friends, who had not been given leave but had taken it, needing, as Johnny Cook said, a bit of a blind after their long ride through this bloody country of bugger all.

In one of these bouts with the brandy bottle Bothma had said, "You like gold, Johnny?" Drink and company had improved his English.

"Who doesn't, mate? Gold is girls and booze. That's what gold is."

"I know where gold is."

"Let's go, then."

"For me half?"

"Half for you, chum, and here's my hand on it. But where is it? Far away, I'll bet. Lord, I've heard the story before. A strike clear out in the bloody bundu somewhere. No water. No food. No bloody nothing."

"Near," Bothma said. "Twenty miles."

"Christ!" Johnny said. "That's not so bloody bad, that isn't."

"It's golden sovereigns buried below a firestone."

"A stone?"

"*Ja,* a stone on which they make a fire in a house."

"A hearthstone."

"*Ja*, that's it, Johnny."

"What sort of house?"

"A farm. Only a woman. We chase her out, take it, and set it to the brand."

That would pay her out. The mean old bitch who thought herself so fine just because she owned a farm and he was only a bywoner. *Ja*, she would see who was baas now. And his wife would see.

Cook looked thoughtful. "Any men, mate? Men at the war, I mean? That'd give us the excuse."

"Two sons on commando."

"Then it's ours, chum. Christ! We'll burn the bloody place and take the brass. Come on, come on, boys. Let's go and you lead us there, matey."

"And half for me?"

"Yes, half for you, my boy. That's fair enough. A fair man, Johnny Cook. Fair's fair, that's what I always says, and the boys'll stick by my word."

It was a fine morning when they rode off from Pretoria, a dozen of them, led by Jan Bothma and Sergeant Cook, all in high fettle at having some sport and getting well paid for it. Sovereigns, bloody golden sovereigns, would soon be clinking in their pockets.

Frikkie Bothma was nearly fourteen when he rode off from Groenplaas to find a commando. There were younger boys than he with them, some actually fighting, but they had gone with their fathers and were among friends. Not alone, not desperate with dishonor, not ashamed to bear their names. Frikkie Bothma, the son of a National Scout. He had taken—stolen really—a good horse from the stables, a bay mare with black points. He had taken his father's rifle. It stuck up high over his shoulder where it was slung on its bandoleer.

He rode northeast, keeping the rising sun at about half right over his horse's head. From what he had heard this seemed the best direction. He did not think of riding into the first clump of trees he came to and waiting there for the night. He rode in full daylight— a big boy with a rifle on a good Boer horse cantering slowly over the veld.

That was the way it went. A peaceful morning, a boy

on a horse, the birds singing their songs in the thorn-bush. A red-breasted shrike, its breast crimson as blood, its wings barred with white, called. Actually it was a double call, for the male and female call together, crying their liquid note as one.

Frikkie heard the crack of a rifle and saw a spurt of dust rise just beyond his horse. He pulled up in astonishment. He was being shot at. It had never occurred to him that he would be shot at. Instead of pushing his mare, lifting her in a gallop, he turned in his saddle to stare. The second bullet got him in the throat and flung him from the saddle. He felt no pain. Only a blow. By the time he had raised his hand to his neck he was dead. He had not got far—only ten miles in distance, only two hours in time, only fourteen years in life.

The mare galloped off.

Two troopers came up at a trot and dismounted at the body.

"Christ, Bill!" one of them said. "We've shot a bloody kid."

"An' 'ow was we to know, chum?" his friend said. "Big, ain't 'e, an' 'e 'ad a gun." He picked it up. There were tears in his eyes. He was only a boy himself, not yet twenty. It was the first man he had killed. He did not know that there had to be a first one, that later you forgot about it. He felt faint. There was a lot of blood running out of the carotid artery. Red blood that was almost black, like those roses his mother had in Devon that smelled so sweet. Red, black, smooth as velvet, sweet in the evenings by the cottage door, with blackbirds singing. Black with yellow bills. Filled with blood too, like a man. Red like a rose.

"Hold my horse, Joe, I'm going to faint." He lay down not ten paces from the dead boy and looked as dead as he, his sunburned face as white as paper.

The red bush shrikes called as one again. They were building their untidy nest of rough grass in the thorns. They and their like had been here forever, for a thousand years and more, unchanged; those of today no different from those of the past, unrecognizable—in the same uniform of gay feathers, of scarlet breasts, and black backs. Singing the same liquid song. They had been here with the first men, the little yellow Bushmen, and the ape men before them. Quite unchanged, as if God, having made them perfect, just set them as bright commas to His creation.

Not in thoughts or in words, but in some other way the two Englishmen were affected by this, by all Africa, its vastness, its silence, its originality. For much of this land was as God had left it. It lay fresh from His hand.

They came from an ancient, cultivated land with sunken roads worn down by wheels, hoofs, and the marching feet of men. From flowery lanes where in the spring men made love to country maids fresh as buttercups, lying on the scented grass. A green, soft land of fat cattle, fair fields of waving wheat and oats, of plowlands, ruby in the setting sun. From Devon, the land of Drake, of seamen, of farmers, where dew dripped diamonds in the dawn and the rain was tender, soft, falling like a child's tears, interspersed with the laughter of the sun.

Not out long, this harsh, savage land was alien to them, inimical. Why not let the Boers have it? They seemed to love it, to understand its moods. This was no plump housewife who banged her pots upon the stove, who shook out her blankets, and set the cream to scald. This was a wild-woman land, armed with storm daggers, with bitter winds, dust storms—twisting red devils that climbed into the air as if the very earth wished to escape.

"We've got to get him back," Joe said.

"Aye." The fainting boy sat up.

"Cover him up," he said. "Roll him in a blanket." Joe was tougher than he, a bit older. Damn it! He couldn't even watch a pig being stuck.

The body was rolled in a saddle blanket fastened with their bandoleers. They tried to put it on a horse in front of the saddle, but he would have none of it. The smell of blood sent him up in a rear.

"We'll have to blindfold him," Joe said.

They tied a white-spotted blue bandanna around the horse's eyes, and still he would not stand.

"A twitch," Bill said.

They made a twitch with a lanyard, pulling out the horse's upper lip and twisting it tight.

"He'll stand now," Joe said. "You hold him and I'll get him up."

The body sagged like a sack over the horse's shoulders in front of the saddle.

"Hold him till I'm up," Joe said. "All right—let go."

The horse shook his head but played up no more. Bill mounted, carrying the dead boy's gun in his hand. They rode back at a walk, silent but for the sound of the horses' hoofs on the hard ground, the creak of their saddlery, and the metallic click of gear—curb chains, spur rowels, a spoon loose in a mess tin.

It was a week to a day since Jacoba had given Catalina the news of her husband's defection. But it might have been the same day. The two starlings still pecked about in front of the house. The black and white shrike still sat on his low branch. The doves still cooed. The insects hummed and the warm air of summer was still perfumed with eucalyptus and sweet orange blossom when the Colonials clattered into the yard. Bothma shouted to the boys, who were eating their midday scoff, to get oxen and inspan a wagon. They obeyed him, knowing him, and not knowing one uniform from another.

Only then, as they were yoking up the beasts, did Catalina appear. She had been in the orchard superintending the irrigation of the fruit trees.

What was going on? Who were these men? Why was a wagon being inspanned? At whose orders? Bothma, what was he doing here?

Bothma in the most hated uniform of all, that of the National Scouts. So Jacoba had been right, a traitor. She had not wanted to believe it, thinking it was just a furious woman's tale. A deserted woman's invention.

She walked up to his horse. Her horse, a Groenplaas horse.

"And what are you doing here, Judas?" she asked. "How dare you come back? And what is this scum?" She pointed to the Australians.

"Doing here, old woman?" Bothma said. "Doing here, you ask? My duty. That is what I am doing. We've come to take you away, to put you where you belong in a camp, and burn this rebellious house to the ground."

"You . . . you . . ." Catalina said. "You ungrateful dog! A cur who bites the hand that fed it. Jacoba spoke truly well when she called you Judas. A Boer man. Man—pah!" she spat. "An ox, a gelding, a *hamel,* a cut thing, *mak,* tame, able only to make war on women."

"I do my duty," Bothma said, half ashamed. Then, recovering, he shouted, "I am a loyal subject of the Queen. Get into that wagon, woman. *Ja,* just as you are. Nothing is to be taken."

"Take her, boys," Johnny ordered. A man dismounted and went toward her.

As he raised his hands to her Wagter attacked. He had stood watching, puzzled by what was going on. All these strangers in the yard. But Bothma was there. He knew Bothma. His teeth ripped through the man's hand as he slashed and let go to spring up at his face.

"Christ!" the man yelled. "Kill him!" Someone fired a shot.

Cook shouted, "Don't shoot, you bloody fool, you'll hit someone."

The man was down on his face with Wagter standing over him when a redheaded man whose slouch hat had fallen off clubbed him with the butt of his rifle.

Catalina stood still, quite unmoved. So this was tragedy. This was drama. My brave dog is dead. I am a prisoner. She was interested in the point where drama was frozen into tragedy. In tragedy there was no action. Tragedy should be preceded by drama, but there had been no time. Given time, given warning, she would have fought or fled. There was still a rifle hidden in the house. But to resist now would only result in an undignified struggle in which nothing would be gained and much lost.

One of the men still had his hand on her arm. She shook him off and walked over to the wagon—my wagon, she thought—where the oxen stood quietly chewing the cud.

Now as she went toward it she found herself listening to the cooing of the doves. A few minutes ago she had not heard them.

It was still unbelievable. It was a dream, a nightmare. A quarter of an hour ago she had been irrigating the orchard. Her shoes were still wet with mud. A film of red dust had settled over them. Her mind seized on the dust, the dust of Africa. What had Boetie's girl said he

said about the dirt on his little Bible. His New Testament
... My shoes ...

The men had tied their horses to the wagon rails and
were going into the house. Bothma was leading them.

"Don't forget our share," the two who were guarding
her shouted. "We want some of the brass too." They
laughed.

"You'll get it," the sergeant said. "Fair's fair. Half for
the Dutchman and half for us. That's the ticket."

The gold. So that was it. Not only a traitor, an ingrate,
but a thief. He knew. How had he known? Then it came
back to her. Bothma had returned wounded from the
war, God save the mark, the night she and Klaas
had buried it. He must have seen a glimmer of light at
the window and come to investigate. But how much had
he seen? What would they find? Would Klaas's plan
with his two kraals work out? Three men came out with
Bothma, went to the tool shed, and came back with picks,
shovels, and a crowbar, the very one old Klaas had used.

Catalina stood leaning against the wagon. The sun
climbed higher and higher into the sky. It got much
hotter. There was no shade here. She felt exhausted but
would not sit down.

Half an hour must have passed before she came out
of her dreams of her own life, of her husband's, of her
daughter and her sons.

Shouts and curses brought her back from the security
of the past into the present. The men came out sweating,
dirty, stained with the yellow subsoil and red earth,
dragging the empty ironbound chest with them. The gold
was safe in Klaas's second kraal. But suppose no one
lived to tell the boys. Klaas was an old man, and she had
little hope of withstanding this transplantation. She
thought of her sitting room, of her carpets heaped with
earth.

"It's gone!" Bothma shouted. "You old bitch—it's
gone!"

"What's gone, Judas?"

"The gold."

"What gold?"

"Don't lie, woman. I saw you bury it, with that old
Kaffir. By God," he said, "we'll find him. We'll burn the
soles off his stinking feet if he won't tell us."

"So you are a Peeping Tom, too. Tell me, Judas, do you always look in at windows? Do you strive to see young maids undress?"

"Tell me! Tell me!" he shouted, raising his hand to strike her, only to find it held. He turned. It was Jacoba. She had come to the house to bring Catalina the news that Frikkie had disappeared since yesterday. But she had not had time. Now she shouted it at her husband. "And your son has gone to fight in your place—a baby to replace a coward."

So this was the explanation of the mare's galloping back to Groenplaas. Catalina had heard her clatter into the yard. Her mare . . . one of her saddles. She had soothed her and put her up herself. It was only now that Jacoba told her that Frikkie had gone that she guessed the truth. The secret would be one more burden.

So Frikkie Bothma was dead, murdered by his father's hand.

Bothma had had no idea that Jacoba was so strong. A man could not have held him more firmly.

"Animal!" she screamed. "Is nothing low enough for you? By God, you are lower than a snake."

"Who's this?" Johnny asked.

"I am his wife. His *vrou,* who never thought to live to see such a thing as this."

The broken chest, patched and stained with yellow soil, lay on its side between the house and the wagon.

"Well, Dutchy," Johnny said, "it was a good try. But someone has been there before us."

"I do not believe it," Bothma said. "It's impossible. There is a trick, *ja,* we have been tricked, *verneuked.*" Where was that bloody Kaffir. "Klaas! Klaas!" he shouted. "Come here before I kill you." Spittle was forming on his lips. It dripped onto his beard. A fortune had slipped through his fingers. There would be no second chance.

Catalina turned to the sergeant and said in English, pointing to the broken chest. "I don't know where this servant of ours heard about the treasure, but he was twenty years out. In the first War of Independence, before he rode off to war, my husband buried five hundred golden pounds in that box. When he came back he dug it up but buried the box with two sovereigns in it again as a joke. We could afford that then." Putting in the two gold pieces before the box was covered had been a good idea. They had been enough to send the men mad and cloud their judgment.

"So you lied, Dutchy," Cook said, and knocked him down.

"I lie?" Bothma said. "Why should I lie?"

"Because he hates us," Catalina said. "He made use of you for his revenge." She laughed. "He has made fools of you."

Cook knocked Bothma down again as his wife looked on unmoved.

"Pack up, boys," Johnny shouted. "Get the bloody women into the wagon. Round up the stock and set the bloody house alight, and we're off," he said. "We've been had. Just a bloody plant."

"My children," Jacoba sobbed, "my children."

"Kids?" Johnny said. "Round 'em up too. Round up the bloody lot and load 'em."

"No," Bothma said, "not my wife and children. They are my children." He turned to Johnny. "Mine," he said.

"Yours or not, they go. That's the orders. You brought us 'ere, didn't you? You brought us on this bloody wild-goose chase because you hate your boss, with a cock-and-bull story about gold. Gold. Two bloody quid! And you'll pay for it, by Christ! Orders is orders. When a farm is burned, take in the women and kids. Can't leave 'em to starve, can we?"

Jacoba, who had got the drift of it, turned on her husband again. "So," she said, "your country is not enough. Your mistress is not enough. You must also betray your wife and children, the fruit of your loins. *Ja*," she screamed, you must drive us all out into the wilderness."

"No, no, Jacoba," Bothma cried. "I did not mean it. I only wanted to make us rich. I wanted to buy a farm of our own."

"*Ja*," Jacoba said, "rich. Richly dead, ruined, with nothing left but our hands, poor whites, poorer than Kaffirs. That is what we will be."

"Pack 'em up," Johnny Cook shouted. "Pack the bloody lot up and round up the rest. There's a couple of houses over there in the trees." He pointed to the chimneys of the bywoners' cottages.

Bothma's other children were there. Catalina wondered

how he felt, his eyes blacked, his nose bloody, his family denying him. He had thought he would be rich and now he had lost everything. His job, his wife, his children, his home and everything in it. Well, perhaps there was some justice after all. But how was it justice? Who would suffer most—he or those he had betrayed?

She saw Martha Prinsloo coming with the children. She was leading Japie by the hand and carrying Jacoba's baby son. The Australians were herding them, almost riding them down, as if they were stock.

"Come," she said, when they got to the wagon, "come, my children. We are all in this together. Let us put our trust in God and pray." She knelt down and they knelt about her. She opened her mouth and began to sing, " 'Oh God our help in ages past . . .' " The women's voices joined hers and the thin piping of the children joined the stream of sound.

Cook shouted, "Take your bloody hats off!" to the astonished troopers.

When they had finished the hymn Catalina said, "Now we will go. Bothma," she ordered, "bring the box so that we may climb up." Martha with Japie in her arms, Sara, Anna, then Jacoba cradling little Flip. Hendrik, Susanna, Catalina, her namesake. Her responsibility, her flock.

Bothma got the broken chest and put it at the back of the wagon, furious at himself for fetching and carrying like a Kaffir. He, Jan Bothma, a master, an independent man. But he wasn't. That had been the dream and she had tricked him and shamed him in front of these damn Colonials. They had struck him. She had turned his friends against him. But such was her authority, such was habit that he had obeyed her. Well, now he was quit of everything. Free to make a new start. He would not make the same mistakes again. Now he would be all out for himself.

As the wagon rolled away Catalina saw the smoke begin to rise from her home. first in a thin wisp, narrow as a ribbon, then in billows. This was the end of the green place, the end of life for her and her people. Klaas had got away. Frikkie was a prisoner or dead, but she would not mention the returning horse to Jacoba.

The horns, the great buffalo horns over the front door on the stoep, were burning. The symbols had gone and,

without symbols, without ties leading from the present
to the past, there could be no future, no life for her. If
only there were some way to tell the boys about the
hidden gold. Some safe way. But she could tell no one.
She could not write. There was only Klaas. And how
long could he live, homeless and unfed?

A kind of fury overtook Johnny Cook. That bastard of
a Dutchman, pulling their legs to get some kind of revenge and getting his own wife and kids into the soup.

The women had upset him. They were not too old,
any of them, and two of the girls were old enough, or
nearly. But by God that was too big a risk. Burn, loot,
but no rape. Not because they didn't think of it or want
to. Christ, how could they help it? But it was a hanging
matter. They'd been out here too long. There had been
no real fighting, just skirmishes, sandwiched in between
great chunks of boredom, and discomfort. Women. Christ,
he was used to going without women at Towoomba, and
there were always the Abos—blacks—like there were here,
till they could get to town. But no whites. It was
months since they'd been near one. The Boer girls just
laughed at them and threw their money in their faces.
Rancor seeped through him, a bitter fury at nothing in
particular. He was not even very disappointed about not
getting the money. They had plenty of money. What they
needed was something to spend it on. If they hadn't had
orders to destroy these farms he'd have pinched a jumbuck
or two and left it at that. But the orders were to kill
everything they could not drive off and burn the houses
down. Christ! They were homesteads. And because he
hated doing it he made a good job of it. God damn them!
He'd show them what a Cocky Boy could do.

Turning his horse away from the wagonload of weeping women and children, he rode back to see how the
place was burning.

Burning bright, sharp, clear and crackling. A real bon-
fire. How the kids back home would have laughed and
danced around it. Kids anywhere, he thought. The rooftree fell and the side walls collapsed inward as he watched,
sending showers of sparks upward like a firecracker, fire-
works, golden rain. If it had not been summer, if the land
had been dry, the veld would have caught. As it was the
gum trees exploded into flame. They did that at home

sometimes. Spontaneous combustion or a spark was enough to explode the volatile oil of eucalyptus that they exuded. And by God these were fine gums and beef-woods—casuarinas, Australian pines as fine as any he had seen since he left home. These trees always brought his heart into his throat, the sight of those smooth white peeling trunks, the smell of them. Bloody well homesick, that's what I am, he thought.

He gave a laugh. That's what I came back for, he thought. Not to see the farm burn but to look at the bloody gums, to sit on me horse and smell 'em all on my bloody lonesome.

CHAPTER 54

A FLOCK OF SHEEP

SIR CHARLES EATON wondered how he had given the orders. It was easy enough to say, "You've got to do it, John . . . It's your turn for duty—you've been away a long time . . ."

Turnbull would do the job he was ordered to do. But the colonel was responsible. But not entirely. He was only part of the chain—just one of the links. Kitchener was responsible. But it was John who would have to do it. The others, himself included, had just used words. Written orders or given them.

He'd said, "You know the language. You may be able to soften it somehow. Explain things to them a bit, John." It had certainly sounded a little lame even to his own ears.

Good God, Turnbull thought, how does one explain burning a house to its owners, explain why one drives off the stock or kills it? How exactly did one do this?

"What do I explain, sir?" he asked. "I mean, how would you explain it?"

"How the hell do I know? You saw the memo. We've got to be more active. Anyway, it's not all burning. Take a troop with you. You won't need more, and you may get some action."

"Will you turn a blind eye to it if I ride out light?" Turnbull said. "Nothing more can happen to me now so I'd like to try out our theory."

"You mean leave a lot of stuff in the lines?"

"Yes, sir. One bandoleer will be enough. Nothing around the horse's necks, no spare shoes, no blankets, just over-coats. We might have a chance of catching a Boer or two if we did that, poor as the horses are."

"Do what you like, John. Here's the map. The Warmel farm's about there somewhere." He made a stab at the linen-backed paper with his forefinger. "Take a wide sweep around and see if you can pick anyone up, then come back and burn the place down."

"Yes, sir." Turnbull paused, then said, "You know, sir, I think these are the strangest orders ever given to this regiment," and went out.

He's not far wrong, either, the colonel thought as he watched John Turnbull stride away. Very queer orders for a regiment of regular cavalry.

When they had been riding half a day, Turnbull saw a farmhouse and went up to it very circumspectly, taking only an orderly with him and leaving his men dismounted to cover his advance.

It was a small, grass-thatched house, whitewashed, with a double door that was closed, flanked on either side by a small window. Bending low under the overhanging eaves, he knocked.

The top half of the door was opened by a fresh-faced Boer girl of about eighteen.

"*Ja?*" she said, and went on to ask in Afrikaans what he wanted, and ended by saying it was no good trying to tell her as she would not be able to understand him.

Turnbull answered her in her own language.

Taken aback and angry, she said, "What are you? A Scout?"

"No, young lady," he said, "I am English but I learned your language when I was hunting in the Transvaal some years ago, and I should like some information."

"Me give you information? Me, a Boer girl?"

"Why not?" he said. "All I want to know is where the Warmel *plek* is—their place."

"What do you want to know for?"

"We are going to burn it down."

"*Magtig,*" the girl said. Then she said, "Wait, I will get some coffee and then I will tell you. I will explain the way to get there."

She was away quite a while. Turnbull smiled.

When she came back with the coffee tray she seemed to have regained her composure. Now she said, "I will tell you all I can because I do not want my father's house burned too." She smiled at him almost gaily and filled his cup. She was going to flirt with him, going to hold him as long as she could.

He was more than ready to play her game.

"You are a *mooi meisie,*" he said, "a pretty girl."

"So they said," she said.

"Said? Who said?"

"The young men said, but there is no one left to say it now, *meneer,* and we pretty Boer maids languish uncourted."

He laughed. "And you blame us for it?"

"Who else?" Her blue eyes were bright, her lips smiling.

Turnbull took her hand. She was unresisting. He pulled her to him and kissed her, not on the mouth as she had expected, but gently on the top of her head.

"You are a good brave girl."

"Brave?"

"Yes. What is your name?"

"Annetta. Annetta Fourie."

"Well, Annetta, do you think I should have told you where I was going if I had not known what you would do?"

"What would I do? What did I do?"

"You took a long time making coffee that is not fresh, and was cooking on the back of the stove. In that time you got a messenger off to the Warmels to say the rooineks were on their way. Then you decided to flirt with me, to let me make a little love to you, perhaps even a lot of love, to give them time to inspan and get away. That is why you are a brave girl, Annetta."

Her jaw dropped, her eyes became as round as blue marbles.

"You knew?" she said.

"Yes, I knew."

"Then why did you . . . ?"

"Why did I let you? Annetta, that is why I came when I saw your house. The Warmels are your neighbors not five miles away. I knew you would send a message to warn them."

"But you might have been shot if my father had been here." She clapped her hand to her mouth. "If anyone had been here. If this had been the house of an enemy instead of a neutral place you might have been shot as you rode up."

"My men were covering me and I had to take the chance."

"But why, *meneer?* Why?"

"Because, young lady, being forced to burn farms is bad enough, but to have to take in women and children is worse. I thought if they were given a couple of hours' start they could get away with most of their stock."

"Two hours you will give them, *meneer?*"

"Perhaps more," Turnbull said. "It is easy to get lost on the veld."

She came to him, putting up her face to be kissed, like a child.

"Thank you," she said. "It was well done, an act of charity for which God will reward you."

"I still have to burn the farm."

"*Ja,*" she said.

"But I may not do a very good job. I am new to such work."

"Your men," Annetta said, "would they not like some food? They can kill a sheep. Though it would take me some time to cook it."

"Since I do not know where I am or even if I am going in the right direction, what does it matter?"

He went to the door, blew his whistle, and, raising his right arm, rested the hand on the top of his helmet. This was the signal to "close in." A moment later his men were at the farmhouse, watering their horses.

"Kill a sheep," he said. "Just one. The girl here will cook it. These people are neutrals—out of the war."

By this time Boer girls were galloping over the veld from farm to farm with the news that the British were going to burn everything in this area, which had, until

now, been immune. When the news was urgent, girls—
the daughters and sisters of the fighting burghers—carried it, if there were any available, as they were considered more reliable messengers than Kaffirs.

The girls rode sideways on a man's saddle with the left
stirrup fairly short. The right leg was crooked over the
pummel with the right stirrup leather let out, coming over
the leg above the knee. The skirt was wrapped around the
left foot, which was jammed tightly into the stirrup iron.

South African ponies usually went dead straight over
the veld, so the girls had little difficulty in keeping their
seats, for they were good riders and used to it. A few
of the richer farmers' daughters had sidesaddles, but most
did not.

Turnbull's troop camped at the Fouries' that night and
reached the Warmel farm soon after dawn. Turnbull reconnoitered it carefully. They knew he was coming and might
have laid an ambush to catch him.

But there was nothing. No one. The front door swung
open on its hinges. There was no sign of life, not a cat,
not a dog, not a chicken, not a sheep or a pig. Only some
white pigeons remained, walking along the top of the red-
painted corrugated-iron roof.

Inside the house was neat, though some of the cup-
boards were open and in one of the bedrooms a drawer
was not fully closed. The Warmels had been well off,
rich. The house was very comfortable in a middle-class
Victorian way. A sofa and chairs covered with purple
plush, a harmonium with music still on the stand flanked
by half-burned candles. The two last songs they had
played were "Where Is My Wandering Boy Tonight?" in
English and "Tafelbaai," a patriotic Boer ditty. There
were two china cats flanking the black marble clock that
was still ticking on the mantelpiece. There were some
bright lithographs on the walls, pictures of the Great Trek
and the burning of Dingaan's kraal among them. On the
floor there was a carpet, some skins—a kudu and four
springbok—sewn together. There were lace curtains at the
windows and heavier ones of purple plush hanging from
wooden rings. On a shelf there were some books in English and High Dutch.

A home. What the Boers called a *woon plek,* a living place, and he had to set it on fire.

Turnbull's sergeant was standing beside him. "Nice place, sir. 'Omelike, ain't it?"

Hawley was right. It was homelike. It could have been a prosperous English farmer's home, except for the skins on the floor, the Dutch books on the shelf, and the pictures.

"Feel like setting it alight, Hawley?" Turnbull asked.

"No, sir. Not even if you tell me to."

"Then I'll have to do it," Turnbull said, and, making up his mind to get it over, struck a wax vesta match—it burned like a tiny candle—and lit one of the curtains. It flared for a moment and then went out, leaving a big brown-edged hole in the lace. God damn it! How did one do it? How did one become an arsonist when one had been trained from childhood to be careful, never allowed to play with matches or fire? How did one undo this disciplined inhibition?

Hawley, who had left the room, came back with a can of kerosene. "How about some of this, sir?"

"I don't know." Turnbull was utterly distracted. "I don't know."

"We've got to do it, sir," Hawley said. "Shall I pour some out on the carpet?"

"Think we can half do it, Hawley?" Turnbull said. "You know . . . not burn it to the ground?"

"I don't know, sir. Everything's so bloody dry out here. Excuse me, sir. Once she takes she'll go."

"I'm afraid so. All right, come on, pour it."

Hawley poured out the oil. The smell of kerosene filled the room.

"Now, sir," Hawley said, "chuck a match down, sir. Strike it, sir, and chuck it." He had taken command. This officer whom he admired, whose men all loved him, was like a bloody child sometimes. No. Not like a child . . . nothing a kid liked better than playing with matches.

The match struck on the box—a long, thin, rasping sound that seemed to them both much louder than it really was. Turnbull held it downward so that the wax dripped and it burned up in a quite big flame. He held it till it burned his fingers, then he dropped it on the darkened patch of carpet—the great wick that would light this enormous lamp. The last fire that would burn between these walls. As he let it go Turnbull thought of the first one, when the house was newly built, of the first cold night when someone had said, "Let's have a fire," and the family that was now in flight had stood around it holding out their hands to its warmth.

The fire ran over the carpet like a living thing, like a carpet itself—a carpet with a think red pile of flame. The material smoldered, the smoke billowed up. The linoleum under the carpet took fire, curling up, crinkling like the skin of an animal.

"Come on, sir," Hawley said, "don't just stand there." Like a bloody child, he was, standing there gaping at what he'd done. Stay there and be burned to a bloody crisp himself if I wasn't 'ere to get him out. He took Turnbull by the arm.

Sergeant Hawley was a man of fifty. He had known John Turnbull since he joined the regiment as a cornet. If he'd had more education he would have been a squadron sergeant major. But he was happy enough as he was, assured of his position, one of the vertebra that formed the backbone of the army, one of the old long-service NCOs who took the yokels and the dregs of England and turned them into men.

Outside, standing by their horses, the troops, mostly green young soldiers, gaped openmouthed as the smoke poured out of the house. First smoke, then flames burst out of the door and windows, licking upward like scarlet tongues.

The rafters caught. The roof iron curled and buckled. The rooftree collapsed and the red-hot sheets fell inward as the flames leaped past them, yellow, red, scarlet, and then disappeared into incandescence beneath a thick cloak of black-brown smoke. Curious how brown some of the smoke was, whirling upward, caught in the draft of its own making, assuming voluptuous, rolling cloud shapes before it became lost in the high sky.

Shocked, maddened by the sight of what he had done, Turnbull rushed into the lean-to attached to the house. It seemed to him that he had to save something. That he had to do something. The lean-to turned out to be a kind of scullery. There were some crockery and a few pots and pans in the sink. As he seized a copper frying pan the gable fell, almost crushing him. Hawley and the two troopers who had followed him only just got him clear in time, but still his jacket had caught fire and his arm was burned.

"You bloody young fool!" Hawley shouted. "Whatcher want ter do? Commit suicide?"

"I got it," Turnbull said. He still held the copper pan. He had saved something. But how much he had lost. Part of his soul, part of the regiment—of the 2nd Hussars— had gone up in the flames.

They got him onto his horse.

"Mount, you bastards!" Hawley shouted. "Trot . . . canter." He had to get them away. To get his officer away —riding at his stirrup to see that he did not fall.

At a hard canter they left the burning farm. The stink of smoke was still in their nostrils.

Then the flank guards let out a yell, a fox hunter's view halloo. In a hidden cup between two little hills, a tiny dell of a valley, they had come across a flock of sheep. The native herder ran when he saw the cavalry on the skyline. The sheep, terrified at the cantering horses, bolted, bleating. The troops, before anyone could stop them, were into them, their sabers out, hacking at them, leaning over their chargers' necks to give them the point.

"Jesus!" Hawley said. "Jesus!" The 2nd charging sheep, butchering them from their horses. That was what happened when troops were ordered to burn houses, homes. It brought out the devil in them, the brigand. His boys, so orderly, so neat on parade, so disciplined, had broken.

"Halt . . . ! Stop! Come back! What the hell . . . !" His shouts, his orders meant nothing to them. He could not stop them. They could not even hear him.

Turnbull had broken down completely and was in tears. Only the trumpeter, Turnbull, and his orderly were still with Hawley. The rest of the troop, when they saw the bloody sabers flashing in the sun, heard the men's shouts and the agonized bleats of the dying sheep, had joined the fun, bursting past him with a thunder of hoofs. The NCOs had gone with them, trying to ride them off and stop them.

Christ, if he couldn't stop the men he'd stop the horses.

"Sound stables!" Hawley shouted.

The trumpeter put the trumpet to his lips. The call,

cool and clear, rang out over the veld, and the chargers, thinking they were going to be fed, pulled up at last; some of them were almost a mile away.

Back over the Warmel place the white pigeons were circling around the smoke, their wings flashing silver white as they caught the sun when they turned. They had no place to rest now but the ground, and would soon be killed.

CHAPTER 55

LONG LIVE THE KING

BY THE TIME Turnbull got back to camp he had pulled himself together somewhat. Hawley had fixed his arm in a sling and accompanied him when he reported to the colonel.

"Back, John?" the colonel said. "What's happened to your arm? Were you hit?"

"A burn, sir. That's what comes of playing with fire."

"So you did the job all right?"

"Yes, sir. I'll send in a report in the morning."

"Good. You'd better go to your quarters and have a rest. I'll send the vet to have a look at you." In the 2nd they always called the doctor the vet and the vet the doctor. It was one of those regimental jokes that are always so inexplicable to outsiders.

In his tent Turnbull fell onto the camp bed. His total world had collapsed. All he had lived for. His squadron had lost their heads and gone mad with an inconceivable blood lust. This might be forgiven, though he doubted it, with the young soldiers who were little more than recruits, but what about the longer-service men? The six or so that were supposed to have stiffened the troop—men who had several years' service? How had they forgotten who and what they were? My God, he thought, they went mad. Mad as foxhounds in full wild cry.

If he closed his eyes he could see them still. The NCOs who had gone after them had tried to stop them, leaning over to get hold of the horses' bridles, shouting orders, riding them off. If they could have stopped half a dozen it might have checked the lot. Three corporals had set their spurs into their horses, got into the lead, and swung them sideways to form a sort of wall, but the troopers had gone to either side of them, nearly riding them down. The men had been demoralized, but so had he in a way, rushing into a burning house like a lunatic.

It was evident that for all men, educated or not, there was a conditioned framework of behavior, a pattern. Everything within the frame, the picture, as it were, was not perfect, but it was not too bad. There were precedents for everything. But when the frame was smashed, the dam broken, the essential savage that lay hidden in every man was freed. Atavism was suddenly licensed instead of being repressed. Every baby was born a savage and had to be trained to fit into its own particular culture. Those were the frames. Each nation, each class, each age, each sex. But they had to be fixed; a man had to know whether he was acting within or without the law and custom.

It was the house that had done it; seeing it burn had sent them mad. If that could happen, anything could happen. Then these cavalry soldiers, with their newly sharpened sabers on their saddles, had seen their quarry. The first one might have been slashed as a kind of joke. They knew all the livestock had to be driven off or killed. But once they saw blood there had been no holding them. He still saw the bloody sabers flashing in the sun as they rose and fell. Still heard the bleating of the wounded sheep. What was he going to put in his report? Not this, certainly. And what was he going to tell Charles in private tomorrow?

The doctor came into the tent. "The old man said I'd better have a look at you."

He dressed the arm. He took his temperature, tested his heart.

"Nothing much wrong, old boy. The burn'll be well in a week. You just need a bit of rest. By the way, I heard some queer stories in the lines. Rumors about a cavalry charge. Light Brigade and all that . . ." He laughed. "Well, boys will be boys, I suppose," he said. "So don't let it bother you, John. They're getting nervous, high strung. It's the altitude partly," and left him. Burton Colt was a good chap and a good doctor. But a civilian could not understand what had happened.

The 2nd had run amok. There had been no real news from Elsie for months. So he'd been wrong there too. There was nothing left for a man to believe in. Nothing at all. Not the regiment. Not his men. Not Elsie. What would have happened if Hawley had not had "stables" blown? And where would he have been if Hawley had not pulled him out of the burning house? I was mad too. I had to save something. The men had to kill something. Two sides of the same penny.

He looked at his copper frying pan. What a return to camp! His men shamefaced, in bloodstained uniforms, their squadron commander with a copper frying pan in his hand. He remembered now that he'd still held it when he had reported to Charles. How had he managed to salute? No wonder he'd sent the vet to see him. No wonder.

Well, there was only one thing to do now. Have a bath, change, and tighten everything up. By God, he'd put the squadron through it now! Tighten everything up. He'd show them who was running the show. Jackson had let them get soft. He tried to pass the blame on to the man who had replaced him, but couldn't. It was the burning order that had done it. You couldn't expect soldiers to be hooligans one minute and a disciplined body of men the next. As for Elsie, he'd forget her, put her out of his head. He did not believe she was in Africa. There must be a thousand Elsie Smiths in the world, several thousand.

It was at this moment, as he sat naked in his green canvas bath, that the colonel came into his tent. "A parcel for you, John," he said. "I thought it might be important so I brought it over myself."

"Thanks, Charles," he said. Important? Nothing was important now. Charles had just taken this opportunity to have a look at him, but it was decent of him to come. He finished his bath, trying his best to keep his bandaged arm dry.

It was not till he was dressed, with the aid of his batman, that he even thought of the parcel. It lay on his rumpled bed. It looked like a shoe box. Wrapped in brown paper and tied with string. The stamps were Free State

Republic with a black surcharge of Orange River Colony. The address was printed.

Lighting a cigarette, he opened it, carelessly, wondering who in Africa could have sent him anything. Di perhaps. Though that seemed unlikely, and she was at the Cape. It was a shoe box. He took off the lid. It was full of letters. Letters from Elsie. Packet after packet tied with ribbon—the kind she threaded in her underclothes. When he saw her writing, the interior of the tent began to blur. He sat down. That this should come now, at this moment. The letters were all in sealed envelopes except the one on top. He picked it up.

"My darling John," he read, "you will be surprised to get this with these new stamps. Aren't they pretty? We were going to Durban in Natal but didn't. Natal is a pretty name. It means birth and has something to do with Jesus. I don't think He was ever here. But I am."

" 'I am,' " he said aloud. Good God, what was the girl doing there? He read on:

"I could not stand doing nothing in London and then they tried to cut me with a razor. They got Betty and I was afraid. Queenie saved my life. She bit the man in the neck and he died, but Vincent saw to it all except for the beautiful carpet in the hall. It was pale, you know, and though we washed it at once the blood won't quite come out. If you did not know it was blood you might think it was the dog, though that's silly because Queenie is ever so clean as you know. . . ."

Somebody had tried to disfigure her! And Queenie, the quietest dog in the world, had attacked a man and killed him. Betty, the girl who had warned Elsie of the plot to sell her, had apparently been dealt with by *them*. My God, he thought, and read on:

"So I joined Lady Finch-Haddley's field hospital with Millie, who can read now, and we're all here with Queenie, who's had lovely puppies. Their dad is a lovely Airedale that belongs to a general. Vincent is taking care of the house and everything so it will be all ready when you come home. . . ."

It went on and on about Lady F.-H., as she called her, the Irish wolfhound Gelert, the doctors, nurses, and other girls. In her usual way she had written a few pages every day.

"Last night," she wrote—they had been at sea then—"a captain in the Welsh Fusiliers proposed to me. Marriage, I mean. He is a very respectable man and I am sorry I cannot marry him if he wants it so much. But one captain is enough for a girl, though it was nice of him to ask me and it just shows how respectable I am now. When you write please write to Miss Elsie Smith, not Mrs. I have put away my wedding and engagement rings. I am sure you will like my engagement ring. Monsieur André, who knows about those things, said it was in very good taste and it was not too expensive. Emeralds and diamonds, three of each. It cost 100 pounds. Do you think that is too much? I hung it on the little china tree on my dressing table at No. 7. It looked so pretty there. I do miss the wedding ring though I bought that myself too, as I told you. It's real gold. Just a plain gold band. Monsieur André said I should get a real one instead of the rolled-gold one Celeste gave me, but I kept that too because it was my first ring of any kind. . . ."

The letters went on, pages and pages of news and love and how she had thought all the girls were pregnant when they were seasick and how awful it would have been but funny too.

". . . I did not tell you what I was going to do because you would have stopped me and I always do what you tell me, but I was too far away in England. In Africa, even if I do not see you, we shall be under the same moon and stars. At night, when you look up you can think of Elsie looking up at the same stars and thinking of you. There is a letter from Millie in with this. She wants to show you how well she writes. I taught her but you know this because you wrote about the blind leading the blind, which I don't quite understand because we both see quite well, but Millie being a country girl can see farther than me. . . . Please don't think I want to bother you out here or make you ashamed. It is just that I could not bear being in a different country and even under different stars, though I did not know that till the first mate showed them to me and told me their names. He showed me the Southern Cross, which is not a cross at all. But it is beautiful because it shines over you, too, for this is the Southern Hemisphere, that is to say, the bottom half of the world. . . .

"What can you think of me not writing for so long?
Except for the letters I sent to Vincent to send you. But
I did. I wrote every day. I just didn't post the letters,
and here they are. They will tell you all that I have done.
I saw you in Bloemfontein. I stood in the street and
watched you ride by."

So it had been she. The girl who had looked like Elsie
had been Elsie.

Miss Elsie . . . Elsie Smith . . . Good God! And he'd
been living for six weeks within a mile of Lady Finch-
Haddley's field hospital. Elsie here . . . Turnbull was
speechless. Elsie, his Elsie, had followed him to Africa.
He must write to her at once. When had she come? Why
had she not come to see him in Bloemfontein? He read
on:

"Knowing you were here at headquarters was awful
but I didn't want you to find out I was here. You might
have been angry and I did not want to make you ashamed"
—there it was again, always thinking of him—"but at
last I could wait no longer, so I asked Lady Finch-Haddley what I should do. I showed her all the letters I had
written. She said, 'Send them, you silly little bitch.' Sometimes she reminds me very much of you in the way she
talks. So here they are. I am very happy in Africa. I am
near you, even if I do not see you. We are under the
same stars and moon. Have you noticed how big it is?
Sometimes it makes me very sad. They say I am a good
nurse and I am happy with the boys. They are so good,
patient, and brave. But operations I do not like. I never
go to them any more. I don't like the blood and knives.
I don't like to see arms and legs like bits of chicken
thrown into a basket. But I have had some news of you
from the men. When you were at HQ we got a sick man
who had seen you. But write, please, John darling. I
can bear this silence no longer. Every your loving Elsie."

Each letter ended with half a page of crosses of various
sizes.

Elsie. How he had misjudged her. Following him out
here on her own. Working as a nurse and making such
a fine job of it that the troops knew her by name. Edu-
cating herself. These were not letters from the Elsie he
had known, except for their childish ending of crosses.

Millie's letter was very short, but she must have spent a lot of time over it. Each letter was separately and beautifully formed. She wrote:

Dear Master,
Miss Elsie has learnt me riting and is very good to me so having no Ma I can't leave her and she took Queenie and me with her wot is nice but hard to leave Mr. Vincent, and the others wot I loves too. Please sir do you not think I rites nice just the way Miss Elsie learnt me? Spelling and rithmetic comes next. Mr. Vincent learnt Miss Elsie rithmetic and she is going to learn me here and then I'll know everything.
  Hoping this ere finds you in the pink as it leaves me,
                                    Your respectful servant,
                                               Millie.

Just fancy them both being out here. He couldn't get over it.

The world was really collapsing around him. Nothing was staying put. How unfair he had been to her. No wonder her letters had been funny. Writing pages each day in her tent and then trying to think of something to send to Vincent so that he could send it on. And Vincent. She had told him to say nothing. He gulped his whiskey. His mind was going round and round. Queenie having lovely Airedale pups. The 2nd losing their heads, going mad. Elsie here. The horror of the farm going up. He thought of the wheeling pigeons, white flashes in the blue sky.

This was not war, not the shouting of the captains, but the sobs of distraught women watching their homes roll heavenward in clouds of stinking brownish smoke. Necessity. He could see the necessity of it. This was the nub of his distress. But was the war necessary? Were soldiers necessary? Had man improved at all over the centuries?

He picked up the white kitten. It purred and made bread with tiny pricking claws. What had happened to the little girl it had belonged to? To the noble old man who had cursed him?

This was not 1870. They were not Germans. They were British. He was a British cavalry officer, brought up in a tradition that made such behavior anathema.

He could not get the pictures of it out of his head,

or the smell of civilian smoke, of burning houses and goods, out of his nostrils. He walked over to the mess tent, where he found everyone in a fever of excitement. Victoria was dead. The Queen was dead, long live the King. A reign that had spanned history, bridging time for sixty-four years, was over. The woman who as a young queen had known Wellington, the Iron Duke, who had lived through most of the nineteenth century and as queen and empress had governed the greatest empire the world had ever seen—was dead.

The reign of King Edward VII had begun.

CHAPTER 56

A KANGAROO COURT

BOETIE now found himself back near Pretoria with a small commando of fifty men. He was riding to a flank alone, his coat collar turned up against the wind, when he saw a movement between two small ridges a mile away. Not a movement but a little low cloud of dust that meant movement. He swung his horse around and rode back to the main body to report. The Boers at once fanned out in a big arc, riding individually, a hundred yards apart, going slowly, partly to make no dust and partly to save their ponies. The dust might mean anything or nothing. There might be guns there, or a convoy, or it might just be a swirl of loose fine dirt caught in an updraft between the hills. When they reached the first ridge Boetie and another man climbed it to reconnoiter.

What they saw delighted them. Below them was a big herd of grazing oxen guarded by half a dozen National Scouts. This was a job they were often given when they joined up. All Boers were good cattlemen and it was some salve to the consciences of these renegades that they should be put on a job like this rather than have to fight their own brothers. Later they would become hardened, but at first it was a good way to break them in.

The two returned and reported to their elected corporal, Stoffel Labuschagne, an enormous, savage-looking man in his forties who was in reality as gentle as a child unless aroused.

What they told him aroused him. He rose in his stirrups, shaking his fist at the sky. "Cattle!" he shouted. "*Ja*, that is good—meat. But Scouts are better."

The plan he made was simple. He divided his men into three parties—two would go around out of sight and on either flank of the grazing herd, get behind them and drive them forward—cattle, Scouts, and all—toward the third lot of Boers, who would be waiting for them.

"Gallop them," Labuschagne said. "In the dust, the British will not know whether the cattle have been stolen or have stampeded. Nor are they likely to shell their own beasts. When the herd reaches here—this side of the *rankie*—we who have been waiting for them will close in from both sides and take the Scouts. A dozen men will drive the beasts on, the others will stay waiting for the British if they try and recover them."

Bothma, one of the cattle guards, was sitting hunched over his horse, thinking about his position, which was poor. Someone else had got the gold. But no one else could have got it. She had dug it up herself with that damn Kaffir and buried it somewhere else. But if they had done that why had the chest been broken open? And how could anyone dig up a woman's drawing room without her knowing, when she was living in the house? Next, with the big house gone, with the taking away of Catalina and his wife and children, he had lost both his job and his family. Also all his possessions, because, as they left, a couple of Australians had gone back to fire all the other dwellings and outbuildings.

Who would have thought of that? How could he have known those damn Colonials would not be satisfied with burning the big house and taking away the deceitful woman who was the cause of all his troubles? And then they had beaten him up as if it had all been his fault.

So things were in a bad way for him. Very bad. He was now completely dependent on the English. He had his five shillings—his two half crowns a day. He was fed, clothed, armed, and mounted. But that was the end of it unless he went out with the fighting forces and could do some looting on his own, steal some cattle, get someone to run them for him till it was over, and then with a land grant from the British start again. A least if he did that he would be his own master, an independent farmer—no longer a bywoner. But again he had his doubts. Was he clever enough to farm alone? How could he get another wife while his wife was still alive? A man couldn't farm by himself and she would never come back to him. Never. His son had repudiated him and ridden off, child as he was, to join some commando. And could he work without direction, without instructions? Bothma knew he had little initiative. He knew he was lazy. With Jacoba and the money the woman had stolen from him it would have been different. Jacoba was clever. She would have managed the money and made him work. She understood a farm as well as he did and had twice the drive. His only comforting thought was that he had done his best for his family, for his country. No man could do more. And if he had failed, well, better men than he had failed.

His dreams ended with the sound of a shot. The Scout sitting his horse, not fifty yards away, shouted, "I'm hit," and fell to the ground.

Galloping Boers approached from both sides. Turning his horse's tail to the herd, Bothma made for the rear. His horse staggered, gave a great leap as a bullet took it behind the shoulder, and fell, throwing him over its head. A minute later a burgher had him by the arms, ripped his rifle from his hand, pulled out the bolt, flung it into the long grass of the veld, and dropped the weapon at his feet.

"Mount my horse," he said, "and don't try to get away."

Once on the horse, his feet lashed beneath its barrel, the Boer mounted behind him, pushing him forward off the saddle onto the horse's withers. The other guards had been captured, tied onto their own horses. Holding their prisoners' reins in their hands, the Boers, with wild hoots and cries, drove the cattle north in a stampede of dust, horns, and tails.

It was a good haul—thirteen hundred head of slaughter oxen and five scouts. When they finally pulled up and Labuschagne and his men joined them, there had been no British pursuit, and they were all very pleased with themselves.

When he went to look at the prisoners Boetie got a shock. These men who stood shambling there were in principle already dead. Living corpses, men living the last few hours, or perhaps even minutes, of their lives. But he had not expected to see Bothma among them. Bothma, their bywoner, his old companion in battle, one of the original Groenplaas Kerels.

Labuschagne towered over the prisoners. He was cursing them.

"Dogs! British jackals! Traitors! Sons of Judas Iscariot! *Ja*," he shouted, "you had better pray, for tomorrow as the sun rises you will die. Because we are Christian men we will give you a night to make your peace with God. Then, like dogs, mad dogs, and dangerous dogs, we shall shoot you dead."

Boetie pretended not to see Bothma. Whether he was a Scout or not, he could not let him be shot if he could help it. Somehow he must contrive his escape.

The Boers put out cattle guards on the captured herd. The prisoners they herded into a small sheep kraal where in some ways, except that their hands were still tied with riems, they were better off than the Boers, as the walls gave them some shelter from the wind.

Labuschagne would allow no fires. He sent a few men forward to act as a picket whose sentries were posted still farther out. He was not going to be surprised if he could help it. It was dark when Boetie got into the sheep kraal, which was inadequately guarded, found Bothma, and cut him loose.

"What shall I do, Baasie?" Bothma said.

"Do, you bastard? How do I know? I only know that because once you were my man, once my comrade, I cannot see you shot without making some effort to save your miserable skin. What would my mother say if she found out I had done nothing for you? Weak, bad as you are, you were once our man."

"Thank you, thank you, *meneer*," Bothma said, almost sobbing. They had crept over the wall of the kraal. The other prisoners had said nothing. If Bothma escaped he might bring help. There was no point in saying anything. To create a disturbance might even precipitate matters.

That big devil who was running the show might decide to shoot them all at once.

"It's no good trying to run," Boetie said. "You would be seen and pursued. There is only one chance. You must hide."

"Hide where? Where is there to hide in the open veld?"

"Here," Boetie said. He pointed to the dark entrance of an aardvark—ant bear—hole. "Creep in, then, pray, and lie low till we have gone."

Bothma made to go.

"There is one thing more," Boetie said.

"*Ja?*"

"Take off that uniform."

"My uniform? But I shall be naked."

"Then be naked, or I give the alarm."

Bothma stripped.

"Now get in there!"

"*Magtig,*" Bothma said, "there may be snakes in there."

"Then by God they'll have good company. Get in and have done. I have finished with you."

Boetie left him and rejoined a group of Boers who were trying to sleep. Overcome by exhaustion, they fell asleep, then, awakened by the cold, they stamped about, beating their bodies with their arms till they were warm enough to snatch more sleep.

Lord, Bothma thought, what luck that he should be here, and what good fortune that that young pup did not know about Groenplaas, the house that had ceased to exist. Or his mother. The hole was very deep. The aardvark had worked hard. And what was more, it was warm underground, even naked. God had not forgotten him after all. Was it not written that the meek and humble should inherit the earth? And what could be more humble than a penniless, homeless bywoner driven by the exigencies of war into this pass? Driven to hiding naked as a newborn babe, like a wild beast, a jackal or a wolf, under the soil of his native land?

In the morning as the sun rose there was a tremendous row with Labuschagne roaring like a bull. "There were five prisoners. Now there are only four of these vermin." There was no sign of the fifth. Some men said there had only been four. They searched the veld with field glasses. None of the horses had been stolen. "All right, bring out the others. Bring out the Judas bastards," Labuschagne roared.

"Can you stand?" he cried, "and be shot like men, or will you lie down tied hand and foot to be shot like dogs? Stand them up, boys," he said, "and bandage their eyes."

The Boers stood the Scouts against the loose-packed stone wall of the sheep kraal, their eyes bandaged with their own filthy handkerchiefs.

"We have not been tried," one of them said in a quavering voice.

"Tried and condemned," Labuschagne said, "condemned by the uniform you wear. Am I right, boys? Shall they die?"

"*Ja! Ja!*" came the rejoinder. "Let them die . . . dogs . . . traitors." Already they were opening the bolts of their rifles. The sound of metal against metal was sharp as they closed them in the thin, cold air of morning. One of the prisoners was whimpering. He had a red bandanna over his eyes. The others were stoical enough.

"That's not a trial," the man who had protested said again. "This is no court."

"It is a court," Labuschagne said, "a kangaroo court, where all have agreed. Now," he said to his men, "five of you to each one." They sorted themselves out into groups of five.

"Ready?" Labuschagne said.

"*Ja*, we are ready."

"You will fire when I say fire. Having fired, you will reload and fire another shot each at the body as it lies on the ground. Ready?"

"*Ja!*"

"Fire!" he roared. The twenty shots rang out in a volley. The Scouts collapsed, their legs giving way under them as great patches of blood burst out over their khaki uniforms. Bits of stone from the wall and ricocheting bullets sang into the air. There was a sharp rattle of bolts, a skimming golden shower of empty ejected cartrige cases in the sunshine, then a second volley, more ragged than the first, another golden shower, and the Boers turned away from the mangled, bloody heaps that lay spread against the wall of the kraal.

Boetie moved off by himself to vomit. His belly was empty and he could only retch, but he gasped and retched and sweated. Now, he thought, I have done everything, seen everything. This was murder. Or was it justice?

He had saved Bothma. He was not likely to be caught now. The men were all saddling their horses. They wanted to get away from here as fast as they could, to forget it in the dust of the cattle they would drive back to Botha.

The men they had killed were not men. They were dogs, traitors, betrayers of their country and their brothers. But they were not quite sure, not absolutely sure, and never in their whole lives would they be certain about what they had done. They had created a nightmare that would haunt them till they died.

This was not a story any of them would be proud to tell. But Boetie had the full uniform of a National Scout, clean and new, rolled in a bit of canvas on his saddle. It was going to come in useful. One day, he thought, it will get me to my love.

CHAPTER 57

LEAVE

THERE was no doubt about Turnbull's condition. He was sick. He could not retain his food. He was running a temperature. He carried on his duties in a kind of stupor. Only Elsie's letters kept him going. The new ones he got each week now, and the old ones. He had numbered the envelopes and read them over and over again.

The colonel was at a loss. He told Turnbull to go on sick leave as a friend. He had refused. He ordered him to go sick. Turnbull had asked if there were any complaints about the way he carried out his duties. There were none.

But the man was dying on his feet. One more thing— a touch of dysentery or enteric—would kill him. Colonel Eaton thought of the girl who was supposed to have been asking about him. There might be something there.

He asked the adjutant if any men had come back from being hospitalized in Bloemfontein.

"There's Sergeant Barker, sir. He only came back last week."

"Send for him."

"Sergeant Barker," the colonel said, "I want to ask you something."

"Yes, sir."

"You're just back from Lady Finch-Haddley's field hospital?"

"Yes, sir."

"Did you ever run across a nurse called Smith? Nurse Elsie Smith?"

"Miss Elsie?" the man said.

"That's it. You did, eh?"

"Yes, sir."

"What impression, may I ask, did you form of her?"

"Wonderful girl, sir, Miss Elsie."

"Did you notice anything about her? I mean did she seem to favor the cavalry in general, and the Second in particular?"

"No, sir. No favorites."

"Let me put it another way, Sergeant. Did she evince any curiosity about the Second?"

"Evince, sir?" The sergeant did not know the word.

"How . . . Did she ask questions about us?"

"Oh yes, sir. She seemed to know Captain Turnbull, sir. She was worried about him."

"Thank you, Sergeant. That will be all."

The sergeant went out of the tent wondering what it was all about.

So that was the way the wind blew. The girl was interested in John Turnbull. That parcel had come from Bloemfontein. He wondered what was in it. I've got to get him away, the colonel thought. A month's leave and he'll be fine. But he would not take it.

The story of the charge had not been reported to him, but he knew about it. In the end he heard everything. That was what had done it. First the job, the horrible job of burning a farm, and then his boys going mad. It had shaken him too. My God, the 2nd Hussars berserk with a flock of sheep, amok, cutting them to pieces as they ran from under the horses' hoofs. For a man like

John, whose life was the regiment, this had proved a breaking point.

He called an orderly. "Give Captain Turnbull my compliments and say I wish to see him."

Ten minutes later Turnbull stood in front of his table.

"I sent for you, John," he said. "There are a couple of things I'd like to discuss with you. Sit down." He pointed to a canvas camp chair.

"Thank you, sir."

"Don't sir me now, John."

"All right, Charles."

"Now, first about this farm burning. We're going to do no more of it. Not in the Second. Let the others do it. Dragoons, Colonials, not us."

"But the orders. They are always specific."

"They are, John, but we aren't. Let's be frank about it. We're a crack cavalry regiment 'second to none,' as our motto says. But at what? At polo, cricket, on parade, in a charge. But with us, and now I'm talking of the officers, soldiering is a way of life. We love it, we love the regiment, the men, the horses, but we're no damn good. See what I mean? Stupid."

"What do you mean, Charles?"

"What I say. We aren't really professional like the Indian Army. We're all rich men. We don't have to stay in the army. So I've decided on something."

"What is it?"

"When we get orders to burn a farm we just aren't going to find it. To begin with, as you know, the maps are bad. Next, except for you and me and a few others none of the officers can really read a map. So they'll go out, find a burned farm—there are plenty about—and come back and report that someone had burned it before they got there. Or they'll just get lost on the veld. Let them say we're inefficient. I'd sooner have that than another battle with a flock of sheep that upsets the whole regiment."

"You found out?"

"Of course I found out."

"I am relieved, Charles. I should have told you about it but I couldn't. It's not the men's fault. They went mad, Charles. They couldn't stand it. They'll fight anything," he said, "at any odds. But they can't burn houses."

"I agree with you, John. And now, something else, and this time you're going to do what you're told. You'll report at Lady Finch-Haddley's field hospital. Here's a chit from me and the M.O."

"That's an order, sir?"

"It's an order. I'll see that your horses are taken care of. And take your man."

"Yes, sir." So it was out of his hands. Charles must know about Elsie, too. Well, it would be a relief.

The situation was beyond him now. She loved him. Whatever she was—or had been—she loved him, and he was lost without her. His world had come tumbling down around him. He hated war and soldiering now. The pleasure of it, the fun of it, had gone, lost in its brutality. It was not even very dangerous. And he had seen what it could do to men. Peacetime, the training of men to be proud and clean and comradely, was one thing. This was something else. The characters of the men ruined, their health undermined with disease, and the frightful wastage of horseflesh shocked him.

When he got to Bloemfontein, Turnbull did not report to Lady Finch-Haddley at once. He went to the Grand Hotel, took a couple of rooms for himself and his man, hired a horse, and rode over to the hospital to see if he could find Elsie.

He sent an orderly in to look for her. "Nurse Smith? Nurse Smith?" he heard someone say.

He heard her voice. Then he saw her and she saw him. She looked beautiful. Cool and dignified in her pale blue uniform, white apron, and cap. This was the girl he'd seen in Bloemfontein, the girl he had thought looked so like Elsie she must be her sister, if she'd had a sister. She didn't run into his arms as the old Elsie would have done. She walked toward him slowly.

"John," she said, "oh, John!"

"I had to come," he said. "Elsie, I want you to marry me. Now—at once."

"I can't," she said. "Not that. We'll go back when it's over, John, back to Number 7 with Vincent, Celeste, and Ellen."

"No, Elsie," Turnbull said, "you're not my little girl any more. Darling, you have grown up. You are a woman, a real person. We couldn't go back to that. One can never go back. We've changed, Elsie. We have both done so much, seen so much. I'm older too."

"I can't stay," Elsie said.

"I've got to see you. When do you get off? I'm at the hotel."

"This afternoon at two. But where shall we go? Oh, John, I want to see you alone."

"Marry me, Elsie."

"I can't. But I want to see you."

"Let's go out into the country," Turnbull said. "I know a place—if only you could ride."

"I can ride," Elsie said.

"Of course you can't. You're just being silly. You think you can just get on a horse and ride because you want to. It's not as easy as it looks."

"I can ride," Elsie said, angry now. "If I say something I mean it."

"How can you ride? Who taught you?"

"Vincent. So there!" She stuck her tongue out at him. "Get two horses," she said. "I'll be there by two."

"They'll not have sidesaddles."

"I can't ride on a sidesaddle."

"What!" Turnbull was aghast.

"I ride like a man," Elsie said. "Like a bloody hussar." And with a swish of starch and linen she left him staring after her.

Now he'd go and report to the old girl, old Lady What-have-you.

When Lady Finch-Haddley saw Elsie's captain she was not surprised at the girl's infatuation, and God knew the girl had had enough experience of men one way or another, particularly the other, to be something of a judge.

She held out her hand. "Captain Turnbull?" she said.

"I'm John Turnbull. I have come to report to you." He gave her his colonel's letter, the M.O.'s report, and a chit from divisional headquarters.

Lady Finch-Haddley glanced at them.

"Come as a patient, eh?" she said. "You don't look very ill to me. I think you just need a rest and a change, John Turnbull. I think you'd do better as an outpatient. Get a room at the Grand."

"I'm there now."

"Oh, you are, are you?" she said. "Well, stay there. And I know someone else who needs some rest and a change too. I'll give her every afternoon off for a week. But no nonsense, Turnbull. Not at the Grand. Can't have any scandals about my girls. You've seen her of course?"

"Yes," he said. "I—" Before he could go on someone flung herself into his arms.

"Oh, Master, Master," Millie sobbed, "you've come at last. She's bin a-pining. I saw 'er," she said, "looking so 'appy. So I said, ' 'E's 'ere!' 'Yes,' says she, so I come to find you." Tears were running down her cheeks. She suddenly realized where she was. In the office tent.

She bobbed a curtsy to Lady Finch-Haddley and was about to go when Queenie, her nose to the ground, followed by six extraordinary-looking puppies, burst in, yelping with pleasure, and jumped up at Turnbull's legs.

"I must say you seem popular," Lady Finch-Haddley said as Gelert, her wolfhound, got up from the far end of the tent and came over to thrust his big head under Turnbull's hand.

The puppies milled about his feet. Queenie sat staring up at him whimpering softly. Millie was sobbing with happiness. The Master was back. Now there was some-one to take care of them all in this horrible country. It was not that she didn't love Miss Elsie. She did. But she had more confidence in a man. He'd take care of them all proper, he would. Me an' Miss Elsie an' Queenie, the pups an' all.

"Take 'em away, Millie," Lady Finch-Haddley said. "You'll see him again—he's staying here for a bit."

Millie was now so happy that she really howled. "Oh," she cried. " 'Ow lovely. 'Ow lovely that'll be. An' 'e can sleep with Miss Elsie again."

"Now, Millie," Lady Finch-Haddley said, getting up to grasp her arm and shake her. "None of that, you under-stand. You know and I know, but no one else knows."

"Miss Elsie knows. She told me. She thinks about it all the time. Misses him, she does. She don't like sleeping alone . . ."

What did one do with girls like this? "Listen, Millie. Just don't say anything about it."

"No, Your Ladyship."

"Just say Captain Turnbull's an old friend, a friend of her father's."

" 'Er dad. 'Er dad's Lord Fenton. Are you a friend of his, sir?" She looked at Turnbull, surprised.

"I'm not," he said.

"Oh, I know I'm not supposed ter know," Millie said. "It's just that I thought . . ."

"Don't think, Millie, and don't talk. If the girls ask you, and they will, just say he's a friend of her father's and he's here for a week or so as an outpatient."

"Yes, Your Ladyship."

"Now get that bloody pack out of here." Lady Finch-Haddley was losing patience. As soon as Millie had gone she turned back to Turnbull.

"She refused you?"

"How did you know?"

"Your face, and what I know of the girl."

"She's a good girl," Turnbull said, "and I want to marry her."

"And she wants to marry you." Lady Finch-Haddley's temper, never very equable and unimproved by the African climate and hospital conditions, flared up. "My God," she said, "you bloody cavalrymen aren't as bright as your own horses. She won't marry you because she knows you'll have to send in your papers. Haven't you had enough of playing soldiers? Do you want to go on burning farms and rounding up women and children all your life? Do you want to sleep with your damn busby and dolman and go to bed in your red pants all your life?"

"I'm going to send in my papers," Turnbull said. "I'm sick of the army."

"When this is over Elsie's staying on here with me. We're going to try to undo some of the harm you've done." By now Lady Finch-Haddley had completely disassociated herself from all the British except for the sick and wounded in her hospital. She had met Miss Hobhouse, who had investigated the concentration camps, and the Boer refugees were her people, or going to be.

"Send in your papers," she said. "Buy a farm and breed horses and cattle. Once you're settled and we've sorted things out a bit you'll get your Elsie. I know her. Good God, man, she thinks of nothing but you. You ought to see her when your letters come and when they don't.

When there's nothing in the mail you'd think she'd got distemper."

"I'll do it," Turnbull said, his face lighting up.

"I'm glad. It would have been a pity to start something like that and let it go. Finch and I had it. But not many do. Afraid of it," she said. "Afraid of love. That's what most people are. And I tell you what I'll do. I'll give you a pair of wolfhounds for a wedding present." She rested her hand on the great shaggy head at her side. "Damned if I don't. And they'll be the first I ever gave away. I sell 'em, Turnbull. Unless people pay for things they don't take care of 'em. And d'you know something? You've paid for Elsie. Paid with thought and love, paid with the King's commission and with people thinking you a fool. Oh yes," she said, "a lot of people know about your setting her up. That Diana Darnley found out somehow. That's a woman who doesn't like you. But I'll tell you this. There aren't a dozen girls like Elsie in all England. You chucked a crust of kindness on the waters and you're getting back a bloody cake. And if you want to get married in London I'll see to it. You can get married at St. George's from my house and half London will be there. They'll come because they're afraid of me, Turnbull."

Turnbull laughed. "I can see why Elsie thinks so much of you. 'A regular madam,' she said you were."

Lady Finch-Haddley caught the word "madam" as a dog catches a tidbit in the air with a snap.

"That's what I'm going after when I finish here—this hospital—the Boer women and children," she said. "Then the madams, the pimps, the whoremasters and white slavers. Got to do something with all the money Finch left me, you know."

"They'd better look out," Turnbull said.

"You're bloody well right, my boy. And when the time comes I may need you and Elsie to help me."

"We'll be there, Lady Finch-Haddley."

"Isobel is the name, John." She took his hand. "And good luck, my boy, good luck."

It seemed to Elsie that two o'clock would never come. She ate no lunch. Then she changed into her riding clothes, had one of the hospital Cape carts inspanned, drove down to the Grand. He was here. It seemed quite

incredible that he should be here. But she had known he
would come. Marry him. How could she marry him, a
girl like her? His career. His friends. She knew there was
talk about her even here. It had leaked out somehow
that she was his friend. Nothing else, nothing beyond
that. Old Lady Finch-Haddley knew the rest. The girls
in the hospital had heard nothing yet, but they would
sometime. Well, to hell with them if they did. It was the
men that mattered; the men loved their Miss Elsie and
she loved them. Was the captain right? Had she changed?
Was she a woman, no longer the little girl he had petted
on his knee, a doll, a loving and beloved toy?

There was a letter from Vincent when she got to her
quarters. She burst out laughing when she read it. He
had said, "You tell the Master, Miss Elsie. Sort of break
it to him. You see, it wasn't exactly my fault. It just
sort of happened." But she was glad. Glad No. 7 was
knowing love again. It was a happy little house, just
made for lovers. And all those people tumbling about in
my bed, she thought. How happy they must be. It was
all so quiet and so pretty and the staff was so nice. Vincent told her about the good wines he had laid in and
Ellen's meals, and Celeste's shop. "A head on her," he'd
said. A head, Elsie thought, and a pretty little bottom,
too. She was the brains behind this little scheme. Celeste
was very romantic. She had even tried to persuade her
to have another lover when Turnbull had gone. She had
said she could manage Vincent. Well, now she'd proved
it. But he had been very honest. All the wages had been
banked. He would take over the lease and pay rent from
the day Elsie had left. He would buy the furnishings at
cost. "You have no idea, Miss Elsie, the money we are
making. It's really very sad to think that people will pay
so much just to be alone with each other for a few hours
without being disturbed. There is so much sadness in the
world that we feel, Celeste and I, that we are doing a
good Christian act of charity to permit meeting of human
beings here under conditions that would be impossible elsewhere!" That was Celeste. That was the way she talked,
always a mixture of Christianity and bedrooms.

But the thing was, how was she going to break it to
the captain? She had said they would go back. That she
would be happy living as she had been. But it would be

impossible now. Too many people knew about No. 7. Vincent would be getting letters every day for rendezvous. Besides, the captain was right. She could not sit still any more twiddling her fingers in that dear little house waiting for him to come to make love to her. Perhaps, as he said, she had grown up. She wanted to do something to help people, to make something. She wanted to help Lady-Finch-Haddley with her rescue work when the war was over, and they had got the Boer women and children in the camps sorted out. There was so much to do. The world was so big.

Turnbull was as excited as Elsie, though he showed nothing, or thought he didn't.

His man made a great effort to restrain himself and failed. "You saw her, sir?" he said. "It's all right?"

"Saw who? And what's all right?"

"Miss Elsie, sir. We all 'opes you're going to marry 'er."

"What did you say, Biglow?" He could not believe what he had heard. We all . . . Who in hell was we all?

"In the regiment," Biglow said. "When we 'eard you were coming 'ere we 'oped you'd marry 'er. She loves you, sir. That's what the boys say wot's seen 'er. Pretty as a picture, too, but they don't know if she can cook. Not that an officer's wife has to cook, that's what I told them, sir." Now he was off he could not stop. "And the dog, the retriever wot killed a man. Did you see 'er? She's not savage, they say—just in self-defense and going to have pups."

"She has pups," Turnbull said. My God, talk about women! The whole army seemed to know about Miss Elsie and him. Must have put two and two together from her inquiries and got a bit out of Millie too no doubt.

But the dog. Everyone knew about her having pups too.

As if he guessed what he was thinking, Biglow said, "It was the general's dog, sir. An Irish terrier. General Forrestier Walker's dog. He done it in the gardens of the Mount Nelson Hotel. That's wot they say, sir."

"They say indeed! And it was an Airedale, not an Irish terrier. Gossip a lot, don't you, Biglow?"

"Yes, sir. We chews the rag a bit. We likes a bit of

news. They'll be glad to 'ear you've seen 'er, sir. Very 'appy they'll be."

"You're writing to the regiment?"

"Yes, sir, to me friends. I got to, about Pretoria for one thing. She's got to 'ave nothing but bully beef and sardines on Sunday. I forgot to tell them. And no 'am. On no account. No 'am."

"Say *ham*, Biglow. You said you wanted me to correct your English."

"Yes, sir, I'd like to talk nice, and that's the way I writes it—h-a-m, 'am."

Turnbull gave up and took out his gold half hunter. Time to get ready for lunch. By the time it was over she would be here. He had picked out two saddle horses from the livery stable and ordered them to be ready by two-fifteen. They looked quiet enough; whatever Elsie said, he was not too happy about having her on a horse.

Turnbull was waiting for her when she drove up. She got down from the Cape cart and took off her brown dust coat.

She looked like a boy in her shirt and jodhpurs, like a beautiful boy. He called for the horses and watched her measure the stirrup leathers under her armpit and adjust them—very businesslike. Then, without any help, without a mounting block, she swung up. He mounted and they trotted out of the yard together. She was right. She could ride. Vincent had taught her well. He really owed Vincent a lot.

Once in the open veld they cantered side by side, silent, just happy to be together. He rode toward a clump of bush and big rocks he had discovered when he was stationed here. There had been a scrap among them; the Boers had held the place for a day till they had been shelled out of it. But it was nice, partly shaded and partly open. The grass between the boulders was cropped smooth as a lawn by the dassies—the conies of the Bible— that lived among them.

He tied the horses to a tree and got out the sandwiches and bottle of cold tea, and put them in the shade. Then, and only then, did he take Elsie in his arms.

When at last they said good-by a lot had been arranged.

He had explained that his career was finished anyway, and that he was going to breed horses somewhere in the Free State.

"Here," Elsie said, "see if you can buy this bit of land. Do you know what I call it, John? I call it No. 7 Africa. I'll come here often after you've gone."

And she did, lying on the lawn-short grass so still that the dassies got to know her and came out to graze in this little open space between the rocks that had within a year known both love and war. There were still empty shell cases lying about, the brass as bright as gold. Sometimes Elsie picked one up and smelled it—cordite, the acrid smell of war—as she lay watching the conies. How long had they lived here? Hundreds of years perhaps. John had shown her the place they went—always in one place—and there the urine was crystallized solid as a block of amber.

The country was taking hold of her; the veld, Africa, its size, its age, struck some chord in her.

She had shown John her wedding and engagement rings, shown him the locket of his hair that she wore on a chain around her neck.

"You were always with me. Always warm and safe," she said.

She had asked him about her nightie. Had he found it in his kit? And why hadn't he written about it?

He hadn't written because he had been too touched to do so and had not known what to say. He had said he supposed the whole army knew about it. They seemed to know everything.

Elsie's mind went back to No. 7. She would not have to break Vincent's news. His philosophy of letting sleeping dogs lie had paid off very well.

John had gone off with the wedding ring in his pocket. "I'll just keep it till it's time to use it," he said.

And the engagement ring he had taken off and put back on her finger. Just fancy that. Him, the captain, doing that. Now she could talk about him, and what a relief that would be.

Charles Eaton had been wrong. It had not taken a month to cure him. A week had been enough.

CHAPTER 58

THE RING

DORA VAN REENAN was worried about the war news. She had been silent and preoccupied all day and her state of mind had not been improved by Carter's call, when he dropped in at the Willows for tea. The girls were out. There was something about his appearance today that disturbed her. Always very neat and well groomed, he seemed to have spent more than his usual time on his turnout. From the top of his dark head to his boots he had a special patina, a significant glow.

"Come in," she said with assumed pleasure. "You're just in time." She pointed to the tea tray.

"Thanks, Dora," he said. He had called her Dora only once before. It was a long time since a man had called her that in this ordinary conversational way. She knew he had done it only because they were alone.

It was curious to be alone again with him; this man with whom she had been so intimate. They had not been alone since the afternoon of the storm. Intimate? Why mince words? She had lain with this man and liked it. Even now as they exchanged banalities her body cried out for him. Her nerves screamed as her manners froze into ever greater formality.

"I knew they'd gone," he said.

"You watch us, Major Carter?" she said coldly. "You watch our movements?"

"You are enemies," he said. "You are suspect." He got angry himself. "You said it yourself," he said. "You hate the English, but not individual Englishmen. Why do you force me to say things like that, Dora? You know I love you. You even know why I came today."

"No," she said. "No, not again. That was an accident." Dora van Reenan felt her voice breaking. "Forget about it. Please. A moment of weakness, and I was afraid—"

"Afraid be damned! You're a lovely and a lonely

587

woman. The storm just gave you the excuse. You're starved, Dora. Starved for a man, for love."

"How dare you say that?" Now she was furious.

"I did not say any man." He had her hand and pulled her to him. "Do you know what I came for, Dora?"

"I know," she said. "To lie with a man-starved widow when her daughters are out. Do you think we are animals? You conquerors. Do you think all you have to do is to take us? First you court my daughter. Then, because she is difficult, you turn to me. Do you think I don't know men and their needs? *Magtig,*" she said, "there are colored girls in Pretoria. There are whores of my own race. Take them," she said, "take them."

"You did not answer my question, Dora."

"I answered it. *Ja,* I answered it."

"No, darling," he said, kissing her gently.

He could have had her then, she knew. On the sofa as he had before. What had happened to her? But he did nothing. Made no further attempt to touch her, but reached in his pocket and brought out a diamond ring.

"Soon," he said, "in a few months all this will be over. There will be peace. I want you to marry me, Dora."

"Marry you?" she said. "With two near-grown daughters?"

"Take it," he said, and before she could stop him he had dropped the ring down the front of her dress.

It would be impossible to fish it out with dignity. Dignity she must now retain at all cost. She could feel the ring's cold hardness between her breasts, held in place by the top of her corset. Cold, cold as ice. Then, gaining warmth from her body, it was only hard, not cold any more, just hard against her stays. She would not find it till she undressed.

Carter was laughing at her gently.

"Dora . . . Dora, darling," he said. "Don't think I don't understand. I am an enemy, a man you are half ashamed and half pleased to see, a man whom you admire but for whom you also have contempt. Do you think I should have made love to you if I hadn't loved you? I did not take you like that, Dora, and you know it."

"Yes, Morgan," she said, "I know it in my heart. It's myself I'm ashamed of, myself. What is a woman? I

sometimes ask myself. A vessel, an empty cup that cries
to be filled. A mindless body that—"

"No," Carter said. "No. My dear, there are things beyond our understanding. I am thirty-seven and never
wanted to marry before. I wanted a woman, a mature
woman, not a girl, and never found one."

"I could still bear you a child," Dora said, "a son."
She knew she could.

"My dear," he said, "my very dear." He took her hands
and raised them to his lips. "I do not think I shall stay
to tea, Dora," he said. "I have done what I came to do."

She watched the door close behind him. My God, she
thought, how I insulted him, acting as if that was all
they wanted of their enemies. The men on their knees.
The women on their backs. But there was more than this
between them. And he was right. They were enemies
and lovers now. But the war would end one day and
then only the lovers would be left. Peace and love. That
was something to pray for. She went upstairs to undress
and find her ring.

If she had been wearing one of her usual high-necked
blouses, this would never have happened. But she had on
a blouse that was high only at the back. It was white;
the neck, embroidered with black, came down in a V
that was fastened with a black and white cameo brooch
and a series of small cut-glass buttons down the front.

But the whole thing was absurd. What a proposal. She
knew that she would never have let him put the ring onto
her finger, but now, in the privacy of her bedroom, she
slipped it on. Its rose-cut facets caught the light—red,
green, prismatic blue . . . She could not keep it and
she had no idea of how to return it. Was she engaged to
Carter or wasn't she? She knew she loved him. But it
was war. How was she to explain it to her almost grown-
up daughters? They thought her old. I'm not old, she
thought. She was in the full flush and power of her maturity. Since this had begun, since the storm and even before it, when she had first felt Carter's attraction, she had
changed almost unconsciously. Her style of dress had
changed, her hair. She had no longer just put on her
clothes. She wore them. And what a difference there was.
Difficult as materials were to get she had got them. She
had had new clothes made. She had taken more trouble

with everything. He had said how wonderful her hair was and had run it through his hands. That was after the first intimacy. A man said, "Let me see your hair down." This was a prelude. A woman who let a man see her with her hair down already in her imagination had let him see much more—see her full and secret beauty. But she had come to him like that, naked under her satin dressing gown, her hair hanging, the whole long glistening black tail of it. Like a young girl, like a wife, like a mistress. For that was what she was. Carter's mistress. It needed only to happen once to make this true. But it had happened more than once afterward in her mind. And did it not say in the Bible . . . ?

That night, after the storm, after the girls were safely home and in bed, was the first time she had slept really well for years. Emotionally exhausted, satiated, happy. If this had happened to anyone else and she had heard of it, she would have been shocked. Such things did not happen to nice women. And he, what had he felt? The ring, still on her finger, was the proof of his feelings. He wanted her. He wanted her for always. Not just as a wartime mistress. Though she knew he could have had that, too. It would have been hard to arrange. But she would have found the means. And she was a spy. There was no doubt about that. She had already used information she had got from him and sent it to the Cape and the commandos. Suppose she was caught. Carter would be disgraced, cashiered. He might even be shot. It was like a cheap romance. A beautiful spy sleeping with an enemy officer to obtain his secrets. That was the way it would read, the way it would appear in the papers. How often it must have happened before. Had she not told her own daughters to use their looks, to ingratiate themselves with the enemy? Distraught now, she took the ring off, wrapped it up in a bit of tissue paper, and put it in the little mahogany and mother-of-pearl box in which she kept her jewelry. With an effort she put it out of her mind.

She had a feeling of unease about Catalina van der Berg. Tomorrow she would take Renata and go to see her again. She must be all right. She must be—the farms near Pretoria had not been touched. This other mother to her new son Louis. His real mother. But I must know, she thought. If he came back, and he would one day whatever the risk, she must have more news for him.

Louisa did not mind being left alone. Quite the contrary. She had seemed almost glad when, with a bag packed and Adam this time in the back seat, she watched her mother and sister go.

Renata was no longer nervous as the old horses plodded off toward Groenplaas. She was looking forward to seeing Catalina again. She brought Louis closer, this woman, his mother. The farm where he had been born, Wagter the dog that was his pet. The dusty road now was familiar. The rocks, the trees, the bush all friendly, all saying, "Here comes that Renata again. We are going to see a lot of her. . . ."

At the Willows, Louisa amused herself for a while at the piano, playing "The Belle of New York." Lance had just given her the music, but she only read the words. Then she played some Boer songs—"Sarie Marais" which had become a kind of national anthem. She was still at the piano when she heard a horse being ridden in. Who has come to see me? Which one of them, she wondered. Lance . . . ? Carter . . . ? Who . . . ? Which bee to her honeypot? Going to the window, she looked out through the curtains.

A National Scout. A Boer traitor. Young, and mounted on a big chestnut horse—an English horse. She saw him go to the stables and offsaddle as if he knew the place. She met him at the back door.

"*Ja*," she said, "what can I do for you? My mother is away. I am afraid . . . Good God! Boetie! Are you a Scout? Have you changed your coat?"

He came in. "Renata?" he said. "Yes, I have changed. Just for the day. Where is Renata?"

"She's away . . . she and my mother." She was not going to tell him where they had gone. "They have gone calling," she said. "They will be back by evening."

She'd have several hours alone with him. They had not been gone long. A plan was forming in her mind. Here was a chance to get back at her stupid, patriotic little sister, to pay her out for her gibes.

"Come," she said, taking his hand and leading him out into the yard. "We will hide the saddle in the loft and turn your horse into the paddock. If anyone comes there will be no trace of you. No one will think anything of seeing an English charger grazing here." There was no mistaking the broad arrow brand of the British Army on its quarters.

They led the horse out and came back. She dismissed Sixpence and told him he need not return till evening.

"Now," she said, "coffee . . . food. You're hungry, I'm certain."

"I'm hungry," he said. "But what bad luck about Renata and your mother."

"I am here," Louisa said. "Suppose I had gone too and there had been nobody? They should be back by teatime." But a lot could happen before they came back tomorrow, she thought. A lot was going to.

When he had eaten she washed up the dishes and took him into the drawing room. "I'll play for you," she said. She had a nice touch on the piano and looked very pretty on the little revolving stool. She played more Boer songs and sang them softly to him, turning to look into his face.

Boetie sat back thinking of the way they sang the same song by the campfires in the field, of the deep bass voices of the bearded fighting men. Of Beyers singing to his wife, of how her face had changed when her eyes met his.

Seeing he was dreaming, Louisa stopped playing. "You're tired," she said. "Come upstairs to your old room and rest. You know," she said, "we call it your room now."

"I am tired," Boetie said, and he was. Tired with what he had gone through, tired with disappointment, tired because Renata was not here. I should not be tired if she were here, he thought. He had time to waste. Time to put in till she got back. He would rest. Like all soldiers he had the trick of it. Taking off his jacket, he folded it for a pillow and in a few minutes was fast asleep.

How young and innocent he looked in sleep. But he was a man. She had reason to know it. This time she had not even kissed him. Not yet. The plan was forming in her mind. She meant to have Carter, to marry him. What business had an old woman like her mother to try to take him from her? For a long time now, at least it seemed a long time, she had thought of seducing Carter. But, and she acknowledged it to herself, she did not know how. Kisses yes, and more than kisses, but that was all. For in this, as for everything else, there must be a first time. There was a trick to it, a skill. And what a way to pay out Renata! The mealymouthed sly little puss.

When Boetie woke, Louisa was beside him on the carpet, her soft mouth on his. He had been dreaming of Renata. Before he knew what he was doing he had pulled Louisa to him. Youth to youth. Boy to girl. Man to woman. More and more inflamed by her, he could not stop. Lost utterly in the arms of this girl who had also been in his mind, even in his dream mixed up with his true love, merging with her. This beautiful bitter fruit was his. His mind repudiated the wild beating of his heart, the pulse of his blood, but could not check them, and then he weakened. No mind was left at all, no time existed, till Louisa got up, laughing, her eyes bright, her lips full and moist.

"You love two girls now, Louis," she said, "or is it only one? The other one?"

What a trick. What a revenge. She was Eve. She had plucked the fruit and stood in the secret garden of a woman's knowledge. She was her mother's equal. Girlhood was left behind.

"Get tidy, Boetie," she said, looking at the rumpled boy. "They may be back any time. My dear sister, your love, and my mother, a woman who at times forgets her age." She wanted to be rid of him. She wanted to think, to recapitulate, to remember. She knew he would not stay after this.

Boetie could not look at her. He could not wait. All this trouble, all these risks for nothing, and worse than nothing. He could never come back now. He had lost Renata, lost the woman he had come to love as another mother, lost a new home, and must once more risk his life riding through the British lines in the uniform of a Scout.

He caught his horse, saddled up, and rode away from the Willows, saluting two British officers he met on the road. Out and on, on toward the Boers, back to the war, his mind burdened with the new knowledge of sin, of lust and its power over the frailty of human will. Evil was now a reality. Nature in its awful, unfeeling grandeur, completely careless of results, played with the hearts of men, who also had the rut of beasts.

His mood, hard and uncaring, may have contributed to his getting clear away without trouble. This young Scout, so utterly absorbed, careless, and speaking good English, was so obviously the genuine article that no one did more than stop him to ask where he was riding alone.

"To Botha," he said. "I have orders to try to suborn some of his men."

"Like that?" an officer said. "Good God, they'll shoot you before you get within a mile of them."

"I have other clothes," Boetie said, and undid the roll fastened to his saddlebags, his own clothes, torn and worn with the usage of war.

"That's the kind of thing those Boers wear," he said. "Rags. I'll get some of them to desert, all right. Never fear. I may be young but I have a persuasive tongue."

"Good luck," the officer said.

Boetie rode on.

By the time the old horses got near Groenplaas, Renata was excited. Catalina might have news of Boetie. She might have heard something. Also, she was hungry. She wanted to get to the house, to have coffee, to wander about the rooms Boetie had known, to be alone in them and feel him with her. Feel his past before they had known of each other's existence. The walls must have something of him. The chairs. His room. The bed he had slept in for so many years . . .

She felt her mother stiffen and the Cape cart pull up.

"What is it, Mama?"

"I don't know, but something is different."

They had turned off the main road and were on the drive, little more than an overgrown track now that led to the great gums and beefwoods that surrounded the farmhouse. As if they cherished it in their arms, the great trees rose like the pillars of a church about it.

But surely from here one should see the chimney and get a glimpse of a whitewashed gable, through the gray evergreen foliage of the gums. Surely . . .

Pulling the whip out of its socket, Dora van Reenan struck the horses. Surprised out of somnolence, even out of old age, they jumped forward in an apology for a canter. On around the next bend . . . the house should be fully visible.

There was no house.

She felt her daughter's hand upon her wrist. "Mama . . . Mama . . . What is it? What has happened?"

"The English," Dora said. "Before God we are too late. The English have been here."

Nothing was left of Groenplaas but a few calcined beams fretted by fire, wrinkled like the skin of an elephant, standing stark, like black bones against the blue summer sky. Just the bones of the house remained, climbing out of the stone foundations like the ribs of some dead beast that were still attached to its vertebrae.

The palms by the back door were dead, the scorched swords of their long fronds rustling against each other like weapons. Dora felt the girl's hand grasp hers more tightly. She felt the bones give under her grip. The girl was so strong. Under the rounded fragility of her small body there was a frame of iron. How little she knew of her girls. How little of herself.

Without another word, she turned the horses. Old or not, they had to manage the round trip.

When they were halfway back Adam outspanned them to drink at the spruit and graze for an hour. There was no need for a knee halter. They were very tame and too tired to wander far.

No one had spoken a word. Renata's soft face was white, hard as alabaster. Her eyes stared, quite unseeing.

Only now did she turn to her mother and say in a voice that was almost unrecognizable, "Catalina. We must find her."

"Yes, Renata," her mother said. "We must find her."

The girl was now in the dominant role. She had grown up in an hour and had taken charge. In a way it was a great relief. Once the girls were women, she would be free. But free to do what? Morgan was English, and the English had burned the house that would have been her daughter's home. It lay dead like an animal, rotting in the veld, surrounded by its offal, its entrails, the remains of the furnishings that only a few weeks ago had made it a home.

When Renata and her mother got back they found Louisa at the piano where they had left her. Time at the Willows seemed to have stood still while they had been on the road and for the first time had actually seen something of the devastation of war. A murdered house. For a house that was lived in was a living entity. There had been the remains of the dead dog lying in the yard. The smell of stale smoke, of death. It could happen anywhere. Even here, at the Willows, in a few hours, if their activities were discovered. They could be prisoners like Catalina and their home a smoking ruin too.

And where was Catalina? How did one find out?

Louisa had taken the news calmly. Since Boetie had not surrendered to the English, this kind of thing was to be expected. It was absurd to go on fighting for a cause that was so obviously lost.

But there was something else about Louisa, some change in her face, about her mouth and eyes. She seemed smug, remote, thoughtful, faintly amused, patronizing, not at all her usual vivacious self as she looked at her sister.

CHAPTER 59

THE CAMP

IT TOOK Catalina and the women and children of Groenplaas more than a day to reach Pretoria in the wagon. They outspanned before dark and sat shivering at a fire built by the roadside, eating some of the chickens that the Australians had lifted, and drinking black, milkless tea. The children cried. The women were beyond tears. In a few hours a world that had taken sixty years to build had collapsed, stone and mortar no more than a house of cards. A man with whom they had lived, one as a mistress, one as a wife, and one as friend, had proved himself to be a traitor and an ingrate. Jacoba was worried about Frikkie. She knew his temperament. To justify his existence, to prove himself more of a man than his father, he was capable of taking absurd risks. Frikkie, who was only just strong enough to raise a rifle. And there was this new child within her that that coward had begun. But, begun as it was, it must go on, must run its nine-month course with seven still to go. There was also the baby begotten when he had left for the war. The women looked to Catalina. She was still Mevrouu van der Berg of the big house, though the house had disappeared. They were still the wives of her bywoners, though one was dead and the other a traitor. Women she had known for fifteen years.

To Catalina, staring into the flames of the fire, nothing was left. Her mind was a blank. Was there no end to misery? First Petrus, then Elsa, then her sons at war— she did not know where Boetie was, Servas so strange that he was lost to her—and now this. What was left? That she was still alive? But what was life now? Her trust, the farm she had held together for her boys, was gone. And what about her pretty daughter-in-law to be, the girl with the yellow eyes whom Boetie loved? Wagter was dead. Her cats would starve. Her poultry they were eating now. Her pot plants destroyed. She thought about the buffalo horns, burned with the rest . . . about the peafowl Petrus had loved going wild in the bush.

At dawn they inspanned and trekked on. By midday the Australians had handed them over and gone off with her wagon, oxen, and all her stock of cattle and horses.

Here she was, with these women and children who were her responsibility, behind barbed wire with two hundred others picked up here and there all over the Transvaal. Women and children the like of whom she had never seen before. Frantic women, furious viragos, disheveled, dirty, savage, almost as wild as the Kaffirs among whom they had lived. Even their language, the words they used, were not hers—a crude patois—a Taal spiced with religious phrases and barroom words. Crude, obscene, brutal, but the story was always the same. The soldiers, the torch, destruction. Their homes in flames, their livestock driven off or killed.

Food was issued to them. Their names were taken and listed in triplicate. The men who did it seemed sorry for them. Sorry . . . If they were sorry why had they not left them alone? Was it not enough to have lost their husbands, brothers, sweethearts, and sons? To have them in the field, not knowing if they were alive or dead?

Their names and the names of their farms were taken by a sergeant, an Afrikaans-speaking Scout. A big backveld Boer woman in her forties sprang at him, held him by the throat, and almost gouged out one of his eyes before she was pulled off.

"The name of my farm?" Catalina said when they got to her. "It has no name."

"All farms have names," the Scout said.

"Only places have names, Judas. I have no place." Catalina spat on the ground at his feet. A few hours only, and she could do that. It did not take long to degrade a person. In a week she'd be like these others: dirty, coarse, crude. She would have to fight it.

The full horror of the burning was beginning to dawn on Catalina. Groenplaas was just one of hundreds, thousands perhaps.

At six they were fed again, a stew that the orderlies who brought it called skilly, and tea with sugar and condensed milk.

By eight they were on a train, herded in with the children like animals, like cows with calves at foot. Their destination quite unknown. To a camp, a refugee camp. But who had made them refugees? To a concentration camp, where they, all vagrants, wastrels now, no longer the wives of solid burghers, no longer women of property, would be crowded together like beasts in a kraal till God knew when.

A girl with a beautiful soprano voice began a hymn. It was taken up by all. A sweet and terrible sound, a song of sorrow, of lament, and prayer to the Lord God, in whom they put their trust, rose over the noise of the engine, of the rattling wheels, and the bang of the couplings as the train pulled out of the Pretoria station.

The camp was a canvas town with streets of white bell tents laid out in parallel lines. To the north, near a clump of blue gums, was a group of marquees, hospital tents, store tents, and so on. The whole area was surrounded by a barbed-wire fence. From a distance it looked like a military camp—which it had been—but now a camp inhabited entirely by women, children, and old men.

From a distance it looked neat, clean, and utterly alien, set down on the bare veld. As they approached its full impact struck Catalina. This was where they were going to live till the war ended. This was a prison. Call it what you liked—refugee camp, concentration camp—it was a prison surrounded by a wall of wire through which they would be able to observe free people, still able to come and go at will. She went over in her mind the events of the last few days. The loss of her home, the impossibility now of getting news of or to her sons, the change in her situation. A week ago she had been well off, rich by certain standards, the owner of a fine farm and a well-furnished house. Now she was penniless—her home destroyed, her stock stolen—naked but for the clothes she stood up in.

It was impossible to believe. Her heart refused to take it in. It was impossible that so much should have disappeared in so little time. Impossible that a man she had trusted, who had been as much a friend as a foreman, should have betrayed her, and with her his own wife and children.

She looked at the people around her, the women and children dragging their feet in the dust of the road. Except for her own people they were strangers, some as unkempt as savages. In rags, their children clothed in half-cured sheepskins, barefooted or in rough sandals of oxhide lashed to their filthy legs—sick, yellow with fever, thin, with the bloated bellies of starvation. For weeks, for months, some of them had roamed the veld in women's laagers, vaguely attached to commandos that could do little to help them. Like herself they were ruined—homeless, stockless. Catalina had never been in the bushveld and had no idea of the primitive way these people lived. One woman, Lettie Strydom—she had been told her name as they came down on the train—was insane. Both she and her daughter had been caught on the veld and raped by Kaffirs. The girl, who was not yet fifteen, must have been pretty once. Now she was like a dead girl, her face bloodless and expressionless, her blue eyes blank as paper, as if she wished to see no more, to see nothing—as if by an act of will she had become blind. She moved with the others, like a heifer heavy in calf with a herd. Pregnant to a Kaffir, carrying his child under her heart. What had happened to the world? Where was God?

Her conversation with Dora van Reenan as they had sat drinking coffee came back to her. "Do you believe in God?" How strange it had been to listen to such blasphemy. Now there was a certain relief in it. If there were no God He could not be blamed. He was let off. There was no case against Him. Perhaps it was better not to believe in God than to believe in one who could permit such horrors. She wished she could talk to Dora again. She tried to recapture the picture of Renata. Her Boetie, her baby, courting a girl. And the five hundred pounds. If anything happened to Klaas the secret would be lost. And Servas? She was afraid the new hardness that he had shown on the farm would be the death of him. A man could not live without humanity. But Boetie must live. Must, must. He must marry his girl and live happily ever after as people did in fairy tales—as she had done till Petrus had been killed.

At last the formalities were over. Their names registered. They were given a blanket and a ground sheet, and stood, the children about them, under the canvas of their tent. Only in the middle by the pole could they stand up straight. There was no furniture. They had no possessions. The red-painted pole was the only piece of wood they could touch. It had never occurred to Catalina that one lived with wood. Civilized men lived with wood, from their beginning in a cradle to their end in a coffin. Furniture. Even a box, a crate. She determined to get a crate, several crates, find an empty can, pick some flowers, anything green. To create a home, to have possessions, things she could clean and move about.

"Well," she said, "here we are."

"*Ja*, we are here," Jacoba said. "Thanks to that bastard I married. The viper! Oh, *mevrou*," she said, "oh, *mevrou*, it is all so dirty." She burst into tears on Catalina's shoulder.

That was it. It was not just the tent, the barbed wire. It was the dirt and the smell. They had been shown the latrines, but many of the women refused to use them. The lines that had looked so clean from outside were foul. There were buckets set out for slops, but they were still thrown out of the tents into the streets between the tents.

And this was where they must live for months. Live, if they did not die, till the war ended and they could begin again with nothing. Even five hundred pounds, if it was still there, was nothing, though it was much more than most people would have.

Luck . . . She supposed they were lucky. At least they were all together. This was the new Groenplaas—bare, sun-baked, empty—where they must try to take temporary root.

At last the children stopped crying—they were cried out—and stood solemn, dough-faced, with big staring eyes, sucking the crusts of bread they had been given by a big, dark, heavy-bosomed woman from the next tent, Nellie Synman. "Pah," she had said, "it is bad at first, but you get used to it. A woman gets used to everything but doing without a man." Her bold black eyes snapped as she laughed.

Used to everything in time, but in how much time? What was there to do? To read? What were the children to do? Where could they play? Where were the veld, their dogs, cats, ponies, toys?

How did one keep the babies clean? How did one wash their diapers? There were girls here and young women by the hundred, menstruating, all modesty lost. Soiled, bloody, half-washed rags had to be watched as they dried or they were stolen.

There was no privacy. No place to weep. The screams of every woman in the agony of birth were heard by hundreds. The insides of the tents were often black with flies and Nellie Synman could still laugh. . . . She always laughed. At the end of a month Catalina knew her well.

"Laugh," she said. "*Ja*, I laugh because it is better to laugh than to cry."

That for the moment was the best philosophy. It was Nellie who helped Catalina get her first packing case and found her a broken vase in which to put the little half-wild brick-red zinnias that grew just outside the wire and could be reached by stretching out one's hand.

Nellie said, "They burned your farm. But they did not take your man, for he was dead, and they were English —the enemy.

"Do you know who burned my home, *mevrou?* The Boers. Our own people. They showed me the orders given to them at Roos Senekal by General Louis Botha.

"They took away my man, who was working in his fields. Burned my house to be an example, dumped me out on the veld with nothing, and told me to find the British lines.

" 'Do everything in your power to prevent the burghers from laying down their arms. I will be compelled, if they do not listen to this, to confiscate everything movable and also to burn their farms.' That's what they read me, *mevrou*. Those were the orders, as if my husband was a traitor or a joiner. He fought and fought well. He was wounded. Then when he saw we could not win he came home to his farm and to me."

Her dark eyes flashed and she stood, legs apart and arms akimbo, her fists on her splendid hips.

Catalina's heart went out to her, to her strong earthiness. This was a true Boer woman, born of the soil, rooted to it by the plows, guns, and blood of her people.

"So here we are, *mevrou*, caught as they say between the devil and the deep blue sea, though I have never seen it," Nellie went on. "Either the Boers get us, the peaceful people who only want to get on with their work, or the English do. First the English pick us women up and then tell us to join the commandos. Then our own people send us to the English. Before God, we women and children are driven back and forth like herds of cattle from one kraal to another." It always came to that. The same simile. People no longer thought of themselves as human beings.

"Starving women to save their children have gone to Kaffir *stads* for food and paid for it with their bodies. Prostituting themselves to the men who were their servants. Others, like the two poor ones here, were caught on the veld and raped. . . . And this is for freedom! That we are homeless and have black babies in our bellies. And here—here," she said, "we starve. Starve for food, for work, for love, for our menfolk. Starve in our minds with worry at being naked and without possessions.

"We fought well and for a while God was with us. Then for some reason He grew tired of us. Therefore we have lost and it must be God's will. For say what you like, we cannot fight them. There are too many of them. Kill one and ten spring up."

It was like living in an endless nightmare of dirt and boredom. At first the numbness of despair acted as a kind of anesthetic out of which Catalina came slowly, having, without realizing what was going on, got into a routine of drawing rations, cooking, and trying to console her tentful of people.

Jacoba's pregnancy was affecting her mind. She sat, utterly apathetic and hopeless. Little Flip was wasting away in her arms, crying, whimpering, dwarfed with hunger. There was no milk. There were no vegetables. The rations barely adequate for adults, were unsuited to small children. Bread was baked in Dutch ovens made of clay. But small children could not live on bread, and on a little gravy once or twice a week. The meat, such as it was, had to be eaten at once before it went bad or became flyblown.

Bugles blew calls, soldiers marched about outside the wire, guards were mounted and changed. News was all rumor. Talk was gossip, reminiscences, questions no one could answer. There were cliques, parties, and quarrels. The joiners and traitors found themselves mixed up with the families of fighting Boers.

Nellie's husband Johan had been impressed.

"He was working on the land and I was cooking when they came. Boers, Catalina," she said. "Our brothers. They took him. They took all our stock, all that was left of it, burned our house, and left me on the veld. A lesson. They said it would be a lesson for the other hands-uppers. They said only the Government could make peace, a burgher had no right to give up on his own. And where is he now, my Johan?" she asked. "And how will I find him when it ends, or even know if he is alive? We have no children. We had two, but the Lord took them in infancy. Never, *mevrou,* till now, did I think that I should thank God for it. Thank Him that they went peacefully, dying in their beds in comfort, and lie buried on their own farm."

As the bushveld Boers had lived for generations in isolation, their children had no resistance to infectious diseases. Chicken pox, whooping cough, measles were all killers.

Flip had not been well for weeks. When Catalina went out to try and get some milk for him, Jacoba was holding him to her bare, empty breast. When she came back he was dead. She saw it at a glance. The little blue eyes were blank as marbles as they stared upward. His mouth sagged, his fingers relaxed.

"It's no good, Jacoba," Catalina said. "He is dead."

"I won't let him go. I'll fight for him," Jacoba screamed as she sprang up, almost her only move for days, the dead child sagging in her arms. Her long, matted hair was down, her eyes wild.

I must get help, Catalina thought. But how terrible it was, all this going on with the other children crying and sobbing about them. Martha put her hand on Jacoba's arm to quiet her and was rewarded with a blow that sent her staggering against the canvas of the tent. The children's cries increased. Two of them began to fight.

"Your ma is mad. She hit my ma."

Susanna tore at Sara's hair and they went down in the filth of the tent floor, rolling over each other like animals. Hendrik was trying to separate them. That was what this life was doing to them all, turning them into animals. Catalina went to find Nellie.

"Nellie, Nellie," she called, "come quick."

She was there in a minute. "What it is?" she asked.

"The baby is dead," she said, "and she won't give it up. She is mad. Insane. She holds it to her—she curses her husband. She says if he had not put her in foal again she would not have been sick, she could have saved Flip, she would have had milk. Come quick, Nellie, we must get it away. The other children must see no more."

It was hot. The sweat was gumming her hair to her forehead. It ran stinging into her eyes. The baby would not keep. A baby—what has it but meat? But it took a camp like this to prove it. Ashes to ashes, dust to dust. Yes, but before that, meat. All of us. Everyone. Me, Boetie, everyone. How horrible it was. Catalina had never thought she could so nearly lose her own self-control, but Flip was like one of her own. All these people—the mad Jacoba, Martha, the other children—were her people, her responsibility. What would happen to them if she broke?

"Come," Nellie said. Big, calm, wide-hipped, a born mother if ever there was one, she strode forward like a great strong mare stepping into her collar and taking the load. Catalina followed her into the tent. She went up to Jacoba, slapped her face, pushed the flat of her hand against her nose so that she fell, and came out with the child.

"We'll take him to the hospital tent," she said. That was where both the sick and the dead were taken.

An hour later Flip was buried in the cemetery with only Catalina and Nellie to attend the ceremony. Martha could not leave Jacoba, who was threatening to kill herself. No one else bothered to come. A baby has no friends, only relations. If they had attended every hurried funeral, the people in camp would have had time for little else. The cemetery was a garden of little crosses. New ones planted almost every day, row upon row of them, the older ones already attacked by white ants.

It was late afternoon when it was done and the parson closed his book. A service in English for a Boer child. The red clay fell in clods on the little wooden box as the Kaffirs shoveled in the earth. No flowers, just a handful of wild red zinnias that scarcely showed up at all on the new-turned ground. The shadows were long, the little crosses immense, big enough to carry a man, a calvary. It was as if everything in the world—the trees, the tents, the very poles that held the imprisoning wire—was mourning for little Flip with long crape streamers.

When they got back Jacoba was calm but tearless. The children squatting on the ground outside the tent, blank-eyed, empty as cups, watched Martha stir a stew in a three-legged black iron pot over a little fire. A scavenging kite flew low over her, looking for a morsel to steal. Its shadow ran like an animal over the bare ground between the tents and up the canvas in an illusion of attack. Catalina shuddered. This was only the beginning.

There were no women of Catalina's class in the camp. They were chiefly share-croppers, bywoners, and bush-veld Boers, from the back of beyond, without education, many of them wholly illiterate. Better-off women, women with means, were allowed to live outside the camp. But she had no money.

This put her in a curious position of leadership, of having to collaborate with the British in an effort to bring some order and cleanliness into a camp of women and a few old men who in all their lives had known no discipline. For this she was hated by most of them. One

woman was furious when she removed the bread dough
she had put in her child's bed, a little girl running a
temperature of a hundred four, to rise from her body
heat. From another woman she snatched a decoction of
boiled horse manure she was forcing a child to drink because it was costive.

"It's clean," the woman screamed, "boiled and filtered
through a cloth. It was hard to get, too. Do you think
I don't know what to give my children?"

Another child, with rheumatism, was sewn up inside
a freshly killed goat, its head sticking up between the
forelegs.

By this time Catalina realized that the British were
doing what they could in the camp and that much of
the illness was due to the complete ignorance of hygiene
of the Boers. The shortage of milk was the greatest cause
of mortality among children. But women fed sardines to
month-old babies. A boy with double pneumonia had his
chest and stomach varnished. A woman whose two children had measles painted them with green paint and they
died of arsenic poisoning. There seemed to be no end
to their stupidity and ignorance.

Catalina had become friends with the nurse at the
hospital, Nurse Norham, and from her she learned how
the British were dying of sickness too. It was the nurse
who took her photo one day, a snapshot of them all
standing in front of the tent with Jacoba trying to hide
her gravid belly behind the children. Only when she
got the print did Catalina realize how they had all changed.
Gaunt, thin from work, worry, and poor food, she looked
sixty.

The fresh meat they got was very poor. There was no
grazing left. Sheep that weighed only sixteen pounds were
slaughtered, and only half was meat.

To buy anything fresh from the hawkers was impossible, even if one had a little money. But camp stores,
whose prices were controlled, sold tinned milk, canned
fish, Worcestershire sauce, chowchow, dates, sweets, and
other luxuries for those who could afford them.

Slowly things improved. They got more and better food.

Catalina made a list of the weekly rations they were
supposed to receive. Sometimes they got full rations. At

others, when the Boers had cut the railway line or there were a lot of new arrivals, they got much less.

Mr. Tucker, the superintendent of the camp, was a kindly, rotund little man who did what he could for everyone. The doctor, Nurse Norham, and her untrained assistants also did their best. But kindness and good intentions could not help the spirits of these imprisoned people, suffering from worry, boredom, and fear for the future. Ruined families, without news of their menfolk for months on end. And then suddenly the monotony of their lives was broken by a burst of rifle fire, the blowing of bugle calls, and before anyone knew what was happening a commando of eight hundred Boers forced the gate and, shouting, firing their rifles into the air, galloped into the camp.

No one was hurt. Mr. Tucker and his staff were taken prisoner. Everywhere men were shouting the names of their wives and sweethearts, for this was a local commando that had made the raid to see how the women were faring. Catalina saw Nellie carried off like a child by her enormous husband. Everywhere girls and women, hysterical with joy, were being kissed and embraced as they laughed and cried. A harmonium was hauled out of the marquee they used for church service and meetings. Two men with concertinas and one with a fiddle began to play dance music. Where an hour ago there had been an atmosphere of desperate gloom there was now one of desperate gaiety. Tents were abandoned to lovers and husbands by those who had no men. Dust rose in clouds from the dancers. Picketed horses neighed, stamped, and reared at the excitement, which lasted till dawn.

There were some children with the commando. Three boys, one of fourteen and two of twelve. When their farms were burned they had escaped, taking horses and riding away into the veld to look for a commando. Catalina talked to the eldest, Dirk van Diglen, who had a rifle nearly as long as he was tall slung over his shoulder.

"I have been in three battles, *mevrou*," he said. "These"—he pointed to the others—"fought too, but they cannot carry guns. They use the rifles of the dead and shoot lying down. As soon as a man is killed or badly hit they take his gun. Also they run messages. They are safe, too," he said, "because the English seldom shoot at children."

All three were exhausted, thin, their eyes enormous in their drawn boys' faces. Her children—she called them that, Sara, Susanna, and the babies—stared at them in awe, fingering their leather bandoleers. They all had bandoleers, even the two younger ones. Children, little boys who should have been learning their letters and herding cattle, had been swept into this bitter world of men. They as much as the burghers, though for different reasons, were glad to be with women again. The smallest boy flung himself at Catalina, crying, his arms around her waist.

"I want my ma," he said, weeping. "My ma. My ma. My ma said, 'Take a horse and ride, Boetie.' So I jumped on old Bles and rode away. I was chased by Kaffirs," he said, "but they could not catch me. Then I found the commando. But I do not know what to do. I am all alone. I have no home place. I am too small to be alone," he sobbed. "*Ja*, I am too small to be alone. I am not a man."

He was a shrimp of a boy. Catalina picked him up and kissed him. He nuzzled his face into her neck like a puppy. What happened in the minds of children who had seen so much? Seen death and wounds? War? Their homes go up in flames?

When she looked around again Dirk was asleep, his head in Susanna's lap, his rifle lying beside them. The girl was stroking his fair, sun-bleached hair like a mother with a child; like a child with a doll that was bigger than herself. Catalina put the little boy down. His name was Carl, he said, Carl Theron. "Danie is my uncle," he said. "Danie, the famous scout. He would have taken me. He loved me."

"Sleep," Catalina said. "Lie down and sleep." His face seemed hot and his eyes overbright. She wondered if he had malaria.

"Kiss me, *Ouma*," he said, "and hold my hand." She knelt beside him, kissed him, and took his filthy little hand in hers. When he slept she left him. She must see if she could get news of Boetie. She looked down at the other Boetie. A pet name. How many were there in

Africa? How many had died? How many on the veld? And where was hers? My Boetie . . . my Boetie. Surely someone would have met him.

Catalina, with other manless women, talked to the older womanless men. The young men had paired off with the girls in the dancing. She went from man to man, asking with the other women about their husbands, brothers, and sons. At last she came across a man who knew something. He had met Boetie van der Berg in the company of a man called Moolman two months ago. He was well and with De Wet. His name was Carl Venter, a Free Stater who found himself with this commando by an accident of war, having been cut off from his own people. Her Boetie was alive. Boetie was well. Catalina burst into tears.

She stayed with Venter and was standing near De Beer, the commandant of the commando, when Tucker, none the worse for his capture, was released.

"We came to see how our women were doing," Venter said, "and it is a good thing they are as well as they are. Had it been otherwise we should have flogged you all. Now we ride away with peace in our hearts."

The Boers were all standing by their ponies, a few already mounted, as the sun began to rise. Catalina got an idea.

"Meneer Venter," she said, "here is a picture of us, of me and our people. Will you try to get it to my son?"

"*Ja, mevrou.* I'll get it to him, the next time we get a messenger from De Wet or send one to him."

"*Opzaal—opzaal!*" came the cry. The dismounted men tightened their girths and jumped on their ponies, shouting, "Good-by—*tot siens*" to the women, weeping and used up by emotion, who watched them ride into the sun with shaded eyes.

The men had come. The men had gone, gone in a cloud of rose-colored dust, in a mist blurred by tears and the light of a new day. But now there was plenty to talk about. The men themselves, the news of the war, of De Wet, De la Rey, and Louis Botha, the heroes who would yet lead them to victory.

A curious calm settled over the camp when the men had left. It was hard to believe they had come and gone, that they had even been here. But for the horse spoor and the high piles of dung where they had stood sleeping it might all have been a dream. The women were very quiet, each lost in the forest of her own thoughts, treading her little forgotten paths. They thought of the men's bearded faces, of their strange clothes—a mixture of rags and English uniforms. Of how thin and hard they were. Some had wounds to show—another inch to this side or that and they would have died. The veld sores on their hands from lack of vegetables and milk, sugar and salt. The smell of their persons, new sweat on old that lacquered them with a new odor.

Nellie confided in Catalina. Catalina told her how Petrus, her own husband, had come back from the war in '81, reliving it all again in painful memory.

There was a hush, an unease over the camp, a before-the-storm calm that was odd because the storm was over. The emotion spent. Catalina seemed more aware of it than the others. She had more education, was more observant, more prescient perhaps. These were good women, most of them. Brave, honest, God-fearing. Stupid only for lack of help, living in the eighteenth century and not the dawning twentieth. The Bible, which not all of them could read, their only guide to the conduct of life.

Then the lightning struck. Susanna, a gentle girl, almost a little woman, became bad-tempered, slapped Sara, cried, and refused her food. She had a temperature. Next day she was covered with a rash. Delirious.

"Measles," Nurse Norham said.

There was very little they could do for measles but let it run its course. The girl's breath came in gasps, her small, budding breasts rose and fell as she fought, choking for air. Bronchial pneumonia. In three days Susanna was dead. She was the first to go. That week eight children died in camp. By the end of a month there were no Groenplaas children. Jacoba miscarried and had no will to live.

"My children gone, my man a traitor, and I have no home. Why live?" And she turned her face to the canvas wall and died during the night.

Catalina and Martha worked with the sick. The death of her children had changed Martha, made her into a fury, defying death, the new enemy, determined to save the other little ones. But what odds they fought. Most of the women believed water in any form to be fatal. They would not wash their children's fevered bodies, sponge their faces, or even give them any water to drink. Dogs were bought from Kaffirs and killed for their blood, which was poured fresh and hot down sick children's throats to give them strength, before anyone could stop these desperate mothers.

Mr. Tucker sent for help, for another doctor, for more nurses, for medicine. He got nothing. The epidemic was so widespread. Death lay like a winding sheet open over the veld. Nurse Norham died. Catalina took her place. There was no rest for her. She knew she would soon die; she could feel her life ebbing away as she gave her strength to others. She even forgot Boetie. Boetie was a man now and must look to himself. A woman's duty was to the young and helpless, the babies, the weanlings, the toddlers that were dying like flies.

More Kaffirs were put to grave digging. Little crosses sprang up overnight like weeds. There was no time to make coffins now, no planks for them. Blankets had to do.

Catalina often thought of her home, her possessions, her furniture. How she had worried about them. But why? Nothing ever really belonged to you. You left everything when you died, or it was destroyed by fire, as hers had been. In the end everything was destroyed one way or another. It was just a matter of time.

Most of all she remembered her little button basket. All the children in turn had played with the buttons. Mother-of-pearl, gilt, glass, enamel, odd buttons, old buttons, ordinary buttons for shirts, for suspenders . . . What woman's work the sewing on of buttons was. Symbolic in a way, as if she with her needle, thread, and thimble held her home together. Making . . . mending . . . Sometimes it seemed to her that her little round Kaffir basket of woven reeds was what she missed the most. There were still buttons in it from her husband's jackets.

The boys had played soldiers with buttons. They had had commandos of buttons, Zulu impis of black buttons. They arranged them in pairs like spans of oxen, with a matchbox for a wagon. She had made a rag doll for Elsa with round shiny black boot buttons for eyes. She wondered if all women were the same, if they ever thought of it, if they realized how much of their lives, how many of their memories were to be found in a little basket that had stood on a table beside them as they held their men's and their children's clothes over their knees, clothes that were like skins, having taken the form of their owners. . . .

There were single survivor buttons too pretty to throw away, buttons that dead fingers had fastened. Come to that, no one ever threw a button away and no one found one without picking it up.

Was she going mad, wanting to sew on buttons again —boys' buttons, men's buttons?

She was living in two worlds now—one of work in a charnel house and one of memory, thought, and speculation—living them simultaneously, jumping from the practicality of work to the dream, so that they merged into a perpetual twilight through which she moved like a ghost. . . . Slipping away from life, which, once this crisis was over, would no longer need her services. Catalina van der Berg was one of the last in the camp to die. Her funeral was well attended. The Boers and their guards standing side by side at her grave.

CHAPTER 60

A SECRET PLACE

Louisa looked at herself in the glass. She looked radiant. She had heard that this was quite usual when a woman became pregnant. It was five weeks since Louis van der Berg had come to the Willows, and she was sure. She smiled at her own reflection. What she had once thought of as an amusing possibility was now a necessity. Now she had to seduce Morgan Carter. He had been pushing her for information, bullying her, threatening her, in a light, offhand, steel-fist-in-a-velvet-glove kind of way. Well, the boot would soon be on the other foot. She not only was going to seduce him, she was going to marry him. Why not? He was rich, good-looking, amusing. He would get her out of this damn provincial society, take her to England, into the world where she belonged.

She knew she could see him at any time. A hint that she had information and he would be there, ready to take her for a ride, to play tennis, or to go on a picnic. But there were some preparations still to be made.

A riding habit would be no good. A tennis dress perhaps. But the place. The place was the thing.

Then she thought of it. His own quarters. He lived in a rondavel, well away from the others, that could be reached through the Willows' garden. Suppose she just dropped in on him? His servant . . . She ignored the possibility. Soldier servants were no fools. If he saw his master was entertaining a lady, he would not come in. But how would he know? That was easy. She would ride her bicycle over. He would see a lady's bicycle outside the rondavel door and take the hint.

She would go tomorrow after tea, take her tennis racket, and say she was going to play tennis with the girls. On the way she would stop at Carter's quarters. Since he would think she had news for him, he would let her in even though he might not welcome her. Once inside with the door closed it would not be difficult.

The whitewashed rondavel wore its thatch roof like a hat, low over its brow. The window was small, the green door low. Against the wall a bougainvillia shed its purple blood.

Louisa leaned her bicycle against the shrub and knocked on the door.

"Come in," Carter shouted.

She went in quickly, closing the door behind her. When he saw her for a moment silhouetted against the bright sunshine, his heart leaped. Slim as a reed. Her mother must have been like her as a girl. They might easily have been sisters. But why was she here?

"What do you want?" he said. "You shouldn't come here."

"Why not, Morgan? If I have news? If I want to see you? I never see you alone now. Don't you love me?"

"I never said—"

"I know, you didn't," Louisa said, "but I know. A woman always knows." She flung herself into his arms.

Her lips were on his. How easy it was. Men, when you were really close to them, had no control over themselves.

Outside a twig of the bougainvillia rustled against the little window. Above her head the round, unpeeled white poplar rafters of the thatched roof rose inward to meet in a little steeple like that of a church, festooned with spiders' webs.

Carter was rattled. The hot little bitch. But how attractive she was. How delectable.

"You shouldn't have come," he said again.

"Why, Morgan?" Her arms were about his neck. The big dark eyes, their pupils enormous, peered into his. "Why not? Didn't you like my kisses?" He shook her off.

"The news?" he said. "You said you had news . . ."

"I have."

"Then what is it? Spit it out." He was getting annoyed with her.

"News. The news is that I love you and can't wait any longer. I suppose you think you are too old for me or some nonsense like that. My father was only a few years older than you and I loved him. I was his pet . . ."

Carter sat down and lit a cigarette.

". . . and I used to sit on his knee like this." Louisa curled up like a kitten in his lap. "Don't you like me on your knee?" she asked. "All right. If you don't like me I won't stay." She jumped up, swishing her long white skirt. She faced him, looking at him, her feet together and her skirt held tight against her thighs. "Look," she said, "look how you've crumpled it." She flung herself onto the bed. "Kiss me," she said. "Be nice to me." She pulled him to her.

God damn this girl. A man should be armored against a woman, be prepared. He should not be attacked in his own bedroom, taken suddenly and unaware. She had seduced him. And here she was, acting as if he had raped her.

"Oh, how could you?" she said, beginning to cry. "Oh, how could you! I'll have to go in the back way," she said, as if this was the end of the world.

"Damn you!" he said.

"Yes," Louisa said, her eyes flashing. "That is love.

This is gratitude. You take all a girl has to offer, her body, her honor, and then you say damn you."

"You . . ." he said. "You . . ."

"Yes, because I kissed you, because I said I loved you. Because you would not declare yourself and I was honest enough to tell you of my love. But was that any reason to . . . to . . . to take advantage of my weakness? I am only a girl," she said. "What do I know of men? How was I to guess what you would do? I hate you," she said, stamping her foot. "I hate you—hate you—"

How funny it was that it should have happened here in this rondavel, where they had played so often as children. But how nice it was to have everything settled. Morgan did not know it, but she did. She dabbed at her eyes with a small scented handkerchief. In a month he would know. What a Christmas present she would give him. The greatest gift a woman could give a man. She was sure it was a boy.

"I'll go now," she said. "Yes, before God, I think I shall kill myself."

"Shut up and don't be a little fool. Do you think you are the first girl who . . . or the last?"

"Suppose," she said, staring at him, her eyes enormous black saucers in her creamy face, her lips wet and half-parted, "just suppose . . ."

"No, I won't suppose, and don't be so silly." The bloody little fool. Did she think . . . ? God knew what she thought or even if she could think at all. But what an enchanting little baggage.

"All right," she said, "I won't kill myself yet."

She had left her tennis racket leaning against a chair. It fell down when she banged the door.

Carter lit another Abdulla and poured himself a stiff brandy, adding cool water from the canvas bag that hung dripping from a rafter.

What now? he thought. He'd heard of men who had affairs with both a mother and daughter at the same time, but that had been in London. Pretoria was not London, not by a long chalk. Besides, he wanted to marry Dora. This would never have happened if the girl hadn't flung herself at him. Damn it, she really had seduced him. By accident, of course. He could not bring himself to regret it. But when he married Dora there would be a curious

situation, living in the same house as Louisa. Still, it
would not last long. A girl like her would soon be married. There was no doubt about that. She was too hot to
stay single long. In a way he envied her bridegroom. If I
were younger . . . he thought.

He wondered when he would see Dora. What she would
say. What had she done with the ring? How could he manage to see her alone?

Going to the door, he shouted for his bath. How much
had his batman seen? How much had he guessed? He
smoothed the rumpled bed and put the tennis racket in a
cupboard. He'd have to think of some way of getting it
back to her. Louisa . . . Dora . . .

A man could certainly get himself into trouble without
even trying. It was really time he got married.

Morgan Carter was neither particularly good nor bad.
He was what the French describe as an ordinary sensual
man, an ordinary man. But men living alone with other
men for too long lose some of their sense and caution.
He could not imagine this having happened at home, no
matter how attractive the girl was. It was a long time
since he had made love to her mother. He had not even
seen her more than once or twice a week and hardly
ever alone. It had been a curious courtship, one of in-
ferences, of looks. She avoided him. By God, if she'd
wanted to tease him she could have made no better plan.
But she had grown more beautiful, dressing with infinite
care, always charming in company and asking him to tea
or to lunch. He supposed that in a year he had seen her a
hundred times. Certainly no more. Why he'd had the ring
three months before he had had the opportunity of giving
it to her. Usually if the girls went out she went out too,
or had some damn woman friend to visit her. It was impossible to think of her as an enemy. It was probably
impossible for a man ever to think of a pretty woman as
an enemy. The British knew that all Boer women hated
them, whatever they might pretend, but they refused to
believe it. This did not apply, Carter was sure, to either
Louisa or her mother. Dora was violently patriotic, but
she disassociated him from the enemy with the curious
woman's logic that could always distort facts to make
them fit into the pattern of love. Louisa was without motives of any kind beyond the excitement of power and the

pleasures of the moment, a beautiful and eminently desirable little butterfly.

In her bedroom Louisa was changing. She looked at herself in the mirror, her small high breasts, her flat belly. She wondered when it would begin to show. Not for three months, she had heard. Not for much longer with a good pair of stays. She stroked herself and smiled. If one knew what one wanted, and was not a coward, things were really pretty simple.

He would make a good husband, a good lover. What a difference there was between a man and a boy. He would show her the world, the great sparkling wicked world that lay over the sea.

Dora van Reenan was dressing too. She had made up her mind. She was going to marry Morgan Carter. She had had him on a string for long enough. Considering what had happened, he had behaved very well, never bringing the subject up, continuing to respect her, though he'd had her. She blushed to think of it. The girls—well, they'd soon be married, they were both ready for it, and then she'd be alone.

But she must get the latest news of the camps off. She must think of a really safe way to send it to her sister Anna. She was overcome at the horror of what she had heard, at the figures she had got. Children's deaths by the hundred. And here she was, being happy, thinking of her marriage to an enemy. There was no accounting for people, for women especially, whose minds and hearts could pull in such opposite directions at the same time.

She dressed carefully. As carefully as if I were going to see him, she thought. He felt very close. Perhaps he was thinking of her. She felt herself blushing like a girl again.

CHAPTER 61

DINNER PARTY

IN THE ineffectual search for Catalina, Dora van Reenan had amassed a great deal of information about the concentration camps. They had failed to trace Louis's mother because she had refused to give the name of her farm, the farm that had ceased to exist. There were many Van der Bergs, and since she had refused to give him a name the interpreting Scout had just invented one to suit the occasion. Van der Berg, widow, two sons on commando —farm, Stinkfontein, Pretroia District." He had thought that a good joke.

But Dora van Reenan now had a detailed report of the camps that must reach both the President in Holland and the English papers. The camps were usually situated near railway lines, often on sites that had been used by British troops and were already infected with disease. Sometimes as many as sixteen people lived in one bell tent that should accommodate six. The tents were bitterly cold in winter and ovens in the summer heat. Children, babies, expectant mothers, and old women all lived under conditions that were indescribable, and died of measles, scarlet fever, whooping cough, pneumonia, and above all of enteric.

The causes, according to her report, were: the hardships endured by the families on their journey from their ravaged farms, which sometimes took three weeks; the poor quality of the food, much of it quite inadequate for children; the fall of the temperature at night when the sun went down; lack of protection against the cold by day in winter and the heat in summer; lack of clothes and blankets; insufficient medical stores or hospital facilities for the sick; ineffective sanitary arrangements.

The figures were appalling. In October, the peak month, the death rate for all inmates of the camps was 344 per 1000. The death rate of the children in that month was

629 per 1000 in the Orange Free State, and 585 per 1000 in the Transvaal.

She had lists of destroyed farms, the firsthand stories of women who had escaped the raiders, her own description of what she had found at Groenplaas—the farm that was no longer a green place. . . .

It took Dora some time to decide on the best way to send this information to the Cape. She made several plans and discarded them. The best plan was another present. But this time it would not be to her sister, it would be to her little nieces at Morningstar. She would send them dolls. There were always people going to Cape Town, and quite by chance she had heard that an Englishwoman whose acquaintance she had made the week before was leaving soon—a Mrs. Frederick Standish, the wife of an officer at headquarters. She decided to call on her, and, dressed in her best, she had the horses put in.

Mrs. Standish, a good-looking, rather fashionable young woman, seemed quite pleased to see her.

"How nice of you to call, Mrs. van Reenan," she said.

"I came to see you because I heard you were going to Cape Town and I wondered if you would take something from me to my sister, who lives there."

"I cannot take a letter that has not been censored, you know."

"There will be a letter," Dora van Reenan said. "Just a note that will not be sealed. But that is not the main thing. The main thing is a parcel for my little nieces. I want to send them each a doll and I am afraid that they will get broken if I send them by post. I suppose," she went on rather bitterly, "there is no rule about a woman, even if she is an Afrikaner, sending a gift of dolls to her nieces?"

"Of course not, and I shall be delighted to take them," Mrs. Standish said, smiling.

"I am most grateful and will bring the parcel in a few days or send it over with one of my daughters."

"They must be the two pretty Van Reenan girls one sees about everywhere." There was a barb in the remark.

"Yes," Dora said. "Girls, even Boer girls in time of war, like to be on the go. Tennis, riding, and so on. I am glad you think they are attractive."

"They are lovely, and one of them is so like you."

"That is the elder, Louisa. Like me?" Dora said. "Yes, perhaps. Like what I used to be."

"I've seen her out with Major Carter quite often."

"They are friends," Dora said. "She misses her father. He was killed at Spion Kop. She likes older men. She says she finds boys very immature." She laughed.

"And the other? The fair one?" Mrs. Standish said.

"Renata? She is much quieter."

"She is lovely too."

"Sometimes I think all young girls are lovely, Mrs. Standish. Youth has a beauty of its own. A beauty of excitement, of wonder, a kind of bloom. I trust you have had a pleasant stay in our town, Mrs. Standish," she said, "and found your husband well."

"I've enjoyed my stay, Mrs. van Reenan. But I do not like the atmosphere of war, and Lord Kitchener does not care for women or like the wives of his officers to visit them. But I was at the Cape. I have a brother farming at Stellenbosch. And being so near, only a thousand miles away"—she laughed—"I thought I'd run up and see how Frederick was doing."

"And now you are off?"

"Yes, back to the Cape. I sail on the *Norham Castle* next month."

Dora van Reenan held out her hand. "Good-by," she said, "and *bon voyage*. I am most grateful about the dolls."

She pulled on her black kid gloves, working them over her fingers. She was glad she had put on the dark blue silk and worn the leghorn hat with cornflowers. Mrs. Standish had been very smartly dressed in a Shantung coat and skirt that fitted beautifully, clinging to her tightly corseted, slim hourglass figure. She had worn a white silk petticoat, with a pleated hem beneath it, that showed very effectively when she sat down or picked up her skirt.

But, considering the war and the fact that Pretoria was seven thousand miles away from the fashion centers of the world, Dora van Reenan felt she had acquitted herself very well and upheld the honor of her people. At least this woman would not go back thinking all Afrikaners were dowdy peasants. And what a good idea to choose an English officer's wife to carry her dispatches.

Two medium-sized, golden-haired German dolls with china heads—heads fastened onto sawdust-filled bodies—

were found. The heads were removed and the sheets of thin paper containing the reports were rolled into pellets and stuffed up the necks of the dolls and into their hollow heads. Now they were ready to start on their way to President Kruger in Holland and Mr. W. T. Stead, of the *Review of Reviews*, the great champion of peace and justice for the Boers in London.

Renata took the parcel over to Mrs. Standish on the carrier of her bicycle and undid it to show her that there was nothing concealed in the packing.

"Just so that you could be sure, Mrs. Standish. My mother said I was to do it. She did not want you to be worried in any way after doing us such a kindness."

"You are a very charming and pretty girl," Mrs. Standish said, kissing her good-by.

Charming, pretty, and full of hate, Renata thought. As full of hate and anger as a puff adder is full of poison. It was not just the English she hated. She hated everyone, including herself. She hated to live a lie. She hated her sister, who was up to something. She had what she always called "that look" on her face. She was too quiet. She even played the piano softly, which was unusual. She also looked astonishingly pretty—prettier than she had ever looked before.

And why had there been no news from Boetie? Of course there was no regular mail from the Boer forces. But notes and letters did get through and eventually reached the person they were written to.

She did not even know if he was alive.

A fortnight later Dora van Reenan's mind was at rest about the information. She had received a letter from Anna saying how much the girls liked the dolls and how well Germans made them, particularly the china heads— the faces were so natural-looking. It was unfortunate, though, that they were china, as almost the first day they played with them Eva had broken hers. But she seemed to love it just as much without a head. . . .

With that settled—at least the world would soon know about the sufferings of the Boer women and children— she felt less guilty thinking about her own affairs. Now that she had made up her mind, she would give a little dinner party and announce her engagement to Major Carter. What a surprise it would be to her daughters.

She would tell them nothing except that she had decided to ask Major Carter to dinner and anyone else they chose to make the numbers even. She felt as excited as a girl. An engagement party. A party at all. They had not given one since the war began two years ago. She began to plan it. Soup, consommé. There would be no fish. Roast suckling pig. She knew where she could get one. Fresh stewed fruit, coffee, brandy, and there was still some wine in the cellar, Alphen, that her husband had laid down.

How lucky it was summer and there were so many flowers. In her mind she arranged the vases on the table. Roses, she thought. Red roses. There was a bush of very dark, almost black, velvety roses that smelled wonderful —General Jacqueminot. It was strange that dark red roses seemed to have more perfume than others.

When she told the girls about the party, they were delighted, Louisa in particular. But anything that gave her a chance to dress up pleased her. She said she would wear her new dark green taffeta. Dora thought it was a little old for her and made her look quite grown up, but then she was old for her age in some ways.

Renata decided on a pale blue sprigged muslin, very full, over a pink silk petticoat. She herself would wear an oyster-gray satin, embroidered and beaded with jet, cut low and off the shoulders, like those of the girls. We will form a pretty trio, she thought, as I stand with my arms around them.

The war was dragging on. Things going from bad to worse, but there was still hope. When the news she had sent reached England, the wave of anger it was bound to produce in a civilized nation might easily bring about an honorable peace. And De Wet was still having successes. Besides . . . besides, one could not live in gloom forever. As a Boer, she had done her best and would continue to do it, but as a woman she had to live, too.

The invitations were sent out and accepted. Major Carter, Lance Bridgewater, and Captain King, riding companions and tennis partners of the girls. The little pig was dead and browning in the oven with an orange—

there were no apples now—in his mouth. The dark red roses in a silver rose bowl filled the dining room with perfume that mixed very appropriately, Dora thought, with that of the orange blossoms, wafted in from the garden. The hanging lamp gave the dining room a soft, warm glow. When dinner was served the candles in the silver candelabra would be lighted.

Then the men arrived, booted, spurred, polished to the point of incandescence. The women were waiting to greet them, a youngish mother flanked by two almost grown-up daughters—a conversation piece in off white, pale blue, and dark, almost rifleman green.

Dora poured out the sherry. The girls each had a glass. She was a little surprised to see Louisa, when she had drunk hers, fill it up again from the cut-glass decanter on the piano. I must speak to her about it, she thought. A young girl should not give herself a drink like that.

She did not know that Louisa was seeking courage, was preparing for the biggest dramatic scene of her life. This was going to be in cold blood. No kisses, no seeking hands. No privacy. And she was playing it alone. They were all—she looked at her audience to be—all enemies. Even Carter.

Morgan Carter looked his best. He had on his brown leather heirloom breeches. They were quite famous in the army. There were only a dozen or so pairs like them, and Dora had never seen them before. He had thought it would be amusing to tell her about them at dinner. They had been made by White of Tarporley in Cheshire, before 1840. He had made no breeches after that date. Though there were some copies in buckskin, none could compare with the originals, which never wore out and were often included in a man's will. Carter's had belonged to both his father and grandfather.

Looking about him, Carter guessed what was coming. Dora had not given back the ring. She was going to announce their engagement.

They had a second glass of sherry, Louisa's third. Her face flushed, her eyes brilliant, she looked lovelier than ever. He wondered what it would be like to have her as a stepdaughter and how she would take it.

What a silly, maddeningly attractive little creature she was. Not little really, though. Quite tall in her high heels.

Slim as a wand, supple, with a waist a man could almost span with his two hands. Carter laughed as he thought back to the afternoon five weeks ago. He supposed all girls were like that, imagining things. Why some young girls even thought they'd have a baby if they were kissed. Still there was a strange feeling in his heart. What a pity Louisa was not a few years older; even two years would have made a difference. What a pity Dora was not a few years younger, say ten years. Dressed up like this, Louisa did not look like a girl of seventeen. She looked twenty at least. Her face, bright with excited laughter, looked more mature; even her eyes seemed to have changed, to have more depth. Her soft mouth looked firmer. Just tricks of light, of course, of the lamplight, and the candles that burned with a still, golden-yellow flame in the warm, rose-scented room.

The dinner was gay, the soup hot—a rarity in Africa —the little pig, nut brown and orange-tipped—delicious. The cold stewed fresh fruit topped with whipped cream and flavored with maraschino—excellent. The wine a little cooler than the summer temperature of the room—just right. 1890 had been a good year at the Cape.

Morgan Carter had told the story of his grandfather's breeches.

"Imagine it," he said, "buckskin breeches made before 1840 being worn by three generations of Carters, and still as good as new, though of course my father told me to use them only on great occasions."

That gave Dora her cue.

She rose to her feet, the diamond ring flashing on her finger.

"I now want to make an announcement," she said, "that will surprise four of you." She smiled at her daughters and their guests. "Major Carter has done me the honor of asking me to be his wife and I have accepted."

Lance, raising his glass, got up as she sat down. "A toast," he said. "We'll drink to—"

"Stop, Lance!" Louisa said, standing up. "And listen, everyone. This marriage will not take place. Major Carter will marry me. I am bearing him a child."

PART EIGHT

THE SCARECROWS

> *"The horses were skeletons, the men starving and in rags. The Boers were defeated but not beaten."*
>
> —BOER DIARY

[*South Africa and England—December 1901— June 1902—Summer, Fall, and Winter*]

CHAPTER 62

THE GREEN BAY TREE

THE DINNER PARTY that had begun so auspiciously had no end. When Louisa had finished speaking she walked quietly out of the room and went upstairs.

Dora burst into tears. Renata tried to comfort her.

Carter stood near them, looking helpless, and said, "I'm sorry. I never knew. It was not all my fault," but no one listened to him.

The other two men had left at once. They drove off in the HQ dogcart. Let Carter walk back. Anyway, it would be embarrassing to be with him now. What the hell could one say? In a way they envied him.

Outside the open window the waxy, starlike flowers of the orange blossoms still perfumed the darkness. The leaves of the orange trees shone like patent leather in the light of the rising moon. A nightjar, swift as a hawk, swooped openmouthed on a moth. What a night for love, for romance. The war and its terrors, the camps and their horrors seemed to belong to another world as, bathed in perfumed silver, its silence, blanket-thick, enveloping it, the night waited for the lovers who never came.

Locked in her room, Louisa sat in her usual position in front of the mirror, her elbows on her dressing table, her head in her hands, her hair, which she had let down, a dark silk curtain framing the white oval of her face.

It was over. She had done it. The plan she had made as soon as she discovered what Boetie had done to her had worked. That yokel. A young stallion. The very first time. It had been unbelievable. The marriage would have to take place at once. Even then the child would be two

627

months premature. A perfect premature child. But if it were born in England, who would know? My little Morgan, she thought, laughing softly. She would call him Dorian, too. Or Dora, if he were a girl, though she knew he would not be, out of compliment to her mother. There was a book—or was it a play?—written by an Englishman—Oscar Wilde, who had been imprisoned for sodomy. It was called *The Picture of Dorian Gray.* The hero had remained young and beautiful with not a mark of his wickedness on his face. Only the portrait, which he kept hidden away, changed, showing the ravages of dissipation. If only a girl could do that, could stay young and beautiful always, see her lovers grow old and have their sons at her feet. Boys whose mother she could be, yet looking like their sisters' friends. Boys—her own sons, even.

Her mind went back to her baby. My little Boer, she thought. A pure Afrikaner born to an unsuspecting Englishman. How she had tricked little Miss Renata, taking her virgin boy. I was the first, she thought. He'll never forget me. She'd never forget him, either. One never forgot the first one—man or woman—because that was the one who changed you, who opened the door. One day, when she was safely married in England, the baby two or three years old, she'd let Renata know. Just with a hint. She could say, "It's quite extraordinary how like Dorian is to Louis van der Berg, a boy I hardly knew and was alone with only once—on the day you drove over with Mama to Groenplaas and found it destroyed. He would not, or could not, wait for you, though he had risked his life to ride into Pretoria in the uniform of a National Scout. I have often wondered why he came if he was not prepared to stay. I never told you he had been, because I didn't wish to distress you and because, like all good girls, you have such a suspicious mind, and besides, you were so upset at finding his mother gone and the farm in ashes. But now it's all so long ago I thought I might as well give you this stale news. But really, if you could see Dorian you would imagine a little Louis— Louis van der Berg in miniature. A real little Boer Boetie that brings my heart into my mouth as I revive the memories of that afternoon, our lovely home and dear Transvaal. . . ." Something along those lines would be good. She'd have plenty of time to think it out.

And her mother. How had her mother—a woman of her age—dared, been foolish enough to try to take a man from a girl like her? Carter would make her a good husband. He was a man who would have his way with her and stand no nonsense, but whom she could manage— wheedle, charm, reward—and could punish by coldness rather than refusal.

How her mother's words, the words that had made Renata so furious, had recoiled on her head. Mix with them, play with them, even lie with them if you must. God knew she had done all that, even the last. Done no more than her mother had said was the duty of a loyal Boer girl. And if she had fallen in love with one of them and allowed him to take advantage of her weakness, who was to blame? No one but her dear mama, who had wanted him for herself. She wondered how far it had gone. This had been another reason for the way she had behaved. She knew now that even if she had not been pregnant she would have made a scene, out of spite, out of curiosity to see her mother's face, out of a desire to make things happen.

There was no danger of his not marrying her. He was an honorable man, and he wanted her. She knew that. She had been able to read it in his eyes every time he had seen her lately. She had pleased him. She wondered if her mother had pleased him too. But it was a good thing the others had been at dinner. It would be impossible to keep it quiet. It was not only women who talked. And suppose she went to the commander in chief, to Lord Kitchener, with her story or threatened to give her version of it to the press. In her mind she saw the headlines. It would be just what the Liberals in England wanted and they would make the most of it. "Staff Major Rapes Pretty Boer Girl at General Headquarters." She would say how she had dropped in to take him a basket of peaches, how he had assaulted her, tearing her clothes off her back, and flinging her down on his bed. . . . Though pregnant by his assault this Boer virgin of a well-known Republican family had been abandoned by him. . . .

But it would not come to that. She knew she would be married by special license within a week. She knew that within a month or so she would be going home.

England was already home to her. Or to the Cape on the way there.

She took off her dress of rifleman green and hung it up. She stroked it as if it was alive. It had done what she had meant it to do, given her maturity, added a few years to her youth, emphasizing the womanhood that would develop. And the color. He had often talked with nostalgia of the dark green uniform of his regiment. That was when she had made up her mind to get a dress made of it if she could find the material.

Someone tried the handle of her door.

"Let me in, Louisa!" It was Renata. There would be a row anyway, so she might as well get it over, once and for all. How she could squash her if she told her about Boetie. But she must not lose her temper. She must remain calm, aloof, grown-up, in front of this stupid child who thought she was a woman. A girl was not a woman till a man had had her.

She unlocked the door and Renata burst in.

"You whore!" she said. "You street girl! How could you do it? How could you?" Her golden eyes blazed with anger. "You knew Mama wanted to marry him. That it had been going on for months. That she only delayed out of consideration for us."

"I?" Louisa said. "I did nothing. I was passing his rondavel with a basket of fruit and I thought I would leave some there for him. I did not even know he was in. I was hardly inside the door before he took me like a mad animal. I was helpless in his arms. He flung me on the bed, he tore my clothes. Look—look—if you don't believe me." And from the bottom of a drawer she pulled her tennis dress, which was torn from neck to waist. What a good idea that had been. She'd thought of it only at teatime today.

"You lie, you lie!" Renata screamed, holding back her blue muslin skirt against her legs and raising it as if she feared contamination. "I know you, Sister. A whore from birth. A whore even with your own father. Always coy, modest, but a coquette. Letting him see this and that. Letting him pet you when you were big enough to know better, while you rolled those big innocent brown eyes at him. Who knows what would have happened had he lived, with an incestuous bitch like you in the house. A bitch in heat. And worse—for even a bitch has seasons.

"*Ja*," she cried, "you will succeed in your designs. You have no heart and a lovely body. As it says in the Psalms, 'I have seen the wicked in great power, and spreading himself like a green bay tree . . .' That is you, my sister, a very Jezebel." Going up to her, leaning forward, her skirts still drawn back tight against her legs, Renata spat into her sister's face.

Dora, sitting in an armchair in her room, had heard it all. The girls had never got on even as small children. And this was the end, the final breach for all of them. And what was worse was that Renata had been right about her sister. There were girls like that, natural harlots, in all walks of life. If we had been poor, she thought, Louisa would have been soliciting on the streets. Renata had been right, too, about her father. There had been something unhealthy, indecent, about their relationship, about the way Louisa had sat on his knee when she was quite a big girl, the way she had rubbed herself against him, almost purring like a cat. If what had happened had happened the way she thought it had, she could forgive Carter. A man was a man, and God knew Louisa was lovely enough to make anyone lose his head if she got close enough to him, if she flung herself at him, if she lay down and offered herself. Renata was nearly right. She knew. As for herself, it had been a dream and it was now over. The next thing to think of was how to get the girl married and out of the house.

She would not see Carter again, ever. But that would not do either. There was no point in having more talk than a sudden marriage would create.

She would see Carter tomorrow. A notice of their engagement must appear in the *Pretoria News* at once. The reason given for this precipitate wedding would be that he was being transferred—he could no doubt arrange it —and wanted to be married before he rejoined his regiment or did anything else that would get him away from here.

She would write at once. She went to her desk.

Dear Major:
In view of recent events your marriage with my daughter

should take place at once. I shall put a notice of the engagement in the paper tomorrow. You will obtain the necessary
permits, procure a special license, and arrange to be transferred out of the capital. There will be a small wedding with a
reception here to a select party of close friends and such officers as you choose to invite. Your transfer is of course the
excuse you will give for this hurried affair. Whether it is believed or not, it is the best thing we can do for all parties
concerned, including myself.

Sincerely yours,
Dora van Reenan

The next week would be particularly difficult to bear,
in a way that only she could appreciate. Her daughter
had stolen her lover practically out of her bed. Louisa
was indeed nothing more than a beautiful, incestuous
whore to whom Carter was more than welcome. She
was sure it would not be long before Louisa made a
cuckold of him, little realizing that he was one already.

Carter, now that he had got over his shock, was half
furious at having been made a fool of, and half delighted
at having so delectable a young bride with an heir already on the way—in the oven, as he put it rather crudely
to himself. He was also amazed at Louisa's courage, at
the way she had stood up to everyone. She had not come
crying to him saying, "What am I to do now you've put
me in the family way?" She had taken it into her own
hands and sprung a trap from which there was no escape.
This way there could be no abortion by some shady doctor in Johannesburg. He was stuck with it and on the
whole was rather glad. How lovely she had looked, a tall,
slim, defiant figure in dark rifleman green, standing in
the candlelight as she flung her bombshell.

He was sorry for Dora, but he realized now that if he
had ever seriously thought he could get the girl he would
never have approached the mother. It was what there was
of Louisa in the older woman that had drawn him to
her. Of course they'd have to be married at once. Babies
just popped out when the time came for them to make
their appearance, irrespective of how long their parents
had been married, or even if they were married at all.

There'd be trouble about it, of course. He'd have a lot
of explaining to do. Officers marrying South African girls,

usual enough in prewar days, was now frowned upon, particularly when they were Boers. He'd probably have to say that she had been working in the intelligence for love of him. They had become too fond of each other and since this little mistake had occurred he had no option. A scandal between an officer on the general staff and the daughter of a well-known Pretoria family must be avoided at all cost. If the newspapers picked it up . . .

He poured himself another drink, pulled off his boots with a bootjack, threw his heirloom breeches over the back of a chair, and turned in, not too dissatisfied with one of the most extraordinary days of his life.

Old Adam brought Dora's letter to Carter in the morning, and he set in motion the wheels that would transfer him back to the 50th.

That dark green dress had been a clever touch. There was more to the girl than just good looks. She had brains. He was not sure if brains in a woman were a good thing, particularly if they were combined with beauty. What he had had in his arms, and on his bed, was just a girl, the shadow, as it were, of what she would become. What would it be like to possess the reality? The woman who in three or four years would create a sensation wherever she went? And she would want to go. He did not feel she'd be happy in his old manor house in Gloucestershire forever. But he'd cross that bridge when he came to it. Skittish though she was, given a bit of luck he would be able to handle her. It would be fun to try, and breeding might settle her down. He felt a strange pride in being a father, as if he was the first man in the world to pull it off. A boy. He was sure it would be a son.

Now that the news was out Louisa was terrified. Carter was well known as chief of the Pretoria Intelligence Section. As she had been his friend, was his fiancée, what would be more natural than the assumption that she had given him information, that this had been the reason for their original association? She might be killed, branded, have her lovely long hair cut off, or be whipped with a rhino-hide sjambok. Carter must get her out of Pretoria and down to the Cape Colony among the loyalists.

General Winters, Carter's immediate superior, showed no great enthusiasm for the marriage, but agreed, when he was told, in greatest secrecy, that the girl had given valuable information and might be in danger, to facilitate a transfer to the Cape or Natal.

This calmed Louisa, who had plenty of other things to think of, with her wedding taking place in less than a week, the reason given out for all this haste being Carter's transfer.

Since the scene with Renata that had followed the dinner party the two girls had not spoken to each other.

Dora, who had to make all the arrangements, talked to Louisa as if she was a stranger for whom she was trying to plan a wedding on short notice. So Louisa's life was divided into two interests: Carter, with whom she now fell in love, and herself, with whom she had always been in love.

She would have no trousseau. There was no time for it, her mother said. She would be able to buy everything in Cape Town, Carter told her. He had a friend there, Mrs. Darnley, Diana Darnley, who he was sure would advise her. Reconciled to making do with what she had and looking forward to the new clothes she would get later, Louisa made the best of it. She had plenty to go on with and it was not her clothes that interested Morgan Carter.

The wedding took place at the Willows. Very few of the friends invited came to watch a Boer girl marry one of their country's enemies. A dozen officers from headquarters were there—still glamorous to Louisa in their clean khaki and shining leather. Her mother gave her away. Renata, a bridesmaid for form's sake, looked as if she was frozen.

The cake had been made at headquarters. The champagne came from the mess. And when it was over the couple drove away in a commandeered victoria behind two fresh English bays. They would not come back. Carter's transfer had been effected.

Louisa sat back in the carriage, smiling as she watched the houses and the gardens go by. She felt stationary. It was Pretoria going away, flowing past her, Pretoria leaving her for good. She felt no sorrow, no feeling of homesickness. She was like a chick that has pecked its way out of the egg and looks out at the world.

A new world was at her feet. She was married. She was going to enjoy that.

The Willows was an unhappy and silent house, with Louisa gone, Dora's dream of romance shattered, and no news of Louis for Renata. As they were deserted by their Boer friends and unwilling to have further dealings with the British, the time dragged. All their inquiries about Catalina had led to nothing. And the war. What hope was there now? The English were too strong.

It was hot summer, a good one, with good rains, that came with almost daily thunderstorms that reduced Dora to near hysterics. To Renata the thunder always sounded like gunfire. Battles . . . war . . . must it go on forever?

This was the third Christmas in South Africa, the Christmas of 1901.

CHAPTER 63

LIES GALORE

In December, Vincent, in Birmingham on business, was feeling pretty contented, though he disliked being away from No. 7. He missed Celeste more than he would have thought possible—both the charms of her person and the salacious wit of her Gallic mind. He also missed his work. He had come to love the variety it entailed. No two days were ever the same. Old clients, new clients recommended by old clients, an endless stream of the rich and well-dressed, gay and beautiful. The pretty women usually in their late twenties or early thirties, quietly restrained, modest, with soft voices and downcast eyes or half-bold, playful as kittens. But each under her polite veneer was excited, eager and, though knowing themselves safe enough in his hands, still half titillated by fear, afraid of discovery. The dinner conversations—tea was seldom served now—were about racing, clothes, the theater, and the ballet, a little discreet gossip with no names mentioned, some talk of horses, of the sales at Tattersall's, the war in Africa, the weather, the shooting prospects—grouse, partridge, pheasant—according to the season. About wines and cooking, dogs, fox hunting, polo, gardens. But under it all, as he served them, Vincent felt the subdued urgency of these lovers to whom a recherché dinner was only the prelude to ecstasy, the air an orchestra played to pass the time in a pleasant manner till the curtain went up and the play began. This occurred when he had cleared away the last plate, left glasses, decanters of port, brandy, and whiskey, and a new, unopened bottle of champagne cooling in a silver ice bucket, and, bowing deeply, said good night. At No. 7 the curtain went up when the door closed and the key turned softly in the well-oiled lock.

Most of the women were very pretty. Some were beautiful. All, naturally, had taken even more than their usual trouble with their appearance. Next morning, looking tired, their lovely eyes bigger than ever, sleek, quiet, smug as cream-filled cats, they chose their hats and lingerie from Celeste's shelves.

Celeste's stories were a real tonic. Some of the young women were so modest that they would accept no help in dressing except for the lacing of their stays. Others even wanted assistance in their baths. Two very rich, middle-class girls who had married well and wanted even Celeste to know it, had coronets embroidered on their underclothes.

Vincent was a Londoner. There was no doubt about that. He missed Celeste in his arms, her stories, Ellen's cooking, and his own wine cellar. He missed the streets, the servants, tweenies, parlormaids, and footmen whistling for cabs—one blast for a growler, two for a hansom. Birmingham was a filthy place, Brennan's Hotel a discreet commercial hostelry where they tried to do their best but failed to achieve their modest ambition. But the property he had bought was splendid. A rabbit warren near the docks with a rent collector on a commission basis who looked as if he was capable of extracting her last sixpence from a consumptive widow. A good buy, without question. Celeste would be delighted.

He had not yet written to the captain about No. 7. He wrote, of course, commenting on the news, the weather, the state of the house and garden, the health of the domestics, his own health, and the condition of the horses, but of the use to which this charming little house had been put not a word. The Elsie cat was out of the bag now, so he could mention her. He wrote to her, too. She knew what they had done, and said she would break it to the captain one day, but there was time enough for that. He had left it so long that a bit longer would not matter. His policy had always been that one might as well be hanged for a sheep as a lamb, and that many problems, if left alone, cured themselves by simply disappearing. He hoped that would happen about this affair. Anyway, least said soonest mended. No one could have said less than he, or let sleeping dogs lie longer. Vincent was a great believer in proverbs, which he described as the "wisdom of the lower classes." His quotations had got him out of many difficulties, as most of these aphorisms were unanswerable.

Coming back from settling his affairs with the lawyer, he had had a small adventure, which, though it had ruined a pair of new gloves, had given him much satisfaction. He had seen a big dray horse slip on a cobbled street and come down, a common enough sight. The carter began to beat it with the stock of his whip as it struggled in the shafts but could not get up. Vincent, seizing its ears and browband, pulled its head to the ground and said, "Sit on it, you bloody fool and stop hitting him."

The man was surprised into doing as he was told.

Vincent undid the girth of the saddle, the breeching, and the traces. The big gray had stopped struggling.

"Let him up," Vincent said.

The man got up. The horse, clear of the cart, gave a plunge, sat on its quarters with its forelegs raised, came up, and shook itself with a rattle of harness.

Vincent patted its sweating neck and looked at its knees. They were unbroken. If a horse breaks the skin on its knees it is permanently scarred, the hairs growing upward instead of down. This ruins its value and the animal, losing confidence in its own ability, having been badly hurt, tends to go on stumbling.

Still at its head, stroking its nose and talking to it, Vincent said, "Put him in. And don't do that again or I'll have the law on you."

He stood back with the crowd that had collected to watch the dray move on.

"You did a good job, guvnor," a man said. "Knows 'orses, don't 'e?"

Know horses indeed, Vincent thought. So I bloody well ought. And, setting his bowler at a jaunty angle, he walked back to his hotel.

It was in this mood of satisfaction, after a mediocre meal of steak and kidney pudding, some Stilton and biscuits, half a bottle of claret, four glasses of port, not a bad port at that, and a brandy and soda reposing under the gold Prince Albert watch chain that ornamented his rounded stomach, that Vincent decided to attend a political meeting. It would give him something to do.

He ordered a cab—a four-wheeler. He did not want to climb the high step of a hansom, nor to have the winter cold in his face. He also thought a man looked silly alone in a hansom. He thought of asking the blond young lady who was sitting alone in the lounge to accompany him, and then thought better of it, though she looked at him with promises of delight oozing out of her limpid, rather bloodshot blue eyes. Those days were over for him.

In the warm recesses of his little leather-upholstered room on wheels that smelled pleasantly of straw and horse manure, both nostalgic odors to an ex-hussar, both overlaid by a heavy musk perfume that was even more nostalgic, and behind the clip-clop of the old horse between the shafts, Vincent's mind grazed over the pleasant pastures of his enterprise. He was a lucky man. There was no doubt about that. But he deserved it. It was no more than his due. He had worked hard and saved his money. He was honest. He went to church on Sunday. He to an Anglican church, Celeste to the Brompton Oratory. When they met at lunch they exchanged the news. He told her about the sermon he had heard. She told him about the sins she had not confessed. Her worst sin was that of envy for some of the young ladies she attended who were younger and more beautiful than she. The afternoon was spent in proving to her how wrong she was. But at the back of his mind Vincent felt that Celeste was also envious of these ladies' intrigues and amours and would have enjoyed the profession of a courtesan. But he was sure of her. Business was too good for her to take risks. Money so often controlled morals, particularly those of women, who became good or bad depending on what they could get out of it one way or the other.

Chamberlain was speaking at the town hall, and the crowd was so big that Vincent paid off the cab and got out before they reached it. Fortunately it was not raining, and in his dark blue melton coat with a velvet collar he was warm enough. With his bowler hat and rolled umbrella he knew he looked just what he was—a respectable businessman, politically conscious enough to wish to hear what the Colonial Secretary had to say.

As he pushed his way through the throng he found that Lloyd George, that damn pro-Boer traitor, was speaking too. Vincent's blood boiled. How he hated that man. All of them. All those bloody traitors, those pro-Boers. Only this morning he had been given a broadsheet describing the British atrocities—rapes, burnings, deaths in concentration camps. Lies, lies, the lot of them. He knew. He had been a soldier of the Queen.

A man with a barrow was shouting, "Three a penny. Lovely 'arf bricks to chuck at Lloyd George. Lovely lovely 'arf bricks. Never get a chance again. Seven for tuppence. Ladies and gents. Chuck a brick for England . . . a coconut . . . every time a bloody coconut . . ."

The crowd was shouting, "Traitor! Traitor! Bloody traitor! Pro-Boer . . . Kill 'im . . . Kill 'im. Kill the bloody traitor!"

Vincent found himself forced up against the barrow.

"'Ave a brick, guvnor. Three a penny . . . seven for tuppence."

The handcart was lit by an acetylene flare. The half bricks glowed pinkish red like a pile of ripe fruit. A nice quality brick, too.

The shouting man, a big rough wearing a cap and a red bandanna around his neck that made him look as if his throat had been cut, was doing a good business. People were leaving the barrow with two half bricks clutched to their chests, the third in their right hands. The coster's face was purple as a plum. "'Arf bricks, 'arf bricks," he shouted. "'Arf bricks to chuck at Lloyd George, the bloody Welshman . . ."

"Kill 'im . . . Kill 'im!" shouted the crowd.

Vincent gave Purple Face a sixpence.

"A tanner, guvnor. You can't carry that lot. Want a boy to 'elp you? I got a kid 'ere . . . reduction on quantity . . ." he shouted.

"Keep it," Vincent said. "Just give me three."

"Wrap 'em up, guvnor?" the man said. "Shall I send 'em? Or will you take 'em with you?"

The crowd laughed as Vincent joined the line pushing its way into the town hall. Chamberlain was speaking on the platform. Then Lloyd George appeared and was greeted with a shower of brickbats. For a moment before they crashed down the air seemed to be filled with red flying poppies. Some thrown from the back landed on people near the stage, who screamed with pain and fury. The bricks thudded on the boards of the platform. A dozen bobbies rushed up to the speakers. One was knocked down. Someone hit Vincent over the head, shoving his bowler down over his ears. He turned around and gave the man behind him the point of his umbrella.

By God this was good. Like old times when he was a trooper, before he got his stripes. By God, he thought, I've not been in a good fight for twenty years. Now everybody was fighting with fists and sticks. Women were screaming and pulling each other's hair. What a show. The claret, port, and brandy had done their work, knocking the years and the respectability off Mr. Vincent as if it was the crust of a pie. He was a happy young hussar again in a barroom brawl.

On that night two thousand windows were broken, one man was killed, and a hundred injured. Lloyd George, the papers said next day, escaped by the back entrance of the town hall disguised as a policeman. What a night it had been. But there was a new problem for Vincent, one that would not cure itself, at least not for a week or more. How was he going to explain his black eye to Celeste?

He picked up the broadsheet again and read it.

Dora van Reenan's news had reached England. The china doll's head had spoken.

He held the broadsheet in his hand. It was headed:

HELL LET LOOSE
WHAT IS NOW BEING DONE IN SOUTH AFRICA.
THE TESTIMONY OF BRITISH SOLDIERS AT THE FRONT.

The lead piece was signed by William T. Stead. Then came:

How we are waging war: the testimony of a British officer.

This was followed by confirmatory evidence—plain answers to straight questions.

It ended with:

READER whoever you may be, what are you going to do to cleanse your hands of your brothers' blood, of your sisters' shame?

Copies of this broadsheet will be supplied for distribution at 2/6 per 100 or 20/ per 1000, and all who desire to arrest the carnival of arson, robbery and outrage are requested to send their names and addresses to the Honorable Secretary, Stop the War Committee, Clock House, Arundel Street, London, W.C.

"Lies! Lies! All bloody lies!"

CHAPTER 64

THE DRIVE

THE 2nd Hussars were standing by, part of the immense cavalry force of fourteen thousand men waiting to begin what was called a model drive, a great battue that was to push the Boers into the bag. French divided his cavalry into seven columns and moved them eastward between the Delagoa Bay and Natal railways. They were to keep in constant touch with each other and drive the Boers in front of them to the frontiers of Swaziland, where they would be forced to surrender or suffer an overwhelming defeat.

But the enemy commandos were not the only objective. Every farm on the line of march was to be destroyed. All women, children, and native servants were to be sent to the rear for internment. All crops were to be destroyed, every bakery and mill burned. All livestock was to be seized or killed, every wagon and vehicle burned. An area of ten thousand square miles was to be ravaged, rendered unfit for life. This great settled area of rich farmland was to be turned into a wilderness.

To Turnbull this was a shocking operation. It was much worse, on a much greater scale, than the operation that had sent him back to the regiment in disgrace after his protest. In the wicked, sweating heat of full summer dozens of wagons piled with women, children, and old men were fleeing before them. The horizon in front of the cavalry was red with the clouds of dust churned up by the hoofs of great herds of cattle being driven by frantic Kaffir herdsmen. Flocks of sheep like woolly mattresses, less fast than the horse and cattle herds, were overtaken.

Behind the advancing line of horsemen a pall of black smoke from the burning Boer homesteads lay over the veld. Over the houses, often a mile or more apart, it rose in dark billows between them. It drifted like a mist, as if the smoke, all that remained of the consumed houses, sought refuge too and was trying to escape.

The troops moved slowly, delayed by the work of devastation, by the business of destroying these farms that had been built with so much pain and trouble on these rolling high-veld plains.

The 2nd took little part in this destruction in spite of orders. There were plenty of people, irregulars and army oddments, coming on behind them who enjoyed the work. But it was done. Locusts in a field of wheat could have done no better, and this, Turnbull knew, was the prototype of all future operations. Only his thoughts of Elsie kept him sane. It was worse than the first drive. The scale was so enormous, success so certain. This was not a war. He was no longer proud of being a soldier. As soon as it was over he would get out, send in his papers, and begin to build up something in this land they were now destroying.

The 2nd ran into the opposition of a weak Boer rear

guard and dismounted and deployed to open fire on them. But it was like a field day with live ammunition substituted for the blanks. It was without reality. No one was hit and he doubted if they had inflicted any casualties.

The Boer forces were fleeing through Ermelo, where the British hoped to trap them. That night, exhausted with the march and the heat, depressed beyond words at the turn of events, Turnbull went to sleep wrapped in his cloak, to be awakened by a sudden burst of furious rifle fire and the wild pounding of hoofs. His first thought was for his horses. The Boers had stampeded them, turning them into the British lines and charging with them, a tactic the Zulus employed, charging with their cattle. The situation was saved only by an infantry counterattack.

Next day the drive continued, but the Boers were neither defeated nor trapped. Botha was back, free, behind the British in the no man's land they had created, and his burghers, digging up the supplies they had buried in the veld, were nearly as strong and certainly more dangerous than they had ever been before. It was difficult for Turnbull to conceal his pleasure.

The great De Wet hunt failed too. General Plumer should have caught him and nearly did, pressing him so hard that the line of his retreat was littered with dead and foundered ponies; but still, even with a large part of his force dismounted, he managed to get away. Without any wagons—De Wet had abandoned his last—without horses, pinned like a butterfly to the board of the Orange, which he tried and failed to ford in thirteen places, he still escaped over the fourteenth drift. Only De Wet could have done it—De Wet, who, a war correspondent cabled home, was reported to be demented.

Mrs. Botha now reappeared on the scene, coming through the lines with a message from Kitchener to pass on to her husband about a meeting to discuss the best way "to bring this bloody struggle to an end."

Botha came into Middleburg under a flag of truce and the two leaders met for lunch. Kitchener said that a British administration would "lead to representative government, that the Boers could keep their rifles under li-

cense, and that British and Afrikaners would have equal
rights."

There were two major points of disagreement: the question of the enfranchisement of the Kaffirs, which the English advocated, and the treatment of the rebel Boers from
the Cape and Natal.

It looked when they parted as if even these major differences could be adjusted, but the picture changed when
Kitchener presented the plan to Milner. Kitchener, the
soldier, wanted the war to end and was prepared to make
concessions, but Milner, the civilian, insisted on an unconditional surrender. The peace terms, modified by
Joseph Chamberlain, that finally reached Botha refused
to pardon the rebels and declined to give way on the matter of native franchise. Though "it was not the intention
of the British government to give such franchise before
representative government is granted . . . and then if so
given it will be so limited as to secure the just pre-
dominance of the white race. . . ."

The letter was sent to Louis Botha on March 7. On
March 16 he broke off negotiations. The war continued
and the English income tax went up to an unheard of
½ in the pound.

On the Boer side both President Steyn, of the Free State,
and Schalk Burger, acting President of the South African
Republic, issued manifestoes saying no peace could be
accepted that did not guarantee them independence. And
De Wet said, "The only object for which we are fighting
is the independence of our Republics."

And the olive branch so hopefully borne over the veld
by the commandant general's wife fell to the ground.

This was the end of March. The trees were beginning to
change color and the chill of fall was already in the air.

When Roberts had handed over to Kitchener in November, saying the war was over and the rest just a question of mopping up—a police operation—neither general
had had any idea of the Boer mentality.

But it was not quite like that. Kitchener had 210,000
troops at his disposal to fight 60,000 Boers, of whom
there were seldom more than 15,000 in the field at any
given time (5000 had been killed or were interned in
Portuguese East Africa, and 15,000 were prisoners of war).

But the Boers were operating in space and every farm was a depot where they could rest and refit.

The conduct of the war was criticized in England, but the Government pointed out that Napoleon had had to employ 400,000 men to cope with the Spanish, and that the Spaniards in their turn had employed more than 250,000 men to subdue Cuba. These were parallels but not answers, and the Opposition had a field day.

Roberts' wishful thinking had allowed the war machine to run down, and when Kitchener started to wind it up again he found the spring weakened. The guts had gone out of the effort.

Officers on sick leave were rounded up, cooks, clerks, and servants sent back to duty. The Remount Service was ordered to produce 8000 horses and 2000 mules a month, as if they could be manufactured in a foundry. The new troops were not as good as the old; the new remounts were animals that had once been rejected. The war was a bore now, and it moved forward in low gear.

Another proclamation was made promising the Boers in the field who surrendered a comfortable life with their families in Government camps and a fair price for any livestock they brought with them. This proclamation was largely the work of the Burgher Peace Committee, a body of captured or surrendered Boers who thought it madness to continue the war and, thinking personal contact with the commandos would help to bring this about, rode out to seek their fighting countrymen.

They were not well received, being regarded as renegades, cowards, and traitors, and those who did not make a run for it and get back to the British lines were sentenced to fines and imprisonment or worse.

The president of the committee was shot for high treason at Ben Vilgoen's laager. Two others were sentenced to death by De Wet. Another was flogged, and one shot.

Their plan had failed in a big way. The Boers were not yet ready for peace, most of them agreeing with De la Rey, who said, "The cause is not yet lost, and since nothing worse than this can befall us, it is worth while to fight on."

The main point of disagreement between Botha and the British, that is to say Milner, not Kitchener—the politician, not the soldier—was the treatment of the Boer rebels, the nominal British subjects of the Cape and Natal who by fighting for their own people found themselves in rebellion against a nationality that had been forced upon their fathers as a by-product of the Napoleonic Wars.

Kitchener was furious and wrote to Broderick, the Secretary for War:

> I did all in my power to urge Milner to change his views, which . . . may be strictly just, but to my mind they are vindictive, and I do not know of a case in history where, under similar circumstances, an amnesty has not been granted. We are now carrying on the war to be able to put 2 or 300 Cape Dutchmen in prison at the end of it. It seems to me absurd, and I wonder the Chancellor of the Exchequer did not have a fit. . . .

Lloyd George, when he heard of the failure of the negotiations, said:

> There was a soldier, who knew what war meant; he strove to make peace. There was another man, who strolled among his orchids, 6000 miles away from the deadly bark of the Mauser rifle. He stopped Kitchener's Peace!"

So the drive went on and the net result read very well —four hundred Boers killed or wounded, a thousand prisoners, eight thousand horses and mules taken, thousands of rifles, hundreds of thousands of rounds of ammunition, uncountable vehicles of every description. Herds of sheep and cattle so numerous that the bulk escaped, it being impossible either to herd or slaughter so great a number. Hundreds of women, children, old men, and natives interned. That was on paper. In actual fact the prisoners taken were unimportant, being chiefly men who had lost their fighting spirit. The interned civil population had now to be kept at the expense of the British taxpayer instead of being self-supporting.

The taxpayer, too, was shortly to be supporting the total Boer fighting force, since, with the destruction of their farms, which had been their sources of supply, they became dependent on what they could capture from the British convoys for everything they ate and used except meat, which they drew from the cattle herds that accompanied each commando. All the uniforms, rifles, and ammunition, saddlery, blankets, and forage used by the Boers were soon to be almost exclusively British. The Boers were now being rearmed and clothed and fed by the British taxpayer, who, though he did not realize it at the time, was supporting two armies—his own and the enemy's, and almost the whole civilian Boer population as well.

Kitchener grasped it. That had been his reason for sending out a peace feeler. Since that had failed, since the great drives had failed, he made new plans, or rather prepared to modify the old.

The policy was summed up in one word: BLOCK-HOUSE.

A blockhouse consisted of two large circular corrugated iron water tanks of unequal size placed one inside the other, the space between them being filled with gravel. They were loopholed and had an overhanging pitch roof with raised eaves for ventilation. They could be mass-produced for about sixty pounds, were easy to transport, being set down without any foundation on the bare earth. They were manned by seven infantrymen and three native night sentries.

The blockhouses were first used only to guard the railways, but before the war was over there were ten thousand of them—manned by seventy thousand infantrymen, all nearly mad with boredom, strung along five thousand miles of barbed-wire fencing. The country was divided into paddocks, camps, turned into a gigantic farm.

CHAPTER 65

THE CLOVEN HOOF

WHILE Miss Hobhouse, whom Kitchener called "that bloody woman," was trying to remedy the evils of the concentration camps, having been stirred to action by the reports in the English papers, Moolman and Melvina Brink were approaching a ruined farmstead whose embers were still smoking. On the short grass around the homestead lay the remains of some half-eaten sheep, pigs, and poultry. Farther away there were dead cattle, horses, and a dozen donkeys that had been shot and left to rot.

Moolman watched Melvina leading her child by the hand, and poking about in the ruins. A day earlier and they would have had mutton, but the sheep were putrid, already flyblown and alive with maggots. There was no game and even if there had been it would have been too risky to fire a shot, especially as they had only one horse and no chance of getting away if they were seen and chased.

The smell was terrible, but still Melvina looked. A fine black stallion lay dead by the door. A horse. There were twenty horses here, but all were dead. All but a foal nuzzling at its dam.

When Moolman joined her, she said, "There is nothing fit to eat. Everything is rotten. I thought there might be a chicken left or a sheep that was only wounded."

"There is something," he said, pointing to the foal.

"One cannot eat a horse, Dirk," Melvina said. "It has not cloven hoofs and does not chew the cud."

Moolman laughed at her. "*Ja,*" he said, "that is in the Bible." He quoted: "'The carcase of every beast which is not cloven footed, nor cheweth the cud are unclean to you. Everyone that toucheth them shall be unclean.'"

"You see, I know it too. But we must have food. Food for you. Food for me to be strong enough to get you out of here. In the wilds, Melvina, these laws have no application. I have eaten elephant and even lion."

"I am a Dopper," she said. "They are very strict."

"Yes," he said, "but I wonder if they are strict enough to prevent your mouth from watering when you smell a roast foal?" And, going up to the trusting beast, Moolman flung an arm around its neck and plunged his sheath knife into its throat.

An hour later they were eating.

Melvina said, "God will forgive me. It is for the child."

"God will forgive you, my dear," Moolman said as he kissed her. This was a good woman. He must get her to Steyn.

At one time he had thought of heading for Pietersburg, where the Boers had established themselves, even running a press for printing paper money, grain mills, and a horse-and cattle-distributing center. This was the only town of any size left to them now, but was likely to be under attack at any time. So, changing his mind, he decided to head toward the Lydenburg, where President Steyn and the other leaders had established a capital at a farm called Paardeplaas—Horse Place. From here they governed what was left of the two South African republics. They appointed magistrates and sent out correspondence that eventually reached Europe. Running the British blockade, it was sent abroad from such intelligence depots as the Willows in Pretoria. There was a certain comic element in this farm headquarters of a fugitive government, in one of the wildest areas of South Africa. A land of wild hills and deep ravines where the lion roared and the elephants still roamed, where giant baobabs—the cream-of-tartar trees of the Boers, fifty or more feet in diameter—had stood witness in this savage land for two thousand years, rooted in these mountain valleys since before the birth of Christ.

This land was home to the hunter Moolman. It was his Africa, still inviolate. No English would catch him here on his way to Steyn, whom he had known as a boy; for though he lived in the Transvaal he was a Free Stater by birth. There might be a predicant on the farm, or a marriage officer. Those officials had been appointed by the Government to marry Boers who found girls lost and straying on the veld and wished to take them as wives. Once married to him, no matter what happened, Melvina would be secure, for he had money—the accumulation of years of hunting—in the bank in Pretoria. He did not even know how much it was, but ten thousand pounds at least.

Moolman had not been surprised at her scruples. He had heard of Boers starving to death before they would eat elephant, hippo, wart hog, or even a hare.

But the foal was not the only thing that was left alive on the farm. The child, who had wandered off on her own after they had eaten, came back with a yellow puppy in her arms.

"Look, look," she said.

"My God," Moolman said, "that is what we need—a puppy."

"We must keep it," Melvina said. "It is a sign from God. He has forgiven us. A puppy. A child. *Ja,* a little child shall lead them . . . Out of the mouths of babes and sucklings . . . Don't you see?" she said. "It was meant. Just look at them, the baby and the pup. They are both young. They are the future. All is not dark while they still live."

There was no answering her. There were great disadvantages to a good and religious woman. To any woman. To them all life was sacred. He was a hunter, a fighter, a killer. She would knee-halter him yet, but he did not care. He had seen enough blood. She said God had sent him to her to save them. But perhaps it was the other way around—God had sent her to tame him. Now she had saved a pup that he would have knocked on the head without a thought. It was surprising what an interest God was suddenly taking in his affairs after so long.

The journey was hard and frightening for Melvina, who had never heard a lion roar before or the laughing scream of a hyena. She was a high-veld girl who had never been in the bush. She was worried by the size of the trees, by the lack of the horizon she was used to. She was frightened at being boxed in like this, enclosed by towering peaks, by the rushing streams, scared even by the barking of the baboons. Most of the way she rode the horse. When the hills were too steep, she walked and Moolman carried the child on his shoulders, her little hands on his head, her fingers twisted in his hair. And he led the horse.

As they marched he told Melvina about the bushveld. He showed her edible berries, taught her how to get water from the hollow to be found in the bole of almost every baobab, told her the names of the birds, and explained the habits of the beasts to try to occupy her mind and distract her. At last, when Melvina thought she could trek no farther, they came to Paardeplaas, the seat of government.

Steyn remembered Moolman well. Yes, they had a marriage officer. But what after that? Would he consider leaving his wife to cook for them? They had brought no woman as they had thought the life too hard for one, but as she was here she might as well stay.

In the morning it was done, with the President and his secretary as witnesses. Later they would have a church wedding, but it was legal now. Melvina had her certificate and was his heir.

"You need worry no more, my girl," he said. "You are provided for."

"And you, Dirk? What about you? *Magtig,* you are more than married to me. You have become my life. You have saved me and my child."

"I will come back," he said. "I will rest here for a few days and then go, but I will find you again."

Just before he left the President, Moolman got a surprise. A horseman whose seat looked familiar rode into the farm and offsaddled. Servas! By God, it was Servas!

"Servas!" he shouted. "It's me, Moolman."

They shook hands and embraced each other. Servas had changed. Always harder than Boetie, he now looked savage. His eyes were as cold as stones.

"What's happened to you, *jong?* What's gone wrong?" Moolman asked.

"This," Servas said, taking out his pocketbook and opening it. "Look. My mother and what is left of the women and children of Groenplaas, my people," he said. "My mother and my people."

The snapshot was bad, crumpled and faded, dirty from much handling, but it showed the women, ill and emaciated to the point of death.

"Two children are dead. The place is burned," Servas said. "It came through many hands, but it reached me in the end. She wanted Boetie to have it, but he could not be found, so it was sent to me here. But they will pay," he shouted. He raised his fist to the sky. "They will pay.

"Moolman," he said, "I'm going to go it on my own. I will raise my own commando, a small one, of men who want to kill."

"Come back with me, Servas."

"No, Dirk. You are too soft for me."

This was new. That he should be too soft for anyone. Did his new happiness show so much? Was that what Melvina had done to him in the few weeks they had been together?

But he was worried about Servas. He had gone sour—he was dangerous, like an ill-treated animal. He had become savage, like a cruelly handled horse. It was not just his mother and his people. Their meeting when he had gone to Groenplaas had not been happy. He had said so himself. It was the property. The destruction of the house, the home of his fathers, that was his, a part of himself—that had done it. He had been a man of property and now he was nothing.

As for himself, Moolman was somewhat amused. No one had ever said he was soft before. But perhaps it was true. Now, after so long, he had something, someone, to live for at last.

CHAPTER 66

THE MADMAN

BEFORE Moolman had gone far Servas joined him, riding a wild-eyed chestnut and leading a pack horse.

"I changed my mind," he said. "Two guns are better than one, four eyes better than two in these times. We shall be safer together. I will go with you to De la Rey, see if I can find the men I need there, and desert with them."

"Desert?" Moolman said.

"Desert to fight my own war. You will hear of us. All Africa will hear of us."

Moolman had little doubt that they might, for this man was mad. The translation of documents and writing anti-British propaganda for Europe from presidential headquarters, where, as if reality was not bad enough, he had magnified every minor incident into a major atrocity; followed by fighting off those who had tried to capture the President, scouting all by himself, alone with his thoughts in this grand but wild and savage country—all this had turned his brain. He was not only mad. He was bad. Moolman wished he had the courage to shoot him. Perhaps Servas was right, perhaps he was getting soft, or, if not soft, at least less hard.

They rode very carefully, knowing there were British cavalry patrols about, doing their trekking after dark, once they were out of broken country.

Servas spoke very little. When he did talk it was about the farm. Moolman had been right. His mother was only the symbol. That she and the others had been taken meant that Groenplaas was destroyed. His home, his patrimony, his beloved soil. The war that he had fought out of a youthful desire for adventure, patriotism, and duty had become a personal vendetta, a private war of unlimited revenge. The farm, always the farm. How he had been going to increase the land under alfalfa, get more pigs and cure hams for export to the Cape. He talked of the big gums and beefwoods, the peafowl, the doves cooing in the trees. All this he had lost, all this the English had taken from him.

"God damn and blast them! God . . . God . . . God . . ." He became inarticulate in his rage. These were the three phases of his life now—silence, reminiscence, and rage.

The first Boers they ran into were scouts from De la Rey's commando, where Boetie was serving. It took them a couple of days to find each other. When Boetie heard a man called Moolman from the north had joined them he said, "Not Dirk Moolman, the hunter?"

"Yes, and he has a man of your name with him."

Servas. At last they would be together again, the three of them, the three survivors of the Groenplaas gang. Boetie went off to look for them. They all saw one another simultaneously and met, shouting and patting each other on the back, each seeking to read the past in which they had been separate in the other's face. War changed men quickly. Wounds and illness, hardship and horrors aged them, altered the expressions of their eyes and mouths.

To Boetie, Moolman looked much the same, a little thinner, a little older, with a new touch of gray in his hair. It was strange to see him without his trade marks— the ostrich plume in his hat, the leopard-skin knife sheath and little all-purpose bowl that had always hung from his saddle. He was still more like a statue of dark wood and stone than a man, except for his eyes, which were no longer cold and sneering. His mouth, too, seemed fuller, the lips no longer a tight line slashed into the mahogany of his face.

But Servas, who now scarcely seemed a brother, stood silent—a grim figure of hate. He was pleased to see no one, his pleasure at finding Boetie had been only momentary. In half an hour none of it was left. He glanced

about him, showing the whites of his eyes like a dangerous horse. Then he burst out:

"I went home, Boetie, but it was not a success. I was
wounded as you know, and Oom Paul sent me back for
a few days' rest. But I had lost touch with our mother.
It was the place that called, the land, the soft, plow-
turned soil, the mealies, the lucerne. Our land, that is
what we fight for." His eyes became quite wild, flaring,
distending, almost popping out of his face. "I saw Bothma," he said, "the dirty malingerer."

"He was wounded," Boetie said. "I saw it. His face
was covered with blood when he rode off."

"*Ja,*" Servas said, "what a wound! He had a nick in
the ear. A nick like this." Drawing his knife he slit the
lobe he held between his fingers. "Wounded," he said,
"blood . . . *Ja,* blood. Look . . . I am covered with blood."
He smeared his hand over his face. "But I am not dead.
I am not even hurt."

What had happened to his brother?

"I saw Bothma," Boetie said. "He joined the National
Scouts and we took him."

"You killed him?" Servas said. "You shot him like a
dog?"

"I let him escape."

"Why?"

"For old times' sake. He was a Groenplaas man. One
of ours."

"All the more reason," Servas said. "By God, this war
will never end if we fight like women. Like little girls.
Sparing this one, letting that one go . . . Soft . . . Soft . . ."
He was almost screaming now as Moolman struck him in
the face with his open hand.

For a moment it looked as if Servas would draw his
knife on him, but Moolman stood unmoving, ready for
him, and he turned and walked away without a word.

"He's mad," Moolman said. "Your brother is mad,"
as Boetie stared at him openmouthed. This was the end
of their reunion.

They saw no more of Servas and ten days later heard
he had led sixteen burghers away, in defiance of all
orders, to go it, as he had said, alone.

De la Rey was less upset than he might have been,
because the men who had gone were bad ones—savage,

half-bandits, border scoundrels, near-slavers, from the Le-bombo Mountains, the Limpopo and Zambesi. No one knew this kind of man better than Moolman, who had often crossed their paths, and it was a measure of Servas's madness that he, much younger than any of them, had been able to impose his will on them and lead them away.

Servas had promised them the world. They were not just going to fight the English. They were going to fight the world, including their own people. These men did not care. They were not real Boers, but fighting adventurers, almost animals, only too glad to find a young leader more energetic and savage than themselves. Servas's scheme was to take his men dressed in British uniforms on a tour of the country, not only burning, but raping and leaving no one behind, not even an outraged girl who could be able to say that the men who had committed these crimes were not English cavalrymen but Boers in disguise. Turning like a wounded hyena that tears out its own entrails, Servas prepared his plan of campaign. The frightful atrocities he would commit would be attributed to the English and would turn the tide of war, and the people of England, overcome with shock and public shame, would bring it to an end.

They would rape and burn and kill. They would shoot a few Boers with dumdum bullets—regular Lee-Enfield ammunition with the steel point of the jacket snipped off with a pair of pliers. They would fight no English, once he had the equipment he needed, unless they could kill them all. No fugitive, Boer or Briton, must escape to tell the tale. All prisoners would have to be murdered.

It did not take the party long to capture a couple of mounted infantrymen. They took their prisoners without a fight since they were so vastly outnumbered. Then Servas ordered them stripped, which they thought natural enough as this was part of the new pattern of war. *Uitschudden,* as this custom was called, served two purposes. The first was to give the Boers clothes and boots; the second, since they could hold no prisoners, was to immobilize them, put them out of action for a few days or longer till they could be re-equipped. Some British soldiers had died of exposure before they got back to their own lines.

But this was not Servas's reason for stripping them.

He did not want anyone shot while dressed. He wanted clean uniforms, but would leave no naked soldiers alive to tell the story.

Servas called Piet Swart and his brother, two giants from the Portuguese border.

"Kill them," he said. They cut the throats of the naked Englishmen as if they were sheep.

He now had two uniforms and two sets of British saddlery, rifle buckets and all. He told a couple of his men to put on the uniforms of the murdered men. They were still warm from their bodies. The English bits were changed to their horses' mouths, their headstalls to their heads, their head ropes correctly tied, the saddles on their folded saddle blankets girthed, the rifles standing in their buckets on the offside of the ponies. Servas was not going to use the captured horses. Someone might recognize them. So they were killed.

Only one thing remained. The two masqueraders must shave their beards. This they refused to do, until Servas told them they would not be the only ones. "We shall all be shaven before long."

At last it was done and the two decoys rode off side by side with shortish stirrup leathers in the English fashion, with their Boer companions riding on their flank a mile or so away.

It took four days for them to find what they wanted—a patrol of twenty men in a little hollow, almost a valley, between two ridges where they could be ambushed. There had been small parties of Englishmen before. There had been splendid places for an ambush before, but never the two of them together until now.

Servas posted his men behind rocks on both sides of the depression. The decoys fired shots to attract the attention of the patrol, followed then with a half-dozen shots in rapid succession, and made hand signals to the British to close in and help them. Then they rode forward toward the valley, firing an odd shot, as if they were pursuing an enemy. When the patrol came up to them they waved their rifles and galloped their ponies down the ambushed valley well in front, hoping their comrades would keep their heads and not shoot them down.

They were in no danger. The shots and cries behind

them proved that, as they swung about to face the surprised British, now surrounded by Boers. Six saddles were empty, three horses down, but they had the rest.

An hour later it was done. Neither a living nor wounded trooper was left in that small depression. The horses, stripped of their gear, were killed, and at dawn the next day sixteen clean-shaven British mounted infantrymen rode out in sections under the command of a young, fair-haired sergeant.

The British atrocities that were to shock the world and change the course of the war were about to begin.

CHAPTER 67

THE IMPOSTERS

SERVAS'S mind was blank as he rode with his men in half sections behind him, as alert as an animal hunting for game, with only his senses active. He had no feeling of good or evil, of time, no memories or hopes. Even the cause of this rapine was lost. The false working of a diseased brain had set him on a course that had appeared logical. If enough atrocities were committed by the British, the news of them when they reached England would cause such revulsion that the Government would fall, and the war be brought to an end on Boer terms. On this assumption he had forged his instrument—the gang of white savages who followed him—and begun his work. Then his mind had slipped a cog. Disguised in the uniforms of the men they had murdered, his men looked, he thought, completely English. But when, with an animal sense of self-protection, he had decided to leave no one alive on the farms he destroyed, he erred. With no one left to tell the tale, no one, therefore, who knew what or who they were. All that was found when Servas had gone were the bodies of the dead, the wrecked houses, destroyed furniture, and broken windows, for he set no signal fires that would alert the countryside. Twice he had seen British troops and avoided them. Nor did they pay any attention to his party. To them they were just another cavalry patrol.

The destruction, the killings, and the women he left to his men, watching them quite unmoved as they shot unarmed farmers and their colored servants; and tied the women's skirts above their heads, so that they looked like sacks with legs, to rape them. They could not see or struggle in the straight jackets of their own clothes, only kick their white legs as man after man took and left them. Before they rode off they killed them with a bullet through their heads. He had watched his men, slavering like hounds, hunt two girls about the age of his dead sister. But no thought of Elsa had come to his mind. They killed the dogs, the stock—horses, cows, sheep—in a wild orgy of blood lust. At the end of it, when they rode away, only a few flustered hens were left alive to scratch and peck among the scattered dead.

That will teach them, he thought. Teach whom? Teach them what? Who was there left to learn or tell the tale? All he knew was that he must drive on like a mad dog, savaging all he met.

They rode up to a farm, collected the inhabitants in a kraal, and dealt with them. On arrival the people neither welcomed nor feared them, believing them to be English, come for water, forage for their horses, a sheep and a chicken or two. These farmers were British subjects, but their hearts if not their bodies were with the commandos. Then, when they heard the men speak Dutch they looked at them with contempt, thinking them traitors who were taking English money to fight their brethren. The men, white and colored, were then tied up and killed, and the women trussed and raped in the soft-piled dung of the kraals, which made, as Piet Marais said, a softer bed than the bare veld. The two girls on the last farm, a place called Tafelberg, had made a run for it. Farm girls in their late teens, active as buck, they had raised their dresses and leaped over the kraal wall with the men in full cry behind them. They had not got far. All this Servas had seen from the back of his horse, not even bothering to dismount, seen, as God must have seen it from up there, utterly dispassionate and unfeeling.

When they rode off after having roasted a sheep and some chickens, he felt the job had been well done and put Tafelberg behind him. Does the lion remember his last kill when he moves on to the next?

Servas's men had destroyed four farms. They were now approaching the fifth, a big property with a plantation of gums behind it.

They were in a good mood, laughing and joking together as they rode. This was better than anything they had known before, hunting and freebooting on the Portuguese border. They had had women, white women, not the black meat they took in the wild north. They had found gold, jingling sovereigns. They had even got used to shaving, dressing neatly, and grooming their horses like Englishmen.

Except for their seats—they rode Boer style with long stirrup leathers, their legs stuck out forward—and the way they held their reins—they were unaccustomed to holding two. They looked like English cavalry to anyone who was not a soldier.

But this time they had made a mistake. The farm had not been reconnoitered.

A troop of yeomanry was bivouacked in the gum plantation. A young officer interested in birds, watching a secretary bird stalking over the veld looking for snakes and young game birds, had just decided that a secretary was a long-legged terrestrial eagle. They could not fly far. They flew and then came down. In open country on a good horse it should be possible to ride one down. He dropped his field glasses, letting them hang in front of him, and looked around to rest his eyes.

He saw a party of cavalry coming toward the farm. He wondered who they were. There was something about them . . . He could not place it—but something . . . He picked up his glasses. They were not British cavalry. They must be the men he was looking for. For, contrary to Servas's belief that these acts would be attributed to the British when they were discovered, the British thought that they were acts of revenge by the Boers who had failed to raise the Cape Colony by appeals to Boer patriotism, and were now seeking to frighten them into participation.

It took only five minutes to get his men into action. Still in their shirt sleeves, their jackets left hanging on the trees, he got them down on the edge of the plantation,

prone, their sights on the advancing Boers. He had to be
certain before he opened fire. Ten men under a sergeant
were ordeerd to mount and stand by, ready to cut the
Boers off if they tried to run. He watched them through
his glasses. They came nearer and nearer. They began to
fan out. He saw how high they carried their bridle hands,
the way they neck-reined their horses, the way they held
their feet in the stirrups. They were not British. They
were not National Scouts. They were Boers in British
uniforms. He had had to make quite certain. These were
the murderers, rapists he was after, who, if taken, would
be summarily shot for their masquerade alone, irrespective of their other crimes.

The attack was sudden. The first thing Servas knew was
the crackle of rifle fire from the plantation as four of his
men fell from their horses. Two more swung around and
began to gallop away. He saw some British cavalry emerge,
charging down on them, their swords flashing in the sun
as they leaned over their horses' necks. Fresh horses,
big horses, fast. Overconfident, they had been surprised.
As he watched, another man was hit, then he felt a blow
on his wrist, as if someone had struck him with a hammer.
How could someone hit him with a hammer on the
wrist? No great pain, just a blow. He looked down. His
arm was shattered, his hand hung limp. Dismounted, hat-
less, the British in gray shirts, their sleeves rolled up,
their rifles at the ready, came out of the little wood
led by an officer. To bolt was useless. This was the end of
his great enterprise. People were coming out of the
thatched farmhouse. Two men and three women, a group
of children. How lucky you are, he thought as he looked
at them, lucky to be alive. He sat his horse passively,
waiting, an observer. All that was going on about him
quite irrelevant. He felt nothing for his men, wounded,
cursing with fury. What were they but scum, instruments
on whom he had played a savage tune?

The British disarmed them, tied their legs beneath their
horses' girths, and prepared to take them back to their
camp, some twenty miles away. The dead were left lying
openmouthed on their backs, grotesque. It was hard to
believe that twenty minutes ago they had been alive
and dangerous.

A bearded man of fifty or so came up to the officer

and said in English, "You saved us, sir, from death. And worse than death for these." He nodded toward the girls and women. "We shall not forget."

A woman accompanied by two maids came out with coffee in a big jug, sugar, milk, and a dozen cups. The Englishmen drank, laughing and joking with one another. The children, hanging onto their mother's skirts, stared up at the big English horses and looked at the dead. Boer children, stolid as dough. A boy of fourteen or so went up to a body and gave it a kick and spat upon it. Above, vultures, recognizing death but timid of people, circled at a great height.

"We'll bury them," the man said to the officer. *"Ja,* before God, my boys will bury them where they lie, their graves unmarked, unfenced, to be trodden by my cattle."

The officer shouted an order. The men, all fully dressed now, formed up. They moved off in threes—two Englishmen to each prisoner and each lashed corpse, one riding on either side.

It was like a dream. Servas's wrist was hurting now. The blow of the bullet, striking the bone and paralyzing it, was wearing off.

He looked at the men on either side of him. Boys. Rooineks. Red necks. Englishmen who went red in the sun and peeled instead of becoming bronzed. He was beginning to feel again. Hatred oozed up with the taste of bile in his mouth. Sense that had been absent for months began to return and with it some appreciation of the enormity of his acts. He felt fear. The fear of the God he had denied. Death, he knew, confronted him. They would be shot. This was his last day upon the earth, his last day in Africa. Tomorrow at dawn he would die against some whitewashed wall. The wounded they would nurse to health and shoot later. That was the English way. But what a waste of energy, good medicine, and bandages. Why not kill them at once? Shoot them lying down if they could not stand up.

Two things were important now: the first to die like a man, facing the black snouts of the squads' rifles, unblindfolded, untied, his arms across his chest. He could support his wounded left arm with his right. The second, to appreciate every instant left to him, every moment in this lovely world, which he had accepted so easily and unthinkingly, which he was about to leave. The sights and sounds and smells of it.

A yellow-green bok-ma-kierie sang on a bush. He did not know the Cape birds. To him it was just a greenish bird, black-marked with a yellow breast, but the voice was the voice of life, of God. The mountains—how lovely they were—purple, Prussian blue, ultramarine in the distance. He did not know the names of colors—only that the mountains were blue and that he would never see or climb another. How wonderful was the movement of the horse beneath him. His last ride. Why had he appreciated none of this before? Did a man love only what he had lost?

That was not so. Groenplaas he had loved, loved the way a man loves a woman. The sweet red earth, rich with unborn crops. The mother of mealies, of alfalfa, of potatoes. There was something beautiful about a potato planted in its earth mother, already sprouted with little buds.

They rode with jingling bits through a valley where green-flowered heath brushed their irons. A rippling, brown-watered stream that looked like velvet ran beside them, patched with arums, their white kid chalices rising on tall stems from the bright green, almost spear-shaped leaves. Shaded by rocks, maidenhair ferns grew on fine black hairlike stems.

Why had he seen none of this before? Why was a man granted sight only when he was about to lose it?

He thought of his mother and the snapshot. Thought of his coldness with her, of the barrier that had grown up between them, of his refusal of her love. He thought of Bothma, the coward and traitor.

And then they were there, at the British camp of neat white tents like paper hats laid out in rows. The horse lines. The smell of smoke and food. By God, he was hungry. They had not eaten because they had expected to eat at the farmhouse. He had forbidden breakfast. Men, like dogs, hunted better and were more savage on empty bellies.

"Eight men," the sergeant shouted. "I want eight men, and as none of you want this detail I'm going to pick the names out of a hat. I've got 'em here." He threw some slips of paper into a slouch hat and stirred them around with his finger as if it was a spoon.

The men's feet moved uneasily. They licked their dry lips. A firing party. Jesus! One man, a Catholic, fingered his beads. God would help him. God would get him out of this. But He didn't. His was the first name called.

"Badley, George . . . Smith, John . . ." was the next. "Herbert . . . Springfield, York . . . Sprat . . . Finch . . . Taylor . . ." Names as English as Yorkshire pudding.

The sun was coming up from behind the mountains. They were outlined black against its gold with great shadows flung down like a cloak before them.

"Don't think I like it, do you, you bloody bastards?" the sergeant said. He was an old soldier with a D.C.M. and the striped blue and white medal ribbon of the Egyptian campaign, but his hands shook. "Look, boys," he said, "I load the rifles. Two blanks, so you'll never know who did it. See? I loads 'em secret-like, puts on the safety catch, and 'ands 'em back to you. An' shoot proper. Kill the poor bugger, see. That's kindest. No bloody mess-up."

There was a firing party for each prisoner. Other parties were being organized.

Badley—he was the Catholic—took his rifle from the sergeant's hand. God would save him from this. All his life he had prayed, had confessed, had gone to Mass whenever it was possible. There was no doubt that he had a blank in the chamber. That would be his reward. The Holy Virgin would see to it. They were the first squad, Servas the first man to be shot. Not against a white wall, against a windbreak of brush, a false hedge supported by horizontal saplings.

The officer in charge, Captain Shakespeare, a man they all liked, stood at their left, his pistol in his hand. If they didn't kill him, he had to finish him off. His face was as white as a bit of paper. The sergeant stood behind him. The prisoner, his head bare, his left arm in a sling, faced them. He seemed the calmest of the lot.

"Port arms!" came the order. Eight rifles came to the port as one. They knew their drill, they did. "You'll never know," the sergeant said.

"Silence!" Captain Shakespeare turned on him.

We'll never know. How heavy the rifles seemed, butt

to belly, muzzle to the left. Death or a blank in the chamber. God, make it blank . . . please, God . . . When would he give the order? When? It came—harsh, hard, like a rasp drawn over iron. "Safety catches off."

Captain Shakespeare had control of himself.

"Aim!" The rifles went up. The barleycorn of the fore sight neatly set, centered between the shoulders of the back. Beyond the fore sight the man. Like one of our own, in British khaki. That would be worse, of course, if anything could be worse, to have to shoot one of your own. The order. For Christ's sake the order! Let's get it over. "Fire . . . !"

Eight triggers were squeezed as eight men prayed.

The man at the fence staggered, threw up his unwounded arm, and fell.

Captain Shakespeare slowly, as if on parade, moved over to him, his revolver cocked. Badley heard it click as he raised it with his thumb.

That was when he turned on the sergeant. "You lied!" he shouted. "I know. I know. If it had been blank there'd have been no recoil." God had not saved him from this. Now this was someone else to pray for every day of his life, the soul of the Boer he had shot. Dropping his rifle, he fell down in a faint.

CHAPTER 68

A DEATH OR GLORY BOY

It was still Boetie's aim to find General Smuts and get to the Cape Colony. Here they were far enough south to be in the winter rain area. The horses were used up, but near here, in the Elandsberg, there were herds of wild horses running and they did not have too much difficulty in driving a bunch into a *kloof* and capturing the replacements they needed. Again they had to be broken and tamed. Boetie got two mares—a black and a bay.

Any rain, even a shower, might make the Orange River impassable, so they pushed on as fast as they could. As they approached it they saw a body of horsemen whom they knew to be Boers from the way they rode and from their formation. Not only was it a Boer commando, but it was the very one they were looking for, and General Smuts, the Transvaal state attorney, riding in the lead, was glad to welcome them into his command.

Next day they saw the dark line of the deep gorge cut through the hills by the Orange, a knife thrust that separated the Free State from the Colony. They also saw the white tents of a British camp and some mounted patrols riding over the country. It was evident that they were expected. Seeing this, Smuts led them back into the hills where a young Boer joined them with fifty men. He said that if they didn't cross at once they would be trapped. The crossing would be difficult because of the steep cliffs and the swift water. But he had a man with him who knew a path down to the river. It was already dusk and the general decided to start at once.

They rode over rough mountain tracks till they came to the edge of the cliff. Below them the river glinted as it boiled in silver eddies through a rocky gut. The path was steep and they went down in single file on foot, their horses stumbling behind them.

The river was not broad here, nor deep, since the winter rains hadn't fallen yet. But it ran fast and strong, tearing at the horses' legs and bellies so that they could hardly keep their feet.

When the sun came up the Boers were in the Colony, invaders, no longer fighting to protect their homes, but attacking the enemy on his own ground. Still leading their horses, they climbed the cliffs on the British side of the river boundary and found themselves on a wide flat where cattle were grazing and native villages nestled in shallow cups among the hills.

This was a Basuto reserve, and a group of men armed with rifles and battle-axes, knobkerries and assagais rode threateningly toward them and watched them ride by. No one thought anything of it till later in the day when the remains of three Boers who had become separated from the main body in their search for tobacco and grain were found dreadfully mutilated by the natives for *mouti*— witch-doctor medicine. The most horrible thing about this was that, for the medicine to be effective, the parts and

the human blood required must be cut and drawn from
the victim while he was still alive.

There was some other action with the hostile mounted
Basutos, and some minor casualties were suffered. Once
out of the native reserve the wounded were left at a
European farmhouse to be taken care of by the English.
This they could always do with the utmost confidence.

And then the weather broke. It rained hard all night
as they lay waiting in mud and water for the dawn. The
next day it still rained and, draped in blankets, since they
had no raincoats, they rode on with chattering teeth.

This was Boetie's first experience of southern winter
rains. In the Transvaal and Free State you froze in winter
but you were dry. If you found wood it was not too wet
to burn. And in summer, the storms born of the heat were
followed by sunshine.

The local farmers, being of Boer stock, were sympathetic, and gave them coffee and sugar, salt and tobacco,
but could spare no clothes, as they could not replace them.
At one halt a woman gave Boetie a slice of bread and
butter, the first he had had for a year, and a cup of real
coffee.

Hearing there were English troops nearby, the commando halted, and Smuts, taking two men with him, went
off to scout their position, saying he would be back before
dark. But he did not return till midnight and then on foot
and alone. His party had been ambushed. Both men he
had taken with him and all the horses were dead. It was
only by the greatest good luck that he had escaped.

That night the horses bolted, thundering off in a wild
stampede, frightened by a porcupine that had come fuss-
ing and rattling its quills through the lines. In the morning the commando was an infantry force—a sitting duck
waiting to be picked up. Not a horse was in sight. But
luckily some burghers out of habit had knee-haltered
their mounts, and as soon as these were found—they had
not been able to gallop very far on three legs—they were
used to track and round up the others. But there were
some anxious hours of waiting.

From now on, as they went farther south, the weather
got worse, colder, with wild storms of sleet and hail.
There was snow on the mountaintops, and no dry fuel to
be found. They spent icy nights huddled in the lee of a

kopje or a patch of scrub. And they were losing horses, leaving some foundered behind them every day. There they stood, dejected, with sunken heads and glazed eyes, waiting for death to come.

The days that followed were no better. More horses were lost. Near Jamestown a British column was sighted and the general drove them on through the black cold night, leading their reluctant horses into a rain that drove straight into their faces.

In crossing a stream Boetie's sandals stuck in the clay of the bank and in pulling his feet clear disintegrated entirely, leaving him barefooted. All he could do was to wrap his feet in strips cut from his blanket and wonder how long they would last. Their guide, a boy from a local farm, lost his way, and after wandering in circles for hours the commando halted. When the sun came up thirty horses lay dead from exposure.

At a farmhouse they got a hot meal, the first in months. The housewife, a stout, friendly woman, gave Boetie a pair of elastic-sided boots and, finding a grain bag, he took it and cut holes for his head and arms. This was some protection against the biting cold.

Before they were fully rested some English cavalry appeared with two fifteen-pounders. They fought them off till dark and then trekked on under the cover of the night.

The next week was a blur of fighting and marching, and then, when they were sure they had broken through the cordon, they found themselves on a mountain plateau looking down at British camps that blocked every road. The white tents were scattered like clumps of mushrooms over the veld that was thick with troops. Another guide was found and he led them by small diverse paths around the British flank and left them at the foot of the Stormberg range. Here, thinking themselves safe at last, they made for a big farm, turned their horses out to graze in a pasture, killed a couple of sheep, and settled down to rest, having been on the move for thirty hours with hardly a halt.

No sooner had they begun their meal than there was a cry of *"Opzaal . . . Opzaal . . .* Saddle up!" as they saw a column of English troops bearing down on them. They escaped up a pass into the mountains and halted on the top, which was, like so many mountaintops in Africa, a flat tableland where the wind roared and whipped grit and pebbles like buckshot into their faces. Reconnoitering over the edge of the berg, they found the British there before them. The gale increased in strength. The men and horses had now been on the move for forty hours and were exhausted from lack of food and sleep. Ammunition too was very short. Boetie had two rounds left. Some men had none.

The British, thinking they had them bottled up, did not attack. Then a crippled man came to Smuts and said he could lead them through the British line by a path that, because it ran through a bog, was not being watched. He led them so near the British that they could hear them talk, and left them on what he said was a path down the escarpment.

The descent was perilous and it was doubtful that in daylight they could have got the horses down. But they are both quieter and more sure-footed in the dark. The mountainside was not rocky. It was just an almost vertical wall, not even a slope, covered with a thick mat of slippery grass down which men and horses slid, glissading together in a kind of wild toboggan run through the darkness, without knowing what was in front of them.

When they reached the bottom they went on, still leading their horses to save them, and in the distance saw the lights of a train approaching them. General Smuts would not let them derail or fire at it, in case they might hurt any traveling civilians. So they stood by their horses in the dark and watched the lighted train go by. The English officers in the dining car were smoking cigars and drinking wine. They could see the silver, the shining glass, and the white tablecloths. Boetie was sure he could smell the food.

Though they did not know it at the time, General John French, the British cavalry commander, was on the train with his staff, going north to plan the capture of the men who stood on the veld watching him go by—General Smuts and his commando, whom the English papers described as having invaded the Colony with the riffraff of the Boer armies.

When the train had passed the commando went on. Whenever there was a check at a fence or a donga, as soon as they halted for any cause whatsoever, the men would sit down and fall asleep.

A farmer gave Smuts a paper containing Lord Kitchener's proclamation, stating that any burgher found under arms after September 15 would be sentenced to perpetual banishment from South Africa. It was now the thirteenth and no one paid the slightest attention to it. Everywhere it was treated with derision and called "the paper bomb."

They trekked on and on, penetrating deeper and deeper into the Colony, and it continued to storm and rain. One night they halted not far from a British camp and looked with longing at the cozy village of tents, at the smoke of the fires, at its ordered streets. Then they moved on before they were observed, but their guide lost his way in the pitch blackness of the night. They marched, dragging their horses by their bridles, through water and mud that was ankle deep. The horses stumbled and fell, some never to rise again. Twice Boetie stumbled over foundered horses that were gasping out their last breath. Then the rain turned to sleet. The grain bag he wore was frozen solid to his body, stiff as armor. Fourteen men were lost that night. There was never a word of them later and it seemed likely to Boetie that they were dead of cold, lying frozen stiff with the horses.

At last they came to a deserted farm and crowded into its rooms and stables, men and horses standing together side by side, the men reduced almost to animals, the animals raised almost to the stature of men, in this strange collaboration of man and mount in war. But by morning fifty more horses were dead, and another fifty Boers were foot soldiers, staggering under the extra weight of their saddlery. As soon as it was light the rain stopped and they broke up the floors, the chairs, and the tables to make fires in the yard to dry their blankets and clothes. Boetie wondered what the owners would think when they came back and found everything combustible burned and the skeletons of fifty horses inside their house.

By now it was September 17. The commando was no longer a fighting force. Had it been led by a lesser man than Smuts it would have been a rabble. As it was it was a ghost commando, a kind of shadow. In front came the few ragged men who still had horses, dragging their staggering, scarecrow mounts behind them. Next came the men who had lost their horses, in groups of twenty or thirty, carrying their saddles. Some held them like hats on their heads, the stirrups dangling like grotesque ribbons over their shoulders. Others had them slung over their backs. The rear was brought up by the only mounted men, the wounded, held onto their horses by friends who marched on either side of them.

But at last the sun was shining. Spring was on its way. The Cape spring with its miraculous carpets of flowers had begun. There were big patches of magenta flowers, patches of yellow. The sun was what they had been waiting for all winter. In a few days the whole world would be covered as far as the eye could see with pink, white, yellow, orange, red, blue, and purple blooms—wall to wall, from horizon to horizon.

In every watercourse and vlei the arum lilies stood grouped, holding up their white cups to the welcome sun. They bloomed all winter, sun or no sun, but now they could be seen in their full beauty, though the Boers called them *varkblomme*—pig lilies—because the pigs were so fond of them, eating both their foliage and bulbous tubers.

Despite their exhaustion, despite the fact that they were practically out of ammunition, the commando was in better spirits. The sun was shining, God and their general would provide.

Punch drunk, content for the moment not to be cold, they staggered and reeled on till a farmer rushed out of a small thatched cottage shouting that a squadron of British cavalry with mountain and machine guns was waiting for them.

Smuts decided to attack. He had no option. He had to have their horses and ammunition. Boetie's section was sent off to scout the position. They splashed through a little river of brown water edged with lilies, the air sweet with the honey scent of *fonteinbos*, and ran slap into a body of troopers. Most of the section was still in the *fonteinbos*. But Boetie and the others who found themselves within ten yards of the soldiers jumped to the ground and opened fire. The British turned and galloped off, leaving four dead behind them. It was here Boetie fired his last two cartridges. Rushing forward, he turned over the body of the soldier he had killed, to get at his bandoleer.

The whole section now pursued the British and hit several more, for though the English horses were fresh they were delayed by a gate where they bunched up. The British left their horses, took cover in the rocks, and opened fire on them. More British joined in the fight and a mountain gun began to shell them.

The Boers crept forward, reached the edge of the hill, and saw below them a British camp only a hundred yards away, heaving like an ant heap that has been stirred up with a stick. Officers were shouting orders, men were running this way and that among the tents as they fell in.

The British had no idea of the Boer strength, but were recovering from their surprise. This placed the Boers in a tight place, as they were now being fired at from all around. Only General Smuts's arrival saved them. He had pushed the commando on when he heard the guns and opened fire on the British from a nearby hill, forcing them to take cover.

From where he lay Boetie and a man called Marko could see the mountain gun that was shelling the commando. They were safe because they were so close to the British that the guns could not fire at them for fear of hitting their own people. Four men were handling the gun. Boetie fired at the man at the breech. He fell with his back to the wheel. The others ran for it. Now a duel began, but at this kind of short-range snap-shooting the English were no match for the Boers. Boetie and Marko killed a dozen men, putting bullets into their heads as soon as they put them up to shoot. Boetie shot a man, hidden behind a rock, in his heel, which he had exposed. The pain and impact of the bullet made him jump up and Marko killed him.

Seeing more British approaching from the rear, the section decided to charge. Yelling their loudest and cheering, they ran down at the British camp. The soldiers, surprised by the attack, bolted in all directions, throwing down their rifles. The commando, seeing what was happening, got their ponies and galloped cheering into the camp.

Thirty Englishmen were killed, fifty wounded, and over a hundred taken prisoner. The force was a squadron of the 17th Lancers, a crack regiment of British cavalry. But it was not the victory that cheered the Boers; it was the loot. Fresh horses, mules, uniforms, ammunition, food, blankets, medical supplies, boots, and saddlery. Every Boer was refitted from head to toe.

Boetie found himself in an officer's long-skirted tunic with chain epaulets, riding breeches, boots, and leggings, with a new Lee-Metford rifle, two full bandoleers, a new saddle and bridle, a neat little gray Arab horse, and a riding mule. A mule for long marches and a horse for action—an ideal combination.

When Boetie got back to where he had left his mare, he found her standing in the same spot, too exhausted to move when he tried to lead her, so he offsaddled her, took off her bridle, and left her. Someone would find her when they had gone. People were always drawn to a battlefield, to succor the wounded if any were left, and to scrounge for anything useful that lay around, even to loot the dead.

The general ordered everything they could not take away to be destroyed. Tents, wagons, guns, rifles, ammunition, and stores all went up in flames, the cartridges popping like firecrackers in the billowing smoke. The prisoners were abandoned, to find their way back as best they might.

Boetie rode off with the commando, king-happy, jaunty on his gray Arab in the uniform of a captain of the 17th, with a silver skull-and-crossbones badge in the band of his slouch hat—a pucka "Death or Glory Boy"—condemned, though he did not realize it, to be shot out of hand if he were taken, for wearing a British uniform, in full accordance with the articles of war. A number of Boers in British uniform had been shot, but the news had not leaked back to the commandos, who, always on the move, knew very little about what was going on.

CHAPTER 69

A NEW MODEL

LORD KITCHENER now realized that the drive system had failed; the fish always managed to slip through some gap in the net. So far his blockhouse system, scorched-earth policy, secrecy, and feints had come to nothing. A new plan had to be devised. It was called the New Model Drive, as opposed to the old-fashioned one. This was going to succeed. It was foolproof and Boer-proof. There would be routes for every single man, halting places, rationing places, watering places. The line from blockhouse line to blockhouse line was going to be so tight that not even a buck or a hare would escape. Only the birds would be safe.

But the New Model Drive could not be begun till the blockhouse lines were completed. There was one line from the Central Railway to Botha's Pass via Frankfort, and another from the railway to Van Reenan's Pass via Lindley and Bethlehem. These were the two east-west fences. The passes across the Drakensberg were blocked, and the Central Railway formed the other, north-south, side of a great rectangular paddock sixty-five miles wide by a hundred sixty-five miles long.

On February 5, in midsummer heat, Kitchener drew up nine thousand men along the north-south line from Frankfort to Bethlehem's fifty-four-mile-long line—one man to every twelve to fifteen yards. They were to move west at a speed of twenty miles a day and would reach the Central Railway in two nights and three days, where the Boers would be caught with their backs to the wire wall, facing such vastly superior British numbers that they would have no choice but surrender.

The advancing line of beaters in the battue were preceded by scouts followed by their guns and transport. Rimington, who commanded one of the units and was the inventor of the New Model, issued the following orders for holding the line at night. No one was going to slip through in the dark this time.

1. Every man from the brigadier to the last native to be on duty and to act as sentry for one-third of the night.

2. *Front Line*—Each squadron to be allotted a length of front, to be covered by entrenched pickets of six men, 50 to 100 yards apart; two men to constitute a double sentry; four to sleep close beside them. Guns loaded with case (shot) to be posted in front line. . . . Transport, artillery vehicles, and all horses to be in small laagers, handy to their units.

3. *Rear Line*—A thin line of rear pickets, each of six men, 500 yards in rear of front line; two pickets to a mile. If attacked, to fall back on the laagers.

4. *Sham Front Line*—A sham line of pickets to be taken up by daylight, a mile or two in front of the real line, and evacuated after dark; fires to be left burning along it. The two real lines to be selected by daylight but on no account to be occupied till after dark.

5. *Cover and Obstacles*—Advantage to be taken of natural cover and obstacles, such as dongas, spruits, and wire fences. Wire entanglements to be used where feasible.

6. *Lights*—After dark no fires or smoking and only whispered talking. Cooking to be done only at midday halt, and as much sleep as possible to be taken then too.

7. *Subterfuges*—Tricks of every sort to deceive enemy as to strength and position of real front line. E.g., [a] supports to be loudly called for when a picket is attacked; [b] gaps to be left in the smoldering fires of sham front line; opposite strong points in real front line.

This mathematical advance of nine thousand men in almost parade-ground alignment over fifty miles of country was a great achievement. Like the Charge of the Light Brigade in reverse, this parade of tortoises over the veld was also magnificent, but it was not war. Mile by slow mile, at a rate of two to three miles an hour, the British pushed forward. Besides the nine thousand beaters there were eight thousand men stationed along the blockhouse fences and seven armored trains puffed up and down, going back and forth, north and south, along the line. These, the armored trains and the eight thousand men, could be regarded as the guns, against whom the beaters would drive the Boer birds.

As the beaters approached, De Wet called in his burghers, but only six hundred men came. The remaining twelve hundred paid no attention to his orders. With the six hundred was an immense herd of cattle, several thousand head, that the Boers insisted on taking with them. With this immense cavalcade behind him De Wet rode toward the blockhouse line between Kroonstad and Lindley.

This was the night of February 6–7, and the seventeen men who guarded the two blockhouses De Wet approached never heard him cut the wire. He got through without a shot being fired. The reinforcements waiting nearby never knew he was close to them till the cattle herd bringing up the rear thundered through the fence at full gallop, smashing down five hundred yards of wire.

And once again De Wet was out and away. But the commandos that had not followed him were not so lucky. One broke through to the north with some loss, but the rest rode up and down in front of the line of advancing troops that was forcing them back against the raking searchlights of the armored trains, whose beams were flickering over the veld in the distance. Driven against them, silhouetted, outlined against the light, they were machine gunned and pom-pomed as they strove to break through. Some did. A few cut their way out, others were shot like game, but the greater part fell back, stunned and bewildered, their horses foundered, their bandoleers empty. . . .

In the end the Boer losses were only three hundred men. Not enough, numerically, to warrant the enormous build-up the British had made, but psychologically important because they were part of the hard core that was being slowly whittled away, peeled off like the skin of an apple.

This was not just a straw in the wind. It was the writing on the wall and the beginning of the end. But the end was still not yet.

Kitchener, after giving his troops a few days' rest, now flung them like a net over the northeastern Free State, which had not been touched by the first New Model Drive.

This was another immense operation, spread over very broken country, but luck was on the English side. This time they had De Wet caught with no avenue of escape, and with him was President Steyn, whom he had joined across the Wilge River. What a catch that would be!

In this vast trap De Wet had three thousand men scattered about. There were also a mass of refugees with their wagons and loose stock who had attached themselves to him, hampering his every movement. By March 3 he had collected about twelve hundred men and decided to attack and break out. His information made him pick a spot twenty miles south of Vrede as the weakest link in the chain.

The moon was full, the wind high, and the sky cloudy, so the veld, almost as light as day one minute, was black a few minutes later as the dark clouds edged with silver shuttered off the moon.

In this strange and bizarre on-and-off light De Wet, in a six-mile-wide cloud of dust set up by his men, moved the vehicles of the refugees and their great herds.

At midnight a picked force extricated themselves from the swirling mob of terrified women and children in carts and wagons and attacked the Australians and New Zealanders who held the line at this point. The Boers broke through the Colonials, wheeled and cut a swath, a bloody gate half a mile wide, for the refugees to drive through with their stock. But they were demoralized with fear and milled about, oxen bellowing, native herders and drivers yelling, women screaming, as De Wet, laying about him with his sjambok, tried to drive them through the gap before it closed. Six hundred fighting men with a bunch of refugee wagons, banging and bumping as their great wheels rolled at a trot, got through, and in the middle of it were Steyn and what was left of the government officials of the Free State.

De Wet and Steyn had escaped again. But the British booty was enormous. Eight hundred prisoners, among them one of De Wet's sons, thousands of cattle, horses, and wagons loaded with women and children. The war of attrition was continuing. The apple was being peeled deeper, deeper.

Steyn now had the idea that if the Government left the northeast Kitchener might leave the area to pursue him. And he asked De Wet to conduct him to the Western Transvaal, where he could get De la Rey's doctor to attend to his eye, which was giving him intolerable pain.

To reach De la Rey, De Wet had to pierce the northern blockhouse line, swing northwest, pierce the blockhouse line along the railway, and then ride southwest and pierce the Kroonstad-Vaal line. This ride, through three blockhouse lines, took ten days, and gives a picture of the man who led it.

Behind De Wet and Steyn, Kitchener was off again, but his troops were exhausted, gaps appeared in the line of beaters, and the surviving commandos either slipped through them or charged at full gallop through the British lines.

But Kitchener was wearing the Boers down. Between

the hammer of his blows and the anvil of their privations they were losing heart as well as numbers. Their leaders knew the end was near, but still hoped for divine intervention, for some act of God that would deliver them. To give up would be to show their lack of faith in Him— in the God of their fathers.

The 2nd had been through all this, losing both horses and men from exhaustion and illness. To Turnbull war was becoming more horrible every day. Chasing these men over the veld, never catching them, just finding their cooking fires and the foundered horses that were left behind them—dead beasts, exhausted beasts. The men who had ridden them must be in just as bad a state. What was it all about? Where was glory?

He felt ashamed of himself, of his feelings. All he could think about was peace and Elsie. Everyone was mad. Unbalanced. Here they were chasing Boers he knew they would never catch. Every time they halted, Biglow decanted Pretoria from her basket and she wandered around the dismounted men, purring and rubbing herself against them. . . .

CHAPTER 70

NO MORE KHAKI

BOETIE, on his gray Arab, wearing an almost new officer's uniform, felt very pleased with himself, pleased among other things to be alive. There had been some nasty moments in the fight. But that was all over and the whole commando, equipped with British lancers' uniforms, horses, and saddlery, turned south and rode toward Bedford, an English-speaking area of the Cape Colony. The inhabitants hardly welcomed them, but put up with them with reasonable grace when the Boers began to commandeer what they wanted.

A pretty, dark-haired girl who reminded Boetie of Louisa said she hoped they would soon be rounded up and caught. Boetie heard her and, laughing at her, said they were not so easy to catch.

"You speak good English," the girl said.

"Why not? My father had us taught when we were children."

"I thought you were all savages," she said, staring at him with big brown eyes. He knew what she was thinking, that if he wasn't a savage, if he spoke English so well, it was a pity he had to go on so soon. Boetie had begun to understand girls a little, and himself, too.

"We are off," he said, "but what about a kiss for luck?" He put his arm around her and pulled her to him. She did not resist. It was an adventure for them both. The kiss of young people in war, enemies without enmity.

Leaving the Bedford district, they rode to the great Winterberg range, which was heavily timbered, much of the forest being primeval, with giant yellow woods twenty feet in diameter that might well be three thousand years old. Here and there roads tunneled through the woods and, piercing the darkness, led toward green fields and white farmhouses that could be seen in the distance.

At last there was plenty of wood for fires and at night the flames leaped high as the Boers piled on the dead branches they dragged in. It was good to be warm at last, and the firelight increased the mystery of the forest that fenced them in with a solid wall of leaves and branches.

Boetie was strangely moved by these forest giants that ran up straight as masts two hundred feet into an invisible sky. For in the deep of the woods no sky could be seen. It had to be taken on trust. Some light filtered down from above, a pale green light, so that as they rode through the forest paths they seemed to be underwater. Nor could the horses' hoofs be heard on the thick carpet of leaves that formed the forest floor.

The old trees impressed Boetie as ancient monuments. These and the cream-of-tartar trees Moolman had told him about in the north. Both had been growing here in Africa year after year since before Jesus Christ was born. They were more than trees, more than lumber. It seemed inconceivable that anyone should ever lay an ax to them.

At the edge of the forest they came upon an inn, and for the first time in a year the commando had beer and brandy. No one got drunk, but one man went to sleep and was left behind when they rode off toward Adelaide, where again they commandeered what they wanted, killing sheep and taking what early fruit there was from the orchards, before making for the great Fish River, Somerset, and the Zuorbergen only fifty miles from Algoa Bay.

Smuts meant to raid Port Elizabeth, but British troops suddenly appeared between them and the town, so they retreated up the berg and camped on one of the hogbacks that formed the edge of the escarpment.

Next day they were engaged and forced to retreat still farther into wilder country, where they found themselves without supplies, except for a wild fruit, called "Hottentot's bread," that resembled a large pineapple. It was edible, but only at certain times of the year, and this was not one of them. Boetie tasted one but did not like it and went back into the firing line, where a desultory action was continuing. There was no great danger in this broken country and they had good cover for their ponies.

Coming back, Boetie found half the men he had left vomiting and rolling on the ground in agony. Some even looked as if they were going to die, and no one seemed worse than General Smuts, who lay as if he was already dead. With half the commando sick and the leader out of action the English were now seen coming down the side of the opposite hill to storm their position. The English were in front of them. Behind them was desolate and uninhabited mountain heaths. They had no food and to move meant abandoning the sick men.

The English by this time had dismounted and were climbing the hill. General Smuts was down, Commandant van Deventer too sick to give orders, and it was left to Ben Bouwer to arrange the defense of the escarpment. It was growing dark and the British, having no stomach for a night fight, turned back and made their way back up the opposite hill, where their fires soon began to twinkle as they settled down for the night.

The Boer situation was far from good. The enemy had gone but would be back. Boetie went among the sick to see what he could do, but there was nothing. They groaned, cried out, and rolled about, worse, if anything, than they had been. General Smuts appeared to be really dead, his eyes closed, his face paper white.

Unless they could move before morning they were

finished. The well men sat beside the sick trying to comfort them and hoping they would be well enough to ride
before dawn broke. A chill wind blew in from the sea.
Boetie had never been hungrier. As the night passed, as
hour followed hour, the sick men began to recover a
little. Two were able to stagger to their feet. Only eighteen
were left prostrate. General Smuts was just able to sit up
and ordered the sick men lashed to their horses. He himself had to be held on his horse. But by the time it was
light enough to see a few yards in the gray predawn the
commando started off down a game track that led into a
gorge, and beyond that into the heart of a range so far
from human habitation that they found Cape buffalo
tracks and mud wallows. This was the first time Boetie
had been near the kind of animal that had killed his
father. It was even possible to smell them, a rank, wild,
cattlelike smell, as in one place they crashed away
through the scrub.

Suddenly, from a grass-covered shoulder, they saw the
white flare of sand dunes and beyond them the blue-gray
of the sea. They were looking at the Indian Ocean.
The sea that neither Boetie nor many of the other inland
Boers had ever seen before. Not that it looked like much
from here, but they could at least say they had seen it.
No other commando had ever got so far south. None
had ever come within sight of the coast.

That night, camped in the mountains, they saw the
lights of Port Elizabeth in the distance, a big town with
hotels, shops, people, food, women.

Some millet had been obtained from a native village,
so, though still hungry, they were no longer starving. They
made their way toward the valley of the Sunday River
through high forest and bush inhabited by both buffalo
and elephant. These elephant in the Addo bush were
small, almost tuskless, but bad-tempered. There were also
some half-wild cattle running here. The commando shot
several, had a fine feed around roaring fires, and lay
down under the trees to doze in the sunshine. They
were ready for a few hours' rest after what they had
been through. All at once the peaceful scene was changed
as a body of English cavalry in fours appeared riding
along a narrow *kloof* not two hundred yards off. They
must have thought the Boers were over the mountain and

not in it, for they were riding in close order without advance or flank guards.

Seizing his rifle, Boetie ran toward the British with the men who had been resting nearby and opened fire. The British could not deploy, being caught between the hills. The leaders turned back as those behind, unaware of what was going on, tried to advance, all becoming a confused, muddled mob of men and horses into which the Boers fired, taking no aim. The target was so big that every shot took effect, probably causing more than one wound as it went into the seething mass. Men and horses fell off the narrow road along the *kloof* into the bush below. Some ran away, others left their horses and, taking cover, opened such a hot fire on the Boers that, though the commando needed them badly, they could not get at the bandoleers of the dead or at the holsters and wallets of the English saddles.

In the end both sides seemed glad to break off the engagement, and the Boers found themselves back in the Somerset district again. Here General Smuts told them that his new plan was to make for the Atlantic coast, on the other side of Africa, clear across the Colony to the old farming districts of the southwestern Cape. To do this, he was dividing his force into two, partly to fool the English and partly because, since they had to live on the land, two smaller forces were easier to supply and would be less of a burden to the inhabitants of the districts through which they passed. Commandant van Deventer left with half the commando and Smuts led the rest. Both were to move west independently of each other.

Van Deventer led them to within a few miles of Aberdeen, then north to the Camdebo Mountains, where they were pursued by the British and escaped only with the aid of a friendly farmer who led them by a goat path over the mountains into a thicket of cactus, almost a forest, twenty feet high, through which the track wound like a snake. This prickly pear, brought from America in the 1850s, had established itself in the Karroo, taking over miles of country.

By dawn they were at the Kareega River, out on the plains again, and here Boetie was sent to scout the position. Seeing nothing of interest, he rode up to a farmhouse to ask if any English had been seen about. There was only

an old woman in the kitchen and she said she had seen no
one but offered to make him coffee. The water was not
hot and so he decided not to wait.

He had hardly got outside before the house was surrounded by British cavalry. It was no use trying to
escape by galloping off, so Boetie just rode on slowly, in
his lancer uniform. The British let him go, but the moment
he was in dead ground he put spurs to his gray and galloped back to the commando, firing warning shots as he
went. He was in time to warn them. Several men were already mounted, and with them Boetie turned back to hold
the cavalry up till the rest of the commando had caught
their grazing horses.

A few days later they got news that left them flabbergasted. The men they had lost had been taken prisoner
and had all been shot. One, Frantz Altman, who had been
taken in the last action while he was fighting in the rear
guard, had been shot that very morning on an adjoining
farm.

"Shot for what?" Boetie said. The British did not shoot
prisoners.

"Shot for wearing khaki," the farmer said.

It appeared that, though the Boers in the field did not
know it, Kitchener had issued a proclamation that any
enemy caught wearing English uniform would suffer the
death penalty. The man had hardly finished talking when
Boetie had his fine tunic off.

"I'll give you an old coat," the farmer said, and
brought out from the house a selection of curious
clothes—a claw-hammer tail coat, green with age, a Norfolk jacket, an old-fashioned short *voortrekker* frieze coat.
Boetie chose the jacket.

All that remained now was the skull-and-crossbones
badge on his slouch hat. Boetie pulled out the pin that
held it, and sent it spinning over the veld. The Death or
Glory Boy was gone, and with him the danger of being
shot if captured.

But it was terrible to think of the unsuspecting men
who had been executed for a crime they did not know
they were committing. Without clothes they had had to
take them from the British or go naked.

It was true that there was no way, when the Boers were
dressed like this, for the British to recognize them, par-

ticularly as the British had given up wearing helmets and now wore slouch hats like the Boers. But it was terrible to think of friends he had thought safe lying buried in nameless traitor graves. In war there was no justice.

They were now near the Swartbergen and the Oudtshoorn area, famous for its ostrich farms. A farmer gave them a good meal of bread, coffee, mutton, and an omelet made of an ostrich egg. He also gave them each a bag with more meat, bread, and an ostrich egg to take back to the rest of their detachment.

As they moved on toward the forests of Knysna, they met several members of the Rex family, descendants of George Rex, the son of George III by Hannah Lightfoot, the Quakeress who was his morganatic wife. He had been given a great estate here in 1775 on condition he did not make any claim to the throne of England. It was a strange and interesting story to Boetie. Here they were, fighting one king of England and being entertained by the illegitimate descendant of another.

Looking for food and shelter and failing to find it, they pushed on in the dark till they saw a glimmer of light in the distance. It was after midnight when they got to the door, which was opened by an English farmer in a ferocious temper. These were his third visitors in twenty-four hours. First some Boers had come and slaughtered his sheep. Then the British had come and settled down to a meal of roast mutton—"My mutton!" he shouted—instead of chasing Boers. And now here was still another lot of Boers demanding more sheep and even getting him out of bed.

It turned out to be Smuts who had been there in the morning. So they were catching up with him at last. Catching up but always behind him, always on his spoor. They went over the "Gough" Karroo, a waterless area, crossed the Dwyka River, where they suffered severely from thirst, having to dig for water with their bare hands in the dry course. But they were reaching a country where there were no railways and where no large bodies of troops could exist. This country was safe for them. To the north, toward the Orange River, there was nothing—a vast desert emptiness.

They halted for some days at Elandsvlei, where there were open water and a grove of palms, and near Van

Rijnsdorp caught up with General Smuts, who had broken
his force up into small groups, operating days apart to
facilitate the grazing and watering of their beasts.

Boetie found himself a dispatch rider, traveling long
distances south of the Olifants River and even beyond
Calvinia. He was seeing Africa all right. The Indian
Ocean and now the Atlantic. Renata and Louisa were a
thousand miles away. God alone knew what had happened to his brother. He wondered if his mother and all
the women and children of Groenplaas were really dead.
Surely some must be alive, something left. But why did he
think that after what he had seen? And Moolman. Where
was Dirk Moolman?

CHAPTER 71

A SOCIETY WEDDING

Diana was excited. Her plans, so carefully laid, though
jeopardized at times by her adventures, had come off at
last. In a few hours she would be Lady Wanthope.

It was spring in England, love time, lamb time. The
daffodils and bluebells were about over, the fruit trees
were in full blossom. The birds were mating and lambs
white as snowballs leaped about their gray-wooled mothers. Pink apple blossom, white hawthorn, the prickly
gorse a golden chrome. Across all England from the Fells
to the Downs there was bird song.

A lot of soldiers were back already and some very pretty
society weddings were taking place, all lace and furbelows,
all morning coats and buttonholes and bridal bouquets,
with carpets spread from the carriage door to the very
steps of the church.

As soon as the carpet was down a crowd collected on
each side of it, a miniature cliff of the curious on each
side of the red valley down which the bride and her at-
tendants would shortly pass.

But some weddings were more interesting than others,
and ladies sometimes went to watch them, standing

among the common people as if they were there by
accident. That was how Mrs. Avery Acton and Mrs. Berke-
ley Fern came to see the Wanthope-Darnley wedding at
St. George's, Hanover Square.

"We'll go and see General Lord Wanthope, pronounced
Wantopp, my dear," Mrs. Acton said, "married to Diana
Henrietta Euphemia, the widow of that gallant lancer
Major Charles Edward Darnley, V.C., who was killed in
action at the Tugela River in the winter of ninety-nine,
right at the beginning of the war. I read all about it last
week. So unfortunate, dear, and of course it was midsummer there."

"That's something I've never really understood," Mary
Fern said. "I mean, if it's winter here, why isn't it winter
there? And how do they do it—hunting and having Christmas in the summer?"

"Well, darling, I don't understand it either and really,
women, as long as they are nice-looking and attractive,
don't have to bother, do they?"

"I don't know. I like to try to understand things."

"I know you do, darling. It's such a mistake. But I do
want to go. I want to see him. He's a magnificent-looking
man, they say, and a monster. They say he likes his fruit
unripe and unwilling." She raised her eyebrows.

"You mean . . . ?"

"Yes, darling. Little girls. Can you believe it? And
boys, too."

"Then I'm sorry for her. What's her name, did you say?"

"Diana Darnley. But you needn't be. There are stories
about her too. They say she pushed him into it, always
saying she wanted to be a hero's wife and so on. Her
husband, I mean."

Eighteen months of widowhood was considered enough,
particularly in wartime, but, to be safe so that there
would be no chance of scandal, they had waited more
than two years. Diana, who had looked charming, like a
pale pink lily shot with gold set against the rich black
loam of a garden bed—she had worn black for a year—
looked even more beautiful in her silk French-gray wedding dress. The bodice clung to her figure. It was without
the frogs and ornamentations usual at the time. The high
neck was edged with lace. So were the wrists of her leg-

of-mutton sleeves, only here there were several layers of
Brussels lace that cascaded onto her white-gloved hands.
The trailing skirt would have swept the pavement if she had
not held it raised, showing the frill of her taffeta petticoat and a glimpse, but no more, of another lacy petticoat beneath. The shoes were gray suède. She carried a
gray suède reticule and a bouquet of white arums and
maidenhair fern, both so common at the Cape but exotic
in England.

An uncle, Sir John Bentley, Bart., a distinguished
bachelor and age-long companion of her husband to be,
gave her away. Top-hatted, spatted, stripe-trousered, and
morning-coated, a dark red carnation in his buttonhole, a
black pearl in his ascot tie, a gold watch chain across
his dove-gray vest, he was the very picture of a gentleman of means and leisure.

The war was not yet over, so although it was not a military wedding the general and his best man and the other
invited officers wore uniforms. And very dashing they
looked in their scarlet and blue, their spurs tinkling and
sabers clanking on the pavement as they marched into the
church.

It was a big wedding, one of the biggest and most fashionable of the season that it opened.

Wanthope had obtained a month's leave in which to
consummate his nuptials. Around the bright uniforms
and black morning coats of the men, the women, in light
summer dresses of muslin, silk, and lace, of Shantung
and flowered French materials, hovered like butterflies
seeking the nectar of male company. They opened long-
handled parasols as they were handed out of their carriages, twirled them a time or two to set their ruffles
while they crossed the pavement and closed them once
again as they went into the church. It was a hot day and
the arm guards did not prevent the perspiration from
darkening some of the new and pretty dresses. From them,
as they walked with swishing, trailing, and raised skirts,
came a waft of mixed perfumes. Lilac, tuberose, violet.
The scents of their time. So that with eyes half closed and
nostrils open they appeared, for a moment at least, to be
a perfumed moving flower bed that merged into a mur-
muration of fluttering, adorable femininity.

The honeymoon was begun at the Meurice in Paris and concluded in the mountains of Switzerland, when Diana's shopping was done, and the heat became unbearable. She bought frothing masses of lingerie, chemises, petticoats, camisoles, knickers, handkerchiefs, corsets, corset covers, silk stockings, and gloves. She spent many hours at fittings and many hundreds of pounds at Paquin and Worth. She bought perfume, powder, which was now coming into more common usage, and even rouge. Nothing was too good for such a customer as Lady Wanthope, no trouble too great. Seamstresses ruined their eyes working half the night to get clothes finished in time. Models paraded creations, walking miles on the carpeted floors of these great establishments, as Milor', who always accompanied Her Ladyship, looked at the girls inside the clothes, undressing them with a practiced and lascivious eye.

To Diana this was the nearest approach to heaven she had ever made, or was likely to make. Her husband encouraged every extravagance, always urging her to buy more, and when there was a choice of two models would make her take them both. The shopping tours amused him. Money was no object and he was a judge of women's clothes, of the smart outer garments and the more intimate lace- and ribbon-trimmed frillies that covered the silken, perfumed skins of the ladies he had chosen as friends and companions since his youth.

These mannequins in their early twenties were too old for his debauched taste, but there had been a time they would have pleased him. There were some pretty fillies among them, though for perfection they should have been younger by six years at least. But in falling in with Diana's whims Wanthope was having the time of his life. He wondered where she thought she would wear the clothes she was buying. He was a man of sardonic humor, a cruel and brutal tease.

The journey from England had been pleasant, the Channel crossing calm. They had been accompanied by his man and Diana's French maid, so had lacked no comfort.

Before they left for Lausanne and Geneva, he sent his valet back to London with most of the heavy luggage, and they traveled light with only three large trunks and six heavy leather suitcases. The maid accompanied the bridal pair.

There were no surprises in this union, for though Wanthope had seen little of Diana in Africa after her husband's death, they had corresponded regularly, his warm sympathy for her loss growing into a genuine affection that ended in an engagement. He had proposed and was accepted by letter. This was the popular story. A war romance . . . general marries hero's widow . . .

Diana, cossetted, petted by this distinguished peer, was contented as a cat. She knew his reputation but was convinced that these follies were due only to his bachelor state, that, married to him, she would soon cure him of these idiosyncrasies. He was a violent man in love as in all else, but as a mature and practiced woman this was no deterrent to their connubial state. Rather the contrary.

She had with Wanthope, as she had with her first husband and her other lovers, avoided pregnancy by following the advice of a Viennese gynecologist in London. Neither Charles nor, as far as she knew, Wanthope was aware of her precautions. This belief was rudely shattered when after luncheon one day her husband flung her down upon the bed and took her. . . . At last, rumpled and furious, Diana turned on him.

"You've made me pregnant," she sobbed.

"Pregnant, Diana? I doubt it," Wanthope said. "But if not today, tomorrow, or perhaps the day after that. That is what I married you for, my dear. I need an heir. Heirs in fact. Did you really think you were going to live in my house in Grosvenor Square, setting London by the ears with your flirting tricks? No, no, my dear. It's Ireland for you, the place in Ulster. A fine climate, if a little raw in winter, but very healthy for children, I am informed."

"My clothes," Diana sobbed, "my lovely clothes."

"Did you expect me to send you to Ireland naked?" Wanthope said. "Though no one can deny your loveliness in that condition."

Leaning against the door, he went on: "'No one else would marry me, my dear. Not with my reputation. No one else at least whose blood was good enough to breed from. You're still young. You have a pretty waist, Diana, a lovely waist, but you're roomy. You have wide hips. I picked you because I knew you were ambitious. You wanted more money than that poor fool Charles had. That poor, brave fool, whom you killed. Not I, my dear. You. You with your gentle gibes about courage, about wanting to be a hero's wife, even if it meant being a hero's widow. How proud you were when the old Queen pinned his cross on your lovely breast.

"You wanted a title. You have one now, and for all I know you may already have an earl in your belly. Fancy that. Just fancy that.

"I know all about you, Diana, all about the men, from your father's groom to the young lancer, to Turnbull and all the others. I know about Dr. Joseph Witteman. I know your life, the whole book of it. I know the names in it, all of them. But I'm the last, the last lucky man of a multitude. From now on you will be faithful because you'll have no chance to be anything else. And I shall be happy leading my own life, with my wife living with my children at my place in Ulster. I shall say I never would have believed it, but some women do change when they marry —even for a second time. But how strange indeed that a titled woman well known for her social activities should suddenly turn domestic, and prefer country life to London. Very odd . . . very . . .

"People will say it's funny, and it is. But only you and I will know quite how funny."

He closed the door quietly behind him as he went out.

Louisa wrote from England every week, not only to Renata and her mother, but to any other friends she had managed to retain in South Africa. It would not have done for the village of Pullmaston to become aware of any breach between her and her family. There was enough gossip anyway. She always used the heavy crested Pullmaston Manor paper. The Carter crest was an eagle with one spread wing, and the motto *"Pas Mort"* seemed singularly apt.

Things for Louisa had not gone quite the way she had hoped. After the wedding from the Willows, where everyone had conducted himself in a most decorous and conventional manner, they had gone to the Cape for their honeymoon, spending the month's leave Carter had been given at the Queens Hotel at Sea Point.

Love and marriage were all they had been cracked up

to be. Now able to let herself go, Louisa did so, gay, charming, and forever amorous.

Carter left her at the Queens with instructions to behave herself when he rejoined his regiment. The 50th Rifles was almost immediately engaged and within a month Carter was back at the Cape again, this time in the military hospital at Wynberg. Louisa moved to be near her husband. Three months later he was invalided out of the army. Still handsome, still apparently in perfect health, he took his wife home to Gloucestershire, but now unable to father another child or even attempt to make one. He continually thanked God for what he called their little mistake in the rondavel.

Celibacy drove Louisa frantic. Flashes of temper followed by nervous prostration kept her in bed for a week at a time. But her looks continued to improve. She was maturing fast and her dark eyes burned with a hidden slumberous rage at fate, at God, and her husband.

The shooting at the manor was good. So was the fishing. In consequence the house, which was large, almost always had guests who came down for the sport old Morgan could give them. A nice chap, very nice. Nice house, good cooking, pretty wife, and some of the best pheasant shooting in England. What more could you want? Many of the men were brother officers. Riflemen. Louisa had to entertain the wives while the men shot and fished. Women! She had always hated women. She watched the men come and go. The bachelors. The married men going into their rooms with their wives . . .

The droop of an eyelid, a look, would have been enough. But she did not dare. Morgan would divorce her and then where would she be—without money or position? A kept woman was all she could become, like some of those adventuresses she had seen at the Cape, looking down her nose at them as she passed them by.

But if it happened, and in her heart she knew it would —she was not yet twenty—she had a card up her sleeve. To begin with, whatever happened would be most discreet. It would be a matter of live and let live. One day before so very long she would face Carter and tell him she was a girl, a woman, who could not live continent, not that he should need telling. She would promise to stay with him and care for his home, but she must have a private life of her own. If he refused she would warn him not to press her. If he pressed her, she would say his son was not his and make it public. Not only would he look a fool but he would lose the heir, even if he wasn't of his own blood, whom he loved.

She knew she would win, and her health took a turn for the better as she played a kind of game with herself, wondering how long she could hold out. Why, she laughed suddenly, Morgan might even find himself with a little girl one day. He had once told her he wanted one.

But it hadn't worked out quite the way she had expected. She did not like the English climate, even in the warm West Country, and she hated country life.

Jan Bothma, when he escaped from his brutal captors, came back a hero. He said that he had not been able to save his companions, but had strangled a Boer and escaped, naked, riding bareback on a stolen horse that had been shot from under him just before he reached the British lines.

He was now promoted into the collecting yard and slaughter section of the livestock operation and found himself almost rich in a matter of months. Hearing his wife had died in camp, something he did not regret, he married a young and docile blonde and started another family.

Bothma was a man who, years afterward, when he was a town counselor, said, "I fought for my country. I bled, I suffered, but I came through a better [much laughter] and a richer man."

Jan Bothma, bywoner, traitor, thief, a town counselor. Who would have thought it? The devil certainly looked after his own.

In the high veld where the 2nd lay, Turnbull, whistling quietly to himself, walked down the lines to the colonel's tent. His mind was made up at last.

"Can I come in, Charles?" he asked.

"Come in. Come in." The voice was cheerful. Everyone was glad the war was ending. The "go slow" was really a stop order. Everyone was sick of it. Everyone wanted to go home.

"Well, John, what's up?"

"I'm sending in my papers, Charles. I've done with soldiering. I'm going to stay on here. And Biglow wants to stay with me. I'll buy him out."

"Going to farm?" the colonel asked.

"Yes. Breed sheep and horses. I'm going to buy every good Boer mare I can lay my hands on. A hundred or so anyway, however bad their condition."

"Why?"

"Because they've survived. Because they are the pick of the horses in Africa, just as the last Boers in the field are the pick of the men. And I'm going to import a couple of Arab stallions and breed from them."

The colonel lit a cigarette and offered Turnbull his silver case.

"I want to go now," he said. "I want indefinite leave, Charles."

"You can have it, John."

"And Biglow?"

"You can take him. He's on leave too, till you buy him out. We'll start things moving at once."

Lady Finch-Haddley was not surprised when Turnbull and Elsie came to see her.

"She won't marry me," Turnbull said. "She thinks you need her."

"Need her? Where did she get that silly idea? *He* needs you, I don't," she said, "and you'd better marry him at once before he finds someone else." She laughed.

"I thought—" Elsie said.

"I know what you thought, but you can unthink it. A hospital wedding. Arches of crutches," Lady Finch-Haddley said.

"I'll see if I can get Sir Charles to come down and give her away," Turnbull said.

"Give me away? Who the hell is he to give me away?" Elsie's ideas of the marriage ceremony were vague.

"Keep quiet, dear," Lady Finch-Haddley said. "Someone always gives the bride away. Her father, an uncle . . ."

"Old Fenton," Elsie said. "That would surprise him, wouldn't it?" She began to giggle.

"I'll send him a signal," Turnbull said.

"Who? Fenton?" Elsie said.

The answer came next day.

MAHOMET CANNOT GET AWAY, EVERYTHING READY FOR RE-
CEPTION OF MOUNTAIN. REGIMENTAL WEDDING ORDERED.
C.O. 2D HUSSARS.

A regimental wedding, an arch of swords, the band.
His brother officers, and Old Charles giving her away.
That was what little Elsa had always wanted. How odd
that Elsie should be getting it. The two girls were becoming more and more like one in his mind. Elsa had given
Elsie her past, and Elsie had given Elsa the future she
had lost. . . .

"You'll ask me, I suppose?" Lady Finch-Haddley said.
She had driven over to the Grand with Elsie when the
signal came.

"We'd better have a drink," Turnbull said, and called a
waiter.

"Brandy," Lady Finch-Haddley said.

"Champagne," Turnbull ordered.

Fizz . . . bubbly . . . a bottle of the widow . . . And
here she was going to be married to her captain in Africa,
sitting beside a real lady who had become her friend. It
was all too much.

Elsie burst into tears.

Turnbull and Lady Finch-Haddley laughed and patted
her.

Drunk, that's what they were. Drunk, the bloody
lot of them . . . And what had Mahomet to do with it?

CHAPTER 72

A MATTER OF SELF-RESPECT

WHILE Boetie and his outfit were harassing the western
desert, Louis Botha, whom the British had been hunting
in vain, arrived in Klerksdorp for consultation with Steyn,
De Wet, Hertzog, Olivier and the other leaders who were
waiting for him.

The meeting began with a hymn and a prayer. Schalk
Burger asked Botha, De Wet, and De la Rey to report on
the state of their men. It took them a day of discussion

before they could agree on what terms to lay before Kitchener. Only Smuts was away. He was at O'okiep in the Cape and a message was sent to recall him.

In Pretoria, Kitchener received them as equals, with the honor that was their due as the fighting generals and presidents of the two republics. This was April 12, 1902, and the disposition of the Boer forces was about as follows when the Boer leaders laid their proposals before Kitchener in his Pretoria house.

The Cape was a stalemate with three thousand invaders and rebels roaming the Colony, but no general uprising seemed likely. The Boer farmers were sympathetic, gave information, food, and remounts to their compatriots, but no more than that.

In the Free State there were still some seven thousand burghers in the field under Kemp.

In the Transvaal there were approximately twelve thousand Boers still active under the command of Piet Viljoen, Muller, and Beyers.

The grand total of the Boers in the field was still about twenty-two thousand, though in the last year they had lost half their strength owing to Kitchener's drives and blockhouse system. The apple was continually being peeled down, but a hard core still remained. These survivors were the pick of the pick, the cream of the cream, the toughest, the bravest, the most resourceful and experienced fighters in the two republics. They could in no way be considered beaten. Their generals had escaped every net and every trap, leading their best men with them.

By the pattern of the logistics they had evolved, they were enabled to trade space for time in a terrible game of tag, while they waited for the British Government to fall. If there were a change of government, the British might give up the war. It was unpopular with many people. So they fought on, living on food they captured, fighting with captured rifles and ammunition, and riding captured horses. This was their point of view. The attitude the Boers took at the meeting with Kitchener was based on these beliefs.

Schalk Burger spoke for the Transvaal. He offered votes for the *Uitlanders,* equal language rights in schools, a commercial union with the British territories, that is, the

Cape Colony and Natal, an immediate amnesty, and an agreement that all future problems should be settled by arbitration.

When he had finished, Steyn, the Free State President, rose. He said quite simply that they had come to the meeting to achieve the objects for which they had fought.

Kitchener could not have been more taken aback.

"You mean," he said, astonished, "that I am to understand from what you say that you wish to keep your independence?"

"Yes," Steyn replied. "The people must keep their self-respect."

Now there was a deadlock. Kitchener knew their proposals would never be accepted, but, wanting to keep the negotiations going, he wired the Boer offer to the British Government, that is to say, to Chamberlain.

The answer was no. But after further wires and further cabinet meetings in London some progress was made.

The Boers wanted an armistice so that they could consult their burghers in the field. This was not granted, but Kitchener agreed to a "go slow" while negotiations were in progress. It was formally agreed that the Boer governments and thirty delegates from each republic would meet at Vereeniging on May 15, to decide if they would make peace or continue the war.

The Boer leaders were all given free railway and telegraph facilities to enable them to round up their delegates.

While all this was going on the war would continue, but no commando whose leader was away as a delegate would be attacked. This would not be cricket.

But both in England and South Africa there were differences of opinion. There were die-hards on both sides. Milner's friends wanted an unconditional surrender, while Lord Rosebery did not want the war fought to an end. He did not want so bitter a finish that cooperation between the two white races in Africa would be impossible. Kitchener agreed with him.

On the Boer side, both Schalk Burger and Louis Botha felt surrender to be inevitable, but Steyn was not ready to give up. For him reason had ceased to have meaning. De Wet was with him and rode over the country addressing commando after commando, making the delegates promise not to agree to surrender unless they got their independence.

Boetie, knowing nothing of the real facts, was not unduly depressed at the situation. The commando held the ground between the Olifants River and the Orange, almost four hundred miles away. They had had a lot of small successes, miniature guerrilla victories that had cheered everyone. They were out of touch with the forces in the north, and assumed that things were going equally well there, saying that soon the British would get tired of pursuing the commandos over the veld and whistling happily in the dark of their ignorance.

Boetie and De Lange lay behind the rocks, sniping at the British posts on the other side of O'okiep. The range was eight hundred yards, and they were not likely to hit anyone. But it was a good idea to let the British know that the Boers were still active, and it was not unpleasant lying in the sandy soil in that early autumn day.

When the light began to fail, they returned to their horses, which were grazing knee-haltered on the sparse grass, half a mile behind them. They had hardly mounted when they saw a Cape cart coming up from the south. The driver had a white flag tied to a whipstock fastened to the hood.

They rode up to it and found two British officers and a Hottentot driver.

"What are you doing here?" Boetie asked.

Both Boers sat their horses with their rifles lying across their saddle bows.

"We have a dispatch," the older of the Englishmen said. He was a major, with gray hair and faded eyes. "We want to see Smuts."

Boetie looked at him angrily. "You mean the general," he said.

"That's it," the younger officer, a captain, said.

"Then follow us," Boetie said.

Long before they reached Concordia, a number of other Boers had ridden up to see what was happening. To see a Cape cart here, much less one with a white flag, was an event, particularly if it held British officers.

"They want to make peace," someone said.

"*Ja*, peace. Before God what else can they do? They can't catch us any more than you can catch fleas in a kaross." There was some laughter. But the faces of the Englishmen, though they denied any knowledge of the dispatch, did not look as if they carried peace terms, at least the kind of peace that would be acceptable to the Boers.

When they reached the dorp and the general's headquarters, they got out of the cart stiffly, cramped by their long drive, and went in.

Boetie watched them with interest. He always found professional soldiers curious. They were so neat, hardly human in some ways.

An hour later the general came out alone and strode slowly over the veld, his head held low, apparently in deep and gloomy thought.

When he came back, his mind seemed to be made up. A few moments later a man came up to Boetie and said, "The general wants you."

"Wants me?"

Boetie left the fire and went to the house.

"The news is bad," Smuts said. "There is to be a meeting of our leaders and the British at Vereeniging. I am summoned to it. I have a safe-conduct for myself and an orderly. I am taking you."

Boetie was silent. Then he said, "What about the men?"

"Say nothing to the men."

In the morning the British officers drove off to Steinkopf to warn the troops there that a Boer delegation would soon pass through their pickets. They looked cleaner than ever. They were fat and well rested. It was a long time since the Boers had seen men in such prime condition.

"Slaughter condition, Boetie," De Lange said, laughing. "Like oxen prime to be killed."

General Smuts sent a message to O'okiep with orders for a cease fire while the congress was going on.

Next day, all men came in from the outposts to say good-by to their commander. They paraded in fours past the courthouse, sitting very erect in their saddles with their rifles on their thighs. Boetie's heart was sore. They did not yet know that the war was lost. They thought that their sacrifice had served its purpose—that they had won through.

There were no fat men here. No fat horses. But there were no beaten men, either. Their bearded faces were hard bronze masks, in which their eyes burned like fires with their pride.

When the parade was over they dismounted and stood by their horses as the general addressed them. Some leaned against their horses' shoulders, some had their arms over their necks.

". . . Do not expect too much, *kêrels.* I will do my best. But be prepared for disappointment. . . ."

But none of them took his words to heart. They were sure of victory, of a negotiated peace that would at any rate restore their free republics.

Boetie rode off with Smuts and their escort toward the British lines, where they were met by the British commander. The escort took their horses, sang the commando hymn, mounted, fired a farewell volley into the air, and galloped cheering back to the commando.

The war was won.

General Smuts and Boetie entrained for Cape Town. At Simonstown they were transferred to the battleship H.M.S. *Monarch,* where they stayed as guests for a week. Then they entrained again for the north, for Kroonstad, where Lord Kitchener met them. He was mounted on a magnificent black horse and surrounded by a guard of mounted Pathans in native dress, with drawn, gold-mounted scimitars.

To meet this enormous mustachioed man was like meeting God or the devil. This was power personified. As Smuts' orderly, Boetie knew he was witnessing a historic scene. His general listened, totally unmoved, as Kitchener told him he had had four hundred thousand troops against their eighteen thousand.

"Twenty to one," Smuts said, "but mercenaries against patriots, and picked men at that." Then he taxed Kitchener with the farm burning and the execution of men caught wearing British uniforms.

But terms were offered. Kitchener said the burghers could retain their horses and saddles and the British would help to rebuild the destroyed farms. The commander in chief then left them with orders to proceed to Standerton, where they would meet General Botha.

At Standerton, on the high veld, General Smuts said, "We have arrived, Louis." It was the first time he had called him Louis.

Boetie looked at him in surprise. Of course they had arrived.

"Of all the things you have seen, of all the things we have seen together, this is going to be the worst." The general's gray eyes, usually so cold, were moist. "Now you must be a man. It is not difficult to be a man in action, my boy. This is going to be much harder, as you will see. Come on, we must get out."

There was a cart with a mounted escort to meet them. A dozen smart troopers stood by their horses. A cavalry officer saluted. These were the conquerors. General Smuts put his foot on the step of the cart, gripped the dashboard, and stared out over the rolling veld at the wide and distant horizon. "Our land," he said as he pulled himself up.

The cart was driven past a number of small British camps, where the guard turned out and presented arms to honor them, past the lines of blockhouses that had ended the war, till they reached the party of Boers General Botha had sent to meet them. They had two spare horses. It was strange to be mounted again, and among Boers. It took two days' traveling across the deserted country to get to the rendezvous.

They rode in near silence through an empty world. They did not see a soul, not a head of stock. They passed a number of ruined farms. Even the birds seemed to have abandoned this stricken area across which the cold wind of war had swept, brushing all life before it.

"A man," the general had said. Yes, I must be a man, Boetie thought, sitting straighter in his saddle; and now, when he saw the delegates from the commandos in the Eastern Transvaal who had come to elect the delegates they would send to the Peace Congress at Vereeniging, the general's words were driven home.

There were three hundred men assembled here, representing the Boers still in the field. This was the pick of the Boer Army. They were dressed in sacking, in the re-

mains of English uniforms, in hides and rags, in the
shreds of patched-up clothes. Their equipment was
mended with riempies and bits of leather. They were
starving. Many were covered with veld sores, owing to lack
of vegetables and salt. These were unbeaten men. But as a
force, the Boers were broken.

Boetie had never seen men in such condition. Their
horses all skin and bones, with matted tails and scrawny
coats, their girths, buckled to the last hole, were still
slack.

It took a day of oratory and wrangling to elect the
delegates. Wild-eyed men, their beards and long hair
blowing in the cold wind, argued and shouted. They were
not beaten! They would fight on! Time was on their side.
There were many in England who were against the war.
World opinion was on their side.

But at last it was over, and those who had not been
elected returned on their hungry horses to rejoin their
distant commandos. Some led their horses to rest them.

The successful deputies started back toward the British
lines, led by General Botha. All the way to Standerton
the British troops fed them, and stood at attention as
the tattered cavalcade rode by. As usual they looked in-
credulous, unable to believe that such men had held
them up so long.

Back at Standerton they entrained again for Vereeniging—a little mining town on the Vaal. Here a camp had
been erected by the British for the delegates from the
rest of the Transvaal and Free State.

Botha was addressing the delegates of the Eastern
Transvaal. They were redoubtable as they listened, unmoved, standing beside their starving horses.

Boetie, looking at them, thought, These are no longer
men. They are fighting scarecrows with nothing left in
them but their courage. The rest had been whittled
away, day by day, by almost three years of war. Their
eyes burned in the sunken sockets of their brown wood
faces. Their mouths were hidden by hair.

Each republic had a tent and a large marquee had been
pitched for their meetings.

General Beyers was appointed chairman. Schalk Burger

spoke. He recommended submission but said the vote must be unanimous.

Botha then said that the vote could not be unanimous as long as the Free State burghers felt bound by their promise to De Wet to go on fighting.

Then Smuts and Hertzog, both lawyers, gave the opinion that it was a principle of law that delegates were more than mouthpieces and must vote as they thought best.

Next Botha described conditions in the Eastern Transvaal. Between where they now sat in conference and Ermelo, a hundred miles away, only thirty-six goats remained alive. There was not a single head of horned stock left in all the area. The few burghers who still had mounts declared them too weak to move. The women were in an indescribable condition, sick and starving, and all but naked. It must be remembered, Botha said, that winter was coming on. It might freeze tonight or tomorrow. The natives were restless and hostile. At Vryheid they had massacred a number of Boer families, mutilating their bodies for medicine. Fifty-six people—men, women, and children—were dead at their hands.

One thing the blockhouse system had done was to cut off almost all communication between commandos in various parts of the country. Delegates from areas that were better off were horrified to find that other commandos were on the verge of starvation.

The natives were an important factor in the debate.

Surrender was inevitable. Steyn was too sick to attend on the second day. But reason also lay sick. Emotion ruled. One old man said, "As far as I am concerned I will fight on till I die."

Others echoed him. Having come so far, having lost so much, why not go on? In this sea of passion, agreement of any kind became impossible till State Secretary Reitz, acting for the sick Steyn, suggested they hand over the Rand with its mines, give up the Transvaal's share of government in Swaziland, and let the British control foreign relations as long as they were left alone to rule themselves.

Smuts and Hertzog drafted out the suggestions in the correct legal form.

Koos de la Rey, the Lion of the West, who had the

strongest force behind him, now spoke for the first time. He said it was not a question of fighting to the bitter end. The end had come and another chance to negotiate might not occur. This was the De la Rey who, in the spring of '99, had testified in the Volksraad saying he was against the war but would be in the field fighting when Kruger and his government had fled.

The effect of his words drove home Botha's arguments. If Koos de la Rey felt the end had come, he was probably right. And suddenly the tide turned, as a tide must, rising to flood, pausing for an instant, and then falling back. The burghers, the spring of their will suddenly released, began to think of their families, their farms, and how they could start again.

But not Christiaan de Wet. To him all this was impious. What had taken place was the will of God. "God is minded by this war to form us into a nation," he shouted. "This is a war of religion."

Every general was here—De la Rey, De Wet, Beyers, Kemp, Brink, Hertzog—all the heroes, many of whom Boetie had heard of but never seen.

Mixing with the crowd, he heard the same story everywhere. Starvation, lack of horses, ammunition, and clothing. The blockhouse system had finally checked all movement. Farmsteads everywhere had been burned, crops stolen or spoiled, stock slaughtered. Twenty thousand Boer women and children dead in the concentration camps.

Some of the Free Stater die-hards wished to go on fighting, and to them General de la Rey said, "Has not the bitter end come?" Boetie was near him when he spoke. It was over. The end had come. He went to Smuts's tent.

"I'll go back with the news alone, Louis," the general said. "You are a Transvaaler, and near home. Go back, and begin to build our land again. *Ja*," he said, "as the phoenix rose from the ashes, so will we rise again. Boy," he said, "we have been beaten, but not defeated, and we have made history."

There were now only two courses: to submit to circumstance or leave the country. It was impossible to think of leaving Africa—and Renata. So, with a hundred or so others, Boetie rode to Balmoral to hand in his rifle.

The day was beautiful, calm, windless, but cold, the sky utterly cloudless, a bowl of blue. The tiny branches of the thorn trees under which the British colonel sat at his table, the kitchen table of some Boer woman, were a fili-gree of black, ancient lace against the winter blueness, caught in the mirror of the frozen pan behind him.

This was a very African day on which their Africa, the republics for which all these men had fought, was dying. This was the last, bloodless, and most tragic field. Freedom had expired. These were her obsequies, these her bearded mourners, the men who had fought so long and hard for her life.

A flock of red-beaked finches landed among the thorn twigs with a rush of little wings, quite fearless, almost defiant of mankind. In the distance Boetie heard the harsh kark-kark cry of a flushed korhaan. The brown reeds broken by winter pierced the ice and stood rooted in the mud bottom of the pan as they had since time be-gan. As they would continue to do. Nature went on, un-aware of man's pain, of broken hearts and hopes.

He wondered if the others felt as he did—isolated, un-participating in the scene before them. Observers merely, this residue of a civilian army that had fought so well. First the scum had gone, the worst, by desertion and surrender. Then the boldest men had been killed, men like Danie Theron, victims of their own courage. Others had fallen out through illness, through the hardships of the long campaign, and this was the bones and the guts of it. Bold but not reckless, inured to all discomfort. Men in their prime, most in their twenties and early thirties, a few much older, a few as young as he. Boys of whom the war had made men. Only now, when there was so little to think about, did he see their clothes in a new way. Tatters that were like flags—rags of glory. Men whose faces were little more than skin-covered skulls. Only their burning eyes seemed alive.

The officer and the handful of Englishmen grouped about the table were men of a different world and breed. Sleek, smooth, clean, well dressed in spotless khaki.

The Boers stood silent, still, as if waiting for something

to begin or to end. As if there must be some drama. As if so much could not end like this with the signing of their names at a kitchen table under a group of gnarled thorns on the veld. They looked like rocks, like stones grouped in dozens, in pairs, or standing alone.

The officer put on his overcoat. The Boers had no coats to put on but were used to it, used to cold and wind and heat, to rain and hail. They stood like animals, did not even turn their backs to the wind that had sprung up, for in the field they had become part of it, of the landscape, as immune to weather as bush and trees, as rocks and anthills.

Boetie held his Lee-Enfield in the crook of his left arm. Soon he would be unarmed. What a number of rifles he had had. His own that he had given up in Pretoria. The Mauser he had been issued. The British Lee-Metfords and Enfields he had picked up. That was what they were here for, to give up their rifles and sign away their freedom. When they left they would be subjects of the Queen or exiled. How many Englishmen had he killed and wounded with the weapon resting in his forearm? How many miles had he carried this English gun? How many salvaged and looted rounds had he fired? In his hands his rifle had ceased to be a mechanism of steel and wood. It had been alive. How well he had tended it, greasing it, pulling it through every day with the brass-weighted lanyard that nestled safe behind the little trap door in the hollow of its butt. How he treasured the four-by-two bits of white flannel that he put through the eye of the pull-through weight, always trying to keep a clean one to give the rifling grooves a final polish. Of the half dozen rifles he had used this one had been the best.

The *rooibekkies* were still chattering in the trees, hopping from branch to branch. They were on their way to the north, to the warmth of the low veld, Moolman's low veld. That was where he was going to go—with Renata if she would go with him. Alone, if she would not. For he was no longer certain of her. It would be British, too, but they would not bother with the wild fringes of the land. If Moolman were not dead he would find him there.

He had wanted to see Africa. Well, he had had his heart's desire. Few men knew it better. He thought of his commander, General Jan Christiaan Smuts, on his way to break the news of defeat to the commando that had seen them off, certain the war was won. What a job, what a thing to face. How would he tell them that it had all been for nothing. He thought of the old President in Europe, away from his beloved land, knowing he would never see it again—not the mountains, the rivers, the wide-open veld, the bush in which he had hunted and fought Kaffirs, the lands he had tamed. Not his old wife or his sons or their sons.

Boetie moved his rifle, taking it in his hands. The butt was warm from his body. But the barrel was like ice. Some men had notched their guns, but he had never been a killer, never pleased to see a man fall to his bullet.

A tall Boer was moving from group to group. He had a yellow beard that looked like gold against the sunburn of his face. His long hair fell in a lion's mane over his shoulders. He heard a man laugh and the metallic click of magazines being loosened as the Boers loaded their rifles.

The British officer looked nervous and moved uneasily in his folding chair.

"Do not be frightened," the big man said. "We shall not shoot you. Don't be *bang*"—the Afrikaans word for fear—"we are not murderers, not even of women and children."

"Load, *jong*," he shouted to Boetie, who was standing alone. He put the last eight rounds he had into his magazine and banged it home.

"*Kêrels!*" the big man roared into the sky. "We will give up no ammunition. We will fire the last rounds of the war. Then we can say we went on till our ammunition was done, our last cartridge spent. So we will greet the end of the war with a volley as we did the beginning, when mounted and armed with our Mausers we rode forth to fight for freedom."

He raised his rifle and emptied his magazine into the sky.

At the first shot the finches rose in a brown cloud. Boetie had had no idea there were so many. All the Boers were firing now, the air about them alive with shining empties that caught the sun as they fell and lay, golden cylinders about their feet. The Boers were shouting, laughing, crying, cursing, human rocks suddenly exploding into life. The bullets fell, spent, from the sky, in a rain of lead on the veld beyond them.

"Now," the big man said. He ran forward, raised his gun by the barrel, and splintered the butt upon a big, nearby rock. The others followed him like hounds, shouting, smashing their rifles, beating the red granite, scarring it with white wounds, and dropping the ruined rifles in a broken heap at its foot.

Now there was no sound but the hammer-and-anvil beat of rifles being smashed upon the rock. When it was over it stood scarred with white wounds above the shattered heap of the Lee-Enfields and Metfords that had been captured from the British.

Du Toit, which was the name of the big, lionlike man who had begun it all, climbed over the wrecked rifles and, standing on the stone, said, "Now we will sign, Brothers."

He jumped clear and led the way to the table, the crowd following him on reluctant, shuffling feet.

A fair-haired man in front of Boetie picked up the pen, dipped it in the ink, and made an X.

There were several Xs on the paper.

"Can't you write your name?" the officer said. The whole scene had made him nervous.

"No," the fair man said in English, "I am only an ignorant Boer," laughing in his face. "That is my mark, a cross to commemorate the dead. My son in battle, my wife and two daughters in one of your camps." He spat on the ground and turned away.

Boetie followed his example, making a neat cross.

"What, you too?"

"A farm boy, Captain," he said, "and I too have my dead."

After that every man signed with a cross. Above them was a clear winter sky, and a bitter wind that rattled the seed pods in the gnarled thorn above the table and sang in the dry, icebound reeds.

After signing, the Boers came together again, but, unable to meet each other's eyes, mounted their tired horses or marched away to pick up such pieces of their broken lives as they could find. No longer cohesive, no longer a body of men, they were individuals, each with his own fears, to whom the horizon called, the wide veld, the rolling hills and plains, the mountains of the Transvaal, which had ceased to be a free republic and was no longer theirs to defend.

Pretoria and Renata were a hundred fifty miles away, but Boetie's mind was made up. He would find her and take her north to the bushveld if she would come. The past was dead. This was the present.

The men who had ridden out so hopefully from their homes, coming in like the spokes of a wheel to the central hub of war, were disbanding. The wheel was broken, had disintegrated, unable to bear the weight of the burden to which it had been subjected. Men who had been rich in family, stock, and possessions were ruined, returning to their devastated homes and weed-grown lands in the hope of finding something left, some testament of their labor. Each thought, Surely something must be left. But for many what could be left, with their wives and children displaced or dead? And what was a place, even if it still stood, if empty of life, with no fire in the hearth, no children's laughter, not even the barking of a dog?

CHAPTER 73

THIS WAS HOME

Now it was over. More than two years of his life wasted, his brother dead, homeless—Boetie assumed Groenplaas was destroyed—an orphan, back in Pretoria on the way to see the girl he had betrayed. She was all that was left now, and old Klaas, if he was still alive, and Moolman in the northern bushveld—the Zoutpansberg—the mountains he loved so much. He had received a message from him. "Come to me, Louis, I am married and have started farming and hunting again. Bring a wife if you can."

A wife. Would Renata marry him? Was she already married?

On foot, unarmed, in the ragged remains of a British uniform, he found his way to the Willows. The British were of no importance now. They could do nothing more to him, these well-fed, red-faced Tommies, the smart officers on their fat, well-groomed horses. Victorious, yes. But he knew and they knew that the Boers had never been properly beaten, had not been brought to their knees. Millions had been spent to bring about an unconditional surrender, but it had not been unconditional. There had been conditions, as there had to be with so many Boers still in the field at the end of it. The very pick of the Boer nation, the flower of it. Yes, that was what he had got out of it, to have been one of them, a "bitter-ender" who had fought under De Wet, Botha, and De la Rey.

Once not so long ago in this town he had wondered what it would be like to be a man and if he would be afraid. Now he knew. He was a man and had been afraid. He had seen war and love. He had known a woman, but the wrong one.

The great weeping willows, bare of leaves, continued to drip their long hair into the dam. They did not change. Wars, sorrows, and joys all passed them by. Unless they were hit, wounded like men by shellfire. He thought of the willow where his companions had taken shelter, bursting like a bomb.

That was over now, all over. The past was dead—the days and the men all dead, gone. In order to live now the slate of memory must be wiped clean. He must think of today, of Renata, and of tomorrow—with or without her.

At the house Renata was waiting, carefully dressed, sitting with her hands in her lap, waiting, as she had waited, scarcely stirring from the window or the stoep since peace was signed.

He would come. "No, Mama, I will not go out . . . No, Mama, I will not do this . . . I will not do that." She was surprised at her own will, at her defiance, but this time when he came he would not find her gone even for an hour.

Only after the wedding, after the whole disgusting affair was over and her sister, smug as a cream-filled cat with the euphoria of her pregnancy, her triumph over the woman who had borne her, and the gifts, clothes, and jewels her doting lover had piled on her, had Renata begun to create a picture of what had happened.

The answers had come by stages. The first after the happy couple had left for a honeymoon at the Cape. Leaving her mother to her own thoughts, which could scarcely have been pleasant, Renata had gone to the spare room, Louis's room, she called it now, to sit and brood. Suddenly she decided to turn it out. Boys, even old Adam, never did a proper job. Suppose he came back. She laughed. As if Louis, back from the war and in her arms, would notice a little dust.

But it was the woman in her, the wife to be. This was his room—their room—where he had kissed her. It had for her the sacred quality of a home. That was the chair he had sat in reading his little Bible. This was the carpet on which he had slept.

She had turned it out once before after he had left in Louisa's clothes, taken everything out onto the landing and swept the floor with a stiff broom. Since then Adam had kept it clean with a lick and a promise.

It did not take her long to move the furniture, but as she moved the chest of drawers to sweep behind it she found a brass button, an English button. It had not been here before. She knew that. And no Englishman had ever been here.

She saved the button, putting it in a little beaded Zulu basket where she kept her "best things," as she called them—the brooches, a turquoise pendant, a pretty pebble she had picked up on the veld. An idea, an impossible idea, was forming in her mind. She could not believe it, could not see how such a thing could have happened. But, half-formed, the idea, the feeling, persisted.

It was not till three months ago that she had grasped the truth. Louisa, who wrote quite regularly though she never answered her letters, had said:

". . . Dorian is very well, a really lovely child, and Morgan is delighted with his son and heir. But you would be surprised to see him, he looks so like Louis van der Berg, a regular little Boer boy. . . ."

That was it. That was it. The Delilah, the Jezebel! Louis had come that day, the only day in all those years, except for the first time when they had gone over to Groenplaas at his request, when she and her mother had been away.

Louisa had met him and seduced him, whore that she

was. That was why he had not waited, why there had been no word of him, no news of him except what she had been able to glean from others—spies and intelligence officers who pierced the British lines.

Poor boy, she thought. Poor lad. A blind puppy in the grasp of a she-wolf. But he must never know she knew. She would never say a word. If he wished to tell her, well and good. Forgive him? What was there to forgive? She was a Boer girl, brought up at the Willows, which was half a farm. Could a bull resist the in-heat heifer? Could a boy, a man, hard and lonely from the war, keep away from a dripping peach thrust into his mouth?

She could not even hate her sister any more. Her hatred had reached its highest point when she had spat in her face. She had no sister. Louisa was a letter-writing ghost, sending news from the nether world. So, day after day, a clean fresh dress every day, she sat waiting like a bride for a lover who did not come, her eyes on the gate through which he must pass.

The lover who did not come, but he would. One day soon he would come. Today, tomorrow, next day. She lost the days, lost count as they merged into each other, but she did not lose patience.

Dora was worried about Renata. Suppose Louis did not come? There had been no letters from him and letters did get to Pretoria, slipped through the lines somehow. Not regularly, of course, but they came all the same.

She had called her a one-man girl, but how far was she going to carry it? Suppose he never came. Was she going to sit forever like a dog on the grave of its master?

And when he came—there was no *if* in Renata's vocabulary—Louis was not to be told of his mother's death or the ravaging of his home. Not to be told that nothing was left, not one stone upon another, not a single head of stock, not a dog, a cat, or a chicken. A few peafowl that had gone completely wild in the neglected fields and had gone back to bush were all that was left of the life that he had known there.

Of herself Dora thought very little. With one daughter a wanton in a foreign land, a little traitoress, a serpent that had bitten the breast that had nourished her, with another all but demented, frozen into a living death of waiting for a man who might never come, with her own hopes of remarriage to a man she had come to love lost in a scene that even now she could hardly believe had really taken place, there was nothing for her to do but wait. She ran the house and garden. She did what she could for refugees and homeless Boer women. She organized a new kind of intelligence, a central depot where news of the women displaced by war and of men seeking families could be collected.

She was lonely and would be more so when Renata went, for inevitably she would go, either to Louis if he came back or eventually to another man.

I might remarry, she thought. It will not be love again. But there will be good men who have lost their all who will be lonely too. The thought was a consolation that she kept at the back of her mind. Perhaps one day she would again make a home for a man.

Then she heard a cry: "He's here! He's come!" and the door of the French window onto the stoep slammed.

Going to the window, she saw Renata running, her skirts held high in her hands, and saw her fling herself into the arms of a ragged, bearded man.

So the girl had been right to watch, to follow her heart, and wait for her heart's desire. Perhaps after all there was a God.

Boetie's wonder at how he would be received, which had made him hesitate at the gates of the Willows, was gone when he saw Renata running toward him. She was waiting for me, he thought. He stood ready to catch her in his arms. Her ash-gold and honey hair had come down and was flying out behind her. She was laughing and crying. "Louis, my heart, my heart. You have come at last!"

"*Ja*, I am here," he said. He could say no more, and together they went into the house.

Leaving them alone, Dora went to prepare some food. Coffee, meat, bread, potatoes, jam, *konfyt*. Brandy. In a few minutes everything edible in the house was spread on the table and Renata was giving him food, spreading his bread, and cutting up his meat as if he was a baby. This was what women gave a man. Love, food, and sons.

When he had done eating, Boetie said, "Tomorrow I will
go to Groenplaas. I can walk there in a day."

"Walk?" Renata said.

"*Ja*, walk. I have no horse. You would be surprised to
know how many miles I have walked. But at least I need
no longer carry my saddlery and rifle. That is over, my
darling. Now I shall walk free as a beggar with my hands
in my pockets."

"We shall ride," Renata said.

"You have horses? Riding horses?"

"No, but I'll get them. I'll get them from the English.
They will lend me two good ones."

Boetie laughed. "That is good—two English horses to
ride over and see what is left of my farm."

"You know?" Dora said.

"I guessed, Mama"—it was the first time he had called
her that—"but still I must see it."

Dora van Reenan was his only mother now. Catalina,
the beloved mother of his childhood, was dimmed by his
long absence. Even by the tragic snapshot. This was not she.

The horses were fresh. Big English chargers. Renata rode
well and looked beautiful on a horse. The familiar road
was unchanged, every landmark the same. They hardly
spoke but touched hands now and again.

Renata looked at the same landmarks—the trees, the
rock outcrops, and the veld. They were her friends. "You
see," she said silently to herself, "I have brought him back
as I said I would."

"So this is Groenplaas," Boetie said. "*Ja*, my heart, I
have brought you indeed to my home at last. So is my
dream realized. Here lie the dead of my race, the dead
of our dreams, and our hopes."

"The trees," she said, "let us go to the trees."

"*Ja*," he said, "the trees." They would not burn. He led
her toward the tall blue gums, their peeling trunks white
in the winter sunshine. The smell of eucalyptus and late
violets was in their nostrils. How long ago it was that he
had said he would one day bring a girl here to propose
to her? A lifetime, or less than three years? The day Servas
had come back from the dorp with the news of the ultimatum. The day Boetie had said, "I am a man; I shall ride
my own horse to war." A man. That pup of sixteen. But

he was a man now, with the full horror of that fate upon him, forced into manhood like a plant with the rich muck of war. The cold, the heat, the reek of blood, and the stink of the putrid dead. Servas shot as a mad bandit. His mother dead in a camp. Their home a ruin, their livestock dead. And he was alone except for this girl at his side. A man who was still a boy.

They were by the great smooth white tree where his father had asked his mother to marry him. Their feet had trodden through the violet leaves where once he had only come unshod.

"I never used to wear shoes here," he said. "Never. Let us take them off, Renata," he said, bending down. He fell on his knees to help her. His hands found her ankles, her calves, the silken warmth of her thighs. Down here below her, grasping her as a drowning man might clasp a floating rose, as a man might embrace the legs of a statue, begging it to come to life . . . The perfume of the violets intoxicated him as if it was wine. Letting go of the girl, his eyes blind with tears, he sought the slender stems of the flowers among the leaves. He would pick her a bunch as he had once picked them for his mother, and give them to her. All that was left, all that was beautiful of Groenplaas, his heritage. He handed them upward, his hand feeling for hers. But she was not there. She was beside him, her lips soft as fruit upon his own.

Only when they left did he wonder how it was that the gum plantation and the violet beds beneath the trees had retained their old perfection. There was not a weed among the flowers.

The water furrows still ran. The doves they had disturbed cooed above their heads.

The answer was old Klaas, his father's boy, who stood beside the horses.

"Baasie, Baasie," he cried. "I knew you would come back!"

"Klaasie," Boetie said, taking the old man in his arms.

"*Ja*, Baasie, it is I. I alone have remained, for where else is there for me to go?"

"You kept the furrows clean and weeded the flowers."

"Those were my orders, Baasie. The old Baas told me before he died to do so. 'Klaas,' he said, 'see to the blue flowers, for that is where I obtained my heart's desire.' "

The old man's voice now rose in anxiety. "The Baasie must not blame me," he said. He waved at the ruins of the house. "When the rooineks came, what could an old Kaffir do alone? But I saved one thing. *Ja,*" he said, "it is the little pot the old Baas used to fill with the blue flowers for the Missus." He fished in his rags and brought out a little white vase with a scattered design of pink roses on it. How strange that his father had picked violets for that vase too. How it must have pleased and hurt his mother when he brought the first ones, clasped tightly in his sweaty little hand, and put them in it on her dressing table!

Boetie took the vase. He held it to his cheek for a moment. It was warm from the belly of the old man. He put it into Renata's hand. "It was my mother's," he said. He smiled sadly. "It is the only heirloom of the Van der Bergs of Groenplaas." She dropped it down her blouse so that it bulged like a third breast upon her bosom. His mother. Tears came into his eyes. How she must have suffered. How wonderful it would have been if she had been here to greet them. But he seemed to feel her presence. She had seen Renata and held her like a daughter in her arms.

"There is something else, Baas," Klaas said. He had dropped the "Baasie." "There is gold. There are five hundred golden sovereigns the Missus and I buried beneath the great stone of the hearth. When that Bothma led the rooineks here—"

"Bothma led the rooineks?" Boetie said. "Bothma! And I had him in my hands and let him go."

"It was Bothma. He knew of the gold, though how I cannot tell. And they dug and dug but did not find it." The old man laughed, showing his pink, toothless gums.

"But if it was there?" Boetie said.

"*Ja,* it was there, but we made a plan, your mama and I. *Ja,* Baas, we buried the gold very deep. Then we filled in the soil with much care and tamped it down with water. Then we put in another box of wood and iron with a lock. This one I smashed open and your mama put in two sovereigns. So when they came they thought it had been looted, though how they could not imagine. Anyway, they rode off."

"They rode off?" Boetie said.

"They rode off with two sovereigns for twenty men—one only, really, because their leader, who said he was a man of his word, gave Bothma one. They had planned to go shares. *Ja, Baas,*" the old man went on, "that was evidently their arrangement. He knew of the gold, led them to it, and was to get half of what they found."

"Bothma," Boetie said again. "Bothma!" He clenched his hands as if he had them around his throat.

Klaas went on: "They put the Missus and the other women and children into a wagon and drove away as the flames rose from the house.

"Baas," he said, "they took Bothma's woman and children too, and it is said that they are also dead with those of Baas Prinsloo. Is this a judgment of the white man's God? That women and children should perish for no cause?

"I saw it all," he went on, "as I lay hidden under a heap of trash. The Nooi silent, still as a rock, the women and the children crying. The dog Wagter dead, clubbed in the yard. The peacocks screaming. Then they left, and in the ashes I found the little vase. I have lived on, Baas, because I had to tell you of the gold and tend the flowers.

"For one day, it was in my heart, the Baasie would return with this maid and bring her here as the old Baas his father did before him."

"This maid?" Boetie looked up sharply. "How did you know her?"

"She came with her mother once to visit your mama."

Boetie knew that, but she had not told him she had seen Klaas.

"They came again three days after the house was no more," Klaas said.

"In the summer, Klaas? Was it in summer?"

"*Ja,* Baas."

Boetie turned to Renata. "How often were you away from home all day? Both you and your mother?"

"Just twice, Louis, when we came here."

"Before God," he said, "you were here then when I came to see you. When I rode to the Willows." Great sobs suddenly racked him. That was how he had missed her. Louisa had said nothing. All that sorrow, all that pain, all that loneliness on the veld could have been avoided if he had seen her, instead of betraying her, his love . . . if he had even known where she had gone. "My God," he said, "I am a Judas too. Louisa," he said. "Louisa . . ."

Renata kissed him.

"I know," she said.

The old Kaffir patted his master's back as if he was a horse. It would do him good to cry in his woman's arms.

They sat on some broken masonry.

"Now," Boetie said, "tell me. Tell me why neither you nor your mother said my home was destroyed, though I had guessed it, knowing my mother had been taken. But you did not say you had been here, had seen it."

"We did not know how to tell you when you came. Then I said to my mother that the best plan would be for me to come with you. It would be better for you if it came with one swift blow, with me at your side.

"As to Louisa, I guessed that too. Listen, Louis," she said, "I have no sister now. She is an English whore."

But one thing she would never tell him—that he had a son. The first son he knew about should be hers.

She patted her breast. "Louis," she said, "this is the beginning of our house. *Ja,*" she said, "one day we will build again—a whole new life about this little pot."

"And the hearthstone," Boetie said. "We will take it north. We will go with old Klaas in a new wagon with stock and tools. We will join Moolman. Let Groenplaas rest. One day when my heart is less sore we will come back and build again. But now we shall go to the bush-veld where Africa still lies untouched. *Ons Land,* my heart. Where we shall see no English flags."

When they had ridden off, the old Kaffir went to the violet bed. Their tracks were easy to follow in the light of the great orange moon that had just come up. *Ja,* he thought, as he looked at the crushed leaves where they had lain, that is the new young Missus. It is good that the Baasie has someone to love, for his heart is sore with hate.

He smiled at the ruins of his master's house. The gold was there. He had saved it for his Baasie. His work was done. There was no need to live on now, no need and no desire. He had seen enough. That was when a man was ready to die, when he had seen enough. Before God he, old Klaasie, had seen too much. It would be easy. It was only the young, the poor young, with so much left to see, who died hard.

AUTHOR'S NOTE

THE BOER WAR has always been of special interest to me. I was two years old when it began and five when it ended. The newspapers in those days were illustrated with drawings, and my father used to color them for me with water color. In spite of having relatives on both sides ours was a very patriotic household. My father had been a soldier.

In the First World War many of my friends were Boer War veterans: Captains Graham Clarke, Chambers, and McCabe, Major Lynch, and many others. The talk in the mess was of Mafeking and Kimberley, of the horses they had ridden and the battles they had fought. None of them survived the war. All were killed or died of wounds.

General Forrestier Walker, who commanded our division —the 20th Light (Infantry) Division—had been in GOC, Cape Town. The commanders of the British Expeditionary Force were Sir John French and Sir Douglas Haig, both of Boer War fame. My uncle, General Francis Stone, commanded the Royal Engineers.

Louis Alphonus Martin, who fought with the Boers and joined the Coldstream Guards in 1916, was my greatest friend. We went through several battles together. Another friend was Colonel Karri Davis, who commanded the Imperial Light Horse, one of the finest and best-found irregular regiments in the British Army.

In Africa I made more friends, many of them Boers. When I ran a cattle ranch, De Wet was a neighbor. I met General Brink and General Hertzog. I discussed the war with Dr. Albert Hymans, who was Kruger's physician. I have walked and ridden over most of the battlefields.

The little girls to whom their aunt sent dolls containing messages for Paul Kruger were cousins. The house and farm that I call Morningstar is Alphen in Constantia. I have taken very few liberties with history. The descriptions of the battles and the life led by both Boer and Briton are authentic. The names of several regiments have been changed. There are no 2nd Hussars, no 10th Black Dragoons, no 22nd Lancers, no 50th Rifles.

Colonel Deneys Reitz, who wrote *Commando,* was a friend. General Smuts was a neighbor of my cousin, A. J. van der Byl of Irene, and I have been over to his place on several occasions.

I am half South African Dutch and half Scottish, and South Africa means a great deal to me, for there lie my dead. Perhaps this is a "Kaffir" concept—that a man is in some way tied to the soil that is peopled by the ghosts of his ancestors. And I have a lot there. Nine generations of ghosts, from the first, Jacob Kloten, who landed at the Cape with Jan van Riebeck to make a garden for the Dutch East Indian merchant fleet in 1652 (Kloten's land grant was the first to any white man on the African continent) to the last of my uncles, who died not long ago.

My great grandfather was Chief Justice of the Cape Colony and the first High Commissioner of Natal. His brother, Sir Josias Cloete, fought as an ensign of hussars at the age of fifteen in the Battle of Waterloo. For three hundred years the family have been lawyers, soldiers, and farmers holding immense blocks of land where they bred remounts for the army, Merino sheep, ostriches, or had vineyards and made wine. Napoleon's last words were supposed to be a request for a glass of Constantia, made on the big Cloete wine farm of that name. It was bought by the Government in the 1880s.

This book has been thought about for thirty years, worked on for more than ten. This was a most interesting war, coming as it did between the American Civil War of 1861 and the First World War of 1914. It has been called "the last gentleman's war" and it began that way, with a great deal of chivalry on both sides. But it resembled in some ways the Spanish Civil War, as a number of weapons and tactical maneuvers developed here were used eleven years later in the battlefields of France and Belgium. Barbed wire and trenches were invented by the Boers. Lyddite, shrapnel, machine guns, and observation balloons were used extensively for the first time. So were the field telegraph and the movie camera. It was the last war in which the cavalry charged with lance and saber. It was the first war in which big guns—at least they were considered big then—were used in "landfare," another innovation of these do-it-yourself soldier-farmers.

Another interesting feature is the number of men engaged who later became famous. General Smuts, who with President Wilson was largely responsible for the League of Nations. Winston Churchill and Edgar Wallace were war correspondents. Conan Doyle was a medical officer. Rudyard Kipling visited the wounded and worked on a paper. Mahatma Gandhi was a stretcher-bearer. Lloyd George became prominent. Cecil Rhodes was active in the defense of Kimberley, and Baden-Powell's messenger boys were the first Boy Scouts.

The war was one of movement. It covered thousands and thousands of square miles. This is a story of marches and countermarches, of barbed-wire fences hundreds of miles long, of burning farms, of epidemics in camps where twenty thousand Boer women and children died. This was a war against space, and typhus, and time. The nineteenth century and all that it represented died in South Africa. The twentieth began with the death of Queen Victoria.

STUART CLOETE

Begun 1950—finished 1962.

Written at:
    Cape Town
    New York
    Johannesburg
    New Orleans
    Prince Edward Island
    Paris
    London
    Nice
    Lausanne
    Atlantic City

APPENDIX 1

*HISTORICAL SURVEY OF SOUTH AFRICA**

At the end of the eighteenth century, the Dutch were still in possession of Cape Colony, where they had established themselves in 1652. Cattle farmers continued to push the frontier of settlement eastward along the coast and northward into the veld. The Orange River was reached in 1760 and the Great Fish River in 1776.

1814, May 30. By the Treaty of Paris the British secured definitive possession of the Cape.

1820. About four thousand British colonists (Albany Settlers) were settled in the eastern coastal region by the British Government, giving the colony for the first time a noticeable English tinge.

1822. A proclamation provided for the gradual establishment of English in place of Dutch as the official language.

1826. The Cape Colony was extended northward to the Orange River.

1834. Abolition of slavery throughout the British Empire, with inadequate compensation to the owners.
    Great invasion of the eastern regions by the Kaffirs, irritated by the constant encroachment of the Dutch cattlemen and farmers.

1835–37. The Great Trek of the Dutch (Boer) cattlemen and farmers to the north and the east of the Orange River. Irritated by the abolition of slavery and by the sympathetic native policy of the Government, the Boers sought new lands and freedom from interference. About ten thousand moved northward. Under A. H. Potgieter they passed beyond the Vaal

---

* Cape of Good Hope, Orange Free State, Natal, South African Republic, Rhodesia, German Southwest Africa. Condensed and reprinted from *An Encyclopaedia of World History*, edited by William L. Langer, Boston: Houghton Mifflin Company, 1940.

River and settled in what became the Transvaal. Those under Piet Retief crossed the Drakensberg and began to occupy Zululand and Natal, regions largely depopulated by the ravages of Chaka, the great military leader of the Zulus.

1838, February. Retief and sixty followers were treacherously slain by Dingaan, the powerful king of the Zulus, who massacred the immigrants and destroyed Durban.

December 16. Dingaan was defeated by the Boers, now led by Pretorius. The Boers thereupon settled in Natal (Republic of Natal).

1840. Dingaan was defeated by his rival, Umpanda, who became king of the Zulus and accepted the rule of the Boers. Immigration of Zulus from Zululand into Natal continued unchecked.

1842. War between the Boers and the British in Natal. The Boers were repulsed and British authority established.

1843, August 8. Natal was made a British colony. Thereupon many of the Boers departed, moving northward over the Vaal River.

December 13. By treaty with Moshesh, powerful leader of the Basutos, Basutoland became a native state under British protection. A similar treaty was made with the Griqua chief. Thus many *voortrekkers* were put under native jurisdiction.

1844, May 31. Natal was combined with Cape Colony for administrative purposes.

1848, February 3. The British governor of the Cape proclaimed as British territory all the region between the Orange and Vaal rivers and the Drakensberg. The Boers were disunited, but some, under Pretorius, opposed the British. They were defeated.

1850–53. Great Kaffir War on the eastern frontier of Cape Colony.

1852, January 17. By the Sand River Convention the British Government recognized the independence of the Transvaal.

1854, February 17. By the Convention of Bloemfontein the British Government withdrew from the territory north of the Orange River. The settlers thereupon organized the Orange Free State, with a president and a *volksraad.*

1856, December 16. Organization of the South African Republic (Transvaal) after years of confusion. Pretorius became President, and Pretoria (founded 1855) the capital.

Self-destruction of the Kaffirs, who slaughtered their cattle in the hope, encouraged by their prophets, that the heroes of old would return and drive out the white man. The population, deprived of food, died of starvation, and in the end was reduced to about one third of the original number.

1857, June 1. The South African Republic and the Orange Free State recognized each other's independence.

1860–64. Pretorius was at the same time President of the South African Republic and of the Orange Free State, thus establishing a close bond between the two Boer states.

1865–66. War of the Boers of the Orange Free State against Moshesh, the chieftain of the Basutos.

1866. Kaffraria was joined to Cape Colony.

1867. Discovery of diamonds near Hopetown, on the Orange River.

1867–68. The Orange Free State defeated the Basutos, who had risen in protest against the cession of territory in 1866.

1868, March 12. The British annexed Basutoland, following a petition by Moshesh. His lands were returned to him, despite the protests of the Orange Free State.

1871. The town of Kimberley was founded and soon became the center of the great diamond industry. The opening-up of this great wealth completely changed the economic setup in South Africa.

October 27. The British Government annexed the diamond region (Griqualand West), which had been under the rule of the half-breed chief Waterboer, under the authority of the Orange Free State since 1854. The Orange Free State vigorously protested this action, which had much to do with stimulating Boer distrust of the British.

1871–72. The efforts of the British to bring about federation of the South African colonies were frustrated by the opposition of the Cape Government.

1871. The government of Basutoland was taken over by the Cape Colony.

1872. Thomas Burgers, a learned Dutch minister from Cape Colony, became President of the South African Republic.

1875. Lord Carnarvon, continuing his efforts toward federation, arranged for an informal conference at London. As a result the claims of the Orange Free State to the diamond country were settled by a money payment.

1876. The Cape Government extended its influence up the west coast of Africa, concluding treaties with native chiefs as far as the frontier of Angola, but this policy was disavowed by the Home Government.

1877–80. Sir Henry Bartle Frere, Governor of Cape Colony. His purpose was to push forward the work toward federation.

1877, March 12. The British annexed Walfish Bay on the coast of South-West Africa. German missionaries had been active on that coast since 1842, and had, in 1868, appealed to the British Government for annexation.

1877, April 12. Annexation of the South African Republic by the British. This was intended as a step toward federation, but was a flagrant violation of the Sand River Convention. The Boers, under the leadership of Paul Kruger, protested vigorously, but without avail.

1877–78. Kaffir War. As a result the British annexed all of Kaffraria, and in the following years (1879–86) extended their authority to the northeast.

1879. The Zulu War, against Cetywayo (king since 1872). Cetywayo had built up again the military power of the Zulus. Jan. 22 he defeated the British in a battle at Isandhlwana. Reinforcements were rushed to the front, and July 4 Sir Garnet Wolseley won a decisive victory at Ulundi. Cetywayo was captured Aug. 28 and peace was made with the Zulu chiefs Sept. 1.

1879. Foundation of the Afrikander Bond, a Dutch group designed to work for recognition of the Dutch language. Under the influence of Jan Hofmeyr it soon rallied most of the Dutch elements in the Cape Colony, but with a much larger program of South Africa for the South Africans, with gradual elimination of interference from the British Government.

1880–81. Revolt of the Transvaal Boers against the British.
 December 30. A Boer republic was proclaimed by Kruger, Joubert, and Pretorius. The Boers repulsed a British force under

Sir George Colley at Laing's Nek, and again defeated and
killed Colley at Majuba Hill. The British Government, under
Gladstone, was unwilling to contest the desire of the Boers
for freedom, and on April 5 concluded the Treaty of Pretoria,
by which the South African Republic was given independence,
but under the suzerainty of Great Britain.

The "Gun War" in Basutoland Colony.

1880. Organization of the diamond industry. Two great corpo-
rations were founded: the Barnato Diamond Mining Company
and the De Beers Mining Corporation.

1882. Establishment of Stellaland and Goshen, two Boer states
in Bechuanaland. This was part of the Boer expansion to the
westward.

1883, April 16. Kruger became President of the South African
Republic.

August. Lüderitz, a German merchant, purchased from the
natives a large tract of territory north of the Orange River.
When Lüderitz hoisted the German flag at Angra Pequena,
there was much excitement in London as well as in Cape Town.

1884, February 27. The Convention of London further defined
the relations of the South African Republic to Great Britain.

May. Fearful of German expansion eastward as far as the
Transvaal and the cutting of the route to the north, the British,
under the influence of Cecil Rhodes, concluded treaties of protection with the native chiefs of Bechuanaland.

August. The Boers, under Joubert, attempted to establish a
republic in Zululand and thus secure themselves access to the
sea on the east.

December 18. In order to frustrate this move, the British
Government annexed St. Lucia Bay to Natal.

1885, September 30. The Bechuana territory was organized as
British Bechuanaland (the region between the Orange and
Molopo rivers) and as the Bechuanaland protectorate (north
of the Molopo).

1886. Discovery of gold on the Witwatersrand in the southern Transvaal. Gold had been found in various parts of the
Transvaal before this, but the rich reefs were opened up only
at this time. There was a wild rush to the Rand. Johannesburg
was laid out. Rhodes and his associates took an active part in
the financing and organization of the industry, and his company
soon controlled a large share of the business.

1887. The British annexed Zululand.

1888. Amalgamation of the De Beers and Barnato diamond interests, giving the De Beers corporation, under Rhodes, practically a monopoly of the industry.

February 11. J. S. Moffat, a missionary and agent of Rhodes, concluded a treaty with Lobengula, King of the Matabele, by which the latter accepted British protection.

October 30. In a further treaty Lobengula gave the Rhodes interest exclusive mining rights in Matabeleland and Mashonaland.

1889. The Cape Colony and Orange Free State concluded a customs union. At the same time the Free State and the Transvaal (South African Republic) concluded a defensive alliance.

October 29. The British Government granted a charter to the British South Africa Company, headed by Rhodes.

1890, July 17. Cecil Rhodes became prime minister of the Cape Colony. He enjoyed the support of the Afrikander Bond.

1891, June 10. Dr. Jameson was made administrator of the South Africa Company's territories.

1892, September. The first trains from the Cape arrived at Johannesburg. An immense traffic developed and the income from the railways came to be a vital factor in the finance of Cape Colony.

In Johannesburg, Charles Leonard organized the foreign (*Uitlander*) element in the National Union, to agitate for better educational advantages, better police, easier franchise requirements, etc.

1893, April 12. Kruger was elected President of the South African Republic for another term of five years.

May 12. Responsible government was introduced in Natal.

July. War of Lobengula against the Mashona. The South Africa Company interfered, defeated the Matabele, and took Bulawayo. The chiefs submitted and the danger passed with the death of Lobengula.

September 25. The British annexed Pondoland, thus connecting Cape Colony with Natal.

1894, November. Rhodes paid a visit to Kruger and renewed his efforts to induce the Transvaal Government to join the other states in a customs union.

1895, May 3. The territory of the South Africa Company

south of the Zambezi was named Rhodesia, in honor of
Rhodes.

June 11. The British annexed Tongoland in order to block
the last possible access of the Transvaal to the sea.

July 8. Opening of the Delagoa Bay Railway from Johannesburg and Pretoria to the sea. This gave the Transvaal at least
an economic outlet free of all British influence.

November 11. British Bechuanaland was attached to Cape
Colony.

December 29. The Jameson Raid.

1896, January 6. Because of his part in the Jameson Raid epi-
sode, Rhodes was obliged to resign as Prime Minister of Cape
Colony.

March. In Rhodesia there was another rising of the Matabele.

March 17. The Transvaal and the Orange Free State concluded an offensive and defensive treaty, a direct reaction to
the Jameson Raid.

September 26. Aliens Expulsion Act passed in the Transvaal. This, the Aliens Immigration Restriction Act (November 26, 1896), and various restrictions on the press and on
public meetings resulted in continuous friction between Great
Britain and the Transvaal.

1897, November 4. The railroad from the Cape reached Bulawayo, in Southern Rhodesia. This line was intended by Rhodes
ultimately to connect the Cape with Cairo.

December ·1. Zululand was annexed to Natal.

1898, February 10. Kruger was re-elected president of the South
African Republic for five years.

1899, March 24. The *Uitlanders* sent a petition with twenty
thousand names to Queen Victoria, recounting their numerous
grievances.

May 31–June 5. The Bloemfontein conference between Milner and Kruger, arranged through the efforts of President
Steyn of the Orange Free State.

October 12, to 1902, May 31. The South African (Boer) War.
By the Treaty of Vereeniging (May 31, 1902) the Boers accepted British sovereignty but were promised representative
institutions as soon as circumstances should permit; the British
Government promised a grant of three million pounds to enable them to rebuild their farms.

1906, December 6. By a new constitutional instrument the
Transvaal was granted responsible government.

1907, July 1. A new constitution, with responsible government, was established in the Orange River Colony.

1908, October 12, to 1909, February 3. Meeting of a constitutional convention, first at Durban, then at Cape Town. The
older ideas of federation were now brushed aside and the
sentiment spread rapidly in favor of union. The convention
agreed on a scheme for a Union of South Africa.

1909, September 20. The draft constitution was approved by
the British Parliament as the South Africa Act. It went into
effect on May 31, 1910.

In 1899, when the Boer War began, world opinion was pro-
Boer and against the British. Now, in 1963, the wind of
opinion has changed and is blowing from the opposite direction against the Afrikaner Nationalist Government of Ver-
woerd.

Yet these are the same people, Boer or Afrikaner. The trouble lies, as it has lain since 1837, with the Boer concept of
segregation and racial inequality. The great Boer Trek was
caused by the liberation of the slaves and the fear that under
British administration the colored people and Hottentots (there
were no Bantu in the Cape Colony then) would be given equal
rights. The same fear animated the Boers in 1880 and 1899.
This remains their fear today, for, isolated from the world,
standing still while the rest went on, the Afrikaner is unchanged—an eighteenth-century man in the latter half of the
twentieth.

Their logic is simple, and arithmetically correct. If the democratic *one man, one vote* were applied, they would be overwhelmed. They were afraid of being overwhelmed by the
Uitlanders—the Outlanders—mostly British, who outnumbered
them in the Transvaal and fought to preserve their racial integrity. How much more would it be threatened by universal
suffrage, where the preponderance of nonwhite to white is
four to one?

They claim, rightly, that the Union of South Africa is the
only Christian and industrialized country on the continent.
The colored people—Bantu, Cape colored, Malay, and Indian
—claim that they have no political rights or say in the country's affairs. They, too, are right. And unless some compromise
is reached, there is more than a possibility of a conflict that
would ruin the country.

Geared to a Western industrial system, and without white
men to run it, millions of African Bantu would starve. In
actual fact neither the white nor the black can get on alone.
Together in symbiotic association, with blacks not held back

because of the color of their skins, and inefficient whites not supported by subsidy in artificially contrived superiority, the country would go forward, exploiting its hitherto untouched riches, and attain its true destiny.

The future of South Africa, and indeed of all the world, is probably colored. Even that of the United States and Europe. Modern technology has made one world. The patchwork of separate cultures created by geographic isolation has already begun to disintegrate. The next stage of our evolution is toward uniformity and equality. This at least is our stated ideal. The haves, both as individuals and nations, are to help the have-nots. All differences are to be ironed out, even those of sex. As we of the West move into automation, produce IBM machines that are smarter than men, and nuclear bombs capable of blowing the world apart, the underdeveloped nations move into literacy and, it is to be hoped, ordered democratic forms of government similar to our own. All this while the world population explodes in an orgy of unprecedented fecundity. That is the present and the future, a time that began at the turn of the century, when the Boer War took place. A war in which some muzzle-loading cannon were still in use and the cavalry still charged with lance and saber. That is its historic interest. There is another—an emotional one. And it was emotion that influenced world opinion in favor of the Boers. It was a conflict between David and Goliath. Between two of the world's smallest nations in alliance against its greatest power—the empire of Queen Victoria.

The Boers lost the war. Goliath won. He could hardly help it, much to the world's regret, and peace was signed at Vereeniging in 1902.

In 1948 the Boers, now the Nationalist Party and then led by Dr. Daniel Malan, took over the Union of South Africa, winning the last battle at the polls.

£25.—.—

*(vijf en twintig pond stg.)
belooning uitgeloofd door
de sub-Commissie van Wijk V
voor den Specialen Constabel
dezer wijk, die den ontvluchte
Krijgsgevangene
          Churchill
levend of dood te dezer kantore
aflevert.* —

Namens de sub-Commis.
                    Wijk V
          Oss de Haas
                    Sec.

<u>Translation.</u>

£25

(Twenty-five Pounds stg.) REWARD is offered by the
Sub-Commission of the fifth division, on behalf of the Special Constable
of the said division, to anyone who brings the escaped prisoner of war

CHURCHILL,

dead or alive to this office.

For the Sub-Commission of the fifth division,
(Signed) LODK de HAAS, Sec.

A BOER WAR REWARD FOR CHURCHILL
DEAD OR ALIVE

APPENDIX 3

LADYSMITH AND THE TUGELA

Looking back today, one can easily see that Sir Redvers Buller's attacks on the Boers investing Ladysmith were one long battle, broken into separate parts and phases by retreats, delays, and armistices to collect the wounded and bury the dead. But to the combatants on both sides there were a number of engagements, each a battle, though the actual fight was never given up. It began with the Colenso disaster (December 15, 1899), which was followed by the British defeat at Spion Kop (January 24, 1900). Then came the abortive action at Vaalkrantz (February 5). The heights of the Tugela finally fell on February 27, 1900.

BIBLIOGRAPHY

Amery, L. S. (ed.): *The Times History of the War in South Africa*, Vols. I–V (1900–09).

Armstrong, H. C.: *Grey Steel; J. C. Smuts.*

Arthur, Sir George: *Life of Kitchener* (1920)

Atkins, J. B.: *The Relief of Ladysmith* (1900).

Balfour, Lady Frances: *Ne Obliviscaris* (1930).

Battersby, H. F. Prevost: *In the Web of a War* (1900).

Batts, H. J.: *Pretoria from Within.*

Begbie, H.: *The Story of Baden-Powell.*

Bell, E. Moberly: *Flora Shaw* (1947).

Bond, John: *They Were South Africans* (1956).

Brandt, Johanna: *Petticoat Commando.*

Butler, Lieut. Gen. Sir William F.: *Autobiography* (1911).

———. *Life of Sir George Pomeroy-Colley* (1899).

Cairns, Capt. W. E.: *An Absent-Minded War* (1900).

Cambridge History of the British Empire, Vol. VIII (1936).

Carrington, Charles: *Rudyard Kipling* (1955).

Carter, Thomas Fortescue: *A Narrative of the Boer War* (3rd edition, 1900).

Childers, Erskine: *In the Ranks of the C.I.V.* (1900).

———. *War and the Arme Blanche* (1910).

Churchill, Winston Spencer: *Ian Hamilton's March* (1900).

———. *London to Ladysmith* (1900).

Cloete, The Hon. H.: *The History of the Great Boer Trek.*

Cloete, Stuart: *Against These Three.*

Columbia Encyclopedia, The.

Colvin, Ian: *Life of Jameson* (1922).

Cooper, Alfred Duff: *Haig.*

Cory, Sir George E.: *The Rise of South Africa.*

Cowles, Virginia: *Winston Churchill.*

Cresswell, W.: *Our South African Empire.*

Cummings, Gordon: *A Hunter's Life in Africa.*

De la Rey: *A Woman's Wanderings in the Boer War.*

Dennison: *A Fight to a Finish.*

De Wet, C. R.: *Three Years' War* (1902).

Dickson, W. K.-L.: *The Biograph in Battle* (1901).

Dictionary of National Biography.

731

Doyle, Sir Arthur Conan: *The Great Boer War* (1903).

Dugdale, Blanche E. C: *Arthur James Balfour* (1936).

Durand, Sir Mortimer: *Life of Field-Marshal Sir George White* (1915).

Du Val, Charles: *With a Show Through South Africa.*

Eade, Charles (ed.): *Churchill by His Contemporaries.*

Encyclopaedia Britannica.

Engelenburg, F. V.: *General Louis Botha* (1929).

Fitzpatrick, J. P.: *The Transvaal from Within* (1899).

———. *South African Memories.*

Fort, Seymour: *Life of Beit.*

French, Hon. Gerald: *Life of Field-Marshal Sir John French* (1931).

Fry, A. Ruth: *Emily Hobhouse* (1929).

Fuller, Maj. Gen. J. F. C.: *The Last of the Gentleman's Wars* (1937).

Garrett, Edmund, and Edwards, E. J.: *The Story of an African Crisis* (1897).

Garvin, J. L., and Julian Amery: *The Life of Joseph Chamberlain*, Vols. I–III (1934).

Gibbs, Peter: *Death of the Last Republic* (1957).

Gie, S. F. N.: *Geskiedenis vir Suid-Afrika* (1927).

Grant, M. H.: *Words by an Eyewitness* (1901).

Green, George A. L.: *An Editor Looks Back* (1947).

Green, Goodwin E.: *Raiders and Rebels in South Africa.*

Green, J. E. S.: *Rhodes Goes North.*

Gretton, R. H.: *A Modern History of the English People*, Vols. I–II (1912–14).

Grinnell-Milne, Duncan: *Baden-Powell at Mafeking* (1957).

Hadcock, A. G., and Lloyd, E. W.: *Artillery.*

Haggard, Sir H. Rider: *The Days of My Life* (1926).

———. *The Last Boer War* (1899).

Haldane, Gen. Sir Aylmer: *A Soldier's Saga* (1946).

Hamilton, Lord George: *Parliamentary Reminiscences and Reflections* (1922).

Hamilton, Gen. Sir Ian: *Listening for the Drums* (1944).

Hammond, J. L.: *C. P. Scott* (1934).

Hammond, John Hays: *Autobiography.*

Handbook for Farmers in South Africa.

Harington, Gen. Sir Charles: *Plumer of Messines* (1935).

Harris, William Cornwallis: *Wild Sports of South Africa.*

Hay, Ian: *One Hundred Years of Army Nursing* (1953).

Headlam, Cecil (ed.): *The Milner Papers* (1931).

Hillegas, Howard C.: *With the Boer Forces* (1900).

Hobman, D. L.: *Olive Schreiner.*

Hobson, J. A.: *The War in South Africa* (1900).

Hofmeyr, Jan H.: *South Africa* (1931).

Hole, Hugh Marshall: *The Making of Rhodesia.*

————. *The Jameson Raid.*
————. *The Passing of the Black Kings.*
————. *Lobengula.*
Holt, Edgar: *The Boer War.*
Hone, Percy F.: *Southern Rhodesia.*
Jackson, Holbrook: *The Eighteen Nineties.*
Jacson, Col. M.: *The Record of a Regiment of the Line* (1908).
James, David: *Lord Roberts* (1954).
James, Lionel: *On the Heels of De Wet.*
Juta, Marjorie: *The Pace of the Ox.*
Juta, Rene: *The Cape Peninsula.*
Keppel-Jones, Arthur: *South Africa.*
Kerr, Montague: *The Far Interior.*
Kestell, J. D.: *Through Shot and Flame* (1903).
Kinnear, Alfred: *To Modder River with Methuen* (1900).
Kruger, Rayne: *Good-bye Dolly Gray.*
Kruger, S. J. P.: *The Memoirs of Paul Kruger* (1902).
Laidler, P.: *A Tavern of the Ocean.*
Langer, William L. (ed.): Encyclopaedia of World History.
Lee, Sir Sidney: *King Edward VII* (1925–27).
Leigh, William: *Frontiers of Enchantment.*
Leslie, Shane: *The End of a Chapter* (1916).
Le Soeur: *Cecil Rhodes.*
Linesman: *Words by an Eyewitness.*
Livingstone, David: *Travels and Researches in South Africa.*
Lloyd, E. W., and Hadcock, A. G.: *Artillery.*
Lucas, Sir Charles: *Historical Geography of South Africa* (1915).
Lucas, Thos. T.: *The Zulus and the British Frontier.*
Lyttelton, Gen. Sir Neville: *Eight Years* (1927).
McKenzie, F. A.: *Paul Kruger* (1899).
Macdiarmid, D. S.: *Life of General Grierson* (1923).
Magnus, Philip: *Kitchener.*
Marquard, Leo: *The People and Policies of South Africa* (1952).
Martin, A. C.: *The Concentration Camps.*
Maurice, Maj. Gen. Sir Frederick: *Life of General Lord Rawlinson of Trent* (1928).
————, and Arthur, Sir George: *Life of Lord Wolseley* (1924).
————, and Groul, M. H.: *History of the War in South Africa* (1906).
Melville, Colonel C. H.: *Life of General Sir Redvers Buller* (1923).
Michell, Sir Lewis: *Cecil John Rhodes* (1910).
Millin, Sarah Gertrude: *Cecil Rhodes.*
————. *The South Africans.*

——. *South Africa.*

——. *General Smuts* (1936).

Montague, Captain W. E.: *Campaigning in South Africa.*

Morley, John: *Life of William Ewart Gladstone* (1903).

Mossop, Dr. E.: *Old Cape Highways.*

Nathan, Manfred: *Paul Kruger; The Voortrekkers of South Africa.*

Newman, N.: *With the Boers in the Transvaal.*

Newton, Lord: *Lord Lansdowne* (1929).

Nixon, John: *The Complete Story of the Transvaal.*

"Old Issue, The"

O'Meara, Lieut. Col. W. A. J.: *Kekewich in Kimberley* (1926).

Owen, Frank: *Tempestuous Journey; Lloyd George, His Life and Times* (1954).

Petrie, Charles: *Joseph Chamberlain.*

Pettman, Charles: *Africkanderisms.*

Phillips, Mrs. Lionel: *South African Recollections.*

Phillipps, March: *With Rimington.*

Pilcher, Colonel T. D.: *Some Lessons from the Boer War* (1903).

Rainier, Peter W.: *My Vanished Africa.*

Ralph, Julian: *At Pretoria* (1901).

——. *Towards Pretoria* (1900).

Regan, W. F.: *Boer and Uitlander.*

Reitz, Deneys: *Commando* (1929).

Robertson, Field-Marshal Sir William: *From Private to Field-Marshal* (1921).

Rorke, Melina: *By Herself.*

Royal Commission on the War in South Africa: Report, Minutes of Evidence, Appendices (Cd. 1889–92), (1902).

Sadoul, Georges: *Les Pionniers du Cinéma* (1947).

Savage, Raymond: *Allenby of Armageddon* (1925).

Scully, W. C.: *History of South Africa.*

Selous, Frederic Courteney: *Sunshine and Storm in Rhodesia; A Hunter's Wanderings in Africa.*

Selwyn, James: *South of the Congo.*

Smith-Dorrien, Gen. Sir Horace: *Memories of 48 Years' Service* (1925).

Smuts, Jan Christiaan: *A Century of Wrong* (1900).

——. *Towards a Better World.*

Smuts, J. C. (son): *Jan Christiaan Smuts* (1952).

South and East African Year Book.

Sowden, Lewis: *The Union of South Africa.*

Spender, J. A.: *Life of Sir Henry Campbell-Bannerman* (1923).

Stathan, Reginald F.: *Paul Kruger and His Times.*

Steevens, G. W.: *From Cape Town to Ladysmith* (1900).

Stevenson-Hamilton, Col. H.: *The Low Veld.*

Theal, G. M.: *South Africa.*

Times, The, 1899–1902.

Trevelyan, G. M.: *History of England; English Social History.*

Trollope, Anthony: *South Africa.*

Tuller, Thomas: *Cecil John Rhodes.*

Van Der Poel, Jean: *The Jameson Raid* (1951).

Viljoen, Gen. Ben: *My Reminiscences of the Anglo-Boer War* (1902).

Vulliamy, C. E.: *Outlanders* (1938).

Walker, Eric A.: *A History of South Africa* (1935 edition).
———. *The Great Trek.*

Wallace, Edgar: *People* (1926).
———. *Unofficial Despatches* (1901).

Webb, Beatrice: *Our Partnership.*

Wells, A. W.: *South Africa.*

Wells, Carveth: *Introducing Africa.*

Wilde, Richard H.: "Joseph Chamberlain and the South African Republic, 1895–99" (in *Archives Year Book for South African History*) (1956).

Wikinson, Spenser: *Lessons of the War* (1900).

Williams, Basil: *Cecil Rhodes* (1921).

Williams, Charles: *Hushed Up* (1902).

Wilmot, The Hon. A.: *The History of Our Own Lives in South Africa.*

Wood, Evelyn: *From Midshipman to Field-Marshal.*

Young, Filson: *The Relief of Mafeking* (1900).

Younghusband, Francis: *South Africa of Today* (1899).

In addition there are the newspapers, magazines, and illustrated papers—*The Times, The Illustrated London News, Punch, Cornhill, Blackwoods,* and a number of family diaries and letters.